IN LOVE
OR IN
THE MORGUE

Rodney H. Washington

DEDICATION

I dedicate this book, to the only one IN THIS WORLD, that, truly sees, what I do. I dedicate this book, TO the only one, that, TRULY SEES, WHAT IT IS, THAT I do! I dedicate THIS book, to the only one, that, truly knows, HOW important IT IS, TO me, TO DO, WHAT I DO!!! I DEDICATE THIS book, to THE ONLY ONE, IN THIS WORLD, that, TRULY believes IN, WHAT I do! (I DEDICATE THIS BOOK, TO YOU, FOR, YOU ARE THE ONLY ONE, IN THIS WORLD, THAT, UNDERSTANDS, WHAT I AM OUT TO ACCOMPLISH, WITH MY WRITINGS!!!!!!!). I dedicate this book, to the ONLY one, that, IS there, WHEN I do, WHAT I do. I DEDICATE THIS book, to THE ONLY ONE, that, I WOULD ALLOW TO BE AROUND ME, WHEN I do, WHAT I do!!! (THOUGH, I DO get more work done, WHEN YOU'RE NOT there:) Though, MOST IMPORTANTLY, YOU ARE THE ONLY ONE, I WANT AROUND ME, WHEN I do, WHAT I do! AND SO, TO my lady, MY LOVE, Tiffany DeVon, I THANK YOU FOR HAVING. MY. MUTHA'. FUCKIN'. BACK!!!!!!! AND!!!!!!!,...FOR BELIEVING IN ME!!!!!!! AND I, Rodney H. Washington, (Rippy, like a motherfucker!), DEDICATE "In Love Or In The Morgue", TO YOU!!!!!!!

ACKNOWLEDGEMENTS

I would like to acknowledge, my lady, Tiffany DeVon, for her skill-set and for her time and assistance, in the formatting of the front and back covers for "In Love Or In The Morgue". And, it is a must that I acknowledge, my lady, for her "photographic eye" and, acknowledge same, with a Photo Credit for the Author Photo. I would also like to acknowledge, Tiffany DeVon, as my Manager, Advisor, and as my Public Relations, for taking the iniative, of doing all the things I don't have the time nor patience to do, and, for doing them exceptionally well. For making the calls. For getting things going and getting things done. For getting book signings scheduled. For making the follow-up calls. And, for the calls after that! For ALWAYS reppin' and promoting my books! For posting and promoting my books on HER OWN top shelf Skincare & Perfume Collection website! - (Tiffany DeVon 1971),(tiffanydevon.com) - For no other reason, than out of love. I thank you, hun! And I Love You!!!

I would like to acknowledge, my friend from way back and boxing sparring partner ("When the sun was at its hottest!"), and an advit "reader of books", Christopher John Lowe, as my Consultant. Thank you for your time and skill-set!

Lastly, I would like to acknowledge,...me! Original front cover art for "In Love Or In The Morgue" painted by yours truly, Rodney H. Washington. Oil and acrylic on canvas.

For YOUR listening and viewing pleasure, please go to my "Brotha Trife" YouTube Channel and check out the music video for "Christmas Mourning"! (Brotha Trife - Christmas Mourning). "Christmas Mourning" is an original song composed and performed by yours truly, Rodney H. Washington! The "Christmas Mourning" music video can also be enjoyed on the Tiffany DeVon 1971 website (tiffanydevon.com). For serious business inquiries, interviews, updates, etc., YOU can reach me directly via email: lonewolflifebrothatrife@gmail.com. I'm also on Instagram: @ rodneyh.washington.

PREFACE

Roughly, a month or so after I completed my debut novel, "Born In A Manger", I found that I missed writing every day. I missed the grind. I missed creating. I missed "the art" of writing. Because, THAT'S WHAT writing is to me. Art.

To me, writing,...is painting. The blank page is my blank canvas. (I know what my painting looks like in my mind, BEFORE I even start painting!). I know what I WANT IT TO LOOK LIKE on my canvas. I know HOW I want my painting TO LOOK LIKE ON THAT blank page! ALL I have to do,...IS GET IT THERE!!! (So that, YOU KNOW WHAT IT LOOKS LIKE!!!)...(So that, YOU see, WHAT I see!).

AND SO...

I bought a couple of those black and white composition books (a.k.a. canvases!) AND, on August 05, 2018, I wrote my first notes (a.k.a. my first brush strokes!), for "In Love Or In The Morgue"! I simply thought to myself, "What do I see? What do I THINK HAPPENED to, of, and, in, the lives of my characters BEYOND THE ENDING of "Born In A Manger"??? WHAT DO I SEE,...the characters doing? What "moves" WOULD THEY HAVE made?? HOW WOULD things have played-out,...in THEIR lives!?!"

And so...

After filling-up several composition books with notes, thoughts, ideas, potential storylines, potential chapter titles, oil paints, brush strokes, etc., (I already knew what I was going to title my book!)...I got back to work! I got back to typing!! I got back to painting! In other words,...I GOT BACK ON MY GIDDY-UP!!!

And...

MAKE NO MISTAKE, typing-up a book IS work, (to be sure!).

BUT...

It's NOT work to me!

(Tapitty-Tap-Tap-B-Bop-Do-Wop-Da-B-Bop-Skipitty-Skap-To-Tha'-Mutha'-Fuckin'-Tipitty-Tap-Tap-Tappin' - WHEN I'm typin' - WHAT I'm writin' - I do it - HOW I do - WHEN I do - AND I DO IT - JUST LIKE a Jazz Singer SCATTIN'!!!),...(with my eyes closed;)

I don't write to offend. I write, to offer. I don't write to appease. I write, to push. I WRITE, BECAUSE, I LOVE TO WRITE! I WRITE, BECAUSE, I NEED WRITING IN MY LIFE!! And,...I WRITE EVERY DAY!!! I write, with the hopes, that, at least one person out there, in the world, reads and loves, what I have grinded on, for so many countless hours!

And so...

I'M BACK AGAIN!!!

(TO push your mind, FEARLESSLY AND UNAPOLOGETICALLY, YET AGAIN, this time!!)...

AND SO...

I PRESENT TO YOU, BOOK No.2, IN A SERIES OF BOOKS, THAT'S GUARANTEED TO BE, THE MOST UNUSUAL!!! YES, INDEED, FOR THOSE THAT GOT IT IN THEM TO READ Part 2 of 3, I'M BACK WITH ANOTHER BRUTAL BOOK...with a soul.

For(You See!)...

"In Love Or In The Morgue", is hard-hitting and fictionally-written, of entertainment, motivation, and information!!!

And...

(Have no doubts!)...

YOU WILL FIND yourself, LAUGHING, SHOUTING AND CRYING ALOUD!!!

(FROM the UNIQUELY-CREATIVE metaphors - AND FROM - the "breaking-down-of-my-mind's" DESCRIPTIVE-DEFINITIONS, OF - AND - FOR - YOUR ENJOYMENT AND DISSEMINATION!!!)

Although...

BE FOREWARNED!!!

FOR...

IT'S A BATTLE OF ENDURANCE reading "In Love Or In The Morgue"!

For...

My chapters end where, and, for, no other reason, than: TO WRITE - TO WHERE - IT FEELS RIGHT!!! (Got it!).

And so...

YOU, THE READER, ARE IN for some chapters that are exceptionally long! *(A-Single-Burst-Of-Hot-Air-Blown-From-Nostrils-Smirk!!)(THIS GUY, doesn't even know THAT long chapters ARE a major turnoff, FOR PEOPLE LIKE ME, WHO enjoy reading books!)*...(I heard you think!).

COULD I have POSSIBLY made, SOME of those exceptionally long-chapters, shorter? The answer to that,...is no.

(NOT in MY book!). (Not THE WAY I write!).

I CHOOSE to make SOME OF my chapters exceptionally long,... FOR a purpose. *(Oh, THIS ought to be good!)(WHAT ON EARTH, could THAT purpose, POSSIBLY BE?!?)*(I heard you think!)...(By the way),... (AS you're reading this),...(I'M also reading),...(YOUR mind!).

AND SO...

(THE SOLE PURPOSE, FOR, THAT PURPOSE, IS, TO PUT YOU THROUGH EXACTLY WHAT, THE CHARACTERS in my book, ARE going through!!)...

IT'S FOR YOU, the reader, TO experience, WHAT the characters, ARE EXPERIENCING, (in real time!). There's no calling "Timeout" in this book! There's no splitting-up of a long chapter, for example, say, into three smaller chapters,...JUST FOR the reader's benefit AND/OR comfort!! *(Huff!!)(I'M NOT reading ANYMORE OF THIS crap!)(Who in the heck does this guy think he is anyway!?!)(WHY WOULDN'T HE PUT THE COMFORT OF THE READERS, FIRST???)*...(I heard YOU think:) Well, (high-horse-smarty-pants!!),...I'LL TELL YOU!!!

Simply put...

It's not fair TO my characters.

I PUT my characters "through it"! (They DON'T GET TO call "Timeout"!). It's a rough 'n tumble book, with rough 'n tumble characters, trying their damn-best (OR WORST!!!), JUST TO GET THROUGH THE WORLD, I'VE CREATED FOR THEM!!!

SO, IF YOU want to get through an exceptionally long-chapter IN MY book? Well, then,...you have to get through it,...WITH THEM!!! YOU HAVE TO GO THROUGH EXACTLY WHAT, MY CHARACTERS ARE GOING THROUGH!!!

I write, to push YOUR mind! I write, to push MY mind! I write, to inform. I write, to entertain. I write, to teach. I write, to learn. I write, to FREE MY MIND!! I write,...TO FREE YOUR MIND!!! WHEN, I WRITE, I'M THERE!!! (I'M RIGHT THERE, WITH MY CHARACTERS!!!).

And so...

WHEN, I WRITE, I WRITE, TO GET YOU THERE, AS WELL!!!

Make no mistake, I place "commas" and "dashes" and "parentheses", wherever, and, however I so chose to, do so! TO BE SURE, I AM NOT A STICKLER FOR "PROPER" GRAMMAR OR "PROPER" SENTENCE STRUCTURE. TO ME, IT'S THE FLOW OF WHAT I'M SAYING, AND HOW THAT FLOW LOOKS ON CANVAS, (Thee "AESTHETICS" of it all!), WHILE STAYING TRUE TO CONVEYING THE MESSAGE, (HOW IT FEELS RIGHT TO ME!), - ARE WHAT ARE - OF FAR GREATER - OF IMPORTANCE, TO ME! AND, IF A MISPELLED WORD HAPPENS TO MAKE IT THROUGH THE COUNTLESS HOURS, OF ME GOING OVER AND OVER AND OVER THIS BOOK?? Then,...SO BE IT;)

And, make no mistake, I am more than capable of writing "proper". But,...THAT WOULD BE SOME BORING-ASS-SHIT!!! This is the style of writing God has gifted me. This is the style of writing I have developed, (a.k.a. "RODISM"). THIS IS THE WAY I LOVE TO WRITE!!! This is the way I CHOOSE TO write. Writing this way, FEELS NATURAL TO ME. (BIG BOLD LETTERS, BIG BOLD PARAGRAPHS, BIG BOLD CHAPTERS, METAPHORS YOU'VE NEVER READ BEFORE, AND ALL!!!)...(AND ALL UNAPOLOGETICALLY AND FEARLESSLY-WRITTEN!!!)... (AND, OH BY THE WAY!)...(I'VE BEEN DESCRIBED MY WRITING AS "UNAPOLOGETICALLY" LONG BEFORE "UNAPOLOGETICALLY" BECAME TRENDY!!!). AND SO, THIS IS THE WAY I'M JUST GONNA' KEEP-ON WRITING!!! And, as such, all of my books are written outside-the-lines and written by an outside-the-lines mind.

In Love Or In The Morgue is the sequel to Born In A Manger. If you became endeared to my characters and style of writing while reading Born In A Manger, I'm very confident in saying, you will enjoy In Love Or In The Morgue just as much, if not more so, than Born In A Manger.

While it's not necessary to have read Born In A Manger for you to enjoy In Love Or In The Morgue and to follow the storyline, I didn't make it easy on you! In Love Or In The Morgue is consciously not burdened by excessive "catch up"! *(And why would I do something like that?)*...(Well,...I'll tell you!). BECAUSE, I WANT YOU TO READ "BORN IN A MANGER" FIRST!!!

So, for my first time readers, enter the world of "Born In A Manger". Allow yourselves to be taken places you've never dared to venture! And THEN, see for yourselves which characters are back for more, to take YOU places, YOU won't EVER forget!!!

Well...

I see YOU'VE stuck around! (So, LET'S GET INTO THANGS!)...

UT-OH! ...SHOWTIME!!!!!!

"In Love Or In The Morgue" begins exactly 1, 261 days after "Born In A Manger" has ended. Pockets, the old school hustler and player turned drug kingpin, is back! And, he's landed in a place where his shiesty and conniving-ways, are sure to make him millions...THE MUSIC INDUSTRY!!! Come! Let us all join Pockets,...ON TOP OF THE WORLD!!! (AS, HE GOES TO WORK, as the Managing Partner of Jettison Records!!!). Shall we? Yes,...I THINK WE MUTHA' FUCKIN' SHALL!!!

STATEMENT

"In Love Or In The Morgue" begins exactly 1, 261 days after "Born In A Manger" has ended. Pockets, the old school hustler and player, turned drug kingpin, IS BACK!!! And, he's landed in a place where HIS shiesty and conniving-ways, ARE SURE to make him millions,...THE MUSIC INDUSTRY!!! Come! Let us ALL join Pockets,...ON TOP OF THE WORLD!!! (AS, HE GOES TO WORK, as the Managing Partner of Jettison Records!!!). Shall we? Yes,...I THINK WE MUTHA'-FUCKIN' SHALL!!!

ABOUT THE AUTHOR

Well-thought-of, or, well, thought of.

Chapter One

DAY 1, 261

In the city of hurricanes, barnacles and social climbers get lapped up upon, by vibrant greens and blues. Of what's left of the oranges and reds, of what's left of the yellows and whites, of what's left of this beautiful Floridian sky, all is beautiful for the beautiful people, and if it's not you'd never know it, 'cause they'd never show it. For the show of See-And-Be-Seen must go on, so the fakery, effrontery, and baffoonery continues, of what's left of this month of April.

Dressed in all white linens, looking down over the white railing holding him back, looking past the silver cross hanging from his long silver chain, Heavy Duty looks down upon the barnacles leeched onto the great white chain keeping him anchored in place, getting lapped up upon, by vibrant greens and blues. The wispy and slimy green algae, teases as it waves, at the ocean, at nothing, at everything, and apparently, at Heavy Duty too, (as far as HE'S concerned!), as he watches it living on his chain, waving at him, teasing him, the chain keeping him in one place. As about as welcomed as humor found within some slimeball too ignorant to know any better, the slimy algae and barnacles, *mark the white chain's time in the marina,* (and, that too, of Heavy Duty!), as he continues, to look down upon the twain, unwelcomed on his white chain, as he watches the acquainted trio, getting lapped up upon, by vibrant greens and blues.

Waving back at Heavy Duty, from a yacht (docked TOO close for the owner's liking!), is a toasted, well-done-in-by-the-sun, wrinkled-up hand, covered in spots and Riesling. Waving "drunkardly" at Duty, the elderly - *old-habits-die-hard* - woman, makes NO attempt, in keeping the Riesling off the deck, as she attempts to wave back in her glory days, while clutching her chalice, of: I-Know-I-Still-Look-Good! NOT the least bit put off, nor surprised, by her antics, (again!), the yacht owner, her husband, looks down at the drink in his hand, clutching and swirling, a too watered down and no diving rock glass, of: THIS-Is-Why-Husbands-Die-BEFORE-Their-Wives! Finishing off his beverage of choice, the yacht owner reaches for his faithful bar cart, (necessitously stocked full of vintage crystal bottles of resolve), looks around the marina and sighs, before pouring himself another strong glass, of: Money-DON'T-Buy-Happiness-OR-Class!

"SHE'S FUCKIN' NASTY, MY DUDE!!!", shots fired broadside by Heavy Duty, across the yacht owner's bow, (and over the brow, of his rotisserie broad!).

From over by the white railing containing him, above the great white chain bounding him down, Heavy Duty looks back over his shoulder, back over at what drove him over here in the first place! Dressed in all white bikinis, seen exposed, through sexy white linen "Swimsuit Cover-Ups", Gidget Cole and her former prostitutes, drink and lounge and reminisce, *about the man that drove them all down here in the first place. (Change is good)…(ESPECIALLY, the type of change, Duty dropped on this yacht, WHEN HE AND THE GIRLS blew into Miami!!!).* Though, habits can and DO get dropped like anchors,…*old habits do die hard,*…FOR street niggas and street urchins, LIKE these!

For…

The streets, are FOREVER talking! (They HAVE A WAY, of calling a nigga or an urchin *back*)…

For…

THAT fickle-bitch, is undefeated!

AND...

(She INTENDS, to STAY that way!!!).

"Whatchew doin' WAY over there, Duty? YOU ain't scared of pussy, IS ya'??", one of the girls belts out, (from too many belts, of: I'm-Gonna-Smack-Me-A-Ho!), WHILE comfortably lying on her back, on the comfort of a deck lounger.

"Eat a bag of dicks, trick.", Heavy Duty, tells the former prostitute, who's mouth has learned to be too comfortable, and has grown too loose, from the comforts, of: caught-fresh-daily-catch-of-the-day - comfort foods. The very same mouth, that, *WITH dick in hand, acquired the taste of somebody's dick for money. The very same money, she then handed over to somebody.* The very same mouth, that, has acquired the taste FOR the entitled rights, OF costly bottles of acquired tastes. The very same mouth, NOW, *lacking the grounding of the feeling, OF WHEN you're ABLE to, add some kind of meat to your "Chi Chi".* The very same mouth, NO LONGER grounded *BY the feeling, of having ENOUGH granulated sugar, to make, your: "Bragging-rights-Kool-Aid!".*

FOR(YOU SEE!)...

Forgetful-eyes, NOW full of brighter days and skies, of oranges and reds, and that of yellows and of whites, and skies of blue, *of eyes,* no longer privy to, *the trash swimming in the gutter waters, flowing down along the track, WHERE the former prostitues, used to scuff up their shoes.* Vibrant colors of greens and blues in ears *gives them amnesia,* filled with lapping waters and of seagulls beating them for a shrimp cocktail on ice or two! OR, MAYBE, they just want to forget *where they came from, of the one or two coldhearted "Johns", that used to beat them for their pimp's money.* ...Blame it on the swimmer's ear THAT gets them through!

And so...

Snapping her fingers one time, (for, JUST one time, IS ALL it takes!), with, NO need to look-up-from-under her oversized white sun hat, Gidget Cole, lets the loose-mouth girl, (and, them ALL know!), *THAT, they AIN'T too far removed FROM the streets!*

FOR...

Loose-mouths CAN (AND, DO!) get cut loose like bait, *and WILL get sent right back to the "lady in waiting".*

For...

THAT fickle-bitch-of-the-streets, SHE IS OUT THERE, always out there running her mouth, and just waiting. On you.

"I need a smoke. I'm outta smokes. I'm goin' for smokes.", Gidget, announces across their yacht deck, over to Duty.

"I'M goin' witchu'. YOU KNOW I don't LET YOU go NOWHERE alone.", Heavy Duty, replies, relieved from the white railing.

"This hat ain't gon' cut it wit this breeze. Gemme a sec, Duty. And, I'll be right back up.", Gidget, tells Heavy Duty, (then, heads inside and, down the steps, to the cabin below, to put on a wig).

Standing before herself and the master cabin bathroom mirror, Gidget Cole reflects *on those days, when she stood looking in a shattered-broken-bathroom-mirror with Brotha Trife.* Looking away, she takes off her sun hat and, puts on one of her many expensive wigs. Wig money (and, so much more!), *compliments of, that, hard-to-close trunk of "Too Cold's" black BMW 750il, that Unc, gave to his Nephew, (which was filled with more stacks of money on top of the stacks on top of those stacks, than, any of them put together, had ever seen before in their lives!).*

Back up the cabin steps, then down the yacht ramp, Heavy Duty and Gidget Cole walk down the long wooden marina dock together. As they walk, they pass the time by talking, as they get passed by warm bay breezes that go through palms. As they walk, they walk past the anatomically-plastically-correct and corrected. (Enjoying life up on their yachts?). As, the correct and corrected "get correct". (AS, they go through frozen Bay Breezes in their palms!). Duty and Gidget left Pa. for this kind of life and weather. Whether or not they know it, there's only one thing that COULD make this life better.

As the oranges and reds of the Floridian sky begins to wane, they talk and walk down the sidewalk, talking and walking their way past the skyscraping resorts. Imposing to some as the resorts impede, the sky's clouds of white, and the bay's breezes, from blowing through the palms. Thoughts impede, into their thoughts, of thoughts they don't want to resort back to, *back to the days and, of the ways, of putting quick cash the fast way, back into their palms. Old habits* outlive their ousters, BECAUSE *they're more patient.* Patience is a virtue. (But,...so is fun).

Just as the blackness of the night impedes down on it all, the two find that their walk and conversations have led them far from the marina's docks, Dockers, AND boredom. (No it didn't!)...(They led themselves astray!!). To enter a gas station, they walk past a rough crowd looking at them hard, (comprised mainly of some hard-looking hookers and a pimp in Jordans!).

Duty and Gidget, step from the - unreasonably-poorly-lit-exterior - of the gas station, and into, the interior, of - a-well-lit-for-GOOD-reason - gas station! (And, in doing so, *they step back INTO the mind-set OF,... the lives they left behind!).* (And, for good reason!). *THEE (at times!), Mentally-Draining-Mind-Set, OF: Maintaining being smooth, WHILE maintaining your cool, all the while, while you HAVE TO watch your back, while watching EVERY move, while maintaining a certain look on your face, while maintaining a certain look in your eyes, while maintaining, NOT looking at anything or anyone in particular, ALL THE WHILE, while YOU'RE looking at everything AND everyone particularly, while acting LIKE you ain't even doin' any of that, while doing this THE ENTIRE TIME while you're in this scene, JUST so that you can get through it all, WITHOUT getting stepped to, WHILE ALL THE WHILE, in your mind, IS just to MAKE IT OUT of the scene alive! AND, all the while, WHILE maintaining THE mental-mind-set, OF: I-AIN'T-here-to-be-fucked-with, SO DON'T fuck with me, AND IF you fuck with me, I'M fucking YOU up! (BUT,...I DON'T KNOW y'all!)...(AND, Y'ALL got me outnumbered!!). AND, all the while, WHILE you're thinking,...(YOU DON'T KNOW... IF their boys...WILL jump in!!!). And, all the while, while this IS GOIN' ON in YOUR mind, you know, THAT, you're TOO-seasoned, AND been through TOO MUCH, TO LET this (OR ANYTHING) shake you! WHILE, maintaining IN your mind, that, the seasoned-look, IN my eyes, AND the seasoned-body-language OF mine, IS what's kept anyone FROM saying anything to me, OR about me, OR stepping to me,...this entire time.*

(BECAUSE, they don't want to step to somebody THAT JUST MIGHT be "seasoned-enough" TO handle, some: "seasoned-shit"). While all the while, while maintaining, in your mind, these-motherfuckers-might-just-look-hard-and-be-soft-as-fuck, while maintaining, nah, they-ain't, these-is-some-loose-niggas. While maintaining, in your mind, if-you-want-my-shit-I'ma-make-you-work-for-it. While maintaining, fuck THESE motherfuckers! While maintaining, I-know-my-town-ain't-soft-but-this-town-is-real-and-hard-as-fuck. While maintaining, I-really-won't-feel-safe-until-I'm-AT-LEAST-several-blocks-away-from-here! While maintaining, I'll-be-watching-my-back-all-the-way-back-to-the-safety-of-my-bed - kind of - mentally-draining mind-set, OF: THIS-Is-WHY-I-Left-Pa.-IN-The-Motherfuckin'-First-Place - kind of - MENTAL-DRAIN. Shew! (AND, OY VEY!!!)

AND(ALL THIS, FROM)...

Just walking through the parking lot!

(The: Unreasonably-Poorly-Lit-Parking-And-Gas-Pump-Island-Areas of, The: Unreasonably-Poorly-Lit-*This-Just-Set-This-Mind-Set-Off*-Exterior-Loitering-Grounds - of, the gas station!). TO, stepping into, The: The-Employees-Could-Give-Half-A-Damn-Of-What's-Going-On-Outside - BUT - The-INSIDE-Of-This-Bitch-IS-Gonna-Be-Well-Lit-AND-For-Good-Reason - gas station! *(WHICH, just added to Heavy Duty's and Gidget Cole's - "old days and ways" - Mind-Set!).* TO, walking up towards the counter. (Where, Gidget and Duty stand several deep, back from the front of the line). While, all the while, while watching their own, AND the other one's back! And MAINTAIN, ALL OF THIS, LIKE it's their duty. Because it is. And has to be. Oy vey.

The two hard-to-hear West Indies accents, coming from behind the counter, (or from whatever island they come), STAY on their island, BEHIND the protective-bulletproof-glass counter window. AND, if they ever do leave their island and come out from behind the counter, it's seldom. A middle-aged couple standing outside, looking like they'd love to score some smack, stands right smack dab in the middle of the store front window. Finally giving in, Duty and Gidget, look over to their left at the middle-aged couple, just to find them staring right back! For your convenience, on the shelves towards the back, for a dollar, only for you to go through faster than a dollar, are paper thin four rolls of toilet paper packs. For sale, right next to, The: We-Love-YOUR-Look-And-Brand-SO-We're-Just-Gonna-Steal-Your-Idea-BECAUSE-We-Think-Everyone's-Too-Stupid-To-Pick-Up-On-What-We've-Done-And-WE'RE-Really-NOT-That-Good-Or-Creative - Boxes, of: off, off, off, Brand Cereal. But, up in front of them, up at the bulletproof window, Duty and Gidget, find it humorous, while asking themselves, "Is this shit foreal??"

While standing two or three deep, while waiting in line to buy smokes, while still being watched by the middle-aged couple in the window, Duty and Gidget, think to themselves, that, *"This HAS gotta be some kind of joke!"*. For, each person in line in front of them, are there to ONLY buy cigars and wraps! And, when who's next, when it's their turn to be at the front of the line, that person then follows suit, (just like all of them that was in line before them!). And, pulls out of their pants pockets,... big bags of weed! (I mean, REALLY, REALLY, REALLY, BIG BAGS OF WEED!!!). Then, smell it. BEFORE placing the big bag of weed on the counter. BEFORE it goes into their pants' pocket. (Then, AGAIN on to the counter, JUST to put it right back!). And, Duty and Gidget, don't even say a word. Not even to each other. *(While, maintaining, KEEPING an eye on EVERY motherfucker!!)*. BUT, Duty and Gidget, DO think to themselves, *"I-guess-they-ain't-the-least-bit-concerned-about-gettin'-popped-for-some-weed-OR-whoever-the-middle-aged-couple-facing-them-in-the-window-is-...THAT-KEEPS-walking-over-to-and-talking-to-WHOEVER-THAT-IS-IN-THAT...undercover-looking-car!"* (parked across the street!).

And so...

Duty and Gidget, to themselves, think, *"Well, either-they're-facing-charges-or-they-think-they're-doing-a-good-deed!"*.

AND...

EACH TIME, the middle-aged couple comes back, they ain't staring at NOBODY from their broadcast booth, right smack dab in the middle, of THAT window, except FOR, AND stare only at,...the two new comers. (That BEING, Heavy Duty and Gidget Cole!!). WHICH, puts the two of them,...on edge a little.

And so...

Right around the time, Duty and Gidget, are just one back, from standing from the front of the line, one of the hard-to-hear accents, comes from around back of the counter, leaving his island. And, just stands over by the front door. Just then, one of the hard-looking prostitues, from out front enters, with a fucked-up looking nose, and it's looking fucking-sore! Looking like a - back-alley-tipping-over-trash-cans-street-rodent - the hooker, is wearing two black eyes like a mask, from taking a punch to the nose, that, MUST HAVE BEEN potent! IMMEDIATELY, she begins telling the man, ALL ABOUT...the man! AND, blaming the man FOR her face! Man, she was yelling at the man! (*For, the man, not doing ANYTHING last week, from not stopping her, from getting hit by a strong pimp hand!*). The man, just looks at her, like, *"That was yours! That, wasn't MY shit!"* And, he looks at her, like, *"Plus, I don't eat where I be crappin'!"* Then, in his island accent, the man, looks at her, shrugs his shoulders, and, asks, the hooker, (with all-too-audibly-clarity!), "Huh? Is THAT, WHAT happened???"

(And, AS FOR, Duty and Gidget??)...

WELL...

THEY AIN'T feelin' THAT shit!!

BUT...

(WHO knows, IF she's telling the truth?!?)(Since, Duty and Gidget, *didn't see that shit happen!!*).

PLUS...

They're, JUST there, TO BUY some smokes!

'Cause...

(*That's-HER-cross-to-bear-not-OURS - is THEIR mind-set!!*)...

PLUS...

(WE just want to get back to OUR life on OUR yacht!! AND, tonight, sleep in OUR comfortable big bed, in OUR own - inside-downstairs-master-bedroom - yacht cabin!!)...

BUT...

Before Gidget can buy her smokes. And, just jet. The hard-to-hear accent, from behind the bulletproof counter window,...just be DRAWIN' on a nigga!

As...

(He STAYS askin' Duty, to hand him yet ANOTHER big-faced-bill!)...

For...

The hard-to-hear accent on HIS island, from BEHIND the bulletproof counter window, to hold up and inspect!

(Drawn in now, 'cause, this is the shit, FROM THAT shit, THAT'S gonna happen!)...

For(NOW!)...

There's a few more faces! On the outside! IN the window! AND, NOW, a few more, standing...BEHIND THEM!! IN the store!

AND(On top of that!)...

THAT, FUCKIN' - smack-starved-middle-aged-couple-from-smack-dab-in-the-middle-of-the-window HAVE, (NOW AGAIN!!), made THERE WAY back across the street, TO THAT, undercover-looking-parked-car! (AND, NO DOUBT, REPORTING ON Duty and Gidget!!) FOR, about the third or forth time now, SINCE they've been in this store!

(Yes indeed!)...(Drawin' on a nigga like a gun!)

And so...

Duty, sways there, as he stays there, side-to-side, irritated. Gonna hold his tongue. ('Cause, from, behind the bulletproof counter window, the hard-to-hear-accent, won't even hear himself being berated!). Good!! You happy now!?! Let's go! Gidget got her smokes.

And...

They step back out the door. (And, back out INTO, The: Unreasonably-Poorly-Lit-Exterior!!!)...

WHERE...

Pimps and hoes gonna be doin' what they do, showin'-they-asses, AND putting on a show!!!

For...

Just out front, parked by the first gas pump, the pimp got all his hoes back in his car, but one, and that one, is slowing down HIS money hunt.

And...

(With all eyes on the pimp out front, this ain't no time for the pimp to front!)...

And so...

The girl, with the raccoon-eyes, the pimp, he, tells her, "YO' ASS, BEST-BE-BACK IN THAT CAR, starting AT five, BE-FO' I counts down TO one!!!"

And...

(Just to, MAKE SURE, SHE KNOWS, WHAT'S, the NEXT step!)...

AND...

(JUST FOR, EVERYONE watchin', OF THAT, NEXT STEP, THAT, HE'S sure!!)...

The pimp,...raises his hand.

AS...

HE begins, HER countdown!!!

AS...

HE, counts down, FROM five, FAST!!! (STEPPIN' FAST, towards her, IN HIS Jordans!!!!)...

And, (by the time, he gets to three)...

(The hooker's raising a defensive-forearm!), PLEADING, AS SHE, CRIES, "NO!!! NO!!! DADDY, NOT HERE!!!"

WHICH...

(GOT, GIDGET, THINKIN', "Her brainwashed-mind, would rather ACCEPT her beating SOMEWHERE ELSE,...just NOT here! WELL,...I'll be darned!")

And...

(EVEN THOUGH, she started walking towards the car)...

The count of five. IS,...the count OF FIVE!!!!! (YOU gotta follow the rules!)...(it's really not so hard:)

AND SO...

A STRONG PIMP HAND smacked her ass DOWN TO the parking lot anyways!!!!!

And(UPON THAT?)...

Gidget, performs the customary *"running of the pockets"*, pointing a pistol of her own, at the hard-looking crowd looking hard, so they CAN'T stop it!

'CAUSE...

(Heavy Duty, pistol whipped the fuck out of the pimp's head!!!)...

AS...

They BOTH reverted back, (being in that environment!) *to, Their: "old ways of the old days"!!*

And? SO *NOW...*

THEY'RE back!! ("Seasoned-shit" popped off!!!)

SO(NOW!)...

(Back to THEIR YACHT, they GOT TO get back!!)...

AND SO...

They ran over the pimp's legs IN his OWN car! ('Cause, after THAT shit? That long walk, IS TOO far!!!).

Duty, whipping the whip, finally felt safe, when he made it back, to the marina's docks, Dockers, AND THE boredom! Gidget, exits the vehicle, with a BIG BAG of the pimp's weed! AND, a big knot roll of the pimp's cash!

(And, as FOR Duty?)...

Well...

Duty, steps out the pimp's ride, with ALL his hoes,...AND his motherfuckin' Jordans!!!

Duty, Gidget, and hookers. Walk down the loooooong wooden marina dock, past all the yachts. Under the eyes of scrutiny, from some, "Well, I never!", onlookers. Then, up their own yacht ramp they go. To some more hard-looks, and, to one, or two, "OH, HELL NO's!!!" Duty and Gidget ain't having it! DON'T need the shit! AND, just head straight down the steps to their master bedroom cabin down below.

MEANWHILE...

(Past AND present hookers, up on the deck,...got titties poppin' out!!)...

FROM...

Hair flippin' and hair tusslin'!!

WHILE...

Old-habits-die-hard - "Ms. Riesling" - next door, pours herself another drink. ('CAUSE, her old ass is READY to come join the show!).

Leading the way down the steps, Heavy Duty, enters the master cabin first. And, proceeds straight into the master bathroom of the master cabin. (Ain't got to piss),(Just pissed,...at himself).

As...

What the fuck just happened back there, at that gas station, starts to hit him. Stole a pimp's whip. After a nasty pistol whippin'!!! And, he's angry. ...At himself!

'CAUSE...

(Unc, told him to leave "THIS" life!).

AND...

(Go to Miami!).

Then...

Just like that, Heavy Duty, punches the bathroom mirror!

'Cause...

(Back to his old life, days-and-ways,...he went slippin'!)...

With thoughts weighing heavy on his mind, and the weight of Heavy Duty's body on his hands, blood from his hand runs down the bathroom sink he leans on. Head down, eyes closed, like he's prayin'. Then, raises his head and, opens his eyes, after, Gidget Cole, who's just been standing there watching him, says, "You're just like him, you know?"

And, upon opening his eyes, he looks at her and, asks, "What were you sayin'?"

"Your Uncle, Brotha Trife, you're just like him.", Gidget Cole, reaffirms.

"More than you could ever know.", Heavy Duty, confirms.

"You miss him, don't you?", asks, Gidget.

"More than you could ever know.", he replies.

"You see, it ain't so bad to reminisce over him. I know that's what got you upset earlier, up on the deck, when me and the girls were all talking about him.", Gidget Cole, consoles.

"It just hurts. That's all.", Heavy Duty, confirms.

"I know.", she reaffirms.

After a bit of thought, Duty, confides, "And you're right, G. Ain't nothin' wrong wit thinkin' 'bout the man. But, the more I think 'bout the man, the more I wanna know,...what happened to the man? Where the man is? If the man's alright? And, THAT'S the part THAT hurts, G."

(Giving Duty that "mom-look", like: *"Now-you-ought-to-know-better!"*), Gidget, replies, "Now, you need to stop wit all that. You know you're Uncle is alright. If ANY man is a survivor, THAT man is!"

"Yeeeaaahhh maaaaaaaan, you got that right! But, me and Unc, that man...that man gave a fuck. When,...so many didn't.", Nephew, tells her.

"Listen to yourself. That's life.", she states.

(NOW, lookin' at Gidget, like: *"Now-YOU-the-one-that-ought-to-know-better!!"*), Heavy Duty, lets HER know, "I KNOW that's life! You know WHO you're talkin' too, right? Maybe, YOU been sippin', on too many, Sangrias and Mai Tais, too much. EVER think of dat?!? Eatin' good! Shrimp and lobster, everything!! YOU forget Heavy Duty, used to be 360??? My dude, I used to be up in EVERYBODY'S HOOD,...sellin' that STICKY-ICKY!"

(Gidget Cole, NOW more than peeved, SNATCHES off her wig!), and, shouts at Heavy Duty, "Nigga, DO YOU forget, MY life!?!", (As, she's fed up with livin' HER life, a life UNDER...sun hats, expensive-ass wigs, and weaves!!!).

Gettin' a lil' hyped himself, yet, Duty, still explains, "THAT'S what the fuck I'M talkin' 'bout, Gidget. LIFE!!! I gots to make sure, MY PEOPLES, THEE: "MOST Triflin' Motherfucker THIS SIDE Of The Mississippi!", is alright. HE changed MY life!"

"Nigga, he changed OUR lives.", somber, Gidget Cole, replies. Then, looks away from Duty, and touches the South Beach plastic surgery repair, *of her grizzly afro puff wounds*, (while looking into - broken-shattered-master-cabin-bathroom-mirror - lines.)

Now, chilled-out, 'cause there's no need for him to get hyped, 'bout how he feels and, on what he KNOWS he's right, Heavy Duty, states, "And, that's what I'm talkin' 'bout, my dude. Life. HOW WE gon' be livin' "the life", and don't even know, if our peoples is alright??"

Coming back down, Gidget, replies, "'Cause, THAT'S the way HE wanted it. *"Go to Miami, Nephew."* Remember?? If any man a survivor, that man is. Remember? We've changed, just how he wanted it too, how he wanted US too."

"Yeeeaaahhh maaaaaaan! How could I forget??, Heavy Duty, says with a smile, *(as he reminisces over the man)*, and, then continues, "BUT, it's MY life to live. And, I ain't gon' be livin' THIS good life, IF I don't know, what happened to Unc. YOU SAW that shit out there, G. I pistol whipped that motherfucker down! What can I say,..."*Old habits die hard.".* AND, you ain't said the word *"nigga"*, SINCE you've been down here, G. *Looks like old habits die hard FOR YOU too, pimpin'!* Plus! MY Uncle, will tell you,..."*MY Nephew's hardheaded!".* And, besides, I told my Uncle, *"I got him in these streets!".* Unc, was a man of his word. And so, I gotta be a man of mines. Me and Unc, we're on some *"Death Before Dishonor",* shit!"

"So, whatchew sayin'?", Gidget, asks.

"I'm sayin', I'M finna' go weigh anchor on this-here yacht. AND GO find my Uncle!", Nephew, tells her.

Then...

(Duty, while holding his trusty pistol - *old-habits-die-hard-style* - in his bloody hand, pistol-whip-style)...

THAT...

Fickle-bitch, called: "the streets", swear fo' God, cracked a smile!

And...

As, she does…

Heavy Duty, *looks away, (from the life Unc wanted for him)* and, looks away from Gidget Cole, as well. And, looks down upon his bloody hand, holdin' bloody chrome, before, he continues to say to her, (but, more so), (for himself!), "Besides, there's someone I've been meaning to drop in on. Trust me. It's long overdue."

"I'm comin' wit you.", Gidget, immediately tells him.

"Death Before Dishonor.", Heavy Duty, lets it be known.

"Death Before Dishonor.", Gidget Cole, reaffirms.

And, then. ON that…

They both walk back up the steps, back up to the deck. And once Gidget's back on deck, she snaps her fingers, just one time. ('Cause, just one time, IS ALL it takes!). Past AND present hookers' titties stop poppin' out. Got some - best-act-right - up on that deck now. 'Cause, Gidget Cole, puts them ALL in check!

Yacht ramp and ropes, brought up in from the side.

Captain Heavy Duty, 'bout to whip this bitch up the East Coast. Takin' past and present hookers, on a time-of-their-lives-ride-of-time-and-tied. And, just fo' flava, Heavy Duty ties the laces together, of that pistol-whipped-up pimp's Jordans. Past and present hookers, Captain Heavy Duty will be escortin'. And, on what he's about to do, this Death Before Dishonor shit, Nephew never waivers.

Thinking of his Uncle, underneath that ol' El Train bridge, of the last night they did stand, Nephew smiles and, tells himself, "It AIN'T over.", then tosses those Jordans, from his hand.

And…

Gidget and Duty watch, as the laces wrap 'round the mast line, way up above the shroud. (Suspending the pimp's Jordans, above the head, OF HIS…drunken Riesling neighbor!)

As...

She looks up at the Jordans hanging on her yacht.

As...

Heavy Duty and Gidget Cole are looking down.

Then...

Duty tips his Captain's hat at her, Riesling from chalice falls to deck. And, let me tell you, the deck, ain't the ONLY thing gettin' wet! *(Old habits die hard,...what the heck:)*

As...

Ms. Take-Me-With-You, at Heavy Duty, she's steadily waving back!

Then...

Chopping blades, launches Captian Heavy Duty from the dock. Can't imagine what would be strong enough, to get in the way of, this Death Before Dishonor shit. Captain Heavy Duty gon' whip this yacht up the East Coast non-stop.

No more vibrant greens and blues.

And...

No more whitecaps.

For...

Back behind Duty's yacht, chopping blades,...cuts through an ocean of blood.

Captain Heavy Duty never looks back.

Chapter Two

ON TOP OF THE WORLD

...**M**eanwhile, as it turns, up on top, where the world turns, Bad Habitz pokes his nose up in the air, (just like, a baby seal in the ocean), trying to breathe. Just like, it's something the adorable lil' baby seal, (by watching his mama!),...just born,...just learned.

As...

Bad Habitz, lies prone. ON the ice. Covered IN TWO FEET OF blood, sea lion and, walrus fats, whale blubber, and...machine-gun-powder burns.

FOR...

Way up on the ice cap, Bad Habitz, he takes a break from all that. THEN, starts chasing baby seals, penguins, and (lest we forget!),...the arctic monkeys. And, then, gets right back...to crackin' they skulls and, splittin' they heads open! (From, the: I'm-Puttin'-This-Bitch-Over-The-Fence! - type-swings!), (of his oft-on-hand,...wooden baseball bat!).

And...

With baseball bat in one hand and, with his Tommy Gun in the other, Bad Habitz, lies back down, prone on the ice, UNDER the two feet of blood, the sea lion and, walrus fats. And, (lest we forget!)...the whale blubber! And, you know how Bad Habitz gonna DO!!!! *(The DUYU CREW cross the globe, then cross it again, DOIN' what they DO!!!!).*

FOR...

Lying prone down in that fatty-blood, Bad Habitz,...lets loose with that Tommy Gun!

And...

ALL those white feathers, AIN'T camouflaging SHIT!!

'CAUSE...

(ALL those snowy owls CAN get it too!)

And, Bad Habitz, he don't need no tire-spikes, on his bright red chopper. And, he don't need no smoke and, mirrors and, Bad Habitz don't need no motherfuckin' wires.

For...

Bad Habitz, is a: I-Can't-Believe-This-Shit-Did-I-Just-Read-This-Shit, *SEASONED*, globe trotter!!!!

'Cause...

(EVERY TIME the DUYU CREW rides out, like some tapeworms on some dookie, THEY be gettin' into some shit! And, DO some shit. Some, Not-To-Us-BUT-YOU-Type-Shit!!!! The, kind-of-type-shit, YOU,... might find spooky!)

FOR...

The HOT animal and, mammal blood, melts the snow. WHICH THEN, flows, into the Arctic Ocean! And, of ALL the blood and blubber, Bad Habitz gets on himself, (AND gets on his vintage bright red Prohibition Era-style gangster suit), well,...Bad Habitz,...rubs it in like lotion!!!!

As, for...

THIS member, OF the DUYU CREW, HE'S waging war, on top of the world. IN his bright red suit! Putting hot Tommy Gun bullets, THROUGH polar bear pelts. AND YOU KNOW, Bad Habitz, don't give a fuck, HOW,...the arctic foxes felt.

And...

FUCK THE caribous!

'CAUSE...

(THEY CAN get it too!)

FOR...

Bad Habitz, is tryin' HIS best, TO TURN, one-third, of the oceans, into the blood of a corpse. (By the time the ice cap melt).

...And meanwhile, as it turns, ALL ships of cargo and, seafaring men, (oh, you can best believe!)...THEY GONNA' LEARN!!!!

That...

Diet, IN his black Prohibition Era-style gangster suit, IS OUT, on the high seas, off the coast of some African country.

And...

He's sinking ships of cargo. (The Diet's, OWN: mass-starvation food embargo!) And, of the ships, The Diet can't make turn away, HE gladly, makes them sink and burn. Black flag flown. Of a staving skeleton, (clutching his rib bones!). MOST SHIPS, turn back. When, THAT flag is shown! And, of the, so-called-brave, seafaring men, that venture onward,...Diet sends down to Davey Jones!

...Meanwhile, as it turns, covered in sand and, dragpipe burns, on a pale colored chopper, kicking up sand, clothed in the desert, IN a pale Prohibition Era-style gangster suit, YOU KNOW, Dead Sexy DON'T give a damn! Dead Sexy, don't give a FUCK, 'bout the price, of the life, of a walrus.

FOR...

Dead Sexy's bringing DEATH TO MILLIONS!!!! STARVING, (from discounted wheat and, barley quarts for a denarius). STAY HUMBLE, 'cause Death's ridin' WITH hell. Where he's gonna show up next? DEAD SEXY WILL NEVER TELL!!!!

For...

You ARE dust.

AND...

(To dust,...y'all SHALL return!)

FOR...

Dead Sexy's BURYING MILLIONS, out in the hot-ass desert, PACKED IN TIGHT, with other motherfuckers...in tiny brass urns.

...And meanwhile, as it turns, Pockets, sits behind a large red mahogany executive desk, and working on new hustles. Of which, the unhip, GONNA' pay the price. AND, of which, THAT OF your feelings, Pockets...has of absolutely NO concerns!

FOR...

Business is business.

AND...

Of the music industry, y'all...'BOUT TO bear witness!

For...

Grapes get mashed, JUST LIKE, your hopes and your dreams. (The music biz DON'T need you!).

For...

YOU'LL get burned and, discarded LIKE trash!

WHERE...

ALL the others before you, hopes and dreams,...churn.

'CAUSE...

There will ALWAYS be another, hopeful, ill-informed artist, (with the stars in their eyes),...WILLING to take THEIR turn!

And so, up in his billion-dollar-view corner office, on the top floor of the music industry titan building of Jettison Records, Pockets, busies himself with his business of, working on new hustles. For, Pockets takes in the billion-dollar-view of downtown Atlanta, like he takes in new artists, with NO appreciation of, the hard work of the creator's creations. And so, in his all red everythang office, Pockets, the CEO, and Managing Partner of, Jettison Records, takes a break, from his conniving-ways. (Then, cocks his custom red custom-made red hat, hard to the side...*just like in the old days!)* And, he looks cross his red mahogany desk and, cross his plush red carpet on the floor. As he, looks up at the flat screen television, mounted on his all red everythang office wall, right next to, his red bathroom door. And, he looks at the breaking news reports, coming in, from ALL cross the world. (Of blood washing-up on the sands of the sea, beaches and, the shores!!!!). And, he just sits back in his throne, of a high back red tufted leather upholstered executive desk chair and, turns up the volume. So, that he can listen to, of what, each news anchor from cross the world, influences us to do...and think. (About seas of red waves).

"AYO!!! Do you see THIS shit!?!", Pretty High, shouts at Pockets, as he comes kickin' in Pockets' red office door, entering from his adjoining billion-dollar-view office. (Wherein, Pretty High, AIN'T been buying into, the mass media report, of the seas, of the blood, of a corpse).

"WHAT I TELL YOU 'BOUT KNOCKIN'?!?" I coulda' been *"auditioning"* a new artist, RIGHT ON TOP, of this fine, illegally-harvested and, imported-Peruvian, red mahogany desk of mine!!", Pockets, PROUDLY boasts,....*(of BOTH, conquests!!)*.

"Yeah, yeah, yeah. WE BOTH know, THAT'S *hoagie oil,* ALL OVER your desk calendar! But, ayo, do you see this shit?? AND, on EVERY television channel at that! MY BOYS, are havin', ALL the FUN!!!! And, I'M stuck in some office! IN some office building! LISTENING TO FUCKIN' DEMOS!!!", Pretty High, lets Pockets know, disgusted, pointing at the TV. (KNOWING the DUYU CREW are out there just TEARING UP SHIT!!!!).

(Speaking on and, with, the voice of reason, *for reasons, Pockets, has NO problems with, justifying in HIS mind. For, the reasons of HIS mind's reasoning, are, the ONLY ONES that matter, in HIS mind!*). And, so, Pockets, so reasons, "NOT just SOME office building, Pretty High. THEE, office building. And, NOT JUST some office, YOU on the top floor, CORNER OFFICE, of Jettison Records. YOU ON TOP OF THE WORLD!!! Yeah, so, well, anyways, Pretty High,...you on a mission to conquer the world, ain't ya'? WELL, what better way to do it...than through music?", Pockets, replies, smilin' all sly.

"Ayo, I know what it's hittin' for.", Pretty High, replies. (Then, looks at the TV screen and, then looks down at his pristine, all-white, Prohibition Era-style vintage gangster suit), and, says, "I'M just used to something more, um,..."*INVOLVED*"."

"OH, so, so, YOU want to get MORE involved, huh? THAT'S WHAT I'M TALKIN' 'BOUT! SHOW SOME DAMN INITIATIVE!! Well, YOU'RE in luck! I got JUST THE THING for you!", Pockets, lets it be known.

"Ayo, so, what the fuck is it?? 'Cause, I AIN'T tryna' be sittin' behind some desk ALL mutha' fuckin' day, Pockets. ...Ayo, I'm 'bout ready to go break Too Cold out of that FUCKIN' bank vault! AND, just go WILD-THA'-FUCK out!!!!", Pretty High, replies.

"HEY! HEY!! HEY!!! NOW, you're just talkin' crazy!!!! OR,...did you forget?? Ma'Ma's STILL in that bank vault prison cell WITH him!!", Pockets,...reasons.

"AYO!!! I know. Fuck THAT shit!!", Pretty High, replies, (coming to his senses!).

"Listen, Pretty High, I just signed these two rappers. Yeah, so, well, anyways, I've been "grooming" them,...so to speak. OH SHIT, YEAH, you just gonna LOVE this shit! AND, I just signed, this YOUNG girl. And, she's got ALL THE TALENT in the world,...but, MAN,...is she

EVER lost. Yeah, so, well, anywaaaaaays, THAT'S where I come in!", Pockets,...reasons.

"Ayo! So, WHERE tha' fuck DO I come in, wit all this?!?", inquires, Pretty High.

Pockets, leans way back in his high back red tufted leather upholstered throne, cocks his custom red custom-made red hat hard to the side, just one of many custom red custom-made red hats that he owns. And then, Pockets, looks up from under that custom red tilted-brim, concealing most of his eyes, before Pockets lets it be known, as he replies, "Back up north, in Pa., I'm finalizing plans. I'm planning-out a dual, debut-concert, slash, meet and greet. Yeah, so, well, anyways, it's for the fans. You know, so, the fans can get to love my new artists. It's my plan, and, it's my intentions, to have and allow, the fans, to get up-close-and-personal, with my new artists. It's my plan, to REMOVE that "veil", which separates the fans from the artists. Yeah, so, well, anyways, I want to allow the fans, to JOIN IN and, to BE APART OF, THE WHOLE EXPERIENCE!!! Yeah, so, well, anyways, I got some business up there, in Pa., don't worry 'bout it. So, I'll be hittin' the highway, with my three newly-acquired artists. You know, givin' them a taste of the life. It's my plan, to see, if my three new artists, CAN hack it on the road. As it turns, Pretty High, the two rappers, that I, JUST SO HAPPENED TO HAVE SIGNED, just so happen to be, FROM Pa. Yeah, so, well, anyways, I'm headed back up to Pennsylvania, I got business and, you know, things to handle up there. Don't worry 'bout it. But, while I'm up there, I'll be looking for a smaller, how can I say, a more, INTIMATE venue...something of tight quarters. Yeah, so, well, anyways, it's for the fans. I, uh, I really want the fans to be apart of it all. 'Cause, THAT'S JUST the kinda' guy I am! And so, Pretty High, while I'm up there on business, I'll be settin' up their concert and, the meet and greet, you know, debuting my three new artists and, yeah, so, well, anywaaaaaays...creating a buzz. Killing two birds, with one stone, so to speak."

"Ahhhh, "creating" a buzz. Ayo, got it.", Pretty High, replies, with his pristine white suspenders outstretched tight, before lettin' 'em fly, back to the chest, of his, pristine white, Prohibition Era-style vintage gangster suit shirt, KNOWIN' he's 'bout to get back to THAT work! (That very same work, AS TO why, *HE WAS PLACED HERE*, ON this earth!!!!).

"That's good. And, by the way, Pretty High, good work by you. That demo, you know, the one you told me to give a listen to? Well, I did. NOT for long, mind you,...but, I did.", Pockets, informs.

"AYO!!!! You TELLIN' me, you actually SIGNED MC Busta-Nut and False Profit??", asks, Pretty High.

(Raising his right index finger while, motioning for Pretty High to provide him with a moment, Pockets, then presses the Intracom button on his Jettison Records Executive Desk Telephone, summoning, Pockets' very own, Jettison Records, music industry, EXECUTIVE, "Personal" Assistant), "Phillip. My files. BRING THEM TO ME!!!", Pockets, demands!

"I got you.", Phillip, replies, (through the Intracom of The-Jettison-Records-Access-Only-Communications-System).

And, before Pockets can EVEN take his finger, off of the Access-Only-Intracom button, enters, Phillip Tate. ("Personal" Assistant Extraordinaire!), "I got you.", Phillip, announces, while placing said demanded files, right down on top of, (AND IN), Pockets', Executive Desk's calendar's..."HOAGIE" OILS. (Oy vey).

"Thank you, Phillip. YOU, may go now.", permission granted, by Pockets.

BUT...

BEFORE Phillip CAN leave, Pretty High, takes ahold, of the white suspenders, of his white Prohibition Era-style gangster suit. And then, he pulls them, far-outstretched, and tight. And then, lets them, sail-back hard, against his chest, as he, lets those vintage white suspenders fly. And then, Pretty High, tilts up the brim, of his, white Prohibition Era-style vintage gangster hat. And so, and so as, (and to MAKE damn sure!), THAT, Phillip Tate CAN ensure, THAT, he's seen WHILE being seen. While, Pretty High, is giving him the once-over. *(As it turns, Pretty High, HAS seen, Phillip Tate around this titan of a building of Jettison Records and, has seen him plenty).* *(However, as it turns, Phillip, is just about the ONLY person, that Pretty High has seen around this, titan of a, newly-built, state-of-the-art building!).* HOWEVER, Pretty High, loves to let, Phillip Tate, exactly know, where PRETTY HIGH believes PHILLIP TATE stands in the pecking-order. And so, Pretty High, does so give, Phillip, a hard look. And he does it, while he does it, nice and slow and smooth. As Pretty High does so, grillin' and mean-muggin' Phillip Tate, from Phillip's eyes on down, to Phillip's black Florsheim shoes. And then, mugs Phillip, on back on up, to Phillip's black dress pants. And, then moves right on along on up to, Phillip's red neck tie. Of which, Phillip's red necktie, all-over, is patterned with, tiny black rowing oars. As it turns, of which is, clipped to Phillip's white dress shirt, by a 24 karat gold tie clip. Of which of Phillip's, his tie clip, is made from 24 karat gold and, displays an open door. And so, and so then, Pretty High gots to make damn sure, that he ain't even tryin' to be Phillip's friend. And so then, glares at Phillip's black with red oars silk pocket square. Of which, is folded of three stairs. And so, and so then, Pretty High, REMOVES Phillip's pocket square, from the left breast pocket of Phillip's black sport coat, wipes his own brow with it, sweaty from the brim of his white Prohibition Era-style gangster hat, and then, announces to Phillip Tate, "Whew, you have a tough job!" And then, Pretty High, refolds Phillip's pocket square into a four peak fold. Just like that of his own. AND, that of which, of all four of which, the DUYU CREW riders' pocket squares, in their Prohibition Era-style vintage gangster suits, are shown. And then, Pretty High, stuffs that four fold pocket square, back into the left breast pocket of Phillip Tate's black sports coat. And then, Pretty High, tilts the brim back down on his white Prohibition Era-style gangster hat and, informs Phillip, "Ayo. YOU don't know what work is. WE don't leave no hope."

And so...

While all of this is going on, (the fuckery of Phillip), Pockets, he just sits there, like he doesn't even care. ('Cause, he don't!). And, besides all that, Phillip, has been disposed of, anyway. (So, what the fuck are you still doin' in my office?!?). THAT shitz on you! ...Motherfucker.

Phillip, always an uneasy one around Pretty High, *(and, for more than one good reason!).*

For...

The ease of which Pretty High can cause Phillip Tate to become uneasy, IS the reason, in for which, (AND subconsciously!), WHICH CAUSES, Phillip, to begin, OUT OF the blue, his nervous whistling!

And so...

Having been disposed of by Pockets, Phillip Tate, exits Pockets' all red everythang office.

And...

Heads on back down the hall. Just to be, (for his sole purpose in life!), IS to be, AT Pockets',...beck and call.

AND...

Phillip, makes himself readily available, to be, at Pockets' disposal.

FOR...

(Future disposals!)

"He ain't no Headslap.", Pretty High, declares, to Pockets, (while laughing at Phillip Tate, while Phillip Tate leaves),...(while nervously whistling!).

"No,...he ain't.", Pockets, replies, (big money kills off loyalty like a disease).

Quickly disposing of the *memory of Headslap*, Pockets, refreshens his memory, by opening the file on his desk and, upon tracing down the papers therein (with his index finger), so, then informs, Pretty High, that, "To answer your earlier question. Yes, it's MC Busta-Nut and False Profit. Those are my two newly-signed rappers."

"AYO!!!! You gettin' UP there, Pockets! YOU AIN'T even remember their names!", Pretty High, laughs, (and, then, becomes very serious, which is rare-territory for Pretty High!), as he, says, "But, ayo, Pockets,... MC Busta-Nut??? I hope, you DON'T plan on makin' ANY money, WIT THAT DRUNK-MOTHERFUCKER!!! ALL, HE DO, IS GET DRUNK, SIP "LEAN", SNORT-UP EVERYBODY'S SHIT, AND SMOKE BLUNTS!!!!"

Closing the file, (AND the conversation!), Pockets, leans back in his high back red tufted leather upholstered throne, cocks his custom red custom-made red hat hard to the side, looks cross his red mahogany executive desk and, then, he tells, Pretty High, his ONE AND ONLY reason, (for, in which, HE reasoned!), in his OWN mind, FOR the reason, OF the signing, of the two newly-signed rappers, "They're marketable."

Chapter Three

BRAIN TUMOR

...Meanwhile, down below, in the under the ground levels, of this newly-built, state-of-the-art building of Jettison Records, of which, a titan building, in that which, appears to be made solely of glass, from the exterior. The, we'll-see-you-first-and-know-who-you-are building, is actually, heavily-comprised of, two-sided mirrors. For so, that of those, on the outside, for so, that of those, on the inside, for so, for that, for them, it becomes the interior. The mirrored-building, of: "Don't-Call-Us-We'll-Call-You!" is, heavily-comprised of, armed guards at the doors. (AND, at the building's perimeter!). For so, for that, for them, TO SO, ENSURE, that not just ANYONE...can come in. SOLELY BY INVITATION AND APPOINTMENT ONLY, with secret handshakes, symbols and, verbage...to keep out the phoney.

For...

Inside of THIS building AND, inside of THIS industry, THERE'S NO SUCH THING...as a crony. *(Get promised the world)*...(Left eatin' bologna!)

For...

If you're in, you're IN. And, if you ain't,...YOU AIN'T!!!

AND...

(YOU CAN stick your loyalties,...JUST south of your 'taint!!)

For...

In THIS industry, if you think you got a confidant? (I think not!). MORE LIKE steal your ideas. FOR, they DON'T plan. (They plot!)... (WITH - nefarious-vigor - OF your dreams and hard work's - burial spot!). YOU, are JUST a pebble, masoned, IN the bottom steps, made of stone. (THE VERY SAME, of which, are keeping them, THE RICH... right where they are). AND THEY, only let up, a select chosen-few. Of which, the very same, *that which, were NEVER made or, meant* for you. (That being, AT the top...of THOSE stepping stones). The very same ones that, you and your broke pockets, ARE NOW AND, forever masoned. (EDUCATE YOURSELVES to the music industry and, your steps,...never hasten).

Hmm...

Strange, you NEVER SEE the men WITH,...the strange nicknames. (The newly-built building of Jettison Records is practically always empty). So, it always practically looks the same!

BUT...

You CAN find 'em! Waaaaaay out on the horizon. And then,...look vertically. *(The Unseen Powers: A Silent-Flight Entity.)*

For...

They hold the control bar of the whole entire world. (And that too of, the whole entirety of...The Music Industry.)

...And so, in the under the ground levels, down below,...are the *stolen.* WHERE, the stolen AND, the exiled, *OF: "Are-No-Longer-Of-Use",* (and/or, of whom), *became, TOO: "Threateningly: 'We-Must-Do-Something-ABOUT-This!' - Influential"*...do so, "exist". And, do so exist, for, the remainder of, their: "This-is-no-longer-working-for-US!" - days, on this planet. Though, you do hear cries. It's a *FAR cry* from, *that world tour life*, that these stolen and stashed in the under-the-ground-levels of Jettison Records, *had known*. (That: *city-to-far-away-from-their-roots'-city tour life*),...*when they used to electrify a live show, of full capacity.*

(I heard he was seen in Cuba. I heard that he ain't dead. Nah, I seen his autopsy photo online,...SO IT'S GOTTA' BE TRUE!!! I saw the pic for myself online, SO HE'S GOTTA' be dead. It sure looked like his tattoos! *With that, "Y" incision of split dark skin, in so, in the skin. Displaying, a layer of contrasting white body fat. Split. 'Cross his chest and running down his stomach)...(WITH HIS FACE PULLED RIGHT DOWN OFF OF HIS HEAD!!!)*

And so...

Down below, in the lower levels...hey, WELL, at least it's really nice down here! In the lower under the ground levels of Jettison Records, (YOU BETTER!), learn to like it!

FOR...

YOU have no voice in your choice. (YOU'RE GONNA' BE down here,...year after year).

(Have no fear? IT DON'T MATTER IF YOU DO!!!)

For...

The string pullers are now in charge of your complete control...*ever since they chose you. (Chose you, based on the naivete, of, YOUR:..."eager-modability")*. And now. Look at you!

For...

YOU,...allowed them too! They brought you into this life. THIS music industry life! (Trust me, if they didn't want you in, you wouldn't be. And now, YOU CAN'T get out!).

And...

(Of all, The: Artistically-Super-Powers, that, *gained TOO MUCH power*, OF the ear?)...

WELL...

The: "Pullers' Of The Strings" WILL,...cut short your career!!!!

EXTRA!!! EXTRA!!! READ ALL ABOUT IT!!!

From RIGHT DOWN IN there. In the lower under the ground levels. You can READ all about it. *OF HOW, your album sales...went vertical.* (Just like, the vertical strings, on that control bar). And, it's all because, you as an artist *WERE*, and have, *AFTER "death"*...become too endeared.

WHICH...

IS the string pullers, number one fear. And...so, now...YOU'RE down here.

(LEARN to like it!)

'Cause...

In the lower under the ground levels, of Jettison Records, IS forever more...where you're going to exist. Year after year. And so, in death, unbeknownst to the world and the rest, you'll exist for the rest of your life, in the lower under the ground levels, I'm sad to report, at the bottom levels of this, Jettison Records resort.

And so, down below...

(It's a regular - who's-who-who-dunnit-off-the-charts-off-the-grid-off-the-meter, just nutt'd my pants, of every conspiracy theorists' murder mystery dinner theater!)

The lower levels of the underground are equipped with bowling alleys and, theater seating of, virtual reality. *(So, that you, can see the lucky stars and, feel the outside world).*

However...

(And, unfortunately), YOU AIN'T FREE!

BUT...

(Hey,...you're free of rent!)

AND...

YOU'LL be provided with, private A-List celebrity chefs (and, all the other fine accoutrements!).

Still want this life?? Still WILLING to roll the dice??? WELL, come take a look, there's more...

And so, right down below, right down in the lower levels of the underground, IN THIS VERY BUILDING of, Jettison Records...LIVES THE ONE!!! (And, many more of, "THE ONE", of many more). As they do, so live. (RIGHT HERE!!!). Right down in the lower under the ground levels, of this very titan of a building of, Jettison Records. But,... NAAAAAAH!!! You wouldn't BELIEVE THIS shit, that, THE ONE, *with the swivel hips*, is rock 'n a gray pompadour? AND, you probably wouldn't buy it, that this ONE over there, *once gleaned TOO MUCH POWER of the tongue. And so, was subsequently, shot through the lung!, (When bullets came through his car door).* AND, OH LOOK!!! Through that other ONE's borough, (you know the one!), THAT borough OF the brave. *In which, the mass news media broadcasted straight from, as they did so document that, long-flowered-procession of a funeral motorcade.* And, take a look at that ONE, THE ONE, "some", would have you believe, *committed suicide...with a shotgun.* BUT, never-not-once, was any ONE of 'um, *ACTUALLY...ever seen dead. But, Y'ALL just drank the Kool-Aid! (Of what, the mass media, had to say!!!).* BEFORE, each ONE of THE ONES, if they ever even really were, *were even really ever...placed down in the grave.*

(But they gotta be dead, it's all over the internet!)...(AND HEY, after all, it's what the mass news media said!)

SOOOOOO...

They GOTTA' BE dead!!! ...(right?).

(But, wait,...there's more. RIGHT DOWN HERE, IN the underground of the, Jettison Records', lower levels. More exist, forever more). Come take a look...

For, it's THE ONE, THAT - *NO-LONGER-even-looked-like-the-same-person-THE-LONGER-he-stayed-in-the-music-industry* - WHO's, personal doctor, *gave him too much, of the wrong stuff!* And, as FATE would have it, that ONE over there, who's name I can't even type or pronounce...*died of the SAME "causes"*...sho' nuff! And you know why he changed his name. (That's not a question. That's a statement!) For, so do I. I know it too! But, as for me, WELL, I read it on the internet. AND, I heard it reported by the mass media,...SO, SO, SO, IT'S GOTTA' BE TRUE!!! Know what I'm sayin'. (NOT a question. ANOTHER statement!) Really?? You want me to believe that, that ONE over there...*choked...in his sleep???* And, you'd lead me to believe, that, that ONE over there, *whom, played soccer every day of his life and, smoked ganja all day* and, (you know what THAT HELPS to fight!) and that, *at the ripe, old age of 33,* you would lead me to believe, that he *died from cancer of...his feet???* (Or perhaps it was the age of 36?)...(According to the scriptures of certain documents). And it's always a mystery. The mega stars of music, if they're alive? How they died? *Of drugs? Murder? Or if, they actually did commit...suicide?* OF WHICH, TO WIT, continues to be...a very long history, OF, AND IN AND, ALL THROUGH...The Music Industry.

But none of this could be possible. ...(right?) But wait...there's more... for...

...down in the under the ground levels, of Jettison Records. Of the underground, you remember, where they have theater seating of virtual reality and the, *you - shoulda-stayed-in-your-lane* - bowling alleys? But wait, there's more. Come take a look...

The List of 27? More, like: The List Of 27-Ways To *Pull The Wool* Over The World's Eyes! *Candlelight vigils in parks. Stuffed animals and balloons tied. To and placed, in front of the gates.* (Of untimely death star's estates). And, of course, *they all went to Heaven!* 'Cause, no one could possibly really believe. All. This. Conspiracy. Shit.

But...but...but...but...AIN'T THAT???

Naaaaaah! It COULDN'T be!! It's GOTTA' BE a dream! Of, two long-gone rappers!! And between them there ain't no beef!! And

THEY'RE NOT rollin' a blunt. BUT, THEY'RE rollin' 'n ballin' n' hoopin' 'n hollerin'. Sharin' a laugh. N' talkin' shit. Over two last-men-standing bowling pins, (like the East and West Coast), on opposite ends. Of a 7 - 10 split.

And, RIGHT DOWN THERE with them, *the definitive - robotic-lackin'-compassion - words* of a doctor, *in Robocall-speech,* CAN be heard, by the dreamer, (each time, he rises up, through the white sheet)...

And so, right down there with them, down below...

In the lower levels of the underground, in the under the ground levels of Jettison Records, in a cold, floor-tiled, long hallway, made of white jade, along an emerald tiled-wall, Trife, rests on his back.

Covered under a white sheet, under the protection of Pockets, removed from resting on his gurney, from resting in his own private room, to now, resting on that same gurney, in that same cold hallway, the one, with the floor, tiled of white jade, and he does so, resting, along the black protective wallguard-rail protecting the white grout and emerald tiles. Trife rests. And does so rest. Covered under a white sheet. And under the protection of Pockets...but he doesn't know it yet. And...he AIN'T resting. For something's going on. *(BEEN GOIN' ON!!!).* But he don't know it yet. And God help you all if he ever fig'a's-it-all-the-fuck-out. Real shit.

For, he's no longer resting. And, Trife's no longer hooked-up to all those wires and shit. For, the intubation tube, was removed, from Trife. (When, he was removed from his own private room). For, in that cold hallway, *the - coldhearted, pre-practiced, detached, robotic-doctor-jargon-speech in, the - Robocall, pre-recorded, harassment-lines - of, what Trife THINKS,* a doctor would have said, lets Trife know, for a second time now...that he's brain-dead.

And he can see it all, when he passes through that white sheet that covers him head-to-toe on that gurney, *and he can see it all,* from out in that hall. *Every speck of texture in the white grout, the floor and the wall tiles, of the long cold hallway, made of emeralds and white jade.* As he hovers there, by the drop ceiling. And, each time he hears the words *IN HIS HEAD,* that he's brain-dead, after which, each time, through that white sheet, his spirit passes, up through and, comes out.

And just like that. He's right back in his body. And once again, Trife don't see nobody. *And then here comes that, now familiar, Robocall-doctor-voice*, not even trying to rescue him. That voice is just there, just to let him know, that he has died, now for a third time, and that he's brain-dead.

"Wha-e-rrr lou-sing-g ha-em. O-kay, tha-at's it. Ha-e's brah-aind duh-ed.", (the words Trife hears again for a third time now), ain't nobody rushing around, ain't no "Code Blue's", they gave up on him, didn't even try to save him, IS WHAT he's thinking. No wonder the floor tiles of white jade are scuff free, 'cause there ain't no stampede. (Of nurses and doctors running down that emerald hall, trying to revive THE ONE that used to appall). That being. THE ONE AND ONLY: MOST Triflin' Motherfucker THIS Side Of The Mississippi!!!

And he can see it all, from hovering up by that drop ceiling in that emerald hall. As he looks back down, and sees, *the form of his body*. (Laying there on his back). Laying there on that gurney. Under that white sheet. And Trife, *does so think*, hovering UP BY that drop ceiling, *"I would swear THAT'S my two favorite rappers of all-times! RIGHT OVER THERE, in a bowling tourney. Hmm...behind locked closed doors with armed guards!!"*

And then just like that, he's right back, under that white sheet.

But he ain't brain-dead, maybe it was all a dream, 'cause he rolls over onto his stomach, with his head laid to his right side. On that gurney. And under that white sheet.

And now, Trife's paralyzed.

AS HE sleeps, with the left side of his face on that gurney. (Head laid to his right side). *"Damn! WHAT was that!?!"*, Trife, thinks to himself. (AFTER what in his head, *he KNOWS he JUST FELT!*).

Trife, from under, that stuck, anxiety-laden, sleep-paralysis-feeling. And, from under the force of paralyzing gravity. And, from under that white sheet. And, from laying on his stomach, on top of that gurney. And, from under the right side of his skull, from overtop of the right side of his brain, *Trife, just felt an explosion*. Not a painful explosion.

But...

(An explosion nonetheless).

And, as Trife lays there, potentially stuck, he tries to artificially imagine, of what the fuck, just happened. For, there's an area, under the right side of his skull and, right atop of the right side of his brain, a cavity of sorts, (subdural is the name). And, in THAT space, what Trife felt, WAS an explosion. And then, what HE FELT was, *the flutter of...warm air escaping.* (But, there's no escaping, for Trife!) AS HE, continues to lay there, stuck, sleep-paralysis-frozen.

"I have a brain tumor! AND FUCK ANY HACK DOCTOR THAT DOESN'T BELIEVE ME!!!", Trife, says to himself, *(with ALL certainty!!!).*

And as Trife lays there. Stuck. He tries to budge. But with no luck. And, as he lays there, stuck, he is fully aware, of his - known-and-familiar - senses, telling him, that, "This is what being in a deep-sleep feels like." However and though, Trife does not feel his eyes, twitch from side-to-side, of and from, deep REM sleep, which he has felt before, but that aside, Trife is aware, that he is aware, OF being aware, OF being awake, WHILE being asleep, of and from and being in, a deep sleep. And, Trife CAN'T move, stuck, nor open his eyes, stuck, no matter how hard he tries, stuck. While & And, paralysis-applied-sleep applies, MORE of its *centrifugal force,* down upon him. (JUST to KEEP HIM there!) Laying there!! STUCK LIKE THAT!!! (JUST...to push out the panic). WHICH it does! Which CAUSES, that SICKENING, *I-can-beat-this-but-I-haven't-been-able-to-do-it-yet,* sleep-paralysis-PANIC, to kick in on him. And, Trife can feel himself laying there and, he can feel the left side of his face stuck to that gurney and, Trife can feel that gurney stuck to his stomach, I'm gonna try to move again, mother fuck it. But, Trife failed to force, himself to beat the powerful force, of sleep paralysis' *centrifugal force,* and is forced to remain forced, to lay helplessly stuck to that gurney, *by, at and in, the mercy* of sleep paralysis' *unmerciless centrifugal force.*

BUT...

AS he does so lay there, *stuck,* as he, (beez and remainz), *forced to stay forced,* to lay there, *stuck,* in that emerald hallway, Trife, HAS NOW become, very much consciously aware of, the power he has been granted. Granted by himself. *(Granted FOR himself!).* THAT BEING, of said *"self-*

granted-power", of such, to grant himself the power, of and by, himself granting himself, through what he believes, just may be, that of his...*third eye vision.* (And as such, THAT BEING, *the ability* to provide himself, *with the vision* OF himself, *by, at, and from,* the *ability* to *look down upon his paralyzed body, from up by that damn drop ceiling.)*

And all the while, Trife DOES SO NOT KNOWING, THAT, from on top of that tiled-floor of white jade, from laying on top of that gurney, from under that white sheet, from just above his brain, from just beneath his skull, *IF he,* in fact, just had, *a brain tumor or an aneurysm explode?!?* Explode. *Just above his brain.* Explode. *Just beneath his skull.* And, of such, Trife is able, and does so, analyze ALL of this, *from under that helpless-panic* of being *matted-down* TO THAT GURNEY...by sleep paralysis' *centrifugal force.*

But. What he does know, is. As he lays there, unable to move. *Stuck.* Though, he's TRYING to move. *Stuck.* Though, HE KNOWS it's from, sleep-paralysis. *Stuck.* But, as he lays there, *stuck, stuck behind the darkness of his eyelids, HE KNOWS* that *he's watching himself, sleeping in his paralyzed body. From up by that damn drop ceiling!*

And, Trife *knows he knows in his mind,* though, not from or due, to this present moment in time, though, *from when he left his body. Not once. Not twice.* (BUT, from a third time, now!). *FROM, being informed, BY a robotic-voice, that, he was brain-dead.* Which, just may all have been, all from, *while he was, (all up and) in, a deep-sleep, of and from, an REM dream.*

"But, this MUST BE from third eye vision.", as, he tells himself, (from that *inner-voice* in his head). The head of which, is *stuck* to that gurney. The head of which, *THAT HEARD,* (but is now, devoid of), that: *robotic - Robocall-doctor - voice.* The head of which, *is filled,* with: *I'M-PARALYZED-PANIC.* (From *being* panic-stricken), (from being under the white sheet). *"You realize that you CAN see yourself.",* from, the *inner-voice* in his head, *(he heard himself say).* NOW realizing, that, HE HAS... *third eye vision.* (MOTHERFUCKIN' OY VEY!!!)

And over the ricochet sounds of an East Coast West Coast 7 - 10 split, Trife, DISTINCTLY hears the laughter of his favorite rapper. *(The laughter from the rapper from his songs and his movies, that, Trife, will never forget).* And does so, and is able too, *feeling the power FROM that feel-good-laughter,* Trife, *feels* that his body, is able to power out from under the sleep paralysis, *FINDING* the power IN himself, *FROM the power IN his favorite rapper's - CAN'T-help-BUT-FEEL-that-same-way - laughter,* TO power out FROM UNDER sleep's POWERFUL paralysis-*applied centrifugal force.* And he rips the white sheet, (of which covered his head, body and feet). Then balls and tosses it, which drapes over when it lands on the Jettison Records Access-Only Emerald Hall of White Jade Security Camera, above his gurney bed. And he tries to speak, but that intubation tube was placed deep, and where the fuck am I anyway, *third eye vision* was clearer than his current vision, *from who-knows-how-long I was asleep?* But. What he does know, is. They, whoever the fuck they are, gonna need a motherfucking army, if in this building the plot on him was to keep! And so, shit kicking back in, though, he ain't familiar with his current surroundings. And can't see more than just a blur, and though his throat is jacked, and he can't even say a word. It ain't where you're from, it's how you move! And, damn. Familiarity of his silent steps, I must be wearing my steel-toe-removed black biker boots, 'cause I'm creepin' smooth. Though many long-term memories of his memory slips him, the short-term memory of his *third eye vision surroundings* is still with him, as *self-preservation begins* to kick in, Trife begins the movements of slippin'. In and out of town like consciousness, moving like a ninja and leaving no fingerprints. Be. Become. And remain. Silent as the wind through a chain-link fence. To do what I do when I do it: Vanish Like Smoke From Nigerian Incense. And for some reason, Trife's thinking, that he *should just listen for the sounds.* And that's how I'm gonna break the hell out, though, I don't know it or how, that of, the lower levels of the Jettison Records underground.

Chapter Four

THREE TEARS

...Meanwhile, DURING an "audition", (THAT AIN'T hoagie juice IS the point YOU'RE missin'!), a billion-dollar-view IS IN full view, WHEN Pockets' red office door, ONCE AGAIN gets kicked open!

"Do you see this shit!?!", is what, Pockets hears, from all-up-under, from all-up-in, from all-up-on top of his fine red mahogany executive's desk calendar. All, right in the middle of his "audition".

"WHAT I TELL YOU 'BOUT KNOCKIN' FIRST?!?", Pockets, hammers out, (NOT missing a beat!).

"I got you.", Phillip Tate, replies.

('Bout to flip out, Pockets, slips out, backing out, then, slips back on his custom red custom-made red briefs, to briefly, flip the fuck out!)...

"WHAT!?!", Pockets,...releases explosively. (Oy Vey).

"Do you see this shit on every security camera??", asks, Phillip Tate.

(Blood pressure subsiding, from his previously, er, um...elevated-state). With it now, just sinking in, that, THAT IT WASN'T Pretty High, kicking in his red office door. (BUT, that, of Phillip Tate!)...('CAUSE, Pockets, failed to hear that cowbell-whistle)...('Cause, he was all-up-in the middle of his "audition"...rough like gristle!), "Wait? What?? Security cameras???, Pockets, begins, "NO, I wasn't lookin' at no-damn security cameras! THAT'S, what MY "Head of Security" IS for!!! I was in the, er, um, middle of a "fucking audition"!! ...Phillllllip? WHERE. THE. FUCK. IS. PRETTY HIGH??? AND!!! What's tha' mutha' fuckin' goings-on is?!?"

(Briefly checking the security camera cluster-monitor, posted-up-on, his red office wall), Pockets, questions, Phillip Tate, "All over,...WHAT cameras?? THAT camera, there??? It's just showing all-white,...must be a malfunction. It's just on that camera, NOT on EVERY camera. Phillip, get Pretty High to take care of that for me, huh?"

"I got you.", Phillip Tate, replies, before looking over at, The: Will-do-ANYTHING-to-get-my-big-break-into-the-music-biz - full-of-hopes-and-dreams - Artist, (and-GOT-full-OF-more-than-what-she-hoped-or-dreamt-for!), before, he then, looks back at Pockets, before, he begins, his nervous-whistling, before, he then, continues, "HOWEVER, sir, the camera IS functioning just fine. What it is you're seeing, on your security-cluster-monitor, IS a white sheet, THAT'S covering the camera...the security camera from The White Jade Hall, sir."

"Camera from the white jade hall? A sheet? So, GO remove it.", Pockets, simply states.

Looking back at, The: I-KNOW-I'll-get-signed-after-THIS-"audition" - Singer, (as, she's CONTENT to remain, ALL-splayed-out, all-up-on... Pockets' desk!), Phillip, then looks at Pockets and, says, "Sir, if we could only speak in private,...that white sheet is the least of our concerns." (And then, after some more nervous-whistling, Phillip Tate, whistles some more!), BEFORE, he continues, "The White Jade Hall, sir. ...With emeralds, sir."

"Ooooooooooo! Emeralds AND white jade! Yaaaaaass!! THAT sounds exotic and sex-say!!!", the "auditionee", would say.

"SHUT THA' FUCK UP, BITCH!!!", Pockets, would say to the "auditionee", (then, continuing back to Phillip), "OH!!! Oh. Oh. Oh. A white sheet IS COVERING a camera IN The White Jade Hallway! ...I see. Have Pretty High go down there and comb the halls, I want my "Head of Security" to take care of that...personally."

"I got you. HOWEVER, sir, Pretty High took off. As did, C. Trife, as you have grown fond of, referring to him as. THAT'S...C. Trife's white sheet covering the camera.", Phillip Tate, bears the bad news. (Then, wipes his own brow bare of sweat,...with his four-fold-pocket-square!).

"BRING HIM TO ME!!!", Pockets, demands!

"I got you. But,...WHO, sir? Pretty High or C. Trife??", Phillip Tate, asks, reluctantly, then, BEGINS TO subconsciously-whistle-out, a: no-name-tune (OUT OF NERVES!!!), (THAT, he, nor ANYONE ELSE, has EVER heard!).

"GET THE FUCK OUTTA' MY OFFICE!!!", Pockets, demands!

"Ooooooooooooooo! Say, sex-say, can I stay?, the "auditionee", would say.

"Phillip.", says, Pockets, simply, (as he, simply cocks his custom red custom-made red hat hard to the side).

AND SO...

AS, Phillip Tate, drags the "auditionee" by her bare-ass feet, bare-ass naked, kicking-and-screaming, DOWN OFF OF Pockets' fine red mahogany wood, right on down to and cross, Pockets' plush red executive office carpet, then promptly, in all one motion, *(as if Phillip has done this before!),* right on out the office and down the hall, the "auditionee's" fingernails would claw, the slick black onxy floor tile, beggin', screamin', cryin' n' pleadin', all the way down, The: On-Top-Of-The-World - Executive Hall. (Can I get a yes, yes, y'all?)...(SOMEBODY SCREAM!!!). Blood from the flesh, of the tips, of her fingers, would stain the black onyx white tile grout.

AND...

(THAT'S HOW, her introduction into a major record label began AND, career in the music biz ENDED, Jettison Records, Black-Onxy-Hall-Black-Listed!)

(Bare-ass-naked-landing-on-the-sidewalk-cover-your-face-here-comes - your - "Don't-get-hit-in-the-face-BY-your-own-demos!" - TOSSED OUT!).

And, as such...

WAS introduced to the ending.

(THAT: TOO-hungry-"child", NEVER saw it coming FROM the VERY beginning!). And as such, began and, so ended. (All on the SAME day!). *Just as, ALL THE OTHER "auditionees" did! Who's fingernails left claw marks. (Past-particles, of: bloody - floor-grout-ENDUCING-sandpapered-OFF-fingertip - smears!). And WHO'S tears, have dried,* in and all, ON THAT, slick-black-onyx-tiled long Executive Hallway floor. And all and all, ALL, just WANTED NOTHING MORE than to be a singer, for the rest of their lives, (THEIR ENTIRE LIVES!!!),...EVER SINCE... *they were a kid.*

(Flesh and blood FROM, their - nails-knocked-off - bloody-fingertips, LEFT scratches and gouges,...BUT couldn't clutch. The: "by-design" - onyx-laid-floor-hall-tiles - WERE too slick! And thus, so proven, so laid, as such).

AND...

They ALL painfully stained THAT white tile grout!

AS...

THEY ALL, all the way down THAT hall, leading from Pockets' slammed-closed executive red office door, did so, IN SO DOING, beg, cry, plead, and shout!

And...

Their dreams have died, long before their tears have dried.

And, ALL...

(The EXACT SAME way!!!).

BUT...

(SOMEWHERE!). Downtown...

...Trife, recognizes, that irrepressible muffled-sound, of: glass in motion, caused by muffled bass. 'Cause, coming from inside of this club, (pulled in like the North Pole!), Trife, KNOWS, *down in his recently-awakened-soul,* "I'll bet strippers are upside down, up inside, up on a pole, swingin' 'round."

(The man, *who once WANTED NOTHING MORE, THAN TO place himself into a Klonopin-enduced-coma FOR three days,* may have gotten his wish...and then some).

As...

Trife had been in a comatose-like "Resting" state, for approximately three years or so now. (Give or Take). And, it wasn't the commotion of bowling pins, and the hoopin' n' hollerin', that awakened him. But, him,...*talkin' to him,...talkin' to him.* (And him, *lookin' down on him, lookin' down on him).*

For...

If he ever had a twin, someone just like him, the world wouldn't know what hit it. And that's some truth and realness, that this world should never forget.

And so...

Trife, still finding it hard to speak, feeling like himself, though, his memory of his memories of himself are weak. Though, clarity of his sight-vision is beginning to grow. Trife, steps into the strip club. (Though, he was able to find and recall THAT bitch!). WHERE INSIDE, the TRUE hustlers...ARE the ones who strip! (And, once they get down from being up on from getting off that pole, YOU BEST tip them for the show!).

...Meanwhile, back at the all red everythang, on his throne, on the Jettison Records Access-Only Communications Executive-Line Phone, in his all red everythang office, Pockets, is in his bag!

AS...

He was JUST informed, by DJ Wood, that, he and his "People", would be on the next flight home...

As, FOR Pockets? Well...

(HE CAN'T even hang up the phone fast enough! And, ends the call quick!)...

Then...

Presses, and, before he can even take his finger off of his Executive Desk Phone Jettison Records Access-Only Intracom Button, into his office, enters, Phillip Tate, "Personal" Assistant Extraodinaire, lickity-split!

Pockets, leaning back in his high back red tufted leather upholstered desk chair, and after some serious face washing, (with his avid powerlifter hands), looks up at Phillip and,...offers him to have a seat. (This is new for Phillip! Phillip, always at the ready, fresh new desk calendar blotter provider, files organizer, pre-"auditionee" "auditioner"-rider, you name it, Phillip Tate, is ALWAYS at the ready!). And, he does so, WITH a professional appearance AND positive outlook! (ALWAYS!).

FOR...

(Phillip Tate, is ALWAYS at Pockets' beck and call,...to facilitate).

BUT...

Never NOT ONCE, has Pockets, EVER offered Phil to have a seat in his, all red everythang office!

And so...

As, Phillip Tate, takes a seat in the left chair, of the two red tufted leather upholstered executive office-furniture office chairs, (so seated in front of Pockets' executive-size red mahogany wooden executive desk), Phillip Tate,...knows that THIS IS serious!

(Leaning forward, elbows on red mahogany wood, Pockets, informs Phillip, about the phone call HE JUST HAD,...with DJ Wood!), "THAT,...fuckin'...bifurcated-tongue - fuck! You know what he MANAGED to convey?? HE'S flying back from overseas on the red-eye. Tonight! Him,...AND his "Peoples"!!! THEY WANT to begin "prepping" for the "pre-production" of the "May-1st-Carving"."

"I got you. BUT,...that COULD BE a problem, sir. Sir, C. Trife, STILL HASN'T been located!", Phillip Tate, replies.

(Elbows off mahogany, hands flailing and "mutha'-fucka's" sailing!), Pockets, goes into a patented "whistle-enducing" explosion, "Listen, mutha'-fucka'! I AIN'T have you come into MY mutha'-fuckin' office, TO mutha'-fuckin' tell me, WHAT tha' fuck, I, ALREADY mutha'-fuckin' know! I, ALREADY-MUTHA'-FUCKIN'-KNOW, IT'S , A: mutha'-fuckin'-problem,...MUTHA'-FUCKA'!! WHAT, I need FROM YOU,...mutha'-fucka',...IS TO mutha'-fuckin' TELL ME, WHAT'S THE - mutha'-fuckin' - timeline - ON, C. Trife!?! ...Mutha'-fucka'!"

(Knocking off his nonsensical-whistling, Phillip, educates Pockets, OF what REALLY goes on IN the under the ground levels OF Jettison Records! *And, AS TO WHY, this building WAS built - IN THE FIRST - mutha'-fuckin' place!!* AND, AS TO WHY, inside AND out, THERE ARE...SO MANY armed guards!!!)

OF...

The weights, temperature and, alarms.

OF...

The nitrogen, incubators, more care,...all harm.

"I got you. The cloning process varies from clone to clone, sir. There's no accurate or scientific way to be absolutely certain how quickly or strained a subject will recover the full memory, speech, sight, OR full strength, and so forth, OF THEIR "donor selves",...IF EVER, sir. We believe, that, the stronger OF body and mind, the donor WAS IN their life, AT the time OF the DNA collection, THEN, THAT, will have an "exponential effect" ON, their full recovery rate. Sir, other factors to consider, ARE, but, NOT limited to: THE METHOD of and, the nature of collection, of the donor's DNA, if the donor was alive at the time of collection and, we believe, that, a prime factor on and of recovery rate, COULD very-well be effected, IF the donor is STILL CURRENTLY alive. Based on, C. Trife's, "ease-of-escape", FROM THE lower levels and, thusly, THIS fortified building, I, sir, HATE TO inform you, that,

I would rate, C. Trife, to, CLEARLY be in, thee upper percentile of rapid recovery rate, to full, and, cognizant recovery."

(Leaning back into his throne, Pockets, washes his face again!), and, then asks, "Which would be WHAT, nigga? WHAT IS,...the upper percentile recovery rate!?"

"Hard to say, sir. We believe, that, the upper percentile can recover almost instantaneously, to, three-to-five, upwards, to, fourteen-business-days, AFTER their "awakening", sir. There are MANY factors to take INTO account, sir. We believe, that, the longer the clone has been in their "Resting State" and, the longer one can PREVENT the clone from coming into contact, with, their known surroundings, such as, people, places and things. THEN, that, CAN prove, great dividends, IN keeping them, FROM learning, that, they aren't actually who they think they are, the donor, but the clone."

"What's, THIS - "we believe" - shit, nigga? AIN'T "y'all's People", doctors and, mad scientists and, shit?? So, EITHER y'all know. OR,...y'all DON'T know!", belittles, Pockets!

"I got you. WELL, SIR, it's a science, BUT,...it's not AN "exact" science. Not yet. I mean, WE ARE good, sir. The best! BUT, "Cloning" HASN'T been around for AS long as, say, extracting teeth or, amputations. SO, what WE BELIEVE, IS, what WE believe. And, THAT'S what we get YOU to believe.", Phillip Tate, replies.

"You hustling me? ARE. YOU. HUSTLIN'. ME!?!", Pockets, would ask.

THEN...

(Pockets, becomes aware OF, the: "fatal-flaw-error", of: ALL TRUE hustlers!)

And, THAT BEING...

Attorneys, (worth THEIR salt!), NEVER, ask a question, THAT, they don't already know the answer to!

And so...

(Pockets, tosses his last question asked, over his shoulder. And, continues back, TO HIS, *old-money-hustlin' WAYS!!*), "Listen, nigga.

Don't talk to me 'bout what is, and, what ain't, a perfect science. The "People", the "Pullers OF Strings", the "They", the "Them", *HAVE been IN power SINCE, the T-Rex had trouble wipin' his own ass!* SO, don't come into MY mutha'-fuckin' office, *talkin' 'bout, "Clonin'" AIN'T been 'round long as, choppin' off a nigga's feet!* Now, SINCE we both *know that to be true,*...you best start talkin' some truth."

"I got you. Sir, there IS NO upper percentile rate. WE,...we work off of a "Three-Tiered System"...1). Controlled. 2). Controllable. 3). Out of Control.", (old school duped!), Phillip Tate, UNCOMFORTABLE, FROM Pockets, TAKING OFF the gloves, OFFERS UP the goods!,... (WHICH, could get him GOOD and killed!)...(OR,...at the VERY LEAST,...get HIS motherfuckin' feet cut off!!!).

(Pockets, *back to, HIS: old-school-old-money-ways, (old habits die hard,* ya dig!!), asks, a question, that he, IN FACT, already knows, the answer to!)...

(Come. Let's listen in)...

"And, C. Trife, would be in the upper Third Tier, isn't that right?", Pockets, asks, (LEADING the witness LIKE a motherfucker!).

"Clearly.", Phillip, replies, then continues, "C. Trife, sir. As in, "Clone Trife"! ...Nice touch, sir!!"

"Nigga, I don't need no pat on the back FROM YOU!! I don't need you to validate SHIT for me,...OTHER THAN the timeline. Trust me, ON this, Phillip. IF, C. Trife, IS ANYTHING *like, B. Trife, was?!?* ...Nigga, LET'S just say,...THAT'S the ONLY REASON why, I'VE managed to prolong, C. Trife's carving, for, AS LONG as, I have! And, TRUST ME on this NEXT shit too, Phillip. Trife, is OF far more "use", than, BEING some - damn "cutting board" - FOR, DJ Wood!!! And,...FOR WHAT?!? SO, THAT, DJ Wood, can feel BETTER...about himself??? Fuck him! AND FUCK his fragile ego, too!! By, YOUR OWN "Peoples'" word, YOUR OWN "The String Pullers", are: *"Allowing, DJ Wood, to get some payback!".* Business IS business, Phillip! YOU, KNOW THAT!! SO, you actually think "The String Pullers", are gon' put business aside, JUST SO, DJ Wood, CAN carve C. Trife tha'-fuck-up WORSE, *than Brotha Trife, carved him tha'-fuck-up?!?* ...Phil, in MY opinion,...THAT'S just a complete-waste of somebody, that, KNOWS HOW TO get shit DONE!!! Yeah, so, well, anyways, for...greater financial gain.", Pockets, tells him, (and, HIMSELF!!!).

"I got you. ALTHOUGH, sir, what Brotha Trife DID, TO DJ Wood, *cutting out his salivary glands like that.* Well, sir, IF I MAY? Might I, remind you THAT, *it WAS live on-air,...during his own "Morning Wood Show".* And, it *WAS,* might I add, *"Bring Your Child To Work Day"*!! The man's embarrassed! BEEN embarrassed, sir. He lost his "Morning Drive Show", AND, the "People", lost a major star, IN A major market, sir. Personally, sir, I'M surprised that you've been able to put off C. Trife's carving, FOR as long as you have, sir. Convincing DJ Wood, and the "People", to wait UNTIL their May 1st Anniversary, to carve up C. Trife,...nice touch, sir. Oh, sorry! But, uh, yes, I agree, sir. Business is business. With that, I do agree. HOWEVER, sir, I AM sorry TO inform you, that, the "People" WANT HIM carved up,...due to the loss of that major morning drive market! And so, that's EXACTLY what's GOING TO happen.", Phillip Tate, replies.

"FUCK THAT!!! Business IS business!! And, I'VE GOT some LONG-OVERDUE business to handle back up north,...RIGHT IN THAT major market of North Juarez! DJ Wood and the "People" want to come back early in "preparation" of the May-1st-Carving? Ok, then. WELL, I've been doin' some "prep-work" of MY OWN,...by having C. Trife's intubation tube removed. Hate to tell ya', mutha' fucka', BUT, C. Trife's comin' WITH me! THAT MAN, knows HOW TO handle business! Well, *B. Trife did,...*anyway.", explains, Pockets.

(Wiping his brow, with his pocket square, Folded-in-4s), Phillip Tate, replies, "I would HIGHLY recommend that you DIDN'T do that, sir. If the "People" return, and, C. Trife, isn't back in his room, in the White Jade Hall of the lower levels, intubated in his "Resting State"?? IT'S very well possible that, YOU WILL BE THE ONE, DJ Wood IS carving ON, COME May 1st!"

(Cocking his custom red custom-made red hat hard to the side), Pockets, hates to inform, Phillip Tate, that, "You can't outwit me, boy. I didn't know 'bout the "Three Tiers" UNTIL YOU told me! NOW, who do you think THEY'LL be carvin'-up, come May 1st? Me? ...OR,

YOU!?! SO, it would BEHOOVE YOU, to start tellin' me, MORE 'bout this "Clonin'-Shit"! 'CAUSE, if I were a betting man? WHICH I AM!!! IT'LL be YOUR salivary glands, BEING dug-the-fuck-out, LONG before mine!"

Mouth too dry to whistle. Phillip Tate, begins,...asking helpful-questions! (Just another pawn, on Pockets' "Hustle board"!)...

(Come. Let's listen in)...

"I got you. The two main things, I'll need to know are, as follows. A). Is, B. Trife, still alive? And, B). What was the DNA-Specimen used, in collection?", questions, asked by Phillip Tate.

(Looking up from under his right brow at his red office ceiling, elbows on red mahogany, Pockets, leans forward after some thought), and then, so reasons, "It's been...what? THREE LONG YEARS or so, SINCE I've seen my babygirl??? *THAT would be the timeline of me not receiving ONE damn word, ON the whereabouts of that MUTHA' FUCKIN' Brotha Trife!* So, NO, I don't know, if he's still alive. If I'm a betting man, which I am, I'd say the mutha' fucka's still alive. ONLY 'cause I haven't killed him yet! My patience HAS been tested. I've been waiting for the right time, THE ONLY TIME, to wake up C. Trife. I NEEDED both DJ Wood and the "People" to go back overseas. AND, I needed to know, if B. Trife was dead, or where he was at, so that I could go kill him. THAT mutha' fucka' cost me a whole lotta' money! HE fucked shit up for me! SHIT!!! *I couldn't get at them mutha' fuckin' North Juarez city pensions!* What good is a horse ranch, without my mutha' fuckin' race track?? DON'T ANSWER THAT!!! Point being, PHILLIP, I ain't wastin' no more time!!! Trust me, YOU see how C. Trife moves, he got RIGHT THE FUCK outta' the lower levels, DIDN'T HE!!? Don't NOBODY need TWO of them mutha' fucka's RUNNIN' LOOSE in the world AT the same time!! Shiiiiiit, *B. Trife* AND C. Trife together? FUCK. THAT. SHIT!!! THAT'S somethin' the world, don't NEVER need!! At-tha'-fuck-all."

"I got you. Well, sir, the Three Tier System is very accurate. Very accurate. However, some of those earlier factors I spoke on, can play a factor. By all means, sir, it would be extremely advisable and advantageous that, prevention of C. Trife, from coming into contact with B. Trife, be paramount. Furthermore, if in fact, B. Trife is deceased, it's extremely advisable that C. Trife not learn of such information. Just one of the many reasons, sir, for by all exigent means of prevention in allowing C. Trife, to come back into contact from such triggers, *as his known-surroundings, persons, places, and things.* You can never be too careful or cautious with, OR around, the Three Tiers, sir! It's far more, than, just keeping C. Trife out of his hometown, and so forth. You never know what *particular scent* will trigger a long-term memory. Such as, something that occurred in their childhood,...*both good or bad,* or trigger something that, occurred *a week or two before their DNA was collected* from their donor selves. In the cases, where, we believe that, the clone, will, in all probability, be classified in the Third Tier, based upon their donor selves. Our team of doctors will surgically remove the clone's olfactory nerve, while they're still in their "Resting State". So, that, the clone's brain cannot detect any scents, smells, or odors. DJ Wood and the "People" opted to forego this procedure on C. Trife. Because, they want him to be able to smell his own blood during his carving. THAT'S HOW badly they want to carve him up! WE'RE talking about, The: "String Pullers", here! Do you understand, sir?? This WILL happen.", Phillip Tate, explains.

"I see. Well, PHILLIP, I WILL BE sending C. Trife BACK INTO North Juarez, TO handle THAT "long-overdue business" that, I NEED TO handle, that, IS...long-overdue. Listen, Phil, I CAN'T go back into the city. SO, sending C. Trife in FOR ME, IS a risk, that, I'M just gonna have to take! You see, Phillip,...B. Trife did some work for me,...in North Juarez, several years ago. Not for long, mind you. It DIDN'T take long for, B. Trife, TO fuck THAT up! Listen, Phillip, keeping C. Trife out of his hometown, IS WHAT I'll really need to do. But, shiiiiiit, C. Trife WOULDN'T even recognize that shit hole, now!", replies, Pockets.

"That WOULD BE a risk, indeed, sir. Third Tier's recover quickly! HOWEVER,...there are ways of reeling him back in. You WON'T have much of a timeline, regrettably, with THIS particular, Third Tier. Getting C. Trife in and out of North Juarez, AND, getting him returned back into the lower levels, intubated, BEFORE DJ Wood AND the "People" return, well, sir, with ALL DUE respect,...I just don't see HOW you're going to be able to do that. I'm sorry to have to inform you, sir. But, it's simply NOT feasible!", Phillip, tells Pockets.

"Listen, nigga. DON'T you concern yourself WITH who-returns-when. ALL I need to do is, to throw a "lil' delay", into that red-eye flight,...buy me some time, so-to-speak. And, I know WHAT buys time MORE than anything!! ...WHERE the fuck did, Pretty High, get off to, anyways?, asks, Pockets.

"I got you. He didn't say, sir. Well,...not exactly. I overheard him, going on-and-on about, *"How bored, he's been, "rotting-away", behind, "some desk" in "some office""*. And, then he mentioned something about, *"Going, "where the four winds meet""*. My apologies, sir, I'm not sure who Pretty High was talking to. BUT, I did hear Pretty High, saying, he'd be coming right back here, with, um, I believe what, he said, was, with...*"The Do-You Crew"???*", Phillip, informs Pockets.

"The DUYU CREW???? OH, NO!!! NOT them nutty mutha' fuckas!!!!", Pockets, explodes!, (elbows off mahogany!!).

THEN...

Pockets, leans back in his throne. Looks up at his red office ceiling, *(from up under his right brow), thinkin', plannin', plottin', schemin' and,...* SPEAKING TO HIMSELF!

(COME! Let's listen in!)...

"The four winds...the four winds...", Pockets, repeats aloud to himself, *(as he's, TRYING to - "fig'a it" - THA' FUCK out!).*

And, so then...

Pockets, cocks his custom red custom-made red hat hard to the side, (having huddled-a-new-hustle in his mind!). And so, Pockets, with elbows back on red mahogany, looks at Phillip Tate, (from cross blood red wood) and, says, "Ok! I got my red-eye delay! NOW, what I need from you, PHILLIP, is to get me some data,...reading materials,...WHATEVER it is you may have, ON HOW to reel Third Tier's back in! Phil, I'm 'bout to raise-on-up. So, GET ME that data, Phillip, while I'm gone. I'M HEADED OUT TO FIND C. Trife!!! And, WHEN I DO find him, I'LL BE bringing him back here. Phillip, contact MC Busta-Nut, False Profit and, Y.S., have them pack for a promotional road trip. Have them in my office and, ready to hit the road with me, by the time I get back. IF, the DUYU CREW returns, before I do,...GOOD LAWD, Phillip,... JUST STAY THA' FUCK OUTTA' THEIR WAY, huh?", Pockets, breaks it down.

(Whistling musically-nonsensically!), Phillip Tate, replies, "I got you. I got you on the data, sir. BUT, there's STILL *data* FROM YOU, that I'LL need! The *DNA source used in collection,* sir. I need to know, *what was the source of DNA collected from B. Trife? And, I'll need to know, if B. Trife was still alive, at the time of this DNA collection?"*

Chuckling, Pockets, replies, *"DNA. DNA.",...*"You *sound like* my fuckin' brother! You know that??"

"Sir??", Phillip Tate, asks, inquisitively.

"It's not important...don't worry 'bout it.", Pockets, replies, *(with memories of his own memories, that, he doesn't care to remember...getting the better of him).*

Then...

Leaning back into his high back red tufted leather upholstered throne, Pockets, *(harkens back in thought, to the day he collected B. Trife's DNA,... WITHOUT Brotha Trife even knowing about it!)...*

AND...

(Harkens back to the day when, due to his own actions, there'd be a very good chance of him being able to collect B. Trife's DNA, without B. Trife, even being aware, that, Pockets, would later be collecting his DNA, all without Pockets, even being aware, that, that's what he had done HIMSELF!)...

FOR...

Pockets, just has a true-knack, for putting plans into motion, directly or indirectly, plans of a personal nature or for others, (by things he's said or done or otherwise), intentionally or unintentionally, without even knowing that he has put that plan in motion, (for he or for others), who he or for who others feel as though they can find financial gain, by and from that plan, by that direct or indirect, word, action or otherwise, of Pockets, personally or for other persons, that was done, intentionally or unintentionally, directly or indirectly, by Pockets. (And, you can best believe!), that, WHEN Pockets, recognizes that the plan(s) that he has placed in motion, HAVE BEEN recognized BY others, (who feel the need to bite his shit!), (FOR financial gain OR otherwise!), Pockets,... becomes patient, (VERY patient!), TO LET the other(s)...gain financially FROM HIS plan(s).

And, then...

Pockets goes and gets HIS taste! (Pockets, IS a TRUE hustler. Indeed!).

AND SO...

Pockets, *IN A daydream-thought,* tapping his right thumb, right index, and right middle fingers *hypnotically, rhythmically,* on his desktop, *staring blankly into the fine woodgrain swirl lines, (which mark it's own time!),* of his fine illegally harvested red mahogany executive desk, *thinks back to earlier days, of days:* before he used his true old school hustling ways, to hustle his way, to damn near the top of the Music Industry Food Chain, *and, back to days: when he had damn near an entire city's police department...AND it's city,...in his pockets:*

"Look, I don't know nothing about no skin cream and I don't know nothing about dyeing my dreads.", "Too Cold", says, to Anna Mossitti, with a red leather toiletries bag held in his hand, complete, exclusively with, the ONLY skincare line therein, THEE: "Tiffany DeVon 1971 Skincare Line", THE ONLY skincare line, that, Anna Mossitti, ALLOWED to touch her FLAWLESS SKIN! And, the reason FOR same! (THAT BEING,... FLAWLESS SKIN!). Bringing out from within, the NATURAL GLOW, of her NATURAL BEAUTY, FROM WITHIN!

Seated on his red throne, positioned behind his red mahogany executive desk, in his all red everythang apartment, up on the top floor, of Precinct One, in the City of North Juarez, Pockets, clutching a cluster of french fries, held by his right thumb, right index and, right middle fingers, dipping said fries, hypnotically, rhythmically, into a pile of ketchup, on a spread out McDonald's bag, spread out atop his red mahogany desktop, begins gettin' in his bag, as he calls over to Anna Mossitti, "Babe, JUST take "Too Cold" into the bathroom

*and, dye the tips of his dreads, AS YOU DID, for Too Cold. And, babe,...
THEN let the man GET cross town, huh?"*

Tap, tap, tap,...

Pockets...

*(Gets himself back, to the days of the "harkenback", to, oh, 'bout, 1 ,260
or so some-odd-days back, as he, remains IN IT, NOT DRIFTIN', FIRMLY,
seated IN place, BACK IN THAT: ALL RED EVERYTHANG - ABOVE
THE LAW - APARTMENT, that he had!)...*

Dip, dip, dip,...

Pockets...

*(For the first time now, now finding he's in that all red everythang
apartment alone, finding Anna Mossitti and "Too Cold" to be now long
gone, all-up-in up top in Precinct One, finding now, there's no one to be
found, within his ALL RED EVERYTHANG - ABOVE THE LAW -
APARTMENT DAYDREAM,...though, he's finding within,...though, not
yet seen,...SOMEONE'S THERE, SNOOPIN' 'ROUND,...just waitin'...
IN THE WINGS!!!)...*

Tap, tap, tap,...

AS...

(POCKETS,...CAN NOW FEEL IT, IN HIS BONES!!!)...

*(NOW NO LONGER IN THE WINGS, NOW ALL-UP-IN HIS
ALL RED EVERYTHANG DAYDREAM, RIGHT NEXT TO HIM,
STANDIN' THERE, POCKETS, FIRMLY IN PLACE, SEATED THERE,
ON HIS ALL RED EVERYTHANG THRONE, SOMEBONE'S THERE
WITH HIM, ALL-UP-IN HIS ALL RED EVERYTHANG - DAYDREAM
- HOME!!!)...*

Dip, dip, dip,...

(Looking up from his ketchup and fries, being dipped inside those red-swrill-mahogany-desktop-lines, standing there,....IT'S THAT DAMN-DIRTY-ASS VICE COP, is exactly-who-tha'-fuck he finds!!!)...

Tap, tap, tap, *dip, dip, dip...*

AND...

(Pockets, CAN damn-near...*SMELL THE "JOOP!" COLOGNE!!!)...*

AS...

Upon his *red-swrill-line* desktop, Pockets continues, to *hypnotically, rhythmetically,* tap, tap, tap, his right thrumb, right index finger, and his right middle finger, as he *continues, to dip, dip, dip into ketchep, the cluster of french fries he's daydreaming about, cluthed in his right hand...*

ALTHOUGH...

Tap, tap, tap,...

AND...

Tap, tap, tap,...

UNBEKNOWNST...

Dip, dip, dip,...

AND...

Dip, dip, dip,...

SURE-AS-FUCK...

Tap, tap, tap, *dip, dip, dip,...*

(NOT APART, OF POCKETS' - *"HARKENBACK-DAYDREAM-PLAN!!!)...*

..."Too Cold", has headed-on-over to Legs' apartment, with Heavy Duty, after leaving the downtown radio station Building of "WILI", after leaving

DJ Wood, aching in pain, leaving him with a reptilian tongue, and,...NO salivary glands!!!)...

AND SO...

Dip, dip, dip,...

(STILL WITHIN THE UNBEKNOWNST!!!)...

Dip, dip, dip,...

...UNBEKNOWNST, TO "Too Cold", The - "Joop!"-Cologne-Bottle-Wearing-Red-Face-Rolex-Wearing-Dirty-Vice-Cop-On-Duty-Prostitute-Poker-Big-Ass-Caddy-With-Big-Ass-Rims-Drivin'-Stayin'-Dressed-Smooth-Head-Shaved-Smooth, Smooth-Brother, HAS headed-on-over to Precinct One! Making his way, directly up the precinct's back staircase, like he ain't got no time to waste, like he's payin' tha' rent, OPENS UP THAT ALL RED EVERYTHANG DOOR, MAKING HIS WAY INTO Pockets' ALL RED EVERYTHANG APARTMENT!!

FROM AFTER, the dirty vice cop sped off, from out in front, of the WILI Building, FROM AFTER, another city cop, pulled up out front! AFTER WHICH, the dirty vice cop, pulled - dirty vice cop - "Rank"! AFTER WHICH, "You don't need to be here! I'LL handle the call!" AFTER WHICH, that other city cop drove off! FROM AFTER, the dirty-ass vice cop, being frank!

AFTER WHICH, while, addressing "Too Cold", this is what, that dirty-ass vice cop, had to say, "Stay in North Juarez for as long as you like! You're gonna make me a very rich man! It's gonna cost, Pockets, plenty! For me, to make, THIS go away!!"

AFTER WHICH, that dirty-ass-vice-cop-"Joop!"-cologne-smellin'-brother, got back in his big-ass Caddy - with the big-ass rims - of undercover. AFTER WHICH,...HE BURNED RUBBER! AFTER WHICH, leaving "Too Cold" and Heavy Duty, standing there, out front of the WILI Building,...IN A CLOUD OF "JOOP!" COLOGNE AND, BURNT RUBBER!!

Tap, tap, tap,...

AS...

(Pockets, wasn't privy, to MOST OF that!)...

Dip, dip, dip...

...."Did you not hear that shit ON the radio?? YOUR boy fucked up!! I HOPE you were listenin'!!", the dirty-on-duty-street-walker-marauder - vice cop, tells Pockets, walking up next to Pockets' illegally-harversted Peruvian red mahogany desk, from after bargin' in!"

Looking up, from behind his desk, from looking down, from working on, figuring out the formula, to crack the code, OF GETTIN' AT THOSE CITY PENSIONS, Pockets, replies, "Nigga, YOU SEE ME, workin' here! Hell no, I ain't listenin' to that corny-mutha'-fucka's Morning Show! He run his mouth, TOO-DAMN-MUCH!! I told my brother, to bring the DJ to me. Why? ...What the fuck my brother do?"

"Cut the shit, Pockets. Me, and you, BOTH know YOUR brother, Too Cold, IS downstairs IN THAT bank vault cell! (Chuckling),...THAT'S where we keep ALL THA' LOONEYS!!! Don't worry 'bout a 'ting, Pockets. It's just ME, YOU, the Commissioner and,...a few others "on the job", that know it. BUT, that's gonna cost you,...IF you want to keep it LIKE that! And, IF you want me to keep quiet, 'bout, that shit spread-out cross your desk, I SEE YOU workin' on?? ...Well, THAT'S gonna cost you too. I want IN, ON that!! Don't be cockin' yo' hat AT ME, Pockets! IT'S a dog-eat-dog world, ain't that right, dawg? BUT, listen up, Pockets. DJ Wood, AND "His People", WANT SOME payback FOR THAT SHIT, your "brother", just pulled ON live air. Shit moves quick in this city, dawg, AND,...THAT'S, GONNA' cost you, TOO!! Dog-eat-dog, dawg. Dog-eat-dog.", the dirty on-duty - strumpet thump-it - vice cop, informs, Pockets!

"LIKE, what?! Money? WHAT tha' fuck "THEM People" want,... MONEY?!? Shiiiiiit,...I'M Pockets! I STAYS-WIT money IN MY, mutha'-fuckin', POCKETS!!!", Pockets, replies, (cocking his custom red custom-made red hat...HARD to the side!).

"Nope,...DNA. "THEM People",..."THEY" WANT that crazy-motherfucker's DNA. It's ME, that WANTS, YOUR money!", the dirty, on-duty - paramour-deplorer - vice cop, informs!

Tap, tap, tap, *dip, dip, dip,...*

AFTER *WHICH...*

(That - dirty-ass-providing-dirty-ass-judges-dirty-ass-money-for-dirty-ass-warrants-of-arrests - vice-cop, provides Pockets, with a North Juarez Police Department manila Evidence Envelope, (containing a surgically-sealed plastic screw-top-lid container), placing it on top of Pockets' red mahogany desk!)...

..."DNA? That's IT??? Noooooo, problem. Narco, I know ALL 'bout, DNA. I read. And, if we're in luck, I just MAY have the next best "source" of that wild-mutha'-fucka's DNA,...besides his blood.", replies, Pockets.

(Making his way from behind his desk, to cross his red shag office carpet, and, into his red-tiled, practically - all-red-everythang - bathroom, Pockets, reaches down into the red marble bathroom sink and,...pulls out the drain-stopper)...

And...

Sure enough! JUST, as Pockets, told Anna Mossitti to do, Anna Mossitti, DID do "Too Cold's" hair the exact same way that, she did Too Cold's hair, (by shampooing it first in the bathroom sink!), before dyeing the tips of his dreads a beaming gold, (assisting in the transitioning, of: Brotha Trife... into..."Too Cold").

AND...

Sure enough! EXACTLY, what Pockets, thought he MAY find, intertwined, (around the white plastic hook of the drain-stopper), WERE...hairs FROM the head of "Too Cold"!! (Some long, some short, several of beaming gold tips, some with, and some without, the follicle).

And so...

After reaching down into the red bathroom sink, Pockets, reaches down into his custom red custom-made red dress pants. And,...pays the dirty vice cop WITH dirty money! (Chain-of-Custody packaged), the, dirty-on-duty-keeping-reports-on-all-escorts - vice cop, gets on his way, (with, WHAT he came for. Pockets' money! And, B. Trife's DNA!).

Dip, dip, dip, tap, tap, t...

Pockets, comes back from his, *Harkening-back-Daydream,* as he comes back from his, *Mahogany - Red-Swirl-Lined - Gaze!*

NOW...

NO LONGER, TAPPING his right thumb, right index and middle fingers, on his Jettison Records executive red mahogany desk, *back in* and from, *thinkin' 'bout the good ol' days, just as if he were DIPPING clutched french fries IN ketchup,* Pockets, is NOW REALIZING, that, THAT'S WHAT, he just did!

'CAUSE...

(Old habits die hard, ya' dig!)

AND SO...

Pockets, looks back up, at Phillip Tate, (from cross that fine illegal blood red wood!) and, says, "It was follicles, from his head."

"I got you. That's good! Blood WOULD have been worse, for, the Tier Three's, as far as, "repercussions" go. The: Tier Three's, have a long documented-history of, well, sir, in layman's terms, "flipping the-fuck-out and snapping", WHEN, they gain the knowledge THAT, their: "donor-source selve's", of their DNA, are deceased. It's NOT pretty, sir. They stop at nothing TO find and kill those responsible FOR their donor selve's death and,...THOSE responsible for the cloning process. The key, to it all, sir, is, in fact, if B. Trife IS deceased, NOT to let his clone, C. Trife, become MADE AWARE of it. C. Trife, is CLEARLY a Tier Three!!! SO, what he doesn't know,...WON'T hurt him. Or, you. Or, US!! ...For, that matter. HOWEVER! SOME clones, your First and Second Tier's, we can use the "known-death" OF the clone's "donor-self", TO OUR advantage. AND, in a case-by-case basis, we DO sometimes, in fact, make the clone aware, that, they ARE, IN FACT, a clone. The: Tier One's and Two's, are, controlled and, controllable. So, WHEN they ARE informed, that, they ARE, in fact, a clone, they, OFTEN TIMES, gain a sense of invincibility and superiority. WHICH, we can manipulate and use TO OUR advantage! For,...financial gain,...OF course. WHICH, sir, encompasses MANY THINGS...as, you are, MORE THAN, aware of. BUT, your Tier Three's ARE different. C. Trife,...is different. It may or may not be advantageous, TO inform him, that, he is, IN FACT, a clone. Whatever it is, that, you're planning ON HAVING him do, for you, up there in North Juarez? YOU, sir, MAY find it advantageous TO, IN FACT, tell him, that, he IS, a clone,...to bring out THAT sense OF invincibility! AND, to use THAT, TO accomplish, your goal. But yet, and still, there's a certain "risk/reward" that MUST be weighed, for such..."potentialities". That, sir, is ONLY SOMETHING, that, YOU will be able to determine, IF, in fact, you WANT to "implement", that ploy. HOWEVER, if you do, so choose, TO GO that route, sir, DO NOT allow him to learn, or, to EVEN think, THAT, his "donor-self" is deceased. In time, things will come back to C. Trife, sight, speech, memory and, so forth. The thing that you do have going for you is that, the clones, regardless if they're a Tier One, Tier Two, or Tier Three, they will have no knowledge of anything, that has occurred, in their donor-selve's lives, OR in the world, for that matter, AFTER the date and time that, their DNA was collected FROM their donor-selves. For example, sir, if the clone DNA was collected the day prior to the Space Shuttle explosion. And, they're cloned the day AFTER the explosion. THEN, the clone will have no knowledge of, and, that, the Space Shuttle, indeed exploded. UNLESS, of course, they are told about it, read about, etc., etc., etc. We like to control WHAT our clones read, AND learn, WHO they talk to, interact with and, so forth. As a matter-of-fact, sir, in most cases, we don't allow our clones to read at all. The Third Tier clones, have a strong - magnetic-like-pull - to their donor-selve's,...like a twin. If they don't know, that, they're a clone, they'll STILL try to seek out their donor-self, without even knowing, THAT, they're doing it! It's like, when, twins are separated at birth and, have no idea that, they are a twin, BUT, YET, they just know it. It's the same principle with clones, sir. Thing is, sir, if a Third Tier clone discovers that, they are, in fact, a clone, WITHOUT first being informed, that, THEY ARE a clone, well, sir, that could be as bad, if not worse, than, the clone gaining the knowledge, be it directly told or otherwise, that, their donor-selve's ARE DEAD! And, SOMETHING ELSE that, you have going for you, sir, is the fact, that, you personally KNEW the "DNA donor-self" OF, C. Trife! THAT being, B. Trife! That'll give you a "clearer-ability", OF THE manipulation, THE control, THE "reeling" of C. Trife back in. What you'll NEED TO do, is, BEFORE the full-recovery of C. Trife's memory takes place, is,...get him to believe you. Sir, you NEED TO gain his trust! During that window, tell him things that B. Trife has done, or things you think B. Trife would have done. In doing so, apart of C. Trife's cognitive-memory will be triggered and, he'll find it believable. And, since he won't know any different, he'll believe it. Trust is important, too. Get, C. Trife, to trust you. Get, C. Trife, to BELIEVE you. And, with that "sense-of-superiority" and, with that "sense of invincibility" that will kick in, YOU could have something incredibly good OR, incredibly dangerous on your hands. But yet, and still, WITH your Tier Three's, sir, such "potentialities", COME WITH, a far greater risk, than reward. Once that full-memory-recovery kicks in, that sense-of-superiority and invincibility doesn't go away, NOT WITH the Tier Three's!!! So, be careful what you create and, be careful who you manipulate. Be careful. Because, your creation will come back to bite you. Hard. I know you don't want to hear this, sir. BUT, you are taking a big risk in taking THIS particular Tier Three, up there, WITH YOU, to North Juarez. Whatever it is, that, you need him to do FOR YOU, IN North Juarez,...I sure hope it's worth it."

Tipping his custom red custom-made red hat up, (to wipe his own brow!), Pockets, looks Phillip Tate, right in his eyes and, says, "She is."

Chapter Five

MR. STEAL-YOUR-SHINE

...Meanwhile. Back downtown. Back at the strip club. Two lost souls are about to meet. Violently.

Inside of the strip club, where the flashing lights, stage smoke and titties in your face, have their own funny-way, of causing one to lose all-concept-of time and money. How long have I been here? (Fuck if I know). How much money have I spent? (Fuck if I know!) BUT, I KNOW I'M STAYIN'!!! ('Cause, I ain't ready to go!) Funny how, there's never a clock posted up on a wall in a strip club. BUT, ain't it funny how, there's ALWAYS an ATM posted in a strip club, WITH an absurd surcharge??? And, ain't it funny how, the bartenders in strip clubs, ARE ALWAYS far more hotter than the ones up on stage, taking off all their clothes? Ain't it funny how, (YOU DAMN RIGHT!) you're GONNA' pay $.5.00, again, to get your OWN money out of their ATM, (again!), just to pay $20.00 for a drink, (again!!), JUST SO you can again, have that brief-interaction, with, THAT hot bartender? (Because, the more you drink,...the MORE you're JUST picturing that hot bartender WITH NO clothes on!!). (BESIDES, you've ALREADY SEEN all of what, the strippers up on stage, (getting naked), have to offer). SO, ain't it funny how, the strip clubs employ the HOTTEST girls,...AS their bartenders, (IN their Fantasyland!?). (And, since you HAVEN'T seen HER naked),...

THAT hot bartender IS, fast-becoming, YOUR fantasy girl! (IT'S the hot bartender, that BECOMES the one, YOU'RE fantasizing about,… IN "Fantasyland"!). AND, the more you drink, (YOU DAMN RIGHT!) THAT hot bartender WANTS you! (I COULD HIT THAT!!!). And, ain't it funny, that, the more you tip the hot bartender,…the more you THINK, that, YOU have - "bettered-your-odds" - OF, hittin' that?

BUT…

The REAL jokes on you! ('Cause, THAT hot bartender, finds it ALL TOO funny!).

'CAUSE…

She thinks YOU'RE a joke!

'Cause…

(SHE AIN'T NEW to THIS three-ring-circus!!!)

AND, (TO her!)…

YOU'RE just, the - "NEXT-warm-body" - sittin' there, ON THAT barstool! And, ALL she can see, (through the flashing lights, stage smoke, AND titties),…is YOUR big red nose AND dunce cap!(OY VEY!!).

But…

You AIN'T dressed in no white clown outfit, oh no!

(Hmm. Now, let THAT SHIT sink in!)

And…

Ain't it funny how, all of the fully-nude strippers, up on stage, are becoming green with envy?

AS…

You're giving more of your attention, and green, to that hot bartender, (who's wearing MORE than them!), wearing somethin' sexy, more so, than, you're giving to the ones (up there on that stage!), WEARING... nothing at all??

AS, (YOU!)...

BLOW your kids' lunch money, sittin' there,...dressed as a dollar bill, complete with a dunce cap and,...a big red nose. (Laugh to keep from crying).

And...

Right up in there with them, in that strip club, ("BITCHEZ"), seated up at the bar, looking at titties and ass,...is C. Trife! He looks like himself, he feels like himself, his vision is nearly all the way back, though, his throat is still on fire and, he's finding it hard to speak. He's even dressed in all black, how he would normally dress. (SO, he doesn't know...he's not him). Black jeans, black biker boots (with the steel toes removed for greater foot-speed and agility in a fist fight), and, wearing a black long sleeve button down dress shirt.

Yes, indeed. He's most certainly dressed in all black,...*just how DJ Wood WANTED him dressed!* (FOR the carving of Brotha Trife!!!). *And,... yes, indeed! If DJ Wood and his "People", had access to Brotha Trife's "Bully Boyz colors", (emblazoned with those famed "double B's" on the back, of that leather vest of black, of those "double B's", the color of "Bully Boy green")??? WELL, C. Trife, MOST CERTAINLY WOULD HAVE BEEN laying there on his back, in the under the ground levels of Jettison Records, amongst and with, all those bells and whistles and shit, and with the blinking lights, sounds and buttons, that intubation tube, and those adhesive EKG Pad Electrode Buttons, for the past 1 ,261 days, laying in his gurney, in his Bully Boyz colors, in "The Hall" of green emralds and white jade!!!*

(Shoot!), DJ Wood and his "People", EVEN TATTOOED - "Proverbs 15:3" - under the eyes of the clone of Brotha Trife!!! (Even though, it had to be redone, a couple dozen different times!)...('Cause, tattoo ink, in clone skin, dissipates,...and sinks in!). SO, just to ensure, on THIS clone, there would be something permanent, laying on his gurney, laying on his back, in the under the ground levels, in HIS OWN room, fully intubated in his "resting" state" and all that, "They" even went so far, as to have - "PUGILIST" - branded

cross his stomach! (JUST SO, the clone of Brotha Trife, LOOKS JUST LIKE Brotha Trife!)...(FOR WHEN they carve him the fuck up, ON May 1st!!!).

And, since, THEE: "Pullers OF Strings" demanded upon Pockets, contingent upon Pockets' Jettison Records hiring, Pockets, "pull some strings". And so, with BIG MONEY TO BE MADE,...Pockets, came clean! And, corroborated that dirty vice cop's story! (That, IT WASN'T Pockets' brother, Too Cold, live on-air,...THAT DID the slicing and dicing!). RATHER, THAT, OF Brotha Trife, a.k.a. "Too Cold", of the ACTUAL Too Cold, Brotha Trife, WAS ACTUALLY JUST PRETENDING!!

AND, WITH THAT, DJ Wood, DOESN'T want to carve-up "Too Cold". (Nope!). DJ Wood WANTS PAYBACK, ON BROTHA TRIFE!!! (*SINCE, THAT'S WHO-THA'-FUCK, actually carved, DJ Wood, THA'-FUCK-UP!!!). And so, DJ Wood, was insistent upon, and, so granted, (BY, THEE: "Pullers OF Strings"!), THAT, the clone, (be, and, to) look, EXACTLY like, Brotha Trife. And, NOT, HIS character, HIS portrayal, OF: "Too Cold".* (Oy Vey!!).

BUT...

(C. Trife, he DOESN'T know anything about ANY OF that!!!)...

AS, HE...

Sits up at the bar catching the show and, gettin' good and fucked up and, catching a GOOD CASE of the rams!(OY VEY!!!).

C. Trife's memory is still shot. It will take quite some time - for his - "recently-awakened" Tier-Three-Mind - to regain, his mental faculties. Though, C. Trife, *being a "DIRECT DESCENDANT" - of, B. Trife,* is WITHOUT prejudice, (in regards to), and, AS SUCH, (and, oh yeah, ...PLEASE, make NO mistake!!!), THAT, C. Trife, AIN'T DOWN WIT NO - time-wastin' - fake-ass - "sometimey"(AND, if YOU "sometimey"... YOU "ALL-THE-TIMEY"!!!) - bullshittin'-ass-NONSENSE!!! (AND, ON THIS, C. Trife, IS WITHOUT...bias or fallacies!!). BUT, then again, *from all the drugs his "donor-self", Brotha Trife a.k.a B. Trife, put into his body, (and from just all the really fucked-up-shit he's seen and done), his brain has taken quite a hit. And, as such, his memory started to become poor a long time ago.* And so, C. Trife, has taken that on, *(a "hereditary demented-dementia" of sorts).* And so, C. Trife, has this whole "Mr. Short-Term-Memory" thing, going on, (AND, he DON'T even know it!!!). SO, C. Trife, don't really know what he doesn't know, he doesn't realize what he's not realizing and, he's not thinking about what he's not thinking about. TO, C. Trife, today is today. And he's in a strip club. And, FURTHERMORE, as far as HE'S concerned or knows, Rae Sremmurd ARE the Beatles,...AND they're BLACK!!!! AND, as far as HE'S concerned, he's NEVER EVEN HEARD this song BEFORE!! *(BUT, he was feeling the fuck outta' it BACK IN 2016!).* But, sadly enough, he doesn't remember that. But, he's feeling the fuck outta' it right now, as it's playing in the strip club. And, as far as he's concerned, he got the fuck outta' a really fucked-up situation...wherever the fuck he was... whatever the fuck that place was all about. BUT HE'S HERE NOW!!! (ALL UP IN BITCHEZ!!!) And, he came in BITCHEZ to get fucked up! *Because,...something in his head, TOLD HIM to come into this strip club...and get fucked up. AND, something in his head, TOLD HIMSELF to BULLY some money...as he was walking around lost! (Old habits die hard, ya dig?).* And, he knows he'll make his way home...somehow...some day,...*(WHEREVER the fuck home is???).* But, AS for right now, AT THIS VERY MOMENT, the ONLY thing C. Trife is THINKING about, is gettin' to know that stripper over there. (Hey, go-eazy on the man!),(He just woke up after *THREE years!)*...(WHAT THE FUCK YOU THINK HE'S THINKIN' 'BOUT!?!). Shiiiiiit. Anyway-Damn-Way!

And so...

The stripper on his mind, is several - warm-bodies-dressed-as-dollar-bills - away. As, she's making her "tip-round". As, she makes her way 'round the bar, collecting tips, from the customers seated up at the bar, (dressed as dollar bills!), that have just watched her - show-it-all-off - up on stage.

When the stripper first came on stage, walked out on stage, took the stage with her grace. The first thing she did was stage herself, in her clear stiletto high heel platform-stripper-shoes, right in front of C. Trife, ignoring all others. As, he in turn, ignored every motherfucker in the joint but her.

And then...

She began to dance. Right in front of him. FOR him. And then, she'd go and work the stage. The poles. And the customers seated up at the bar, gettin' that tip money. From them. BUT, after her first song ended and, as her second song began and, WHEN it came time for her to take off her top, when she took off her top, guess who she came back to AND, took her top off for? For him. And, after "first-dibs" were given to him on them titties, she left. And, got back to working the stage. And got back to working the poles. And got back to working more tip money out of the - warm-bodies-dressed-as-dollar-bills -, seated up at the bar. And, when her second song ended and, when her third and final song began, when it came time for her to work that G-String down her tone thighs, take a guess who she got back to and, worked them shitz off for? For him! And, NOW that her three-song-set is finally over and, now that she's finally down from off of that stage, (taking with her, money and grace) and, now that she's finally making her tip-round 'round the bar and, now that she's finally just a few barstools away from him,...some dickhead is being disrespectful to her. And C. Trife is peepin' this shit. And that ain't good for him.

This guy, the dickhead, dressed in a gray, well-worn-thin t-shirt, pleated eggnog shorts and, navy blue low-quarter slip-on Nordstrom Rack tennis shoes(with no socks!), is PURPOSELY rockin' the trendy, dressed-down-look, of: I-Ain't-Got-Money. (BUT, got more money in here THAN everybody!). But, NOW, he's got to TURN-UP his "snot-attitude", (BECAUSE, he's GOT TO let EVERYBODY in here know, THAT,...he's GOT a lot of money!). BECAUSE, the trendy, dressed-down-look, of: I-Got-A-Lot-Of-Money-But-I'M-Going-To-Dress-As-Though-I-Ain't-Got-A-Lot-Of-Money-Because-THAT'S-What's-Trendy-RIGHT-NOW-Between-The-I-Got-A-Lot-Of-Money-Folks - (thinking they're being so smart and clever) - ISN'T enough, for THIS guy! Nope! *(AND, the ONLY reason WHY, he beat the Dress Code and, got in here in the first place is,...he's got a lot of money!).* BUT, he's a cheap-fucker AND, feels entitled NOT TO tip the strippers, (and so, THAT'S WHY he's still got a lot of money!!). Cocky. Rich. Entitled. Jerkoff. Piece of shit. Fuckin' drunk, strip-club-dickhead customer. Yeah. That guy.

And so...

While, C. Trife, remains seated up at the bar and, as he continues to ignore every stripper in the joint except for her, he looks over to his left and watches, as: Mr. Eggnog Shorts, STEADILY continues to fuck up!

(Come! Let's take a look!)...

AS...

He continues to make the stripper stand there, in front of him, during her "tip-round", with her boobs "at-the-ready", (as she, continues to stand there, in front, of: Mr. Drunk No Socks Special Motherfucker), as she, continues to WAIT for him, to tip her, (as he, CONTINUES to completely blow her off!). As she, continues to wait for him, TO acknowledge her presence! (SO, THAT, HE CAN THEN, RESPECTFULLY...place a single dollor bill tip, BETWEEN her boobs!!). AS her, bare breasts, continue to be held by her hands. As, she's continued to be MADE to stand there, and wait, TO BE TIPPED, a single dollar bill, between her bare breasts. As he, KNOWS THAT she is standing there. As he, knows AS TO WHY, she IS standing there! As SHE knows, HE knows, as to WHY, she is standing there! *As she, has seen him tip, all of the other strippers, that have come down off of the stage, after having danced their three-song-sets. As she, has already seen him tip them all, RESPECTFULLY, a single dollar bill, between their bare breasts, as they made their "tip-round". (As he, didn't fuck with them!!).* As he, has now decided, to single out, THIS ONE particular stripper to (AND, TO!) fuck with her! As he, continues TO pretend, THAT, there ISN'T a female standing there, (RIGHT IN FRONT OF HIM!!!), HOLDING her bare breasts!! (As he, CONTINUES TO THINK it's funny!). As he, stands there, with his rich-drunk-obnoxious-quartet. As, Mr. Dickhead, continues to look at his obnoxious-quartet and, around the bar, FOR approval OF, his: DRUNKEN-DICKHEADISH-ENTITLED-BEHAVIOR!!! As she, HASN'T DONE DICK, to THIS dickhead, TO WARRANT SUCH dickheadish-treatment! As she's, CONTINUED, TO BE MADE, TO STAND THERE,...and wait, (amongst and with!), the drunken-entitled-dickhead quartet, OF: Joe & The Jerkoffs! As her, bare breasts, continue to be held in her hands. As her, bare breasts, continue to be neglected! As her, bare breasts, continue to be denied being squeezed. (As, Mr. Rich Drunk Entitled Prick, has still YET TO PLACE, a single fucking dollar bill, BETWEEN her bare breasts!!). As her, bare breasts, continue to be held in her hands, as they, continue to be neglected, a single dollar bill, being place between them. As they, continue to be denied, being squeezed together, (so that, the stripper, can collect her dollar bill tip and,...JUST BE ON HER WAY!). As, Joe Jerkoff, and his jerkoff friends, CONTINUE to have, a good laugh, AT HER expense! As, Mr. Needs A. Smack, has finally caught the eye and, "the look", from,...C. Trife. (As, WITH "that look", it HAS finally made Mr. Pleated Shorts, find ENOUGH good-sense, IN THAT DRUNKEN-HEAD OF HIS, TO reach into his pants pocket AND,...pull out his wad of cash!). As, Mr. You 'Bout To Get Fucked-Up, continues to, shuffle through, all that cash in hand. As he, continues to, search for a single dollar bill, (amongst and with!), ALL THOSE $20s, $50s AND $100 dollar bills, in his hand! (As she's, continued TO BE MADE, TO stand there, AND WAIT,...with boobs "at-the-ready"). As, Mr. Bad Shitz Comin' Your Way, continues to take his good ol' time. As he, continues to slowly fold a single dollar bill in half...(lengthwise). As, C. Trife, continues to peep this shit, continually becoming more and more pissed-off and yet, happy at the same time, (damn near giddy!). AS he, *CONTINUES to, think of ALL the bad shit, HE'S GONNA' DO,* TO: Mr. Yeah I'm Definitely Fuckin' You Up!!!

HOWEVER...

AS her, bare breasts, were NO longer BEING neglected and, as her bare breasts were no longer being denied, being squeezed together, to take the tip, BEING PLACED BETWEEN her tits, (TO collect her hard-earned tip!)(SO, THAT, she can just be on her way and, be done AND away FROM, THIS drunk asshole!), Mr. Needs A. Smack, goes and...PULLS THE DOLLAR BILL BACK OUT, (FROM BETWEEN HER TITS!!)...IN LAUGHTER!!! And, C. Trife, just peeped THAT shit! AND, that AIN'T good for him!

AS...

THIS - Rich-Drunk-Dickhead-Strip-Club-Customer - HAS, NOW, done this FOR...a SECOND time!! As, IT'S NOW old...(and, WAS NEVER funny FOR the stripper!).

As...

(C. Trife, DON'T find this shit funny either!)...(And that AIN'T good for him!).

And so...

As the stripper, looks around the bar for a bouncer and, as none are to be found, (none that are paying ANY attention to her anyway!), she continues to look around the bar for assistance. As, her eyes find that C. Trife's, have already been locked on her's. And in "that look", so much is said. But, the most important thing, C. Trife, hears, is, "You got this for me?"

So...

C. Trife, shoots up out of his barstool! (Which gets the attention of the stripper! The dickhead! AND, most of the warm-bodies-seated-up-at-the-bar-dressed-as-dollar-bills!). And, it gets the attention of the strippers, UP-ON-STAGE, STRIPPING! And, it gets the attention of the strippers, seated on barstools, seated up at the bar, drinking drinks, (bought for them, by the warm bodies - seated up at the bar - dressed-as-dollar-bills)...(spending their kid's lunch money!!).

BUT...

(BEFORE, C. Trife, can say OR do anything, to: Mr. Nordstrom Rack Tennis Shoes)...

Mr. Steal-Your-Thunder, (who's seated across the bar!), SHOUTS ACROSS THE BAR and, across the strippers up on stage stripping, shouting over to AND directly at, Mr. Nordstrom Rack Tennis Shoes,

"YO! WHY YOU BEING A DICK???", (feigning his voice TO SOUND LIKE, he ACTUALLY gives a fuck!).

C. Trife, taken aback a bit, by someone, NOW wanting to SAY OR DO something (IN defense of the stripper!), looks over at that guy, seated across the bar, *who, apparently, DIDN'T feel the need, TO do or say ANYTHING,* until now, (UNTIL he saw C. Trife stand up!). WHO, THEN, to C. Trife, apparently, this guy, *MUST have seen THAT dickhead, BEING a dickhead, TO THAT stripper, BUT, didn't do a damn thing,...*'cause it ain't his problem! (BUT, NOW, wants to LOOK LIKE the hero!!!) *AND, WORSE THAN THAT, it just would've killed that guy, TO HAVE SEEN, C. Trife shine, INSTEAD of him, IS the impression, that, C. Trife, is getting!* So, he steals C. Trife's shine, by stealing C. Trife's thunder, so that C. Trife couldn't shine, so that the guy could be the hero, so that only he would shine. Yeah. THAT guy.

Still standing there in - *"Stolen-Thunder-No-Man's-Land"* - C. Trife looks, as Mr. Trendy Dressed Down Dickhead, standing there in no socks, looks over at the "thunder-stealer" seated cross the bar, (seated directly cross the stage from him), seated there, with a couple of his buddies, and, with, a couple of strippers. And then, from - *Stolen-Thunder-No-Man's-Land* -, C. Trife, stands there, and, watches as, Joe Jerkoff, shouts over cross the bar (and, cross the stage), to the *"thunder-stealer"*, (announcing, to the entire bar, as, well as, to the *"thunder-stealer"*, himself), "MAN,...I WAS JUST PLAYING AROUND!!!"

And...

With theft of thunder complete...

C. Trife, takes a seat back down on his barstool. And, starts patting his pants pockets for a pack of smokes that's not there, *(NOW realizing that he's a smoker!),* NEEDING a smoke, WANTING a smoke, from being the victim of *"blatant thunder-theft-bullying!"* (A Bully Boy, *who currently has no remembrances of having ever been a Bully Boy,* but, still instinctually retains, *that Bully Boy attitude and mentality,* HAS BECOME, the victim, OF: *"Thunder-Thievery Bullying"!!!)*...(Ain't THAT some shit!?!)...(AND, A MOTHERFUCKER!!!).

HOWEVER...

C. Trife, does so, for the stripper, (AS, MUCH AS, for himself!!), looks over, at: Mr. Rich Drunk Trendy No Socks Wearing Special Motherfucker, and, shouts, (the best THAT HE CAN with, His: Rough - Gravely-Throat-On-Fire-*Been-Intubated-For-The-Past-Three-Years-Or-So* - Voice, "NAH, MAN, YOU DON'T PLAY GAMES WITH HER!!! YOU GIVE HER THAT, FUCKIN' MONEY!!!", (And, C. Trife AIN'T feigning shit)...(for, C. Trife MEANS that shit!).

(Being rich and drunk, don't mean you can't get your ass kicked)...

SOOOOOO...

C. Trife, watches, as Mr. I Was Just Playing Around, changes that one-dollar bill, INTO a twenty-dollar bill, folds the twenty down the middle lengthwise, then, just holds the bill by his right thumb and index finger, (ensuring, there's plenty of bill, BETWEEN his hand and her's!). And then, he tips the stripper, by holding his hand outright for her to take it, WITH her hand, (and, NOT by her boobs!!),...*because, HE ALREADY fucked that up,*...(THE: Hand-Down-The-Boobs-Cheap-Thrill - Tip!!), WHICH, she, so then collects, (Her: Nineteen-Dollar-Turn-Around-Come-Up - Tip!), WITH, her hand. And then, does what, *she's just been standing there being made to wait to do.* (And THAT'S, just be on her way and,...AWAY from the dickheads!). Though, Mr. Dickhead, not the least bit put off that, the whole bar, NOW *thinks he was being a dickhead. Because, he IS a dickhead!* But, since he's a dickhead. *(And, KNOWS that he's a dickhead!).* He, looks over at C. Trife, *like: "Are-you-happy-now?",* before, he goes back to his conversation, with his hot girlfriend, and, with, the other two dressed-down-trendy motherfuckin' dickhead-buddies of his (that, between he, his dickhead girlfriend and, his two dickhead friends, makeup and comprise, the dickhead-quartet, of: Joe & The Jerkoffs!).

And so...

Joe Jerkoff, his dickhead-jerkoff of a girlfriend and, the two other jerkoffs that, he calls friends, get back to, as they, continue to, stand there, up at the bar, and, swill $20 drinks, after $20 drinks, but, ONLY want to tip the strippers a buck. (AND THEN - fuck with them - AT THAT!!). WHICH, really isn't all that hard TO FIGURE OUT why *or imagine! BECAUSE, rich-dickheads, have hot girlfriends, who, have no self-respect for themselves. Which, makes them, shitty-people too! And, most likely, have more problems and, more of a fucked-up life than, the strippers do.* And so, dickhead-jerkoff girlfriends (like herself!), take their - shitty-ass problematic-lives - out on strippers. And since, dickheads, know they're dickheads. And since, dickheads, hang with dickheads. (And that girlfriend's a dickhead too!). 'CAUSE, she's a female, *and, she JUST STOOD THERE, thinking it was funny, along with all the other dickheads, in their dickheadish-group! As she, watched her dickhead-boyfriend, BEING a dickhead to that stripper, a fellow female, instead of, speaking up and, telling her dickhead-boyfriend that, he's being a dickhead right now! (And, NOT TO make, that stripper's life, any harder than, it ALREADY is!).* Yeah. THEM dickheads!

And so...

With a kiss on his cheek and, a pack of smokes in his hand, the stripper, tells C. Trife, "Smoke these, I'll be back to talk with you." And then, places her purple velvet drawstring Crown Royal bag, (FULL of her hard-earned tip money!), up on the bar, next to C. Trife. And, then she walks off. (KNOWING,...ain't nobody gettin' THAT money!). And, after a few minutes, she returns. And, takes a seat in the empty barstool, next to C. Trife. And, after a few drinks, tension in the strip club increases.

(Let's have a look!)...

Mr. Dickhead, keeps looking between the strippers' legs, as he keeps looking cross the stripper's stage, as he keeps looking cross the bar, looking over at, Mr. Steal-Your-Thunder. And, every time that he does, it certainly would appear, all that, Mr. Steal-Your-Thunder, (does in reply), is to look back at Mr. Dickhead and, tilt his bottle of beer (way up high in the air!), as he takes a sip of beer. (But, Mr. Steal-Your-Thunder,...got some shit to him!). SO, as he, does so, (places that bottle of beer up to his lips, to take a sip), there's a purpose FOR tilting that beer bottle WAY up high in the air, EACH time that he takes a sip, (after, each time, he's prompted to do so!).

'CAUSE...

(AFTER each time, Mr. Pleated Eggnog Shorts, looks over at him from cross the bar, WHAT appears to be, an innocent sip of beer, ISN'T what it appears to be at all). (AND, CERTAINLY, not AS INNOCENT as it WOULD appear!).

For...

(Appearances ain't everything. *And, everything AIN'T always as it appears!)...*

And so...

HAVING some shit to him, Mr. Steal-Your-Thunder, is actually fuckin' wit Mr. Dickhead. (BUT, nobody in the bar knows this,...except for he and the dickhead!).

And so...

(Since Mr. Steal-Your-Thunder got some shit to him)...

He uses that tilted-way-up-high-in-the-air beer bottle of his, to conceal his right eye from the rest of the Jerkoffs, that makeup and comprise, the dickheadish-entitled-drunk quartet, of: Joe & The Jerkoffs. And, from behind that - tilted-way-up-high-in-the-air-beer-bottle - of his, Mr. Steal-Your-Thunder gives, drunk-ass Joe Jerkoff, a cocky, sarcastic-wink - with his right eye. Which he does, *(AND HAS BEEN DOING!!),* each time that he takes a sip!! (WHICH, he conceals behind that - tilted-way-up-high-in-the-air beer bottle - of his!) Which he does, *(AND HAS BEEN DOING!!),* so that NOBODY ELSE in the club, EVEN KNOWS that he's giving, Mr. Dickhead, that - cocky, antagonistic-wink!! (Of which!), AFTER each time, Mr. Dickhead, gets winked at,...IT JUST sends Mr. Dickhead through the roof! (EACH TIME that it KEEPS happening!)... (AND it keeps happening a lot!!)...(THAT'S WHY Mr. Dickhead KEEPS looking over cross the bar at Mr. Steal-Your-Thunder!!!). Mr.

Steal-Your-Thunder keeps baiting him in! AND THAT'S THE ONLY REASON WHY MR. STEAL-YOUR-THUNDER KEEPS TAKING A SIP OF BEER!!!...(TOLD Y'ALL Mr. Steal-Your-Thunder got some shit to him!).

BUT...

(Being drunk and a dickhead as he is!)...

Joe Jerkoff, also keeps looking over at, and keeps staring at,...C. Trife as well! *(Having seen the stripper buy C. Trife, the first of several drinks, that she's now bought for him). The FIRST drink, being bought WITH that $20 bill C. Trife, MADE him give to her!* And, EACH TIME that she buys him another drink,...THAT JUST SENDS Joe Jerkoff through the roof EVEN more!!(OY VEY!!). HEY!!! JOE JERKOFF!!! You're rich and you have a hot girlfriend. AND she's in here with you, looking at you, looking at titties. AND she's NOT jealous! HEY!!! DICKHEAD!!! You're ahead of the game! Just leave it at that. (But, NOOOOOOOOOOO!!!). Mr. Entitled-Fuckface, *thinks that his money,* (no, strike that), *his mother's money,* (no, strike that), *his STEPDAD'S MONEY,...('cause mommy, got his future-stepdaddy...sprung on swallowing nutt, WHEN she was trying to land her next "wallet-and-benefits". Which she did so...successfully!* Which SHE NOW feels as though, she's NO LONGER ENTITLED TO DO, swallow his nutt...so she don't! Mission accomplished you stupid motherfucker!). STUCK with another wife that, ain't swallowing nutt no more...(not his anyway!). AND padding a secret-nest-egg for herself! AND stuck with some smug jerkoff-stepson, who CAN'T EVEN DRESS HIMSELF!!! *Who THINKS that his money,* (no, strike that), *his mommy's money,* (no, strike that), *HIS STEPDADDY'S MONEY,...can get him out of ANY situation, even fucking around with killers.* Which it won't.

And so...

*With rams caught a long time ago, and, with those stares from Joe Jerkoff caught a long time ago as well,...*well, C. Trife, has a decision to make. And, well, C. Trife's either gonna keep working on trying to leave this club with this girl, or...leave that guy KNOWING that C. Trife, DON'T play tha' bullshit!! *Because, all that eye-balling-shit, IS beginning to work on C. Trife's LAST-damn-nerve!* (AND, it's beginning to fuck C. Trife up on, working on, by last call, HIM working on...leaving with this girl... after last call!). And so, *after some thought,* C. Trife, *being B. Trife, being Brotha Trife,* BEING himself, *decides...,* "FIRST *I'm* GONNA' *leave this - squirrelly-mutha'-fucka' - IN a puddle of his OWN blood! And, THEN I'm gonna leave WITH this girl!!*"

And so...

When - Mr. Mommy Lay Out My Clothes For Me For Tomorrow Alright Mommy Thank You's - NEXT stare, is met BY "a look" from, C. Trife, of: *"I'm-Going-To-Open-Up-Your-Fuckin'-Head!",* C. Trife, hollers over, to: Mr. Can't Dress Himself, as he, says, "All this fuckin' starin', yo! You wanted to do somethin', BITCH?!?" And the SECOND the head nods "yes", (which was done with the SLIGHTEST of nods!), a nod, of: *"My-Head-Nod-Is-Telling-You-"Yes"-But-My-Heart-Is-Telling-Me-"NO" - 'Cause-You-Done-Took-That-Shit-A-Long-Time-Ago - (AND, FUCK) - Did-I-Just-Really-Nod-My-Head-"Yes"-To-THIS-Guy? - (FUCK ME!!!")* - C. Trife, flies out of his barstool and, is met by the dickhead's hot dickhead-girlfriend ('cause she's a dickhead too!), runnin' FULL SPEED at him, WITH HER HANDS OUT, while pleading to him, "NO!!! NO!!! NO!!!", (for C. Trife, NOT to fuck-up, her: eggnog-pleated-shorts-wearing-dickhead of a boyfriend!).

What to do?... What to do!?... (Come! LET'S have a look!)...

C. Trife straight hits her with a quick-shake-and-bake-dip-down-low-left-spin-right-spin-back-left-followed-up-with-a-"swim move"-left-coming-right-off-her-left-hip and, ends up in dude's face much faster than, and, before, either the dickhead or his hot dickhead of a girlfriend, knows what the fuck JUST happened!!! "You wanna fight, bitch? Let's take the shit outside!", C. Trife, barks at the guy, *with, his: Tier-Three-Mind, NOT even remembering that, his line before (and, TO instigate!) a fight - ALWAYS, was: "You wanna fight? Swing." -, cutting right to the chase, eliminating ALL pre-fight talk! 'Cause, either you WANT TO fight OR you don't. 'Cause, I want to fight. And, we ain't gotta' take shit outside! 'Cause, I don't wanna go nowhere. 'CAUSE, I WANT all these motherfuckers in here TO SEE, me, bust you, the fuck up! Sooooooooooo? IF YOU wanna fight? Then, swing. (Yeah. THAT'S what I thought!!).*

HOWEVER...

C. Trife, is surprised, *that, after SUCH A - sheepish-head-nod - at* HOW pissed, AND EAGER to fight, the guy has NOW become! ESPECIALLY NOW, THAT, C. Trife, is IN the guy's face!!! DARING HIM!!! CHALLENGING HIM!!! STARING HIM RIGHT IN HIS EYES!!! SEASONED!!! A *seasoned* fighter, *though, with his recently-awakened-Tier-Three-Mind, he doesn't even remember that, he is,* but, yet, he is. And yet, he's ready, able, AND WILLING, to handle, some: *"seasoned*-for-this-shit!"...*(BROTHA TRIFE BLOOD, YA DIG!!!).*

HOWEVER...

Coming as, MORE OF A surprise, to C. Trife IS, the guy's ANSWER, TO, if, he wants to take the fight outside? *(ESPECIALLY CONSIDERING how, Mr. Dickhead's feet, remained FIRMLY-planted in place!), especially after such a bullshit-head-nod, of: ""Yes"-I-Wanted-To-Do-Somethin'" - especially after it was his "dickhead-of-a-girlfrind"* ('CAUSE SHE'S A DICKHEAD TOO!!!) - *AND, NOT HIM - who came running full speed, at C. Trife, especially after, C. Trife, closed distance on him FAST!*

(Soooooo? What the fuck was his answer? I'll fucking TELL YOU!) Come. Let's listen in...

"NO! I WANT TO FIGHT, HIM!!!"

Wait? WHAT?? *Unbeknownst to C. Trife, and to Mr. Dickhead's hot dickhead of a girlfriend, and to the rest of Mr. Dickhead's dickheadish-crew, is that, EVERY TIME, Mr. Steal-Your-Thunder, tilted that beer bottle of his way up high in the air, ONLY he and Mr. Dickhead knew, that, in ADDITION to, using that - tilted-way-up-high-in-the-air beer bottle of his, to conceal that - make-you-come-unglued - antagonistic-wink - of his, is that, he was ALSO resting his right middle finger alongside of that - tilted-*

way-up-high-in-the air beer bottle - of his, as he, kept subtly giving Mr. Dickhead the middle finger, EVERY TIME, he took a sip of beer, from that - tilted-way-up-high-in-the-air - beer bottle of his! WHICH WOULD ONLY MAKE MR. DICKHEAD LOOK CROSS THE BAR EVEN MORE, TO TRY AND FIGURE OUT, IF, IN FACT, MR. STEAL-YOUR-SHINE, WAS ACTUALLY GIVING HIM THE FINGER!!! OR, IF, IN FACT, MR. STEAL-YOUR-SHINE, WAS ACTUALLY JUST RESTING HIS MIDDLE FINGER ALONGSIDE OF HIS BEER BOTTLE EACH TIME HE TOOK A DRINK!!! WHICH WOULD MAKE MR. DICKHEAD, TRY TO FIGURE OUT, IF, IN FACT, MR. STEAL-YOUR-SHINE, WAS ACTUALLY FUCKIN' WIT HIM!!! WHICH WOULD MAKE MR. DICKHEAD, GO FROM LOOKING AT MR. STEAL-YOUR-SHINE'S MIDDLE FINGER, TO LOOKING MR. STEAL-YOUR-SHINE IN HIS EYES, TO TRY AND FIGURE OUT, IF, IN FACT, MR. STEAL-YOUR-SHINE, WAS ACTUALLY FUCKIN' WIT HIM!!! ...BY GIVING HIM THE FINGER!!! WHICH, WOULD BE CONFIRMED, BY, MR. STEAL-YOUR-SHINE'S, - ANTAGONISTIC - MAKE-YOU-COME-UNGLUED - WINK - OF HIS, THAT, MR. STEAL-YOUR-SHINE, KEPT GIVING TO HIM!!! WHICH ONLY MR. DICKHEAD COULD SEE, THE FACT, THAT, HE WAS REPEATEDLY BEING GIVEN THAT - ANTAGONISTIC - MAKE-YOU-COME-UNGLUED- WINK - OF HIS!!! CONFIRMING THE FACT, THAT, IN FACT, HE WAS, IN FACT, BEING GIVEN THE MIDDLE FINGER BY MR. STEAL-YOUR-SHINE!!! WHICH WOULD ONLY SEND MR. DICKHEAD THROUGH THE ROOF EVEN MORE!!! EVERY TIME!!! WHICH WAS IN ADDITION TO, THAT - MAKE-YOU-COME-UNGLUED - ANTAGONISTIC-WINK - THAT, MR. STEAL-YOUR-SHINE, KEPT GIVING TO HIM!!! CONFIRMING TO MR. DEADHEAD, THAT, YES - YOU STUPID-DRUNK-ENTITLED-DICKHEAD - MOTHERFUCKER - I AM GIVING YOU THE MIDDLE FINGER!!! WHICH IS WHY MR. DICKHEAD KEPT LOOKING OVER CROSS THE BAR AT MR. STEAL-YOUR-SHINE IN THE FIRST MOTHERFUCKIN' PLACE!!! (TOLD Y'ALL MR. STEAL-YOUR-SHINE GOT SOME MOTHERFUCKIN' SHIT TO HIM!!!). *And, poor C. Trife, he had no idea! THAT, all the while, while he was just sitting there, smoking that stripper's cigarettes and, drinkin' that stripper's liquor and, actually getting to know and growing fond of that stripper, Mr. Steal-Your-Shine WAS, fuckin' wit Mr. No Socks! (AND, ADDITIONALLY, UNBEKNOWNST to everyone else in the strip club, EXCEPT FOR Joe Jerkoff AND Mr. Steal-Your-Thunder, that IT WAS even being done! AND, (TO MAKE MATTERS WORSE),...UNBEKNOWNST to C. Trife,... HE was actually gettin' ready TO BE cock-blocked!! (THAT MUTHA' FUCKIN' THUNDER-STEALIN' MUTHA' FUCKA'!!!).*

And so...

Taken aback. Again. Back to standing in - *"Stolen-Thunder-No-Man's-Land"* - AGAIN!!! C. Trife, takes a look around the club, to see - WHO THE FUCK - Mr. Dickhead - NOW - wants to fight...MORE THAN HIM!?! (ESPECIALLY NOW, that, HE is THE ONE - standing face-to-face - WITH the guy!). AND...ESPECIALLY NOW, THAT, it's actually HIM - who's is in the guy's face - CHALLENGING HIM TO FIGHT!! *ESPECIALLY NOW, that, HE was ABLE to - make it over to Mr. No Socks* - THIS TIME!!! - (WITHOUT) - ...having his MOTHERFUCKIN' SHINE STOLEN!!!

(Oh, NO! ...Not THIS motherfucker AGAIN!!!)

And so, from - *"Stolen-Thunder-No-Man's-Land"* - C. Trife, spots Mr. Steal-Your-Shine, grabbing his cell phone from off the bar and, standing up and, saying, "No Problem.", (accepting the fight being challenged to him). And then, Mr. Steal-Your-Shine, begins making his way around the bar to fight - Mr. Drunk Rich Trendy Dressed Down I'm Just Here To Be A Dickhead To The Strippers - Strip-Club-Dickhead-Customer - Motherfucker. Yeah. That guy. *"OH,...HOLD UP! AWE, HELL NAW!! AND, AIN'T THIS SOME SHIT?!?",* C. Trife's, Tier-Three-Mind, *generates such thoughts, (as it,* and he) then, *generates, some mo', "This is the SECOND TIME NOW, that, Mr. Steal-Your-Shine, has stolen MY thunder! ...AND, MY motherfuckin' SHINE!!! Nah, fuck THIS shit! I ain't lettin' this tall-skinny-lanky-motherfucker, steal MY mutha'-fuckin'-shine! I'M kickin' tha'-shit - outta, this: NO-socks-wearin' - rich - drunk - dickhead-motherfucker,... MY-DAMN-SELF!!!"*

AND THEN. ALL HELL BREAKS LOOSE!!!!!!

(Come...let's take a look!)...

As, Mr. Steal-Your-Shine, is making his way around the bar, all of the strippers, that, were sitting over there cross the bar with him, all jump up off of their barstools and, start running in their high stiletto stripper-heels! (To get in front of him!). To BLOCK him. To prevent him FROM reaching, Mr. Drunk-Entitled-Dickhead! *Because, this WON'T be the first time, Mr. Steal-Your-Shine, has been in a fight, IN THEIR strip club. For, they've all seen Mr. Steal-Your-Shine, almost kill a man, in that club before.* (And, shit like that, TENDS to chase off, ALL of, the: Dollar-Bills-Seated-At-The-Bar-Dressed-As-Dollar-Bills!). And, THAT'S just bad for business. (AND FOR, JOE JERKOFF!!!).

And so...

(There were high heels breakin' and girls stumblin'! And drinks spillin'. And customers getting knocked into. And I'm pretty sure a bitch even hit a bitch for calling a bitch a bitch!),(HEY, the strip club IS called BITCHEZ! What the fuck you want from me???:)

But, (through the onset, *of hell being broken loose)...*

The stampede of strippers, WERE able to finally, head Mr. Steal-Your-Shine, off at the pass! (As, Mr. Steal-Your-Shine, stands there, buffered behind boobs and butts!). And, as C. Trife,...stands there,...(WATCHING THIS SHIT!!!) *he, thinks to himself, "Welp. I GOTTA' give it to the guy... HE CERTAINLY KNOWS HOW to steal a motherfucker's shine, with style!!"* And, as C. Trife, is standing there - *in "Stolen-Thunder-No-Man's-Land"* - (WATCHING THIS SHIT!!!), Mr. Steal-Your-Shine, does something, *that, C. Trife, NEVER thought Mr. Steal-Your-Shine, WOULD do.* (What he do?!?)...*(Served-up some SHINE on - a silver-fucking-platter - FOR - mutha' fuckin' C. Trife!!!).* "AIN'T NOBODY STANDIN' BETWEEN YOU AND, MY BRO!!! OH, YOU FUCKED NOW!!!", Mr. Steal-Your-Shine, shouts, from cross the bar. *(Serving, Joe Jerkoff off to C. Trife!)(While, serving C. Trife up some shine, on a silver-platter!)...* (WHILE, shouting overtop of the gaggle of girls, that surrounds him!!!).

While, even managing to serve himself up, SOME MORE SHINE!!!...(BY SERVING, C. TRIFE, UP SOME SHINE!!!). WHILE, HE REMAINS,... safely-tucked behind butts and buffered BY boobs!!...(AIN'T THIS SOME MOTHERFUCKIN' BULLSHIT!!!)...*(NOT ONLY, DID, Mr. Steal-Your-Shine, GAIN, EVEN MORE SHINE, BY GIVING, C. Trife, some shine)...*

BUT...

He did it,...in a way, that,...*NOW HE AIN'T EVEN GOT TO FIGHT NOBODY!!!*

AND...

STILL GOT, MORE SHINE, OUTTA' THE MUTHA' FUCKIN' DEAL!!! (YOU SEE HIM, standin' over there, surrounded by all them strippers, DON'T YOU???). AIN'T THIS SOME MOTHERFUCKIN' BULLSHIT!!!

And so...

As, C. Trife, returns his attention, upon Joe Jerkoff, *('cause,...FUCK IT...might as well SHINE!)*, one of, Joe Jerkoff's "Jerkettes", (feeling drunk AND brave) attempts, to tackle C. Trife! As, he comes from 'round back of Joe Jerkoff and, CATCHES, C. Trife, GOOD in the ribs with his shoulder! (Digging, his right shoulder, HARD into the upper left side of, C. Trife's, rib cage). While, wrapping his arms, around C. Trife's torso, (AS HE DOES SO!!). AND,...SQUEEZES HARD!!! (Bringing, and forcing, C. Trife's, rib cage, down EVEN MORE INTO, this asshole's shoulder!). Pressing, his shoulder bone, more and more, into C. Trife's ribs, AS IF HE KNEW what he WAS DOING. *(Because, C. Trife, COULD FEEL when his rib snapped!)...(RIGHT ON TOP of that motherfucker's shoulder bone!).* THAT, dickhead-friend, of: Mr. Dickhead, was PURPOSELY forcing his shoulder, INTO C. Trife's ribs,...right above his heart.

Broken rib and all, C. Trife, was able to fight off, being taken to the floor, by the sneak-attack-tackle. And, was able, to wrap his OWN arms around the torso OF his tackler! And,...pick him up. AND, THEN, violently-slam - the tackler's body - INTO the side of a pool table!!!

(Shifting the massive slate-top pool table, OVER SEVERAL FEET, by the shear force of the tackler's body being slammed, into the side of the pool table alone!). Violently knocking over barstools, when and where, the pool table, comes to a rest, up against the bar, and, up against the barstools, *that, once lined the bar,* BUT, NOW, litter the floor!!! Then, the blaring music gets cut! AND then, the bright house-lights come on!! And, from under the glare of those bright house lights, and, from under the glare of every set of eyes in the joint,...*it's time for C. Trife to shine!*

The two then regroup. And reposition their hands, grappling while standing. *("Dude is short, BUT dude is strong!", is what, C. Trife's Tier-Three-Mind, is thinking).* And, each time, Mr. Dickhead's - drunken-buddy - *THINKS, he's got, the upper hand on ol' C. Trife, and, can take C. Trife, down to the floor,*...C. Trife, muscles him RIGHT BACK the other way! And, each time, C. Trife *THINKS, he's got, the upper hand and, can take this - short - strong-dude - down to the floor,*...THE LITTLE-FUCKER, MUSCLES HIS WAY-BACK,...to having the upper hand!

(And, as Joe Jerkoff, and, his last remaining - rich-no-socks-wearin' - dickhead - drunken-jerkoff-of-a-friend - AND - Mr. Steal-Your-Shine's crew, ENDS UP, MIXING-IT-UP,...a machete gets pulled from a pants leg,...OH-MY-DAMN,...someone's finna' get cut!!!)...

Well (On THAT note!)...

C. Trife, DECIDES, that, it's time to end this shit! As, he, and, the guy he's been grappling with, are beginning to edge-their-way-over - closer-and-closer - over to, a set of tall bar tables. (AND the tall bar tables' tall barstools!). BECAUSE, seeing those tall bar tables AND those tall barstools, *TRIGGERS* - C. Trife's, Tier-Three-Memory! *(Of a bar fight, Brotha Trife, was in...sometime...someplace...somewhere).* C. Trife, can't recall everything, *but, WHAT his "recently-awakened" Tier-Three-Mind, DOES know, is, "GETTIN' CAUGHT-UP in, all these tall-ass bar tables. AND, all of these tall-ass barstools,...AIN'T NO-WAY TA' GO 'BOUT WINNING A BAR FIGHT!!!"*

And so...

C. Trife, takes his left hand and, places it behind the guy's head and, then pulls the guy's head down. (AND forward!). And, then, holds the guy's head steady, with just his left hand. And, then,...WITH his right fist,...C. Trife, proceeds to - T-THE-FUCK-OFF - on this guy. Hitting him eight times. Just eight times. With each punch landing, on a different place, of the guy's, head and face. (And, C. Trife,...did this on purpose). So, that, the guy, NEVER knew WHERE,...he was going to get hit next. (JUST TO MAKE IT IMPOSSIBLE, FOR him, TO defend, himself!!)... ('CAUSE, THAT's some shit, Brotha Trife, WOULD do!!!). Twice to the top of his forehead, he gets hit. Twice to the side of his left eye, he gets hit. And, with four rapid-fire-HARD uppercuts, (THROWN LIKE he's TRYING TO fuck a motherfucker up), ('CAUSE, HE WAS!), the guy, gets hit, once in the nose and, the final three-shots,...he takes right ON his chin. Digging, the big - walnut-size-knuckles - of his right fist, RIGHT INTO THE BONE, (of the tip), of, his, motherfuckin', ENTITLED-chin! JUST AS, the "little special-motherfucker" - DUG HIS SHOULDER into, C. Trife's ribs! (STRAIGHT-UP cracking one of C. Trife's ribs)...(IN A STRAIGHT-UP CHEAP-SHOT-SNEAK-ATTACK!!!). Before, C. Trife, in turn, ends-up breaking the guy's nose and,...UNHINGING HIS JAW, WITH, the last of those, three, NASTY, uppercuts!!!! (THROWN LIKE, he was TRYING TO, fuck a motherfucker up!). Because he was. And so. He did.

And...

With the fight won. *AND, with it FINALLY being, C. Trife's time to shine,* (in front of every set of eyes in the house, from under those bright house lights),...C. Trife, LOOKS UP AT those bright house lights, (BLINDED, by those bright house lights!), AS, HE'S looking up at THOSE bright house lights,...FROM LAYING FLAT ON HIS BACK! (AND, WITH the guy he just beat up, lying on top of him). *AND, WONDERING to himself, in his Tier-Three-Mind,..."HOW THE FUCK - THIS SHIT - JUST HAPPENED?!?!?!"*

(HOW could - this shit - POSSIBLY have happened? YOU wanna take a guess??) I'll wait...

AS IT TURNS OUT, in TRUE Mr. Steal-Your-Shine fashion, *Mr. Steal-Your-Shine decided, that,…NOW it's a good time,…(FOR him!) to show, what HE can do!* Hmm.

AND SO…

Mr. Steal-Your-Shine, gave the guy (C. Trife, WAS going toe-to-toe with!), some-kind-of a martial arts kick,…FROM behind! (Taking out the guy's LEGS!!). SENDING the guy, DOWN to the floor. And, when he did, he ended up taking C. Trife,…DOWN TO THE FLOOR WITH HIM!!!!!! ("AIN'T this SOME shit! AGAIN!!! THE SHIT HAS HAPPENED TO ME,…AGAIN!!!", racing-thoughts in a, recently-awoken - Tier-Three-Mind!!!). AND, JUST FOR GOOD MEASURE, (AND, just to MAKE sure!), that, if ANYBODY HAD - ANY DOUBTS - as to, *WHO SHINED the MOST* that night?

Well…

IT WAS A MUST, (FOR MR. STEAL-YOUR-SHINE, TO LEAVE NO DOUBTS!!), THAT, IT WOULD BE HIM,…*THAT SHINED THE MOST!!!*

AND…

Just to make sure, that, if ANYBODY was going to be talkin' 'bout, *WHO SHINED that night?*

Well…

(YOU KNOW HOW MR. STEAL-YOUR-SHINE'S, GONNA' DO!!! HE'S, gonna make DAMN sure, *that, IF ANYBODY was talkin', 'bout, ANYBODY SHINING,…THAT IT WAS HIM,…that, THEY'D be talkin' 'bout!!)*

AND SO…

Mr. Steal-Your-Shine, being the *"empathetic-sort"* that he is, *('cause, when it comes to stealing your shine),…(it's fuck your feelings!).* And so, he pauses for a moment, SAVORING the moment, OF being center stage, UNDER those bright house lights, (MAKING DAMN SURE that ALL EYES in there are all ON HIM!!!). And so, as C. Trife is still down on the floor (and, has just about wrestled this dude off of him!), Mr. Steal-Your-Shine, comes up on dude from behind, and CATCHES dude right in the back of his head, with some crazy-looking martial-arts-kick, knocking dude out cold! (THAT MUTHA' FUCKIN' MR. STEAL-YOUR-SHINE!!!). Ya' gotta give it to him. ...*He sure knows how TO steal a mutha' fucka's shine with style!*

LOST CHILD

Pockets, following his instincts, *headed out into the City of Atlanta and, headed to where he believed, C. Trife's Tier-Three-instincts, would have lead him.* (A strip club). *And so, after Pockets drove around town for awhile, in his all red everythang Dodge Challenger, Pockets, retraced his travels, doing drive-bys past the strip clubs, he'd already driven-past, (and, or), actually stopped at, (to poke his head inside of it quickly), for a hot minute, to see, if he could see, C. Trife.* And so, as he continues to drive around, Pockets sees, just up ahead, (outside of that strip club up there), NOTHING BUT cop cars. Ambulances. And, not much more than, a whole lotta flashing lights, under a sea of blues and reds. And, continuing to follow his instincts, Pockets, indeed, heads towards THAT strip club. (Due, solely to, Pockets' instincts, telling him, just ONE thing,...*C. Trife WAS here!*).

Pulling to a stop, after pulling into the strip club parking lot, Pockets, is met with an excited, "Hey! Pockets!", *from a stripper known to him, and she of he,* (just getting off work and, being walked through the strip club parking lot over to her car, by a bouncer).

The stripper, after telling the bouncer, "I'm good.", the bouncer, then, walks off back towards the strip club and, goes back inside, (leaving the stripper alone by herself outside with Pockets). After asking the stripper if she's seen the man, that, he then describes, the stripper, standing, talking into Pockets' rolled down driver's window, with Pockets, still seated inside, replies, (ALL disgusted and shit!), "Yeah. He WAS here! NASTY motherfucker!! He got in a fight, fucked some - rich-motherfucker - up. Broke his jaw AND his nose!", (And then, ALL DRAMATIC AND SHIT), the stripper, *pantomimes the fucked-up guy's injuries, while she uses her fingers to manipulate her nose and, uses her hands to demonstrate, HOW - fucked-up - the, rich-drunk-guy's unhinged-jaw, ACTUALLY looked,* by saying, "THAT motherfucker's JAW was ALL HANGIN'-DOWN-LOW *like this here,* all hangin'-down-AND-TO-THE-SIDE, *like this here,* and the motherfucker's nose, WAS ALL PUSHED-TO-THE-SIDE, *like this here!!!*" And then, she continues, by telling Pockets, "I heard the paramedics saying, *they called-ahead to the hospital and, that rich-dude, is going straight into surgery.* Babe, the motherfucker YOU'RE looking for, SHOULDN'T be TOO HARD to find! HE got blood, ALL OVER his face!"

(And Pockets sits there, in his car, looking up at her, like, *"OH SHIT!!!"*). And then, he asks, "Blood? All over,...his FACE?? *MY...MY boy,...LOST???*"

"Sweetheart, YOUR boy, AIN'T lose shit!!! *HE, was fuckin' dude UP!!* And, THEY BOTH ended up on the floor. And then the dude your boy was fightin', straight-up - got KICKED in the BACK OF his head! AND THEN, ALL this blood came pouring out, *like this here,* out that guy's broken nose, *like this here,* down ALL OVER your boy's face, *like this here!* I'M ALL freaking-out and shit! Pockets, I ran up to your boy, tryna' give him a bar towel, so he could wipe his face, from all that blood and shit! And he was like, *"I got blood all over my face???".* Pockets, sweetie, HE DIDN'T EVEN KNOW IT!!! SO THEN, YOUR BOY, walks over to the big mirror, by the stage, *like this here,* and checks-out his face in the big mirror by the stage, *like this here.* Your boy sees all the streaks of blood running down his face, *like this here,* AND THEN...just calmly walks back over to me, *like this here,* hands me back the bar towel, *like this here,* and then, says to me, *like this here, "I'm good. There can NEVER be, too much blood, love!",* the stripper, standing there, tells Pockets, (*pantomiming C. Trife, the best she can and, imitating C. Trife's, rough-gravely-throat-on-fire-long-standing-intubated-voice),* before, she then, turns around, unable to see not much more than an ocean of flashing red and blue lights, on top of all the emergency vehicle rides. Then, turns back to Pockets and, says, "All that blood, all over HIS face, *like this here.* Ewwwwww!!...Pockets. Babe! YOUR BOY,...YOUR BOY, is triflin', AS FUCK!!!"

Pockets, (just BUSTS-UP LAUGHING!!!) while, looking up at the stripper and, says, "YEEEAAAHHH!!! SOMETHIN' LIKE THAT!!!", then, peering through the flashing reds and blues, (the best THAT he can), Pockets, asks, "IS HE,...under arrest?", scanning the back seats of the cop cars, STILL lookin' for the man.

"No. He left with, Me. Me, got him out of here. He, left with Me and, his crew.", the stripper, informs Pockets.

"Me?", a very-puzzled Pockets, replies.

(Looking at Pockets, like, "You KNOW, Me!"), the stripper, provides, "Not me. Me. You know, Me. M.E.? *"Mr. Empathy".* You know, Mr. Empathy. They be callin' him, M.E., but, he be goin' by, Me. He don't like, M.E. He's all about some, Me."

(NOW just getting it!), Pockets, laughs-out-loud (again!), and, says, "Ooooooooooooh! Me! THAT, *"SHINE-STEALIN'"*, MOTHERFUCKER!!! WELL, why DIDN'T you, just SAY so? Yeah, I know "of" him. Good lawd! Yeah, words goin' 'round he tryin' to get signed, but, THAT SHIT, AIN'T HAPPENIN'!!! I mean, he got a star "look" about him, but, if he thinks THAT'S enough to get him a deal? HE'S foolin' more than himself! Look-here, sweets, I'M IN tha' mafackin' "Game"! I know EXACTLY what, he needs! A). Learn to shut tha' fuck up and listen! B). Get dedicated. C). Get vocal lessons. And, with his "look"? Who-tha'-fuck knows? He MIGHT just land himself a record deal! But, it's whatever, I AIN'T SIGNIN' HIS ASS!!! ...HEY,...did they say, WHERE they were headed to??"

"You know, Me. *They ALWAYS be headin' back, to Lost Child's crib, when they be, leavin' the club. Gettin' they, smoke on!* You KNOW HOW Me's, gonna do!", the stripper, tells him.

"And, you say, he went with Me,...to go-'n-get smoked-up, huh? *SOUNDS 'bout, right!"*, Pockets, says to the stripper.

"Hey, babe. You know where, Lost Child, lives?", the stripper, asks.

"Yeah. I do. 'Cross town. I KEEP an eye on "certain-mutha'-fuckas", in MY city! ...Tha' Spanish-brother needs'a briefcase in his hand, NOT a machete,...I can make some money WITH him.", Pockets, replies.

And then...

The stripper, looks down at Pockets, VERY SERIOUSLY, *like, she's ACTUALLY sincerely-concerned and worried for, (AND ABOUT!), Pockets' welfare. (AND SAFETY!!!).*

(And, even perhaps,...Pockets', mental-state-of-mind)

FOR...

(Fuckin' WIT, some dude LIKE this!)

BECAUSE...

ALL that she, (or anyone else, in Atlanta, for that matter!) really knows, about Pockets, is, he's some sort of "big-wig", that works at Jettison Records, *for the past three or so years now. And that, no one had ever seen the man that stays dripped in red, in Atlanta before, he landed that "cushy-gig" at Jettison Records' - recently-built-state-of-the-art - titan of a building. And, that, prior to that, he must have worked for Jettison Records at their other location, and/or, he must have been, some kind of big-wig for a long time, for some other record label, before that.* And, that's all that they know-the-fuck-out-of his business! 'Cause,...THAT'S HOW Pockets likes it!! (AND, it's gots-to-be THAT way!...Outta NECESSITY!!!).

And so, then...

The stripper, asks, Pockets, "Sweetheart? How do you KNOW this guy, anyway? That, nasty-triflin'-motherfucker! Are...are you, alright? He, left with, Me and them. I think YOU should just let him, STAY GONE! NOBODY wants him comin' back, in this here club, 'cept, for, lil' homegirl, your boy, was rappin' too,...I can tell you, THAT much! Tha' cops can't EVEN arrest him, can't make ANY arrests, 'cept, for, arrestin' them, rich boys. 'CAUSE, one of them rich boy's, hit your boy, first. Them - rich-motherfuckers - were, fuckin'-wit US strippers ALL NIGHT,...before YOUR BOY, showed up! Your boy, DIDN'T like it. They started some shit with Me and, your boy. SWEETIE, Me and YOUR BOY, DON'T PLAY!! THEM TWO motherfuckers, don't play!! I'm sayin',...ON MY MOM'S, Pockets!!! ON GOD,...them two, DON'T play. AND, them rich-boys got, fucked-the-fuck-up, FOR it. THAT shitz, ON them!!! *Cops said, they don't know WHO, your boy is, NEVER seen him 'round before.* They be, lookin' for him, though. Pockets, babe, they don't want to arrest him,...CAN'T arrest him. *Cops said, he was just defending himself.* I even heard, *one of the cops saying, someone said, that, he heard YOUR boy's rib snap, WHEN THAT - rich-DRUNK-fucker - ATTACKED him.* I heard, *the cop saying, that, he was putting in his report, that, your boy sustained, "A broken rib, in self-defense".* So, babe, they don't want to arrest him. They just wanna FIND him. And,...GET HIM THE FUCK OUTTA' TOWN!!! Noooooobody, WANTS HIM 'round here, Pockets! 'Cept, for, lil' homegirl, of course!"

THEN...

The stripper, (gets all nosey and inquisitive and shit!), givin', Pockets THAT eye, stating, "Seems to me, babe,...seems like, YOU'RE the ONLY one, that knows him! YOU sure, YOU good?? Sweetie, I DON'T THINK you, should go lookin' for him. Dude's bad news! Baby, HOW you know him,...ANYWAY???"

And...

Pockets, just looks up at her, (cocks his custom red custom-made red hat hard to the side!), and then, simply states, "Don't you concern yo' self with me, baby cakes. It's a long story."

Then...

Reaches down, deep into one of his custom red custom-made red suit pants pockets and, pulls out a money clip, made of nothin' but ivory. (Nothin' but poached). Filled-up with, NOTHIN', BUT: brand-new-crisp-FRESH-makin'-Pockets'-custom-red-custom-made-red-pants-pockets'-interior - AND - Pockets'-red-everythang-car-interior - filled-up - with-the-SMELL-of - NOTHIN'-LESS-than - brand-new-CRISP-fresh-cash-money! (Just like, his OTHER money clip, IN the interior, of his OTHER, custom red custom-made red suit pants pocket!!). ALSO made, of nothin' BUT ivory. (And nothin' BUT, poached!). And, filled-up with, NOTHIN' LESS than, one thousand dollar bills! (Filled-up with, nothin' less than, ONE HUNDRED of the fuckers!).

And then...

He peels one of them fuckers off! And then, balls it up. And then, with one hand, pulls the stripper's hand (AND HER) forward! (ALL rough-like!)(OY VEY!!).

AND THEN...

With his hand, (with the money in it), CRAMS that "fresh-crispy-fucker" down INTO her palm! (Cramming in her skin "THE BARBS" of, that: balled-up-CRISP-FRESH-BRAND-NEW $1,000.00 bill!).

And then...

He GIVES the stripper, NOTHIN' LESS than,...an EYEFUL of AN EYE OF HIS OWN! Before he drives off. Off to continue his pursuit... of FINDING C. Trife!

MEANWHILE. (SOMEWHERE!)...In the City of Atlanta...

C. Trife, finds himself entering a street-level apartment door, *after finding himself for half the time trying to endure, the big talk of half-truths, while being couped up next to Mr. Empathy, in the back half of a Crysler Concorde coupe, finding himself HAVING TO, HAVE TO HELP HIMSELF PASS THE TIME, by spittin' a free-style rhyme, (inside of his Tier-Three-Mind!!!), after finding there's just no end to these pipe dreams, (of Mr. Empathy, being some-kind-of-self-professed-open-mic-kareoke-king!), though, after Mr. Empathy, finally started to sing, (after he FINALLY stopped talkin' 'bout himself!), C. Trife, did find, that, he didn't sound half-bad, (when he was tryin' to sound like someone else!).*

AND SO...

FOR, NOW, *(after the throw-down!),* C. Trife, finds himself, apart of a new crew! *And, he's thinkin' to himself, these white dudes are pretty cool, (for having his back!). And, mad-respect goes out to the Spanish cat, that brokeout a machete, (during that strip club scrap!).*

And...

As for, his best-interest? *(C. Trife, thinks it was for the best!)*...

'CAUSE...

If they didn't get him out of BITCHEZ?? *(C. Trife, thinks he'd be under arrest!!)*

And so...

(With that street-level apartment door closed, up a narrow staircase, these are the three, he follows)...

Lost Child, the lost one, finds himself lost, at the ripe ol' age twenty-one, and, at the rate he's goin', he's gonna live a short life, for following after the lead of the likes, of the one that's ALL about some "Me", (a.k.a. Mr. Empathy), and, he'll lead him there, (for he's dangerous!), (and this is the crew C. Trife is hangin' with!) for, Mr. Empathy, is somewhere in his thirties, for he is WAAAAAAY TOO proud, for, to him, he ain't lost, (he just ain't tryin' to be found!), and, some cat named Machete Steeze, and, he's workin' with more than just an "Ace" up his sleeve, and, rest assured, he knows EXACTLY, how many years he's been alive, 'cause, Machete Steeze is a "numbers guy", and, he "biddy-bops" wit a noticable-limp, from the machete, running down the pants leg, he got concealed inside of it!

With, C. Trife, still in the process of being the last one, to file into Lost Child's apartment above, with his final step that flight's last step has finally come, with them all then entering with a sharp-right, the first thing in C. Trife's sight, is a HUGE fish tank in the living room, with variously-different kinds of fish stocked tight. Some big. Some small. With his apartment still filling-up with the whole team, Lost Child, with remote control in hand, with-all-be-damned - with no one else even thinking to bother, they better get to it - before Lost Child can get to it - on the arm of his recliner, turns on his large flat TV screen, mounted above his fish tank, on the wall. With a narry-disapointed-nor-relieved-

Machete-Steeze, with his machete's tip now stuck in the carpet still clean, with placement of his machete's handle - leaning against the arm of the sofa - at a 45-degree angle, with Lost Child and Machete Steeze, now being the only two, remaining in the living room, with Lost Child reclining in his recliner, elevating his feet, with Machete Steeze next to his weapon-of-choice, is where he takes a seat.

And so...

(With Mr. Empathy and C. Trife, adjourning to the kitchen),... (waddaya' say we all go in there, with THOSE TWO, and have a listen!!)...

Once in the kitchen, Mr. Empathy, breaks out a small glass vile of hash. And, then, unscrews the vile's tiny plastic black cap. And then, says to C. Trife, "Smell this. Let THAT *tag* ya'!"

C. Trife, leans forward and, takes a big long sniff, off that open vile of hash, being held up to his nose by, Mr. Empathy. And ONCE, that smell, *(of THAT hash!),* travels-up-out of, that tiny glass vile, AND ONCE, C. Trife gets, *TAGGED* IN THE NOSE *(by THAT HASH!),*...C. Trife REACTS. (Pulling back!). And, says, "DAMN!!! THAT'S, some: *POTENT-ass SHIT!!!"*

(PLEASED by C. Trife's reaction and, by the *QUALITY* of his shit!), Mr. Empathy says, to C. Trife, "You think the SMELL of that hash, *TAGGED* ya'?? JUST WAIT, til' ya' SMOKE IT!", (then Mr. Empathy, peeks his head out of the kitchen real-quick, looking into the living room), and then, asks, C. Trife, "You see that fish tank out there? *I smoked this hash, after we left the strip club, last night. And, I GOT STUCK, on that sofa, out there, STARING AT that fish tank, for, THREE-fuckin'-hours, straight!!!"*

"FOR, THREE HOURS, my man??? Break THAT shit - THA'-FUCK - out!!!", C. Trife, replies.

"I HOPE, you don't plan on goin' anywhere for, awhile! 'Cause, you gonna be stuck right here, with us.", Mr. Empathy advises, him. (then, studies C. Trife's face for a few), BEFORE, asking, "I've never seen you 'round, before. WHERE tha' fuck, you from?"

And...

Mr. Empathy, just stands there...watching.

As...

C. Trife, has trouble in determining, exactly where it is, (the fuck) he is from!

And...

After, sufficient-time, has lapsed, (enough for Mr. Empathy to get pleasure outta watchin' C. Trife, wrestle with that question!), Mr. Empathy figures,...he'll fuck with him some more! "What the fuck DO I care, where YOU'RE from!? Tell ya', what. I'LL give ya', an EASY one! WHAT'S your name, man?", Mr. Empathy, asks, (hoping to get a rise, out of another beleaguered-answer,...to such a simple question).

With no hesitation, C. Trife, blurts out, "I'm the most triflin' motherfucker THIS SIDE of the Mississippi!", *(but, his Tier-Three-Mind,...has no idea where the fuck that came from!).*

Busting-up laughing, Mr. Empathy, says, "You know what? FUCK IT!!! Let's JUST smoke this, shit! What the fuck I care, what YOUR name is!?! I'll just call you, Triflin'...or, would you prefer,...Trife? I'm Me."

"Holy shit! That's my name!", C. Trife, exclaims, (knowing that, he is who he is!), *but, didn't even realize, that, he wasn't even aware of, not being aware of, what his name was,* right until right now. *Or was.*

"You're Me?", Mr. Empathy, replies.

"No! No, I'm not you! I'm me!", C. Trife, tells him, (more so, for himself!), (after the realization of what his name is), *but, without the realization of, why he wouldn't have realized, what his name was.* Or is.

"So, you're Me, too?", asks, Mr. Empathy, for clarification.

"No! No, motherfucker! I ain't you! I'M ME!!!", C. Trife says, emphatically.

"Relax, man. It's all good. I've just never met, another Me, before.", Mr. Empathy, tells him as it is.

"Listen, I ain't you, motherfucker! I'm me!", explains, C. Trife.

(Getting hyped himself!), Mr. Empathy, says, "I ain't SAY, you was me, motherfucker! All, I SAID, was, I just never met, another Me, before!"

"Don't be callin' ME, motherfucker!", C. Trife, snaps!

(Things NOW getting heated, Mr. Empathy, claps back!), "You been callin' ME a motherfucker, and that's exactly what the fuck I'ma call you right back! I don't know why you gettin' all-the-fuck pissed off, motherfucker! I ain't know you was Me, until you told me, you was Me!"

"Listen, motherfucker! I ain't never SAID, I was you! I SAID, I was me!", C. Trife, fires right back!

"EXACTLY!!! So? WHAT the fuck is, YOUR problem!?! You're Me. And I'm Me, too. Oh, damn.", Mr. Empathy, says, (smiling that, shit-eatin'-grin, of his!), then, holds that, little glass vile full of hash, up to his own nose. And, then takes a nice big ol' long sniff! And once, the smell of *that hash* has traveled up outta that, lil' glass vile and, *tags* him in his nose, Mr. Empathy, catches a nice big ol' long wiff, *(of THAT hash!)*, and then, (LACKING the least bit of empathy!), says, "Like, I was sayin'...", *(fuckin' bustin' up laughin' to what, HE finds funny inside!)*, "You're Me and I'm Me, too."* THEN, quickly holds *that hash* up to C. Trife's nose, (lettin' it *TAG* him real quick, too!!), then, (cracking himself up!!!), Mr. Empathy, announces, *"Hashtag, Me, too, muthafucka'!!"*

AND...

C. Trife, just stands there,...*wondering what the fuck is so funny???* (That, Mr. Empathy, is cracking-himself-up over!). *LAUGHING, at something he finds,...NO humor in!).*

As...

(C. Trife, stands there, watching Mr. Empathy, having a good ol' time!)...

As...

C. Trife, is finding no rememberances, of: #'s.

OR...

Having ANY knowledge of, (or hearing about!), the: "Me Too Movement"! (C. Trife, just figures, that, it's just something, that, some MAY find funny and,...SOME may not:)

'Cause...

(He's been in a coma for the past three years)...(And he doesn't even know it!)

(Having heard things get heated in the kitchen), Lost Child, gets up off the sofa and, walks on over, to see, what the hell is going on. (And, more importantly than that!), WHAT he REALLY wants to know is,... *HOW COME AIN'T NOBODY SMOKIN' ANY HASH YET!!!*

Entering the kitchen, (all-giddy and shit!), Lost Child, beginning to giggle, asks Mr. Empathy, "What the fuck's, SO funny???", then looks, and sees, that, Mr. Empathy, is STILL holdin' the lil' glass vile, *(of THAT hash!)* and, HASN'T EVEN packed-up ANY OF IT to smoke, yet! And then, Lost Child, announces, "Oh, y'all JUST in here catchin' *TAGS*, off that shit, huh? *THAT'S, the: best-worst-smellin' shit, EVER!! Like, touchin' the tip of your tongue, wit' a 9 Volt battery, or some shit!* Me too, dammit! Y'all, just in here gettin', *hash tags!* I wanna *hashtag, me too!* Bitches!!"

"Oooooooooooooooooooooo!!", Mr. Empathy, cracks up laughing, *(knowing Lost Child has NO IDEA, what the fuck it is, he just said!)*, then, holds that tiny glass vile *(full of THAT hash!)*, up to Lost Child's nose, and watches. As, *the: "best-worst smellin' hash EVER"*, makes him react, pulling back, *(like a hand touching the element of a hot stove!)*.

While...

C. Trife, just stands there. STILL PISSED!!! *(And...still puzzled)*.

(Finding it funny, that, C. Trife, doesn't find ANY of this funny!), Lost Child, asks Mr. Empathy, "What's HIS, problem? What the fuck's he-all pissed-off, fo'??? AND, why was y'all hollerin', all-up-in MY 'partment, fo'!?!"

Mr. Empathy, points at C. Trife and, says, "It's, THIS guy! HE'S, all-pissed-off, for some reason, 'cause, we got the same name."

(Looking at C. Trife), Lost Child, points at C. Trife, and, asks, "You're Me?"

(Looking up at the ceiling and rolling his eyes!!), Mr. Empathy, announces, "Oh, YOU just asked HIM, the WRONG damn question!!"

"I AIN'T YOU, MOTHERFUCKER!!! I'M ME!!!", C. Trife, starts going off again!, (THIS TIME at Lost Child!).

(Too lost and mellow in his mind, from pills 'n shit all the time), Lost Child calmly, replies, "Keep it chill, man. It's all good. I just never seen two of Me's in the same room at the same time before. I've never met another Me, before.", (then, points at Mr. Empathy), and, says, "Except for him. That's the only other Me, I know. This is pretty fuckin' cool!!!"

(Waaaaaay too much mental-stimulation for, his recently "awakened" mind!), C. Trife, rubs his head, and, says, "I'm lost."

Getting all happy and shit (over something so simple), Lost Child, smiling, beginning to giggle again, (all silly and shit!), asks, C. Trife, "You're Lost, too!?"

"Yeah, I'm lost. Straight up lost me, is that alright with you?", C. Trife, replies.

Gettin' all happy and shit, Lost Child, replies, "Lost Me!?! Is that ALRIGHT, with me??? Are you fuckin', kiddin' me, man!? THIS, is the greatest day, OF my life!! I'm Lost, too!! You're Lost AND YOU'RE Me!?! Ain't THAT, some shit! What ARE the - motherfucking - odds!!!", Lost Child, says,...*all lost and shit.*

Getting hyped (all over again!), C. Trife, explodes, "Nah, motherfucker! I ain't, YOU! I'm ME!", (then, points his finger into his own chest), and, says, "Me? I'm still lost, like a motherfucker!!"

All giddy and shit, (with the laugh of a simpleton going on!), Lost Child, points his finger at C. Trife, and, says, "Yeah, you Lost Me!! This is fuckin', awesome!! You, fuckin' Lost Me!!"

"BOTH y'all, motherfuckers lost me!!", Mr. Empathy, tells both of them, (ALL disgusted and shit!).

"Nope. Only he, Lost Me.", Lost Child, tells Mr. Empathy, (through the tears of his simple laughter).

"Motherfucker, you lost me a long time ago!", C. Trife tells, Lost Child.

"Nope! YOU, LOST ME!!! I'm, Lost Child. But, we both Lost, keep it chill, it's all good!!", Lost Child, tells C. Trife, (cracking himself the-fuck-up).

(From hearing all the commotion 'n shit!), from the living room, Machete Steeze, gets his "biddy-bop" on, and, upon arriving at the doorway to the kitchen, asks, his team members, "So, what's the motherfuckin', hold up?", inquiring upon ANY unfathomable-reason why, ain't NOBODY lightin' up *(THAT hash!)* yet!

Mr. Empathy, turns to Machete Steeze, (and, says of C. Trife), "He's all-pissed-off, 'cause, me and him, got the same name!"

(Looking at C. Trife), Machete Steeze asks, him, "You're Me?"

Looking up at the ceiling and rolling his eyes (again!!), Mr. Empathy, says, (all sarcastic and shit!!), "OH, YOU JUST ASKED HIM, THE. WRONG. DAMN. QUESTION!!!"

"NAH, MY MAN! I AIN'T, YOU!! I'M ME!!!", C. Trife, goin' off, gettin' set-off, again!!!

"Yeah? That's cool. You're Me. And??", Machete Steeze, with a shrugging to his shoulders - two-hands-raised-up-like-so-what - and, with - an-and-what-head-shake - from - side-to-side, all-unfazed, replied, *(all chill 'n shit, dude's legit, handles his shit, far from chicken shit, never sweats irrelevance, but tha' type to swing a machete at your fuckin' head, fo' fuckin' wit his "chicken" 'n shit!).*

"Yeah. AND, HE'S Lost!!!", Lost Child is all to happy to tell, Machete Steeze. ('Cause, IT DON'T TAKE TOO MUCH!)...(For, Lost Child is, easily amused:)

"You lost, man?? Yeah, you could be. I've never seen you, 'round.", Machete Steeze, asks of C. Trife.

Jumping back into the conversation, *(AGAINST HIS BETTER JUDGEMENT!),* Mr. Empathy says, to Machete Steeze, "Yeah, I already asked him. He's gotta be lost."

(Feeling all drained and confused), C. Trife, just shakes his head, while staring at the kitchen floor, and, says, "Yeah. I'm lost. I'm DEFINATELY lost."

(Getting all happy and smiley and shit!), Lost Child, tells C. Trife, "HEY!!! I'M LOST TOO!!!"

"OH, WILL YOU TWO JUST KNOCK-IT THE-FUCK-OFF, ALREADY!!! LOST CHILD, GO SIT IN YOUR OWN-DAMN LIVING ROOM!!!", Mr. Empathy, explodes!!!

(All smiley and simple and shit!), Lost Child, gives C. Trife, a light, backhanded-slap, on his chest, then, leans forward and, whispers to C. Trife, (all proud and shit!), "He's talkin' 'bout me!", just to give C.

Trife, some clarification! *(JUST in case, C. Trife, wasn't sure, WHICH OF THE TWO of them, that, go by Lost, Mr. Empathy, was talkin' 'bout!)*(OY VEY!!!).

Just shaking his head at Lost Child, (as Lost Child leaves the kitchen), Machete Steeze tells, Mr. Empathy, "Pack that shit up, already. In here, actin' like, it's your first day on tha' job."

And so...

Once the normalcy sets back in, *(which normally occurs INSTANTLY!)*, *after, Mr. Empathy, sends Lost Child, out of the room,* Mr. Empathy, pours a small portion *(of THAT hash!)* into a glass hash pipe, and, says to C. Trife, "You see just this small amount? That's enough to get, just me, AND YOU, fucked-up, ALL night!!" Mr. Empathy, then packs the hash pipe, full *(of THAT hash!)*. After which, C. Trife, Mr. Empathy and, Machete Steeze together, walk back into the living room.

Where...

Mr. Empathy, tells C. Trife, to take a seat on the sofa next to him, (the three, take a seat, on the sofa), with, Machete Steeze on the far left, C. Trife on the far right, and, with Mr. Empathy taking a seat in the middle. Lost Child, (having been, stretched out in the recliner chair), to the left of the sofa, *(ever since, having been, kicked-out of his OWN-DAMN kitchen!)*, with, remote control in hand and,...STILL hasn't found anything good to watch on TV!

"Go ahead. You can get greens.", Mr. Empathy, tells C. Trife, handing him the hash pipe *(packed tight of THAT hash!)* and a lighter.

C. Trife, takes the hash pipe and the lighter and, (without hesitation!), fires it up. *(And fills his lungs with mustard green hash!)*. With smoke held, then blown out his lungs, C. Trife, passes the lighter and the hash pipe to his left, to Mr. Empathy. Who, then asks, "Yeah, what you think 'bout that shit?"

"Good shit.", C. Trife, replies.

Mr. Empathy takes a hit, and, then, says to C. Trife, *"THIS hash* will keep burnin', ain't no need to light it again, once it's been lit. It'll keep, burnin' 'til it's done.", (then, places the lighter in his pants pocket, before passing the hash pipe to his left, to Machete Steeze).

"Good shit, my man.", C. Trife, replies, *(of, the: "continual-burnage")*, as Machete Steeze, takes a hit. Who, then passes the hash pipe to Lost Child. Who, then places the remote control down, just long enough to fill his lungs *(with THAT hash!)*. Who, then passes the hash pipe back to Mr. Empathy. Who, then passes the hash pipe, right back to C. Trife, telling him, "Go ahead and fill your lungs, buddy. You gonna be *stuck* here,...just LIKE us." (Hmm).

And...

Without another thought, C. Trife, does just that. Takes another hit. And DOES, fill his lungs up. *(With more of THAT hash!). That hash,* of his newfound friends. (That: *"newfound-kind-of-friends"!*). That, *"newfound-kind-of-friends",* that, out of life, just may want more, but, *if strip clubs 'n gettin' high,* is all they're living for, *his life is gonna get stuck there...*just like them).

After taking his hit, C. Trife, passes the hash pipe to his left, back to Mr. Empathy. Who, then YELLS cross the room at Lost Child, "YO! TURN THIS SHIT!!! Find SportsCenter or somethin'! We can't watch THIS shit, *on THIS shit!!",* with, Machete Steeze chiming in, *"THAT hash,* ain't *NEVER* lie.", in agreement!

(Lost Child, who had finally settled on, what program to watch), replies, "Man, it's JUST some bugged-out horror movie, watch. This goblin, climbs out from under the crib, and snatches-up, this baby!"

C. Trife, *(not tryin' to EVEN see, no baby, being, snatched-out of no crib, by no damn goblin!),* chimes in, himself, *(on the subject),* "Yeah, TURN this shit, man!"

And, *(on that!)...*

Mr. Empathy, turns to C. Trife, and, asks, "You gettin' fucked-up, off THIS shit, AIN'T YA'!?! YOU can't, watch this shit, *on THIS shit,* either, huh? *This-HERE-shit, AIN'T-that-shit, TO BE smokin' on AND, watchin',* THIS-HERE-shit!"

And...

C. Trife, replies, "Yeah, my man. I'm gettin' fuck-up, *ON this shit!* BUT, I ain't down with, NO BABY SHIT, man.", (then, C. Trife, turns to Lost Child) and, tells him again, "Turn that shit to somethin' else, holmes."

And, *(ON THAT!)*...

C. Trife, then, settles back into the sofa and...begins to stare at the fish tank. And for whatever reason, be it *(THAT hash!)* or, the fish inside of that tank, but,...*FISH HAVE NEVER BEEN SO INTERESTING!!!* And as C. Trife gets *stuck* on that sofa, staring at that fish tank, just as Mr. Empathy did the night before, *(just as Mr. Empathy TOLD HIM he would!)*, C. Trife sits there, *stuck* on that sofa, watching the fish dance. (Just as, with the flow of traffic, is a dance). And so, and, as such, off *THAT HASH, the fish, so dance.* A big truck comes up an on-ramp, moving, pushing, forcing, the car in the right lane over into the left lane. But there's a car in the left lane, been in the left lane, and that car in the left lane speeds up. That car that's been in the left lane speeds up when the big truck coming up the on-ramp is coming up the on-ramp. 'Cause the driver of the car that's been in the left lane is a prick, and it's human nature, (and that driver knows the traffic dance!). The dance of traffic. The on-ramp shuffle. Big truck comes up on-ramp. Car in right lane moves to left lane. Car in left lane speeds up. 'Cause the driver of the car speeding up in the left lane is a prick, and it's human nature. (And that's the dance of traffic). The traffic dance. The on-ramp shuffle. (And though the dance has commenced, not all have yet begun to dance). The dance of traffic. The traffic dance. The on-ramp shuffle. Those on the wall not yet dancing, the wall of traffic, have seen that those three, (the big on-ramp truck, the right lane to left lane car, and the prick that's been in the left lane now speeding up), have all broken the ice, and have begun to dance, the dance of traffic. The traffic dance. The on-ramp shuffle. And so they all grab a dance partner, and exit the wall and enter the dance floor, gettin' down with the dance of traffic, the traffic dance, the on-ramp shuffle, speeding up and maneuvering to avoid or stay ahead of, stay in front of, don't want to be behind of, the big truck, the right lane to left lane car, who's also speeding up and maneuvering for, the big truck, and speeding up and maneuvering for, the car that's been in the left lane, but is now speeding up, 'cause the driver's a prick. And it's human nature. The dance of traffic. The traffic dance. The on-ramp shuffle. The car that's been in the left lane and been speeding up doesn't want the big on-ramp truck, or the right lane to left lane car, to be in front, to get ahead, to be first, 'cause the driver's a prick, and it's human nature. And onward goes the dance of traffic. The traffic dance. The on-ramp shuffle. The left lane car that's been in the left lane speeds up, the big on-ramp truck moves from the on-ramp to the right lane, THEN ONCE IN THE RIGHT LANE THE BIG TRUCK SPEEDS UP, 'cause the driver of the big truck doesn't want the car that's maneuvered from the right lane to the left lane, being pushed over by the big truck, avoiding the big truck, so that the big truck can maneuver, from the on-ramp to the right lane, to get in front, to be in front, to be first, in front of it, in the right lane! 'Cause the driver of the big truck is a prick, and it's human nature. So the right lane to the left lane car then speeds up, and goes back to the right lane, getting in front of the big truck, that was on the on-ramp, but that's now in the right lane. 'Cause the driver of the right lane to left lane back to right lane car, doesn't want the big on-ramp truck, that's now in the right lane, to be in front, to be ahead, to be first. 'Cause the driver of the right lane to left lane to right lane car is a prick, and it's human nature. The dance of traffic. The traffic dance. The on-ramp shuffle. The car that's been in the left lane, that's been speeding up, stays in the left lane, and stays speeding up, staying ahead of both the big truck that was on the on-ramp but now in the right lane, AND the right lane to left lane back to right lane car. 'Cause the driver of the car that's been in the left lane, and that's been speeding up, doesn't want the big on-ramp truck that's now in the right lane or the right lane to left lane back to right lane car, to get ahead, to be first, to be in front, 'cause the driver's a prick AND it's human nature! The dance of traffic. The traffic dance. The on-ramp shuffle. And up ahead, you just know that there's a speed trap, up ahead. Hiding. Hidden. Harboring. But the driver of the car speeding in the left lane, that's been in the left lane, isn't thinking about the possibility of something hiding up ahead, possibly a speed trap. Hidden. 'Cause, the been in the left lane, been speeding up driver, just gotta be first, just gotta be ahead, that driver just can't be behind. 'Cause that driver's a prick. And it's human nature. And you know there's just gotta always be that one on the dance floor, you know there's just gotta always be that one driver, there's always one, that just says, *fuck it!* And doesn't move the fuck over or speed the fuck up! And just fucks up the dance. The dance of traffic. The traffic dance. The on-ramp shuffle. And that's what C. Trife sees as he sits there. *Stuck.* On that sofa. Staring into that fish tank. *Stuck.* As the largest by far of three catfish, swims from one side of the tank to the other. Back-and-forth, back-and-forth, back-and-forth. Over and over and over again. Pushing the two far smaller of the three catfish, to the opposite side of the fish tank, avoiding the far largest of the three catfish, maneuvering to get away, and stay away, from the far largest of the three catfish. And there ain't no wallflowers in this fish tank! The far more largest of the three catfish won't allow it! For, as the far largest of the three catfish swims, back-and-forth, back-and-forth, back-and-forth, from one side of the fish tank to the other, over and over and over again, a multitude of even smaller fish, of some kind of species, all swim to the opposite side of the fish tank as the far largest of the three catfish, avoiding the far largest of the three catfish, maneuvering from the far largest of the three catfish, WHILE STILL having to, and trying to, avoid and maneuver around, and away from, the far smaller of the two catfish! Back-and-forth, back-and-forth, back-and-forth. Over and over and over again. (Those multitude of smaller fish of some kind of species don't have an easy life!). And all the while, a BIG funky-looking fish, that could PROBABLY fuck-up the far largest of the three catfish, just stays hidden, harboring, holed up, in a rock cave, down amongst the sediment and the fish dookie. While, a gigantic algae eater fish, just says, *fuck it,* staying on the glass, in one spot. *STUCK.* Back-and-forth, back-and-forth, back-and-forth. Over and over and over again. The largest of the three catfish moves the fish along. Back-and-forth, back-and-forth, back-and-forth. Over and over and over again. 'Cause he's a prick. And besides,...it's only nature!

That's some *good* ass *hash,* huh?

MO' BITCHEZ!

"**A**yo! TRIFE!!!", (is, what C. Trife is, met with), after having, Pockets, pulling-up on him, after, pulling-up in, the apartment complex's parking lot, after - having-popped - some, old school rap, in his car's CD player. (Pockets, after having, thought about it), *that, THAT'S how HE first pulled-up on, Brotha Trife, (after, Brotha Trife, stepped-out of Precinct One). After having, stepped-out of, that bank vault prison cell, after having, met with Too Cold and, the DUYU CREW, (for the first time).*

And so...

After having thought about using that ploy, to help reel in C. Trife, with, something *known and familar* to him, (connecting he to C. Trife, and C. Trife to he). As with*, after pulling-up and, bumping old school rap, connected B. Trife to Pockets, and Pockets to B. Trife, (the first time that they met, in North Juarez).* Pockets, dually uses music to cover, yet, deploy, his bullshit. (And, FROM his, all red everythang Dodge Challenger, bumps some deep cover shit!). To, deeply cover-up, yet, uncover, his bullshit, (after, pulling-up in front of, Lost Child's closed street-level apartment door).

AFTER...

(Having seen, C. Trife, having stepped-out from, after having pulled-up from, and from after, having closed Lost Child's street-level apartment door. From after, pulling-up from, THAT sofa!).

Whereafter...

C. Trife, pulled-up from Lost Child's apartment. After *having, triggers, trigger thoughts,* on that sofa. *After having, stared at that algae eater long enough!* Whereafter, having *(triggered)* thoughts, OF that - *wild-intense-dream* - of his, that he had. Where, he was able to see himself sleeping, from after having been asleep. *(And yet, known to him, that he was awake, while being asleep).* From after, having felt some kind of aneurysm, or brain tumor, *explode in his head!*

Whereafter...

He was finally able to break free. *Of the pushing, depriving, THE PRESSURE, of sleep paralysis' gravity.* (And thoughts of how it felt to be *stuck!*).

Whereafter...

(After having, thought about all that!), C. Trife, pulled-up from Lost Child's apartment. (After having, pulled himself up from, being *stuck* on that sofa, LIKE that!).

BECAUSE...

(C. Trife, might not know where he's going and, *he might not know where he's from* and, he might not know how he's even going to get there and, he might not know what the hell he's going to do if he ever makes it there, *wherever the hell there is,* but what he does know is, he no longer wants to be *stuck!)*

And so...

"Pockets???", a VERY highed-up, (off *THAT HASH!),* C. Trife, asks, *after having the recognition of the sound, of Pockets' voice,* after Pockets, turned down the song he was just bumping. After having, to peer through the darkness and, the glare, of the apartment complexes' parking lot's lights.

After peering into, the dark interior, of Pockets' car interior. After peering into, Pockets' rolled-down, front passenger's side car window. All while, peering, from over by, Lost Child's closed street-level apartment door.

"MY BROTHER!!! MY BROTHER!!! IT IS, YOU!!! HOW YOU DOIN', MY BROTHER!?! GET IN!!! I'll get you outta here, man. Whatchew' doin' on, THIS side of town, my brother? THIS ain't for YOU, Trife. Not, no more. I've been lookin' YEARS, for you, Triflin'!! Get in and, I'll get you right, man. Get your life, back on track!", Pockets, calls out, from his rolled-down, front passenger's car window, (laying on the bullshit)...(THICK!).

(With a serious case of amnesia going on, but, C. Trife, KNOWS that, he - kinda-knows - WHO, Pockets is), *C. Trife's, recently-awakened-mind, wrestles to unstick, stuck memories.* 'Cause, the whole scene just seems eerily-similar, (for some reason), to him! From when, *he was around some fucked-up cats, who he didn't even know. (And there, was nothin' but, a whole lotta misunderstandings-goings-on!).* To, stepping-out a door. Back to the outside world. To, having some cat, he didn't even really know, pull-up on him... BUMPING some old school rap!

"And damn!", C. Trife's - recently-awakened-mind - begins, in cognitive dissonance, "Wasn't this...the same song...that was playin'??? AND THEN, the motherfucker, calls over to me, out his car window,...tellin' me to get in. JUST like tonight! Just like, RIGHT now! Yeah...YEAH, I know THIS, motherfucker! THAT'S, POCKETS!!!!!! Don't, NOBODY rock a hat, cocked haaarrrd to the side, LIKE, the nigga, Pockets!! I bet, the nigga's still rockin', all red everythang, too!! Wait?? Didn't I decide to stop using the word "nigga"? Wasn't there some loud-ass-bullhorn, broadcasting some loud-ass-message, commanding motherfuckers, to stop calling each other, "nigga"? Didn't I have beef with them? But,...yeah...YEAH, I know, THIS nigga!! WAIT??? ...Didn't we have beef?? BUT,...didn't this nigga have,...a different car? A Buick or some shit?? Oh, well. Look. Guess I'm just high as fuck...OFF THAT MOTHERFUCKIN' HASH!!!"

And so...

(C. Trife decides that, he's gonna take that ride!)

And...

Gets hit in the head with somethin', before he gets inside.

And...

(Takes that ride, 'cause, his - recently-awakened-Tier-Three-Mind - has so decided), "'Cause, I'm TOO motherfuckin' high TO walk! AND, I ain't stayin' motherfuckin' here. *Stuck.*"

And so...

(As C. Trife gets in Pockets' car and, sits down in the front passenger's seat and, then closes the car door, Pockets, tries *to prevent the look that must be clearly in his eyes, from traveling to his face.* Because, as C. Trife is putting on his seatbelt and, checking out the all red everythang interior of Pockets' 2018 Dodge Challenger, Pockets, lets C. Trife get about as acclimated as he's gonna let him get, but, first,...he just has to ask)...

"Um. Hey, uh, Trife. You want a towel or somethin'??? I...I got a roll of them blue shop towels, in the trunk of the car.", (a mystified!), Pockets, offers.

"Nah. I'm good, my man. ...Why? Wassup???", C. Trife, replies.

"Daaaaaaaayum! THIS nigga's TRIFLIN', AS FUCK!!!", Pockets, thinks to himself, "He MUST still WANT all that BLOOD, all OVA', his face!! OH, HOLD THE FUCK UP!!! THIS nigga's been like THIS,...the whole time??? YOOOOOOOOOO!!!!!! DON'T tell me, Lost Child and them, ARE AS FUCKED-UP as, THIS nigga!! Good! ...It's good, to keep, niggas like them, on standby. Ain't NOTHIN' my POCKETS, can't buy!!", (Pockets, huddled-up in his mind, cookin' up new hustles, with and for, Mr. Empathy and them Lost Child boyz!), while he, just remains staring at all that blood, (transfixed wit tha' shit)...(All-OVA', C. Trife's face!). From forehead to chin. (This WHOLE mutha' fuckin' entire time!!!). And, so then, Pockets, replies, "Nothin', man. You good."

"No doubt.", C. Trife, tells him, (then, goes back to checking-out the car's all red everythang interior), and, then, asks Pockets, "New whip??"

"Noooooooooo. Same one.", Pockets, replies, cocking his custom red custom-made red hat hard to the side.

(And, on that note)...

First, Pockets begins to drive. Then, throws his bullshit into overdrive! Monopolizing the conversation, as they drive back cross town. Sinkin' his hooks in 'em. Makin' the most of, his: *"window of opportunity"*. Pockets, is a true hustler foreal! (So, he's just rollin' wit' shit). Playin' his part, doin' his part, OF playin' HIS part! *(To reel C. Trife in!)*. Just gonna hustle his way through this shit. Before he can get back to his office. (AND READ UP ON THIS CLONING SHIT!!!). Pockets is a gambling man. And so he's rollin' the dice. 'Cause, that money, off the backend to be made, off that, back up north trip? Is worth THIS price! And besides. What he got WAITIN' on him. *(BEEN waitin' on him!)*. Back up north. On that...you can not put a price! So, Pockets gotta do THIS shit! This HERE shit! (OH LAWD!!!)...before, THIS HERE "Tier Three", (WHENEVER the fuck THAT may be!?)...figa's shit the FUCK out!! (Can I get a, "OH LAWD!!!").

And so...

(As they ride, as Pockets drives, as Pockets drives C. Trife back to Jettison Records, they come up on the pink flashing neon sign for the strip club BITCHEZ)

As...

The last of the flashing reds and blues gets cut. (As the first of the last of the emergency vehicle rides begin to ride out of, the BITCHEZ parking lot). Headed their way! Peeping the scene, C. Trife, looks and, turns to Pockets, and, asks, "Damn! What happened here??? Shit mustuv' popped-the-fuck-off!"

"THA' FUCK??? "SHIT" mustuv' "popped" the-fuck-off??? Oh,...shit! HE don't even REMEMBER, this shit!", is, what, Pockets thinks, (as he, huddles back up in his sharp hustle-mind), KNOWING how he's gonna spin this shit! (IN record time!).

(Come. Let's have a look)...

"Triflin'! MY BROTHER!!! Quick!! Lay your head back on the headrest, WITH your face TOWARDS your window, WHEN we pass by the strip club!! Act like, you're asleep!!", Pockets, barks out, (his instructions OF bullshit!).

"Do WHAT, now??", a highed-up (and, "huh"-looking), C. Trife, asks, snapping his head to the side, as he turns his face to face Pockets. A face, covered in tacky, (yet, cracked and creased) on and about and around the eyes, the lids, tops, bottoms and, the sides. AND above, AND on the corners of, his mouth. AND, ALL DOWN AND ALONG his nasolabial folds!! (Where, MOST of the blood has flaked, or IS flaking off).

"MY BROTHER, MY BROTHER!!! YOU SEE ALL THEM FUCKIN' COPS UP AHEAD, DON'T YOU, MY BROTHER?!? LAY YOUR FUCKIN' HEAD BACK ON THE SEAT!!! PRETEND THAT, YOU'RE SLEEPING, MY BROTHER!!! SHIT!!! NO!!! NO!!! TURN YOUR HEAD, THAT WAY!!! THAT WAY!!! TURN YOUR HEAD, TOWARDS YOUR WINDOW, MY BROTHER!!!", a shouting Pockets shouts, while turning towards C. Trife, (while placing a reassuring hand on C. Trife's shoulder), while Pockets spews-out, more of the laying-on-of-the-spreading-of-the-bullshit, (while the bullshit gets laid on thick), while BITCHEZ get approached!

(With BITCHEZ on his mind, with BITCHEZ up ahead, with BITCHEZ on the side of the road, Pockets gets back to checking out BITCHEZ, on the side of the road ahead. After having spread, laid and spewed, Pockets is feelin' pretty damn good 'bout the quick work he just put in. However, the quick sharp mind of Pockets, is always workin'. Always puttin' in work. And he's quick wit the shit).

And so...

After he checked BITCHEZ out. After he gave BITCHEZ the once-over. Pockets has a few options with BITCHEZ. *(Might breakout some of his ol' standby moves that he hasn't done in years on BITCHEZ!)*. Has to make up his mind on what he wants to do with BITCHEZ! And so, after chosing and deciding on BITCHEZ. (BUT, before he approaches BITCHEZ), Pockets is gonna make damn sure,...that he uses the proper precautions for BITCHEZ!

'CAUSE...

Pockets knows, what he's gonna do, before THIS night is through. He's gonna end up ridin' all up on BITCHEZ. (And he knows, that,

THAT it's ALWAYS the case, *that, all the fun starts and stops, with strippers and cops!).*

And so...

(Pockets knows how he's gonna play BITCHEZ)

FOR...

He's gonna hasten his pace, just a little bit more, but not too much, but just at the right rate. (As he's ridin' on BITCHEZ). And by doing that, before he knows it, BITCHEZ would've came. (And he would've came on BITCHEZ).

But...

This old school playa' and hustler doesn't want to come on BITCHEZ too fast! So, when Pockets does, (hasten his pace), it won't be too fast. It'll be just at the right rate. (So he'll make BITCHEZ come faster), as he's ridin' on BITCHEZ. So he can come on BITCHEZ, faster.

All the while...

WHILE keeping in his mind, not too come on BITCHEZ too fast! Which, brings to HIS mind. *Of how, all of his favorite baseball players used to take the diamond.* At just the right pace. (And NEVER, at TOO fast of a rate!).

AND SO...

Pockets, begins increasing his pace. And, does so, at just the right rate. So that, he can do, ultimately, what he just wants to do! And that being, after ridin' up on BITCHEZ, ridin' all up on BITCHEZ, once a nigga, done rode on BITCHEZ, ALL Pockets really wants to do, is to keep it pushin' on BITCHEZ! (And then eat a turkey sammich or some shit:)

'Cause...

He's really not tryna' be stressin' BITCHEZ. (Pockets ain't stressin' BITCHEZ). Pockets just ain't tryna' put in too much work on BITCHEZ! *Don't want to really have to dig into his bag of tricks,* while he's ridin' all up on BITCHEZ.

And so...

Pockets, cocks his custom red custom-made red hat hard to the side. (And grins satisfyingly). As he picks up his pace, but just the right rate, while ridin' up on BITCHEZ. And as he does, Pockets begins to grin satisfyingly some mo'...as he watches BITCHEZ coming.

AND SO...

Feelin' the moment, being in the moment, reading the moment, stayin' in the moment, Pockets decides that he's gonna pick up his pace...just a lil' bit mo'...just to make BITCHEZ come, faster, some mo'. (And he, does just that!). Make BITCHEZ come, faster, some mo'. (All from just, picking up his pace). But, just at the right rate. (For, Pockets knows, just the right rate, to make BITCHEZ come faster, some mo').

And so...

He watches, (with that grin of satisfactory). As he looks at BITCHEZ beginning to come. That he MADE, BITCHEZ come. (More and more). (Faster and faster). The more he picked up his pace! (But, just at, the right rate). All from, and, all the while, just ridin' on BITCHEZ. The more he rides up on BITCHEZ.

All the while...

WHILE keepin' in mind. He's using protection on BITCHEZ! (And WHY he's using protection on BITCHEZ!). *To protect C. Trife, from catchin' a case!* All the while, while keepin' in mind, as *ALWAYS* is the case. *All the fun starts and stops, with strippers and cops!*

So...

(It's a good thing for Pockets that, he was no longer ridin' up on BITCHEZ. Already did his ridin' up on BITCHEZ. No longer was all up on BITCHEZ. That he had already seen BITCHEZ coming. That he'd already seen BITCHEZ come. That a nigga had already done rode on BITCHEZ. Finished up on BITCHEZ. And that a nigga kept it pushin' on BITCHEZ! Didn't just say FUCK IT, and ride all up IN BITCHEZ, AGAIN...SOME MO'!!!)

'Cause…

After Pockets seen BITCHEZ come. (From after he rode up on BITCHEZ). For after BITCHEZ came. (From, for, when and) while, Pockets was still coming. (For then and then). Pockets subsequently came. (Substantially Pockets came on BITCHEZ). For then. (AND then). And only then. Again. Pockets cocked his custom red custom-made red hat hard to the side. And KEPT it pushin' on BITCHEZ.

'Cause…

(Pockets was finished coming, finished up, and was finished with BITCHEZ)

For(YOU SEE!)…

Outta' all those cops, that had already been all up in BITCHEZ, out of all those cops, that Pockets saw, (as it turns out), more than too many of the last remaining of all those cops, he saw them as they were pulling out of BITCHEZ. A whole lot was coming out of BITCHEZ!!! (And THAT'S just somethin' he wasn't tryna' see at all!!:)

HOWEVER…

There were, STILL some cops in BITCHEZ. There were, cops that, had already been in BITCHEZ, already came in BITCHEZ, *(took another call, rolled out),* just to come again, in BITCHEZ. (To BITCHEZ, seemed like half the police force was all-up, in BITCHEZ!).

And so…

(Good thing for Pockets, too!)…

'CAUSE…

Once he had already rode up on BITCHEZ, Pockets (looked to his left), out his driver's side window, and saw, the last of the cops, pulling out of BITCHEZ. (But it was all good).

'Cause…

Back when BITCHEZ was still coming. (In fact), Pockets was still coming.

'Cause...

Essentially, one could argue, dependant upon your point of view, one could say, they were both coming at the same time. (One could say).

'Cause...

(After BITCHEZ came, Pockets kept it pushin', but one could argue, that they came at the same time:)

And...

Pockets was good, ("gooder than good":), the motherfucker was the goodest of good, ('cause the motherfucker was feelin' damn good, motherfucker!).

'Cause...

(THAT'S the last time Pockets saw, them pullin' outta' BITCHEZ cops BITCHEZ!)

And so...

Pockets kept it pushing. And kept it pushing towards his destination. (That being, Jettison Records). And Pockets had C. Trife sit back upright. Another "awakening" one could say. (One could). 'Cause, Pockets and C. Trife, had already came upon and, finished up on BITCHEZ. And, C. Trife didn't know, what the big deal was, (why Pockets reacted they way that he did!). And, Pockets continued to take advantage of, the (still somewhat) early stages of, the recent awakening of, a Tier Three. (As he), additionally, continued to still take full advantage of, the potent mind under the potentness of, *(THAT!)* potent *hash*.

And...

Pockets, continued to take full advantage, of his monopolization of, his type of "conversation" with C. Trife. The mastery of vagueness, prompting leads to further questions, leading to promises of future answers, that never come. As he, continued to take advantage of C. Trife, fully, as a true upper echelon, music industry type.

And so...

It's dark, and well after working business hours, upon arrival at Jettison Records. Then again, there's never really anybody there, ever to be seen, working in that "front" of a skyscraper of a building. (Not seen, above the lower under the ground levels, anyway).

Pockets' headlights lead the way, while pulling up, in his all red everythang ("Buick or some shit"). Headlights glance the front of security fences and, the guardhouse, of the fenced-in and guarded, Jettison Records parking lot. Pulling up, in the direction of the swinging-barrier gate arm, of the guardhouse (and, once there), Pockets is met with more than one swinging arm and, plenty of directions.

Arms are pulled, armed guards pull and swing their arms, swinging firearms out of the guardhouse like they're fencing. Armed guards swing and point their arms, pointing firearms, in Pockets' direction, directing Pockets to remain seated, giving orders for C. Trife, to exit the vehicle, arms up. Not one in a position to take directions, though, in a position to do as directed, Pockets, swings his car door open, hops out, and, says, "WHAT THA' FUCK!?!"

"Pockets, it's not you!! It's, HIM!! He's, THE ONE, we've been looking for!! He broke out of the under the ground levels of Emerald Hall, made it off-site, BEFORE we could "doublelock" the building down and,... secure its perimeter.", an armed uniformed guard, explains, (his excuses to Pockets).

"MUTHA' FUCKA'!!!! Lower y'alls mutha'-fuckin' weapons!!! Pointin', your mutha'-fuckin' guns, at my FINE red everythang automobile!?! Tha' fuck's wrong, wit y'all??? Pointin', yo' shit, AT my shit!", Pockets, barks at the armed guards, (then, flicking his right thumb, over in the direction of C. Trife, Pockets, asks of the armed guards, "Who tha' fuck you think, he is? Bill Cosby or, some shit!?!", (of C. Trife, still seated in the car). (AND, THEN, Pockets gives some directions of HIS OWN!), "NOW, open that fuckin' gate! He's, with ME. I!!! ME!!! MUTHA' FUCKAS!!! Found him, for YOU. NOW, you mutha' fuckas, just shut-the-fuck-up, be cool, run them tapes back and, AIN'T NOBODY gotta' know, he was gone, AND, OH, BY THE WAY, THAT I DID, y'alls job, FOR y'all!!! YOU hear me!?!"

"What tapes!", an armed guard, replies, (while holstering his service revolver!).

"Cute. Now, open that gate. And, stand 'side.", Pockets, responds, (before getting back behind the wheel). Burns rubber to enter the lot. Narrowly missing the guardhouse's barrier gate arm (as it's on the up swing!).

The laugh of luxury. The luxury laugh. Laughing THAT expensive laugh! (The one that costs). Laughing the laugh of at the expense of others, Pockets, tears through the sprawling gated parking lot, fuckin' up,...('cause, C. Trife's givin' him THAT eye!).

Pockets enjoys breaking the armed guards' balls, *(ALMOST, as much as Pretty High, likes fuckin' wit Phillip Tate!)*. A firearm don't mean shit when power pulls the trigger. Power don't mean shit to a hair-trigger mind.

Parking his car, next to his prized possession, his very own, Jettison Records RV. (Though, not all red-equipped). It's CERTAINLY equipped with everythang! And, Pockets picked it out himself, personally, an all black 2018 Thor Motor Coach, for himself, personally. Just 'cause, it was the "Vegas" model. (Just 'cause, HE'S a gambling man:)

For...

ALL THAT studio time, advisory work AND engineering, *(you see, for it was hard work that, PAID for THIS ride!)*. Some sad-sucker, NOW GOING THROUGH major depression,...NEVER DID GET radio airplay...OR their CD pressed!

FOR...

(ALL OF THEIR MONEY - went towards - con men and bums, to be sittin' pretty!)

And...

In THIS ride,...Pockets, BE sittin' pretty!

(Hopes 'n dreams 'n money BURNED!!!)

Some sad-sucker, "turned-out" BY "the biz", (TO BE!!!) just ANOTHER statistical-tragedy! ...Just another music biz sad-sucker... (RIPPED-OFF!!!!!!)...on the sly.

Chapter Eight

THE WELL

Pockets ain't "Them People", (no facial/ocular recognition-entry-access-data on file for him), on the "outside", to enter, it's hold his Jettison Records Photo ID's chip, up to the sensor. And it would behoove one, to be known, to the armed guards, once inside. And, it would behoove them armed guards, to swallow their pride. C. Trife, unmoved, by some clown ARMED guards, (and, it would behoove one, NOT to step to him hard!). *You see, THIS AIN'T THE FIRST TIME, guns have been pointed at him!* (Well,...at least,...that's the feeling, that HE'S gettin'!)...

For...

On a night of loss, S.W.A.T., LIT UP Brotha Trife! ON a night of loss. Lost his mind. Down an empty bottle of vodka, LOST HIS MIND!!! Blacked out, zzzzzzzzzzzzzzzzzzzzzzzzzzzz...

AND...

Woke up to a commotion outside!

(Come. Let's take a look back, *in a TIER-THREE-MIND)...*

"I...I...I guess...I musta'...did some shit...to have...warranted all of... this???", (C. Trife's Tier-Three-Mind, steps back in time),...LIT THE FUCK

UP, AS HE STEPPED OUTSIDE, by 12 gauge shotgun projectile-cartridge tasers!...(And, OF COURSE, rubber bullets and sin:)

And so...

C. Trife, is just doin' what's coming natural to him! *(Peepin' shit, THE FUCK out!).* JUST IN CASE, he's got to BREAK THE FUCK OUT... ALL OVER AGAIN!!!

FOR...

(THIS building could NEVER hold him!)...

These armed guards, THINK they gonna come and,...serve C. Trife???

Yeah. OK.

(Oppositional-DEFIANT is what, HE'S gonna order!!)...

So, C. Trife, *(as with B. Trife!),* AIN'T GON' LISTEN, *(to what, THEY got to say!!).*

And...

He ain't feelin' the looks, *from the guards that HE embarrassed! (Yeah, try it if you want too!).* C. Trife, *gives the guards the eye,* while Pockets, leads the way.

AND SO...

Up the elevator, down the Black Onxy Executive Hall, (C. Trife's, *Tier-Three-eyes-'n-mind, observes-n'-peeps it all),* "LOOK AT THAT!!! *Streaks of blood! And, fragments from fingernails.* Fuck all these *"distractions",* anyway! I'm steppin' into Pockets' all red everythang office for a reason. Get my life right? Fuck it! I'LL listen to WHAT, my long-lost-friend, HAS to say!"

Instinctually taking a seat in Pockets' office, once offered, once seated, *(eyed-up the one of the two),* on the left, from his view point, (of the red tufted leather upholstered chair), *the one, instinctually,* that'll get him the quickest out, that, closed all-red office door! *(The one, that'll grant him, HIS NECESSARY vantage point).*

'Cause...

His instincts are telling him to listen for, what YOU don't listen for.

Like...

(Appropriate business attire shoes, and boots of armed guards, ON that Executive Hall Black Onxy Hallway floor!)(OY VEY!!!).

And so...

Seated in front of Pockets' huge blood red mahogany executive desk, once after, once removed, reading materials Pockets, so desired, from off of. Immediately placing several hardbound books, (immediately bringing to mind!), they are thick, like college curriculum, of which, immediately go behind his desk, and, upon his plush red carpet office floor. Immediately upon seeing them! Immediately upon opening up his all red everythang office door. Pockets, takes a seat, upon his high back red tufted leather upholstered throne and, states (his verdict), "You're high as fuck, so I know, for something to munch on, you're jonesin'."

And so...

(Pockets, takes the liberty of deciding WHAT, C. Trife, will eat).

'Cause...

That's what he does, takes liberties. Liberty taker. (And liberties he takes!).

Enters...

Phillip Tate, "Personal" Assistant Extraordinaire, carrying two china white plates. (Droplet moist from the coldness). Takes the liberty of (and, slight enjoyment in!), placing both plates down, right on top of hoagie oils. Bon Appetit! Mangiare!! (AND, Bust-A-Grub!!!). On two turkey clubs!! *(Fuck tha' fries,* chips this time!). And, one crisp and chilled pickle spear, each for each to dine. (And ALL BEFORE, Pockets, can lift his finger off the Jettison-Records-Access-Only-Intracom button, on his all red everythang, executive desk telephone!).

"Phillip? Aren't you forgetting something?", asks, Pockets.

"Sir?", Phillip, questions, upon stopping his nervous whistling, (intiated upon seeing, for the first time, an upright sitting Tier Three!!!)...*(AND,... the blood ALL OVA' his face!!!)*. Then Phillip, continues,...nervously, "Oh, yes. MC Busta-Nut, False Profit, and Y.S. are enroute. I have to say, sir, you made it back much faster th", Phillip Tate, gets abruptly cut off! (And not from Pockets' or his own foot, in his mouth!).

"The hot sauce, Phillip? WHERE is my Tabasco, for MY turkey club?!? You KNOW I won't eat THIS, without spittin' on it wit-some Tabasco first. AND YOU, KNOW THAT!!!", Pockets, replies, disgusted with Phillip, for speaking on his comings-and-goings, ESPECIALLY in front of C. Trife! (Almost, as much, AS he's disgusted, THAT, he, his hot sauce, AND his turkey club, have been neglected!), (All while, trying to maintain, an "appropriate business decorum", of: a big time music executive). And, ESPECIALLY in front of C. Trife, sitting IN his all red everythang office, that HE'S FINALLY in. (And, ESPECIALLY NOW, that, he HAS - music-industry-exec.-hustle-bullshit - TO spin!).

C. Trife, sits there quietly, patiently, looking 'round, *half stuck* off *(THAT hash!)*, diggin', yet, takin' in the scene. In less than one business day's time, C. Trife sits (amongst, and) with, all those framed double platinums, displayed in red, framed, famed, and hanging on red. And, he's hanging with the man, in that red-walled on top of the world office, (that took him in record time!), from the bottom to the top. *"But this is three times now, that I've seen an "ugly side" to Pockets.",* C. Trife's, Tier-Three-eyes-n'-mind - continues to - peep-n'-rationalize, *"Hey, but,...I'm SURE there's an "ugly side" TO this music industry shit. But, hey, my long-lost-friend SEEMS sincere. AND, he says he WANTS to help me! I...I should be alright. Right?"*

Ready to hear what the man has to say, and ready to dig into that sammich. (But, just like Pockets, he too, will wait on THAT hot sauce!). Two orange sodas, the Tabasco and, hesitation, facilitated. Phillip Tate, provides the drinks and condiment. (But, with C. Trife in the room, Phillip Tate, cannot provide further comments, to his boss!).

Phillip, though, will take the iniative, giving Pockets a look and, the remote control to Pockets, he also gives. *(What had he learned?)*...(The price of hot sauce going up??)...*(The fuck is the goings-on???)*.

With TV on, is that a tear, in Phillip's eye? Did he really just blow his nose, in his four fold pocket square???? *(Pockets' face, says it all)*, (As, soon as, his open mouth fell!). Open mouth, turns, to: *"Oh shit!"*, turning on the news!

C. Trife, sees and hears, then, looks over his shoulder, over his back, at the talking heads, playing THE game, of: "well-chosen pick-and-choose", (From all cross the world), reporting on, WHAT mass media wants, you TO think, ABOUT a London to New York red-eye, somewhere over the Atlantic,...BLOWN-OUT the fuckin' air!!! (NOW,...listen to what, they WANT YOU, TO think!).

"Them...fuckin'...DUYU CREW...motherfuckers...Well, how's THAT for a delay!!", Pockets, mutters to himself, under his breath, (of a red-eye flight, under an ocean of red).

"Excuse me, sir??", Phillip Tate, asks, (of what he thought, of what he just heard).

Pockets, gives Phillip Tate a look. (Of which, for Phillip, he keeps in store). Stay on my good side. And, AS YOU turn, that red knob, ON your way out,...STAY on THAT SIDE of my, all red everythang closed office door!

And, in turn, C. Trife, takes some initative! (AFTER, giving a look, of his very own, as well!). Little red cap, off that, Tabasco, he unscrews. AFTER, havin' been eyeing up his sammich,...(more so than the news!).

Tier-Three-Mind, CAN'T remember the last time, he's even HAD a turkey club, or if he even LIKES turkey clubs?? (But, THE WAY he's "housing-it", one could NEVER tell!).

And so, (on that note)...

As the two, sit there, eating their dinner, Pockets, makes dinner conversations, over the crunch of potato chips, and over the sound that they make, (when being gathered for consumption), on a cold china white condensation-moistened dinner plate.

And Pockets, gets right into his bullshit, over the rough-gravely sounds, of C. Trife's *"Yeeeeeeaaaaaaahhh's", in agreement, over agreements, over the agreements,* Pockets, only goes over, (in which, over which!), Pockets knows, C. Trife will be in, over agreement, over with!

Over three years, C. Trife's throat, got fucked-up, from being over-intubated. (Over vocal cords that intubation tube was situated). Over promises, vaguegrandeurs and, information. *Over agreements* with Pockets, *are:* throat-on-fire, *"Yeeeeeaaaaaahhh's", (on occasions).*

Over the sound, of Pockets, actually stopping to take a breath, on occasions, is the mastery of vagueness. Of which, he spins so well. Of which, quick-sick-wit-it music-biz-bullshit, of which, ain't no limitations!

And, as such, Pockets, gets into his bullshit. (Come. Let's take a listen)…

"I see that you're hungry, that's good. My most "moldable-artists" make my BEST artists. BECAUSE, they are hungry! The key ingredients to that turkey club is the Tabasco…and of course, the Duke's mayonnaise. I'ma southern boy, so it's gotta be Duke's! But listen, that's what I do. I know the right ingredients, to put together, to make a bangin' sammich. AND, a banger, of an album! Trife, take the common housefly. It wants in, so badly. For example, to land on your turkey club, just to get a taste, of that, incomparable Duke's mayonnaise. It has the drive, perhaps, it even has the know-how, TO GET into your house, just to get a tiny-taste, of that Duke's mayonnaise. BUT, that's ALL it has! The common housefly, Trife, has no vision of its future. It has no vision, even with those big ol' eyes of his, of how to move on to the next house. The fucking thing, is named for, WHAT the fuck it does! BUT, its best course of action, is to keep banging against that window, over and over again, trying to get out! And,…it does it backwards. You ever notice that, Trife? A trapped fly, banging itself, over and over again, against a window, is doing it, BY flying into it, with his tiny lil' fly legs facing away from the window. Kinda crazy, huh?? Even with those big ol' eyes of his, and even after being named for what the fuck it does, it still can't figure out how to fly outta the house. Trife, if a fly gets into your car, you ever notice, it can't find its way out? You can roll down all the car windows. And, you think the fucking thing, is no longer in your car, 'cause, you no longer see it. But several miles down the road, you're stopped at a red light,…and there it is. STILL in your fuckin' car! You try to wave at it, swat it out the window, but it don't leave. It's named after what it does. But it can't figure out how to fly out the fucking car window! Now, you take a football player, a linebacker, a defensive end. If he can get to the quarterback and sack him, great. If he can do it every game, even better. If he can do it more than once a game, say, two or three times a game, even better still. And, if you have a defensive coordinator that can game plan and, develop schemes to put that defensive player in a position, and his surrounding cast of defensive players in a position, to put that star linebacker or defensive end in the best possible position, to get after the quarterback, to get that sack, then, even better still. It's all recognition. It's all read and react, Trife. Wouldn't you agree? And, if that linebacker or defensive end has the wherewithal, the know-how, that "it" factor, to, NOT ONLY sack the quarterback, BUT, to make the most of his EVERY opportunity, when he's around the quarterback, THEN, even better still. For you see, Trife, it's one thing to lay a big hit on a QB. But, if you take advantage OF EVERY OPPORTUNITY you come in contact with the quarterback, then, that's what makes you a star. The linebacker or defensive end that can get to the quarterback and, strip the ball loose from the quarterback, while he's sacking him, for a "strip sack", then, even better still. And, if that linebacker, or defensive end, can recover that ball himself and, create a turnover and, get the ball back for the offense, then, even better still. And, if that linebacker, or defensive end, can recover that ball and, take it straight to the house, then, even better still. If that linebacker, or defensive end, can do that and, do it every game and, do it more than one time a game, well, that's when, that linebacker or defensive end, will GET PAID the REALLY BIG BUCKS!!! Now, if you have a general manager, that recognizes, that, you have THAT type-of-player on your team, well, it doesn't take a genius, YOU draft AROUND that player! Wouldn't you agree? You BUILD around that player and, you restructure contracts AROUND that player. And, the ugly, BUT, necessary part, of: "the business side" of it all is, SOMETIMES, Trife, you have to cut certain players, BECAUSE that star player, IS THE TYPE-of-player THAT, comes along, once IN a lifetime. AND, THOSE are the type-of-players, Trife, that put asses in stadium seats and, win championships. And with both of those, Trife, THAT'S WHEN the REAL MONEY, really starts, rollin' in! But, it takes the right general manager...or, the right Managing Partner,...as it were. My brother, I don't think, I KNOW, that, I have TWO OF THOSE-type-of-players, on MY team.", Pockets, bullshits completely, (Big-Hustle-Wheels turnin' throughout, his, oft, at times: just-likes-to-hear-HIMSELF-talk - soliloquy!).

"Who then? MC Busta-Nut and, False Profit??", C. Trife, replies, *in his: That-Tobasco-Sauce-AIN'T-Doin'-His - Been-Intubated-FOR-The-Past-Three-Years - Throat-On-Fire - Deep-Rough-Gravely-Speaking-Voice - ANY-Justice!* (Or is it?).

"Nigga, PLEASE! They houseflies! Their offspring feeds off the dead. IT'S, YOU!!! You and, Y.S.", Pockets, rebukes.

"You think so, huh?", C. Trife, queries.

"I don't think. I know!! BUT, WHO people THINK, they need IN their lives to be a star, IS THEIR star! And, BELIEVE ME, I CAN make YOU a star! Stick with me. Don't worry 'bout it. I'll be your Head Coach, Defensive Coordinator AND, General Manager, all rolled into one.", Pockets, lays the groundwork, (then, goes right back into, Some: Music-Industry-Exec.-Bullshit - Shit!)...(Vagueness at its finest, as, ONLY) Pockets, knows how, "I am business. And business, is just like me. And, it's all just like football."

Over the crunch of potato chips and, *(with a warm washrag over his brain!)*, C. Trife, just sits there, listening, still willing to give it a chance. STILL doesn't want to be *stuck!* BUT,...still trying to understand...*(what the fuck the music biz gots-ta' do-wit a quarterback, gettin' the ball knocked out his hand!).*

"Listen, Trife, no matter what team a player gets traded to, you have to have all the bases covered. You have to know the "cover three's", the "cover two's"...", Pockets, explains, (while showing three and then two fingers on his right hand)...then, Pockets, holds his hand up and, with all five of his fingers, (as if, he's holding a gun!), aims his hand, at C. Trife, and, says, "The nickel package."

C. Trife, unmoved, (and not due to *THAT hash!)*, the gun, he looks past and, directly into Pockets' eyes, (in which), Pockets tries, to clean it up by saying (and, BY lowering his hand!), "You have to know all the schemes. I'm always scheming,...so to speak."

"Mmm-hmm, yeeeeeeaaaaaahhhhhh.", C. Trife, replies, *(intubation-voice-amazin'!).*

And, (on that NOTE!)...

(Pockets gives it to him). "You hear that, Trife? How you just said, "Mmm-hmm, yeeeaaahhh." Shiiiiiit, I can't even do it ANY justice! Stick with me, Trife. That voice of yours. Magic! Yeah, so, well, anyways, I was gonna groom you to work as an engineer, for Jettison Records. Perhaps, even send you off to college, pay your full tuition, so, that, you could become an agent for my artists. Told you! Told you, Trife, I was gonna get your life right, my brother! But,...that VOICE of yours, Trife. Money!! The industry HASN'T had anything like THAT, since, Leonard Cohen or Tom Waits. Not SINCE, dare I say,...Teddy Pendergrass!!! PLUS, you're all dressed in black. I'm seeing a whole - "Buddy-Guy-thang" - happening here, RIGHT before my eyes!!", Pockets, tells him, eyeing up money!!, (I mean, C. Trife sitting there!).

"Tom, WHO???", C. Trife, asks.

(Pockets' Big-Hustle-Wheels are always turnin', ALWAYS churning full throttle...)

And so...

Pockets, NOW realizes, that, he has TWO "windows of opportunity" TO,...roll them bones on!! (First things, FIRST though!) *Pockets, gots-ta'-get - THAT VOICE - of his on wax, (pronto!). (But, it's GOTTA' BE a hit!!!). Being intubated, for three plus years, has given C. Trife the voice, OF...the next great blues singer!*

BUT...

His voice won't stay like that forever...(once his throat recovers:(

AND, (as FOR)...

That, OTHER *"window of opportunity"*? Well? THAT WON'T stay open forever, either!! Gambling man gonna roll the dice, on this one! (Hey, EITHER it's gonna workout. Or? It's not).

BUT...

What Pockets, DOES - *"got-goin'"* - FOR him, IS...*Pockets knows,... what C. Trife, doesn't.* (And, THAT'S what, Pockets, IS fearful of!)

'Cause...

(Pockets KNOWS, how B. Trife was!!)

And so...

As, Pockets huddles-up, in his *Big-Hustle-Mind,* *"OH LAWD, don't let THIS Tier Three, SITTIN' HERE before me, FIND OUT all this "Tier-Three-Shit",...ON HIS OWN!!! Yeah? well? What tha' fuck? I'MA gamblin' man! It's BEST, if he HEARS IT FROM me, for himself. AND, MORE IMPORTANTLY, THAN, THAT,...IT'S what's best, for ME!! Hey,...it's not like I gotta convince Brotha Trife that, he's a clone. Well,...essentially, it is. I JUST, gotta convince this clone, that, he's a clone! Shiiiiiit, I'M POCKETS!!! Gift of THE gab, baby! I GOT THIS!!! ...I hope."*

AFTER ALL, what's the worst that could happen? (Let's find out)...

"Tom Waits. Don't worry 'bout it.", Pockets, begins, by answering C. Trife's earlier question and, (then, gets right into, as he, gets right back to, His: Music-Biz-Big-Wig-Exec.-Power-Move-Mass-Manipulation!), "Stick with me. I'll be your Head Coach, your Defensive Coordinator AND your General Manager, all rolled into one. That's what, I'll do for you, my brother!! That's what, I'll BE, for you! ...And for, Y.S., of course. BUT,...I'm gonna need you, to do something, for me.", Pockets, begins, what's probably, the most important conversation that, he's ever had in his life, as it, just might be his last one. *(Fuckin' Tier Three's, man!).*

"Oh, *yeeeeeaaaaaaahhhhhhh?* Like, what?", C. Trife, inquires, (as if he KNEW, there was more too, all of this, "my brother" shit!).

"My brother!! My brother!!", Pockets, starts out, then, softens his voice and body language, in his attempt (in presence, and presentation) to, sound solemn, "All I need from you is, not to mind my liberties."

"Your what?", C. Trife, asks.

(With a deep breath taken), Pockets, gets into it, "My liberties. Look, Trife, I'm at the top of the world, right where you are now, physically. Although, not financially, but, you CAN be. ...WITH, my help! Now,... this is going to be, a lot for you to take in, BUT, I took the liberty of cloning you."

"You did,...WHAT??? My man, YOU motherfuckers ARE ALL the same! Talk MORE SHIT than, a used car salesmen! That's a good one,

Pockets. Never heard, THAT one!! What else ya' got, for me??", C. Trife, quips!

"Hang on there, a second. You see HOW hyped, you JUST got? Over NUTHIN', at that! You was probably ready, to whoop my ass, too, huh?", Pockets, admires.

"Ain't no probables, 'bout it, Pockets.", C. Trife, admits,…*(yet, still seated)*.

(Thinking back, to how Brotha Trife used to sit there just like that, in front of his desk, get all pissed off, while flyin' off the handle and, flying out of his chair)…

Pockets knows, C. Trife, *still ISN'T fully back to being, B. Trife!*

WHICH…

Gives Pockets, THAT MUCH MORE confidence, FOR this conversation! *(CONSIDERING, C. Trife's sitting there, WITH a face FULL of blood!)*, Pockets, then asks, the magic question, that, JUST COULD,… get his ass kicked!

But…

Still, he, cocks his custom red, custom-made red hat, hard to the side, 'bout as cocky and hard, as he's ever cocked it hard to the side before, then asks, "Then, WHY didn't you?"

"I…I…I'm not sure. Some…*somethin' tells me…I woulda' already BEEN UP OVER your desk…before.*", C. Trife, comes clean, while sitting there *(WITH a face FULL of blood!)*.

"MY point, exactly! *I knew, your brother,* well. Damn, *not your,…* yourself. Damn, wait, not YOU, *I knew you…before.*"

"Huh??", C. Trife, asks.

"What?", Pockets, replies.

"Motherfucker, I asked you, a question. Don't be asking me no-damn-question TO, MY question!", C. Trife, tells Pockets.

Spinnin' shit, *workin' on a groggy-mind,* Pockets, *(goes to work!),* "You're confused. That's, alright. You said before, *that before, you would've "whooped my ass",* ain't that, right? Soooooo, why didn't you?"

"Motherfucker, that's TWO questions now, that you asked me to, MY question. Don't be, askin' me, no more damn-questions, JUST ANSWER, my damn-question.", C. Trife, replies.

"Which? Was?? What???", Pockets, asks.

"Motherfucker! What I tell you, 'bout that shit!?!", C. Trife, gettin' hyped.

"Listen, my brother, just calm down a minute and, DON'T strain that voice of yours! You didn't want me asking you, no more questions but, I HAD to, ask you, another question, 'cause, at THIS point, my brother, I don't remember what the question was, that, you wanted me to answer! ...Know what, I mean???", Pockets, says, *(AND ASKS!!)* STILL workin' on him *(with NO let-up!!).*

"ANOTHER question! I'M gettin' the fuck, outta-here!! YOU AIN'T, serious people. You...FUCKIN'...car salemen!", C. Trife, (somewhat!) explodes.

Then he...

Sits there. Looking around. (At the fine, red, EVERYTHANG!). And, at ALL the double platinum albums, (on the all red everythang walls!). And then, thinks about where the hell he's going from here. (Can't remember!). *(And,...doesn't know where the fuck home is).*

And then...

While rubbing his head, says, aloud, to himself, "I feel like I have, *a warm washrag, that's been wrung out and, placed over my brain...I...I can't, think straight...I feel dulled-down. Muted.*"

Throwin' in a quick face washing, with his large avid powerlifting hands, (just to try and, sell his *bullshit of concern!),* Pockets, looks C. Trife, square-in-the-eyes, and, states, *"You had, the same problem before. Before, you, were you. You, before you, were, you. KNOW WHAT,* I mean???"

"Another, damn-question. No! No, I don't know *WHAT,* you mean!", C. Trife, replies, *beginning to rub his head,* through his thick dreadlocks *(again!).*

Pockets, going to work on, *(soaking that washrag, with MORE warm water!),* tells, C. Trife, "Listen, *you, before* you, were, you, *had* "CTE",... Chronic Traumatic Encephalopathy."

"C.T. *what,* my nigga???", C. Trife, asks, having no idea what the hell that is!

"CTE, Chronic Traumatic Encephalopathy. You know, it's what all these NFL players are being afflicted with, from all of the head trauma and, concussions they endure. Well, before the NFL ruined the game with, the "softening" of, the sport! I mean, what tha' fuck?? There's STILL punching in boxing! There's STILL fightin' in hockey! Right OR wrong?? Shiiiiiit, you can volunteer to be in the military and, get shot at, or shot. BUT, if you voluntarily sign up for football,...YOU CAN'T even really hit nobody NO MORE! What kind OF BULLSHIT is that??? Look. *You, before* you, were, you, *fought all the time,...*I mean, *ALL the time!* For *something,* for *nothin',* for *everything,...you fought. A "fly-off-the-handle-at-split-second's-time, motherfucker".* And? *Over,* what? *Some "cooze" at, some bar?!?* Listen, I knew you well. Well, *I knew you, before* you, were, you, *well. I looked out for him, he looked out for me.* I mean,...you. Listen, me and *you* were cool for years. But, we grew apart, lost touch. I went *my way, and he,* I mean you, *went yours.* I got into the music industry. And, worked my way up to the top. But you, *I mean, him,* went down the wrong path and, got into a lot of bar fights. Just as, you, I mean, *him,* I mean, you, did tonight! WHEN, I was finally able to, locate you, I mean, *him,* years later,...it was too late. The CTE, from, too many devastating blows to the head and, concussions, had, already taken hold,...taken its toll. You, I mean, *him,* wasn't the same man. ...Just not the same, man. *He,...*committed suicide. And, one night, I received a knock on my door and, it was two cops, standing there, when I opened the door. And, I AIN'T got to tell you,...well, maybe I do, that, WHEN out-of-the-clear-blue-sky, you open your door, and, there's two cops standing there, well, they AIN'T got good news, for you! And so, they proceeded to inform me, that you, I mean, *that he,* had committed suicide and, asked me, to come down to the morgue, to identify *him.* I loved your brother, I mean, *him,* I mean, you. Listen, I went down to the morgue with them, to identify you, I mean, *him,* which, I did. WHICH, was VERY hard, FOR me. BUT,...I had to do, the right thing, by you. AND, pay my final respects, to you. I mean, *him.* And so, while standing there, in the morgue, with the two officers, after I, positively identified you, I mean, *him,* I asked, the two cops, if they wouldn't mind stepping out of the morgue, for a few minutes, so, that, I could have a moment of silence with you, I mean, *him,* alone. And so, when, they complied with my wishes, I pulled a few strands of hair from your head, yeah, so, well, anywaaaaays, to keep in *remembrance of you.* Well, that was going to be my excuse, to the cops, if they didn't step out of the morgue. Because, what I actually wanted the hairs from your head, I mean, *HIS head,* was to clone *you.* Listen, this music industry is MORE corrupt and fucked-up than, you could EVER imagine. And, since I worked my way up to the top, well, I know what the rest of the world, DON'T know! THAT, if I pull a few strings, for the "String Pullers", then, a few pulled hairs, from your head, WILL give me, what's worth more, than, ANY of these double platinum albums, on MY office walls.", Pockets, informs, C. Trife *('s facial expressions),* knowing, he COULD keep runnin' WITH, His: *Music-Biz-Straight-Off-The-Top-Gift-Of-The-Gab - BULLSHIT!).*

"Yeah? And, what's that??", asks, C. Trife, believing the believability (of, some of), of what he's being told.

"YOU!!! ...I mean, *him.* Right downstairs, in the lower levels of this place, the underground levels, that, you escaped, um, walked away from, there's a lab. A BIG, lab! And, in that lab, "ALL SORTS OF THINGS" are done and, take place. Downstairs, in the lower under the ground levels of this building, there's a team of doctors that, have the ability to do cloning. And so, I pulled some strings, for the String Pullers, yeah, so, well, anywaaaaaays, I can't go into that, and, had you cloned! I felt a horrible guilt, over the fact, that, I didn't do right by you...I mean, *him.* I made it big, in the music industry and, when I finally caught up with you, I mean, *him,* years later, it was just TOO late for me, to save you. I mean, *him.* So, BEGIN BELIEVING that, you're actually a clone, 'cause, that's what you are. So, stick with me, I'll show you the ropes to this shit. I don't know if, it's *the acoustics* in my office, or what, but, *that rough-gravely voice of yours IS, absolute money!* Yeah, so, well, anyways, fuck being a music agent, that's what I REALLY wanted to groom you to be, send you to college. You always loved music, I mean, *he did,...was always into old school rap.* Think about it, for a minute. The way you were freestyling tonight, over that "187" jam I was bumpin', in my Buick or, some shit? You got it in you, my brother!", Pockets, informs C. Trife.

"Yeah, I think, I *remember* that. *I was always spittin', freestyle raps, with my boy,*...what the fuck was, *his name??*", C. Trife, replies, to Pockets (and himself).

(Getting C. Trife, *off the topic of Brotha Jester!),*(While, still trying to get *into, AND, work the mind,* of THIS-HERE Tier-Three!), Pockets quickly, says, "Don't worry 'bout it. Just spit me somethin'. Right here. Right now. GO!!!".

"Narcissistic delusional diluted, his brain was so polluted, green gills filtered bong waters filled wit mustard green hash, narcotics, and cough syrup flavored-vermouth, the professional bridge burner, the steadily clout chasin' claimin' never earner, was NEVER gonna follow thru, his NEXT boo-hoo IS his excuse, couldn't hold down a job, couldn't hold it together, could care less to uphold the word of truth.", after which, a surprised C. Trife, just sits there, looking cross that huge red mahogany executive music industry desk at a very surprised-looking Pockets, (looking VERY impressed and shocked!), from after having been put on the spot, after showing NO fear, (but VERY fearful of being *stuck!),* so, C. Trife knew, he COULDN'T freeze-up or fuck-it-up, with *NEITHER of them knowing, WHERE-THA'-FUCK that shit just came from,* from C. Trife, *UNABLE to realize,* that, all he did *was spit, a version, of a few bars, of the free-style rhyme, he was rapping earlier tonight, inside of his Tier-Three-Mind!!!*

"That's what tha' fuck I'm talkin' 'bout! VERY few can "go", WHEN it's "Go Time"! So, who knows? If, you got it in you to spit on the spot, then, you got it in you, to write some shit down! But, AIN'T NOBODY tryna' listen to no twenty-eight-year-old rapper! I mean,...WHERE'S the "sense of urgency" WITH SOME of these motherfuckers out here, talkin' 'bout, HOW THEY GONNA' blow up??? ANYWAY!!! Since, you're well past that "twenty-eight-year-old - rapper-mark", and, *got that blues-voice LIKE-a-motherfucker,* well, it's simple then, write me a blues song. Just make it a hit. It's gotta' be a hit, my brother!! And, WHAT MAKES for a hit song, IN THIS industry, my brother? *BRAINWASHIN'-SHIT!!!* Just throw in some *"black on black" violence,* some *self-degradation, "shameful-shit",* you know,..."SHIT" THAT'LL BE SURE TO GET PLAYED ON THA' RADIO!!! "SHIT", that these sheeps and robots *will buy* into! And, MOST IMPORTANTLY, "SHIT",...that people *WILL buy!* And,

I WON'T have it, any other way. ...Yeah, so, well, anywaaaaaays, don't worry 'bout the session artists. I'll reach in MY pockets and, I'll get you all the best session artists, money can buy! My brother!! My brother!! Just write me the lyrics, write me a hit song and, so, yeah, anyways,...I'll take care of all the rest."

Rubbing his head, (with BOTH hands this time!!), through his, head full of thick dreads, C. Trife, confides, "Listen, my brother, after, of ALL that,...I...I...*I feel, like,...I gotta' washrag, that's been pulled fresh outta' a pot of boiling water and, its been laid over my brain.* I...uh...I don't know which, of this shit, that, you just told me, is harder, for me to believe?? That, I'm ACTUALLY a, motherfuckin' clone. Or, that, you're gonna get my foot in the door, WITH THIS music shit! That...that...that I'm ACTUALLY... gonna be a star?? And that, all this "music shit", is just gonna workout for me,...IN MY favor. I mean, you hear some crazy-ass shit 'bout, the music industry, Pockets. Like, how hard it is to break into, and, how motherfuckers are constantly gettin' ripped off...da...dying, being owed millions and shit. I don't know, man...I mean, it...it's...it's, like this, my brother...and,...and, don't take no offense to this...BUT, I'd believe I'm a clone, before I'd believe I'd make it into the music industry...and,... and,...that, everything's gonna work out for me with this, music shit. You know I LOVE music, my brother. Write you a, hit song? No. Fuckin'. Problem! I ain't even sweatin' those "sell ya' soul" lyrics, YOU WANT in tha' damn song. ALL, I KNOW, IS...YOU, BEST-NOT-be, bullshittin' me, holmes.", C. Trife, tells him.

(Pockets, smiling intently, *thinking* to himself, *"I'll be damned, I'm still alive.",* with, a sense-of-relief, and, strangely, with a renewed- love of, for, the: "renewed-understanding", of: a full new sense, of: the power, and, the poise, in which, he did it, of: his - "I'm-A-Professional - At-This-Shit - And - WITH-THIS-SHIT - With-My - Look-A-Man-In-The-Eyes - LYING-WAYS")...

And so...

Pockets, FULL OF HIMSELF, FEELING himself, (more so, that, he's pulling this shit off, than, C. Trife, buying into THIS shit!), Pockets, believes that, he IS, TRULY,...on TOP of HIS GAME!!!

AND SO…

Pockets, keeps pushin' HIS bullshit, *keeps pushin' that hot washrag down, (WON'T let it up!), the one laid atop this Tier Three's brain,* "I know, I hear you, my brother. BUT, on my MA'MA, my brother, yeah, so, well, anyways, EVERY word I've said to you, IS true." (And then, Pockets, cocks his custom red custom-made red hat hard to the side and, continues…), "Me and you, DO go back years and, I WAS, searching for you, FOR years. Look at me! I've done quiet well, for myself. I DID make it big, IN the music industry. And, take a look around, my brother, THOSE platinum plaques all around you, AIN'T fake. But, I get it. I get it, my brother."

And then…

Pockets, begins to chuckle, a bit. (NOT nervously, mind you!).

RATHER…

As an agent. (An agent to aid - in this - Agent, of: "bullshit's dissimination" - OF bullshit!)(OY VEY!)(NO shame!!).

Before, continuing…

"If I was you, sittin' there just like you, I probably woulda' laughed you right-on-out the room, if you, were to tell me, the same shit that you've just heard. But, think about it, my brother. I want you to, really think 'bout it.", Pockets, begins, before he pauses, (mind you, not a pause 'cause, he don't know what to say next).

Rather…

A pause 'cause, he KNOWS EXACTLY what HE'S doin'! And, the pause, was 'cause, the pause, like the chuckle, are his agents (of) to aid, to he, an Agent. An agent, to aid…BULLSHIT!

And so…

Pockets, begins again, (after he began), 'cause, he's done with his agent of pause, his pause, (of and, cause), of…BULLSHIT, and, so then, continues, ('cause, he's ready to get back into his bullshit)…('CAUSE, that's what he REALLY LIKES to do!), "You ever see some shit, like that, in your life, the...under the ground levels? YOU WERE THERE!!! THAT'S WHERE...The. Shit. Goes. Down! LOOK, I'M an OPEN BOOK!! YOU need more proof, or some shit??? GO 'head THEN, ASK ME anything! And if YOU, like my answer, then,...good. And, well, if you DON'T, well, the sun will still come up tomorrow and, we'll both be alright. Well? At least, I know, I'LL be!", Pockets, (in love with himself!), cocks his custom red custom-made red hat hard to the side and, (challenges!), as he, continues, "Open book, my brother. Open. Mutha'. Fuckin'. Book. AND, I BET, I GOT an ANSWER, for you!!"

Reaching past the few remaining chips on his plate, C. Trife, picks up his pickle spear, bites the thing in half and, in between crunches, (and in between - *collecting his thoughts*...the best, that he can!), DOES SO, in fact, HAVE a question FOR his brother! And so, does so ask, Pockets, "Downstairs...earlier...whenever, that was...Look, Pockets,...I've heard some wild-ass, unbelievable-shit...tonight...today,...but, *WHAT WAS that-shit, you said,* WHEN, we had guns pulled on us, BY them armed guards, outside?? Yo, Pockets, my man, I don't know what, to tell ya', but,...*DON'T BE TALKIN' SHIT ON, BILL COSBY!!!!!!*"

("OH FUCK!!! HE DON'T KNOW!!! I GOT 'EM!!!", a Big-Hustle-Mind huddles-up!)

Smiling ear-to-ear, Pockets, states, "MY BROTHER!!! MY BROTHER!!! I KNOW you're STILL "up-in-the-air" 'bout, some of this, shit. BUT, WHAT IF, I COULD PROVE TO YOU, that, Bill Cosby, IS doin' "state-time", RIGHT NOW, as we, mutha'-fuckin'-speak!?! WOULD ya',...believe me then?? AND, I ain't EVEN-GON - tell you, *what, THEY SAY, he did!* BUT...what, if??? WHAT IF I CAN, prove this shit to you? That, you ain't EVEN KNOW a thing, 'bout it, *'bout, this, Cosby-gettin'-locked-up - shit. 'Cause, while all that shit was goings-on, shown all over the world, by just 'bout every mass media outlet, paradin' the man! Paraded the man, ON SOME town square shit, hands bound, MADE 'EM do tha' "perp walk" while, an angry mob cursed him and, cheered, at the same-damn time!* What, if, I could prove to you, that, that's what they did to the man? I'm tellin' you, right now, my brother, you ain't see NONE of this shit, *'cause, yo' ass been sleep, fo' tha' past, three years! ALL, that shit happened, while, you was bein' cloned, AND after you was cloned, 'cause you been down there, in them lower under the ground levels, OF THIS place EVER since,...* would you believe me then???"

"Pockets, my brother, I'm givin' you a pass on this shit. And it's all because. Um, yeah. And, it's all because. 'Cause...um...'cause...FUCK!!!... THA' FUCK was, I sayin'??? OH, YEAH!!! And, it's all because, *we had guns pulled on us. And, they wanted me, NOT YOU...and,...and, you ain't leave me hangin',...you...You ain't run off, like a bitch!...So,...so,...I...I* figure,...you REALLY DO, got my back! But, yeah, I got a couple questions, for ya'...shit...that'll, come back to me...But, yeah, *that COSBY shit,...*like, C'MON, MY MAN!!! NEXT thing you'll be tellin' me, be some-OUTLANDISH-shit, LIKE, Trump is the President of the United States, or some shit!!!", C. Trife, replies, busting himself up, (laughing at the end!), over some-shit, he would find tooooo, UNBELIEVABLY-OUTLANDISH!!!

("OH, FUCK!!! 'DIS NIGGA!!! I AIN'T, EVEN-GON' TELL HIM, THAT, THE PHILADELPHIA EAGLES finally WON THE SUPER BOWL, while his ass was in the under the ground levels, AND FUCK ALL THIS SHIT, THE-FUCK-UP!!!!!!, a Big-Hussle-Mind,...so reasons!)

Pulling out his cell phone and, *pulling up what mass media wants you to think about the Cosby case,* Pockets, seated on his big hustle throne, seated behind his big hustle desk, holds his phone out facing C. Trife, who, *reads what it says, 'bout Cosby.* Then, C. Trife, snatches the phone from out of Pockets' hand! *(Feverishly-clicking on links!) AND SCROLLING, UP AND, DOWN PAGES!* (JUST TO MAKE SURE, for HIMSELF!!!) WITH, Pockets, looking on intently, of course! (Readying himself, to snatch his cell phone back!). In case, in the event, C. Trife, stumbles cross something, while he's surfin' the net, that, Pockets, doesn't want C. Trife to read, or know. (Hmm).

Just 'cause...

It could fuck shit up! (AND, BESIDES!) ...Pockets hasn't USED IT AGAINST HIM, YET!!!

But, THEN...

C. Trife, says to Pockets, "Alright, my nigga. ...Damn, Bill.", (WHICH, relieves Pockets, a lil')...(But still!), C. Trife, *lookin' at the cell phone screen,* as he's, handing Pockets' cell phone back to him, C. Trife, cries out (fanatically!), "YOOOOOOOOOOOOO!!! *THA' RAIDERS GOT GRUDEN?? CHUCKY'S COACHIN' THA' RAIDERS, AGAIN!?!* YOOOOOOOOOOOO!!! *THE SILVER AND BLACK* ARE BACK, BABY!!!!!!!"

"Man, 'GIMME my phone!", Pockets, says, snatching the phone outta, C. Trife's hand! Then, explains to C. Trife, "You've had too much *mental-stimulation,* for one night. Yes, the Raiders *got Chucky,* back. LET'S, JUST SAY,...the Raiders, *had a VERY interesting offseason.* I...I don't think you're ready, *for all that.*"

"Why? *What HAPPENED???*", asks, C. Trife.

Just then...

Enters, Phillip Tate! ...("Personal" Assistant Extraordinaire!)

"Pardon me, sir. MC Busta-Nut, False Profit, and Y.S., have arrived. Shall I, lead them to your office?", (Saved by the bell! Or, by the whistle,... as it were!).

"No, no, put their bags in the RV and, then have them wait for me, in the studio lobby. And, Phil, pack Mr. Trife here, a bag. Go to wardrobe and, pick out a couple of all black outfits, suits, some "bluesmen shit" and, a black Stetson. You know, how to do it, Phil. Then, place Mr. Trife's things, in my sleeping quarters for me, huh? Oh, and Phil, go to Procurement and Supply and, get Mr. Trife here, one of those black and white composition books, and, an ink pen and, put it in my sleeping quarters, in the RV, along with the rest of his belongings. Mr. Trife here, is an extremely-talented singer/songwriter, WITH very thought-provoking lyrics! Phil, you should hear him freestyle, sometime! He'll be, writing us, our NEXT big hit, for Jettison Records! Yes sir, just a matter-of-time, before, Mr. Trife here, adds MORE double platinum plaques, to MY, lush, all red everythang, office!", Pockets, instructs, and, does so inform, *(ALREADY in "Promotor- Mode")* FOR, his NEXT big artist, *speaking on,*

WHAT he WANTS others to believe (and, doesn't necessarily care to believe, himself). *Just as long as it sounds good!* Just as long, as the one HEARING, *(the bullshit!)* just, nods their head in agreement and, not necessarily, that they believe, *(in the bullshit!),* themselves.

And, (on that note!)...

Phillip Tate, facilitates Pockets. (Providing WHAT HE requires!). *Providing, what he has facilitated for Pockets, many a time now! For, and, in front of,* many an artist. Booking agent. Venue owner. Some, overpriced-diva-bitch. "Metroid". Frizzy-haired(with NO "d.o." FOR the "b.o."!) types. *AND, FOR, (and, IN FRONT of!),* The: THIS-black-mesh-baseball-snapback-hat-to-the-back-wearin'(and-oh-hey!)-I'll-try-TOO-hard-AND-WEAR-this-black-bandana-beneath-it - types(SHOULD-make-me-look-cool,...right?)(YOU KNOW THE ONES!!!)(THE: "Hey, I'm a rockstar,... right?")(the: studio session artist - GLORIFIED-SELF-RIGHTEOUS-original-band-member-"fill-in" - types!)...(Yeah. That guy).

And...

Phillip, does so, BY, the nodding of his head, *(in: silent-agreement!).* DOING his part, (HIS duty!) of, doing WHATEVER! *...(to help SEAL the deal!).*

AS...

"Mr. Trife" (as he, goes by NOW!!!)(OY VEY!!!)(WENT ALL "HOLLYWOOD" WITH THA' SHIT!!!), *looks on, in: Silent* - I-Know-Pockets-Is-JUST-Makin'-Shit-Up-On-The-Fly-With-THAT-"SALES-PITCH"-But-I-Know-He's-Right-EVEN-IF-He-Don't-Know-It-TO-BE-The-Case-BUT-I-Know-It-To-Be-The-Case-SO-I'll-JUST-NOW-Nod-My-Head-IN-"Silent-Agreement"-TOO - *type of -* Silent Agreement!

FOR...

The world needs ditch-diggers and head-nodders too! (Nothin' wrong with being a ditch-digger).

HOWEVER(!)...

Pockets, (and, Pockets' ALIKE!) need, festor 'round AND upon, NEED and require, *The: Silent-Head-Nodding-In-Agreement-Silent-Head-Nodders(of, signing-on AND selling out!!)-Of-The-World,* TO feel special, TO feel superior, TO pump the love(fuck the heart!) into THEIR heads, so, (that!), they, can carry-on, (in, their: "shallow-bullshit-lives"), so, (that!) they, can feel better ('bout, what they KNOW they lack!) IN their lives, TO justify "the bullshit!", *(but, MOST are far gone, and removed),* from, the: "requirement of the justifications".

'Cause...

(They ARE, THAT shallow!)

BECAUSE...

They live, RETURN TO, bathe, eat and, provide nutrients from, THAT bottomless, three toad, swarmin' of green-backed-flies, "Well of Bullshit".

And...

FUCK YOUR feelings, motherfucker! *(DON'T BE A: Silent - In Agreement - Head Nodder - of the Head!).*

And, (ON THAT NOTE!!!)...

Pockets, is pleased. *Of, saying it, what he said, AND, HOW he said it.* In that, *TO pull out of, not, but one, BUT, that, of TWO - Silent-In-Agreement-Head-Nods!* And, as far as, Pockets, IS concerned, *he had, everyone in the room,* (though, JUST two!), *in his office,* (at, and), *buying into,* MADE them *"give and provide",* made them - *OFFER UP, The:* (MUCH coveted!) *Silent Head Nod of Agreement!* (And, for this!), Pockets, believes, (scratch that!) he, doesn't think, (for, HE KNOWS!), that, he is on top of his game right now and, (for that!), can do no wrong. *(Got people TO buy into his bullshit!!).* And, for this, (and, this alone!), Pockets, is in love with his rocketship-fast and, powerful, fuck your feelings, next hustle/new hustle mind! But, before Phillip Tate, is allowed to, (and, or) is ABLE to run along, (to facilitate!), Pockets, loves to hear himself talk! (And, loves to hear himself giving, orders and demands!) And so, (and, for THAT!), he, gets right back to talking, "And Phil. Give my RV, a "quick-once-over", for me. This'll be, the first time, that, I've actually taken it off the lot! Just, check the tire pressure for me and, shit like, that. And, check the oil level, too. And, don't let me catch you using a funnel or, spillin' any oil on, MY engine!! And, oh. Phil. Find out, which company, it was, that, installed the custom-vinyl-wrap on the, private helicopter and, get that lined-up, for me. I want, my RV wrapped, exactly how, the private chopper is wrapped, with, "Jettison Records" in "big white script lettering", cross my RV, upon, MY return! Oh. And, Phil. Make sure, Y.S., and them, remain in the studio lobby until, Mr. Trife here, gets showered-up in my RV's sleeping quarters and, changed into his new wardrobe.", (Pockets, then, turns his attention to Mr. Trife), and, says, "Mr. Trife, you're gonna HAVE TO get, all that blood and shit, off your face. I can't have Y.S. seeing you, like that. She's tough,...but skittish,...more like damaged, been through a lot.", (then, Pockets, gives C. Trife a quick-look, before he leans over in his high back red tufted leather upholstered throne). Then, gathering in, his large avid powerlifter hands, Pockets, collects up his reading materials (from off the plush red carpeting behind his desk), while, calling Phil, over to his side, "And, oh, hey, Phil. Take these down to my RV for me, if you would?"

"I got you.", states, Phillip Tate, then, exits Pockets' office, closing the red door shut, behind him.

Reaching for one of the last remaining chips on his plate, C. Trife, asks, "So, *what were we, talkin' 'bout?*"

(Changing gears, of his Big-Hustle-Gears, the ones, that are always turning, always churning, of and in, his New-Hustle/Next-Hustle-Mind!)...

Pockets, switches gears!

And...

He's quick wit tha' shit! (Gettin' the hell *off the topic, OF the Raiders,* with C. Trife!).

And(THEN!)...

Pockets, so, informs,..."You were asking me, how you died?"

"Yeeeeeaaaahhhhh??...Yeeeeeaaaaahhhhhh?...Yeeeeeaaaaahhhhhh,...I...I was. So? What the fuck, I do? I gotta tell ya', my brother, THIS is some, fuckin'-trippy - fuckin' - messed-up - shit. But,...I'm STARTIN' TO dig-the-fuck outta it! A clone? FUCK IT!!! Sounds 'bout right. If not ME, then WHO!?", replies, C. Trife, with a laugh. Smiling hard. (And, beginning to feel...*Invincible).*

As, A-Matter-Of-Fact, as he can muster, Pockets, with the art of the lie, and quick wit tha' shit, looks C. Trife, right dead in his eyes, and so tells him, *"You blew your head off. Stuck the barrel of a thirty-aught-six in your right eye, blew your fuckin' brains out. And peeled your face off in the process.* Make no mistake about it, my brother. A 12 gauge shotgun will do massive damage, this I am sure of. A 12 gauge will blow the top of a nigga's head clean off, leavin' brains and shit, all OVER the place. But that thirty-aught-six, my brother? THAT-shit-PEELS-faces!! *And, THAT'S why the cops needed ME...to, identify you.* You AIN'T have no FACE, MY brother!! Now, *you asked...*I told you. Yeah, so, well, anyways, I would NEVER bullshit you. *Never have,* never will. *It's* REAL!!! *THIS shit DID happen!! EXACTLY how* I am tellin' you *it happened...*my brother...*is the fuckin' way it went the fuck down.* Like,...how'd you think *that made me feel...*seeing you, I mean *him...layin' there in the ma...morgue like that...in that bloody FUCKIN' WHITE disaster bag??"*

Chuckling, *(while tryin' to envision it all!),* C. Trife, then looks at Pockets, smiles, and, says, *"Sounds like some shit,* I would do!!! I bet,...*it didn't even hurt.* Sorry *to have* put you through it, Pockets. *Still some shit I wudda' done tho'.* Damn. *That musta' been some gun.* What I do *that shit* with,...a *30...30,* what?"

PLEASED. That he's now got his hooks down in 'em good. *Had 'em in. When. He bumped that "One-Eighty-Seven" - shit! Looked out for 'em. With them. BITCHEZ cops. AND. When. Them. SERVICE REVOLVERS. Were ALL POINTED down on 'em.* And might I add? *From a POSITION of ADVANTAGE!* Pockets. *LOOKED THE FUCK OUT!!!* (Which ONLY helped!) *Puttin' Pockets' hooks in 'em down in 'em deeper. (A lot!).* BUT. AND HOWEVER!!! C. Trife. *Buyin' that. ($traight off the churnin' gears dome shit!).* CERTAINLY, has Pockets,...IN LOVE with himself! That, *his Sharp-Hustle-Mind, quick wit tha shit,* and all in due time. *Was able* *to manipulate the mind. OF A TIER THREE!!! ALL AND WITHOUT!!!* Having to have read. All those DAMN text books and reading materials. Yup. *Them fancy-pants fuckin' doctors downstairs in the lower under the ground levels,* AIN'T GOT SHIT ON OL' POCKETS!!!...*Or so he thinks....*And would PROUDLY let PHILLIP TATE know *that shit* in an INSTANT. Yes. Pockets TRULY is. In love with himself. At this very moment. *At his conquest. With his sharp mind. Quick wit tha shit. And did it all,* in due time. *While looking C. Trife right straight dead in his eyes.* Why-Yes. Pockets *thinks he can damn near do ANYTHING.* AND. *Get away with it!!* Do or say...whatever...AND *HOWEVER!!!...*he *motherfuckin' pleases.* Pockets, certainly is in. *The right industry for THAT.* With that. *Fucked up. Fuck YOUR FEELINGS. Mentality.* And so, does so, elaborates, *"30-06 deer rifle".* But them white boys call it a "thirty-aught-six". It's just some old-timey whiteboy shit, their great granddaddy's used to call it. You know. *When them good ol' boys were out, er, huntin'.* You know,... *runnin' through the woods and swamps.* That's what *some old brother told me one time,* anyway. Don't worry 'bout it. I'ma country boy, so I get my hunt and fish on, but that's whatever. Hey, let's get this wrapped up, and, get you on the road, huh? Maybe we'll get some fishin' in or somethin', at my horse ranch, in Tennessee. I got a large man-made pond there, wit-a thick sticky-mud bottom. I got that pond stocked wit all kinds of shit. BUT, just be careful, if you do, do some fishin', at my place. 'Cause, if you slip in and, your boots fill up wit them pond waters, and your boots get stuck, down deeper and deeper in that mud, let me tell ya', my brother, the more you struggle to free yourself, well, let's just say, MY pond WILL BE STOCKED wit MORE THAN catfish and snappin' turtles! But that's whatever...don't worry 'bout it. Listen, I'm takin' all y'all on a road trip, give y'all, a taste of that "roadlife". I'm taking all my new artists, my TOP artists, on the road with me. THAT INCLUDES you too, my brother! GOTTA' lookout for my new artists and, create a buzz FOR y'all! You know how it is, do my part to, uh, get y'all to blow up. I'll be settin' up a show, and a meet and greet for y'all, up in Pennsylvania.", (then, *feelin' the love,* though, not the falseness of the good vibes that, he has created, in his, On Top OF The World - Executive Music Industry Office),...*(and, under C. Trife's scalding hot washrag!)*...(MOREOVER, *the love,* of *being in love,...*

WITH HIMSELF!!!), Pockets, the gambling man, rolls tha' dice, goin' for *"mate, checkmate"*, then, states, "Yeah, so, well, ANYWAAAAAAYS, I had you, I mean, *him,* cremated. And, I made ALL of the arrangments MYSELF! I had to pull some strings, for the "String Pullers", strings, they needed pulled for a while now. So,...I pulled them. Don't worry 'bout it. BUT!!! I had the Jettison Records private helicopter, fly your remains ALL THE WAY OUT to California, my brother.", (and, then, *pantomiming with his right hand, coming from way out here, then swoopin', comin', in, down low, to here, left hangin', right above* that fine red mahogany wood!), Pockets, *makin' the sounds, with his mouth, of the blades of a chopper cuttin' the air,* (castin' soggy potato chip particle projectiles cross his desk as he does it!), and so, then, Pockets, continues, as he *describes the chain of events,* that so then followed, *in his lie-churning-mind and, occurred IN his bullshit subdued,* (YET dramatic!), SELLING tha shit, *"And then. Then, that private helicopter. Well, that private helicopter flew directly over top of, NONE OTHER, TRIFLIN'!!!...Than. The......Oakland......Alameda...... County......Coliseum...And once we were there.* Trife, my brother, *once we had arrived, I instructed that pilot...to hover down low...directly over top of the 50 yard line.* And don't you know...*with that private Jettison Records helicopter...hovering down low...I and I alone,...scattered* your...I mean...*his ashes...all out onto that football field... from THAT private chopper."*

With a hush and a pause coming over the room, Pockets sits, *fully in love with himself,* fully perched up high upon his high back red tufted leather upholstered throne, *not knowing if* he went to *"The Well"* too deep, that time. *THAT stinkin', Well. That, bottomless, endless, unrelenting, and uncaring, Well. That, swarmin' of green-backed flies, Well. That parasitic, maggots and brain-eatin' amoebas, molds and three toads, Well. (Swimmin', livin', down deep, down in the mystery-waters of that bullshit, Well). THAT WELL!!!* (YOU KNOW *THAT WELL!!!*),(DON'T ACT LIKE YOU DON'T!!!). *THAT WELL!!! THAT WELL,...packed with nothin' but LIES and BULLSHIT, WELL!!!* (THAT'S THE MOTHERFUCKIN' WELL, MOTHERFUCKERS!!!). *That Well. The shiesty,* "out-for-me-and-fuck-you's", (of the world), *use and use you, to build their homes, clothe their children and, feed their fuckin' kids from, Well. The Well, their kids* (essentially) *feed directly out of, Well. The Well, they feed their kids directly out of, Well.* (Yes, *THAT Well*). And, on that, *scattered-his-ashes-line-of-bullshit,* Pockets awaits, with bated breath, to see, *if* C. Trife *took the bait,* *(that being, a 30 gallon steel drum burn barrel, attached to a great rusty chain, hoisted up from the depths of THAT Well,…and, if he jumped the fuck inside!).* With C. Trife, *rubbing his head, (trying to rub free from the heat of that washrag!),* C. Trife, finally gives his approval, with a simple, "My man.", (and a smile).

(A custom red custom-made red hat gets cocked hard to tha' side)

"Good. Ok, *ease your mind,* my brother.", Pockets, begins, *"THAT'S far too much stimulation, for you to take in, ON the FIRST DAY of your "awakening".* Stick with me. I'll walk you through the *"Cloning Recovery Process"* but, as for now, I just want you *to ease your mind.* I don't want you to think too much. We have a long drive up to my ranch. And, we'll be making a stop along the way. So, get as much rest as you can, in the RV. I don't want you talking too much with, the other artists, um,…rest your voice. Yeah, THAT'S WHAT, I want you TO do! Get your rest! So, that,… you can rest your voice. Yeah, so, well, anyways, *I gave you life,* a new life, so that I can give you a better life, *in your second life.* You feel me?"

Just then, *(so much for NOT wanting C. Trife's mind, to get OVER stimulated!!!!)…*

ENTERS(!!!!)….

THE DUYU CREW!!!! Kickin'-in Pockets' all red everythang office door!!!! (And, STILL covered IN *"the art of their concerted-works"*!!!!) AND,….stinkin' of *commercial flight fuel!!!!*

Bad Habitz, clothed in his bright red Prohibition Era-style vintage gangster suit , the same color of which, *(that BE),* matchin' his skin!!!! *(FROM the frostbite and, gangrene that, HAS set in!!!!).* Wearin' his - bright red - gangster derby, *(bloody feather of, a snowy owl,* jammed in the band!), with, tha' jacked-up brim all-jacked, (like, the four, by ALL four!!!!), they be rockin' their, matching vintage hats. *Jet fuel fumes, insulated in* his bright red clothes, *by the bloods of the arctic, frozen in repose. Lookin' fucked-up, like,* A - From-The-Back-Of-The-Cage - From-The-Back-Of-The-Blowing-

Feathers-All-Over-Windshied-Tractor-Trailor - AND IN JUST 30 DAYS - Straight-TO-The-Table-FROM-The-Egg - This-IS-Their-Life - DON'T know NOTHING else - ALL-JUST-FOR-YOUR-CONSUMPTION-AND-GNASHING-PLEASURE - Chicken!!!! *BLOODY arctic snowy owl feathers,* to his suit, they be *stickin', to the whale blubbers,* AND of the cute, little adorable, *big baby-eyed baby seal - fats!!!!*

Diet, stays dressed, head-to-toe, in all black. (He too, with, his derby brim all-jacked). (BUT, still wearin' it like a boss!). *Upon, the high seas, unfathomable-amounts of dead bodies overboard, he tossed.* And, his black Prohibition Era-style vintage gangster suit, looks more white than black, *(as he's, covered head-to-toe, in high seas sea salts).* And, *he's GOT deep painful long cracks,* (far from chapped!!!!), *IN BOTH corners of his mouth. Lookin' like a marooned pirate,* (AND, I think he likes it!!!!). *('CAUSE, his nasty-corner-cracks makes it look like, he's forever smilin'!!!!).* (OF WHICH!), when he talks,.....it *MAKES THEM gape!!!!* And, tied cross his throat, (chokingly-hard!!!!), *bearing the marks, of ligature strangulation,* hangin', down his back, Diet wears his - *high-winds-of-the-high-seas - tattered pirate flag -* as a cape!!!!

And, (oh boy!!!!),.....THEN you have Dead Sexy!!!! Rockin' his Prohibition Era-style vintage gangster suit. Pale is the color. (OH SHIT!!!! Not his face, oh, no, not his face!!!!)...*BUT, the rest of him, is in, desert sands and, poisons of the skin.* (And, from head-to-toe, with, the shit, Dead Sexy, is covered). *By blisters, rashes and, redness. AND, the shit is flakin'!!!! From, burying millions in the desert, in tiny brass urns,* (got the earth, SO shook!!!!), Mother Earth, just might start quaking!!!! *And, he did it ALL BEFORE, he tore, outta' the desert, on his, chopper of pale. Leaving behind, buried in the sands, his shovel and pale.* (To, meet up, at the four winds, with Pockets' - "red-eye-flight-delay" - HOOLIGANS!!!!). *And, of those, that, Dead Sexy left, buried in urns???? DEAD SEXY, LEFT 'EM, WHILE HE WAS LEAVIN' 'EM, ALL FEELING FORSAKEN!!!!*

Pretty High, clothed in his - *(NOW-far-from-pristine!!!!)* - white Prohibition Era-style vintage gangster suit. *Tattered. Ripped and shredded. Head-to-toe imbedded, with passenger airline fuselage shrapnel.* (Lookin' fucked-up like scrappel!!!!). For, in his degloved right hand, *for which was able to withstand,* (the explosion!), he holds, his prized possession. *Of the efforts, of the DUYU CREW, successfully concerted.* (Of a London to NYC red-eye flight...deverted).

Pretty High, *tossin' (which, would you believe, is actually red not black) just to make sure it, comes crashin' down back,* (upon, fine illegally-harvested artisan cut grains), *PERMANENTLY DAMAGING,* Peruvian red mahogany wood(JUST SO, THAT IT, MOTHERFUCKIN' WOULD!!!!)fuck-up, Pockets' music industry executive desk, (of red artisan cut grains, of the very same!), JUST SO, IT WOULD, drive Pockets the fuck insane!!!!

And, with Pretty High, with that, lil' laugh of his and, with the skin-burned-off-down-to-his-skeletonized hand, (NONE OF THIS SHIT was APART, of POCKETS' PLAN!), watches as, *comin' crashing back down,* (upon and on red mahogany wood!), *was the, flight's recorder black box, of the flight, of DJ Wood.* Along for the ride, of falling from the sky, *(WERE)* some very-much-so-in-power "People", that *(WERE),* on THAT red-eye London to NYC flight. *(What the sharks don't gorge themselves upon, as they devour the living and the dead, well, the bottom-dwellers and the birds of the sea...WILL BE eatin' good tonight!).*

"YOU FUCKIN' DUYU CREW MUTHA' FUCKAS!!! ARE YOU SERIOUS, WIT-THA'-SHIT, RIGHT NOW!?! I ASKED YOU TO *"DELAY"* THE FLIGHT,...NOT BLOW-IT-OUT THA' FUCKIN'-AIR!!! AND THEN!?! YOU BRING *THE FLIGHT RECORDER,...* HERE?!? MY NIGGA, WHAT-THA'-FUCK IS WRONG, WIT YOU??? LOOK AT MY MUTHA'-FUCKIN' FINE, RED MAHOGANY DESK!!!", Pockets, blows-the-fuck-up!

(B. Trife, never-not one - FOR OTHERS' - "sudden-moves")...

HOWEVER...

C. Trife, ain't *there* wit it yet. Plus, *(THAT!) hash,* has kicked-in for a second wave! *(And, you know how that goes!).*

And so...

C. Trife, just sits there, with his back to the crew. Unmoving. And unmoved.

"AYO!!!! Pockets! *Long-time-no-see,* mutha' fucka'!!!!", Bad Habitz, belts out, as the DUYU CREW breaks out...(into laughter!!!!).

Talking to the weaving-head, and, of the face being washed, hidden and buried behind massive avid powerlifting hands, elbows on *(NOW-not-so fine!)* illegally harvested and imported Peruvian red mahogany wood, Pretty High, tells Pockets, "Ayo, Pockets, you know we ain't one for followin' YOUR instructions. You CAN'T BE askin' US to *"delay-some-shit"!* What tha' fuck IS wrong, WIT YOU?? *"DELAY-SOME-SHIT",* to US, means, to mutha' fuckin' *"DESTROY IT"!!!!* But, ayo... no hard feelings, huh? So, waddaya' got for us, Pockets? What's good wit this - *"CREATING A BUZZ"* - shit????"

"HEY! HEY!! HEY!!! Don't BE speakin' on that shit, right now!", Pockets, abruptly objects, snappin' out of his "Why-ME-funk", (eyes widened!!), observed, between, face washing fingers, with a look in them, like, "Yo! What's wrong wit y'all???? Talkin' this, loose-shit, in front of the man, sittin' wit his back to y'all, in front of y'all????"

AND...

Here they go! (Right on cue!) The DUYU CREW, *doin' WHAT they do!!!!*

(The art of the chaos)...

"AYO!!!! PRETTY HIGH!!!! *You brought Pockets back a souvenir, from OVERSEAS!!!* AND, HE don't sound like he APPRECIATES, THA' SHIT!!! AIN'T THAT, RIGHT, Dead Sexy!?!", Bad Habitz, *stirs the pot first!,* (while, pointin' at that black box!), (while, resting in the valley, of fucked-up blood red mahogany artisan cut grains!), while, lookin' at Dead Sexy, *(while, INSTIGATIN' shit!!!!).*

"YEAH, HE DO!!!! AYO!!!! *HE don't sound like he, appreciates, the KIND gesture!* Kinda FUCKED-UP on your part Pockets,...on-some, REAL shit. AIN'T THAT, RIGHT, Diet?!?!", Dead Sexy, *adds his ingredients to their fucked-up gunk.*

"AYO!!!! POCKETS!!!! You know *the TROUBLE, Pretty High had to go through???? To get that black fuckin' box, THROUGH CUSTOMS?!?!*

TELL 'EM, *WHAT KINDA' TROUBLE you had to go through*, PRETTY HIGH!!!!", Diet, *adds some salt,* makin' Pockets salty. *(HIGH SEAS sea salt, that is!!!!).*

(And as C. Trife sits there, in that chair, facing Pockets, with his back facing the DUYU CREW, *there's just somethin' 'bout their madness). There's just somethin' 'bout the way they talk and interact with one another. AND there's DEFINITELY somethin' 'bout the way they FUCKIN' WIT POCKETS!!!! AND, on that note, maybe it was just one of those somethin's. OR maybe, it was ALL THREE SOMETHIN'S. BUT, SOMETHIN' has JARRED this TIER THREE'S MEMORY!!!* AND, ON THAT NOTE, C. Trife, turns 'round in his chair, to see if he knows these guys. And, as he does, The DUYU CREW, ALL stop in their tracks, stopping their chaos, thinkin' they've seen a bloody ghost!!!! *1). Bloody: 'Cause, they were just in London, and, over in London, they-be-kickin'-that bloody slang shit. 2). Ghost: 'Cause, they're not sure if they're actually seeing, what they're actually seeing. 3). Bloody ghost: 'Cause, well, you remember C. Trife's face is still all covered in blood, right?)* Good. Let us proceed...

And just like that, there's, itchin' kickin' in, like, from the mere mention, of someone merely mentioning, that, they found a tick on themselves yesterday, and,...picked it off. (And you know, that, that tick, is no longer around!)... BUT, WITH THAT mere mention, YOU begin itchin'!!!!! And so, Dead Sexy begins, *(with his memory and itchin' kickin' in!!!!), his reactionary-rubbing of his eyes,* (THEN, blurts out as he cries!), "AYO!!!! POCKETS!!!! I HOPE like a MOTHERFUCKER, you ain't plannin' on US, *WORKIN' wit THIS GUY again!!* I AIN'T WORKIN' wit *HIM!!! HE'S GOT PINK EYE!!!!"*

And just like that, (and, on that note!), Pockets, with elbows, on fucked-up red mahogany, leans forward, (past the black box:) and, squints his eyes, staring at the eyes of the man, that smoked some *strong-ass(THAT!)-hash,* several hours ago. And then, with assessment made, and convinced, Pockets, leans back into his high back red tufted leather upholstered throne, looks up at Dead Sexy and, then, does so state, "He ain't got pink eye. He's just pretty high, that's all."

"AYO!!!! DON'T BE CALLIN' HIM, PRETTY HIGH!!!! I'M, MOTHERFUCKIN', PRETTY HIGH, MOTHERFUCKER!!!!", Pretty High, begins goin' off!!!!

(A quick flash, of a glimpe of his past, of a memory, of an interaction)...

C. Trife, sees the view from above, *in his mind's eye, looking down upon, looking into, that bank vault cell, of his, of B. Trife's, so, of his, as well, of THEIR, FIRST ENCOUNTER, with none other than, the DUYU CREW!!!!*

But...

"WHEN did that happen??"

AND...

"HOW do THESE CATS,...KNOW ME???"

And...

"I HATE that SHIT!!"...("Don't be SLIPPIN', nigga!!")("Havin' cats know YOU, but YOU AIN'T SURE, HOW YOU know THEM!!!").

THAT'S...

("The definition of "SLIPPIN"', nigga!")...

SOOOOOO...

"They HAD you, IF they wanted you!"

(Time to clear your head and get focused, brotha!)...

BUT...

All, THAT - "Don't be callin' him, Pretty High!" - SHIT????

Well(as for *that!*)...

C. Trife, *speaks on it,* "Oh, hold up! I...I...I can't do this shit *again.* ...Listen, motherfucker. I ain't Pretty High! ...I'M ME!!!"

Chapter Nine

MACCHIATO

The next morning...

*T*he career choices made, the families one was born into, of those playing the game, and, making all the right moves and decisions, proceeds. Proceeding, all across America, the sounds of the morning are taking place. (What's that sound?). The sound any working man would know. The sound any roommate, wife, child, or significant other of a working man would know. (What's that sound?). The sound of a razor being banged against the upper area of a bathroom sink bowl, just to the right, OR left, of that tiny - this-is-to-prevent-the-sink-from-overflowing - drain, as razors get banged, after several passes, several times, several times over, for several more passes, according to the amount of - shave-by-numbers-real-estate - on the faces and necks, there is to be shaved, and then banged, repeatedly, again, against the upper area of bathroom sinks, all across America, just to the right, OR left, (as the case may be), knocking free, fresh cut stubble and whiskers, from the ridiculous amounts of blades, where fresh cut stubbles and whiskers get impacted and sandwiched, and packed in place, in between all those ridiculous blades, right in there with the bloody foam of shaving cream.

The cadence of it all, the running waters, the splashing of the waters in the bowls of sinks, of the rinsing and banging free of the mortar-like hardened pink-tinged cream and of the stubbles, mud, grasses and twigs, cautionary log cabin-esk sidings, which requires more intensified banging, providing more intensified ample-audibles, through closed bathroom doors, if one so gives a fuck or has the time, of the banging of the razors, all across America, of the sounds of morning.

Of the sounds of morning. All across America. Of the banging on the bathroom doors. Of the, "MOM, SHE'S STILL IN THE BATHROOM!!!" Of the, "MOM, SHE USED UP ALL THE HOT WATER!!!" Of the, "YOU'RE GONNA' BE LATE FOR THE SCHOOL BUS!!!" Of the, "IF YOU MISS THE BUS, I'M NOT DRIVIN' YOU TO SCHOOL!!! Of the, "YOU'LL BE WALKIN'!!! AND DON'T LET ME GET A CALL, AT MY NEW JOB, THAT YOU WERE LATE!!!" Of the, "I told you, you were going to be crying in the morning. Tonight, you're going to bed at seven." Of hot water being poured into hot cereal. Of the spoons in bowls stirrin' it up! All across America. Of the sounds of morning.

Of the sounds of morning. All across America. Of the unmistakable-feeling of the sound, (to some), the feeling of the sound of two pieces of styrofoam being pressed and rubbed together, of the sound of hardened lifetime brake pads being pressed and rubbing against blued - from-heat-and-wear - rotors, all across America, of the morning rush, of turnstiles and of tokens, of the sounds of morning. Of the sounds of morning. All across America. Of commentaries made. Of, "That guy has a loose serpentine belt." Of, "That asshole shouldn't be in the carpool lane! Where's a cop when you need one!?" Of commuters bitching about the car in front of them, not having their money ready at the toll booth! Of the sounds of morning. All across America.

Of the sounds of morning. Every morning. But, in America. This morning. In Pennsylvania. In the city of North Juarez. *No longer in,* but, as of EVERY morning, (as is, the case!), *from within, to the mandatory-adjourning thereto,* to the front, to outside, out front, of La Alla Banca, (North Juarez's I.A. Club), (no, you are not welcomed!), the sounds of morning,...are quite different.

For Skin's crew, meets every morning there, for, (well?),... FUGGETABOUTIT! For Skin's, don't give a DAMN 'bout YOUR problems! For, that's what they are. YOUR PROBLEMS!!! (For Skin's, got problems of HIS OWN!). For Skin's, don't give a fuck 'bout your "negligible carpool lane issues", your lukewarm-at-best morning showers, OR if your lil' rugrat-crumb-snatcher, has some Wheatena to eat, for breakfast. For Skin's, HATES RATS!!! For Skin's, GOTTA' EAT TOO!!! So, FUCK YOUR crumb-snatchin' rugrat! (Foreal).

But, as for this morning, THIS morning, has adjourned to early afternoon, (as light envelopes, don't go unaddressed and, priority is placed upon them!). For this morning, has turned to early afternoon, for Skin's has no desire to get clipped, for Skin's wants to keep what he's got, for Skin's wants to keep what's his birthright! For Skin's, wears his concerns heavy like a hood. For Skin's, wants to protect his head like a condom.(oy vey).

As for THIS morning? Skin's is in rare form! As for Skin's, some might even say he's raw. But, as for Skin's, he don't give a FUCK how raw he may be, or how raw he may be coming across. As for Skin's, he knows what to do with friction, as for Skin's he don't care how it makes you feel, or how you feel about it. As for Skin's, you don't say peep and take it. For Skin's is a raw fucker! And he don't give two fucks!!

And so...

It's now the early afternoon, so caffe correttos get sipped in small white porcelain cups, at two small white round metal tables, as polyester knees avoid one another under same, repulsed at the very thought, of same, and so, repel one another like the North and South Poles. As the crew sit and sip, on white metal chairs, on the sidewalk, out front, in front, of La Alla Banca, North Juarez's I.A. Club. (And no, you are not welcomed!).

For Skin's, light envelopes aren't the only thing he has to lay down for the crew, for Skin's has been rubbed the wrong way. And so, as for Skin's, he's now been irritated. And so, as for Skin's, he's gonna have to spread some irritations of his own. For nobody likes for Skin's to be rubbed the wrong way, for Skin's to be irritated, (and, subsequently!), for Skin's to be rubbed raw.

Skin's, *(as he is so affectionately called by his crew, and "friends of theirs"),* is the boss of the "5th Avenue Boys", (though, no longer boys). For, the crew, has been around for a long time. (They have just about seen it all!). *From the days of North Juarez being how they wanted it to be, how they maintained it to be,* how, to them, *it SHOULD STILL BE, how they, guarded it against, how, before, all of - "those kind of people" - rolled into the city, like Dodge vans.* (And, as such, *being named* and known as, North Juarez!).(OY!). *Back when, the city, was still the crime capital of the world. Back when, keeping an Irish flag from moving next door and, being flown in front of THEIR stoop, (RIGHT NEXT TO "OUR" STOOPS!!!), was, just about, the only conflict, there was to have, for guys like "US". (Of course, EXCEPT for someone's little sister BEING - "Waddaya'-stupid!?!" - ENOUGH - to, bring home one of the "darkies"!)(OY VEY!!!).*

Yup. The 5th Avenue Boys have seen it all. (From before Legs, was known as Legs). *From Legs, being the crew's enforcer, to Skin's personal driver and bodyguard, (to Skin's, ordering the first of two failed car bomb hits on ol' Legs!).* Yup. The 5th Avenue Boys have seen a thing or two. *Like: How the hell did that blackass Pockets, set up shop in OUR city anyways??? (AND LIVE to get away with it!?!). How did we not see that coming???* And, how the hell come none of you's, can locate Legs? And Pockets, better NEVER show his blackass in THIS city again! (For Skin's, has been rubbed the wrong way this morning, for Skin's would love to *pull back time and expose Legs to be, the dickhead-rat, he always suspected he to be).* For Skin's is irritated. And NOBODY likes for Skin's to become irritated!!

Skin's, as he goes by, is actually NOT skinny. *Like all great mob names, it's just something in particular about him, that, the rest of the crew,* (and, you best be, a "friend" of his, AND THEIRS TOO, if you wanna break-his-balls, about it!), *choose, just so, they, can break-his-balls, about it!* Skin, or Skin's, (as, everyone calls him), goes about 5' 8", 5' 9" or so, salt and pepper hair, of more gray these days than black, *which when his crew or wife puts him through it, over his forehead, hangs down like bangs, no longer combed slicked back,* a bit of a belly, more girth of waist, (these later days), and, he'd rather have it, so, he doesn't spend wastefully on his clothes, gettin' up in age, a man's-man-dirty-work-man, *many a day, spent at construction sites and on the docks, or from laying-low, for many an hour, casing joints to loot,* didn't give him his dark olive complexion, *for that came from the boot.*

"...and, YOU'S call yourselves, "soldiers"! AND, YOU THERE,... YOU'S got a Roman soldier tattooed, on your right forearm. For what?!? IF YOU'S A SOLDIER?? THEN, SOLDIER, DAMMIT!!! Shoulda' got some *"chink-writings"* on you's arm instead, like, what's off'a tha' menu, where you's fuckin' goomah works. ...Fuggetaboutit!", Skin's, tells his crew, (and, one member of his crew, in particular!), causing Skin's, to place his tiny white porcelian cup, back down on the table, before he can even take a sip, (as, the crew, found the ball-breaking to be funny!),(as the crew, broke out into laughter!), causing Skin's, to swipe-away the salt from out of his bangs, (AND, his "saltiness"!), as he, swipes back,..."YOU'S *think THAT'S funny,* DO you's??"

"Sorry, Skin's.", the soldier of ink, contends.

"Skin's, MY ass!! "Sorry", IS WHAT you's wife's GONNA' be, *IF I hear ONE MORE TIME* from Philadelphia that, we gave up on, locating Legs. *'Cause, YOU'S lost your touch, when it comes to, makin' car bombs!* I know that fuckin'-junkie, degenerate, herion-addict-asshole, dickhead, rat-fuck-Legs, is STILL in MY, fuckin' city! Its'a - spit-in-MY-face - to, haveta' hear HIS name mentioned,...*after all, this time.",* Skin's, lays it down!

"I hear you, Skin's. And, you're right. But, that's NOT right, talkin' 'bout my wife, that way. That's my WIFE, Skin's. ...The mother, of my two kids, Skin's. The mother, of my SON.", the inked-soilder, rebukes.

"Right? I don't need *you's to tell me,* what's CORRETTO!! I'M the ONE, that tells YOU'S what's right and, what is not. AND, THAT GOES FOR ALL, OF YOU'S!!! You's think, Legs, is the only one, that can get clipped?", asks, Skin's, then lifts his cannoli off his small white porcelain plate, a big bite he then takes, then once back in place, (cannoli back down on porcelain plate), with mouth full, with bangs full, Skin's, he then, states, "You's think, Skin's, is the only one, that's gotta eat?? Now, GO FIND ME that gimpy-mudda'fucca'! And I don't care, HOW it gets done. JUST, GET IT DONE!!!", then, takes a little sip of his caffe corretto, then continues, (after little thought!), "AND 'DAT fuckin'-moolie, too!! ...Pockets,...HE'LL *come for that, "macchiato."*

After another big bite of his cannoli, yet, before he can wash it down, (with another much needed and desired sip!), Skin's, looks up to see his tables still to be full, (full of his crew still seated there), then, fully goes off again, (with mouth FULL of cannoli!!), "WHAT THE FUCK ARE YOU'S DOIN', STILL SITTIN' HERE??? GET TA' WORK!!!!!!"

Polyester knees slam together like magnets, as mobsters in dated suits scramble up from the tables, as porcelain cups and porcelain plates tremble, as leather shoes and metal feet scuff and scrape the sidewalk, as muscle remains, holding up La Alla Banca, as the boss remains seated. And takes a sip. Of the sounds of morning.

Chapter Ten

CROSSED LEGS

After, *a first night, of this: "roadlife".* After, *a night, of too much coffee...*

After, *a night, of too many bathroom breaks, at too many service plazas, and, oh hey, what the hell, y'all hungry, (don't matter!), there's a Huddle House just off this next exit, so we gon' stop, (again!), 'cause Waffle House, ain't got NOTHIN' on Huddle House, and the boss(Managing Partner of THIS HERE shit!), wants to eat Huddle House, so, guess what y'all, we makin' another stop, at this exit just up ahead. And I suggest that y'all, bust a fat grub. 'Cause, when the boss is payin', (with this Jettison Records' travel per diem, of course!), it don't make NO kind of sense, for y'all NOT to eat sumthin'! 'Cause, you NEVER know if this is the last time you'll be gettin' off THIS here RV! And, hey, let me make this VERY clear. If y'all gotta take a shit? Take a shit! 'Cause, there AIN'T NO blowin' up MY DAMN RV!!! Or the one that blew it up, gon' be walkin'! Soooooo, err'body off tha' bus, stretch yo' legs. Take a shit! Smoke whatever it is y'all be, smokin' on. And, let's GET at this Huddle House, y'all!*

And so, (after *a night of, THAT!!!)...*

A night of, Pockets driving like an old man, a night of, driving a big ol' RV that he's never driven before, a night of, "Oh shit! I forgot! I'ma jump

159

off this highway up ahead and, buy me a big ol' bag of Twizzlers, a big box of Mike N' Ikes, some beef jerky, a gallon of distilled water AND, another extra large black coffee for the road. 'Cause, that's how I BE travelin'! And I NEEDS all that! (WHEN I BE travelin'!). (And besides, Jettison Records is payin' for ALL MY SHIT!!!). So? I'ma get me a big ol' bag of that expensive-ass, gas station beef jerky, too!"

And so...

A night of, blaming every driver for driving like a bonehead, (even though, he was the one AT fault!). After, a night of, his night vision makin' it hard for him to see, the lines and signs, this - stop-n'-go - road trip from hell - has adjourned into,...the sounds of morning.

(And, as such, so too, now continues)...

As to, what it now has become. A road trip from hell, in the early stanza hours,...of early afternoon:

C. Trife, all showered and cleaned up, AND rested up, *did so, as Pockets desired. And did so, take a hot shower and, wash all that blood from off his face, (as to not freak, Y.S. out!). And did so, proceed with Pockets, straight from Pockets' all red everythang office, down to the - let-a-guard-point-another-gun-at-me - parking lot, (of Jettison Records!). To, C. Trife, proceeding immediately thereto, (to inside of Pockets' RV). And then, as Pockets went back inside the double-sided double-mirrored-building, (to speak AT Phillip Tate!), one last time, (just Pockets' way, of making way, for another opportunity, just for Pockets, to hear himself talk!). As he, gave Phillip Tate more directives. As he, retrieved HIS artists from the studio lobby. As they, needed to be talked to! (And, as Pockets did),...C. Trife, did so, proceed, past the chairs and, past the sofas that transform into beds, (through the kitchen area) and, did so, as, he proceeded to, the back of the RV.* Back where, Pockets' sleeping quarters has its own door, its own bed, its own closet, its own bathroom, its own shower, its own television AND, its own mobile studio. *(FULLY paid for and installed BY AND AT, the expense of SOMEBODY'S studio time!), (SOMEBODY'S CD, that NEVER GOT PRESSED!!),(at the expense, of SOMEBODY'S project, that NEVER GOT COMPLETED!!!).(And, at the EXPENSE, of SOMEBODY'S precious*

TIME!!!!). (AND, LEST WE FORGET, *AFTER ALL THAT, BIG-MUSIC-BIZ-TALK!!!!!),*...JUST, for Pockets, to be able to "make magic happen", on-tha'-go! Fuck your feelings.

After taking that hot shower, C. Trife hit the hay. And after a sound night's sleep, a night of sleeping off and away the effects of (THAT hash!), a night of sleeping so sound that he was oblivious to all of the frequent stops, at all the service plazas, that he was unaware that he was even at, Mr. Trife awakens, feeling like a new man. (And,...then *it* hits him!!!). *That FEELING,* of waking up in a place, where, you've slept, *FOR...the...VERY...FIRST... TIME!!! That feeling of,* ok, I think I'm in a safe place,...*but,...WHERE the fuck am I??? That* - crashed in someone's back guest room *after a night of heavy drinking - feeling.* And with *that feeling, (that* - just opening your eyes and *not seeing anything that looks like your own - feeling!). That* - waking up and *not seeing anything that looks familiar - feeling. That EXTRA tired feeling. That feeling you get* when you first wake up, and you're so damn tired, yet slept so sound, that upon *opening your eyes, and blinking, for the very first time, you can feel them sting.* (Yeah, *THAT feeling!). That feeling of, when you're not sure of,* that if by blinking, *you're actually causing your eyelids to sting, by bringing them together,* when you blink, *or if it's actually your eyeballs, that are what's stinging,* AND *BY* blinking, all that you're really doing is, *actually causing your own eyeballs, to sting even more.* Like, you ain't doin' yourself no kinda favors! (Damned if you do and damned if you don't type shit!!). 'Cause, upon waking this way, you find yourself in a true no-win situation. So, fuck it. Might as well stay the fuck in THIS bed, AND WITH my eyes closed! 'Cause, I could sleep another 5-6 hours easy! And, hey, with my eyes closed, *at least my eyes NOR my lids, will be stinging like this,* REGARDLESS of why they're stinging, *REGARDLESS of which ones are actually doing the stinging!* ...FUCK!!! This ain't MY bed! *And, where the fuck am I again??* (YEAH. *THAT fucked-up, feeling!!!). That feeling, of...*damn, I musta' really been out! *'Cause, I haven't felt my eyes sting like this, since the LAST time I was so tired, and, slept SO SOUND, like THIS. That* - waking up your freshmen year of college *in your dorm room for the first time, BEFORE you can fig'a-it-all-out - feeling! That feeling, of that moment, that you feel,* when it takes you a few-sleepy-seconds, *to get it all worked*

*out in your mind, (and the disorientation that comes along with it, feeling).
THAT FEELING!* And, *THAT DISORIENTATION!!* WHICH, *kicks-in,*
THIS recently awakened Tier Three's "natural" progression, *OF a recently
awakened Tier Three's disorientation!!!*

And *that* could be detrimental to all!

(Am I movin'? *Nigga, was that turbulence??? Or, was that a pothole, I
just felt?? And, WHO'S fuckin'-voices ARE THOSE I hear, on the otherside of
this, motherfuckin'-bedroom door???* I DON'T KNOW THEM!!! *I DON'T
KNOW YOU!!!!!!* And now,...*I DON'T feel SAFE!!!!!!* 'Cause, *I don't be
sleepin' where, I don't be trustin' motherfuckers! I don't be closin' my eyes
'round motherfuckers, I DON'T KNOW!!!!!!* Alright, fuck ALL THIS shit!!
I'm gettin' up, gettin' dressed AND, I'MA see what's REALLY GOOD
with these voices, I'm hearin', on the otherside, of this MOTHERFUCKIN'
door!!!!!!)

And *with those thoughts, on that note,* C. Trife, gets up outta *somebody's
bed...*

And, *makes his way over to somebody's closet,* and *opens up somebody's
closet door,...*and likes what he sees. "Oh yeah, that's right! *What was that
motherfucker's name, again? Phil??? Phil?? Phil? Phillip,...*or some shit. Ok,
I'm cool. *Whew!* THAT'S good! *Glad we got THAT,* worked THE FUCK
OUT!!! Ok. Chill, brotha. Breathe. Just, chill.", C. Trife, says to himself,
breathin' n' chillin' n' gettin' it worked out. (Unzipping the black garment
bag hanging in the closet, Mr. Trife is pleased to see several black suits),
"And, I'll be damned, looks like the sleeve lengths and inseams, might
fit just right! Ok, Phil!! I see you!! Think I'll put on the black Perry Ellis
suit!"

Looking down on the floor of the closet, (first once hidden by the
hanging garment bag), C. Trife, discovers a suitcase. Which he partially
unzips and, takes a peak inside. (Big number on a small price tag!). *"Who
tha fuck is, Jimmy Choo??? THAT'S pimpin', tho! I see you, Phil!!",* C. Trife,
thinks to himself, thinkin' to himself, "Yeah, I'm likin' this music industry
shit, ALREADY! THAT Pockets, is ALRIGHT! Damn,...A MAN OF HIS
WORD!!! He SAID, he was gonna lookout for me...and, he has. He SAID,
he was gonna make my life better...AND, HE HAS ALREADY!!! A lot of*

people say, a lot of shit, but, what he's been speakin' on, wit me, I gotta say, I gotta give it to him, he's comin' through, wit tha' shit! I gotta, give it to him. Everything, he said, was gonna happen, IS happenin'! Last night, I had Atlanta PD, lookin' for me. Had guns, pulled on me. AND, laid up in some tiny apartment, HIGH AS FUCK(off THAT hash!), face all bloody n' shit, wearin' ripped n' torn clothes n' shit,...AND WANTED by, the law! AND, THAT MOTHERFUCKER came, got me!! Yeeeeeaaaaaahhhhhh, FUCK-THAT, LIFE!!! AND, NOW, I'm on a road trip! A...a...a business trip. MY TRIP!!! CHECK ME, THA'-FUCK OUT!!! Goin' on tha' road, TO MY OWN SHOW!!! ...Shit! I better come up with some, fire-ass shit! I know I got it in me, to write some, fire-ass shit,...some shit, ain't NOBODY EVER-CAME-UP-WIT before!! It'll hit, me. I ain't worried, 'bout it. I ain't sweatin' shit, I know, I got, a hit song, in me. AT LEAST, ONE!!! The best shit, just comes to me. Once I get that first line, BAM!!! IT'S, ON!!! I'M OFF-N'-RUNNIN', WIT IT!!! Just like, back when me and,...what'sa-name...were, spittin' freestyles. Ok, I GOT THIS!!! Wait. Shit. That's, right. So,...I'ma clone? FUCK IT!!! I'd rather be a RICH-CLONE, than be BROKE, like back when I, was HUMAN!!!"

Then...

Looking down on his pile of clothes, *(from where he dumped them on the floor last night),* C. Trife looks at, his bloodied shirt, the one with holes in it, *(from last night's fight!).* Then, takes another peek, at his sharp, black patent leather, (stylishly-trimmed with tiny gold stars!) Jimmy Choo shoes. And, C. Trife, *thinks to himself, "I'M ON TOP OF THE WORLD!!!!!!! AND,...ain't even haveta' pay my dues! Yeah, FUCK tha' bullshit,...I'M ridin' out, WIT Pockets!!"*

(Then he removes the suitcase from the closet, and tosses it on the bed. Then gathers up his bloodied clothes, to cram into the back of the closet, but becomes intrigued by something he's just read)...

Stacked behind the suitcase, on the closet floor, C. Trife, finds Pockets' reading materials! *"Hmm, ok, let me find out. What tha' fuck he needed THESE, so bad for!",* C. Trife, *says to himself, (in his intrigued - Tier-Three-Mind!!!).*

BUT...

A knock on the bedroom door, got C. Trife quickly placing the books in his suitcase! *From outside the door, from Y.S., "Mr. Trife, you good?"* ..."Yeah, I'm good. I'm gettin' dressed. I'll be out after I brush my teeth and, wash my face!", then he places the bloodied clothes in the closet, (this closet ain't short on surprises!). Leaning in a back corner,... *"Thirty. Ott. Six.",* Mr. Trife, *says to himself,* as he marvels at it, (of the rifle being held in his hands!).

Lights. Camera. Action.

Mr. Trife steps out of the private sleeping quarters, after some time, CLEAN AS FUCK. (Hey, GOTTA' look the part!). First impressions begin, from the VERY start! (And Mr. Trife is ALL about it!!). His thick long dreads, hang down the back of his black Perry Ellis suit, fittin' him just right. *And he don't know it,* (or he might!), but, he's wearin' shit that he's only seen on TV, and in the movies, and dressed better than he's ever been dressed in his entire life! Pockets at the helm, gettin' closer to the ranch, MC Busta-Nut and False Profit, breakin' weed up in the kitchen, (just a couple of skinny niggas in skinny pants!). Y.S. with her headphones on, *stays in her own mind, singin' her OWN songs!* And MC Busta-Nut and False Profit, best not even try it, 'cause with that look Y.S. keeps on her face, them two skinny niggas don't stand a chance! Y.S. looks up at Mr. Trife, as he makes his way up to the front, MC Busta-Nut saw that shit, hatin' and shit, as he's rollin' up his blunt. $ix hundred dollar yellow hoodie, custom red-laced Doc Martin boots, just given to her, which isn't rare, and she's only 16, Y.S., young singer...and she can kill you with that stare! *And ALL she's ever wanted, is to be the biggest singer in the world,* and she's got NO problem, lettin' YOU know, that she's a star, as she lets her fingers flow through her long curly light brown mermaid-like hair! *And there ain't no need for you to even think, 'bout talkin' to her, 'bout a part time job, or even school.* (In one ear and out the other?). (Shiiiiiit, it won't EVEN get in the FIRST ear! YOU FOOL!!!). So just save it. ('Cause trust me)...*(SHE WON'T CARE!!!)*. So, once at the front, Pockets offers Mr. Trife, the big cabin seat of the co-pilot. Mr. Trife, lookin' fly, takes his seat, and from behind, MC Busta-Nut, (your TYPICAL music indusrty PROFESSIONAL hater-type),(the - EVERYONE else is GARBAGE - type), for, Mr. Trife, can just feel it, that MC Busta-Nut DON'T LIKE IT!!!

"Weeeeeell, HELLO THERE, sleepy-head!! So nice, of you to join us.", Pockets, says with a light chuckle, then continues, taking his eyes off the road, (for a split-second), "OH-KAY!!! OH-KAY!!! I see YOU, Mr. Trife! You clean-up, alright, playa'!"

"Yeeeaaahhh, weeeeeell. What, can I tell ya'? *THAT HASH...*was A mutha' fucka'!!", Mr. Trife, replies, *(intubation voice amazin'!),* then continues, (with a light chuckle of his own), "And, YES!! I DO!!!".

(As, MC Busta-Nut, just hates)

Pockets, then points to the Smoky Mountains, ahead in the distance, through that huge RV windshield, at those beautiful mountains of Tennessee, and, says, "You see that pinnacle? That's where I'm headed, you feel me?"

"Yeah, I feel ya', my brother. That's where I'm headed, too. Do YOU, FEEL me?", Mr. Trife, answers.

"Yes, I do, my brother. Yes, I do. And I'M tha' one, that's gonna get you there!", Pockets, replies, ALWAYS one for the "upsells" of "salesmanship", of the - what-he-can-do-for-you - the - steady-and-constant continuance, of it all, OF: WHY YOU NEED HIM!, (and he's QUICK, wit tha' shit),...(at all times!).

(And, MC Busta-Nut, just hates!)

Then, there goes MC Busta-Nut, firing up his blunt. The distinct aroma of dank, wafts up to the front! And, gettin' that smell of potent, *brings Mr. Trife back to that - "Yeeeeeaaaaaahhhhhh, FUCK THAT LIFE!!!" - moment! (That, he just had, in the back!). Of, NOT gonna be wearin' no more rags! Of, NOT being ALL fucked-up and, of no more ripped-up clothes. And, it brings him right back,* as that dank hits, and, then,... travels up his nose!

And so...

(As Mr. Trife turns 'round, of which, he HAS absolutely NO doubts!), as he, tells MC Busta-Nut, to, "Put THAT shit, THE FUCK out!!!"

And...

Pockets, just looks over to his right, at Mr. Trife, (nigga-are-you-crazy!?), that's what that look LOOKED like!

THEN...

Pockets, hits him with some levity. (Slapping Mr. Trife's left arm playfully!).

Mr. Trife, *checking out* his suit's arm, of his brand new *of any harm,* of wearin' this shit for the very first time, with that - *don't-be-gettin'-no-beef-jerky-pencil-shavings - on my, fly-ass, - I'm-just-wearin'-this-Perry-Ellis-suit-of-mine - for-the-very-first-time - ...*(is WHAT *that look* looked like!). And then, Pockets, explains, "Listen, my brother. I know you're new to the music industry. So, I'm just gonna go-'head and, break-it-down fo' ya'! You know,...MAKE YOU AWARE of THE inevitable! The music game, AND the drug game, ARE one in the same! WHERE you find music, YOU FIND drugs! YOU FEEL ME?!? SO, get used to drugs BEING AROUND. 'CAUSE, if you can't? YOU WON'T be around! And, it won't be me, firing you. I'M the one, that's trying to help YOU! It'll just be YOU, NOT seeing, the big picture OF THIS industry. Drugs...drugs will be EVERYWHERE, my brother. JUST get used to it. You feel me?". (And then, slapping Mr. Trife's - brand-new - just-wearin'-these-fines-for-the-VERY-first-time - purposely-gettin' - fine-expensive-ass-gas-station-beef-jerky-shavings - on the sleeve of his suit), - Pockets, continues, "Listen, my brother. It's the inevitable. YOU WILL run into it! Let me tell you a lil' funny story, to help put this music-biz-drug-shit into perspective, for you. Yeah, so, well, now, anywaaaaaays, YOU should know by NOW,...I got you WIT THIS music industry shit! Now, pay attention. MY time, AIN'T cheap!! *Back in the day, right before I first cut-my-teeth in this industry,* green-as-fuck like you, *this cat approached me in a strip club one night, struck up a convo wit me. You know, just politickin'. We was just shootin' tha' breeze and shit.* Dude was cool "enough", ya' know.

Kinda' shot-tha'-fuck-out. But, dude was real chill...real chill. But, you know how it go, I don't KNOW this white man, you feel me? *AND, we ALL UP in this club and shit,* you feel me? So, I wasn't feelin' that shit at first, see what I'm sayin'? *So, we gettin' our drink on and shit. Checkin' out the strippers and shit. Listenin' to tha music and shit. He could tell, I knew my music! We was feelin' some of tha' same shit bein' played in tha' club. And, after a couple mo' drinks, dude starts goin' on and on 'bout, how he was some "Master drummer", or some shit. Dude WOULDN'T shut tha' fuck up 'bout some,..."Moeller Method",...some...drumming-technique,...of some kind. He...he...JUST WOULDN'T SHUT THA' FUCK UP, 'BOUT IT!!! Playin' the drums ON the bar with his two fingers, DEMONSTRATIN', this, fuckin' Moeller-Method-shit TO me, leanin' over talkin' to me, WHILE he's explainin' this shit to me, just to make sure, that I COULD make sure, that I could hear him soundin' LIKE an expert ov'a tha' loud-ass music playin' tha' club!* But, the mafucka' keeps sprayin' me wit spit, WHILE he's doin' it! Fuckin' guy GOT annoyin', right? So, he could tell I'm startin' to not feel his ass no mo', right? SPRAYIN' me wit spit and shit, right! GOOD THING my brother wasn't wit me, that night! Baby bro wouldn't be feelin' that shit, AT all! BUT, this is WHAT makes tha mafucka' SO DAMN chill! *He says to me, "Heeeeeey, maaaaaan, you smoke reefer?". "Shiiiiiit, DO I!?!", I says, to tha' mafucka'. So, we down our drinks real-quick-like 'n shit and, head-out to his car in tha' mafuckin' parkin' lot. And, I'm sittin' in this hippy's car and shit. And, he turns on some ol' Motown-shit and, pulls out a pack of Zig-Zags. So, he's rollin' tha' shit up, and we politickin' and shit and, groovin' off a some old Smokey Robinson and shit.* Like I said, this white dude was a real chill dude! I could fuck wit 'em! *So, he twists tha' shit up nice and tight and, lights tha' joint, takes a few drags, then, passes tha' mafuckin'-shit to me.* BACK in THEM days, Mr. Trife, I was all 'bout some reefer! *So, I takes me a couple drags, off that bitch and, pass it on back to him, right?* BUT, THIS TIME, Mr. Trife, tha' mafucka' don't take no couple drags, off tha' mafucka'. *THIS MAFUCKA', hits that shit just one time and, THEN starts to get this weird-puzzled-look come over his face, as he's holdin' tha' joint out in front of him, starin'-hard at tha' shit! So, tha' mafucka' goes to take another hit,...but stops! And, then, all serious and shit, tha' mafucka' turns to me and, NOW tha' mafucka' begins starin' at me!* NOW, this is some strong-ass reefer, for BACK in them days! So, I'M ALREADY high-as-shit, off a just takin' them, lil' couple of drags! *SO, I don't know IF IT'S tha' reefer, OR if it's just me, but, I DON'T KNOW what this mafucka' is starin', AT ME fo'!!* And, you know WHAT this mafucka' *says* to me, Mr. Trife?"

"Nah. What he *say*?", Mr. Trife, inquires.

Pockets, cracking himself up, beginning to laugh out loud, says, "THIS mafucka' says to me, *I KNEW you was gay! I could taste it on the joint, AFTER you passed it back to me!!!*'"

"How observant.", a deadpan, Mr. Trife, replies.

And Pockets, with his eyes back on the road, staring down the highway, *(staring back in time)*, just shakes his head, smiling, and laughing to himself, *as he reminisces, and talking to himself, as he thinks back, "Man, THAT SHIT used to fuck-me-up, EVERY TIME!!! ...every time...",* And then, Pockets, eats some more beef jerky, (slaps Mr. Trife back on his arm again!), looks over at Mr. Trife, and explains, "Mr. Trife, you're really gonna hafta' lighten-tha'-fuck-up, IF you're gonna be in THIS industry. You're missin' tha' WHOLE point, son! *Me and this hippy-biker-drummer-mafucka',...became good friends. 'CAUSE he, WAS loose!! He was always playin' some kinda' practical joke, sayin' some, crazy - off-tha'-wall - shit.* He was good people! And, he was chill-as-fuck. *We'd get together most nights. Get HIGH-AS-FUCK all night! Talk music all night. Listen to music all night.* YEAH, we WAS high-as-fuck, BUT, WE WAS SERIOUS-as-fuck, 'BOUT this music-shit, too! *All but, once,...maybe,...he'd come over to my crib. And, we'd ALWAYS end up wit tha munchies, like'a mafucka'! And, just like clockwork, we'd jump in his ride and, he'd drive like a lunatic down tha' street a few blocks and, we'd tear-tha'-fuck-up-outta' some pizza and wings!* You know, wash 'em down wit'a couple of cold brews. ...MAN, *THOSE WERE THA' DAYS!*" (Then, eatin' some more beef jerky and, slapping Mr. Trife AGAIN on his arm!!), Pockets, busts-up laughing, *as he recalls, "WE COULDN'T EVEN dip-off into tha' men's room and, do a couple of lines! I'm talkin' 'bout, NOT EVEN, a bump! IF YOU WAS doin' blow, wit THIS mafucka', YOU HAD TO do it wit him, BEFORE he got tha' munchies! 'CAUSE, THIS MAFUCKA', would just let all that grease from tha pizza get all over his hands and, LET THAT SHIT run-tha'-fuck all the way down his arm! HE AIN'T GIVE A, FUCK! I'M TELLIN' YA',*

MR. TRIFE, THIS MAFUCKA' AIN'T GIVE - NOT-ONE-DAMN - FUCK!!! *He ain't NEVER wipe that shit off, either!* I mean, it was his coke and all. And, yeah, if you're offerin',...I'M DOIN'! *BACK IN THEM DAYS, I'M DOIN' UP ALL YO' SHIT!!!* But, it's kinda hard to do some lines, *when tha' shit, looks more orange than white,* you feel me? BUT, *with all the drugs and, liquor and, women,* guess what, Mr. Trife?? *ME AND HIM could STILL take care of AND, handle OUR business.* MUSIC BUSINESS!!! *HE taught me, 'BOUT THIS, music shit! Taught me, 'bout, all the - "behind-the-scenes" - shit, THAT goes on IN, THIS business.* You know, *pointed me in the right direction, with, some contacts of his, in the biz. He was gonna be my contract guy,...we was gonna start a label together,...* but,...THAT SHIT didn't work out. One day, he was here. And then, the next,...*he was gone.* Fuckin' musicians, man! NOTHIN' BUT head cases!! SO, I got back to doin' what I was doin', got back on my grind, *grindin' and, buildin' up my empire in Hard Times. This hippy dude was always talkin' music or drugs. He'd be always tryna' to get a lot of shit from new drug connects and shit.* Dude used to *tell* me all tha' time, *"If you're gonna' get in this "Drug Game", then, "GO BIG!!!", or, DON'T get in it AT ALL!!"* He damn-near *pointed me down THAT road!* So? *THAT'S what I did,* Mr. Trife! *I got in "Tha' Game", by settin' up a meeting wit one of his connects, shortly after dude just-straight-jetted on me.* And,...*I went BIG!!!* But, *that hippy fucked-up.* I caught him slippin', Mr. Trife! *One time,...he told me his connect's name, when he was all fucked-up on blow!* BUT, if you've noticed Mr. Trife, I AIN'T drop NO *names* this ENTIRE conversation! And, THAT'S WHY I ain't NEVER get busted! ...Shit, maybe *I wouldn't have even gone that route, IF dude stuck around and, we got into this music shit together.* BUT, he was tha' one that, *hipped-me to this shit,* Mr. Trife, that, the "Music Game" and the "Drug Game", is one in the same. *Where you find music, YOU WILL find drugs,* Mr. Trife. You feel me?"

And, on that note...

(Pockets is done with the conversation. Pulls an Earth, Wind & Fire CD from out of his CD book and, upon giving "his brother" a look, Mr. Trife, makes his way out of the co-pilot's seat, to make his way to the back, to sit amongst, and to get to know, his brand new label mates, as the first track Pockets blasts)...

"What's your name, brother? I'm, False Profit...'*CAUSE, YA' CAN'T STOP IT!!! I'm burnin' rubber, straight-out tha' cockpit, I'm out ta' get, ALL that I can git, makin' money tha' fast way, that's a SURE bet!*", (False Profit, spits his "*customary-introduction*"), then, follows it up with his *standard follow-up of,* "*Yeah, yeah, I know, I know. You WAS feelin' that!*", as False Profit, introduces himself to Mr. Trife, as Triflin' takes a seat.

"I'm, Mr. Trife.", he informs, (as the two shake hands).

"That's my boy, MC Busta-Nut and that's Y.S. ...She bad!", as informal introductions by False Profit are made, with neither of the two, extending a hand, Y.S., because she's damaged. *(And, still listening to herself sing in her headphones!).* MC Busta-Nut, because he's an arrogant conceited-fuck. *(And not hardly the big star he believes himself to be).*

"You smoke?", False Profit, asks, taking a hit off the blunt, (then, holding it fire-side to palm), prompting, both Y.S. and MC Busta-Nut, to look at Mr. Trife, (on his answer they wait upon).

"You DAMN, right! Gimme 'dat.", Mr. Trife, replies, then, takes the blunt from False Profit, takes a pop, *(gettin' that fire back in his eyes!).*

"You know somethin', Mr. Trife? Pockets *said, our underground-mixtape,* "*The Spermicidal Tendencies*"*, was straight-garbage...but,* I NEVER doubted that, we'd make it. Can't nobody spit LIKE my boy, Busta-Nut. AND, ain't nary a mafucka' out-here touchin', MY beats! You, needa' beat? I got you, ON beats! My nigga, I got beats on TOP of beats! I got BEATS for DAYS.", as False Profit, tries to do his part, to welcome Mr. Trife into the fold...(or is it into the fray?).

"Tha' fuck?? Nigga. *We sold 400,000 on that mixtape!* Don't be talkin' bad on MY mixtape, Profit.", MC Busta-Nut, snaps!

"*Maybe it WAS straight-garbage. Maybe it was.* MAYBE,...your listeners don't know good music. I don't know. Maybe not, but maybe.", Mr. Trife's attempt, to enlighten MC Busta-Nut, (looking right at him), while making a no-look pass of the blunt, to his left, to Y.S.

"Tha' fuck, you talkin' 'bout? *We was independant. AND got on tha' radio! After we was on the DJ Wood show, our shit blew-up and, sold 400,000 on a mixtape, nigga.* What tha' fuck, you ever sell?? What kinda' numbers, YOU workin' wit!? Yeah! THOUGHT, SO!!!", MC Busta-Nut, tells Mr. Trife, then, tries to take the blunt from Y.S., but, *with that look of her's,* he knows! *(She ain't done with it yet!).*

"Young boy, slow your roll. You don't know me. ALL I KNOW IS, Pockets, is playin' Earth, Wind & Fire, RIGHT NOW and, I don't hear YOUR shit. And, that's why, I said that. So, stop and think, before you open your mouth, young boy. 'Cause, MAYBE your shit, *WAS shit!* And, as for me? It ain't gonna be 'bout numbers, for me. Quality over quantity, ya dig?", Mr. Trife, replies. "Say what??", questions, False Profit.

"Quality. I don't give a fuck if my song sells five records or five million. DON'T get it twisted, I ain't gonna turn tha' money down! ...We all got somethin' to say. Every one in the world, got somethin' to say. Though, most just keep it in. I ain't built that way. I got somethin' to say and, you can best believe, I'MA say it! ...I just wanna get my word out. ...Whateva' tha' fuck it is? ...Put it in a song, ya' dig. And make it some fire-ass-shit! But I can tell you one thing, the energy I put into the song, it could sell five million copies. And the song WILL be good, 'CAUSE I'LL make it good! So, the song will be good enough to sell five million copies, ya' dig. But honestly, I don't give a fuck about the five mil. If five people buy it, and I've reached five people, then, THAT'S my five mil right there. But trust and believe, young boy, it'll be good enough to sell five mil. So, one way or the other, I'll still be on top of the world.", Mr. Trife, breaks it down.

"Yeah...yeah, I feel you on that.", agrees, False Profit.

"What!? Nigga, you crazy. Both y'all crazy. Shit, my nigga, I'm tryna' get paid. Get money!", explains, MC Busta-Nut.

"So what are you, a producer, a rapper? Singer? What?", False Profit, asks.

"Nigga, ain't nobody tyrna listen to no fifty-year-old rapper!", MC Busta-Nut, letting Mr. Trife know, (while letting that dank out his lungs).

(Holding up his black and white composition book), Mr. Trife, says, "I'm a writer, a poet, and can hold my own in a cypher, young boy. Sure, I could rap it. But first, I gotta write it! Never thought I was much of a singer, but, you know what?? I bet I could sing it, too. Might make it a blues song, or I might just come wit some new-flava'-shit. Gotta bring somethin' new to the conversation, if ya' wanna make it in THIS biz.", Mr. Trife, explains.

"Yeah, I dig. That shit might be tight.", False Profit, signs on.

"Now there, YOU go!", MC Busta-Nut, comments, on False Profit's comment, then turns his comments on Mr. Trife, "THOUGHT I already, told you! AIN'T NOBODY tryna to listen to, NO fifty-year-old rapper!!"

"I ain't fifty.", Mr. Trife, says, (then, *thinks* to himself,..."Am I?"), then, continues, as he, speaks his mind, gonna use his mind to make it in this industry, instead of relying on VIOLENCE this time, (as he, continues with his reply), "...and, if you ain't got nothing positive to say to me, then, keep it TO yourself!"

"Mr. Trife, you sure got MAD-SHIT to learn, 'BOUT 'DIS industry!", MC Busta-Nut, says, (with the laugh of a dickhead)...(as Y.S., continues to play-it-off, *as if, HER songs in her headphones were still playing!*).

Once at the ranch...

MC Busta-Nut and False Profit pile off the RV, (like two kids from an inner city elementary school, on their first field trip to the country!). "Ain't you comin'?", Mr. Trife, asks Y.S., even offering, to carry her bags off the RV for her, prompting Y.S., to tell him, *she's got it,* bringing her bags *(and attitude along with her!)*(OY VEY!).

(Pockets, the gambling man, lucked out!)...

AS...

His sprawling horse ranch came with, the best view in Tennessee!

Though...

Pockets, couldn't get at those pensions, (from North Juarez City!).

SO...

(There are NO horses to see!)(Oy vey!).

White 3-Rail Horse Fencing surrounds the grounds, dead center is a huge man-made pond, but just watch that thick sticky-mud bottom, (bless your heart!), or your ass will be gone. From the ranch porch it's picturesque, from the white rocking chairs, the view of the Smoky

Mountain pinnacle is the best. (And the view changes!). Big blue way-up-high sky with big white fluffy clouds, it amazes. (And there ain't nothing like a Smoky Mountain sunset!), reds from the veil above cut-through tree-covered-mountains, (cut-like, the sky was bled). In the evening, when the sun is goin' down, white and yellow lights speckle the mountain ranges, from distant towns. Red lights of towers can be seen, and ain't nothin' to hear some "traveling" gunshots,...(if you know WHAT I mean!). And, if you look close, and know what to look for, (then, you'll know what you're looking at!). AS, *bright blue tiny lights, accent the mountains,* with that - illegal - *"my-daddy's-daddy-taught-my-daddy"* - and - (I'MA just leave it AT that!) - *and - "I'm just keepin' it in the family" - and - "YES our shit is boobytrapped!"* - ('Cause, THAT'S - "Our heritage" - shit, IS go down!).

And, after a day of fishing, (and, NOPE, nobody came up missing!)...

(Y.S., MC Busta-Nut and False Profit, catch some shut-eye in the ranch, Pockets leans on a porch post, as Mr. Trife, rocks on a rockin' chair, and they're both sippin', got Mr. Trife high again, and, NOW sippin'! *Got 'em again!* So, NOW *it's time to REALLY get in Mr. Trife's ear!* BUT,...it's gonna be risky! But, Y'ALL know Pockets! So, fuck it! Big brass balls gamblin' man! So NOW, here's his chance!)

Both gettin' lit, Pockets, decides to open up a bit...*about his past.*

"You know, Trife.", Pockets, begins, taking a big swig outta his rock glass, before continuing, "You see all of this? The horse ranch, the fly - fancy custom-made custom-tailored red suits - of mine, my successes, my status, my stature, *it didn't come easy,...it didn't come without a price.* I've lived *"that"* life. Then, *moved on from it,* went legit, and now - I wanna make sure YOU live a legit-life, too. But, *there's unfinished business.* YOU SEE there's *no-damn-horses* on THIS horse ranch, don't you?? THIS RANCH, *was 'SPOSED TO BE* yours...I mean, yeah, yours,...*motherfuckin' B. Trife's,* nigga! But,...*shit got fucked-up.* You,... no, *Brotha Trife, fucked-shit-up for me...*for you. AND, THAT'S *WHY there's unfinshed-business,* for me,...AND you.", (then, takes another sip, swirling his swill 'round and 'round amongst the rocks), then, gets back at it, (hustle-game NEVER stops!), "But, *back before all this, the horse ranches, The: Top-Of-The-World-Music-Industry-Offices, I was a street-nigga. Always been a nigga,* DON'T get it wrong, STILL a nigga, to this day. But,...*BACK THEN!? BACK when, I was JUST comin' up,* shiiiiiit, *I built an empire, Mr. Trife, straight-up street-nigga-style...*

(Come). (Let Pockets take you back in the day)...

...You see, *my baby brother used to drive 'round the city in an old white primered-up and rusted-out conversion van, ain't-have-no seats in it,... OTHER than the one he was drivin' 'round on. And, he'd go to ALL THA' spots,...out where, grown men would be standin' together, a couple together at a time, all leaned tha'-fuck-over,...MORE helpless than infants! They'd be slumped-up against a building. Or, laid-out on tha' sidewalks. And MY brother, DIDN'T give a FUCK,* my G! *My brother, would get 'em ALL, in THAT van! And it didn't take much, NOT the way MY brother handled business!!* And, them fiends? SHIIIIIIT, *them fiends would ALL pile-in! And, my brother, he'd break-it-down for 'em, as ONLY HE could! How'd they, ALL best lay-down-silent on the floor, all pile-in and on top of one another and, HOW'D NOBODY best-not even THINK 'BOUT poking they head up OR make a sound. And once that van was full,* shiiiiiit,...*it was ALWAYS full! We ripped-out every fuckin' seat in that van, 'cept fo', the driver's seat, TO make the most of EACH trip,* my G. *My brother would drive them all back to the block, back down this alley, and they'd all pile-out that van, and into an open door, where MY bodyguard was just standin' there all imposing n' shit, just waitin' on them. My brother drove them all to me. And if anyone talked, if anyone didn't move fast enough, my bodyguard would SLAP-THA'-FUCK outta the back of they heads. Right on that notch! And he's DARE THEM ALL to, "Say somethin', again!"* ...*And then, my brother would wait out in that van, and keep a lookout, as my bodyguard followed all them fiends up the steps, to where I was waiting on them. And at the top of the stairs, they'd all wait for my bodyguard to get up to the top of the steps, where he'd open the door and let them all file-in. And then, once all in, my bodyguard would file-in too. And close and lock the door.",* (and then, Pockets, swirls his Grand Marnier, and, stares out at the red tower lights gracing the summit of the Smoky Mountain pinnacle),... (*reminiscing, in his glory, of recollections, of his glory days!),*...takes a sip and then, continues, as he, looks down at Mr. Trife just sittin' there, slow rockin' in that rocking chair, back to looking up at Pockets, (taken away from*, the mountain range's tiny bright blue lights, that shine like the moon!),* with a rock glass of Grand Marnier of his own in hand, (in the darkness of the horse ranch porch), as Pockets, continues,..."*And I'd be sittin' there, occupying my time, while I waited on my brother to get back, reading a good book in the back of a room, on the third floor in the ghetto, sittin' there, at a round wooden table. And, I'd be there, just waitin' on 'em all, just sittin' there, just to tha' side of that table, with just my right arm restin' on tha' tabletop. And I'd be sittin' on an old wooden arm chair that was missin' an arm, and, wit a couple of them - "back-spoke-thingies" - missin'. But, I'd be sittin' there like a boss, with my legs crossed. And, all laid out on that table, I'd have a snifter. Wit a bottle of E&J next to my glass. With an old Army .45 handgun laid out on its side, next to that bitch. And next to that, I'd have the strongest bundles of hog, that my city had EVER seen! And after I served those sheep, my bodyguard would lead my flock away. And then, my brother would run 'em all back from whence they came. And drop 'em off. And leave 'em. Grown-ass men and shit. My brother would leave them right there on them sidewalks. Standin'. Leanin'. Doubled-tha'-fuck-over! ...The ones, that, COULDN'T make it over to a building, anyway!* You know, *to lay down on the sidewalks, to lean up on the buildings. So? SO, THAT THEY could just NOD-THA'-FUCK-OUT...and MAKE all their problems GO AWAY!! BUT, those ones, my brother would just leave, standin' there on tha' sidewalks, while, everyone else was just out tryin' to enjoy a beautiful day?* Shiiiiiit, you gotta realize, Mr. Trife, *you had grown-ass-men standin' there in the middle of tha' sidewalks, in tha' middle of tha' damn day. All bent tha' fuck over. Like they was tryin' to suck they own dick!* AND it was all because, *I HAD tha' strongest hog, that MY city had EVER SEEN!!! THAT SHIT, used to crack my brother tha' fuck up!!!* THAT nigga's just TOO-DAMN-COLD!!! *And then,...'bout an hour or so later, my brother would be back wit more. And I served them.*"

"Damn, Pockets. That's deep. You *lived that* shit, huh??", Mr. Trife, replies, as they then both share a laugh, finishing off the Grand Marnier in their glasses, before loading them back up, and the dank, and the booze, (though, Pockets, *tryna' keep* Mr. Trife's brain *scrambled on the drugs and on the liquor)...*(BUT, *it's got* this Tier Three's memory...*kickin' in a little quicker!).* As, Mr. Trife,...does *a lil' reminiscing of his own!*

(OH SHIT!!!)...(NOT *THIS TIER THREE* MOTHERFUCKER!!!)

Come! (Join Pockets on that dark horse ranch porch, in the foothills of Tennessee...as we take a listen!)...

As(WE)...

(Enter a Tier-Three-Mind, as it takes us back in time, where we'll arrive in the world, of a young Brotha Trife)...

"Ok, my brother, I GOT a story of my own for you.", Mr. Trife, starts out, takes a drink, as Pockets stares, *oh good Lord, (what tha' fucks gonna come out HIS mouth!),* before, Mr. Trife, gets back at it...

"I was a young kid, well, seemed like just a kid, *compared to how I was at the end of THAT day. Where was it? Where was it?? Where was it??? Ahh, fuck it, it'll come to me. But anyway, in my hometown, I had just stepped outside of my house and my Mom told me, to come back inside and put on a jacket, because it just started beginning to rain. It was kinda fucked-up, never seen anything like it in my life. On my side of the street it wasn't rainin', but, on the otherside of the street, it was. Yeah, yeah, that's right...and...and it was sunny out. Didn't make no kinda sense! So I turned 'round, and told my Mom, "Awe, Mom, I'll be alright, I don't need a jacket, I'll just stay on our side of the street. And after my Mom went back inside, all hell broke loose. The whole otherside of the street got shot the fuck up! Shit, EVERYTHING got shot the fuck up! Houses, mailboxes, squirrels, wasn't nothin' or nobody that wasn't a target on my block! Dogs and shit were runnin' 'round loose attacking people, draggin' people back to this man for him to shoot them. Yeah...yeah... it was fucked-up. And I saw those dogs...and I ran and hid. And my whole block got shot up by this man. I couldn't understand it, why the fuck would he do something like that??? And I heard the man whistle for his dogs...and I heard their paws jumping back into the back bed of that pickup truck...and I heard that pickup truck drive off. And I could hear the next block gettin'*

shot up. And I could hear the people screaming as those dogs attacked them and drug them down the street, back to that man…and that man just blasted them away. And I was so scared. And…and it wasn't until it sounded like that truck and those dogs were far, far, away, before I came out of my hiding place. And I just stood there…in the sun…on my side of the street. And I just started walking. I walked directly cross the street. And a dead baby was laying there. And…and…and it was gettin' rained on. 'Cause it was still raining on just that side of the street. And it was crazy. Nobody came outta their houses. It was just me…and all these dead people… laying all around me in the street. And I'm just standing there…looking down at this dead baby girl…laying face down in the street…up against the curb…with the rain water ready to wash her away. Turns out her mother got blasted and flew up into these bushes. But I didn't see her. Turns out…a lot of mothers died that day.", then, Trife, *drifts off* a bit, and…just kinda *mumbles to himself,* (but, Pockets, *heard every word!),* "My Mom died on a rainy day, when the sun was out, her great getting up morning, she used to tell me, "I won't be around for ever.", "Mom, thanks for the warning.",* (and, then, Trife comes back from it), *reminiscing into deeper-remembrances while reminiscing, (dangerous recently awakened Tier Three shit!),* and, then, he was back, as he looked back up at Pockets, and, continued,…"*And it was just me out there, well, the only one that wasn't dead. Just me out there with the dead…just me and the dead gettin' rained on. And I just looked around and started pickin' up some of the bullet shells…but that wouldn't be the only thing I collected off the streets that day. I had this big ol' knife,* you know? *Used to keep it hid, 'case anything crazy happened.* And it did! *AND ALL I DID WAS RUN AND HIDE!!! So I ran to where I was hiding. AND I GRABBED THAT KNIFE!!! And I came back over to where that little babygirl was laying…and I cut her head off. It took me seven cuts…stop and start…stop and start…stop and start…stop and start…stop and start…stop and start…, JAGGED, cross her throat…I cut that little babygirl's head clean off!* Don't ask me why I did it? *…I just did it.* Maybe, 'cause, *I was upset with myself?* Maybe, 'cause, *I was ashamed that all I did was run and hide?* Maybe I did it, just to see *if I could do it?* But I did it. And then I got pissed. *Pissed at myself. Pissed at the world. Pissed at everybody on my block and in my neighborhood, that did exactly what I did. Ran and hid! And they was all STILL hidin'!! And then my boy came 'round* *to check on me. Finally!! Saw me with that bloody knife and baby's head, in my hands, and he yelled out, "YO'!!! THAT'S TRIFE!!!" And...I just looked at him with no feelings at all, thinkin' 'bout a rainy day when tha' sun is out, and, take a blade, and, go cross his throat in seven cuts...stop and start...stop and start...stop and start...stop and start...stop and start...stop and start...cut his head clean off too, and, then, I told 'em, "Yeah. Something like that."... and that day made me...from that day on, I only answered to Trife. On that fateful day, that's when I learned how to move in silence...and stay in blind spots...and learned how not to die. And then me and my boy went 'round and, got all the neighborhood kids, even motherfuckers a couple grades older than us, they was comin' with us...they didn't have a choice! And we went up to the school yard. And me and my boy...one at a time...took them all on... SWINGIN' JACK!!! And if you could hold your own, if you could hold your hands, then you could be one of us."*

"Hey...hey, uh, Trife, my brother...damn. *That's some* deep shit. Fuck. Listen. But that's what I'm talking 'bout, NO MORE *hard livin'*, huh? So listen. There's some things I need to talk to you about.", Pockets, stammers, as he begins, (and sure AS FUCK, *gettin' the HELL off the subject of Parkinson's City, Gun Battle Bradley AND the Bully Boyz!)*(OY VEY!!!).

"Oh, hey, Pockets, my brother, don't even sweat it. I got you on a hit song! I'm more concerned 'bout me being ABLE to sing it, than me, comin' up with some fire-ass-lyrics, for you.", Mr. Trife, replies.

"No, no, that's not it.", Pockets, reassures him.

"Then? What is it? OH, what? *Slippin'-back, to tha' "old ways"??* Nah, you won't hafta' worry 'bout me, *goin' back to tha' "old me".* I'M all about, this music shit! Thanks, Pockets. Thank you, again, my brother. I really do, appreciate you believing in me and, givin' me a shot.", Mr. Trife, confides.

"Weeeeeell, ya' *MIGHT hafta'*...a little. *"Slip-back",* that is. You see, *there's unfinshed business. Your brother,* well, actually you, *B. Trife-Brotha Trife, who* you were just speaking on, well, actually, *who* I WAS just speaking on earlier too, *was supposed to be posted-up on this horse ranch,*... just as you are now. I was trying to *give him a better life back then,*...just as I'm trying to give you a better life now. Yeah,...so...well...anywaaays,

I built my empire,...moved up north. Got into some major hustles. But, my main goal, my main objective, was to leave that street life behind. *Build my own race track,* here in Tennessee and, give the State of Kentucky a run for their money! All "legal-like". But, as you can see, by the lack of horses on my ranch, *that never happened. Shit went down,...as it ALWAYS seems to do, WHEN you're in that street life and, well, SHIT GOT fucked-up. I had to leave town...in a hurry...and, did some unbelievable-shit, in the process.",* Pockets, says.

"Yeah? *Like what??",* asks, Mr. Trife.

Taking a real big drink of his drink, (then, filling it right back up!), Pockets, confides in Mr. Trife, *"I blew town,...and left my lady behind."*

"Damn, Pockets. Ain't gonna lie, my brother, *that IS* fucked-up.", Mr. Trife, lets him know.

"I agree. And I'm glad that, you agree too. 'Cause, when we head back up north to Pa., you're goin' into the city and, gettin' her back for me.", Pockets, unveils his plan.

"I'm gonna,...DO what???", inquires, Mr. Trife.

"Like, I said, my brother, a lotta'-shit - *gotta' - whole-lotta' fucked-up.* I CAN'T go into the city! Like, I was, sayin', *I had some MAJOR hustles goings-on, with, some heavy people.* There's a price on my head. So, I can't go back into the city...the City of North Juarez.", Pockets, informs.

Snapping his fingers, *(trying to recall some shit!),* Mr. Trife, repeats the name a few times, *"North Juarez...North Juarez...",* then, says, (unable to recall), "I'm with you, my brother. Just show me where the city is and, consider it done. So,...what's up? *WHO* ARE these people that, want you dead?", (then, swirling his drink and going to take a sip), Mr. Trife, continues, (before, he takes that sip), by asking, "So, *who is it?* The mob?", Mr. Trife, asks, jokingly.

Deadly-serious, Pockets, replies, point-blank, "Nope. The cops. The ENTIRE fuckin' police force!", (WHICH, stops the brim of Mr. Trife's glass, from ever touching his bottom lip!).

"Oh shit.", states, Mr. Trife, *now realizing the seriousness* of what he's being told...(AND,...*the enormities OF* THIS business trip!).

"Yeah. *"Oh shit",* is right. You think, I like, ANY of this!?? LEAVIN' MY lady behind??", (then, Big-Hustle-Gears of Big-Hustle-Mind...

grinds), "Yeah, so, well, anywaaaaaays...I probably feel, *how you musta' felt, that day, YOU RAN AND HID.* SO,...there YOU go! So? Are you gonna help me,...or not?"

Insulted. Mr. Trife raises up outta his rockin' chair, (spillin' Grand Marnier!), stands before Pockets, and, says, "Don't ever ask me anything like that again, in my entire life."

Not knowing how to take that, (with *"Brotha Trife"* closing distance on him like that and all!), Pockets, goes the "levity-route" again, (but, you know he really meant it), "What!? You're not gonna help me??", then looks down and away, then looks back up at Trife, (with a sly-look in his eyes!!) and, replies, "It's not like, I asked you to kill some cops for me. THERE'D be half-a-mil. in it for you, IF ya' did."

"Nah. Fuck that. I ain't killin' no cops. They ain't did shit to me. Get your lady back for you? That I CAN do. You're givin' me, a better life. SO, I figure, YEAH, I'll go into that city and, bring your lady back out, for you. That'll be my way of givin' you, a better life too."

"Awww, bless you, Brotha Trife...bless you.", Pockets, says, in reply, (in relief), in all seriousness, giving Brotha Trife a hug, then, tells him, "...but, there's more."

"Oh, yeah? *Like, WHAT?!?*", a now distrustful Mr. Trife, asks.

"Take it easy, my friend, take it easy. My lady, she has a HELLAVA' set-of-pipes on her. You get her out of the city for me and, I'll tell you what. I'll help you out. That song you write, I'll tell you what, I'll put her on that song with you. Whatdaya' say?", Pockets, presents.

"MY MAN, I don't even know how I'M gonna SOUND, singin' on that song, yet!!! But,...ok, if she can sing it WITH soul? FUCK IT! I'm down! ...She'll ONLY make MY song better.", Mr. Trife, replies, shaking hands with the man on the deal, (*wow...a record deal,* talking music, talking business,...about MY FIRST SINGLE!)...(*I'll drink to that!*).

"Alright then. We'll talk more about this. But, AS for me? I'm headed into this ranch and, gonna lay-me-down. YOU SHOULD get some shut-eye, Mr. Trife. We'll be back on the road in the morning.", Pockets, informs him.

"Yeah, I'ma get-me-some shut-eye, in a bit.", Mr. Trife, lets him know, (then, swirls his liquor), continuing, "But, FIRST,...", then, he takes a drink, before, saying, "I'm gonna sit here and, finish my drink. And look-up-at ALL these beautiful stars. Never seen a night sky LIKE this before... ever. *...I don't think!?!"*

"Alright then, my brother. Have a good night.", Pockets, tells him, then heads on inside the ranch.

"No doubt, my brother. You do the same.", Mr. Trife, replies, before taking a seat, back down in his rocking chair.

(Just he and his drink, and the pond, a toad or two or three, *and some time to think)...*

And Mr. Trife, just looks up at all those stars, like *(as if) at some point in time, millions or billions of years ago,* like *(as if) they were (at some point in time) in a great giant palm, and smeared cross the sky.* And the more Mr. Trife, looked into that night sky,*...the more that was exposed.* (You see), to Mr. Trife, you have the stars that, seem bigger and far more closer to the earth, (almost like you could reach out and pluck them outta the sky). And then, there's all of those other stars, (that you could just tell), were way-up-high and, so VERY far. And then you have, all of those tiny pinhole stars, (that just seem to appear outta nowhere!). The ones, that, make you think,...WERE THEY ALWAYS there?? (The ones, that, make you think, I can't believe I'm EVEN ABLE to see these tiny specks of light, WITH the naked eye!). The ones, that, just breakthrough the - upper-dark-outer-shelf - of outer space - and, poke through (like little tiny lights of pinholes). The ones, that, make you feel at peace (and, give you a sense of grace). AND THEN, Trife *sees it!! (WAY UP there!!), flying cross the, outer - way-out-there-way-up-there - outer-upper-shelf - of the night sky (and of outer space). And, it was EVERY bit the brightness AND size* of those pinhole stars. As Trife *sees something, tiny and bright, crossing the outer upper-shelf. It did race.* And, Trife, stands up outta his rocking chair, spilling Grand Manier! *And, just watches this thing makin' tracks!! (THOUGH, leaving no tail or trail, this tiny bright pinhole light, was on its motherfuckin' GIDDY-UP!!!!!!).* And, Trife, took notice as to, *HOW quickly it closed distance on the other stars, (before coming to, and then, PASSING those stars!),...every star,...any star. (And realizing, how far apart those stars actually are!). And, at how, that tiny bright pinhole light,* *blew past them all,…(like it was nothing!). Traveling in a straight line, (as it came from over the roof of the ranch).* As Trife, *watched it travel that - upper-outer-dark-shelf - of outer space.* And, Trife knew, that, *he was witnessing something special!!* UNTIL, this big walnut tree, (to the right of the man-made pond) obscured his vision, *of that, tiny bright speeding flying light,* (until he could no longer see it, from that tree by chance).

(And so, then, Mr. Trife, *got this idea. Figured with everybody in the ranch knocked out, nobody would know. And so, it would be no big deal. And so, Mr. Trife, hustled over to the RV. Quickly and quietly)…*

And…

Snuck into the private sleeping quarters, in the back of the RV. And,… retrieved that gun! (OY VEY!). *(Gonna use that rifle scope,…as a telescope!), AND FOLLOW THAT tiny bright pinhole light. (AS IT WAS, out makin' its' - cross-the-dark-outer-reaches-of-outer-space - run!).*

And as Mr. Trife, stood back up on the porch and, held that deer rifle scope up to find, *that tiny bright pinhole light, (racin' cross the sky!)… he felt, what felt like, some deja vu.* And, felt something unexpectedly hit him, on top of his head. Something tiny, perhaps. (Something, perhaps something, *that fell to earth FROM THE night sky!).* And, as he got hit, (just a reaction), (nothing he meant!), Mr. Trife, unexpectedly,…pulled that trigger. (That thirty-aught-six, got a KICK!!!). And that deer rifle scope, took out his right eye.

And, as Mr. Trife, flew back, *unconscious,* landing on the porch of the ranch, (on his back!). *Out there in the black, (just above and to the right), of that pond, (just above and to the right), of that big walnut tree…WAS A BIG GIANT FACE IN A BIG GIANT CLOUD!!! Kinda gray in color. Kinda, but not so much, eerie. (And, that face in the cloud, WAS THERE, to check ON him!). And then, it scrolled up. And, leveled-out flat. Before drifting off. And then, floated off to its' left.*

As it traveled on.

Chapter Eleven

Y.S.

The next day...

Back on the road. Though, later than initially intended. Pockets at the helm. Draped in custom red custom-made red everythang. Witha' wireless white earpiece-jack in his ear. Handling music-biz business. On the road. On his phone. (This-here shit, IS life!). MORE THAN a career!

In the back...

Mended. Laying in bed. Laying on his back. (For YOU, and, for ALL intensive purposes, this *inanimate "being"*, alive *but not alive,* but then again he is, *this Tier-Three-Clone of Brotha Trife,* alive, but yet, *not as* nature *intended,* and so, here we are and here we go...), *inanimate,* yet, a - beyond-at-times - EXTREMELY-animated - *"being",* but yet, and so, he does *so lay* and does not lie. (ya' dig?). And so, and as such, Mr. Trife, does so lay and does not lie, in the back private sleeping quarters. Frozen hand. Held to frozen eye socket. Witha' bag of ice.

In the kitchen area...

Y.S., showin' False Profit a thing or two. ('Bout this-here music-biz). As, MC Busta-Nut's breakin' up weed. Music-money, drugs, and girls.

STAYS ON Busta-Nuts' mind! HOWEVER, payin' attention to Y.S., (ON THIS music-biz tip!), IS WHAT he really needs!!

Back up in the Captain's chair...

"No. Listen to me! HAVE THEM go through the main 800 number. Have them go through the prompts 'til they get to, The: "Employee Directory". MAKE SURE, they tell Phillip Tate, THAT, I SPECIFICALLY referred them, to: "Artist Development". You got that? Ok. Good. Alright...alright...uh-huh...ok...alright, then,...let me know.", Pockets, speaks into his - feel-the-need-to-look-like-the-need-to-stay-in-constant-contact - white-wireless-earpiece-phone-jack.

Then, moving back, towards the back...

Y.S., is showing False Profit, on her phone, how to Google "ASCAP". And telling him what they're all about. And, as to, WHY, HE NEEDS TO KNOW these things for himself for! And, she's keeping her voice down! (So Pockets, doesn't hear!). ...As, Mr. Trife emerges, from out the back, stepping out the private sleeping quarters' door.

"What's all that??", Mr. Trife, asks, (of Y.S., False Profit and, of ASCAP). As, the two, are all huddled-up together on her phone. False Profit breaks-out. To join Busta-Nut. As, MC Busta-Nut, fires-up, the broke-up weed. Mr. Trife, (witha' bag of ice!), sits down next to Y.S.. To see-what's-was - the-going's-on!

"Uh,...you GOOD, Mr. Trife??? That...that gun blast scared me! We thought you WERE dead!! Pockets, THOUGHT, you stuck that rifle in your eye! AND pulled the trigger!! Wait. Like? WHY tha' fuck would he think, YOU'D do somethin', LIKE that?!?", Y.S., asks, informs and, inquires.

"Hmm? ...Good question...*no idea*...but yeah, I'm good.", Mr. Trife, replies, as he removes the bag of ice from his right eye. (Swollen and stitched closed!!). *Had emergency surgery.* Then, got RIGHT BACK on the road! 'Cause, if he can't go,...NEXT MAN UP goes in the game! 'Cause, THAT'S HOW that goes! (Poor Mr. Trife, just can't seem to keep,...blood off his clothes!!!).

(AND, the motherfucker is recovering QUICK)...*(on some: clone-regeneration shit!)*

Though...

He DON'T REMEMBER THAT fact!!!

FOR...

That gun blast, *knocked him unconscious,* landin' him on his back. Poor ol' Mr. Trife...*(HE don't remember NOTHIN' 'bout this "Clone-Life"!).*

BUT...

(HE STILL FEELS...*INVINCIBLE!!!)*(OY VEY!!!).

"EWWWWWW!!! That's TRIFE!!!", Y.S., announces, at the sight, of his right eye, (PAINFULLY-SWOLLEN and, stitched-closed TIGHT!!).

"Yeeeeeaaaaaahhhhh, somethin' like that!", Mr. Trife, replies, *intubation-voice-amazin',* witha' laugh and smilin'!

(And, wouldn't you know?? Pockets DON'T mind! *GOT those PAIN PILLS CLOUDIN' Mr. Trife's recently awakened Tier-Three-MIND!!! SO,* that trip to the E.R., AND that script of 90 Oxy's,...*WAS RIGHT ON TIME!!!)*(OY FUCKING VEY!!!)

"What's good on them Oyx's, Mr. Trife!? You holdin' out?", MC Busta-Nut, asks.

"BOY!!!", from Y.S., (AND that LOOK of her's!), dead's all that!

Then, back up to the front...

Pockets whippin' it. (And you would think it!), BUT, that earpiece in Pockets' ear, ISN'T just to front! As he, finds himself, in JUST ANOTHER music biz phone call! Just, another day. (OF, The: "Music Biz Life"!)...

"Phil, now pay attention, IT'LL work. We'll get it back in "session files". And then, we can mix and master it...", Pockets, explains, cockin' his custom red custom-made red hat hard to the side, (WHILE looking AT Mr. Trife, in his rearview mirror, in the back of HIS ride!).

And, once again, past the kitchen...

(Past - False Profit and, MC Busta-Nut, gettin' fucked-up, cuttin'-up n' fuckin'-up!)...

Y.S., and Mr. Trife, are seated in the back. And, get into a deep conversation. As Pockets, remains engrossed. On the call. On the phone. (On, his: white - wireless-LOOK-AT-ME - earpiece-jack!)...

"Well, to answer your earlier question, Mr. Trife.", Y.S., begins, showing Mr. Trife her phone, and, (Y.S., DON'T talk to NOBODY!), BUT YET, she continues, "Well, at least HE gives a fuck, tryna' learn some shit, 'bout this biz. NOT LIKE, that - FUCKIN'-idiot - nutjob!", Y.S., says, of False Profit and, (the nutjob Busta-Nut!), then, sadly-enough, finishes off her statement, WITH, "Not that, him, TRYNA' LEARN THIS business,...is gonna make a bit of fuckin' difference."

"Waddaya' mean?? So,...whatchu' sayin'? Pockets told me, that, he'd handle everything, FOR me.", Mr. Trife, replies.

(Laughing RIGHT AT Mr. Trife!), Y.S., let's him know, "YEAH! It all, SOUNDS good...TIL' it don't happen!", and then, knocks-off her laughter, ('cause, AIN'T a FUCKIN' thing funny!)... (AND YET, continues...), "I know MORE 'BOUT this biz, than, Profit and NUT-JOB, EVER will! Learned, some-shit...A LOT of shit,...from my sister,... twin sister, that is. I OUTTA' HAVE my fuckin' head examined, to STILL BE chasin' THIS dream! But,...I'm chasing it for her, at this point. Damn. You know somethin', Mr. Trife??? THEY, WHOEVER the fuck "THEY" are, but, "they" really should tell you, THE SHIT you're GONNA' BE gettin' yourself into, BEFORE you get into THIS business.", Y.S., confides.

(Placing the bag of ice, back up to his eye), Mr. Trife, replies, "There's shit to everything."

Turning off her phone, (AS NOW, she feels as though, she's just wasting her time!), Y.S., let's it be known, (as she's QUICK to SPEAK HER MIND!!), "You soundin' stupid, right now. Yeah, THERE'S SHIT to everything! I'm only sixteen and, I fuckin' know THAT already. And you, you're the fuckin' perfect candidate, FOR this shit. I got you pegged already, Mr. Trife. YOU'LL do ANYTHING for this shit...JUST LIKE MY TWIN SISTER!!"

"So, WHAT'S good?? She couldn't make the trip? Prior commitment or somethin'??", asks, Mr. Trife.

"MY SISTER is in the morgue!! Damn...THAT'S fucked-up...I keep forgettin'. She's FINALLY buried! SHE, WAS in that FUCKIN'-MORGUE, long enough tho'.", (STRAIGHT-GRILLIN' Trife!!!), Y.S., let's it be known, with great hate and sadness.

Removing the ice bag from his eye, for better or for worse. (But, he wants to show Y.S., how he TRULY FEELS about, WHAT he's just learned...), "Tha' fuck, you talkin', 'bout?? Your TWIN sister's... dead??? THAT'S horrible, Y.S.! I'm so sorry for you. GOD BLESS.", sums-up, Mr. Trife.

"Thank you, Trife.", she says, in reply.

"You're welcome, Y.S.. Hey, um,...what happened? I mean,...like, what the fuck, Y.S.?? That's fuckin'-horrible, on my part! Sorry Y.S., it's none of my business. Your business is YOUR business, ya' dig.", as Trife, stumbles all cross that.

"No. It's fine. I WANT TO tell you, what happened. So,...so, that it wasn't in vain.", Y.S. explains. *(And then, explains...), "My sister died FOR this dream. Taking reckless and risky chances, with all the - "next-big-things-in-the-music-industry" - with a - studio-in-their-bedrooms. Gullible,...found raped, beaten all-about her face, wit' her teeth knocked-out and dead in a skate park."*

"'Cause, THAT'S HOW *THAT* life ends.", Mr. Trife, confirms, repositioning the ice bag over his eye.

"Yeah. Exactly! *Nobody knew where she was,...her body in the morgue, went "unclaimed" and unidentified. The city, stuck her in a pine box and buried her, ON her side,...to save space. Buried AND stacked - side-by-side - ON their sides, with ALL THE OTHER "unclaimed" people in the city morgue that, no one ever came to the morgue,...and signed for.*", as Y.S., tells it. Jaded.

(Staring into the RV floor), in the back, *looking back, thinking back,* Y.S. continues for Mr. Trife, *and FOR her twin sister,* (but perhaps, more

for herself...), *"She loved to sing...THAT'S ALL she EVER did...all she ever wanted to be. All she ever wanted to do, was to get signed by a major label and, she died for it. Her love for singing and, her love for being a "big time" singer, took her life. Because, EVERYBODY told her everything they wanted her to hear...for THEIR benefit. She was in love with this whole idea, of making it big in the music industry,...in love with it more than she loved herself, and that kind of love took her life."*

"DAMN...", Trife, thinks to himself, while looking at her, with his one good eye, with her head down, as she *stares at the floor.* (And THANK GOD, Trife, DIDN'T let, THESE NEXT WORDS, come out HIS mouth!). As he, continued *in thought,* *"...Unsigned in life and death. That was her hell."*

Then, back to the wheel, (ON TOP OF THE WORLD!!)...

The man, (for HIM), life IS good, makin' money from what othermotherfuckers sang, stayin' draped, in custom red custom-made all red everythang, as he, continues to: Wireless-Wheel-And-Deal, "... by mid..."

But...as it is. In the RV. In the back...

The tension. The depression. The anger. The let-down. OF TRUST...that was NEVER there! The money spent. The money, SO freely-invested. Of, her Dad, HAVING TO keep reminding himself, that: "You'll get ALL THIS money back, just SAVE all your receipts!" (Of: The Start-Up Costs)...(Of: The - fuck-you - IT-AIN'T-MY-money!!)...(Of: The - "For-your-best-interest")... (THAT,...WAS NEVER THERE!!!).

OF:

The, "Oh, just wait 'til tax season, THIS year!" (Of: The fat return!!!). Of: The BAD ADVICE. (OF: The ILL-PREPARED tax preparer). THAT HELPED TO...lead us all down the road to ruin!

OF:

The more, BAD - "I-Shoulda'-Looked-Into-All-Of-This-A-Lot-More-FOR-Myself" - "ADVICE". Of: The "fuck it". Of: The realization. OF: The

- *"Once-All-The-Money-Is-Gone"… - …"They'll-Stop-Asking-FOR - IT!!!". Of: The phone, that no longer rings or notifies. OF: (AND, ON THAT NOTE!) - All-On-My-Own-All-By-Myself - DISPARE!*

And, *(on THAT note!)…*

Then coming back, *(from her head)*, head back up, Y.S., looks directly at Trife, and, just feels the need to continue. *(Of: Her thoughts). To vent, for herself. And, FOR her twin sister!! Of: Her and, FOR her, sister's journey. OF: What she found to be, THE MOST FUCKED-UP THING OF ALL!!!*

(Come. Y'all wanna have a listen??)…

"You know, Trife. *My Mom died, and, finally, after fighting with the insurance company and, having my Dad callin' them every day on the phone,* you know, Trife, *it took my Dad askin' them, what was their corporate street address, that, he was gonna have to come down there in person,* and, in these days of "Post-Columbine", NOBODY wants somebody showin' up pissed-off AT THEIR place of business! And so, you see, Trife, it wasn't for us, it WAS for THEM, *that, they FINALLY came-on-up-off a THAT money! But, my Dad, believed in me and my sister. And, he believed in our talents. And, he invested ALL that insurance money into us. But…WE DIDN'T KNOW! None of us knew!* What didn't we know?? *WHAT WE WERE gettin' ourselves into! BUT, these "MUSIC INDUSTRY BLOOD SUCKERS", SAW us comin' and, sucked-up on every drop of my dead Mom's money! And, we started our own label, my twin sister and me, our own publishing company. My Dad thought it best that, we do it all on our own. But, we didn't know what, we didn't know. But, these music MOTHERFUCKERS knew!!! And…they were soooooo smooth with it! One playin' the other! NOBODY on the same page! "Oh, I worked eleven whole hours yesterday, layin' down electric guitar traking, for your debut album. So, I'm CHARGIN' Y'ALL - TIME-AND-A-HALF - for all my work, instead of the daily $800-a-day session-artist - rate."* Like, WHAT KINDA' BULLSHIT is THAT, Trife?!? I'M TELLIN' YOU, THEY WERE JUST MAKING UP THE SHIT, AS THEY WERE GOIN' ALONG!!! *So, THE OWNER of the studio that we were using, said, he talked to the session guitarist and, told him, "No way! You're NOT charging* *them, time-and-a-half.* "BUT, who the fuck do you believe, Trife??? *So, the fuckin' - ass-eatin'-studio-session - guitarist - was like, "Fine! I'LL just work for three hours tomorrow. And then, I'll just work three hours the day AFTER that!"* AND, HE CHARGED US $1,600 FOR TWO DAYS WORTH OF WORK!!! Like, WHAT kinda' bullshit is that, Trife??? But, what tha fuck could WE do!? *We hired him at $800-a-day session-artist-rate. So, we had to pay him the $1,600.* Which was TOTAL BULLSHIT!!! *We had the money, but, with SHIT LIKE THAT constantly goin' on, THOSE BLOOD SUCKERS sucked all our money right up!!* Like I said, THEY saw us comin'. And...they did it to us, anyway. *So, all the money was gone. And so, then my sister started runnin' with all these so-called managers and rappers and next-big-things,...walkin' 'round late nights by herself,... from one sofa to the next, from one home-studio to the next and, we never knew where she was, or who she was with. And, she fuckin' died FOR this bullshit love affair, WITH GETTIN' SIGNED to a major label!* AND, WE STILL AIN'T GOT SHIT, TO SHOW FOR IT!!! Mr. Trife, I carry me and my sister's thumb drive 'round with me, EVERYWHERE I GO! 'Cause, I don't trust leavin' it nowhere!!! I walk 'round, EVERY DAY, with $60,000 in my pocket and, all this fuckin' thumb drive has on it *is drums, guitar, and bass from the studio sessions we paid for.* And, ALL those motherfuckers are havin' a good laugh at OUR EXPENSE!!! I SWEAR I WANNA' KILL EM ALL!!! But I won't. *I wanna ride this dream out for my sister!* And, you know somethin', Mr. Trife? *WE didn't even authorize, the bass-guitar-studio-sessions! THE ENGINEER OF THE DAMN STUDIO, authorized it ON HIS OWN!!! AND THEN, TRIED SAYIN', HE WAS GONNA' HOLD OUR MUSIC, FOR "LACK-OF-PAYMENT", FOR THE BASS SESSIONS, THAT, WE NEVER AUTHORIZED!!!* FUCKIN' BULLSHIT, TRIFE!!! But...THAT'S this fuckin' music industry, for ya'! *And the studio, and, all the "hired" session-artists, WERE ALL singin' a different tune. EVEN TO THEMSELVES!!! AND, THEY WERE ALL, IN ON IT!!! Even, this, tryin'-to-be-lookin'-like-Rick-Rubin-lookin' - BLOOD SUCKER - motherfucker, that, came cross all SOOOOOO sweet and sincere-like. "Hermet-Boy", was some "Music Contract Advisor".* MOTHERFUCKIN' BLOOD SUCKA'!!! *But, HE WAS all in it together WITH - all them - studio motherfuckers AND session artists, too! And, I ain't* tryin' to be defending them, Trife. *But, they were saying, they didn't want to work with my sister no more. They were saying that, since she showed up at a production meeting all fucked-up, and, noddin'-out - seated at the table, wit 'em all, that, in their own words, "Nobody wants to work with a drunk or a junkie."* I mean, I get it. *But, they were never really about it. They were just, all about getting our money.* So, yeah, *HE got his money, too!! HE helped to bleed us dry, too!!* BLOOD SUCKER!!!"

And all Trife can say is, "Damn.", as he can feel her pain.

"DAMN, NUTHIN'!!!", Y.S., begins, (as she snaps!), as Trife, HAS YET, to hear *the MOST fucked up part!* "Mr. Trife, *a song writer, came to my house, with promises of getting me into a Disney movie. Talked ALL THIS SHIT, 'bout, me doin' the voice and singing the songs of the MAIN character! He said, that, the animation, was being held-up, by a "contract dispute" in Japan. But, THIS MOTHERFUCKER sat there, IN OUR LIVING ROOM, REASSURING me and my Dad that, THIS WAS really going to happen. Said he, had written songs for Bruno Mars and, ALL these people! Said, he didn't even have to work anymore, due to all the royalties he was collecting, from all his sucessful-song-writing-work. I WAS SO EXCITED...so hopeful. Turns out, it was ALL BULLSHIT! AND A WASTE OF TIME!!!...totally broke my spirit. And, the worst part is, the guy, this "successful-song-writer", turned-out to be an undercover vice cop! JUST PLAYIN' a young girl, a YOUNG SINGER, to get closer to my Dad, to see what he was all about! EVEN had the NERVE, came to OUR house JUST DAYS before Christmas! Sat there, in our living room, with me and my Dad. And, he kept looking up at the lighted angel, GRACING the top of our Christmas tree... AND, HE sat there, and LIED to us. TOTALLY ruined my Christmas! And, the fucked-up thing, the phone calls stopped being returned and, we waited months!! BECAUSE, the guy was so FUCKING believable! And, THAT FUCKING PIECE OF SHIT VICE COP, WAS WILLING to hurt a little girl...just to lock my Dad up.* FUCK YOU!!!!!!"

"SOME muthafuckas, AIN'T-GOT NO shame! Y.S.,...*you figured all that out on your own,* huh?? You're pretty smart, you know that!?!", Mr. Trife, reacts.

"I am...and, thank you...BUT smart enough to know, *the motherfucker COULDN'T even sing! BWHAAAAAA!!! My Dad, asked him to sing something, I think he was feelin' him out, as the prick cop sat right there in our living room...lookin' up at our angel on the top of our tree. And, the motherfucker sat there, stutterin' and stammerin', TRYNA' THINK OF somethin' TO sing! AND THE BEST THIS BLACK MOTHERFUCKER, COULD COME UP WITH to sing, was, some, old Negro spiritual! AND, THE MOTHERFUCKER, WASN'T EVEN ANY GOOD!!!* YEAH, some BIG "song writer" HE turned out to be! FUCKIN' CLOWN!!!", Y.S., confesses.

"YEAH, straight CLOWN-MATERIAL, if ya' ask me!! If you're a vice cop. And, your "cover" is TO BE a song writer. YOU SHOULD AT LEAST - MAKE-DAMN-SURE - YOU CAN CARRY A FUCKIN' TUNE!!! STRAIGHT CLOWN-MATERIAL-ASS-NIGGA!!!!!!", Mr. Trife, says, (gettin' "*THAT look*" on HIS face AGAIN!!!), as Y.S. and Mr. Trife, BOTH SHARED A GOOD LAUGH AT THAT NON-SINGING-BLACK-ASS-VICE-COP'S EXPENSE!!!!!!

(Then, coming back from, *her "momentary-lapse"...into happiness*), Y.S., confesses, "*A few days later...on Christmas Eve, my Dad got "detained" on some civil-rights-violatin'-bullshit and, my sister never came home. I lost them both. It was the worst Christmas EVER!!!* I got nothin' or nobody. JUST POCKETS and, my twin sister's dream. Oh yeah, AND this fuckin' $60,000 thumb drive in my pocket! You wanna know somethin', Trife?? THERE *was so much wheelin' and dealin' and double-talk goin' on, DURING the makin' of me and my sister's debut album* and, it turns out, IT WAS ALL BULLSHIT!!! NOBODY, AND I DO MEAN NOBODY, WAS "ALL IN" AND COMMITTED,...'cept for me and my Dad and my sister. They, GOT their "session artist" money! They, GOT their "studio time" money! EVEN, THAT BULLSHITTIN' - comin'-off-ALL-SWEET-and-nice - HERMET-BOY - TRYNA' LOOK LIKE RICK RUBIN - lookin'-BLOOD-SUCKER - who "CLAIMED" to be "OUR MUSICAL ADVISOR" - AND, charged us mad-money - to type up ALL KINDS OF CONTRACTS and shit for us- AND,...IT ALL WENT NOWHERE!!! Yeah, EVEN HIM! HE WAS IN IT TOO, WITH THEM!!! THEY ALL, GOT PAID!!! And paid well.* AND, WE AIN'T GOT shit to show for it. AND, EACH AND EVERY LAST ONE OF 'EM, CAN ALL EAT A DICK!!! So, Mr. Trife, I'm STILL CHASIN' this dream for my sister. Nobody cares, Trife, nobody in the entire music industry cares. *They GOT their money!* So, they don't care if your CD ever gets completed and pressed. Or if, one of your songs even makes it to the radio. AND, WHY SHOULD THEY??? *They got their money, they got paid already,* so FUCK IT. Know what I mean? And, you know what the kick-in-the-balls is, Trife? *The funky-smellin' engineer, WHO went ahead, AND took it upon himself, to schedule the BASS-guitar-tracking-sessions, WITHOUT even asking my Dad first if it was ok, 'cause, like, my Dad's the one that would have been payin' for it, so you'd think they'd check with him first,* right? WRONG!!! Not THESE PEOPLE!!! Fuckin' BLOOD SUCKERS!!! *So, the fuckin' body-odor-like-a-MOTHERFUCKER-engineer, tried to hold our music from us! Talkin' 'bout, WE OWE him for the unpaid bass sessions. My dad told him, he wasn't payin' for bass sessions that he never authorized and, that, the shady-engineer and, his bass player would get a taste, you know, a percentage, on the back end, AFTER the album was released.* And, you know what this motherfucker, told my Dad?? *He said, "A percent of nothing is nothing."* DID you catch that, Trife?? *HE KNEW, our album, would NEVER be completed! HE KNEW, our songs, would never hit the radio!* AND HE STILL TRIED TO BLEED US DRY!!! All these supposedly "BIG TIME" artists, we were workin' with, studio heads and engineers, even that fuckin' BLOOD SUCKIN' "music industry advisor" - *ALL talked a good game,...how connected in "the biz" they were and, all that they have done.* But, you know somethin', Trife?? *NOT ONE of 'em, EVER mentioned ANYTHING, 'bout gettin' our record on the radio!!!* EVERYBODY'S funny, Trife. But, DON'T YOU EVER FORGET THIS,...the BIGGER the money,...the FUNNIER they are!!! I'm so fuckin' sick of this shit."

Just then, back up at the wheel, (back up at the TOP OF THE WORLD!!!)...

Pockets, makes some announcements, pulling into a lot, that, "WE'RE ALL gettin' out and, havin' a lot of drinks!"...(Leaning forward, to look out the side windows, from seated way in the back, Y.S. and Mr. Trife can spot the infamousness of the sign: "BITCHEZ". Illuminated. In neon. Pink. And pulsating. And against the sky of black)..."This is how we get down at Jettison Records! "Roadlife" and partyin'. Handle YOUR business. AND THE REST is a dream! Mr. Trife, here. Wear these sunglasses! And, I know, you're only 16. But, Y.S., I know the manager of these here BITCHEZ. So, we're all gettin' down off this here bus and, walkin' in together like a team!"

AND SO...

"Oh! I get it now!...", Mr. Trife, says, to Y.S., behind a revelation, said aloud, as the two, follow behind Pockets and HIS crew, through the lot of BITCHEZ. Behind 24 Karat gold lenses. Of limited edition. Cazel's hide. Mr. Trife's eye...(well, for the most part!). (But, the fresh weepings of blood, on his fresh new suit, IS the telltale!). And, as Y.S., asks Trife, "Triflin'??? What???", (Mr. Trife, gets back at it!), (of finishing off his revelation!), *(all charasmatic!)*, "...The name. *OUR NAME!!!* Jettison Records...*jettison*...as in... *"down"*...as in, *"this is how WE get down"! THIS* life. You see *HOW* we rollin', Y.S.?? So,...FUCK IT! *It's time TO party!!!"*

And, as Pockets overhears, he turns his head to holler back, (as he, AND THOUGH, keeps-on-steppin' towards BITCHEZ!), "I like *that vision,* in you, Mr. Trife. I LIKE that, *YOU like that!* Stick WITH me!! And, I'LL get YOU there!! HOWEVER, Mr. Trife, Jettison Records, means: *"WE BE DROPPIN' ALBUMS!!!"*, Pockets, *in love,* with hearing himself talk, (made, YET, ANOTHER announcement to HIS team!).

And, just as Pockets' team, approaches the strip club door, a stripper in tears, back in her street clothes, kicks it open with force! Followed closely by her manager! As he's, reaching for her arm. AS SHE, makes an announcement of HER VERY OWN,...of warning and harm: "THEY REALLY SHOULD TELL YOU, ABOUT ALL THE FUCKED-UP-SHIT YOU'RE GONNA' SEE, BEFORE YOU START WORKIN' HERE!!!", shouts, the stripper in tears!!!

"Get control of your bitchez.", Pockets, coldly, told the manager. (As Pockets, Busta-Nut, and False Profit...enter BITCHEZ).

And (on THAT note!)...

Y.S. SNATCHES her arm away from Mr. Trife!, (as she, was helping him through the lot of BITCHEZ!).

(Having heard AND seen enough!)...Y.S., heads back towards the RV. Parked waaaaaay in the back. Way in the back of the lot. *(But, SINCE she's seen, and BEEN THROUGH a lot!)*...Y.S., turns and, yells at Mr. Trife, "IT'S ALL ONE BIG HUSTLE, TRIFE!!! IT'S ALL JUST ONE BIG FUCKIN' HUSTLE!!! JETTISON RECORDS DON'T STAND, FOR: "WE BE DROPPIN' ALBUMS". JETTISON RECORDS STANDS, FOR: *"DROPPIN' ARTISTS - AFTER WE BLEED YOU DRY!!!"* YEAH, SO, WELL, ANYWAAAAAAYS!!!", Y.S., schools Mr. Trife, tryin' not to cry!! (And, she don't talk to NOBODY!!!!!!).

(BUT, YET!),...one, NOT trying TO stay *stuck...*

AND SO...

AS Trife, enters the club, he don't let the bouncers pat him down! Getting on his giddy-up! (Catching up!). With Pockets, False Profit and, MC Busta-Nut. In the VIP area. Just gettin' setup! Once settled. Out come the finest girls in the joint. (That would be the bartenders, IS my point!). And they're ALL coming out in, somethin' sexy and shit! Coming out with bottles of Dom. In ice buckets. Illuminated champagne labels fluorescing, off the sparklers and shit! But, as for Trife, he AIN'T feelin', all those damn sparklers and shit! ('Cause of his stitched-up and stapled-shut eye, with the fresh blood weepings and shit!). But, his 24 Karat gold lenses, from his Cazel's, (of limited edition!), well,...THEY be deflectin' THAT shit! And so, Mr. Trife, takes a seat. (Right there, ALL UP IN, THE MUTHA' FUCKIN' VIP!!!)(I SEE YOU MR. TRIFE!!!) (YESSIR!!!). And he does it, sittin' damn-near-directly cross, the round table of, their VIP section-sectioned-off, as he does it, sittin' damn-near-directly-cross from Pockets. As Pockets, sits there, slightly to the left of the table. As he does it, *as he used to do it,* on the table, *with his right arm restin'! (Old habits and hustles do die hard!).* And so now, as he does it, *as he used to do it,* he does it, with his right arm restin', *though, no E&J,* SO UNDER bottles of Dom! Labeled-White-From-The-Black-Light-Labeled-Up! Sparklin' and fluorescin'! As he does, with his custom red custom-made red hat cocked hard to the side. (No question!). As he does it, as he sits there, sittin' there, like a boss. As he does it, as he sits there, *with his motherfucking legs crossed!* As MC Busta-Nut, checks out a stripper, in particular, up on stage. As False Profit's tellin' a bartender, nothin' but false shit, in her ear, that's what he's speaking. As, Mr. Trife, sits there. All up at their sectioned-off-round-table-section of the VIP. With eyes of fire. Beaming like the sun. With his eye of blood weeping.

Strippers on laps, making their laps, while making their rounds. (Of and in and all through the VIP). *Are these guy's rappers? Who's-who? Girl! Just back-it-up and drop-it-down!* And with a stripper on his lap, ignorant-ass Busta-Nut, STILL gon' clown AND get his laughs! THAT expensive laugh. The laugh of luxury. (ALL UP IN THE VIP!!!). Laughing the laugh to hurt your soul. The laugh at the expense of others! *On this,* False Profit *will tell you* the truth, *"Busta-Nut ain't nothin' but, an ignorant-ass-motherfucker!"*

Looking up on stage, wide hips sway, healthy woman, thick through the haunches, coochie hangin' like a hammock, and MC Busta-Nut hollers at her, diamond encrusted grill gleaming of karats, cross the club, all up IN AND FROM, (THE VIP!!!), all highed-up on weed, silly and simple, *"BITCH, YOU LOOK LIKE YOU GOT LONG HANGIN' DOWN LOW TITTIES, WITH FRIED-HARD-AND-BURNT AREOLAS, FO' YO' NIPPLES!!!"*

(And, ya' just gotta feel bad for the stripper). 'Cause, she DIDN'T deserve all that! And, the stripper storms off stage! AND, she was just THROWIN' that! (What was she throwin'??? Well,...oh boy! Here it comes...) She was just throwin' that uterus, WITH the precision of a computerist!! AND, she was throwin' that "anchor", WITH the anger of a "Gamer"!! ('Cause...SHE. Didn't. Deserve. THAT. Shit!).

And, *on that note...*

Some - businessmen's-night-out-in-the-big-city-for-suburbanites - sitting in the VIP booth next to Pockets to his right, all start crackin' up laughin', *AT Busta-Nut's snappin'!* And, one of 'em stands up. Laughin' out loud. (AND holdin' his gut!). And, he was laughin' so hard that, he JUST COULDN'T hold it down. And, too many shots and vomit, came up through and out, shootin' outta his nostrils and, shootin' outta his mouth!! (And, wouldn't you know? Where ALL THAT vomit came down??). With SO MUCH force! *AND makin' a GUTTURAL sound!! BURNIN' FROM the Fireball!!! WITH the TASTE of sour cream,* from the potato skins, *AS the PUKE shot out his throat!!!!* Damn. *Sigh* Here we go... *IT ALL CAME DOWN ALL OVER POCKETS' CUSTOM RED, CUSTOM-MADE, RED SUIT COAT!!!!!*

Which...

...makes Pockets PUKE! Which, makes Busta-Nut BLOW CHUNKS!! Which, makes False Profit VOMIT!!! DAMMIT!!!(oh shit... here we go...wait for it...wait for it...)EVEN - "PLANTAIN TITTIES" - LOST HER LUNCH - EVENTUALLY!!!!!! Which, makes Busta-Nut BLOW CHUNKS all over again! (WHEN he got a look AT the - "wiry-hairs" of her's - poking out - ALL around - JUST ONE - fried-plantain-nipple - like the hairs SCRATCHING grandbabies - on-some-old-woman-from-Brussels chin!)(OY VEY!!!). *Which,* made the drunk-suburbanite-businessman, lean back over the brass bar, separating the VIP sections, again! (Living dangerously!). *From, smokin' a lil' bit 'o weed, a couple times, got baked twice, out in his car, followed-up by too many shots,* got him leaning back over the - Sectioning-Off-Between-The-VIP-Booths-Sectioning-Brass-Bar! And ONCE, his mouth filled-up with, THAT: *"watery-pre-puke-slobber"* - (THEE: "telltale" - THAT - YOU'RE GONNA' BE PUKING IN JUST A LIL' WHILE!!!) - AND, AS SUCH, - THUSLY FILLED-UP - *WITH the TASTE of sour cream MIXED with Fireball, ALONG WITH HOT stomach bile!!!* Well, *TOO much VOMIT,* from too many shots, came back up, through and outta his nostrils, and back up outta his mouth! Came back up outta his nostrils. And, back up outta his mouth, again. *Comin' right up and back down on Pockets', custom red custom-made red suit's left arm...ALL OVER AGAIN!!*

Which...

...only makes Pockets PUKE...ALL OVER AGAIN!!

And so(and, BUT!), (Stayin' "CRISPY" is a must!)...

"This is DISGUSTING!!! I think, I JUST pissed on nut!!! Yeah,...I...I...I think, I just did.", MC Busta-Nut says out loud, while his piss is hittin' the back of a Men's Room urinal cake, while gettin' hit with the taste of BLOWN CHUNKS back in the back of his mouth! As, some hot-chunky-vomit, hits him ONCE AGAIN, at the top of his esophagus! *(From, having the realization, OF having just pissed ON nut! From, some nasty-Men's-Room-strip-club-customer - that - "shook one out" - and - had "finished-up"!).* As, Pockets, False Profit and MC Busta-Nut, had adjourned into BITCHEZ' Men's Room, to freshen-up!

And...

...by the time, the three had finished cleaning-up, mouthful of mints, smelling of Polo cologne, to help with the freshen-up, (and, you KNOW, False Profit gripped-up, ALL the money, outta the bathroom attendant's tip cup!), Mr. Trife, HAD ALREADY handled his business! And, broke that - Ultimately-Twice-Puking-Up-Shots-Of-Fireball-And-Ultimate-Twice-Baked-Crispy-Potato-Skins-Chunks-Suburbanite-Businessman - FOR - $2,000.00 crispy cash money bucks!!!

In all brand new Absurd-Sur-Charge-Strip-Club-ATM-Crispy-Hundreds, Mr. Trife MADE him pay!! (Even though, the suburbanite-businessman made an offer, to buy their VIP section, four bottles of "Dom Rozay"!!!!). But, Mr. Trife told him, that, "It WASN'T enough!" Told the man, "Pockets' custom red, custom-made red suit coat was, gonna cost him, two-thousand bucks!" Told the man, that, "Pockets' suit coat, was custom-made of - handwoven Italian - linens!" And then, he broke that motherfucker, for two grand in cash, (in front of strippers and,) IN FRONT OF ALL of his Suburbanite-Businessmen friends!! (And, thusly declined, his offer of, the luminously-labeled-up, four bottles of, the Roses of Dom).

And, all it took, was, just that look, in Trife's eye. (And, him, gettin' that, arch in his back!)(oy vey!). WITH his chest out. And, with his shoulders reared-back! And, it just may have been, Trife's double-clinched fists! With, his, walnut-sized knuckles, ALL-ASKEW and shit! And, with all his businessmen-buddies watchin', (the strip club manager, and ALL the strippers in the club too!!), Trife made him peel off 10 - $100 bills. Made him put it in his hand. Then told him that it wasn't enough. And then, made him peel off another, 10 - $100 bucks. On-demand. All crisp and shit. From the club's - absurdly-high-sur-charge - ATM - and shit. Crispy-bills, makin' *that, Embarrassing: MAKIN'-ME-Peel-Off-Twenty-$100-Bills-In-Front-Of-EVERYBODY - Sound! ('Cause, Brotha Trife be Mr. Trife! AND, that's how, THEY BE, gettin' down!!).*

Not once. BUT twice!! (Did Trife, MAKE HIM, put that money in his hand!!). MADE HIM, make "payment-made" for damages. Made Payable, To: - Pockets' - Custom-Red-Custom-Made-Red-Suit - of - Handwoven-Italian - Linen. And then. (ALL-IGNORANT and shit!). Mr. Trife,...leaned into him.

And, while motioning with his right hand, (JUST LIKE, a whirlwind!), Mr. Trife, told the man, right dead IN his face, "AND, I WANT MY FOUR, BOTTLES OF, THE DOM ROZAY!!!" ('Cause, THAT'S SOME - ignorant-ass-Bully-Boyz - shit - THAT - Brotha-Trife - woulda'-do - back-in-the - day!!). And, in front of the whole club and, in front of all of his friends, wouldn't ya' know...HERE COME ALL THOSE FINE-ASS-BARTENDERS AGAIN!! WITH the sparklers and shit!!! (AIN'T THAT a bitch?!?). FOUR bottles of the Dom, wit tha', labels fluorescin' white and shit!!!!

(Hey, what can I say? *Mr. Trife, REALLY rocked THAT club's world!)*

WHEN...

He, SMACKED THE SHIT outta some Professional-Dickhead-Strip-Club-Customer! For, making some - STUPID-ASS - comment, about one of the bartenders. For, sayin' some DUMB-ASS shit! That, she was pretty... for a black girl!

(FOR, THAT'S *MR. TRIFE'S LEGACY, from here* and from here on out! *In THAT particular BITCHEZ...*TO THIS VERY DAY!!! *The man behind the 24 Karat gold limited edition lenses of Cazel. WITH club lights and, with sparklers and shit, MAKIN' them glint! The man with the eyes of fire. The man who's eyes WERE blazing like the sun! For, that was the man...* they call Mr. Trife)

And so...

By the time the odd-trio, came out the Men's Room, with Pockets, holding his custom red custom-made red coat, (still covered in slop!).

Well, Mr. Trife, was no longer sittin' in their - Stageside - VIP - Section! *(For, you see, the manager, DIDN'T want NO MORE problems! And, was showing the label and, the artists, some love.)* For, the odd-trio, in custom red and skinny jeans, found that, Mr. Trife, had been moved to the - VIP - Up-The-Stairs - Section. With, Mr. Trife, lookin' down over the stage! From the - Above-The-Stage - Levels - of the - VIP - from WAAAAAAY up top! (Found him with four strippers)...(All grindin' on him and shit!). Found him with four bottles of Dom Rozay! With bottle tops leaning over the top of the sides - yet packed in tight - of silver champagne buckets - filled up with ice - with Rozay labels fluorecin' - FROM - the Above-The-Stage - Levels - of the - VIP Section's blacklights - which got those champagne labels poppin' in the dark - LIKE - glow in the dark - tan lines!!! AND, WITH the sparklers and shit!!! (And, well, of the sparklers? Well, Mr. Trife, DIDN'T mind!). For, you see, Mr. Trife, had four strippers on him...and he was GETTIN' ON his grind! And besides, from those 24 Karat gold Cazel lenses, (of limited edition!), (turning his eyes to fire and shit), well, they deflected those sparkers, so that his wounded-eye wouldn't get hit!!!! And, he sat there in his glory. And, he sat there feelin' like an *invincible man!* And, they found him up there like that. Above the stage. In the - Above-The-Stage - Levels - of the - VIP - with a - motherfuckin'-bottle-of-Dom-Rozay - in one hand! And, in the other hand? Well, Mr. Trife, was grippin' a FINE ass! Fucked-a-round and smacked a second! And, with fine-ass-number-three? Well, Mr. Trife, he poured some Dom Rozay down the crack of her ass! As for, the fourth-wild-ass? Well...IT WAS RIDIN' HIS DICK! And he sat there with his eyes, beaming like the sun.

And, as Pockets, led MC Busta-Nut and, False Profit, up that flight of stairs. Pockets, shouted-out-loud upon the wide-eyed club patrons! The bouncers. The bartenders. The businessmen. The manager of BITCHEZ. (Even under the DJ's stare!). And, as Pockets, reached the top, (to the one and only) - Above-The-Stage - Level - of the - VIP - , Pockets, cried-out, "WE'RE ON TOP OF THE WORLD!!! JETTISON RECORDS, BABY!!!". (As, *an Invincible man,* sat there). With his hands full of ass and Rozay. And with his eyes, beaming like the sun.

And then, Mr. Trife stood up. And, he approached Pockets. Then, reached in his Perry Ellis suit pocket. And then, handed Pockets all

$2,000.00 dollars of that crispy cash! Placed it right in the man's hand. Straight from his pocket. And then, he leaned into Pockets. And, once with his lean on, he said, "This is for your suit. AND I broke that fool off for, four bottles of Dom Rozay, too!!!! Plus this VIP upgrade. 'Cause, that's how WE be gettin' down. JR4L: Jettison Records 4Life, baby!!!! 'Cause, *THIS IS HOW Jettison Records be gettin' down!*"

And, Pockets just looked. He looked at the man. And, he looked at all those crispy $100 bills in his hand! He looked and saw, all the bottles of Dom. And then, he looked back down at all that crispy cash in his palm! And, he looked at all the strippers, (JUST WAITIN' to grind on a nigga!) (OY VEY!!!!). Private party style! IN - The-Above-The-Stage-Levels - of the - VIP!!!

And, Pockets didn't even know what to say. And, all Pockets could ask was, "You did all this for...me?"

And, Mr. Trife, simply replied, with the - blood-from-fresh-weepings - coming down outta his - swollen-and-surgically-stitched-shut-right-eye - was, "Yes, my brother. I did this for you and, the label. THE WHOLE CLUB is breakin' they necks! EVEN the girls dancin' on tables! I got 'em ALL lookin' up...TO Jettison Records. WE UP HERE in the - Above-The-Stage - VIP - Levels - OF THE - VIP. Pockets, my brother!! Take a look around and see! That,... we are on top of the world."

(And,...*MC Busta-Nut, just stood there hatin'!*)

And then, Pockets, turned to Busta-Nut and False Profit. Upon his head, his custom red custom-made red hat was hard to the side. 'Cause, that's the way he cocked it! Before he said, "Pay attention, YOU TWO. In THIS industry, THIS IS *HOW,* you get ahead!"

And then, Pockets, turned to Mr. Trife and he said, "Now, I'ma show YOU some love." (Handed Mr. Trife ALL that money right back!). And then, he told him, "Now. Go on. AND, create your *OWN* buzz."

And then, Mr. Trife, walked over to the railing of - The - Above-The-Stage - Levels - of the - VIP. And made it rain two grand worth of crisp hundreds. (Came down all over the stage!). And, looking up at him, was...EVERYBODY!!! In awe at what they saw. As they witnessed. As he stood there. At that railing. Located from, WAY UP above! From the stairs, that led, directly from the stage, to the - Up-Above-The-Stage-

Levels - of the - VIP. Fittingly located! NOWHERE ELSE!!! But, (take a guess!) AT THE TOP of the club!! And he did it, with, the fresh weepings of blood. And did it, while his eyes looked, like the sun, was fully ablaze!!

(And MC Busta-Nut, just stood there hatin'!!)

And then, as a new gaggle of girls, exited the stage. And, headed straight up those steps, towards the man. (Who's eyes, shown like the sun, was, fully ablaze). Mr. Trife, told Pockets, "You enjoy, I'ma check on Y.S." And, with bottle of Rozay in hand, walked on down, the - Above-The-Stage - Level - of the - VIP - steps. With Rozay bottle in hand. Mr. Trife, walked STRAIGHT OUTTA' BITCHEZ. Hatin' ass customers, tellin' the bouncers and manager! (THEY just some hatin'-ass snitches!!). But, it didn't matter. (Mr. Trife, AIN'T WORRYIN' 'BOUT some BITCH-ASS HATIN' chit-chatter!!). And, with bottle in hand. He stepped cross that parking lot like the man! To check on, his homegirl, Y.S.

Upon reaching the back of the BITCHEZ lot, Mr. Trife opens that door to Pockets' brand new RV, *and thinks to himself, "I CAN'T wait to see."(this RV, when we get back to Atlanta). Pockets gettin' this entire vehicle wrapped, black and white like a panda. (And Mr. Trife can see it all now!!). Gonna be decked-out in big white letters. So when we be gettin' down out on tour, the whole world can see, that WE are Jettison Records. And Mr. Trife is just fantasizing, that on both sides, of OUR ride, and EVEN on the roof! So that people in skyscrappers, can look down, and see that shit too!* But Trife can't see, inside the RV, and it ain't from the 24 Karat gold tint, as inside the RV, it's dark as shit. And he's callin' her name, "C'mon, Y.S.!! Quit playin'!!" (Oh yeah, she's probably listening to her OWN songs, if I know my homegirl Y.S., she's got on her headphones). And damn, where's a light switch, all up in this motorhome??? (And damn, mixin' this Rozay on top of them Oxy's, is startin' to give Mr. Trife's gate, a bit of the wobblies). As he's still feelin' good. As he's still feelin' on top of the world. As he's feeling his way through the RV's dark kitchen area, to check on his homegirl. And hmm, I guess Y.S. is way in the back? It's dark as fuck in here, she's probably just takin' a nap? And as Trife reaches Pockets' private sleeping quarters bedroom door in the back, he knocks on it lightly a couple of times, before opening it up a slight crack, while fumbling for the light, "Y.S., you good? I came to make sure my homegirl is iight". And he opens the door, while calling her name. And there's Y.S. on the floor, (on her back she's just layin'). And she's just layin', to the right of Pockets' bed. 30-06 layin' on the otherside, layin' on the floor, *from layin' cross Pockets' red custom suits, layin' cross Pockets' bed. Laid that rifle cross Pockets' suits, after she laid Pockets' suits cross Pockets' bed. Got down on her knees, beside Pockets' bed, like she was prayin'.* (DOUBT that she was. But I swear to God, I PRAY THAT SHE WAS PRAYIN'). *Then Y.S. laid her body cross the suits cross Pockets' bed. Cocked one of Pockets' custom red custom-made red hats hard to the side. On top of her head. At the tip of that 30-06 barrel, she placed her forehead. She struggled and strained, with the passion of a lover. And once she reached that trigger, she pulled that motherfucker.* (Don't nothin' kick like that, all that must have made a horrible sound). *When that deer rifle went off, sending through Pockets' hat and her head, a 30-06 round. Blood. All different sizes and shapes of her brain. Teeth. Skull-the-fuck-fragments. And most of her face. Was simply blown, all the fuck over the place. It was all the fuck over. TOLD Trife she was sick of this shit!...she just wanted it over.* Is that skull?? Holy shit!! I think that is skull!! (The ceiling of Pockets' private sleeping quarters, Trife looks up and sees up above). Too many, some bloody, some white, all jagged. From all different shapes and sizes, of Y.S.' skull fragments. Big clumps of brain everywhere. (And the more Trife stood there and looked, the more Trife became aware). Of the floor. Of the walls. Of the ceiling. Of the big pool of blood. *(That drained through Pockets' oh best believe NOW THEY'RE "custom red suits"). And drained ALL THROUGH the MATTRESS too!!* Of the more Trife inspected. STILL pooling and forming. *Of the drainage.* Under Pockets' bed it collected. *And she was only 16.* Laying there in the all red. EVERYTHANG!!! (With everythang red). On her back. What a sight. *30-06 round went through Pockets' "buttery" mobile studio mic!! Peeled off everything from the top. (Of her right). From the top of her right, cheekbone, on up.* (And I give her credit for her guts). *Y.S. took control of her life.* (By controlling when she'd be dead). *Peeled her fucking face off.* (Ever see a 16 year old female laying there like that?)...(Missing her face and her head?). You have now. Welcome to Mr. Trife's world. *And she was only 16.* And Trife *says to himself and Y.S., "They can't take you away from me, homegirl."* 'Cept for what was left. Of her right cheekbone. From her bottom lip on up. That shit was gone. *Y.S. took a hardline.* And was left with a hardline cut. (Of partial facial bones). (Beneath where her right eye socket *was).* Was only, what was left, of her facial flesh. Wasn't nothin' left to see anyway!! Brain sniglets in her long beautiful curly light brown mermaid hair. Just above the back of her neck. Were gettin' in the way. (Sorry. I lied. And try not to cry). Trife knelt down next to her, removed the 24 Karat gold lenses from his eyes. And when Trife removed her hair from what was left of her face, that's when Trife was met with inner peace and grace. For the only eye that Trife had left, was looking directly into, the only eye that Y.S. had left. Of not to cry. Do your best. Nah, it's alright now. (Go on and cry). A mix of blood and tears came from Mr. Trife's eyes. Fresh weepings of blood streamed down Trife's face. And of her face. Trife never did see it. (But its gotta be SOMEWHERE 'round this place!!). From that jagged cheekbone on down. Of what was left of her head. What a hollowed-out-mess. And laying there like that. Was his homegirl Y.S.

"Thirty. Ott. Six.", Trife, said, with the words of no breath, lowered his head, closed his eye in prayer. And down Trife's face fresh blood wept.

(Damn. Trife's gonna miss his homegirl Y.S.)

Chapter Twelve

IT AIN'T PRETTY

Looking up at Mr. Trife looking down, Pockets leans to his right, (to look past all the hair in his eyes), blocking his sight, from the stripper wit tha' platform heel behind his head, grindin' him right!

Come! (Let's have a look!)..

"You damn right we have a problem, Mr. Trife. WHY-THA'-FUCK you got my custom red custom-made red hat on for, all cocked hard to the side, cocked hard to the right??", Pockets, says in reply. Busta-Nut grindin' wit a stripper. Bust a nut? (Shiiiiiit, he's gonna try!!). False Profit gotta face full of false tits, with nipple ring spikes, fake tit in his mouth, the other tit in his right. Pockets seated there, checks out the face of Mr. Trife. (Staring at the fresh tracks of blood and tears that have dried). *After Mr. Trife re-entered BITCHEZ, got on his old Brotha Trife stroll, wearin' Pockets' custom red custom-made red hat, cocked hard to the side, cocked hard to the right, fully equipped in the front, with a bullet hole. Then back to the top of the world, in the top levels of the VIP, filled-up with nothin' but naked girls, Mr. Trife stood overtop of Pockets, (like he was standing center stage), "We have a problem.", and he told Pockets that shit, while wearin' his custom red custom-made red hat cocked hard to the side, cocked hard to the right, while his eyes shown like the sun fully ablaze.*

(Then once again, it's back out tha' door)...

Pockets, Busta-Nut and False Profit, have no idea, what they're in for. (And yeah, I know these boys are straight off the block, *and have all done some shit, and have all seen a lot*). *But Y.S. was Pockets' #1 artist*, I know he'll be in for a shock. And just as Mr. Trife is leaving BITCHEZ, some *deja vu hits him...(A bouncer stands on a top step, throws a pack of smokes, at the back, of someone's head). And he would swear that he's lived that before. As the deja vu hits him, as he's walking out the strip club door.* And then just like that. Something small falls from the sky, hitting Mr. Trife, on the top of his hat. And he *thinks to himself. That, that's been happening a lot!* And as the four continue walking towards the RV, parked at the back of the lot, *he's thinking about what he was just thinking about.* (And has no idea...*that he was just thinking about Tick-Tock!*).

"Damn, nigga! YOU coulda' left some lights on, up in this piece!", MC Busta-Nut, says for the group. (Feeding off a TRUE businessman's annoyance, for Mr. Trife). For, AND from, Pockets, having been DENIED! (What has Pockets BEEN denied?)...(His TRUE, and RIGHTFUL FULL VALUE, out of - The - Top-Of-The-Stage - Levels - of the - TOP LEVEL - of the - VIP - UPGRADE!!!)...(It's all quite that simple!). EVEN WITH, two hundred grand, in the pockets, of his, custom red custom-made red suit pants. One hundred grand in each. EACH clipped in a separate money clip! MADE FROM, illegally-poached and imported, endangered African elephant tusk ivory... (Pockets, IS STILL tight with'a nickel).

"First of all, SHUT THE FUCK UP!!!", Mr. Trife, tells MC Busta-Nut, on behalf of the group. 'Cause, the way he's feeling RIGHT ABOUT NOW??? (THEY CAN ALL shut the fuck up too!!!). And then, he continues, "It was dark as fuck up in here, for me too. What tha' fuck you want me to do??? I COULDN'T turn ON any lights!! I DON'T KNOW where any of THESE motherfuckin'-cocksuckin'-light-switches are at, up in here!!!"

"You gotta' point, Mr. Trife. Ain't NONE OF US EVER been on the road in this thing before.", Fasle Profit, chimes in, (to the "pissedoffness" and *hatery* of MC Busta-Nut!).

"I got it. I got it. I got everythang! So, I got THIS too.", Pockets, says, turning on the light switch, located on the wall, just inside, just to the left, of the RV's door.

And, as they all step up into the RV, Pockets, gets a *hint* of something! (Of what???). It's kinda' hard for him to tell. Then, turns to Mr. Trife, and, asks, *"You burn somethin'?? Rest of y'all, smell that smell???"*

And then, Mr. Trife, just lowers his head, and, says, "Pockets...you better come with me." And then, Mr. Trife, leads the way through the RV's kitchen area...followed by all three.

(And, when Mr. Trife opens Pockets' door, to Pockets' private sleeping quarters)...

The bitch comes out of Busta-Nut! *Thinkin' 'bout his court orders!* False Profit don't say shit! *BUT the look that came over his face, FALSE PROFIT WASN'T FAKIN' IT!!!* And, Pockets,... just stands there. Standing there, next to Mr. Trife, in the open door. LOOKING DOWN at HIS star! WITH HER face peeled off! Laying there LIKE that. Dead!!! ON HIS mobile studio floor!!! And, as it turns out. It was Mr. Trife. That had NO idea. What HE was IN for!!!

"YOU DID THIS!!!!!!!", Pockets, shouts, (looking up INTO the 24 Karat gold limited edition Cazel lenses, worn by - THIS - homicidal - TIER-THREE - I-shoulda'-listened-to-Phillip-Tate-he-tried-to-WARN-me-NOT-to-take-him-ON-THE-ROAD-FUCK-I-GOTTA'-READ-THOSE-FUCKIN'-READING-MATERIALS-BEFORE-I'M-NEXT - murderin' - motherfuckin' - TIER THREE - fuckin' C. TRIFE - MOTHERFUCKER!!!).

"MOTHERFUCKER!!!", False Profit, shouts, then CHARGES towards the doorway, (from standing a few feet back), to get at Mr. Trife, but is easily restrained by Pockets, the avid powerlifter, holdin' him back!

"Calm down, calm down. I got this. I got EVERYTHANG!!! So, I got THIS too.", Pockets, tells Fasle Profit. Then, once calm, releases False Profit from his grip, after gripping him up.

"SO, let me ask you somethin', MR. Trife!", Pockets, starts out, "If you DIDN'T turn on any lights, 'cause, as you've already so *eloquently said,* *"You don't know where any of these motherfuckin'-cocksuckin'-light-switches are at, up in here.* "Explain to me then, how come THIS "motherfuckin'-cocksuckin'-light", is on?!?"

"Whoa! Whoa!! Whoa!!! Pockets!!!! Hold up, brother. You gettin' waaaaaay ahead of yourself here. I DIDN'T DO THIS!!! I FOUND her LIKE this!", Mr. Trife, says in reply, pleading his case, (as False Profit, looks on with murder in his eyes!), (as MC Busta-Nut, straight WANTS, NOTHIN', to do with THIS, hangin' back, hands in pockets, don't EVEN want to see!), already gettin' - HIS-OWN-FUCK-Y'ALL - alibi ready!, (then, takes another quick-peek in tha' door, Holy Shit, Y.S.,... better YOU than ME!!!).

"BROTHER, MY ASS!!!", Pockets, shouts, (then calms down himself), and then, asks, "What about the light then?"

"Oh yeah, well,...I...I turned this one on.", Mr. Trife, confesses.

"OOOOOOOOOOOOOOHHH!!! Ok!! I see. So, YOU DID turn THIS motherfuckin-cocksuckin'-LIGHT on!! OTHERWISE, that would mean, YOU GOT - some - crazy-kinda-super-hero-night-vision-eye-sight - or some shit - AND - were able to discover her layin' on the floor, WAY-THE-FUCK-BACK-HERE-IN-THE-DARK!!!", Pockets, says, (ALL SARCASTIC and shit!)...before, *thinking to himself, "... Oh, hold up. Wait. MAYBE, HE DOES - have some - crazy-kinda-super-hero-night-vision-eye-sight - WITH - ALL THIS - MOTHERFUCKIN'-COCKSUCKIN' - "THEM PEOPLE" - X'n MOTHERFUCKERS - AND - SHIT!!! FUCK!!!!!! I GOTTA' get up with Phil on this shit!"* (But then, gathers himself). And, then continues, "So, first you didn't turn on any lights. AND THEN your story changes, to: *"Oh, yeah, well, uh, I turned this light on, Pockets."* So, why the fuck should I believe you then, Mr. Trife? That, you didn't peel this poor girl's face off?" (Then, Pockets, takes a look around), and, says, "Seems to me, it's just Y'ALL TWO, covered in blood. What tha' fuck is it WITH you? THAT, you can't seem to keep blood, off a your face?? Oh. Hold up, wait...NEVERMIND!!!"

"Wasn't you tha' one fuckin' wit that rifle, JUST LAST NIGHT, Mr. Trife!?! Gotcha' fringerprints ALL OV'A that bitch!! AIN'T lookin' too good fo' ya', homie!", False Profit, says, while recalling some shit, while breaking down shit even further.

AND THEN, here comes MC Busta-Nut, (FINALLY speaking up!), got his *ALIBI*, LINED-UP, goin' down FOR Y'ALL??? (NOT A CHANCE!!! GOT ME FUCKED UP!!!), "My nigga, ALL I KNOW is, LAST TIME I SEEN HER, SHE was walkin' WITH YOU!!! AND!!! She NEVER MADE IT, INTO tha' club!! YOU was tha' LAST ONE to SEE her ALIVE, my nigga. AND tha' FIRST ONE to KNOW she was dead. I AIN'T KNOW SHE WAS DEAD!!! Profit, AIN'T know she was dead. Tha' nigga Pockets, HE AIN'T KNOW she was dead. So, what that sound like to you, my nigga? And my nigga, WHAT-THA'-FUCK you got me, all up IN THIS TRAILER fo', wit lil' mommy's wig - PUSHED-ALL-THE-WAY - back!?! ...Mat'r fact, I ain't EVEN here, RIGHT NOW!!! *MY ASS, was up in tha' "V.I.P.'S", YOUR HONOR!!!!!!*"

"AIN'T lookin' too good FO' YA', homie!!", False Profit, speaking to Mr. Trife...(on nothin' BUT tha' TRUTH!).(Ain't that SOME shit!?!).

"Alright, alright. Calm down, calm down, y'all. And, that's ENOUGH outta' you, wit that, *"your honor"*, shit.", Pockets, tells Busta-Nut and False Profit, following it up with, "I'm Pockets. I GOT THIS!!! Ain't NOBODY goin' fo' no DAMN judge.", (before, turning his attention back on Mr. Trife), looking up into those 24 Karat gold lenses, covering his eyes, then looks up at what's perched, on top of Mr. Trife's head, wearin' HIS custom red, custom-made red hat, cocked hard to the side, cocked hard to the right, SATURATED, wit ALL KINDS of shit, comin' FULLY EQUIPPED, in the front of HIS hat, of a bullet hole of the dead! And then, Pockets, stands up straight, (this is gonna decide your fate), got his shoulders back, hard to the side, on top of HIS OWN head, HE cocks HIS OWN, custom red hat, telling Mr. Trife, as-a-matter-of-fact, "You better start makin' a whole lotta' sense."

(Under murderous and eyes of alibis), Mr. Trife, presents Pockets with a dare. To: Come enter the room with him. He wants him to see *what he saw for himself. But didn't see. 'Cause it wasn't there.* And wants him to see for himself, what he won't be able to see. 'Cause, it won't be there, for him to see either.

(Make sense?)

Well...

GO AHEAD then! AND, enter THAT room, WITH MR. TRIFE!

(If YOU dare!!!)

AND, take a look, WITH Mr. Trife, for YOURSELF!!! And, LET him, show YOU, *what HE SAW, what WASN'T there.* And, SEE if YOU can see, *what you can't see,* for yourself!!!

And, as you do, follow Mr. Trife, into THAT room, he's gonna WARN you too, as to what, YOU'RE gonna HAVE to do! (And, since you're still reading, I give YOU credit for YOUR guts!!).

AND SO...

WITH warning heeded. Then as, both you, and Mr. Trife, proceeded, is that what you NEEDED, to do, as you go, you're GONNA' damn near HAVE to, TIPTOE, into, through, and around, this - ALL-RED-EVERYTHANG - MINEFIELD - ROOM!!! (JUST to get to, Y.S.' SIDE of the bed!). Brain sniglets in clumps. Of varying shapes and sizes. Blood. Teeth. And...flesh chunks!! Will be ALL OVER this - all-red-everythang - minefield - FLOOR!!! BUT, don't YOU forget to: ALWAYS LOOK UP!!! 'Cause, ALL THAT SHIT, is ON the ceiling too!! And, if YOU ain't payin' attention, WHEN some of that shit breaks free, (and comes down!), well, it's GONNA' be YOU, NOW YOU'RE the one with, the FACE-FLESH-CHUNKS!!! AND WITH THE BRAIN SNIGLETS!!! (ALL UP in YOUR hair!!!). AND DOWN the BACK of YOUR NECK!!! ON top of YOUR head!! (But WHATEVER you do, WATCHOUT for the brain sniglets!!) (If you don't know what you should be looking for, have no fear, Mr. Trife ain't LETTING you, ain't NO turning back you see!) *DON'T turn YOUR back on MR. TRIFE!!! (WHAT THE FUCK IS WRONG WITH YOU!?!)(Turning YOUR back on Mr. Trife and shit!?)* For, Mr. Trife's got you! With, ANOTHER warning: They're kinda pink or kinda gray. Might kinda be red from blood. (And THIS next part of Mr. Trife's warning, SHOULD make YOU happy!) *They might kinda remind you of your childhood!* (AWWW). 'CAUSE, *brain sniglets, ALSO kinda look like TAFFY!!!* And, WHATEVER YOU do, DON'T STEP ON them!! OR get them ON your clothes!! (Worse than dog shit!!!) *YOU'LL have a hell of a time, diggin' them out, the bottom tread, in your shoe soles!* ('Cause, brain sniglets, are ALSO kinda STICKY and TACKY!!!) AND ALL THAT, is what, YOU'LL be SOOOOOO TUNNEL-VISIONED on! As YOU, TIPTOE through THAT room. As YOU, follow Mr. Trife. (In, painstaking-avoidance). Of the teeth, of the sniglets, the blood, the chunks AND, the lumps. And, lest we forget. You AIN'T gonna be able TO avoid… *THE SMELL!!!* BUT, WAIT!!! (THEN it's gonna hit YOU!!!!!!) THE very reason: YOU ARE IN THE ROOM. The reason in the first place. You DARED to, follow Mr. Trife into! And all this time, YOU'RE DEALING WITH ALL THIS SHIT!!! Trying YOUR best, NOT TO STEP, on the…brain sniglets. Or, on the massive blood loss. As YOU, tiptoe around facial flesh. (Shiiiiiit, YOU'RE even trying to avoid the teeth!). And, WITH ALL THIS SHIT IN YOUR HEAD… and when you see her again, you're like, oh yeah…there's a girl laying here dead. (And THAT'S the most fucked up part of it all). As Pockets hangs back a bit. Having met the dare. And heeded the warnings. And did follow Mr. Trife into THAT room. As Mr. Trife is once again…back with his homegirl Y.S.

After confirming, what he knew what he saw, *that he didn't see.* ('CAUSE, it wasn't there!). Mr. Trife, asks of Pockets, "You see, *what's missing?"*

Craning his neck to see around Mr. Trife, (not that he was really trying to get that close to Y.S.)…(OR even step into the room!), Pockets, replies as he shouts, "YEAH!!! *HER MOTHERFUCKIN'-FACE,* NIGGA!!!!!!"

"Naaaaaah! Look here…look close.", instructing Pockets, instructs Mr. Trife. Prompting Pockets, to tiptoe closer, (to a dead body).

(And then Pockets and Mr. Trife, both bend down, and, take a close look)…

At what's left of, the bottom of, Y.S.' face.

And then, Mr. Trife points out, "No tear tracks. Not a trace. Which means, *she had gotten to HER point in life, where SHE wanted to TAKE her own life.* Right here, right now. And I don't know, *if she knew…or even cared…of what she was about to do to her face. But she wanted to leave this world.* Right here and right now. *And did so...without a tear. Not one trace."*

(And then Pockets stands back up right, takes a look around his mobile studio, and actually looked more upset, when he discovered, that, *after the bullet went through and left Y.S.' head, it went through and left a bullet hole,...IN his "buttery" studio mic!)*

And then Pockets looks over at Mr. Trife, sees *the tracks of blood and tears that, ran down his face,* that had dried. And then, Big-Hustle-Gears begin to grind. Spinning inside of a Big-Hustle-Mind. (For Pockets,...just gotta alter his plan!). The plan of this - gamblin' man. ('Cause the world DON'T stop spinnin', over some dead girl). *Just 'cause, SHE was READY to leave,* THAT DON'T MEAN, I'M READY to leave THIS LIFE,... AT the TOP of the world!! (And yeah, that's fucked up)...(BUT!!!)... The music industry: DON'T GIVE A FUCK!!! (And, because of THAT fact!), Pockets, takes his eyes off of Y.S. Then, looks at False Profit and, at MC Busta-Nut. Then, looks at Mr. Trife. And, THAT'S WHEN he decides...Mr. Trife IS the next man up!(OY VEY!!).

(Come. LET'S have a look AT this shit!)...

"Alright, you two. Y'all go have a seat up front and, light one up. DON'T go outside!! And, DON'T BE burnin' MY seats!!! I gotta have a word, with Mr. Trife.", Pockets, tells his two rappers.

"I'M sittin' in the DRIVER'S SEAT!!!", MC Busta-Nut, tells False Profit, (as if False Profit really gives a shit right about now!). With, right about now, being the first time since being shown Y.S. laying there, dead like that, that, MC Busta-Nut has shown as if, he really gives a shit,... about ANYTHING at all.(Damn).

And so...

(Pockets, watches the two, as they make their way back through the RV's kitchen area, back to the front. And, once he sees, MC Busta-Nut, taking a seat behind the wheel, Pockets closes that door, to his mobile studio)...

AND THEN...

It's back to business!

(Blood and whatever else - is-and-may-be - on THIS floor - be damned!)

FOR...

Pockets, walks straight cross that - all-red-everythang - MINEFIELD - floor, leans over Y.S. and...STARTS RUNNIN' HER POCKETS!!!

"What the HELL you doin', Pockets!!! LET her rest, man.", Mr. Trife, laments, (transfixed with, what HE decides and, deems to, be: "THAT BULLSHIT"!!!).

With no slow down, AND with NO care, Pockets, continues to run through Y.S.' pockets! Moving and manipulating her body! AS she's laying there dead like that! But, progress needs to be made, so the follow words, Pockets, does say, "Yeah, so, well, anywaaaaaays, she had this thumb drive that she wanted me to have...you know...in case ANYTHING ever happened to her! Have you seen it? *Y'all two, were rappin' for a minute there, in the back of the RV. She ever mention anything 'bout a thumb drive, to you???*"

"Naaaaaaaaaaaaah, I ain't seen it. What?? She got HER lyrics saved on it or somethin'?", Mr. Trife PISSED, as he's replyin', looking down upon his homegirl, (having her pockets ran!) and, KNOWIN' POCKETS' LYIN'!!!

"Nope. *Her music. Ten tracks. All instrumentals.* Songs we were both working on together, right after I signed her to Jettison Records. I invested heavily into those tracks! Paid for everything MYSELF, straight outta my OWN pockets!", Pockets, gives his account.

"Is that right??? Naaaaaah, Pockets, she ain't never mention a thumb drive to me. *Yeah, me and Y.S. was rappin'...she was sayin' somethin' 'bout her contracts being fucked up.*", deflects, Mr. Trife.

And on that note...

(Still all bent over and hunched, Pockets pops his head straight up, from looking down and through, Y.S.' pockets, EVEN halting the PROCESS, of the running of the pockets! Which you just KNOW,

Pockets HATED to do! BUT, I can make A LOT of money with Mr. Trife)...

So...

This TRUE "music industry businessman"...has to prioritize!

(Come. Let's listen in!)...

"I KNOW *she wasn't talkin' 'bout*, MY contract guy!?", Pockets, persuasively states, damn near, "leading the witness", HOPING *that she wasn't*, (but FOR Pockets!), this IS top priority, ON a need-to-know basis, AND Pockets NEEDS-TO-KNOW, so he needs-to-know *IF she was!* (And he needs-to-know RIGHT NOW!!!).

"Naaaaaaaaah, *she wasn't even talkin' 'bout you OR your contract guy.* WHOEVER he is??? Why? YOU know WHO I'm talkin' 'bout or somethin'?!? *ALL Y.S., was really talkin' 'bout, was, somethin' 'bout, being charged a WHOLE LOTTA' MONEY, for her contracts, that were drafted-up. AND, HOW, her contract guy, turned out-to-be - NOTHIN' - but a RIPOFF artist!",* Mr. Trife, replies, gettin' tha' hang of this "music industry SHIT", MAKIN' SHIT UP,...on the sly!

AND (on THAT note!)...

The "Oh." (of relief, AND), of pleasant-surprise, comes out the mouth of Pockets, in relief, in reply, BEING pleasantly-surprised! (And AS it does, THAT'S the time, that, Pockets is realizing, that, THAT SHIT, JUST came out of my mouth!!!). AND of how, IT MUST HAVE been received! (BECAUSE, I KNOW, the way it sounded!). And so and then and now, it's time to clean THAT shit up...Pockets is realizing! And, in NO time, Big-Hustle-Wheels, of a: Big-Hustle-Mind, begin to grind. As, Pockets, gets RIGHT BACK into a: *"PREVIOUS-phantom-conversation"*, with Mr. Trife. *(As if, the two, were in a previous conversation, to begin with!)*...OF WHICH, *he's ABOUT to start getting BACK, to him about!* With, Pockets, playing as if, AND playing Mr. Trife, *like, Mr. Trife, was JUST STANDING THERE, ON HOLD! Just waitin' ON: "The Speakers' CONVIENCE"!!! LIKE, as if he told, Mr. Trife, "I'll be back to finish telling you, of WHAT I began, telling you earlier."* (BUT, until then, *YOU JUST WAIT RIGHT HERE!*)...(Yeah, just like that!). THAT'S how Pockets IS playing it! AND playing Mr. Trife...alike. (Kinda insulting really. STRAIGHT playin' Mr. Trife, like, HE WON'T pick up on the fact, THAT, it's ALL bullshit!) And, as Pockets plays it, he works THE SHIT, OUTTA' HIS bullshit! (With, just the VERY presentation of HOW, Pockets BEGINS!). The: *"getting back to"*, of: *"THEIR"*, *"previous-phantom-conversation."* Played it, AND Mr. Trife, *like, and as if, Mr. Trife, WANTED to know, OF the "continuance", of some shit, HE was NEVER EVEN IN, a conversation with, or was having with Pockets, IN THE FIRST PLACE, for Pockets, TO EVEN, get back to him ABOUT!!!* (POCKETS GOT SOME SHIT TO HIM!!!)...(Don't he though!?).

AND SO...

(With NO shame, OR threat, of "insulation", to Mr. Trife)...(OR, to his intelligence!)...

Pockets, (does JUST that!), as he gets back, as Pockets, continues..., "Yeah, so, well, anywaaaaaays, AS I was sayin',...*you can't take it personal, when someone in the music industry, doesn't call you back."*...(WAIT!!! WHAT??? WHEN THE FUCK WERE WE TALKIN' 'BOUT THAT!?!) (SEE what I mean??)(OY FUCKIN' VEY!)..."THAT'S JUST THE WAY IT IS, MR. TRIFE!!! HAPPENS all the time. USED TO,...happen to me, TOO! THAT'S, just the music biz, for ya'. You feel me? Mr. Trife, WHATEVER you hear in THIS industry, EXCEPT FROM ME, just think the COMPLETE opposite!! 'Cause,...it ain't happenin'! And, you'll NEVER get THAT phone call, or text, or email, from them. AND, you WANNA' KNOW why??? 'CAUSE, everybody's lyin'!!! Yeah...so, well, anywaaaaaays, as I was sayin', don't read into all that. As, a matter-of-fact, I DON'T want you reading into anything. And, quiet frankly, Mr. Trife, I DON'T want you reading ANYTHING at all. YOU, BE the artist! And, write me, uh, US, a hit song. You be the artist, that, I'm gonna be PAYING YOU, HANDSOMELY, to be! And, I'LL take care of ALL the reading, FOR you. I'LL get you there. Stick with me! Yeah, uh, so, well, anywaaaaaays, I have an excellent contract guy. NOTHIN'

LIKE, Y.S.', contract guy. MY GUY, is the BEST, in THE BUSINESS! I'll have Phillip Tate make some introductions, once we return to Jettison Records. I'll delegate that off to Phil, to see to it, that, ALL the contracts you'll be needing, do so, in fact, get drafted-up in YOUR favor. You know, the royalties, the LLC's, etc., etc., etc. I'ma businessman. YOUR businessman. LET ME handle, the: "business-side-of-things" - for you. And, YOU JUST write hit songs! Record. And, perform them. Simple. You feel me? YOU WON'T have to WORRY 'bout transportation! Where tha' fuck YOU'LL be staying?? Is it five stars? OR, is it a four star hotel? WE'LL have ALL THAT covered for you! YOU feel me!?! WHICH, reminds me...", (and then, just like that, Pockets, immediately goes into one of his pockets. And, retrieves his cell phone. And IMMEDIATELY starts scrolling-down-through his MANY contacts!). All the while, and while and, AT THE SAME TIME, he's explaining to Mr. Trife, (the efficiency of business!), that, "I'm going to connect with PHILLIP, right now!! And, see WHERE he's at, with solidifying a venue UP in Pa., for YOU, MC Busta-Nut's AND False Profit's: "Meet N' Greet Show"!!"

AND...

Pockets, does it all, all the while (and while!), WHILE both of his feet, ARE on BOTH sides OF Y.S.!! (STRADDLING THE POOR GIRL!!!!!!).

All the while (and while!)...

(Standing there - ALL-HUNCHED-THE-FUCK - overtop of her - LIKE that!)...

AS...

All the while (and while!)...

(Pockets, is STILL in, the, VERY SAME position, of the: running of the pockets!)...

ALL THE WHILE (AND WHILE!!!)...

Being watched, (WITH AND BY!), that one eye, that,...Y.S. has left.

AS...

(ALL THIS TIME!!!)...

Y.S.,...is still laying THERE prone! (TOLD Y'ALL POCKETS GOT SOME SHIT TO HIM!!!!!!).

"Right, now? REALLY, my dude?? It CAN'T wait, 'til LATER!?!", A - couldn't-be-more-DISGUSTED - Mr. Trife, asks, of Pockets, (OF his bottomless soul). And, it ain't got nothin' to do, with all - the kinda' grayish-pink-and-tacky - brain sniglets, (the reason being!), all-up-under AND IN, (the bottom of the soles), of his Jimmy Choo's.(Oy Vey!).

Standing back up straight, (while STILL), straddling the poor girl, Pockets, looks into those 24 Karat gold lenses and, directly tells Mr. Trife, "Business, AIN'T pretty. But, yeah, IT CAN wait, til' later!", (then, looks down, at his pants pocket) , as he, puts his cell phone back inside! Then, looks right back up into, those 24 Karat gold lenses, that he gave Mr. Trife, (TO cover his eyes!)(Hmm).

Then...

(Cocks his custom red custom-made red hat, hard to the side)...

And...

GETS RIGHT BACK TO, THE RUNNING OF THE POCKETS!!!!!!

Chapter Thirteen

MIC CHECK

It's all just a matter of opinion, opinion based on perception, perception based on one's mentality, one's mentality, for which they stand. Summoned by Pockets to return, though and through, no dare to meet, with no warning to heed, MC Busta-Nut and False Profit, for reasons of their own, for in their own minds, as for, and as to why, they have agreed, have done just that, and have returned to, THAT room. For which they stand. For which they ALL stand. As MC Busta-Nut and False Profit, stand there next to Mr. Trife, in THAT room. And, for Mr. Trife too. For he is not immune. To what's right and to what's wrong. And to get along, sometimes in life, you got to go along. Even if you KNOW it's wrong! And that's what he wrestles with in his Tier-Three-Mind, *under that HOT washrag,* top-shelf opiates AND top-shelf champagne, and all this death and blood at his feet, *got him feelin' like a sunny day when it rains.* As he stands overtop of AND on, the tacky-taffy-sniglets, of HIS homegirl's brain! As he's been awake and seen and heard and learned and observed, enough now to know, with this music shit, it's all just BUT a game. And, the ONE thing, that, he knows, he AIN'T tryna be wearin' no more ripped-up and tattered clothes! And so, I'ma stand here. And listen. And, then, MY path, I'LL choose! 'CAUSE, I ain't tryna be *STUCK* no more, LIKE, what's stickin' to the bottoms of these Jimmy Choo's!! And so, as they stand, AND, for WHICH they stand, REMAINS, dependant upon, their OWN individual mentality. Whether or not, for each one of the four, as they all are, as they currently do so, stand in the same room, and if so, they're actually standing, in the same room at all. For one's mentality, can be a wicked thing, a wicked place, and can be, based on, so many different fucked-up factors, that one has experienced in their lifetimes, or have been the victim thereto. As to why, they can all be standing in the very same room, but yet, can still be standing there, all alone. So can any one of the four, really be at fault, or faulted, or blamed, for their OWN opinion, of their OWN perception, for their OWN mentality, for which they stand, as they stand, together, all four collectively, concurrently, but yet, individually, as they all stand alone? As for False Profit, for which he stands, False Profit is standing, in the back private sleeping quarters of a luxury RV, *a room in which and where, quite possibly, a homicide has occurred,* just not too long ago. As for Mr. Trife, for which he stands, stands in *a room where a 16-year-old female,* not just ANY 16-year-old female mind you, but, HIS homegirl, Y.S., *where she, just laid a deer rifle cross a bed, and, blew her fucking head off.* As for Pockets, he knows EXACTLY where HE stands! As Pockets stands in HIS mobile studio, and might I add, *a mobile studio, where HIS "buttery" studio mic, has been damaged by a bullet hole.* And as for MC Busta-Nut, well, for which HE stands, MC BUSTA-NUT has NO opinion on the matter! HIS perception of things, from where HE stands, HE'S not EVEN standing in the room, NEVER EVEN WAS in the room, AND, mat'r fact, *HE don't EVEN know WHAT-THE-FUCK THEY'RE TALKIN' 'BOUT, YOU HONOR!!!* As far as HE'S concerned, HE DON'T GIVE A FUCK, if for THOSE THREE, for which THEY stand, if the three of THEM, are standing in, a private sleeping quarters, a mobile studio, *or a room where some 16-year-old girl placed a deer rifle cross a bed, and, blew her fucking head off, OR, as it may be the case, if for THOSE THREE, THEY are actually standing in, a homicide scene.* HOWEVER, having been given and complied with the directives of Pockets, Busta-Nut and False Profit, returned back to the back of that RV, to stand collectively, concurrently, as they, stand there in THAT room, next to Mr. Trife. And it's CRYSTAL CLEAR, to ALL three, individually, from THEIR perceptions, standing there together, collectively, concurrently, EXACTLY, where THEY stand with Pockets. As all three, collectively, concurrently, stand before the barrel of that 30-06. As Pockets stands there. Before them? Or in front of them? Either way that it's perceived, Pockets stands there, standing behind the trigger of that gun.

"Alright now, and LISTEN UP my people! WE, have a situation here, US, together. THIS, RIGHT HERE, is "gut check time". And, I'M checkin' each and every one of ya'! Y'all ALL wanted IN ON this "music industry shit". Y'all ALL wanted to make it big, and, to be a STAR. AND, ALL Y'ALL, signed on with Jettison Records. And by signin' on with Jettison Records, let me tell you somethin', you ALL, have signed on with ME! You wanna LIVE this life?? You want the tricked-out Audis, to drive through your hoods, to park out in front of the studios, to make everybody think that you're REALLY doin' some shit special??", Pockets, addresses the three, lined-up side-by-side-by-side, (like some fucked-up firing squad line), while Pockets, points that rifle at them, straight from the hip, then takes a look around HIS mobile studio, (making sure to keep his rifle fixed "down range"), and then gets a glance at HIS "buttery" studio mic, as he then, standing there with that rifle in hand, checks it out, the one fixed with a bullet hole, the one mic chosen and favored by ANY artist "in-the-know", (THAT wants to make THEIR voice sound "buttery"), and then, gets right back at it, as he once again, fixes his eyes "down range", as he continues to, shoot from the hip, "Well, I'M here to tell YOU, THAT SHIT, comes wit a cost! And so, here at Jettison Records, I'ma show ALL Y'ALL, how it REALLY go down!"

AND SO...

(As MC Busta-Nut and False Profit, remain as motionless as Y.S.)...

Mr. Trife, has a smirk in his eye, BEHIND those 24 Karat gold lenses, of Cazel's limited edition. As, he knows, FIRST HAND, what the other two don't! Though, THAT Bolt Action 30-06, currently has a round in it's breech, each one, concurrently, as we stand, one can die, but, not one of each! And, BESIDES, that bolt action has seen no action, though tragic, yet, *that 30-06 round went through Y.S.' head with no traction.* And so, (and, as such!), Pockets, ain't killin' not one of us! So, it's THOSE TWO that, HE'S foolin'! 'Cause, I ain't see no spent shell casing, down on the floor, amongst and with the teeth, the blood, (NOW beginning to turn dark AND stink!), as, it's coagulating right before my eye, down on this rug! NOR stuck, to and in, as it, just possibly, would be to see, sticking out of, as if, IF it were, *stuck* to and in, the sniglets and ruin! And so, since I'm an entertainer now,...I'LL entertain this shit! AS, 'Nut and profit, NOT in the know, HAVE NOW become, MY entertainment! SO, Pockets, can go on foolin' THOSE TWO some more being fooled!! BUT, I KNOW, ONLY a fool, entertains, some foolishness! (Damn, this music shit, is a FUCKED-UP game!).

And so...

Then Pockets, continues doing, what he LOVES to do, (and that's hear himself talk!), "You see, gentlemen, the way it works in the world, if you're in the right hunting cabin, during the right hunting season, with the right people, then, THAT'S HOW, you get ahead in the world. THAT'S how, you get that promotion and, KEEP GETTIN' those promotions! THAT'S how, you MOVE UP in the world! Fortunately, or...unfortunately, as the case may be, for ALL of you, we're not standing in some hunting cabin, way-the-fuck-up in Mercer County somewhere, wearin' orange hats and, huntin' turkeys! Though, you are in the right room with the right man. As fate,...WOULD have it, all of you, ARE standing here WITH ME, in this bloody fuckin' mess of MY mobile studio. WHICH, really ain't doin' me no good, right now! 'Cause THIS GIRL HERE shot a hole in my microphone! You see, gentlemen, there's several things a man should be able to do. And, several things, a man SHOULD be able to do, WITHOUT doing something at all.", Pockets, states, of facts and vagueness.

"Like what???", False Profit, asks, after he, and MC Busta-Nut, look to one another for the answer. ('CAUSE, unlike MC Busta-Nut,...False Profit would actually like to know!).

"Like pour oil in your engine, without using a funnel, or without spilling a drop.", Mr. Trife, replies, smirkin', behind those 24 Karat eyes.

Snapping his head towards Mr. Trife, (with a look of surprise!), Pockets, replies, "Yeah! That's right!! Ok, Mr. Trife, *you WERE payin' attention.*", (and then Pockets, with *the feeling of pride, with his ego off the charts, FULLY, in love with himself,* for and with, *PROOF POSITIVE,* that, *all his - Grindin'-Gear-Talk - back at his - all red everythang office - with, Mr. Trife, DID make it's way through that HOT washrag, placed on top of that Tier-Three-Brain!),* and does so ask, while pointing his gun at MC Busta-Nut's gut...checkin' it, enjoying himself fully, fuckin' wit heads, fuckin' wit minds, lovin' every second of it, listening to himself talk, while fuckin' wit the minds, while gettin' INTO their minds, (the conformity of it all!), "MC Busta-Nut, you're first. What do YOU think, we should do, with Y.S.?"

Nervous and shit, MC Busta-Nut blurts out, "My nigga, whatever the fuck you tell me to do, my nigga!"

"Good answer. But I want to know, what YOU think, WE should do with Y.S.!?", Pockets, explains.

Thinkin' 'bout his parole, *(and how the charges got bumped down after he "rolled"),* and how, now, his P.O. got him on a "tight-leash probabtion", *(after, that beating he took, back at the station!),* and, of how, he ain't tryna' be back in tha' box, (under key and lock!), all Busta-Nut, is really thinkin' 'bout, is how, *he shouldn't have EVEN left the state of Georgia, (in the FIRST DAMN PLACE!!!),* and so, thinks to himself, that, he just wants to make ALL THIS go away, (AND FAST!), and how, he ain't gon' let Y.S.' stupid-ass, ruin his chance at riches and fame! And so, MC Busta-Nut, replies, "Pockets, my nigga, I say we dump this bitch out in the parking lot! And let's just get the fuck outta here!"

"Hmm. If THAT'S what YOU think is best. Ok, then, False Profit, what say YOU? We dumpin' this bitch out in tha' parking lot, like your boy says? You down wit that?? You down wit Jettison Records? You down wit tha' way "certain thangs" GOTTA' go down, HERE at Jettison Records?", Pockets, checking in with False Profit on the subject, gun barrel fixed on False Profit's gut,...checkin' it!

Nervous and shit, with ALL THAT, murderous look in his eyes, leavin' REAL quick, when that gun, on Pockets' hip, is pointed right at HIS gut,...checkin' it, False Profit, well, says what he HAS TO SAY, to survive, 'cause sometimes you gotta go along to get along, TO JUST GET BY, "Um, yeah, yeah, I like THAT idea, Pockets. I'm down wit THAT shit! Yeah, what Busta-Nut just said! Yeah, let's just roll-her-ass ON OUT the RV door, let her fall down on that parking lot below. AND LET'S GET THA' FUCK OUTTA' HERE!!!"

"I see. I see. If THAT'S what YOU think is the best option for US to do. You can't think of ANYTHING else?? Anything else at all??? That would be best for US and for Jettison Records? Nothin' else at all comes to your mind, huh? Ok, then, False Profit, if that's the BEST that can come outta your mouth, well then, hey, that's the best you got.", Pockets, says to False Profit, (fully enjoying himself!), before turning the gun on Mr. Trife, 30-06 deer rifle pointed directly at Mr. Trife's gut,...checkin' it, straight from his hip, and then continues, as he continues to shoot from the hip, "Ok, then, Mr. Trife, what say YOU on the subject?"

Checkin' Mr. Trife's gut??

Well?...

HE'S gonna let YOU know!

For...

Mr. Trife, AIN'T right in the head! (And,...ain't tryna' be!).

And he, STEPS to Pockets. *And SNATCHES that gun outta his hands!* And, says, *"First of all, don't you EVER in YOUR motherfuckin'-cocksuckin'-life, point ANOTHER motherfuckin' GUN AT ME!!!"*, before, Mr. Trife, *levels off that rifle, right at Pockets' eye, and, pulls the trigger,* to a False Profit and MC Busta-Nut flinch! As Mr. Trife and Pockets, share and enjoy a good laugh, with that same feel-good-feel, *they both shared together on the porch, back at the ranch. Though,* Pockets is laughing at the boys expense!! (*As, Pockets, IS reassured, THAT, Mr. Trife is the RIGHT man, TO SEND into North Juarez!*). As, MC Busta-Nut and False Profit, DON'T EVEN KNOW what to think, and don't give a fuck what ANYBODY says. *MR. TRIFE IS CRAZY!!!* ...(Until, Mr. Trife, *LET'S THEM KNOW* just that!).

Come! (Let's have a look!)…

"The gun ain't loaded boys! Well, NOT with a live round, anyway! Y'all some funny motherfuckers! Yeah, ok. *Gangstas!!*", Mr. Trife, *chastises* the boys, (none-the-least-bit-happy with the two, that, *THEY were JUST willin' to, throw Y.S. away LIKE trash!!!*), as he, ejects that spent shell casing, as he, opens the breech, as it, made a loud "CLACK", as he, ran that bolt action back, as that, spent shell casing got perfectly *stuck,* as it, *stuck* out of, as it, got *stuck* in, a thick dark glob of "jellified" coagulated blood, down on, that HORRIFIC-TOOTH-FILLED-MINEFIELD-RUG, disturbing, like a for-no-reason rash, and so, as it, was so "puzzling-seen", like a, perfectly-cut-potato-square, stickin' out of a glob of hash!

"Bring it in boys, bring it in. HUDDLE UP!!!", as Pockets, as the Head Coach, did so begin, under a skull-fragment-imbedded-ceiling, as False Profit and MC Busta-Nut do just that, DOING as they're told, and do bring it in, and do huddle up with, Pockets and Mr. Trife. And then, Pockets, joins Mr. Trife, in HOLDING THAT 30-06, as he, tells, his: Two - *(I-don't-know-what-to-think-at-this-point - 'BOUT-this-music-industry-shit!)* - Rappers, to hold that 30-06, just the very same. And then, Pockets, *recites some crazy-ass-shit, in SOMEONE'S name!!!!!!* (And, in doing so, *TURNS the TIDE, IN ALL THREE of their brains. EVEN the Tier-Three-Mind!).* With, THAT - *"Recitation"* - of some - *Crazy-Ass-IN-Someone's-Name - Ritualistic - Music Industry - SHIT!!!!!!!*…(THEE *conformity* of it all:(…While, he then, TELLS them all, that, "NOW, we're all in it TOGETHER!!! Me AND Y'ALL!!! …JUST THE SAME!!!"

THE brainwashing:

(Pockets, *implements*), That: *WE ALL got our fingerprints ON this gun - Shit!*

(And Pockets, *uses*), That: *WE ALL done-stepped on Y.S.' brain sniglets - (AND whatever THE FUCK else - ALL THOSE - chunky-lookin'-fleshy-residuals - ARE supposed to be) - Shit!!*

(And Pockets, followed that up, *with*), That: *NOW we ALL have Y.S.' BLOOD on OUR hands - Shit!!!*

(And Pockets, *EVEN CAME WITH*), THAT: *HOW, after he's done tellin' them, what he's 'BOUT to tell them, (of how THEY'RE ALL gonna follow his lead and),...lick their fingers clean! - SHIT!!!!*

('Cause, after all,...how bad DO YOU want it?)...(WELL??)

AND SO...

With, all their hands AND fingerprints all over that gun. With, Y.S.' blood, on ALL OF their hands, Pockets, can now begin...

"Alright y'all, listen up! AND pay attention! 'Cause, THIS is how WE gon' play this shit! My team, my studio, my music! So, I CAN make the rules up AS I go along, HOWEVER-tha'-fuck-PLEASES and BENEFITS ME!!! And besides, WHAT-THA'-FUCK - y'all gon' do, 'bout it?!? THAT IS, if y'all, still WANT "IN" on this, "music industry shit"!?! So, I'M callin' an audible on, this - "Road-Trip-Meet-'N-Greet" - since, Y.S. here, FLAKED-THA'-FUCK-OUT, on us all! So, what we gon' do is, WEEZ still gon' have our show. 'Cause, I'M STILL gon' lookout for y'all! And, weez still gon' have our "Meet 'N Greet". And, Y.S. here, she's STILL gon' come wit us...AND be RIGHT THERE wit us! BUT, will you LOOK AT her fuckin' head?!? ...THIS IS FUCKIN' PERFECT!!!!!! At the show, Busta-Nut and Profit, y'all gonna go out first and be the opening act, for our headliner here, Y.S.. Y.S., is gonna be backstage... you know, warming-up her vocals,...sippin' on hot tea and shit. AND, right in the middle OF Y'ALLS' hit song, Y.S. backstage, WELL, she's GONNA' GET SHOT IN HER FACE - by some - LUNATIC - "stalker-fan-type" - gunmen! AND,...*VOILA!!!* NOBODY goes to jail, AND we "CREATE A BUZZ", FOR Jettison Records!!!!!! SO, does POCKETS, got you?? OR, does POCKETS, GOT YOU!! NEVER said,...it was, gon' be easy. Never said, it was, gon' be PRETTY!! BUT, if you're down for whatever, AND you do, WHATEVER you're told, WHEN YOU'RE TOLD, well, at the end of the day, and, at the start of THAT bitch, YOU TOO, WILL BE, "IN" this music industry! And, YOU TOO, will have some coins, in YOUR account! SO,...if you're down wit me,...IF you're down wit Jettison Records,...*sign your names cross Y.S.' body,* WIT YO' bloody-ass-fingers...AND THEN,...LICK THEM SHITZ CLEAN!!! *DO IT NOW!!!!!!"*

(And then,...*that's what they all did)*...

As...

Pockets, stood there. *And, watched them all do it.* FULLY IN LOVE WITH HIMSELF!!! (*WITH, AND, OF,...*"the conformity" of their minds!)...

As they...

ALL then,...*SIGNED THEIR NAMES IN BLOOD!!!*

AND(THEN!)...

Behind THAT, closed mobile studio door, (in THAT - *massive-bloodloss-WHAT-THE-FUCK-AM-I-STEPPIN'-ON - WHERE-THE-FUCK-IS-THE-REST - OF-HER-BRAIN-AND-FACE??? - mobile music studio* - of Pockets)...

Pockets, the man, draped in ALL RED EVERYTHANG, STOOD there. And, WATCHED them,...*do that and more!* (THAT: Jettison Records - *Ritualistic - The-Music-Industry-IS-Creepy* - SHIT). ...*In SOMEONE'S name!* (The CONFORMITY of it all). SHAMEFUL. SHAMELESS. *AND,...WITH NO SHAME!!!*

AS...

The all-too-eager - too-moldable - too-easily-influenced - BUT - "LUCKY-ENOUGH" - to EVEN be IN this position - OF BEING IN - the "right hunting cabin", *ALL SIGNED THEIR NAMES IN BLOOD,* (for, The: "THE."). ...THE riches and fame.

('Cause, after all,...HOW BAD DO *YOU* WANT IT!!!!!!).

Chapter Fourteen

BLUE DIAMONDS
IN SAWDUST

And so, they continued on. All in it together. *With foul shit done. Massive amounts of drugs done too! TO KEEP 'EM in, (and for the purpose of!), more need and love in the boss.* But hey, like the man in all red say, *"THAT SHIT, comes WIT a cost!!!"* AND SO, up the East Coast they go. (CAN YOU handle THIS life on the road??) All four of them. Manipulation and sin! *WITH, foul-shit done.* But maybe not so much by each one of 'em. (Doesn't really matter, anyway. Does it really matter, anyway??) 'Cause, this one fact, remains as such: THE WAY Jettison Records *gets DOWN - IS - creepy-as-fuck!!* (But, hey, *THAT'S the music industry, fo' ya'!) GET ON BOARD!!! YOU SEE HER dead on tha' floor! ('Cause, IN THIS BIZ, ain't NO SUCH THING, as motherfuckin' luck!!).* And so. Now. They're ALL in it together! Blood on hands. Blood on their tongues. With dead body juices...*FROM the FOUL SHIT they had done!* 'Cause, *this - "music industry shit" - IS NOT -* just a way of life. *THIS IS YOUR LIFE NOW!!! AIN'T no playin' in THIS music industry shit! DON'T get in this shit for fun!* And, if you make a couple of coins... well, hey, for YOU, then, ALL THE BETTER!!! *BUT, with FOUL-SHIT - RITUALISTIC-SHIT - "MUSIC-INDUSTRY-SHIT", already done, IN*

"SOMEONE'S" NAME, well, hey, - MIGHT AS WELL - NOW GO OUT AND GET THIS CHEDDAR!!!!!!

And up the East Coast they have arrived, did it under a midnight black sky, Pockets and them, well, hey, we'll get back to them, for I'M talkin' 'bout, Heavy Duty and HIS crew! *As they've left the plush life, of the oranges and reds that wane into a starry night, to seek out and to find, his long lost brother...Brotha Trife!! (Damn, what would Nephew think? If he only knew, that his one and ONLY true UNCLE, was now DOWN with, AND runnin' wit, THIS crew!). Yacht docked some place. Got to North Juarez someway.* C'mon girls, follow me, Heavy Duty be 360! I got the lay-up and lay-low place! And, well,...*old habits die hard as you know.* So we'll start lookin' for my Uncle tomorrow,...or,...the next day or so...but, as for right now, on THIS day, and besides, *AFTER that LONG boat ride,* I feel like stoppin' by my ol' peoples Legs' place,...fo' a taste!

(The reasoning AND bargaining of it all! IN one's mind! 'Cause, after all,...*THAT'S HOW BAD YOU WANT IT!!!)*

Arriving at Legs', do you know the spot? Cross from the post office, where the back door is kept locked? (You remember now?)...(Don't you!?). That third floor apartment. *Out the window hung a key, where Unc caught it, down on the corner, when Nephew let it drop. Then 'round back, used the key to get in. Then up those back wooden steps.* (Can't you hear them now, *with each step of the warning creekin'?).* You know the place! *Where the outside seemed like the inside. Where the walls, of the halls, of the interior, sure seemed to be,* (well, it sure seemed to me!), that, *THESE walls, should have been, and, maybe WOULD have been, brick and window sills,...of the exterior!* Yeah! THAT funky place!! (BETCHA' CAN *still smell that old musk!). Where evil lurked, 'round each cornered-hall, hidden, latent, and when you would walk on by, that shadowy-evil, BEHIND YOUR BACK, would REACH out and touch!* YOU know the place! YES YOU!!! *Where it JUST had some SHIT to itself!! And the more you walked, felt like a presence was stealth, but there you were, ALL ALONE, in them halls, WITH nobody else!* You remember the halls, *those narrow white halls? Where they just kept going and going, and kept going and going, until they ran, straight into, another white wall! And then just like that, you're bangin' yet another hard right. Takes you forever to get there, but, hey, yet to you, it was worth the walk. And yet, for you, they were there, you were oblivious AND too damn ignorant, that YOU NEVER heeded the warning, from those old creeky wooden stairs.* Yeah, THAT place! THAT PLACE is *stuck* in YOUR head!! (I know YOU remember THAT shit, right?). *As you continue on, you're thinking, that you're pretty sure, this place don't look THIS big from the outside does it?* And then with either and or both, the endurance of man, and or and with, the patience from up above. *Is that why you made it, as you FINALLY reach that door you're there for? For, waiting for you behind THAT door, is that of what you were in love?* You know the one, right? YEAH YOU DO, *afFIXed with the No.33! If need be,...YOU'D crawl!!* I KNOW YOU DON'T WANT TO REMEMBER, AIN'T THAT RIGHT, *on the third floor, at the end of yet another long narrow white hall?* (Well, THAT'S the place WHERE...Heavy Duty put ALL on hold:(SO that he COULD go get himself a *taste!* And with that key, enters, Heavy Duty. In tow, with HIS gaggle of girls! *(Came up to do right! AND, find his Unc, BROTHA TRIFE!!!).* But, as you all know...*hard habits die hard...*so it's back to this 33 world.

"Alright girls...keep it down...can't knock on the door...OR Legs, WILL BE throwin' MORE than a fit!", as Duty, says it.

Key in door.

"Hmm. NOW ain't that some shit!? Locks were never changed. And the key, it still fits!", Heavy Duty *in thought, as he begins,* (then, *gets back to it, after a bit),.... "I KNOW, my boy, Legs,...must STILL BE hidin' out, up in here! EVEN THOUGH, ain't no one, GOT SHOT through the door, yet! It's quiet in here,...hmm,...if I know, MY BOY, Legs,...he MUST BE on them Benzos - IN HIS bedroom - IN THE back! Hmm,...hope, THAT means,... Legs, got his "works", out on the table,...YEAH, HE DO!!! ...AND witha' candle, STILL flickerin'! I KNEW, my boy, Legs, WOULDN'T disappoint! Legs, GOT tha' table FILLED, with, ALL the fine FIXin's!!"*

..."Alright girls,...keep quiet,...Legs, is knocked-out on his back. Which, SHOULD keep him stayin' back in the back...ON HIS back - IN - the back bedroom.", Heavy Duty, says, from the living room, (as he, comes from the back bedroom!), *(as his, shadow morphs of doom!!), (AS IF, HIS shadow WAS on shrooms!!!), FROM THAT - candle's flickerin' -* as HE, RETURNS to the kitchen!

..."Alright girls,...Legs stays, being: *"back-at-it"*. 'Cause he's, *STILL stayin' ON them BENZOS!"*, as Heavy Duty, let's the girls know,..."Hmm. BUT he, left ALL of his shit, ON *the turning table.* Mi casa, su casa, your shit, *IS MY shit!"* (FUCK LEGS!!!)...*('Cause, THAT'S the way it goes!).*

AND SO, (this is what, Heavy Duty, propose)...

"Gidget, we'll get to Parkinson's City and, we'll find my Unc... tomorrow,...or the next day. But FIRST, let's all *spike-up,*...you know,... *KNOCK-OFF some rust!* Hmm,...MAYBE, that's the REAL reason why,...I came back up? SO, let's ALL get a *taste!* And, by the time...them Benzos - Legs shakes,...we woulda' already done-up ALL of his...my bad, MORE LIKE - *MY SHIT,*...and, GOT-THE-FUCK-UP-OUTTA' - HIS place! 'CAUSE, Legs be doin' a BOTTLE of Benzos at a time! Mi casa, su casa, AND, what's Legs', *IS what's MINE!!!* And, if you don't know *HOW to spike-it*...DON'T WORRY...Heavy Duty got you! *LEGS, USED TO shoot me up! Legs, turned me on to it, TOO!!* SO, if you need the help, *JUST WATCH* how Heavy Duty do. *'Cause, THAT'LL BE THE WAY, Legs taught me, how it do!"* (Sittin' *RIGHT HERE...watching the table "turn")*

MEANWHILE...

Back out on the road, gettin' closer to his home, *(though, Mr. Trife, he don't know it!).* Mr. Trife, sold his soul, for a chance at fortune and fame. But first, he's gotta make it in and outta North Juarez. (After he grabs Pockets' girl!). Before, the whole world, can know HIS name!

BUT FIRST...

"Hey Pockets, I've been doin' some thinkin' and, I don't think your plan's gonna work! *You asked Profit and MC,* but, you didn't hear it from me.", so Mr. Trife, (behind 24 karats) turns to Pockets, (behind the wheel),...and, does so, witha' one-eyed smirk!

"AYO! Pockets, MY DUDE! 'Bout this, whoooooole "Y.S. situation", I've been doin' some thinkin'. She's in the back...AND, she ALREADY stinkin'!! So, HOW-THA'-FUCK - you think, YOUR plan's gonna work??? AIN'T NOBODY gonna buy, the fact, that, a lunatic-fan got backstage, and JUST shot her!!!", Mr. Trife, collaborates, from the co-pilot seat, as a co-conspirator, (all in it together now!)(OY VEY!), as Pockets, travels down - busy Business Rt. 36 - at night, *(as Mr. Trife, don't know nothin' 'bout, being too far from the place, where he buried a gun in ice, after he shot Headslap in the face!).*

AND...

He DON'T know, that: "AYO!" and "MY DUDE!", was from, some of his "past life", BREAKIN' ON THRU!!! It just felt natural, for Mr. Trife, to say it like that. *(BUT, poor ol' Mr. Trife, HE ain't even REALIZIN' that!!). That, THAT was, from...a subliminal-life. That, he's lived 'bout, oh, 1, 260 days-or-so back! (THAT HOT WASH RAG ON THE BRAIN WAS A MOTHERFUCKER!!!!!).*

But...

Even with that, Pockets nor him, are realizing, that, more of THIS - Tier-Three's-memory - IS BEGINNING - TO come on back!!! And, neither one of them realize, that, Mr. Trife, DON'T realize, THAT, he's a clone!! AS, A result - FROM WHEN - that, "Thirty. Ott. Six.", knocked him - THE-FUCK-UNCONSCIOUS - just a few days back!!!(OY VEY!!!). Poor ol' Mr. Trife, that Tier-Three-Brain of his, really took a hit! Tier-Three-Brain covered in greenback flies from Pockets' "WELL of BULLSHIT"!

FOR...

HE THINKS,...he's REALLY Brotha Trife!

And(that!)...

Pockets is tryin',...to give him a better life!

But,...what he REALLY wants to know...

WHERE THA' FUCK IS MY PAIN STICK AND MY HOME?!?

AND...

(NEITHER ONE OF THEM realize, what's WAITING on them, up in,...North Juarez!)...

AS...

Pockets' lady, (THE ONE AND ONLY!!!) Anna Mossitti, is and has been...being used as bait!! (Witha', - house-arrest-ankle-bracelet - AFFIXED to her leg!!!).

(*BUT, all Mr. Trife REALLY KNOWS is, what HE REALLY wants to do! And, THAT'S to do right by Y.S.!* And then, to do, of what remains. THAT BEING: 1). Get in. 2). Get Pockets' girl. 3). And then,...make it back out. So that, THEN, *WITH the POWER of his pen,* the whole world's...gonna know his name!)

"What I tell you, 'BOUT THINKIN', Mr. Trife?!? LET ME, do ALL the thinking! What do YOU think, Mr. Trife? YOU THINK, ol' Pockets here, don't realize, I never received an answer FROM YOU, on the subject?? YOU THINK, Pockets, is just some tour bus driver??? YOU THINK, ol' Pockets here, AIN'T ALREADY have a plan in place, TO create a buzz??? HOW MANY platinum records YOU GOT, up on YOUR walls?????? YEAH! THOUGHT SO!!! Don't worry, or think 'bout, WHAT I KNOW!!! What I KNOW, is, what, I KNOW!!! AIN'T, FO' YOU, TO KNOW!!! DO SHIT, MY WAY, NOT, YOUR WAY!!! I got this! Pockets, got EVERYTHANG!!! SO,...I got THIS too!! AND, HOW COME I ain't seen you AS SO MUCH AS crack-open THAT composition book that, I gave YOU TO WRITE me, a hit song?!? You "in". BUT, you ain't - ALL-THE-WAY - *"in"* - YET, Mr. Trife! Yeah,... *"foul-shit" WAS done.* BUT, I ain't REALLY have you BE *'PART OF all that "Ritualistic-Shit".* YOU, SIR, STILL have, some work to do!! Before I LET, you *climb on top OF a dead body!!!* Tha'-fuck you think, THIS HERE SHIT, is hittin fo'?? SO, why don't you enlighten me, WITH, what YOU think, is THE BEST *"course-of-action"* with, this - WHOOOOOOLE - *"Y.S. situation"!?!",* Pockets, breaks it down, while breaking down some - tough-ass - expensive-ass - gas-station-beef-jerky

- *(with hostility!),* while holding a gallon of distilled water by its handle, while FIGHTIN' THE WHEEL!!!

"Ayo, Pockets, my man,...you tryna' be cute? ALL Y'ALL, wit this "Mr. Trife", shit! I'M the MOST TRIFLIN' motherfucker THIS SIDE of the Mississippi, YA' DIG!!!", Mr. Trife, goes off!

As...

Pockets' *Big-Hustle-Gears get to spinnin', "I gots'ta' get my hands on those reading material books, crack them shitz open, and take me a look! LOOKIN' LIKE that head trauma, might'a jarred his Tier-Three-Brain!!! Til' I read them shitz? ON them pain pills and mo', I'M GON' KEEP HIM HOOKED!!!*

As...

MC Busta-Nut, *gets to thinkin', "WITH, Y.S. dead, SHE WON'T be gettin' in MY WAY! (Of hittin' Mr. Trife up, for some of his Oxy's!) 'Cause, I WANT MY head, SPINNIN' JUST LIKE HIS HEAD!!!!!!"*

As...

False Profit, *gets to thinkin', "'DIS nigga's, SPUN-THA'-FUCK OUT!!! What-tha'-fucks, wrong WIT him???*

As...

Mr. Trife, *continues in thought, "Oh! So, so, so, so...NOW, I'M "Mr. Trife!" - WITH - all his, "Mr.-Trife-shit" -, CUTE-FUCK!! THIS MOTHERFUCKER, HERE!!! Tryna' BE - ALL "cute" - n' shit!", Mr. Trife, thinks to himself!*

AS...

(That - concussed-Tier-Three-Mind, has him really thinking that he's REALLY Brotha Trife!)...

THOUGH*(Fortunately enough!)...*

(That - *Tier-Three-Brain*, has been able to maintain, being *STUCK* ain't the life he wants for himself!)...

But...

Pockets, holds the keys to his life.

'Cause...

(Pockets, GOT "record label wealth"!)(OY VEY!!!).

FOR...

(Being knocked unconscious, has put it into his brain, that he's been "signed-on" to write hit songs, poor ol' Mr. Trife, he don't know that he's a clone, or if he can even sing, 'CAUSE he don't know if he's ever sang!)

And so...

Then, he CONTINUES, as he, (THINKS *FOR* HIMSELF!), *"NO WONDER, Y.S., got sick of, ALL THIS SHIT!!!",*...(Y.S....Y.S....Y.S...., man, the love he had, and still HAS, for his homegirl!)...,*"Man, I'MA DO what's best for Y.S. But, still, I ain't gonna, fuck MY shot up!"* And so, then, with that thought-process in mind, (layin' down some groundwork of his own THIS TIME!), Mr. Trife, asks Pockets, "WHEN'S this, Meet n' Greet Show gonna be, anyway??"

"Ain't NOTHIN' jumpin' off, MR. TRIFE, TIL' you get me MY woman, OUTTA' North Juarez!", Pockets, snaps!

"THAT'S, what I'm sayin'!", Mr. Trife, snaps back! (And then, - this here Tier Three - plays it *COOL*)...(*COOL as the washrag THAT'S been COOLING on his head!*), as Mr. Trife, informs, Pockets, of such, "ALL I'M sayin', Pockets, is...we GOTTA' keep Y.S. "fresh" FOR the show."

"HUH??? Ok,...ok, you DO have a point there, Mr. Trife! Yeah,... yeah,...you're right on this one,...I suppose. AND besides, I FIGURE it's gonna take you AT LEAST A WEEK, to work your way into and, around the city, you know, peep-the-scene, BEFORE you'll be able to make your move and, get my woman OUTTA' the city.", Pockets, *painfully* replies, *(HAVING to actually ADMIT,* that someone, actually THOUGHT of some shit that,...*HE hadn't ALREADY thought already, HIMSELF!!).*

But yet *(AND, but STILL!)*...

With, the - *BIG-HUSTLE-WHEEL-GRIND* - (tryna' PLAY Mr. Trife with, That: *"AT LEAST A WEEK"* - Shit!)...

For...

(Pockets KNOWS, Mr. Trife, WILL TAKE THAT SHIT, AS: a "personal" challenge!)

For, *(you see)*...

Pockets, *is just straight-up TRYNA' PLAY, Mr. Trife! TO get him, TO get in, and outta' the city, MUCH faster THAN, "AT LEAST A WEEK"!* (DAMN, THAT MUTHA' FUCKIN' POCKETS, GOT SOME SHIT TO HIM!!!)(AIN'T NO-LET-UP, TO HIS BULLSHIT!!!).

AND SO...

(Pockets, *causing and creating himself EVEN more anguish and pain. Having to actually ASK someone else FOR advice! Causing his throat to tighten and voice to strain. BUT, he's gonna-haveta' - ask-a-way - ANYWAY!* 'Cause, gettin' his woman back IS toooooo-damn-important! (To be, and for, FUCKIN'-UP THIS road trip!). YEAH, SO, WELL, AND - ANY-DAMN-WAAAAAAYS,...Y'ALLS "Meet N' Greet's" - gonna-haveta' - WAIT!!!)

And so...

Pockets, with the *"tonsillitis occurred"*, (AND ACCRUED), (from and of), *"swallowed-pride"*, RIPPIN' RAW *Pockets'* esophagus, IN THE back, AND on BOTH SIDES, Pockets, then does so, *(punts to Mr. Trife!)*, AS he, replies, "Yeah, yeah, uh, yeah, well, uh, so, well, uh, anywaaaaaays, MY plan woulda' worked-out just fine, IF Phil HAD my venue booked ON TIME! SO, yeah, well, uh, anywaaaaaays, *(DAMMIT!!!)...what do YOU suggest???"* ('Cause, Pockets, really WOULDN'T mind...keepin' Y.S. FRESH!!!)...('CAUSE JETTISON RECORDS IS CREEPY AS FUCK!!!)...(BUT HEY!)...(THAT'S THE MUSIC INDUSTRY FO' YA'!!!).

And then, Mr. Trife, uncovers his eyes. Removing those limited edition gold lenses. And, he turns to Pockets with a menacing look IN his ONE eye. With the other, STILL swollen and shit from his surgery. *(And, then asks, Pockets, some shit YOU AIN'T NEVER heard of!)*, "AYO!!! Pockets!! MY MAN,...you ever break into a morgue???", *(OR, for, THAT matter, NOR ME!!!)*.

Spittin' distilled water ALL OVER his big-ass Vegas windshield, with beef-jerky-shavings and red bits of Twizzlers-particles, obstructing his poor night vision of the road ahead. Pockets, turns to Mr. Trife, with an emphatic, "FUCK NO!!!!!! WHY?!?!?!", *(WISHING he didn't punt to this here - Tier-Three-Motherfucker - and, kept the ball himself instead!)*.

"I have.", Mr. Trife, sheepishly-replies, *(really thinking he's really Brotha Trife!)* and, then covers with limited gold his eye. While, Pockets, ignores the road, *thinking to himself, (head ready to explode!)*, "THIS IS Brotha Trife after all!! Shiiiiiit. WHY am I the LEAST BIT surprised!?!"

Pockets, with eyes back on the road, *so reasons with himself*, "OK!!! SHIIIIIIT!!! Here we GO! Gotta keep it GAMBLIN'...MAN!!! Gotta keep Y.S.' body FRESH...fo' tha' show...and, if she stays fresh "enough"? Well, shiiiiiit...POSSIBLY SOME MO'!!!", ('CAUSE, SOME OF THESE MOTHERFUCKERS IN THE MUSIC INDUSTRY, ARE CREEPY AS FUCK!!!!!!), *"But. Hmm.*", Pockets, *ponders to himself,* as he, continues down Southbound Business Rt. 36 at night, *as he, continues his ponderings,* and, continually, continues his continual-battle of the glare of the lights, the continuance of, his poor driving at night, due to his, poor night vision eye sight, *"AIN'T that shitty-ass lime green roadside motel, right up ahead here on the left, right??"* (As, Pockets, ain't seen that shitty-ass lime green Buena Vista, since he seen Brotha Trife putting Headslap on ice!), *"Ok, Pockets, you got this! You got EVERYTHANG!!! And so,...you got this too! Go 'head brother, just roll them dice!! Ain't no other way to do it, just make it do what it do! Just eeeaaassseee on past the Off-Track Gambling Spot. Then, eeeaaassseee on 'round back behind the Mark Meharg Memorial Hospital. And, I HOPE fo' God, that, Mr. Trife's - Tier-Three-Mind -, ain't recognizin' NONE OF THIS, as we go!! Just remember, my brother, don't be buggin'-out - all these - Triflin'-mafuckas-rolled-up-into-one!!! Brotha Trife NOR his clone - AIN'T 'BOUT NO - "rapid-motions"! So, AIN'T no other way for you to do it, you Gamblin' Man...BUT to make it do what it do...niiiiiice 'n slooooooow!"*, (then, turning to Brotha Trife's clone, Pockets, let's it be known, "Mr. Trife, you BETTER know what tha' fuck you're doin'!! OR this WHOLE entire ROAD TRIP could be ruined!!"

And, Mr. Trife, just simply points his finger towards that big-ass windshield, and, states, while cocking to the side, his bullet hole hat, "The sky is black. So, YOU just park o'va HERE - outta-the-way - of the cameras! AND YOU, just LEAVE, the rest to ME! 'Cause, TRUST & BELIEVE, them security cameras will spot your RV, looooooong before they could EVER spot me!", (and then, turning towards Pockets, Mr. Trife asks, while cocking even harder to the side, his bullet hot hat!),..."Are you forgettin' somethin', Pockets?? YOUR - under the ground levels - couldn't EVEN hold me!!", (and then, Mr. Trife, let's Pockets KNOW, as Pockets is forced to listen on with envy, "'Cause, I stick to tha' back roads. AND I stays IN the shadows! Ain't nobody in this hospital ever gonna hear me walkin' in my Jimmy Choo's. I STAY light on my toes!!! *I done crept on my foes, WITHA' line of meth up my nose.* MY brother! Up IN HERE?? My brother,...I MIGHT even fuck-'round, *AND hit the "rock-ninja technique"...I learned IN the dojos!* Pockets, my man, have no fear! My dude, I'M THAT dude, TO, slip-in-and-outta town AND FROM this-here hospital, like consciousness! PLUS, I move like a ninja. AND, I leave NO fingerprints! My dude, I'm silent like the wind, through a chain-link fence. And then, I can simply disappear...LIKE smoke,...from Nigerian incense!!!"

(THAT MUTHA' FUCKIN' Brotha Trife blood, JUST GOT some shit to it alright!! For, Brotha Trife, just always seemed to have the ability, to be in a room, for five minutes WITH ya', BEFORE YOU...even knew he's in there! He ain't have no keys jinglin'! And, Mr. Trife, is...The. Exact. Same. WAY!!! For, HE AIN'T' steppin' on no twigs! THAT triflin' mafucka', ain't scuffin' or shufflin' his feet! And, it ain't no accident, Mr. Brotha Trife, DON'T BE steppin' on no tiny broken pieces of glass, on the pavement. And, when he walks, HE DON'T KICK NO pebbles by accident! The mutha' fucka',...IS silent AS FUCK!!! He LOOKS FOR the shit! (AND THAT, MY FRIENDS, AIN'T-NO MOTHERFUCKIN' ACCIDENT!!!). AND THEN, the mutha' fucka's gonna STAY in your

blind spot! (JUST SO, in 'bout five minutes or so, Mr. Trife CAN WATCH YOU JUMP OUTTA' YOUR SKIN!!!)...(*'Cause Brotha Trife was a prick like that!*)...

(*Hating to admit it!* BUT,...KNOWING that, Mr. Trife, *IS* right!!)...

Pockets, flustered, angered, *THAT he HAS TO admit some-shit,* (*fucks-up, AS he replies!*), "YEAH, YEAH,...I KNOW,...I KNOW,...I know, you be THAT DUDE, to get in and out of a town undetected! And, THAT'S, the ONLY reason WHY, I HAD you,...uh,...yeah, uh,... um. (*SHIT!*) Uh, so, yeah, well, uh, anywaaaaaays. Um, YEAH, THAT! AND, uh, FOR THE PURPOSE OF, DON'T FORGET, uh, you know, *haha(nervous chuckle)* giving you a better life! You feel me, right, Brotha Trife? Uh, I mean, C. TRIFE. (*FUCK!!!*) MR. TRIFE!!! MR. TRIFE!!! Uh, yeah, FUCK, SHIT, you know what tha' fuck I mean! ...*WANT some, jerky?!?!?!*", a stutterin' and stammerin' (*AND fuckin'-up!*), Pockets, does say, placing down the gallon of distilled water, in order to hand Mr. Trife that big-ass - expensive-ass - bag of - gas-station-beef-jerky! (PAID FOR by the Jettison Records' travel per diem of course!).

"MMMMM HMMMM,...YEEEEEEAAAAAAHHHHHHH!!!", (INTUBATION-VOICE-AMAZIN'), Mr. Trife, replies, (though, snatches that big bag of Twizzlers instead!). But yet and but still, STILL suffering some of the effects of being earlier-concussed, that clone-shit, DOES make it under that washrag! But yet and but still,...it STILL goes right over his head!(OY VEY!).

THEN, (upon hearing *THAT voice!*)...

EVEN, MC BUSTA-NUT is forced, to make his way to the front! Coming up from the kitchen area, False Profit, asks on behalf of he and 'Nut, ('cause, well, HE WOULD actually like to KNOW what's up!), "So, what's the moves?? We here AT the venue!?! We heard, Mr. Trife warmin' up! Pockets, I been workin' on some new FIRE shit! Y'all, wanna hear?", (THEN, without waiting on an answer, in ERR'BODY'S ear, False Profit, begins to spit, his new - "Mumblized" - hit!)...

..."Ain't bad, Profit! Ain't bad, at all! WHATCHA' gonna' title that track??", Pockets, asks.

"Hot Cold Dead Girl"! Kinda' catchy,...don'tcha' think!?!", False Profit, debuts.

"Young boy, I couldn't understand a FUCKIN' word!!!", a - couldn't-have-been-MORE-disgusted - (ALL OVER AGAIN!!) - Mr. Trife, replies!, (then, glares through his 24 Karat lense at Pockets)...(WITH his ONE good eye!).

THEN...

(OVER Y.S., IN SADNESS, IN DUGUST, FIGURING THAT SOME "SELF-MEDICATION", TO GET OVER THAT TYPE OF PAIN, IS A MUST)...

Mr. Trife, breaks out those Oxy's, passin' a couple to MC Busta-Nut, to crush up!...(old habits die hard ya dig!)...and, once lines have been laid, all four of 'em, ripped them motherfuckers, ('cause, well,...THEY ALL IN IT TOGETHER NOW!!!), and, that's EXACTLY WHAT they did!!!

And(THEN!)...

After, they all got on their snort, (though, Pockets ain't rip that shit! Well, he did a lil' bit. THAT DECEPTIVE MOTHERFUCKER made sure, most of his, wound up on the floor!), Mr. Trife, does so, inform - (after the land - has been laid!), "DROP me off here! Kill the engine. Kill the lights. You see those five cement steps over there, back in the cut? Back over there, back in the cut, back there, on the right? THAT'LL be the back entrance, TO the hospital's morgue!! Now, pay attention, 'cause, in five minutes, WHEN you see that light go out, over there. THAT MEANS, I'll be standin' on that lil' cement loading dock, at the top, of them five steps. It'll be just me, AND ONLY ME,...back there,...in the cut!!", Mr. Trife, directs.

"How tha' fuck you know somethin', like that???", MC Busta-Nut, cuts in, (peering through the kaleidoscope of beef jerky and Twizzlers). And then, sure 'nuff! (Tucked back in tha' cut). There IS a lil' cement platform. AND, it is AT the top, of five cement masoned steps!

"Enough!! Enough!!", Pockets, himself cutting in, cutting off Busta-Nut, NEEDING to maintain leadership - (of and about) - This - "back in the cut" - Shit!

Yet...

Pockets IS,...OUT OF his depth here! SO, once again, *Pockets is forced, to force on through - THAT tonsillitis - of which - IS NOW - becoming chronic!* And so, he asks, as he defers, - (TO SOME - Mr. Trife LOGIC!!!), "After, the light goes out?", Pockets, questions, Mr. Trife, *BEING about the most Pockets CAN muster!*,(WITHOUT tacking on, The: *",...then what?"*)...('CAUSE, THAT SHIT, *WOULD'VE BEEN toooooo painful!!*).

And...

Mr. Trife simply, replies, like it ain't no thang, ('cause it AIN'T to him!), "Then, fire the engine back up. Cut your headlights, back on. And, just back the RV up to tha' dock, like you 'sposed to, fuckin' be there! I'LL direct you back in. JUST DON'T hit the overhang, overtop, of the loadin' dock!! Know WHAT, I'm sayin'!?", Mr. Trife, directs.

"LIKE I'M,...'*SPOSED TO BE THERE???* You ain't makin' NOOOOOO-kinda'-sense, ALL OV'A AGAIN, Mr. Trife!!! Ain't NO WAY, I'm gonna be able to avoid the security cameras! In THIS big-ass RV??? Backin' it up to, THAT dock??? You CAN'T be serious! LISTEN, we'll just stick wit, MY plan! 'Cause, YOUR plan, AIN'T gon' work!!!", Pockets, replies. (And, IF NOTHING ELSE...*trying to alleviate THAT strep throat of his!!*).

AND THEN...

Mr. Trife, removes those gold lenses from his eye (and, of his socket!). THEN, looks directly into the right eye of Pockets! And, asks, him solely, (though, wholly) of them all, "Where's your faith?"

And then...

He dips the-fuck-on-out the door, WITHA' few of them - long-ass-big-bag-of-Twizzlers - Twizzlers - HANGIN' the-fuck-out the corner of his mouth, (to be sure!).

AND...

(He does it in silence)

And then, as Pockets, Busta-Nut and, False Profit, sit there in the dark. They take turns, as they, take turns lookin' through that - big-ass - kaleidoscope-of-a-windshield - sprayed 'n matted WITH - beef-jerky-shavings - AND - big-ass-red bits of - Twizzlers-particles! And, as they do, they hear some RUSTLIN' goings-on! (JUST outside the RV, from where they are parked!).

THEN...

SURE 'NUFF!!! THAT, dock light went out! AND, it went out IN - PRECISELY - five minutes!!!!! *(JUST LIKE, Mr. Trife, SAID it would!)* BUT,...if YOU'RE *A HATER???* (Hmm!) Like, MC BUSTA-NUT! *(YOU, AND Busta-Nut, WERE hopin' THAT it WOULDN'T!!!)*... (LOOKATCHA'!!!!!!!!!).

(But, LET US, *move on from the hate!*)...

'Cause...

Standing there. Atop of that dock. IN the darkness! For, there stands...a wheeled-gurney. ('CAUSE, standing IN the darkness, OF that dark dock, for standing there, next to that, well, THAT'S Mr. Trife!). *Off camera. And, he's directing like a movie!* 'Cause, HE KNOWS Pockets' night vision WILL BE the cause. (For what???) THE cause OF HIS plan gettin' - ALL-KINDZA' - fucked up!!! And so, well, *the director... he directs. Off camera. And, he's directing like a movie.* Backing up Pockets as Pockets backs up! *Directing Pockets to give that big-ass steering wheel a HARD cut! (For, IT AIN'T in the script, for ALLOWING that RV to hit, that overhang, atop, IN the darkness, overhead!).* As he, stands there. IN a white lab coat. In the darkness. Holding a white disaster bag. Used to zip up the dead. And, as Pockets hops out. Pockets, snatches out. (OF the darkness!). A white lab coat to put on. (OF his very own!). Adorned, with: *"Medical Examiner"*. Embroidered in blue. IN script. ON the left breast. Once tossed down. *SNATCHED OUT OF THE DARKNESS OF THOSE FIVE MASONED STEPS!!!*

(For now and, for then, for Pockets and Mr. Trife, it's)...

Silent night flight movements time! AS they do so! IN the mobile studio! ZIPPIN' Y.S. UP AS Y.S. GETS ZIPPED UP!!! (As for, Mr. Trife, for Y.S., he's STILL got mad love!) BUT, he AIN'T down wit - NO-shit-OF- being - *MOTHERFUCKIN' STUCK!*

(Dually now. And, *AIN'T THIS SOME SHIT???*), *FOR...*

Suitin' up in two uniforms, of two gripped-up and slumped security guards, Profit and 'Nut are, gettin' uniformed-up! *(Gripped-up and slumped, compliments of, that of none other than that of the no other than that of Mr. Trife, gripped-up and slumped!).* And then, just like, Mr. Trife, said unto them, "Just do it, like, the MOST trife. Like, that's what, YOUR PURPOSE is here for!" And then, the four of them, hop down, lower and hoist, (all in it together now, they ALL made their choice!). So then, the four of them, IN THE DARKNESS, roll Y.S. on in, of that loading dock door, that leads to the morgue. For, the four of them, have made it to the top...of those dark masoned steps. WITH False Profit puttin' on THAT *fake-face* on himself! *Of, the: seen-too-much-death. Of, that: Foolhardy - "This don't bother me!" - Mechanism - of Self-Defense.* (WELL NOW!!!)*(Ain't THIS some shit!?!)...* As, the "false one", is now... *FOOLIN' HIMSELF!!! To wear a stiff upper lip. AND A strong chin!* For, to prevent, in the event, someone were to question him, *False Profit, WILL fool them! ("You sure you ain't some rapper in a hospital security guard uniform?") For, False Profit gonna look, talk and act, like he's been here before!* (For, False Profit gonna come cross real legit, like he ain't new to this shit!). For, False Profit, IS and WILL be,...*fake to the end!*

And so...

(As the four hospital "employees", wheel Y.S. down that bottom-level hall)...

False Profit, under a stiff upper lip, decides to make some small talk, "Mr. Trife? HOW THA' FUCK you pull THIS shit off???"
Mr. Trife, real quick to reply, lets it be known real quick, "WE ain't outta here YET, boys! We AIN'T pull off shit! But, ALL Y'ALL gonna

know, WHEN I'm pullin' THAT shit off, THAT'S HOW, I was able, TO pull off this shit!!!"

And, Pockets, ONCE AGAIN, *got himself thinking,* (AGAIN!!), *"FUCK! Phillip Tate, WAS right 'bout, THESE Tier-Three-Mutha'-Fuckas!! Damn THESE, "recently-awakened" minds! Mr. Trife, ain't makin' NO KINDA' sense! I BEST read-up on ALL THOSE reading materials! Shiiiiiit, the FIRST chance, I got the time!"* And then, ONCE AGAIN, Pockets, JUST GOTTA' let Mr. Trife know, (AGAIN!!!), "Mr. Trife, you best know where we're headed! 'Cause, YOU AIN'T makin' NO kinda' sense,...ALL OVER again!!!"

BUT...

(Mr. Trife, ain't stressin'!)

As...

(The two doctors and, the two security guards, continue to wheel Y.S., on down the hall)...

For...

Dr. Trife, hips them to some shit, as he gives them this lesson, (just a lil' somethin' to reassure, as they reach the door of the morgue), "As you can see, the door to the morgue, looks like just any other. Ain't nuthin' special to it. It looks just like an unassuming door, on the front of an unassuming house, next to some shutters. BUT, there's just SOMETHIN' 'BOUT, that lil' plastic black sign, with "MORGUE", engraved in white recessed lettering, that MAKES people shudder! Ain't NOBODY in this entire hospital dyin' to get in here! And, THAT'S what separates it, FROM all the others!"

And so...

(Knowing, that, he'll have - "enough" - "uninterrupted-time", TO DO what the fuck, he came there TO DO!)...Once again, Mr. Trife, gains entry. ...(But "Reader" BEWARE!!!)...(If YOU AIN'T used to this life, if YOU'RE NEW to THIS life??)...(REASONS for YOU to SHUDDER are plenty!!!!!!).

FOR...

Once Y.S. gets wheeled in and, for once they are all inside, Dr. Trife, closes and locks that door, to the hospital's morgue, LOCKING them ALL inside. And then, Dr. Trife, well...he turns on some lights. And, to the others' surprise, (ANTICIPATING seeing some dead bodies!), finding themselves standing in a small office, is ALL THAT they find! ...(Followed by the relief, of a *BIG COLLECTIVE-SIGH!!!*)...(As they, feel that elephant, step from off of their chests!). And then, that elephant... steps RIGHT back on! As they, watch Dr. Trife, walk towards another door, that's being partially obscured, (by some tall filing cabinets, next to a small wooden desk). For, on the otherside of that other door, well... *THAT'S WHERE the smell freezes and hangs! Your mettle it will test.* For, JUST THROUGH this small office...*IS the hospital's sarcophagus!*

And...(OH YEAH!!!)...*(Of THAT smell?)...(THAT, freezes and hangs??)*

Well...

YOU CAN TRY to shower THAT shit off!! (OH, you can TRY!!) And, when you TRY, *DO TRY, to do YOUR best!* BUT, THAT *distinct smell* (of the morgue) IS *STUCK TO* your *mucus membranes!* (AND, *stuck* IN *your mind!!)* DON'T be scary!!! (HOW BAD DO YOU WANT IT???) THAT'S just the *SMELL,* of the *DEAD BODIES at rest!!!*

Just put on that stiff upper lip. (And, do try and act like, you AIN'T posin'!). For, IT'S JUST *chemicals and shit. Hangin'. FROZEN!!!* IN THAT *"atmosphere"* of a cooler. AIN'T LIKE when, the Medical Examiner's assistant, *(WITH PRECISION),* hits that decedent WITH a "Y" incision! (Opening up that perMEATion!). *OF the decedent's, LAST SUPPER and shots! (Of some, dead motherfucker, that GOT SHOT DEAD from some shooter!).* 'CAUSE, THAT'S some *nasty-ass SMELLIN'* shit! So, TRY as you might! *(BUT, ALL the alcohol, drugs and shots, YOU'LL NEED TO DO, TO FORGET that shit),* well...IT AIN'T GONNA' WORK!!! *For, NONE of that shit can make YOU forget!!!!!!*

OH, you CAN wash it out your clothes. (HOWEVER!!!) *IT AIN'T gon' wash THAT smell out YOUR...mucus membranes! Fo', THAT SHIT, gon' STAY, THE FUCK UP YOUR nose!!!* ('Cause, let me tell ALL YOU

MOTHERFUCKERS something!!)...For, Pockets, well, HE'S a gamblin' man! And, he DON'T roll how YOU roll!! (AND, he BE on some *"OTHER"* shit!)...(SOME..."*music industry shit"!!!*) But, FOR YOU, "the reader", well, for YOU, I have a *SAFE BET.* THAT *"skulldust sawdust" that, THE MOST TRIFLIN', momentarily WILL BE kickin' up, (from when he starts diggin', an oscillating autopsy saw, deep-down-and-grindin'-away, IN a dead motherfucker's SKULL!)...*well, ...*THAT SHIT, WILL BE stuck up in ALL Y'ALLS mucus membranes!* (WELCOME TO DR. TRIFE'S WORLD - YOUR LIFE WILL NEVER BE THE SAME!!!) (NOPE!). For, THAT'S SOME SHIT YOU AIN'T NEVER GONNA' BE ABLE TO LIVE WITHOUT!!! (For, that *SMELL is embedded* IN that *"SKULLDUST-SAWDUST".*) AND,...THAT SHIT, *WILL BE embedded IN YOUR mucus membranes (that lines the insides)*...OF YOUR FUCKIN' SNOUT!! (And, oh yeah, HEY READER!!!!!!)...about that *smell?* (DON'T YOU EVER - have NO doubt - about it!)...'cause, *NOT EVEN hard liquor (can OR will!) make that smell, leave YOUR mind.* (HA! YOU WILL NEVER - EVER - LIVE WITHOUT IT!!!) *For, THAT'S SOME SHIT - YOU AIN'T - NEVER - EVER - EVER - gonna be able to FORGET!!!* But, hey reader,...LOOKATCHA'!!! YOU KEPT ON READING!!!...(didn't YOU!?!)...(EVEN AFTER, THAT *SAFE BET!!!).*

And so...

(As Mr. Trife gets busy, doin' what he came there to do, now elbow deep, *triggers get triggered,* in that *recently-awakened-mind,* of this here Tier-Three)...*under the grinding-sound of that oscillating saw, that saw blade moves, side-to-side, fast as the wings of a hummingbird's beat! Under that ever-cooling-washrag, memories, of the mind, of Brotha Trife, into the mind, of Mr. Trife, begins to creep. Side-to-side, right-to-left, side-to-side, right-to-left. Triggered-mutterings of triggers get-muttered under his breath,* "*The destruction of it all. That part, never got to me. It's just...that surgical shit. THAT, "Y" INCISION, - SHIT!!! THAT PRECISION SHIT...of an autopsy. THAT SHIT...got to me...*"

And, as *those horrific-triggers, trigger,* Mr. Trife, to continue *muttering to himself, JUST LIKE Brotha Trife USED to do!* (psst! hey reader, guess what???)...

THAT'S THE ROOM YOU'RE IN! YES YOU!! RIGHT NOW!!! *For, YOU ARE IN, that autopsy ROOM!!* (I SEE YOU!!!)(AND YOU SEE YOURSELF THERE TOO!!!)(AND AT THIS MOMENT OF TRUTH, I'LL PROVE IT TO YOU!!!) For, *a subconscious-reaction, ALREADY happened, when YOU breathed IN, all those fine sawdust-like-fragments of skull.* (Need MORE PROOF???)(Hold on tight, as I make you *CONSCIOUSLY-AWARE!!!*) For, that *"tingling-sensation" you're about to start feeling, tingling IN the bridge of YOUR nose.* Well, *that's from when you breathed in all that skulldust-sawdust!* And, the reason being, *YOU CAN NOW FEEL THAT TINGLING, growing stronger* NOW is because, THAT *SKULLDUST-SAWDUST has been EATING AWAY at your mucus membranes, THIS ENTIRE TIME,* after all! And, you wanna know *WHY, YOU CAN FEEL,* all that *microscopic-skulldust, EATING AWAY AT YOUR NOSE???* (oh shit...HERE IT COMES!!!) 'CAUSE, *skulldust-sawdust* - LOOKS A WHOLE LOT LIKE - *dust mites* - when you get up close! *(AND THAT'S THE SHIT YOU JUST BREATHED UP YOUR NOSE!!!).* AND *ALL OF THOSE AIRBORNE DUST MITES* AIN'T COMIN' BACK DOWN!!! And, I-KNOW-YOU-KNOW, *you can feel* ALL of those *airborne skulldust dust-mites, THAT YOU BREATHED IN!!!* *'Cause, YOU CAN JUST PICTURE all those skulldust-dust-mites -* (UP IN YOUR NOSE RIGHT NOW!!!) - AND THAT'S WHY *YOU CAN FEEL THAT SHIT TINGLING!!!* (Welcome to Mr. Trife's world!) *OH, YOU'RE IN IT NOW!!!* SO, DON'T TURN BACK NOW!!! *For, there's work to be done!* Dirty work! "Jettison Records" - *KIND of work!* For, if you turn back now, YOU'RE leaving too soon! Don't YOU WANT TO SEE what happens ON THAT *silver stainless-steel autopsy table???* Don't YOU WANT TO HEAR the gurgle?? Don't *YOU WANT TO SMELL what's GONNA' run down THAT floor-drain,* in the middle of that room???

(Well, I SEE YOU *stuck* around!)

'Cause...

Ain't that YOU, with Mr. Trife? Can't YOU SEE that dead guy lying there on his back, on top of THAT autopsy table EQUIPPED WITH HOSES

AND DRAINS!?! Can't YOU JUST IMAGINE, what IT MUST be like, with NOTHIN' but a white towel covering YOUR privates, AS YOU lay there NAKED and COLD as ice!? Can't YOU SEE that GRAY postmortem skin?? And how, AT UNNATURAL ANGLES, HIS knees and elbows are BENT!?! Can't YOU SEE that, this IS FROM, the RIGOR MORTIS, that HAS set in?!? Can't YOU SEE YOU GOTTA' HELP out, Mr. Trife, (to FORCE those JOINTS back in the OPPOSITE direction, TO BREAK that rigor mortis, RIGHT???) Can't YOU SEE that orange block of rubber?? (UPON WHICH, the BACK of that dead dude's head is at rest). NASTY SOUND, as the rigor, GETS SNAPPED IN HIS NECK, as his CHIN gets buried in his CHEST!!! Can't you see, Mr. Trife, with scalpel in hand, 'bout to give a deep long slice?!? As he, (starting in the back of that dude's head!), Mr. Trife, drags that blade IN the skin, AS THOSE open dead eyes say unto YOU, "I WANT TO DIE, ALL OVER AGAIN!!!" Ain't that you, then as your eyes, following that blade, AS IT SLICES, around the ENTIRE circumference OF HIS head??? And, ain't YOU THE ONE that just VOMITED IN THE BACK OF YOUR MOUTH??? AT THE EASE, of the way, that RAZOR sharp scalpel blade, SPLIT OPEN WIDE THAT GRAY FOREHEAD!?! (But you're not alone!) ('Cause you're being followed!) FOLLOWED BY that scalpel blade, *is THE FLOW of the DANK DARK BLOOD OF THE DEAD!!!* And, WATCHING along in there WITH YOU, *in that: skulldust-sawdust-airborne-dust-mite-cooler-of-a-room,* YOU'RE BEING WATCHED - *BY THE SPIRITS - OF THE DEAD!!!* And, AS YOU ARE BEING WATCHED, all this time, YOU'VE BEEN WATCHING ALONG *with, Pockets and his men!* (For, ALL this time, IT'S *BEEN YOU,* right in there *WITH them, IN THAT ROOM!!!) And, RIGHT ABOUT NOW, Pockets would count his chips and place a bet!* Place a bet that, right about now...*YOU COULD USE A SHOWER!! As, UPON YOU, countless microscopic skulldust-sawdust-dust-mites HAVE landed!* (And, UPON YOU, they HAVE *BEGUN to devour!!!!!!). For, IN THAT ROOM, YOU ARE BEGINNING TO GET covered!* (TAKE A LOOK ALL AROUND YOU!!!) Can't YOU SEE THEM in that *microscopic cloud, AS they hover???* (And here's a lil' hint)...ON YOUR CLOTHES, they may look like LINT!*(BUT they're even smaller!)*...'CAUSE,... *YOU'RE STILL BREATHING THAT SHIT IN!!!* (And, I'ma let you in on a secret!)(*Though, I hate, and ain't, a snitch!*), BUT,...YOU'RE GONNA' hate yourself, WHEN YOU feel yourself, FINALLY giving in! And, you're probably gonna be on some - *"How'd he know this SHIT?!?"* *(And AT YOURSELF, YOU WILL GET pissed!)*...WHEN YOU HEAR yourself, saying, *"Now, AIN'T THIS a bitch!"* When YOU FEEL that YOU COULD NO LONGER fight the URGE, to SCRATCH YOUR HEAD and, that, YOU COULD NO LONGER RESIST!!! ('Cause,... *skulldust-dust-mites MAKE YOUR SCALP ITCH!!!!!!!).* And YOU WILL be thinking it, EVEN IF, YOU don't say it aloud, *"HOW'D HE KNOW, I'M gonna fight the urge, to fingersweep out my ear?!?"* (Well?)...(I'll fucking tell you!)...(*'CAUSE, there's one or two of them lil' fuckers - RIGHT-THA'- FUCK-NOW - that got all the way down,...IN YOUR EAR CANAL).* And, I bet YOU didn't even realize, (but, YOU WILL!),(WHEN YOU catch yourself sniffin'!), *but, YOU'RE BEGINNING TO get the SMELL OF DANK dead blood ON YOUR SKIN!!!* And, ain't that YOU, that's ABOUT TO FEEL, go through YOUR body, *A DEATH-COLD CHILL?!* *(WHEN YOU REALIZE, THERE'S TOOOOOO MUCH DETAIL, FOR BROTHA TRIFE'S WORLD, TO NOT BE REAL!!!).* So, there ain't no use in YOU screamin'! *YOU IN THAT ROOM, WITH dank dark dead blood...AS IT'S STREAMIN'!!* So, *HOW DO YOU FEEL, BEING IN THAT ROOM, AS THAT STENCH, BEGINS TO HANG IN THE AIR FREEZIN'?!?!?!?!* (And, to Mr. Trife, ain't that dead man bound!?). *As* (starting at the temples), *YOU WATCH, Mr. Trife, perform TWO LONG SLICES DOWN!!* As, all this time, *YOU'VE BEEN IN IT WITH HIM!!* As, YOU get *SICKENED BY THE IMAGE, OF THE CONTRAST,* of the graying, of the gaping, *of that dark dank dead blood, of those two long cuts,* (starting at the temples!!), *split* in the skin.

(After, and then, Mr. Trife, a helping hand TO HIM, YOU LEND!!! As YOU...*assist him!*)

As...

YOU KNOW, IT'S NOW ON YOU! *To lend, Mr. Trife, a helping hand!* There's SOOOOOO much blood *and, IT'S COMING OUT THICK! AND YOU KNOW NOW, YOU GOTTA' DO SOMETHIN'!!!*

(THIS ain't no TIME FOR YOU TO BE gettin' SICK!). *So, DO WHAT YOU CAN, to keep them - hot-nasty-bitter-TASTING-stomach-biles - DOWN SOUTH!* (YOU don't WANT TO TASTE THAT SHIT *again IN the back of YOUR MOUTH!!!*). So, IN YOU, YOU FIND THE STRENGTH!!! *As, YOU BEGIN to wipe and rinse! (That dead man's blood, YOU BEGIN to wash away!) As, IT'S streakin' down BOTH SIDES, of his DEAD-GRAY FACE!* (If YOU WOULD SEE that LOOK IN YOUR EYES RIGHT NOW)...*then*...(YOU WOULD SEE LOVE!!!)(*'Cause, Mr. Trife HAS NOW, GOTTEN INTO YOUR MIND!*) (And, YOU don't even REALIZE)(YOU ARE NOW SEEING, things differently IN TIME!)(YOU NOW HAVE BEGUN, TO THINK fondly upon, all THAT *dank-smellin' DARK streaks of blood!*) CONTRASTED *upon a canvas of gray! 'CAUSE, there ain't no life, IN that dead man's face!* (OH, YOU'RE IN IT NOW!)(So, HERE COMES the REALLY fucked up part!)(AS YOU REALIZE...THAT YOU ARE BEGINNING...TO SEE...those streaks of blood as art)(AND, because of that, OF yourself, YOU BEGIN *TO FEEL disgrace!*)(As, YOU NOW BEGIN TO SEE ALL THAT BLOOD...*as finger paint!!!*)(So, GO AHEAD!)(DON'T BE SCARY!)...*FEEL THAT cold-wet-dead-skin in YOUR bare hands!! As, YOU ASSIST, Mr. Trife, AFTER HE GAVE (BOTH sides OF THAT dead motherfucker's head) TWO LONG DEEP SLICES!! AFTER YOU WATCHED, Mr. Trife, take THAT scalpel and, SPLIT THE SKIN (of that dead motherfucker's head) ALL THE WAY AROUND!!!!!! WITH A nice tight grip, of cold wet dead skin, YOU give a GOOD TUG, AS YOU HELP Mr. Trife, PULLING the dead's FACE, RIGHT ON DOWN!!!*... (YOUR stomach is gettin' a bit jacked NOW, ain't it?)...(YOU'RE feeling a bit dizzy and lightheaded OF YOUR ACTS SO HEINOUS!!!)...Can't YOU JUST *IMAGINE THE TASTE???...Of that DANK DARK DEAD BLOOD,...AS IT,...gurgles down,...that autopsy room's floor grate of center drainage!*).

(And,...oh yeah. HEY READER! YOU CAN wear a mask!) And, I give you credit, for YOUR guts! ('Cause, YOU are STILL READING!!!) For, YOU MUST BE up for the task! (YOU, triflin' mutha' fucka', YOU!!!!!!)

But, *(even WITH a mask!)*...

If YOU'RE STILL GETTIN' A HINT OF THAT STENCH,... guess what?? (OH, AND YOU, BEST BELIEVE!!!)...*SOME of that microscopic "skulldust-sawdust" WILL FOREVER get stuck, (TO YOUR mucus membranes!),....AS YOU BREATHE!!! (For, 'round that mask OF YOURS, it WILL FIND its way 'round!)...Kicked-up from that autopsy saw! MAKING that AWFUL WOODSHOP SOUND! (And, THAT'S what YOU ARE breathing in!)*(And, now ain't THIS A bitch!?)*('Cause, STILL eatin' away AT YOUR SCALP, ARE YOUR tiny-skulldust-dust-mite FRIENDS!)*(And, hey reader, I KNOW WHAT YOU'RE THINKING!) *THIS MOTHERFUCKER ACTUALLY GOT MY SCALP ITCHING!!!* (GO ON AND ADMIT IT!) *'CAUSE, YOU KNOW THAT'S WHAT YOU'RE THINKING!* (AND YOU'RE THINKING, THIS MOTHERFUCKER, BETTER NOT REMIND ME OF THE BRIDGE OF MY NOSE AGAIN!!) *'CAUSE, THEN YOU WILL START TO GET THE INKLING, THAT, I CAN ACTUALLY FEEL THE BRIDGE OF MY NOSE...TINGLING!!!* (told y'all *Mr. Trife HAS TAKEN OVER your brain!)*...(and YOU didn't even realize it but...YOUR FACE AROUND YOUR NOSE...*just started itching again!).*

For, (THEY'RE STILL ALL UP IN YOUR NOSE RIGHT NOW!!!)...

THAT'S WHERE ALL of those "tiny-sawdust-like-skull-fragments-of-the-DEAD" WILL BE FOUND!!! Kicked-up and breathed in, (as that AWFUL WOODSHOP SOUND IS being made!). Kicked-up and breathed in, BY A quick-as-shit-HALF-MOON-thin-lookin' blade! MOVIN' side-to-side! Left-BACK-TO-right! Such a DANGEROUS-COMBINATION!!!(that saw and Mr. Trife!). *For, they both got precision and speed!* (YOU BEST WATCH YOURSELF 'round Mr. Trife!) *FOR, THAT BLADE IS FASTER THAN a hummingbird's wings can beat!* (Stay at a safe distance WHEN YOU SEE MR. TRIFE!!!). *He got that oscillating autopsy saw of bone and meat.*

"DAAAAAAAYYUUUUM!!! YOU SOOOOOO TRIFLIN', MR. TRIFE!!! WHAT THE FUCK YOU DOIN' NOW!?! GRIPPIN' UP...supplies??? Whatcha' GONNA' DO WIT that big red spool of thread?!? I don't know you that well, Mr. Trife. BUT, for that - BIG-hooked-sewing-needle - I'm sure YOU GOT SOME PLANS, IN YOUR HEAD!!! GOOD LORD, MR. TRIFE!!! Are you REALLY gonna take THAT SAW!?! And, WHATCHA' NEED those viles wit tha' red, purple, and gray rubber-topped-stoppers, fo'??? Mr. Trife, you is a VILE motherfucker!!!", a fearful panic-strickened Busta-Nut shouts, (and on, MR. TRIFE'S SOUL!!!), not even FALSE PROFIT CAN LIE, "Nah, nigga, HE AIN'T vile! THAT nigga is TRIFE!!!".

"*Yeeeeeeaaaaaahhhhhh, SUMFIN' like dat!*", Mr. Trife, replies, *(INTUBATION VOICE AMAZIN'!!!),* like the sun, eyes blazin', CHEWING HARRRRRRD on a Twizzler, hangin' out his mouth - (out tha' side!!!).

"Enough, y'all, enough!", Pockets, chimes in!, (with HIS own stiff upper lip!), (Of, His: While-I'm-in-this-morgue-Self-Defense!). *With dead bodies zipped-up on gurneys to the left of him. With dead bodies zipped-up on gurneys to his right. With one poor-wet-cold-dead-blue-motherfucker, (left layin' there!), DEAD NAKED! With a whole lotta other dead-motherfuckers behind those silver stainless heavy-handled doors. (WHERE, other dead-motherfuckers, FEET FIRST, were SLID inside!).*

AND THEN...*YOU GOT THE FREEZER!!!*

(Come! YOU'LL WANT TO have a LOOK AT THIS!)...

FULLY STOCKED, WITH (AND OF!), compound fractures and overdoses!! ENCASED WITHIN their zippered-cocoons...(retaining thick-stenches and odors!) THICK-stenches and odors, (OF their own!), AND OF those, "previously-cocooned", IN same! (THOSE COCOONS DON'T GET WASHED OUT!!!)(So, YOU GET ZIPPED-UP, LAYIN' ON TOP OF, ANOTHER DEAD-MOTHERFUCKER'S, FLUIDS AND JUICES - simple and plain!). *ENCASED WITHIN, (OF AND, WITH!), the THICK stench, OF hard liquor and bowels! And, Mr. Trife, JUST MIGHT go IN there!* (IN THAT freezer!)...(THAT, TRIFLIN' MOTHERFUCKER!!!) *AND...lay HIMSELF on down!*

Lay himself on down...

ON THAT slippery cold floor! (Amongst THOSE filthy "roll-'em-in-roll-'em-out" MOISTENED, condensation, dirty-gurney-tracks!). AND TAKE HIMSELF A NAP!!! In THAT freezer!! AMONGST HIS FRIENDS, a.k.a. The Dead. ('Cause, Mr. Trife's a crowd-pleaser!).

But...

(He DON'T!)

'CAUSE...

There's WORK to be done! (DIRTY-WORK!!!) "Jettison Records" *kind-of-work!* And so, (COME!!! Let's have a look)...

AS...

(Mr. Trife, directs False Profit to write, some false-shit, on a toe tag)...

Pockets, (UNdirected), *UNZIPS Y.S.' - "postmortem-cocoon" - OF HER - white disaster bag! As, MC Busta-Nut, reads what's written on the containers, (positioned up on a shelf). Containing the final meals, of sick stomach contents collected, (of internal organs removed AND inspected!).* (AND, as for, MC Busta-Nut?). Well?...(THE WAY - Jettison Records - "GETS DOWN"...well, *This - "Road Life" - Shit,* IS STILL worth it to him!)('Cause, MC Busta-Nut STILL WANTS, that "Audi A8 status", AND wealth!). *BUT, he knows, before he can make it rain on bitchez, by throwin' up nothin' but C-Notes. That, FIRST, he's got to pay these music industry dues, as he gets hit with the HOT taste of his own "stomach-content-waste" - IN THE BACK OF HIS THROAT.* (And, yes, HE'S beginning TO FEEL a lil' bit SICK TO HIS STOMACH, himself!!).

FOR...

(MC BUSTA-NUT'S UPCHUCKING IN THE BACK OF HIS MOUTH!!! AND SWALLOWING THOSE SLOBBERY-HOT-CHUNKS RIGHT BACK DOWN!!!)...

And so...

(With Mr. Trife's work here ALMOST complete)...

Though, exactly why he did, the things that he did, the reason being, what he came here to do, (TO YOU, THE READER)...have NOT YET QUITE been revealed. *TRUST & BELIEVE, those bodies that, Mr. Trife, JUST WENT TO TOWN ON, WERE sewn closed - WITH THAT - thick red UNWAXED autopsy thread! And, THEY WERE SEWN UP NICE 'N TIGHT, by none other than THE ONE - Mr. Trife! TRUST & BELIEVE, he did so choose to use - THAT BIG-HOOKED-silver-DURABLE-stainless-steel-sewing-needle - to poke through and loop - cold wet skin - of the dead. AS HE, COMPULSIVELY DID SO, OVERDUE,...AS THEY WERE SEALED!!* (MUTHAFUCKIN'-RED-UNWAXED-AUTOPSY-THREAD-OY-VEY!!!!!!).

Though, zippered twice.

FIRST, their chests and torsos. THEN, that of, their: "postmortem-cocoons". And, (OF that, white disaster bag?). Well, (From the outside, IT'S APPARENT, it's transparent and weird!!)...'Cause, YOU CAN SEE *the opaqueness, of the bloodied-insides!...(STREAKED AND SMEARED!!!)...WITH THAT COLD ASS dank dead BLOOD!...* (STREAKED AND SMEARED!!!)...*of the bloodied-insides...(AGAINST, AND UP!!!)...(though, on the bottom)...YOU WILL FIND "ponding"...* (THOUGH FROZEN!!!), *though zippered, and not open, YOU CAN SEE, to the sides, it's the same, thereto!...(FROZEN AGAINST, AND UP!)...* (STREAKED AND SMEARED!!!)...*(Deep)...(Dark!)...(AND, ROUGH!!!).* *...As they. Lay alone. IN BLOOD!!! Of,...dark maroon.* (Go 'head!),(AND, TAKE A LOOK!!!)*(AT THAT "ponding" OF the blood!!).* (AND MAKE DAMN SURE, YOU TAKE A GOOD LONG HARD LOOK, AT THEM TOO!!). *Laying there! DEAD!!! All alone! And,...marooned.*

Then, it's...

Back into the freezer or in a silver stainless-steel heavy-handled drawer they go! (Can YOU handle THIS life on the road???). (DO YOU want it THIS bad!?!). WELL? DO YOU??? Well, then...

Go 'head!! TAKE A LOOK!!! For, THIS music biz SHIT, JUST MAY HAVE YOU *layin' there, LIKE THAT!! As they, CONTINUE to - LAY-THERE-layin'-there - LIKE that!! Layin' IN that white disaster bag!!! As Pockets, gets RIGHT back to...THE RUNNIN' OF THE POCKETS!!!*

AS...

False Profit, WRESTLES blue diamonds off a BLUE FINGERS!!!! ('Cause, OF THE false profit, YOU CAN'T stop it!!!!) *AND, YOU JUST KNOW, THAT False Profit, GON' BE stealin' they necklaces AND LOCKETS!!!!*

AS...

MC Busta-Nut, is thinkin' to himself, "Hmm...you know what??? Hmmmmmm,...FOR being cold and dead,...SHE IS a HOT GIRL!!!"

AS...

(Mr. Trife, THROUGH THOSE limited edition Cazel gold lenses, GRILLS Pockets!)...

AS...

Pockets, STAYS in love with his love affair! OF, RIPPING-OFF (while rippin'-through, the pockets of), THE GIRL with the peeled-off face!!!! (The girl...with the mermaid hair:(

FOR, Pockets IS...

THE art lover! (In love WITH the art.) The art: OF the music biz gank! The art: OF no shame! (OR DISGRACE!!!!) The art: OF STEALING your ideas AND YOUR music!! (ALL while, AND ALL THE BETTER)...THE FINE ART: OF financing THAT SHIT through someone else's bank!

As...

...Pockets, grills back!

AS...

His custom red on top he cocks! (The, runnin' of tha' pockets, he NEVER stops!!). *$TRAIGHT grillin' Mr. Trife! Like, YEAH, YOU'RE gettin' it now!! THIS industry ain't pretty! BUT it's pretty AT the top!!!* (WELCOME to this music biz world!!) *STRAIGHT GRILLIN' at him, like, "YEAH, I KNEW what I was gettin' you into, and it now looks like, you NOW know it too!! A straight up - I-didn't-see-this-shit-comin'-how-bad-do-YOU-want-it - trip to the morgue!"*

(Though, after some time, though, not so much time, Mr. Trife indeed, did his shit)...

AND...

Handled his biz!

Though, he did, remove his bullet hole hat. (Though, behind sun-blazoned eyes). He did, as he, indeed, lowered his head, in prayer, for Y.S. Then, just like that, ('cause, after all, HOW BAD DO YOU WANT IT?), it's back, to this music biz grind! ('Cause, after all,...how bad do you want it?). THEN, the odd four, goes steppin' back out THAT back door! (The one, at the top, of five masoned steps).

THOUGH...

Bagged-up, back in the morgue. Was an extra-thick, extra-husky, extra-red, plastic trash bag. Left tied up. (RETIED up!!). Previously,...tied up. PREVIOUSLY, left labeled up: "INCINERATOR". (And, placed at the bottom, of an wheeled-industrial-strength-canvas laundry cart, in that bottom level hospital hall, just outside the door, with that recessed-white-lettered-plastic-black-sign, labeled: "MORGUE"). WITH EVERY ITEM, white coat and uniform, in its proper-local, it was back. (JUST AS it was before!)(Though, NOT the items that Mr. Trife gripped!!). And, Mr. Trife, is MOVIN' how HE BE movin' jack!(BURNIN' that Nigerian incense!).

AND, as for, THAT TRIFLIN' SHIT, Mr. Trife did, back there, in the morgue??

Well...

Y.S., was zippered thrice. First, there was the removal of her internal organs. But, you have to understand, it wasn't til' after Mr. Trife, with a scalpel in a steady hand, gave Y.S. a "Y" incision. He made a clean run. Her blood ran. And, don't get it twisted, Mr. Trife's scalpel point positionin' - in the vicinity of her collarbone's "AC joint" - was just the beginnin'! As, Mr. Trife, made layered flesh, fat, and red meat, gape. As, the splits in her pecs of her chest flesh met, one at a time,...just below her breastplate. After, and then, Mr. Trife, twisted that scalpel blade, AS HE MADE IT - MAKE ITS WAY, all the way down 'n 'round her navel, Mr. Trife, DID SO, MAKE IT SNAKE! After, and then, gaped-layered flesh, fat, and red meat, hung down over the sides, two at a time, to at a time, knowing together he'll have to heft them shitz back up together, knowing he'll have to pull them shitz together, of her flesh, knowing he'll be sewing together. As, Mr. Trife, had already made his decision, that he'd be givin' Y.S.' "Y" incision, A-"THICK-RED-MAXIMUM-TRACTION-UNWAXED-AUTOPSY-THREADED-STAINLESS-STEEL-STURDY-HOOKED-NEEDLED-BACK-TOGETHER-SPLICE",...(COMPLIMENTS, OF MR. TRIFE!!!). But, you have to understand, THE process OF the plan, OF Y.S.' autopsy,...YOU attended! Didn't none of that happen, til' after, Mr. Trife, implemented, the use of a white-'n-wide - red-numbered-'n-lined - "barrelled-of-circumference" - long-'n-thick - needled-syringe, for the drainage of urine, into Y.S.' bladder, Mr. Trife, punctured dead skin, as he, stuck it deep down within. And then, with that, THICK 'N RED - UNWAXED - AUTOPSY THREAD, Mr. Trife, USED IT to tie off the ends, once removed, of Y.S.' large intestines, to ensure the containment, OF ALL OF HER excrement. THEN, what Mr. Trife chose, back in that room,...(STILL BEING WATCHED),...(BY THE SPIRITS THAT ROSE!), as he, STILL breathed in, STILL TO BE - forever-without-question-mucus-membrane-embedded - ALL UP AND IN, the linings of his sinuses, (BACK IN THAT COOLER OF A ROOM)... (WHERE THE STENCH OF CHEMICALS 'N BOWELS)...(HUNG AS IT FROZE!!!),....Mr. Trife, of her fingers and toes, down to and through and off the bone, snipped! Then, he moved onto her palms and the soles of her feet, as he: "scalpelled-them-off", dead skin split, peeled and lifted-off, clean! And, there will be NO indentifying Y.S., through her dental records. ('CAUSE, Mr. Trife, removed ALL OF HER teeth!). And, ALL OF THAT,

WAS PLACED INTO THAT RED "INCINERATOR" BAG! BUT, NOT UNTIL, AFTER THE REMOVAL, OF EVERYTHING, SKELETAL AND REMOVABLE! (Of, SOME - Layin'-There-Cold-Wet-Blue-Naked-And-Dead - MOTHERFUCKER - LAYIN' THERE - DEAD-NAKED - FULL FRONTAL!). (OH, YOU'RE IN IT NOW! HOW BAD DO YOU WANT THIS "MUSIC-BIZ-LIFE"?!? AIN'T NO TURNING BACK NOW! AIN'T NO TIME TO BE A COWARD!!!)...'CAUSE, BY MR. TRIFE, EVERYTHING REMOVABLE AND SKELETAL, WAS OSCILLATED-AUTOPSIED-SAWED-UP - SLICED 'N DICED, DOWN TO A - fine-skulldust-sawdust-dust-mite-particle-powder!!! (With Mr. Trife - not being new to this - didn't take him NO MORE than an hour!). Which led, to as much DNA, out of Y.S.' jugulars, by Mr. Trife, EACH ONE, BEING BLED!! WHICH LED, to Y.S.' blood, deep-dark-and-dank, flowin' down til' it reached, that autopsy table's drain, positioned down,... by Y.S.' TOELESS FEET!! WHICH LED, AS THAT - DANK-DARK-DEAD-BLOOD - STANK, FLOWED, AND STREAKED - DOWN TO AND THRU, THAT AUTOPSY TABLE'S - WHY'D-THEY-HAVE-TO-MAKE-THIS-SO-THICK-'N-ODDLY-TRANSPARENT - DRAINAGE TUBE! OF WHICH, WHEN SEEN THROUGH, BY WHICH, ALL IN THE ROOM, ALL BUT, Mr. Trife, IT ALL BUT, KICK-STARTED GAGGIN'-ACTIONS AND HURLIN', FOR CERTAIN!!! BUT IT ONLY GOT WORSE WHEN - Y.S.' DANK BLOOD - CAUSED THAT AUTOPSY ROOM'S CENTRALLY LOCATED - ROUND-ESTUARY-FLOOR-GRATE - FOR DRAINAGE, TO FLOOD! BUT IT GOT WORSE WHEN, THE CENTRALLY-LOCATED-ROUND-ESTUARY-FLOOR-GRATE-FOR-DRAINAGE - STARTED WITH ITS SPITTIN' 'N SPURTIN' - OF "SHEETS OF DANKNESS" (AND LEST WE FORGET!) THE "BLOOD CURTAINS"!! AND FOR CERTAIN, IT GOT MUCH WORSE WHEN, THAT ESTUARY-OF-A-FLOOR-GRATE MADE - POCKETS, BUSTA-NUT AND FALSE PROFIT CAPITULATE!!! 'CAUSE, THEIR FUTILE ATTEMPTS TO NOT START HURLIN', WERE NO LONGER WORKIN'!!! (FROM JUST THE SOUNDS ALONE BEING MADE!!!). CAUSE THAT DAMN DRAINAGE GATE WOULDN'T STOP...REGURGITATIN' 'N GURGLIN'!!! After, and then, there was the placement of in, that RED

"INCINERATOR" BAG, of everythin'...but tha' skin,...OF THAT - COLD-WET-BLUE-NAKED-HOLLOWED-OUT - MOTHERFUCKER, THAT Y.S., WAS 'BOUT TO GET ZIPPERED-UP IN!!! Though, NOT BEFORE SO, with that UNWAXED THICK 'N RED AUTOPSY THREAD, Mr. Trife, ZIPPERED-UP Y.S.' CHEST AND TORSO - WITH MAXIMUM TRACTION OF HIS SEWING ACTION - NICE 'N TIGHT - HE DID SO!!! And, then Mr. Trife "Cocooned her" inside, sealed all-up-in, THAT - HOLLOWED-OUT-MOTHERFUCKER'S - COLD-WET-BLUE-SKIN!! (AND HE DID SO, NICE 'N TIGHT!!)(WHICH LED, TO Y.S., BEING ZIPPERED twice!!). And so,...THEN,...Mr. Trife,...ZIPPERED HER THRICE!!! For, once back in her white disaster bag, she got zipped back up, BUT,...THIS TIME,...Y.S.,...EVEN HAD,...HER VERY OWN...TOE TAG! (WRITTEN WIT SOME FALSE SHIT ON IT!). And it was hangin' off just the lil' bit, of what was left of her right big toe - gingerly-looped-over-and-placed - as such, by Mr. Trife, he did so! After, and then, she was slid in, a heavy handled stainless steel drawer, (bless her heart!),(and try not to cry!), as Y.S., by Mr. Trife, FEET FIRST,...WAS SLID INSIDE!!!

AND...

(With all that done, with not Pockets, MC Busta-Nut, nor False Profit, having not one clue or a guess, that Mr. Trife, was actually doing right by Y.S.!)...

FOR...

(It wasn't all that skulldust-sawdust-dust-mite-ass-power, kickin' up in their eyes, makin' them blind!)...

RATHER...

(It was their "creepy-music-industry-ways" blindin' Pockets, Profit and 'Nut!)...

FOR...

(ALL THEY COULD FORESEE, THROUGH ALL THE SKULLDUST-DEBRIS, WAS MR. TRIFE BREAKIN' BACK IN TO

GET - A KEPT-FRESH Y.S. - FOR AT SOME POINT IN TIME - FOR POCKETS 'N FALSE PROFIT - FOR AT LEAST ONE MO' TIME - FOR THE PURPOSE OF FEEDING THEIR CREEPY-MUSIC-INDUSTRY-LUST - AND - LEST WE FORGET - BUSTA-NUT!!!)...

RATHER...

(Mr. Trife, did all that he did to ensure, the music indutry, couldn't fuck with her no more!)...

AND(BESIDES!)...

(Let 'em eat ass!)...

'CAUSE...

(Mr. Trife, ain't breakin' back into this-here morgue!).

BUT...(as for, RIGHT NOW!!)...

AS,(FOR, Mr. Trife???)...

Well...

HE-BE-ON-SOME: *"Silent-Night-Flight-Movements"!!!*

And...

(Vanished up above into the sky of black!). And, once again! Some DEJA VU sets in! As, something "like a pebble", (from the black sky above), hits him (ONCE AGAIN!!!) on the top of his bullet hole hat!

"Mr. Trife, I can't EVEN hate! But,...HOW-tha'-fuck DID YOU pull THIS shit off?!?", (with RARE props given!), from MC Busta-Nut, he questions, *from the darkness,* of THAT platform, at the top, of those five masoned steps.

"It's all in how you move, Busta-Nut. NOW, move your ass on down them steps! And, gemme' a hand removing those reflective strips, off a BOTH SIDES, of OUR Jettison Records RV and, THEN let's get on our mutha' fuckin' GIDDY-UP! How I pull this shit off??? *I pulled the reflective strips off the sides, of that ambulance over there.* TOLD YO' ASS!!! ALL I NEEDED was five minutes! Had to make our RV, look like, some big-time "Mobile Command Center", first!! LIKE, I said, *just back tha' FUCKIN' RV up to the dock, LIKE YOU IS 'sposed to be there!* Like, I said,...IT'S ALL in how you move!", Mr. Trife, spits knowledge AND game!!!

And...

Mr. Trife, did it all, COOL as shit!

WHILE...

Chewin' HARRRRRRD on a Twizzler, hangin' out tha' side of his mouth, (hangin' over his lip!).

WITH...

Guts forged from mettle. (HARDER THAN a cast iron kettle!).

AND...

That slight-one-cornered-smile that he gives, is Mr. Trife's way, of letting them ALL KNOW,...*they WERE NEVER on his LEVEL!!!*

Chapter Fifteen

ICE GIRL

After some time on the road. Of: The Most Triflin's life, (ALL IN it TOGETHER now!), they all HAVE, NOW been exposed! (And, that of, YOU TOO!!) *AIN'T NO ventilation system BACK THERE in that AUTOPSY ROOM! For, FOREVER STUCK up IN YOUR nose,* (WILL BE AND IS) *skulldust-sawdust, hard liquor and BOWELS!* JUST LIKE, the HAIRS on the BACK OF YOUR NECK, sittin' up, THEY WILL BE, FOREVER STUCK, like a catchy tune. *Skulldust-sawdust. A DECEDENT'S, hard liquor and bowels.* In ALL their mucus membranes, (AND,...ALSO YOU!!!). For, YOU CAN'T SHAKE THAT SHIT, like a stripper's glitter and perfume!!

"Lemme' get some of them Twizzlers, Mr. Trife!", (breakin' the silence and ice!), asks, a hard-to-impress, MC Busta-Nut!

"Nigga! YOU GOTTA' better chance of gettin' a SINGLE piece of BEEF JERKY from Pockets! THAN you got, GETTIN' a Twizzler, FROM MY nigga, MR. TRIFE!!", (a DUALLY-IMPRESSED!!) False Profit, SPEAKS-ON, OF the latest OF goings-on's, witha' a rollin'-laugh to boot!

"So, WHAT NOW, Pockets??", MC Busta-Nut, asks, (AS his quest, for a Twizzler, was given the boot!), as the RV rolls on down Southbound Business Rt. 36, as Pockets, GOTTA' KEEP himself a safe distance, (FROM North Juarez's city limits!)...(OY VEY!).

"WHAT NOW!?! DON'T-BE MUTHA'-FUCKIN'-ASKIN' ME, *"WHAT MUTHA'-FUCKIN'-NOW?"!!! I'M THA'* MUTHA'-FUCKA', THAT, BE-TELLIN' YOU - *"WHAT - THE-MUTHA'-FUCKIN'- WHAT-NOW?" -* BE!!!", Pockets, goes off, *still and after, Mr. Trife's movements back there at the morgue,* GOTTA' show that HE'S, (still and after!), the mutha'-fuckin'-boss, cockin' his custom red custom-made red hat hard to the side, before distilled water gets swallowed hard, as he, has too (ONCE AGAIN!),...swallow his pride! "Uh, yeah,...uh, yeah, well, so, anywaaaaaays, "you triflin'-mutha'-fucka'",...WHAT-NOW?!?", Pockets, *painfully-asks, causing him - induced-tonsillitis-of-swallowed-pride* - (like a MUTHA'-FUCKA'!!!).

(Of land laid, of kid in a candy store, of HIS playground, of his: "morgue-arcade"!), Mr. Trife, tells Pockets, "To bang this right, cut your lights, stay on this winding driving-path, til' we make it to the rear and, just drop me off here!"

"HERE??? You TRIFLIN' mutha' fucka'!? WHAT IS IT wit you...wit, tha' dead!?! NEVER MIND!!!", Pockets, expounds, as the RV comes to a rolling stop, *at: Brotha Trife's "known"-Section "MM", (in the back in the dark), of his: "beloved burial grounds".*

"Yeah. Here. RIGHT, here!", Mr. Trife, replies, EVEN IN his *"weakened-memory-state",* (yet and perhaps!), *from, the: "sporadic- shit" falling FROM the sky,* (on top of his hat striking!), has yet, (but perhaps!), *JARRED his memory OPEN slightly,* (like an ajar door, shits coming back to him!), *MORE and MORE!!* But, of: being dropped off, "RIGHT, here!",(AND RIGHT NOW!), of this: *awakened-after-three- years-strapped-down-at-his-feet-and-his-wrists,* (Mr. Trife), has never been MORE sure!

"DAMN, my nigga,...*you IS a TRIFLIN' mutha' fucka', OF THA' MOST TRIFLIN', there IS NO oth'a!!",* MC Busta-Nut, *spits!*

"WHO tha' fuck, YOU tellin'!?!", (a: in FULL agreement!) Pockets, *says,* then, cocks his custom red, custom-made red hat hard to the side, on top of his head! (As, it's time FOR HIM to show: who's-who-who's tha' boss!). And so, of words, Pockets, is NEVER at a LOSS, "'Nut and Profit, Y'ALL TWO head-on back to tha' studio and, start cleanin' all that blood and ALL THOSE brain sniglets off'a EVERYTHANG! 'Cause, me and Triflin' here, WE gots'ta discuss SOMETHANGS!"

(Then. Looking. Studying. JUDGING!!! Questioning. BETTING,...on Mr. Trife! Two custom red derbies face off "face-to-face" in the dark. And BOTH...cocked harrrrrd to the side! Then. Pockets. "Mr.-If-I'm-A-Gamblin'-Man-In-Which-I-AM!!",...rolls them mutha' fuckin' dice!!)...

"Ok. Listen up, Mr. Trife. I don't need no explanations, as to WHY, you want to be dropped off here. JUST, from HERE, make your way into the city and, DON'T fuck up! YOU feel me!? From HERE, and, from HERE, ON OUT, I want RESULTS!! NOT, explanations! YOU FEEL ME??? Yeah, so, well, anywaaaaaays, I KNOW, that, you've NEVER BEEN to North Juarez before. SO, you WON'T KNOW those streets! BUT, you'll HAVETA' find a "lay-up-and-lay-low-spot", you know, for a few days or so. Think YOU CAN handle that???", Pockets, questions (AND, lays it down WITHOUT QUESTION!).

"It ain't where you're from. It's how you move.", Mr. Trife, replies, out the corner of his mouth, hangs down, a long red Twizzler, he chews, chewin' like, *he ain't,* lookin' like, *he ain't,* ('CAUSE, *he AIN'T!*), 'cause,... *HE ain't got shit to prove!*

"Exactly! So. Make your way into the city. Lay-up somewhere. Lay-low! AND, peep tha' scene. MAKE your move! GET MY WOMAN!!! And then,...GET THA' FUCK outta' tha' city! Simple.", one red derby in the dark explains to the other one, (which then, nods that it is understood),(the red derby in the dark, wit'a bullet hole!). And then, Pockets, continues, "Listen. I AIN'T tryna' insult you, Mr. Trife. I DON'T have to tell you what to do, 'cause, you wouldn't be sittin' here right now breathin', if I didn't think you COULD pull THIS-SHIT off! Look. The worst you could get, for helpin' me out on this shit, is an "aiding and abetting" charge. BUT,...NOT really!! 'Cause, "They", being: *"THE ENTIRE - mutha'-fuckin' - North-Juarez-police-force" -* AIN'T lookin', to BOOK me! And, NOBODY, in North Juarez, wants YOU dead. IT'S THE POLICE, THAT want, ME dead! *THEY AIN'T, in Pockets' "pockets", NO mo',...you feel me?!?* AIN'T THAT some, MUTHA'-FUCKIN' shit!?! *YEAH, UH, SO, WELL, ANYWAAAAAAYS,* SINCE you'll have some TIME on your hands, IN the city, whilst you be layin'-low,...SEE WHATCHA' CAN DO wit, comin' up wit, a hit song. And, just keep in mind while you're layin'-low, that, me and the boys, back there, well, we'll be 'round. You know, checkin' on some venues, keepin' up wit tha' ponies. HEY, what can I say!? I'MA gamblin' man! But,...seriously,...I'ma get me a, NEW "buttery-mic" for my, uh, yeah, so, well, anyways, OUR mobile studio and, I'ma get them two layin' down, some new tracks. Might have 'em, lay down that new jam, "Hot Cold Dead Girl"! Anyway, Mr. Trife, TIME-BE-MONEY, my nigga! And, you'll have some time. Work on that song. And, if IT'S fire?? I give you my word! I'LL have it ALL OVER FM radio! AND STREAMING, all over tha' world, fo' tha' end of THIS year! ...ANY questions??", Pockets, *(yeah, so, well, anywaaaaaays!),* reassures.

"Yeah. I DO! JUST one! WHY you keep that gun loaded for??? I lost an eye! AND I LOST my homegirl, Y.S.!! WHAT THA' FUCK, MAN?!?", a-none-too-happy, Mr. Trife, demands!!

"NOW you got ME, givin' explanations!! AIN'T doin' ME no good, Mr. Trife, TO HAVE a gun NOT loaded! OR to have tha' shit ON safety! I DON'T roll like that!! YOU FEEL ME??? THAT'S how, I LIVE!!! Mr. Trife, WHEN it's "go-time"? IT'S "GO-TIME"!!! ...YOU feel me?? AND, my lady, shiiiiiit, SHE BAD LIKE my gun!! SO, just look for tha'-baddest-woman in tha' city, that kicks it like my gun and, THAT would be tha' one, you've found her! And so, NOW, FOR YOU, my nigga, IT'S "GO-time". So, as you would say, *"Get on your Giddy-Up!",* Mr. Trife!", Pockets, explains.

"Bet.", Mr. Trife, replies.

Then...

(Makes his way, to the back of the RV. Grabs his suitcase)...

And...

His autopsy room supplies!

Then...

Walked back up on Pockets, *(Pockets never heard him walk!),* Pockets flinched, *but tried to play it off,* then, before Mr. Trife, takes the field, you know Pockets GOTTA' hear himself talk, so Pockets, gives Mr. Trife, one last pep talk, "Listen, Mr. Trife, it's all gonna workout just fine. You don't get nowhere in life, without taking risks. So, is this risky? YOU DAMN-RIGHT, it is!!! BUT, the reward in this, faaaaaar and away, SUPERSEDES the risk! YOU'LL LEARN exactly what I'm talkin' 'bout, Mr. Trife. You'll see. When you FIRST get a taste, of big money, YOU'LL see! After all this, once you get my lady back for me and, we REALLY get this music thing rollin', shiiiiiit, you'll KNOW what I'm talkin' 'bout. Trife, once you get a lil' taste of big money, you can never have enough. 'Cause, THAT'S when survival and quality-of-life, REALLY kicks in. Well,...it did for me, anyway. You start tellin' yourself, *"Ok, I got this much money."* And then, you set a certain amount in your mind, and, you tell yourself of, *"Out of all that money you have, if I never go UNDER this certain amount of money, well, I'll ALWAYS be good. My lady, my kids, whatever, WILL always be good. My kids, will never know what it's like to go hungry."* And so, you NEVER stop thinkin' 'bout money! It's ALWAYS on your mind!!! So, you think to yourself, *"Ok. NOW I got to go out and, make MORE money!!"*,...it's never enough, Mr. Trife. I'm tellin' you right now, IT'S NEVER enough! Once you get that "initial-taste" of, what it's like, to have big money, shiiiiiit, YOU can never have enough. 'Cause, you'll start tellin' yourself, *"IF I ALWAYS HAVE, THIS AMOUNT of money in the bank, I'LL NEVER again, know what it's like, to get my lights cut off by the 'lectric company! If I always have this much money in the bank, I'll never again, know what it's like, to NOT HAVE a car!"* And, Mr. Trife, AFTER you get that first initial-taste OF big money, you'll be tellin' yourself shit, like, *"If I always have this much money, I'll never again have that feelin' you get, when you're standin' up at the counter payin' for somethin',* (AND you got the store clerk just lookin' at you!)(AND YOU GOT a line of NOSEY MUTHA' FUCKAS standin' behind you!) (LOOKIN' at you!)(JUDGING YOU!!!)(AND, they're all thinkin' the SAME THING, as YOU!!), *AS YOU, stand there...lookin' down...at that lil' key pad...wit yo' debit card stickin' outta it. And, YOU'RE JUST standin' there...waitin'...watchin'...hopin'...DAMN-NEAR PRAYIN', that, THAT MOTHERFUCKER says, "Approved" AND NOT "Declined"!!!"* 'Cause, THAT'S A fucked-up feelin' to have!! 'Cause, THAT'S SOME SHIT, I DON'T NEED, in MY motherfuckin' life, EVER again!!! So, you SET that amount in your head, Mr. Trife. And, you NEVER go

UNDER that amount, NO MATTER WHAT!!! And then, all you do from there, IS THINK 'BOUT, HOW, you gonna' go out, and, GET SOME MO' MUTHA' FUCKIN' MONEY!! SO, GET OUT THERE, MR. TRIFE!!! GET OUT THERE AND, GET MY WOMAN!!! Yeah, so, well, anywaaaaaays, AND THEN, ME AND YOU, WE GON' GET OUT THERE AND, GET THAT MUTHA' FUCKIN' MONEY!!!!!!"

And *(on THAT note!)*...

(Ali steps through the ropes, Evel Knievel heads down the ramp, the Raiders light the torch, and smoke begins to blow, as THE "U" takes the field!)...

Triflin', steps down out of the RV and, steps down into a dark cemetery at night. Light from the RV's interior backlights Mr. Trife, as he stands facing the tombstones and the dead. (Odd for some). (BEYOND uncomfortable to others!). But, for Mr. Trife, he FEELS right at home.

(Tossing down a cell phone and, a stack of cash to Mr. Trife), Pockets, tells him, "THAT's an early "advance" on your future record sales. Don't be no big-dummy and run through it like, some of these mofo's out here that AIN'T NEVER had nuthin'. BE SMART, wit THAT BREAD!! You feel me?? And,...Mr. Trife,...hit me up when you got MY lady OUTTA' the city,...lemme' know where you be at. And I'll come get you."

"Bet.", Mr. Trife, replies, then...*feels the sense of deja vu again. (Just something about Pockets, giving him a cell phone, feels VERY familiar to him!)...(BUT, whenever that deja vu's been hittin' him, somethin's BEEN hittin' him FROM the skies!)*...BUT, that didn't happen THIS time! SO, all that - *deja-vu-cell-phone-shit - he's feeling* - Mr. Trife, don't really know why!

And so...

(As, Mr. Trife, stands there, watching that RV, winding its way back down that winding path, back out towards those tall-spike-wrought-iron-cemetery-gates. Leaving him there. Alone in the cemetery)...DAMMIT... *is this fate!?*

AS...

Mr. Trife, gets hit in the hat AGAIN!

Though...

(The BACK of the hat!)(NOT the top this time!)...

But(STILL!)...

Hit at a high rate!

AND SO...

(OUT OF the darkness of the cemetery, as Mr. Trife, stands there alone, with nothing but his suit case standing by his side, Mr. Trife,... *hears a voice come out of the darkness!)...*

And...

It speaks TO him!

"You be SLIPPIN', Triflin'!"

(OH SHIT! IF that ain't a ghost, THEN, that could only mean,... maybe,...I ain't standin' here alone!!!).

Spinnin' on his heels, Mr. Trife wheels 'round, squints INTO the darkness, AND deducts,..."JESTER??????"

"I said, YOU BE slippin', Triflin'!! THE Triflin', I KNEW, would NEVER LET NOBODY, roll-up-on-him, like this! MUCH-LESS, let a mutha' fucka' THROW A ROCK, at the back of his head! YEAH, B. TRIFE!!! IT'S ME, JESTER!!! HOW-tha'-fuck, you KNOW it was me???", Brotha Jester, replies, *EMERGING out of and up to Trife, from the darkness and the tombstones.*

The two give each other a big hug and, a few punches to the shoulders and ribs, like they've never been apart like before, (ALL HAPPY N' SHIT!), like - two-reuniting-on-the-first-day-of-shool-kids, before, Mr. Trife, *provides his deduction, "HOW-THA'-FUCK, I know it WAS YOU???"* ...'CAUSE, YOU PLAY TOO mutha' fuckin' MUCH!!! Jester, WHAT-THA'-FUCK are you doin' OUT HERE, ANY-damn-way???"

"THA'-FUCK, YOU MEAN???, *"Tha'-fuck, I'm doin', HERE?!?"*, LAST TIME, I seen you, *WAS right HERE!!!* MAN, 'Triflin', I've BEEN waitin' for you TO show THA'-FUCK back up HERE!! B. Trife, let me tell ya' sumthin'. I make my way, BACK TO THIS cemetery, EVERY night, JUST TO SEE, if you'd SHOW tha'-fuck BACK UP! Motherfucker, IT'S BEEN three years!!! THREE-motherfuckin'-YEARS!!! *WHERE tha'-fuck, you BEEN, son!?!"*, Jester, replies.

After some thought, (peeped through the darkness, by Jester), Mr. Trife, answers, "Good question!"

"Uh, B. Trife,...*you good??"*, Jester, asks, *(WITH the concern of an old and TRUE friend).*

"Yeah. Yeah, I'm good. You know me, Jester,...I be iight.", Mr. Trife, tries to assure him, (by playing it off like he's good).

Then, taking a GOOD HARD LOOK (through the cemetery's darkness), Jester, asks, "Fucks-wit-dem threads, 'Triflin'?? AND, THEM SHOES!?! Feelin' them shades though, son! Rockin' them old school Cazel jawns. You BULLIED them-shitz off a some pimp, DIDN'TCHA'?? *SAME OL' mutha' fuckin' B. TRIFE!"*, Jester, *deducts.* (THEN,...gives his assesment, *OF some more deductions,* of HIS own!), *"YOU DON'T dress like that, B. Trife,...SURE you good??? ...Tha'-fuck, you been up too? And, WHO was that MUTHA' FUCKA' that, dropped you off here???"*

"Who?? Oh, him? JESTER! THIS is GONNA' bug-YOU-tha'-fuck-out! THAT CAT, is some BIG TIME "Record Producer", FROM Atlanta! Jester, my man, HE'S one of tha' MAIN mutha' fuckas! *You STILL BE rappin'? You still be gettin' them, CYPHERS goin'??* MY MAN, if you WANT IN on this "music-shit",...I CAN GET YOU IN!!! Got ME, a deal! Gon' be singin' tha' blues, MY MAN!!! I got me a *"stage name"* 'n *EVERYTHANG!!!* Check it, YOU'RE JUST GONNA' BE IN TOO-DAMN-MUCH-LOVE, WIT THIS SHIT! ...Jester,...*I GOES by tha' name of, MR. TRIFE!!!"*, Mr. Trife, says, *with TOO MUCH pride!!!*

(Jester, just gives Mr. Trife, the "once-over")...

And(THEN)...

(BREAKS-IT-DOWN for him!!)...

"T, after you left, I GAVE UP on rap. You damn-skippy, I WANTED TO BE a rapper!! BUT, while you WAS gone, I saw this video on Youtube."

Then...

(Jester, *leaves claw marks* in the cemetery's darkness *shaped like "quotation marks"*)...

As...

He, *restarts*, " "Mr. Trife", you GOTTA' sell your soul, TO make it big. "They", GOT cats out here, wearin' dresses and CLUTCHIN' PURSES!!! That ain't, for me, T. That AIN'T, for YOU!"

(Mr. Trife, just stares through that 24 Karat Cazel gold lense, of limited edition, of his, standin' there, in his Jimmy Choo's, and, not sayin' one damn word).

SO...

(Jester, continues FOR him!)...

..."YOU gotta' sell, YOUR soul. I know how much you love music 'n shit. *And, me and you, we ALWAYS got the cyphers goin'! SHIT, T, I'd text you some shit, on your cell phone, gettin' tha' cypher goin' through text, when I'd be all-fucked-up 'n shit. And, YOU'D hit me back, texting me YOUR rap! AND, we'd just keep that cypher goin', texting back-and-forth, OVER tha' phone!* 'Member that shit!? SO, I don't want to kill your dream of makin' music, T. BUT, I'm tellin' you RIGHT now. THAT - *"SHIT"*? THAT - *"Music-Industry-YA'-GOTTA'-SELL-YOUR-SOUL" - BULLSHIT??* Listen to me, T! THAT - *"SHIT"*, ain't FOR, me and you!!"

"Damn. ...I hear ya', Jester. And, me and you, *we been done rap'd 'bout, certain shit, back in tha' day too,...rappin' 'bout "life 'n shit",...TRYNA' get it ALL worked out!* Jester, you 'member back in them *"cypher-days"*, BACK WHEN, my babies were, just lil' guys? My two puppy pits, Cash and Tatum! AND Ice Girl! She was gettin' up in them years. And, SHE was undersized! ...But, SO beautiful."

"T, how could I EVER, *forget that???* THOSE were some of the best days of my life,...when you took me in,...got me off tha' streets. Those pits were, my *babies, too. Tatum, was a fuckin' ninja, THA' WAY he moved! He'd FUCK, Cash, up!!"*, Jester, would say, *with a fond laugh.*

"Yeah! And, THEN, *Tatum, would use Cash as a pillow at night! BUT, my baby, Cash? Fuck-tha'-bullshit! When he got older? GOT bigger? MY baby, Cash, started holdin' his own, wit Tatum! And, when Cash got that temper, of his, goin'? FUCK-THA'-BULLSHIT, MY MAN!!! There was NO stoppin', MY BABY!!!"*, T, replies-back, *with a fond-back-in-tha'-day-laugh of his own, (WITH, more and more of his memory, from this convo,...* becoming his own!).

"Yeah, and, *didn't matter how big, nee'ver-one-of-'em got! THEY didn't fuck-wit, Ice Girl!"*, Jester, *tells it, as it was!*

"Fuck-tha'-bullshit! Who you tellin'!?! *Ice Girl, was startin' to get old, but, THAT ol' girl would, get after 'em!"*, T, tells it.

"Yeah, *she'd lay up on the sofa, and, watch them two, chewin' they rawhide bones, down on tha' floor. And, she'd just lay there. And, WATCH 'em! Boffum bein' watched!! Up on that sofa, T, she'd watch 'em work tha' first knuckle, off they bones!"*

(Laughing!), T, replies, "Yeah, *SHE would! And, which ev'a of dem two, would finally, work tha' knuckle off a they bone, first?* (Cracking-up laughing!), FUCK-THA'-BULLSHIT!!! *Ice Girl, would come flyin' down off a tha' sofa, AND, BULLY THEIR BIG PIECE of bone away!! She'd just, STRAIGHT-UP, leave'um-wit, JUST a fuckin' knuckle! Ice Girl, LET THEM do, AAAAAAALL OF the hard work! She'd be plottin', tha' whole DAMN time! She AIN'T want it til' AFTER, one of them made it soft enough for her to chew on! And, tha' mutha' fuckin' shit is,...she already HAD a bone! She had HER own-damn-bone, laid right-tha'-fuck-up-there wit her, on tha' mutha' fuckin' cocksuckin' sofa!!! BUT, she AIN'T want to chew ON NO, hard-ass-bone! Ice Girl, WANTED Cash AND Tatum's bones, AFTER, they done-worked tha' shit outta' it!* THAT'S SOME FUCKED-UP SHIT!! Fuck-tha'-bullshit, I'D be pissed! Damn,...*Ice Girl, HAD some shit to her!!!"*

Cracking-up, (laughing himself!), Jester, *continues the reminiscing,* "YEAH, *SHE WOULD!!! And, they would just look up at her, back up, on* that sofa, chewin' on one of they bones! And, SHE AIN'T even pay nee'ver one of dem no mind! And, they'd just have a look on their faces, like, "DAMN!!! That's some cold-ass shit!!!""

"Yeah, *wouldn't they tho'!?* But, *they WOULDN'T DO SHIT about it,* WOULD they!?!", T, replies, (thru he and Jester's laughter!).

"HELL NO!! *Boffum wasn't, fuckin' wit Ice Girl!!*", Jester, tells it!!

Then...

(Gettin' a bit solemn)...

T, states, "DAMN, I miss those dogs. *In the history of the world,* Jester, *there's NEVER been three better pits. Ever.*"

"You got that right, T.", Jester, replies.

(As they, both drop their heads in remembrance)...

Then...

Jester, lighting up a cigarette, causing T's eyes to blaze like the sun, (like the sun...at night...in a cemetery), Jester, leans forward a bit, (after, catching a glimpse, of T's fucked-up-stitched-up-AND-swollen-up - right eye!), "DAMN, SON!!! THA'-FUCK, SON!!! *THA'-FUCK, YOU DO, TO YOUR EYE???*"

With no hesitation, T, replies, (WITH TOO MUCH PRIDE!!), *"Shot my eye out, JUST LIKE I always, said I would!!"*

"Hey,...Triflin',...*WE never, fucked wit guns.*", Jester, let's him know, taking another pull off a his smoke, lighting up T's eyes once mo', (allowing, for Jester, to get another, yet, brief-illuminated-look, at T's "Get-up"). Jester, HAS seen quite enough already! *AND figures, that:* "Mr. Trife" ("AS he GOES BY!") is "ALL IN", On: THAT - "Music-Industry-YA'-GOTTA'-SELL-YOUR-SOUL" - BULLSHIT!

AND SO...

Jester, says, to "Mr. Trife", *(with the care of an old and TRUE friend),* "Yo, T. *That story you just told me, 'bout Ice Girl.*"

"Yeah?", Mr. Trife, asks.

Jester, just dips off into the night.

(Back into, his love affair with the night)...

(*Back, to fall back, in love with The Cut!*)...

Old habits die hard...

Chapter Sixteen

SEVEN FUCKED-UP MEMORIALS

Of the next day, of a cool morning of May, of his beloved burial grounds, Trife awakens, atop on his back, of his beloved wooden cemetery picnic table. (Or,...so HE thinks!!) Sitting up, looking around. Getting acclimated, through his 24 karat golds, Trife sees, his suitcase standing, in the cemetery grass below. But, that's about ALL he sees, (that's remotely close!), of how he remembers things, *(USED TO be!)*. Who tha' fuck? What tha' fuck?? WHO AND WHAT THA' FUCK???

"Ok. NOW. This...THIS, is a bug out!", Trife, says to himself aloud. (And, he don't know that, *his memory has been slowly coming back!),* "BUT, I'm pretty-damn-sure, THESE weeping willows, *USED TO weep more proud!"*

Trife, sitting up, on the picnic table top, Jimmy Choo's flat on top, knees bent, and, 'round those knees, his arms he wraps 'round, to steady himself. And, through those karat golds, Trife, takes a look around. "These trees *were humongous!* AND NOW,...they're just saplings!", Trife, says to himself, aloud again, "THESE dogwoods *were much bigger* than these! *WHAT THE FUCK HAPPENED!!!"*

And...

275

With VIGOROUS-ENERGY, as with the twitch of meth, (though, he's not on it!), though, what Trife IS on, IS THAT picnic table!

AND...

(He LOOKS 'ROUND his beloved cemetery LIKE that!!!)

"And, WHERE THA' FUCK are MY swans!?!?!? *Where tha' fuck HAVE they gone?!?",* Trife, asks himself, in and from amazement, and, in and from, his 24 karat golds, the cemetery's morning sun, got his limited edition's blazin'!!

But...

(THAT'S NOT the best part yet!)...

FOR...

Mr. Trife, *IS in for MORE amazement!*...(Come with me! As WE,... join Mr. Trife!)...

AS...

(HE,...*finds out!!!)*...

And, then it hits him. *(For, THEN he sees it!),* "My...MY...beloved pinetree line! Ain't THIS, some-motherfuckin'-SHIT!!!", Mr. Trife, barks out!!!(from table top hops down!). *Thousand yard stare,* deep breathes in his lungs, (out of necessity!), to catch, some of the cool morning cemetery air! (And, as he walks 'round, HIS: beloved DEHYDRATED-pond!!!), *"NO more muddy banks! AND...AND...AND,... the Kraken's...LONG gone!!!",* Mr. Trife, shouts aloud!!!*(FEELING besmirched!),* and, upon arrival, *at where he performed, ceremonies like church,* Mr. Trife, just looks down upon the...parched burnt earth!

Seven glorious and GLORIOUSLY-TALL evergreen trees. Gone.

UNlike, the dogs of wood. And, the willows that weep. *The cemetery's gravedigger and, "the powers that be", well, THESE trees, Brotha Trife's BELOVED PINETREE LINE, WELL,...they NEVER replanted. (They just left the burnt stumps there!)* And, from time-to-time, (WHEN the wind hits you just right!), well,...YOU can *STILL smell BURNT DEAD BODIES* in the air!!! *(For, the cemetery and, the township and, the "powers-that-be"), just left those CHARRED-STUMPS-there, like seven fucked-up memorials! (Of which, there WERE plenty, of write-ups and, editorials!!!!!!!)* BUT, (and, EVEN still!), those SEVEN trees were NEVER replanted! *FOR, NO ONE DESIRED a "curtain call", (OF the "triflin'-shit"!) ONCE discovered, (ONCE the flames went out!), DAMMIT!!!*

HOWEVER...(AND WITH, SOME DOUBT!!!)...

Some would say, "the powers-that-be", just LET the trees burn!

SINCE...

No one knew WHERE Trife was! Some would say, (the feds) NEVER EVEN called in the fire department! ("THEY" were hoping, that,...the fire would take him!).

BUT...

They were wrong. (Dead wrong!).

'CAUSE...

The bones they found, WEREN'T of Brotha Trife's!

For...

(Brotha Trife's BEEN bringing HIS enemies HERE for years!)...

FOR...

The bones they found, ARE OF TRIFE'S ENEMIES!!!

AND...

(YOU MOTHERFUCKIN' RIGHT - "The Most Triflin'" - brought 'em here!)

For...

Once the flames went out, (long after the swans did!), ALL that the authorities, and, the cemetery's gravedigger found, were, the bones of his enemies, "sentenced to THAT death"!!! (That, The MOST Triflin', brought here and hid!).

AND(TO them)...

(DID THANGS!!!)...

(WHAT COMES 'ROUND, GOES 'ROUND!!! MOTHER FUCKERS!!!).

For...

Of those, Brotha Trife, left there under HIS BELOVED treeline of pine, for of his distrust, IN them, HE could no longer take it! And so, he brought them there. And,...LEFT THEM THERE!!! LIKE SOME borrowed insect, hibernating under the hard frost covered ground of winter. And to, the rejuvenating warmth of spring, they didn't make it.

And so...

As, Mr. Trife, just stands there. Staring at the parched-burnt earth. (AND, AT the fucked-up and, seven charred-memorials!!!!!!!!). He then, upon kneeled knee, sifts through some of the scorched earth. And, sifts through, of what debris remains.

(And, of what comes next, I put this on HIS name!)...

And then, THAT Triflin' motherfucker...collected some teeth!!!

AND...

A smoked rib bone or two!!

(HEY! The motherfucker's name IS "The MOST Triflin'!!!)...

(WHAT THA' FUCK YOU THINK HE'S GONNA DO!?!)

And so...

Trife, looking at the collected teeth and, of the rib bones, that, he's holding in his hands, Triflin', gets this *WICKED-SMILE* come cross his face. *('Cause, he can't remember their names and, HE CAN'T even, picture their faces!)* Although, he don't remember he's a clone, *HIS Tier-Three-Mind, back in time, it traces. (So, as far as HIS Tier-Three-Mind goes,... he's THE ONE that brought them there!),(And, PUT ALL OF THEM THROUGH THAT - Begging-God-To-Take-Me - SHIT!).* And,...he DON'T remember their faces!

"YEEEEEAAAAAAHHHHHH, WEEEEEELLLLLL!", Trife, says aloud, *INTUBATION-VOICE-AMAZIN',* (in and of, His: "Oh well, fuck it!" - Conclusion!). Then, back to the other side of the pond he goes, (KEEPIN' IT the fuck PUSHIN'!).

Mr. Trife, back on the other side of the pond, sits down at "his" picnic table. *(As, plenty-of-times prior, as he has done).* However, NOW, he - ain't-got-no - *BELOVED pinetree line,* OF WHICH upon to look! So, NOW, HE'S gonna do something constructive,...WITH his time! (As he's, trying to keep-it-pushing on the alcohol and them drugs!!).

And so, Mr. Trife...

Opens up...his black and white composition song book!

And...

As he sits there, thinking of what to write, *He FEELS as though, he is being watched,...FROM THE SKY!* And, so, he looks up. (And, as he looks up, there HE SEES,...*a gigantic face in a gigantic cloud!*). AND, he *thinks* to himself, *"Could this,...REALLY be??? THAT, THERE'S A gigantic face, IN a gigantic cloud! AND IT'S, RIGHT ABOVE,...directly, above where, MY FAVORITE OF my gigantic pinetrees,...USED TO BE!!!"*

AND...

He keeps looking up, *at that gigantic cloud, BEGINNING TO BELIEVE,* there certainly *APPEARS* to be, *(yes!), there's REALLY a gigantic face, IN that gigantic cloud,* more so, than, there is not! (And, after some time, one would think, *that cloud,...*WOULDN'T still be, right IN

THAT very SAME spot!)...(THAT, BY NOW, it SHOULD HAVE,... *drifted along!*). ('CAUSE, that WAS, *his VERY NEXT thought!*). And, at the VERY LEAST, *it WOULDN'T* (STILL!) *look EXACTLY the same!!* And, as he, continues sitting there, looking up *into that gigantic cloud,* (he *becomes more and more sure!*) that, he IS looking *INTO a gigantic face!* And, *it kinda' freaks him out* (a bit), *thinking,* to himself, "*THERE'S, a face IN that cloud! Yes! This IS real!*" (And, he *KNOWS*, as though, AS HE IS watching, THAT,...HE *IS being watched!*)...(THAT'S just *HOW* he *feels!!*).

(And these are *Trife's thoughts!*)(OF: *His vision!*)...(COME!)...Let's go *inside his mind:*

And, it's a beautiful day. Bright blue beautiful sky! Kinda' chilly. Kinda' breezy. Which makes the stratus clouds, TRAVEL SLOWLY, from left to right, in the sky. (BUT, not this cloud!). THIS is a cumulus cloud! (The one that, kinda' looks like, it DEFINITELY has two eyes!)...(A nose!!)...(A mouth!!!)... (AND, a jaw-line!!!!) And, I ain't never seen a cloud that big, AND BE SO LOW, to the ground!!!!!

And, of this, I AM sure, as I first sat there, that giant cloud, WASN'T there before! And, as it's presence was felt, I felt as though, I WASN'T sitting there by myself. And, as I looked up, all of the other clouds, WERE gently traveling-on, from left to right. (BUT, NOT THIS CLOUD!!!) For, THIS cloud, STAYED in that very same spot! (And, besides that, IT WAS all by itself!) And, no other cloud, traveled in front of it. (Of that face, no other cloud, obscured my vision and sight) As, all of the stratus clouds, (on THAT morning!) traveled-on, FROM left to right!

And, as I sat there, I became deep in thought. And, I thought of what to write. After I kept looking up at that cloud, this is what, my deep thought brought: The cloud was either the Virgin Mary, Jesus or my Dad. (But, by Dad, perhaps, I was actually thinking, Father God).

And so...

In his song book, Mr. Trife, began to write:

FOR, WHEN

I was born a shy and, withdrawn kid,
Had no idea, of the things, the world, would have did,
Kept a carved-up Bible and, a BIG knife hid,
You think THAT'S harsh???,
THIS world is VICIOUS!!!,

SO, I learned! THAT,...
...the world, was FULL of strife,
DAMN RIGHT! I became!! Brotha "MUTHA' FUCKIN" Trife!!!,
BUT hangin' ONTO bitterness,
IS a waste of life!,
I KNOW Y'ALL WANT to live this,
BUT y'all BETTER think twice!!,

AIN'T no shame, IN MY, mutha' fuckin' game!,
Live with regret?,
OR keep it FUCKIN' pushin'?,
For, IT'S ALL the same!,
YOU learn, if YOU live,
So, I'MA break it down, simple and plain,
The world's GONNA' know me,
Just as long as GOD KNOWS my name,

IF YOU EVER want to know what Heaven looks like,
Just look up at the morning sky,
And look up at the bright son light,
And look up at that, bright blue screen of blue,
And look up at those, big white clouds of fluffy,
And I have no fear,

For, when I meet God,
There will be no lie in me,
No lie in me,
No lie in me,
I HAVE NO fear of thee,
For, when I meet God,
There will be no lie in me,
No lie in me,
No lie in me,
I have NO fear of thee,
For, when I meet God,
There will be no lie in me,

(My Mom died on a Sunday,
Her great getting up morning,
"I won't be 'round forever.",
"Mom, thanks for the warning.",
She said, "I won't be around forever.",
I said, "Mom, thanks for the warning."),

And so, I look up at the sky, EVERY morning,
'Cause, I KNOW He checks on me,
'Cause, THROUGH those fluffy clouds,
I KNOW He takes a peek,
And, when I see big fluffy clouds,
I KNOW THAT'S Heaven coming through!,
And, I look for the son shining down,
Against a screen of morning blue,
AND, when I look at the morning son,
I KNOW what I HAVE TO DO,

I say, "Good morning, Jesus!",
For, the morning son has returned, to see...
IF OUR Faith IS true!,

WHO to trust? Who TO trust?? Who to TRUST???,
NEVER rush! Never RUSH!! NEVER RUSH!!!,
IF IT looks like what it is,
THEN it is,
If it SOUNDS LIKE what it is,
You're BEING disrespected!,
And so, for that, IF I don't HAVE,
YOU GO ON AND KEEP YOUR "illusion" OF love!,
For, I KNOW, in who, I TRUST!,
"Good morning, Jesus!", said, EVERY MORNING, to THE Son,

And,...IF YOU'RE FAKE-AS-FUCK??,
KEEP YOUR OLIVE BRANCH AND YOUR FUCKIN' PEACE
DOVE!!,
AND YES, I AM A SOLDIER OF, THE ONE UP ABOVE!!,
BUT, DIG IT, WHEN IT COMES TO REAL SHIT?,
YES, I AM A WITNESS,
BUT DON'T GIVE A FUCK,
ABOUT NO WITNESSES!!,

So, I don't GIVE A FUCK, 'bout your rejections,
For, NOW,
I'M callin' tha' shots,
AND I'M MAKIN' tha' selections!,
And so, NOW...
I'MA break it down, simple and plain!,

THE world's gonna know me,
Just as long as GOD KNOWS my name,

IF YOU EVER want to know what Heaven looks like,
Just look up at the morning sky,
And look up at the bright son light,
And look up at that screen of blue,
And at the big, white clouds of fluffy,
AND I have NO fear!,
For, when I meet God,
There WILL BE no lie in me,
NO lie in me,
NO lie in me,
I have NO fear of THEE,
For, when I meet God,
There WILL BE no lie in me,
NO lie in me,
NO lie in me,
I HAVE NO FEAR OF THEE!!!!!!,
For, when I meet God,
There WILL BE no lie in me.

And, on that note, *(upon completion of the world's MOST FUCKED-UP gospel!),*(though, a gospel, ALL the same!)...

...Mr. Trife, closes his song book.

(DON'T JUDGE!!!)...*(He wrote it, HIS WAY!!!)...(AND, HE DIDN'T LIE!!!)*

AND...

(IF YOU CAN'T RESPECT THAT???)...

THEN...

(OH-FUCKIN'-WELL!!!).

And so...

With, song book closed, he looks back up at *that cloud*. And, *that cloud,* IS STILL in the exact same spot! And, when Mr. Trife, tried to take a picture of it, with the cell phone Pockets, gave to him, *that cloud, made this EVIL frown! (It WAS a look of PAIN AND HATE!!!). THAT cloud, WAS NOT meant to be photographed!!!...*(oh damn!)...Mr. Trife, PUSHED his luck! *(AND, was tempting FATE!!!).*

And so...

With, his continuance, *of that face in that cloud,* of looking back up into it, UPON Mr. Trife's face, *WAS A LOOK OF FEAR!!! ('CAUSE, he KNOWS, that cloud, DIDN'T like that shit!)(AND, WITH SENSES, OF: "FUCKING-UP"!),...He's sensing, something bad happening in his life, WAS NEAR!!!*

And...

With, his continuance, of sitting there silent and motionless, looking up at *A CLOUD* OF THAT SIZE, *A CLOUD,* BEING SO LOW AND NEAR, well,...*THAT CLOUD'S FACE MORPHED!!!* (And, it was PRETTY FUCKED-UP!). (BEING SO LOW AND SO CLOSE!). AS, *THAT CLOUD GAVE* Trife, *an EVIL snear!*

AND THEN...

That clouds eyes turned INTO the shapes of triangles...as it smiled AT him! Which shocked Mr. Trife! He was alarmed by that! But, Mr. Trife, *felt a SENSE OF PEACE come upon him, from that cloud's* (almost-playful!) - *"I'M-JUST-FUCKIN'-WIT-YOU!"* - GRIN!

And then...

The bottom of the cloud scrolled up. And then, it leveled out flat. (And, the cloud kinda' looked the color of gray, as it did that).

And then...

It traveled FASTER THAN ALL THE OTHER clouds! (As it, traveled to its right).

Until it was...

As, Mr. Trife, watched it, (as it traveled away!), and was, out of Mr. Trife's sight!

And...

With no fear and with no lie, Mr. Trife, *gets hit with something once again, fallen from the sky!* (And, Mr. Trife, wasn't sure what hit him, as he looked around). And, he ended up, picking up, a small *white stone,* from off the ground.

Before he traveled on.

Chapter Seventeen

TEN DAY TRIAL

Down the road a ways, on the shoulder of a loooooong road, tearing-up and getting beaten-up, and accompanied by barking dogs, Mr. Trife, makes his way, in a pair of (TORN-UP AND BEATEN-UP!!!) dusty, Jimmy Choo's!!!

For...

Mr. Trife, traveled on.

And...

Got HIS giddy-up on!

FOR,(YOU SEE!)...

(Mr. Trife's - GOTS-TA'-PAY - HIS - music industry "dues"!!!)...

AND SO...

With, suitcase in hand, to North Juarez, he makes his way. Making it to, and, gettin' in-and-out of North Juarez, figures it shouldn't take him, no more than a couple of days. ('Cause, he *KNOWS* he GOT *SOME* shit to him!). And, though, *he feels invincible, (GOT THAT: Tier-Three-Mental!!!),* HE DON'T remember that he's a clone! EVEN

SO, he CAN'T WAIT to come on through, (to lay-up and lay-low at Legs' place!), *where, it once, so felt, like home!* And, besides, gettin' Anna Mossitti, (ALL he REALLY wants to do!), IS lay-up and lay-low at Legs' place,...SO THAT HE CAN reunite with HIS Nephew!!!

And so...

(As, his - Dusty-Jimmy-Choo's-Giddy-Up, continues)...

Mr. Trife, comes upon, a gas station lot, of which, he begins to make his way on through, at which time, *the onset of deja vu, into that Tier-Three-Mind, makes it's way on through!* Making his way on through, that gas station lot, *that onset, of more deja vu, got him thinking some mo' a lot,* "*DAMN! I'm pretty sure, that, THIS was the spot! WHERE, I ran outta' gas. And where, Nephew, TOLD ME 'BOUT...Tick Tock GETTIN' shot!!!*", Mr. Trife, *thinks* to himself, (*as that, deja vu of him, and that gas station lot of he, travels on through, of thoughts, of and by, his travels, of which, both of which, continues),...*"*Yeah,...yeah,...THAT'S right! YEAH!!! More and more IS COMING BACK to me! Damn, WHEN did my memory...GET so poor???*", Mr. Trife, *thinks* to himself, (as he, steps up onto the curb, in front of the gas station's front door).

AND SO...

"So, what's your bag, Daddy-O? Did'jah order, *Ew-ber?*", (*is what it kinda'-sounded like!*)...

AS...

(Some guy calls out, from the rolled-down passenger's car window, pulling up to Mr. Trife, in a 1983 Cadillac Seville, painted silver and black, with tire walls of white!)...

AS...

"*Ew-bah? Ew-ber?? Uger??????* Whatchew' *say???*", Mr. Trife, *questions,* in reply!

AS...

(Poor ol' Mr. Trife, *DON'T 'member the FIRST THING, 'bout NO "Uger"!!*)...

OR...

(TO HIM, *this - "newfangled-way" - OF PAYING TO SHARE-A-RIDE!!*)...

AS...

Mr. Trife's, *Tier-Three-Mind, is thinking, "What-THE-fucks-up, wit THIS guy??????"*

And so...

..."Hey, buddy! I'm NOT tryin' to bug you,...BUT,...ARE YOU GOIN' to North Juarez? ...OR NOT?? So, lay it on me! IF I drove ALL THE WAY out here, for nothin'? Well, IT'S GONNA' BE a MAJOR bummer!", asking (AGAIN!), is the *"Uger"*-driver-guy!

THEN...

(Getting hit in the back of his bullet hole hat! ...With a stone! ...From behind!)...

Mr. Trife, spins 'round QUICK!!! Expecting to see, Jester!

BUT...

(To HIS surprise!)...

IT'S a trio of lesbian-lovers!!! Stepping-out of the gas station!!! With, all three, sayin' AT the same time, "Nah!!! That's US!!! HE AIN'T CALL FO' NO RIDE!!!"

HMM...

"North Juarez, you say?? Yeah, THIS is me! I ordered, *Uger!* Drive ME to the city!", Mr. Trife, says, (on a dime, turns his attention back on, the *Uger* driver guy!), WHILE, bein' shitty, throwin' his suitcase in the back seat, WHILE jumpin' in the front seat quickly!

"Far out! Let's MAKE some tracks!", the *Uger*-driver-guy, of Mr. Trife's reply, replied back!

"OH, NO, HE DEH-ENT!!! HOLD UP!!! GET THA' FUCK OUT OUR CAR!!!", as, ALL three lesbians..., (ALL three dressed the same!!!), (and, AIN'T not-a-one of 'em, GOT ON clean clothes!!!),(BUT, they all sure BE, LOOKIN' DANDY!!!), (For, they all be ROCKIN' them "daisy dukes"!!!), (And, they all be ROCKIN' tube tops - wit they - nipples showin' through!!), (And, they all be SHOWIN' off they midriffs!!!), (WITH, each one of these smokin' hot girls, SMOKIN' they own - "Full of 'dat" - "Good-Good" - SPLIFF!!!), (And, rockin' a pair each, rocked by all three, rockin' 'em on they feet, are wooden platform sandals, clogs, and wedges, and, they all be rockin' "Candies"!!!)...as, all three did shout!!!(TELLIN', Mr. Trife, AGAIN, of their car), "TO GET THA' FUCK OUT!!!" (And, did I mention, AIN'T not-a-one of 'em, got on CLEAN clothes???)...(BUT, they all SURE GOT ON...a sexy pout!!!).

"Foxy! Foxy!! Foxy!!! Mamas!!! TAKE a chill pill. *Mellooooooow out.* I've been "bookin' it" all day, drivin' 'round like a chicken, with my head cut off! So, be cool, mamas,...it's casual. I didn't check the "rider's info", when THIS fare came through. ALL, I did, was, just to take a quick-lookie-loo, at where the next gig was. So, *relaaaaaax.* It's ALL good vibes!", the *Uger* driver guy, begins, (before, he breaks it down, for them!),..."And, besides! THIS groovy guy, was standing between me and you foxy mamas! Mr. Groovy-Guy here, was blocking my view! And, it's not like you could see me! ...OR, my "Ride Share sign", ON my windshield! So? It's really quite simple! It's NOT your fault, foxy mamas! But,...YOU GOT TO BE MORE CAREFUL!!! The three of you were just ready TO JUST hop on in! You CAN'T just GET IN any ol' car!!!", (chuckling, before, beginning again, the *Uger* driver guy, tries to "keep it casual", while, continuing),..."BUT, I SHOULDA' known, it was the THREE OF YOU, WHEN I saw "Land of Liberty Petrol", pop-up on my Ride Share App. So, mamas, take a *quaaluuuuuude,* 'cause, it ain't that big of a deal, now is it really? So, check-it-out, mamas. This cool cat here, he's headed to North Juarez, too! So, pile on in you foxy mamas and, we can all boogie on down up to North Juarez together! ...Oh, and mamas,...THIS ride's ON ME,...contingent upon, of course,...a gracious tip.", the *Uger* driver, explains. (Creepy MOTHERFUCKER!!!).

And so...

After, Mr. Trife, *eyes-up* the girls and, after the girls *eye-him-up* RIGHT BACK!!! *("Yeah, they're cool."), ("Yeah, he's legit."),* Mr. Trife, hops out, to make some room for them.

'CAUSE...

(AIN'T - NOT-A-ONE - OF THEM - TRYNA' BE - PEDESTRAINS!!!!)

And so...

(Mr. Trife, removed himself from the front seat, to put his suitcase in the trunk, removed from the back seat, after the *Uger* driver pops the trunk, although, before the trunk gets closed)...

Hmm...

(Mr. Trife, just *PEEPED* some shit!)...(Come! Let's have a look!)...

Of how: THERE'S faded-green-oxidized-paint-chips on the trunks upholstery! AND, of how: THERE'S "perfectly-fine" manufacturer's trunk-lid-hinge-holes! (Hmm.)(I SAID, MOTHERFUCKIN' "HMM!!!"). *"So, then, WHY don't the trunk's hinges AND holes MATCH UP?? NICE lookin' car, any-damn-way!",* Mr. Trife, *thinks* to himself, *"Musta' been in an accident...I SUPPOSE?!?"*

And so...

"Great! Just great!", Mr. Trife, *thinks* to himself!

'Cause...

(NOW, Mr. Trife, is IN the middle!!!!)...

Finding himself, in between, two of those three smokin' hot girls, sittin' in the back seat, BEING silly, (messin' with Trife!!), the girls,... BEGIN to wiggle!!

'Cause...

(While, Mr. Trife, was peeping-out the "suspicious"-trunk, the other lesbian lover, hopped-in the front seat, of the brother!)...

"Lovely! JUST lovely!" Mr. Trife, *thinks* to himself, "*THIS, Uger ride, up to North Juarez, IS gonna be, a motherfucker!!!*"

'Cause...

(Mr. Trife, AIN'T down for, and, AIN'T TRYING TO entertain, NO BULLSHIT!!!)

'CAUSE...

Mr. Trife, IS on a mission!

'CAUSE...

(Missin' tha' boat, on THIS - "music-industry-shit"?)...

Well...

Mr. Trife, AIN'T TRYNA', BE MISSIN'!!!

However(AND SO!)...

(Down the road a ways, introductions are made, once they hit the bypass for Route 36)...

And...

NOT ONLY does, Mr. Trife, find himself, with some fly bitches, in a fly ride, *(oddly-enough, Brotha Trife, being a "Buick Man", that he was!),* Mr. Trife, is finding, THIS Cadillac to be something, his *Tier-Three-Mind, wouldn't mind drivin'!!!).*

AND...

(NOT ONLY does he find himself, on a return to the city)...

BUT...

Mr. Trife, ALSO FINDS, that, HE's on a return, To: *The-Old-Ways-And-Of-The-Old-Days!*

As...

Mr. Trife,...gets thrown into *the mix!!!*

FOR...

(Old habits die hard! YA DIG!!!).

And, BESIDES...

(They might be dirty girls, he's hangin' with)...BUT...(THEY SURE ARE BANGIN'!!!)...

And so...

After, a quick "hand-to-hand", between the *Uger* driver and the girl sittin' up front, she turns 'round and, to Mr. Trife, extends her hand, saying, "That's McDusty, she's McCrusty, and, I'm Scabby McKnees. You seem cool enough. You down to get fucked-up???"

"Scabby...Mc...Knees. Well, damn!", Mr. Trife, replies, (shaking hands with ol' Scabby!), before, continuing, "Sure. I'MA NEED ME some medicine,...RIDIN' wit Y'ALL THREE!!! Yeah, I'M down! So, what's good? What's up??"

And so, it begins. Mr. Trife, the *"Uger driver"* and, his three new friends. As, Scabby McKnees, puts fire to the tip of a glass stem! And, they all do hot rails of meth to the city limits, (after drivin' 'round FAST and RANDOM!), TWEAKED-AS-FUCK, the *"Uger driver"*, drops them all off at...a house that's abandoned!!!!

And, over the course of the next ten days, Mr. Trife, STAYS meth-crazed! Smokin' 'n snortin' 'n doin' hot rails of meth! (He came back up north, to be a big music star! But, NOW, he's NOTHIN', BUT just a BIG OL' MESS!!!). Ain't no hot showers, 'cause there ain't no 'lectric! Feels like he's been up for weeks! And, he's beginning to feel desperate! Ain't nobody thought about food! So, ain't NOBODY ate! Shit IS gettin' bad! *'Cause, he's beginning to hallucinate! (EVERY ROOM, IS a room, FROM a room, of room and board, in and of which, he USED TO habitate!)(And, HIS CONCERN, AIN'T of HOW, "they" cut all of his old houses apart! Hammered them shitz back together! AND LED HIM TO THIS HOUSE!!! And, fed him drugs! TO FUCK UP HIS MIND!!! For, HOPES&WISHES, in entrapment-crimes, in so to participate, in so TO incriminate!*

(YOU DICK-LICKING MOTHERFUCKERS!!!)

Yeah.

For...

"They" *SPUN* HIM OUT GOOD!!!

FOR...

(HIS MIND, to manipulate!)...

For(HIS ONLY CONCERN IS)...

WE RUNNIN' OUTTA METH ON THIS PLATE!!!!

AND(BESIDES ALL THAT!)...

His hallucinations, ARE REALLY BEGINNING, TO PUT HIM THROUGH a test!

'CAUSE...

(Outta the three, ol' Scabby McKnees, is STARTING TO LOOK the best!!!).

Can't charge his phone, his phone has BEEN dead! And, he's *so fucked-up,* he ain't EVEN *THINKIN'* *('bout Pockets comin' unglued and goin' outta his head!).* And, THE really, really, really fucked-up part, *(*SPOLIER ALERT*: You know, BESIDES undercover cops, KEEPING HIM fucked-up on meth! Yeah, well, we ain't get to THAT PART yet! But, KEEP THAT IN MIND, lest YOU forget!!!)(Don't worry. I'll let YOU KNOW WHEN!),* IS he, CAN'T WAIT 'til it's dark! *('Cause, THAT'S WHEN the REAL peepin' 'n creepin' starts!)* And, yeah, he's been outside. And, yeah, he's been around the block a couple of times! And, yeah, he's walked a bit 'round. But, he ain't tryna' be seen, *all fucked-up* IN public LIKE this! (ESPECIALLY in THIS town!) So, he heads right back, JUST to find, *that shitz BEEN moved-tha'-fuck-around!!* For, at night, he BE *peepin'* outta EVERY window! And, he be *peepin'* EVERYTHING in sight! On the tenth day, on the third floor, on the floor, next to the window, he opens his song book. *And, of the madness. And, of the methamphetamine-psychosis. And, of the WHIRLWIND!!! And, of NO CONTROL (OVER OR OF!!!) repeated-actions OR thoughts!! (The devil GOT this brotha SPUN SON!!)(Brain FULLY COOKED!!!)(He WON'T remember ANY of THIS shit!)* And so, *of his: out-of-control plight,* ALL DAMN NIGHT, he begins to write, by street light:

(((FEEL the MADNESS!!!)))(((FEEL the WHIRLWIND!!!)))...

THAT'S WHAT IT DO *(Slight Return)*

That's what it do *(that's what it do),*
That's what it do *(that's what it do),*
i said, that's what it do *(that's what it do),*
i said, that's what it do *(that's what it do),*

i've been up for weeks *(i've been up for weeks),*
i've been up for weeks *(i've been up for weeks),*
i said, i've been up for weeks *(i've been up for weeks),*
i said, i've been up for weeks *(i've been up for weeks),*

It's the night of the freaks *(it's the night of the freaks),*
It's the night of the freaks *(it's the night of the freaks),*
i said, it's the night of the freaks *(it's the night of the freaks),*
i said, it's the night of the freaks *(it's the night of the freaks),*

'Cause, that's what it do *(that's what it do)*,
i said, that's what it do *(that's what it do)*,
That's what it do *(that's what it do)*,
i said, that's what it do *(that's what it do)*,
And, when i tell u, that dirty little whore, is the devil *(she is!)*,
U BEST believe THAT shit! *(BELIEVE it motherfuckers!!)*,
'CAUSE, that shit is true! *(i SAID, that shit IS true!)*,

U know what that dirty little whore, said unto me? *(that whore, said unto me?)*,
That dirty little bitch, was talkin' shit! *(MUTHA' FUCKIN' TRICK!)*,
U know WHAT i SHOULDA' told, THAT dirty bitch??? *(WHAT i SHOULDA' SAID!)*,
SHOULDA' told, THAT dirty little bitch, TO hit the bricks! *(HIT tha' FUCKIN' bricks!!)*,

THAT dirty little whore, said unto me *(whore, said unto me)*,
She SAID, "I SEE ur BACK on THEM rocks!" *(BITCH U TALK A LOT!!)*,
U know WHAT i told, THAT DIRTY bitch??? *(OH SHIT! HERE IT COMES!!)*,
i SAID, "BITCH, i AIN'T NEVER STOP!!!" *(((("BITCH!!! i ain't NEVER stop!!!")))*,
And so NOW, i'm on the run *(WHATCHU' runnin' FROM???)*,
MYSELF AND THE COPS!!! *(((i SAID, the MUTHA' FUCKIN' cops!!)))*,

The block is still hot *(the block is still hot)*,
The block is steel hot *(the block is steel hot)*,
i said, the block is kill hot *(the block is kill hot)*,
i said, the block is real hot *(the block is real hot)*,
Peeping tha' fuck outta', tha' lights IN the shadows! *(((lights IN the shadows!)))*,
AND i'm, checkin' tha' locks! *(((i'm CHECKIN' the locks!)))*,

i sit in the dark *(i sit in the dark)*,
i said, i sit in the dark *(i sit in the dark)*,
i sit in the dark *(i sit in the dark)*,
i said, i sit in the dark *(i said, i sit in the dark)*,
Starin' out the window, AT THE MAN *(out tha' window, AT the man!)*,
Sittin' in a clever unmarked! *(((i say, tha' shit was UNMARKED!!)))*,

There's an army of cars after me! *(((it's GONNA' TAKE an army!)))*,
AND, traffic AIN'T MOVIN' RIGHT! *(((shit AIN'T movin' right!)))*,
Stay in YOUR lane *(i say, STAY in YOUR lane!)*,
i STAY, wit'a KNIFE! *(((U should see tha' mutha' fucka'!!)))*,
And so NOW, i'm sittin' in the dark *(i say, i'm sittin' IN the dark)*,
Pennin' THIS shit BY street light! *(i CAN see the light!)*,

i remember food *(i remember food)*,
Yeah, i remember sleep *(i said, i remember sleep)*,
But, that was a long time ago *(long, long, time ago)*,
'Cause, i've been up for weeks! *(((i said, i've been up for weeks!)))*,

'CAUSE, that's what it do! *(((that's what it do!)))*,
That's what it do *(that's what it do)*,
i said, that's what it do! *(that's what it do!)*,
i said, that's what it do *(that's what it do)*,

i've been up for weeks *(((i've been up for weeks)))*,
i've been up for weeks *(i've been up for weeks)*,
i said, i've been up for weeks *(i've been up for weeks)*,
i said, i've been up for weeks! *(((i SAID, i've been up for WEEKS!)))*,

It's the night of the freaks *(it's the night of the freaks)*,
It's the night of the freaks *(it's the night of the freaks!)*,
i SAID, it's the night of the freaks! *(((it's the night of the FREAKS!!!)))*,
i said, it's the night of the freaks *(it's the night of the freaks)*,

'Cause, that's what it do *(that's what it do)*,
i said, that's what it do *(that's what it do)*,
That's what it do *(i said, that's what it do)*,
i said, that's what it do *(that's what it do)*,
And, when i tell u, that dirty little whore, IS the devil *(((she is!)))*,
U best believe that shit *(BELIEVE that shit!)*,
'Cause, THAT SHIT is true! *(SO, SO, mutha' fuckin' true!)*,

i ripped a fat yacker! *(ripped a fat yacker!)*,
It BURNS like a mother! *(((U FEEL that motherfucker??)))*,
Got THAT drip in the back! *(AYO, i GOT that drip!!)*,
And, Y'ALL THOUGHT crack WAS fuckin' whack??? *(((all of it is!)))*,
'Cause, that's what it do! *(i said, that's what it do!)*,

i'm so dehydrated *(i remember water!)*,
Got cottonmouth so bad *(((FUCKIN' breath stinks!)))*,
i'd talk back to the voices *(i hear U in tha wallz!)*,
BUT, i can't hardly speak *(((i'd just tell U, i'd kill U!)))*,
'Cause, that's what it do *(i said, that's what it do)*,

Got dark circles 'round my eyes *(((circle the wagons!)))*,
And, i SHOULD BE tired *(i remember sleep!)*,
But, SINCE i'm ALREADY high *(((the bargaining in one's mind!)))*,
Oh, what's ONE MORE line! *(((ATTA' boy!!)))*,
'Cause, that's what it do *(i said, that's what it do)*,

Gots-ta' FORCE myself to eat! *(((HERE, chew on these nails!)))*,
Tryna' get'a few hours of sleep *(TRY TO get to sleep!)*,
Paranoid as fuck *(paranoid as fuck)*,
i said, i'm paranoid as fuck *(((i'm paranoid AS FUCK!!)))*,
OUTTA' money and luck! *(NO money NO luck!)*,
'CAUSE, that's what it do! *(i said, THAT'S what it do!)*,

And, everywhere i go *(((And i mean, EVERY-DAMN-WHERE i go!)))*,
i KEEP seeing the SAME red truck *(DUDE'S pushin' HIS luck!)*,
And, i see, that blue one, over there *(i see u MOTHERFUCKER!!!)*,
So i walk by, like, i don't care *(AS IF i GIVE a fuck!)*,
'CAUSE, THAT'S WHAT it do!! *(i said, THAT'S WHAT it do!!)*,

The block is STILL hot! *(((the block is STILL hot!)))*,
The block is STEEL hot! *(((the block is STEEL hot!)))*,
i said, THE BLOCK is KILL hot! *(((THE BLOCK is KILL hot!)))*,
i said, the block IS REAL hot! *(((the block IS REAL hot!!!)))*,

i remember food *(i remember food)*,
Yeah, i remember sleep *(i said, i remember sleep!)*,
BUT, that was a long time ago! *(SO, SO, long ago!)*,
'CAUSE, i'VE BEEN UP FOR WEEKS *(((i said, i BEEN UP for weeks)))*,
'Cause, that's what it do *(i said, that's what it do!)*,

'CAUSE, that's what it do! *(that's what it do!)*,
That's what it do *(that's what it do)*,
i SAID, that's what it do! *(THAT'S what it do!)*,
i SAID, THAT'S WHAT it do!! *(((that's what IT DO!!)))*,

i'VE been up for weeks! *(i'VE been up for weeks!)*,
i've been up for weeks *(i've been up for weeks)*,
i said, i'VE BEEN UP for weeks! *(((i've been up FOR WEEKS!!)))*,
i said, i've been up for weeks *(i've been up for weeks)*,

IT'S THE NIGHT of the freaks!! *(((IT'S THE NIGHT of the freaks!!)))*,
It's the night of the freaks! *(it's the night of the freaks!)*,
i said, it's the night of the freaks *(it's the night of the freaks)*,
i SAID, IT'S THE NIGHT of the freaks!! *(((IT'S THE NIGHT of the
freaks!!!)))*,

'Cause, that's what it do *(that's what it do)*,
i said, that's what it do *(that's what it do)*,
THAT'S what it do! *(that's what it do!)*,
i said, that's what it do! *(i said, that's what it do!)*,
And, when i tell u, that dirty little whore, is the devil *(((she is!)))*,
YOU best BELIEVE that shit! *((((WHAT THE FUCK i JUST SAY!?!)))*,
'CAUSE, THAT SHIT IS TRUE!!! *(i said, THAT SHIT IS TRUE!!!)*,

i'm losing mad weight *(i'm losing mad weight)*,
i said, i'm losing mad weight *(((i'm losing mad weight!)))*,
My clothes are all baggy *(((FUCKING DISGUSTING!!!)))*,
Ain't seen McDusty, McCrusty, or Scabby!!! *(((were they EVEN REALLY EVER here???)))*,
'CAUSE, that's what it do! *(i said, THAT'S what it do!!)*,

i'm all alone *(((FUCK Y'ALL, anyway!!!)))*,
'Cept for, the lines, on the plate! *(lest WE forget, the meth mites!)*,
Err'body's ur best friend, when ur holdin' *(ever see an enemy fall in love?)*,
BUT, when u AIN'T, THE stingy, CHECKMATE!!! *(((‌"Awe man, I only got a lil' bit left!")))*,
'Cause, THAT'S what THEY do!! *(i SAID, THAT'S WHAT THEY DO!!)*,

And, i DON'T HIDE shit! *(((oh, check THIS SHIT, out!)))*,
On me, i GOT my shit! *(((U wanna KNOW why??)))*,
'Cause, i DON'T TRUST SHIT!!! *(((i SAID, i DON'T trust shit!!!)))*,
AND, stingy-ass-niggas, AIN'T TRYNA', throw in! *(((Yeah! THAT fucking guy!!!)))*,
'CAUSE, that's what it do! *(i SAID, THAT'S what it do!)*,

Now i got fangs, like a lion *(u wanna know why??)*,
FROM grindin' my teeth!! *(((i'll bite UR fuckin' neck!!)))*,
And i got, tracking devices *(((i said, i got TRACKING devices!!)))*,

IN the SHOES, ON my FEET!! *(((RIPPED them shitz OPEN to see!!))),*
'CAUSE, THAT'S what it do! *((((i SAID, THAT'S what IT do!))),*

The devil's an artist *(((that DIRTY LITTLE WHORE is an artist!))),*
She's drawn in my face!! *(DRAWN IN my MUTHA' FUCKIN' FACE!!),*
She's sculpted, my cheekbones *(my MUTHA' FUCKIN' cheekbones!!),*
INTO the WALLZ of a MAZE!!! *(((OF WHICH, there AIN'T NO escape!!!))),*
'Cause, that's what it do!! *(i said, THAT'S WHAT it do!!),*

i REMEMBER food! *(i remember food!),*
i remember sleep *(((i said, i remember sleep!!!))),*
But, that was a long time ago *(SUCH a long, long, time ago!),*
'CAUSE, i've been up for weeks!! *(((i said, i've BEEN UP FOR weeks))),*
'Cause, that's what it do! *(i said, that's what it do!!),*

That's what it do! *(that's what it do!),*
i said, that's what it do! *(that's what it do!),*
i said, that's what it do! *(that's what it do!),*
i said, that's what it do! *(that's what it do!),*

i'VE BEEN UP FOR WEEKS!!! *((((i'VE BEEN UP FOR WEEKS!!!))),*
i'VE BEEN UP FOR WEEKS!!! *((((i'VE BEEN UP FOR WEEKS!!!))),*
i SAID, i'VE BEEN UP FOR WEEKS!!! *((((i'VE BEEN UP FOR WEEKS!!!))),*
i SAID, i'VE BEEN UP FOR WEEKS!!! *((((i'VE BEEN UP FOR WEEKS!!!))),*

IT'S the night of the freaks! *(IT'S the night of the freaks!),*
IT'S the night of the freaks! *(IT'S the night of the freaks!),*
i SAID, IT'S the night of the freaks!! *(IT'S the night of the freaks!!),*
i SAID, IT'S the night of the freaks!!! *(it's the night of the freaks!!!),*

'CAUSE, that's what it do! *(THAT'S what it do!),*
i said, that's what it do *(that's what it do),*

That's what it do *(that's what it do)*,
i SAID, THAT'S what it do! *(that's WHAT it do!)*,
And, WHEN i TELL U, that dirty little whore, IS the devil *(((she is!)))*,
U BEST BELIEVE me! *(BELIEVE that shit MOTHERFUCKERS!!!)*,
'CAUSE, THAT SHIT is true!!! *(i said, THAT SHIT is true!!!)*,

i have NO IDEA what day it is! *(((NO MUTHA' FUCKIN' IDEA!!!)))*,
AND i DON'T really care! *(((i mean i, DON'T GIVE A FUCK!!!)))*,
'Cause, i've been up for weeks *(i SAID, i've BEEN UP for weeks!)*,

'Round this house, i KNOW people BE sneakin'! *(i said, PEOPLE BE SNEAKIN'!!!)*,
THEY AIN'T GOT NO love for me! *(((AIN'T GOT NO MOTHERFUCKIN' kind of love!!!)))*,
'CAUSE, i'VE BEEN UP FOR WEEKS!!! *(((ima COME KILL U in a week!)))*,

There's a cat on the roof *(((i SAID, THERE'S A MOTHERFUCKIN' CAT ON THE ROOF!!!)))*,
PUT THERE BY YOU KNOW WHO!!! *(((ITS GOT CAMERAS IN ITS EYES!!!)))*,
i'VE BEEN UP FOR WEEKS!!! *(((i SAID, i'VE BEEN UP FOR WEEKS)))*,

THAT cat IS a spy *(((i SAID, THAT COCKSUCKIN' CAT IS A SPY!!!)))*,
PUT THERE by the F.B...oh, nevermind:) *(((YOU KNOW WHO!!!)))*,
i'VE BEEN UP FOR WEEKS!!! *(((i'VE BEEN UP FOR WEEKS!!!)))*,

And, i've BEEN SEEING shadows of people *(MUTHA' FUCKIN' SHADOWS!!!)*,
JUST outside my windows! *(((i mean, ALL OF THEM SHITZ!!!)))*,
THAT i've BEEN WATCHING for weeks! *(((ima come KILL U IN A WEEK!)))*,

i'm CHECKIN' tha' house FOR peep holes! *(for MUTHA' FUCKIN' peep holes!)*,

And, EVERYTHING'S bugged!! *(i said, EVERYTHING'S bugged!!)*,
So, i don't even speak *((((i'D JUST TELL U, i'D KILL U!)))*,

My cell phone IS tapped! *(((i HEAR THAT STATIC AND CRACKIN'!)))*,
With devices in my shoes, they be trackin'! *(((D'Z MOTHERFUCKERS WANT ME BAD!)))*,
They've been AFTER ME for weeks!!! *(((THEY'VE BEEN after me FOR WEEKS weeks!)))*,

AND, i *peep* the whole scene! *(((i said, i PEEP THE WHOLE SCENE!)))*,
If u know what i mean? *(Do u REALLY KNOW motherfuckers?!?)*,
THIS SHITZ LIKE a BAD dream! *(((WAKE THA' FUCK UP!)))*,

If ur out there, i'll see u *(i said, IF ur out there, i'll SEE U!)*,
U CAN'T HIDE FROM me! *((((i SAID, U CAN'T HIDE FROM me MOTHERFUCKERS!)))*,
i'll *peep* U, AND UR team!!! *((((U AND UR WHOLE ENTIRE COCKSUCKIN' TEAM!!!)))*,

i stare INTO shadows AT night! *(IMAGINE that shit for a moment!)*,
AND, *peep* the SLIGHTEST of motions!! *(((ALL. FUCKING. NIGHT. LONG!!!)))*,
i *PEEP* THE WHOLE SCENE!!! *((((i SAID, i PEEP THE WHOLE SCENE!!!)))*,

i stare INTO THE DARKNESS of trees! *(the darkness OF trees!)*,
Mean-spirited-faces, formed by the leaves! *(((THEY AIN'T GOT NO LOVE FOR ME!!!)))*,
THEY BE starin' RIGHT BACK at me! *((((i PEEP THE WHOLE SCENE!!!)))*,

Cars park on the street for hours (((*AND i BE WATCHING 'EM FOR HOURS!!!*))),
And nobody gets out (((*THEY BE THERE FOR, MY BENEFIT!!!*))),
i *peep* the whole scene (*i peep the whole scene*),

i've been *peeping* tiny bright lights (((*IN THE MOTHERFUCKING DARKNESS!!!*))),
They turn from red to orange. To blue. To white. (((*SOMEBODY'S THERE!!!*))),
i *peep* the whole scene!!! (*i peep the whole scene!!!*),

There's birds chirping at night (*i'll say that again*),...
There's birds chirping AT NIGHT (((*i SAID, THERE'S BIRDS CHIRPING AT NIGHT!!!*))),
YO! SOMETHING'S NOT RIGHT!!! (((*wassup wit dem red to orange to blue lights!?!*))),
i *PEEP* THE WHOLE SCENE!!! (((*i SAID, i PEEP THE WHOLE SCENE!!!*))),

AND, i'm in love with the neighbors' dogs!! (((*MOTHER FUCKIN' DOGGIES!!!*))),
They let me know, someone's lurking outside!!! (*Good dog! GOOD DOG!!!*),
i *peep* the whole scene! (((*i SAID, i peep the whole scene!!!*))),

i'll stare at shit U WON'T think of (((*OPEN UR MIND!!!*))),
And, SEE UR REFLECTION!!! (((*EACH AND EVERY MOTHER FUCKIN' TIME!!!*))),
i *PEEP* the whole scene!!! (*i SAID, i PEEP the whole scene!!!*),

i'm a master of patterns (*a motherfuckin' MASTER!*),
i know UR next move! (((*i KNOW UR NEXT MOVE!!!*))),
i *peep* the whole scene (*i peep the whole scene*),

One car turns off *(oh there he goes!),*
ANOTHER one follows! *(((JUST LIKE motherfuckin' CLOCKWORK!!!))),*
i *peep* the whole scene *(i peep the whole scene),*

Same damn big black bird, soars in the sky *(((its GOTTA' flap its wings SOMETIME!!!))),*
THAT SHITZ A DRONE!!! *(((ITS GOT CAMERAS IN ITS EYES!!!))),*
i *PEEP* THE WHOLE SCENE!!! *(((i PEEP THE WHOLE SCENE!!!))),*

AND, i KNOW my shitz bugged!! *(i SAID, i KNOW my shitz bugged!!),*
WHEN i SPEAK ON SHIT, THEY DO SHIT DIFFERENT!!! *(who tha' fucks playin' who:),*
i *PEEP* THE WHOLE SCENE!!! *(((i PEEP THE WHOLE SCENE!!!))),*

And, i SWEAR these wallz, ARE ALIVE!!! *(((THERE'S doors BETWEEN these doors!!!))),*
BEHIND THESE WALLZ...THEY HIDE!!! *(((i'ma come KILL ALL Y'ALL!))),*
i *peep* the whole scene *(i said, i peep the whole scene!),*

i remember food! *(i said, i remember food),*
Yeah, i REMEBER SLEEP!!! *(((i SAID, i REMEMBER SLEEP!!!))),*
But, that was a long time ago *(((SUCH A LONG LONG TIME AGO U MOTHERFUCKERS!))),*
'Cause, i'VE BEEN UP FOR WEEKS!!! *(((i'VE BEEN UP FOR WEEKS!!!))),*

The block is STILL hot! *(((the block is STILL hot!))),*
The block is STEEL hot! *(((the block is STEEL hot!))),*
i said, THE BLOCK IS KILL hot! *(((the block IS KILL hot!))),*
i SAID, the block is REAL HOT!!! *(((THE BLOCK IS REAL HOT))),*

'CAUSE, that's what it do! *(((i said, THAT'S what IT do!)))*,
THAT'S what it do! *(i said, THAT'S what it do!)*,
That's what it do! *(i SAID, THAT'S WHAT it do!!)*,
'Cause, THAT'S what IT do! *(((i said, THAT'S WHAT IT DO!!!)))*,
AND, WHEN i TELL U, THAT dirty little whore, IS the devil! *(((SHE IS!!!)))*,
ON UR LIFE, U BEST BELIEVE!!! *(((WHAT THA' FUCK i JUST SAY???)))*,
'CAUSE, THAT SHIT IS TRUE!!! *(((i SAID, THAT SHIT IS TRUE!!!)))*,

i look in the mirror *(i said, i look in the mirror)*,
And, i DON'T look the same! *(((i said, i WON'T EVER look the same!!!)))*,
'Cause, THAT'S WHAT it do! *(i said, THAT'S WHAT it do!)*,

i said, i LOOK IN THE MIRROR!!! *(i look in the mirror!)*,
My nostrils, are EATEN AWAY!!! *((((on u THE DEVIL WILL FEED)))*,
'Cause, that's what it do *(i said, that's what it do)*,

My nose LOOKS FUCKED-UP! *(my nose IS fucked-up!)*,
And, my hairs TURNIN' gray! *((((THAT dirty little whore, Crystal, IS MAKIN' me AGE!!!)))*
'CAUSE, THAT'S WHAT SHE DO!!! *((((i said, THAT'S WHAT SHE DO!!!)))*,

My eyes BEGIN to squint! *(((i CAN'T help it!!! THEY BE SQUINTIN'!!!)))*,
IN WHICH, THERE'S an EVIL gaze!!! *(((THE DEVIL'S INSIDE ME!!!)))*,
'CAUSE, that's WHAT it do! *((((i said, THAT'S WHAT IT do!!!)))*,

i look in the mirror *(((i SAID, LOOK IN THE MIRROR!!!)))*,
The devil tells me to carve up my face!! *(((THAT DIRTY STINKIN' LITTLE WHORE!!!)))*,
'Cause, that's what SHE do!! *(i said, that's what SHE do!!)*,

THAT dirty little whore! *(i said, THAT DIRTY little whore!!)*,
GOT ME LOOKIN' FOR MORE, ON THE FLOOR!!! *(((OH, THAT DIRTY LITTLE BITCH!!!)))*,

CAUSE, that's what SHE do! *(((i said, THAT'S WHAT SHE DO!!!)))*,

EVERYTHING IS TAPPED BY THE COPS!!! *(((EVERY MOTHERFUCKING THING!!!)))*,
THEY AIN'T GOT NOTHIN' BETTER TO DO!!! *(((AIN'T GOT SHIT ELSE TO DO!!!)))*,
'CAUSE, THAT'S WHAT THEY DO!!! *(((i SAID, THAT'S WHAT THEY DO!!!)))*,

i might drink or, might smoke *(sip me on sumfin'!)*,
But, i'm good, WIT'A 'nother LINE OR TWO!! *(((Yo, i STILL GOT SOME MO'!!!)))*,
'Cause, THAT'S what it do! *(i said, THAT'S what it do!)*,

i stare at that whore and, think *(she'll DO THIS WHEN ur DOIN' GOOD!)*,
She came back to you *(((JUST TO FUCK UP UR LIFE!!!)))*,
'CAUSE, THAT'S WHAT SHE'LL DO!!! *(((i said, THAT'S WHAT SHE'LL DO!!!)))*,

i get less paranoid when, the nighttime is over *(((i REMEMBER SLEEP!!!)))*,
And when the sun, begins to shine through *(((GOOD MORNING, JESUS!!!)))*,
i made it on through! *(i said, i MADE IT ON THROUGH!!!)))*,

i bust open my shoes *(((OH, NO, NOT THE JIMMY CHOO'S!!!)))*,
LOOKIN' FOR a hidden recording device OR TWO!! *(((RESTITCHED AND GLUED!!!)))*,
'Cause, that's what THEY do! *(((i said, THAT'S WHAT THEY DO!!!)))*,

i TRY TO save some for later *(i said, i TRY to!)*,
BUT i ALWAYS end up, doin' that shit up too! *(((i said, i RIPPED THAT SHIT TOO!!!)))*,

'CAUSE, THAT'S what it do! *(i said, THAT'S what it do!)*,

And my EARS, begin to RING! *(((THEY RINGING RIGHT NOW!!!)))*,
NEEDS TO get me a DEGAUSSER or two!! *(((THEY BE TRYIN'!!!)))*,
'Cause, that's what THEY do!!! *(i said, that's what THEY do!!!)*,

i try to shit, but i can't *(i TRY to shit, but i CAN'T!)*,
'CAUSE, i ain't eat no food *(((i remember food!!!)))*,
'Cause, that's what IT do! *(i said, that's what IT do!!)*,

i CAN'T be 'round THIS shit! *(if u got that shit, DON'T come 'round!!)*,
'CAUSE, IF IT'S 'ROUND, then, that's what i'll do! *(((i said, THAT's
WHAT i'll do!!!)))*,
'CAUSE, that's what IT do! *(i said, that's what IT do!)*,

Cops, Feds, AND ALL THESE low-life neighbors! *(((ALL Y'ALL
MOTHERFUCKERS!!!)))*,
AND I'M bein' sweated-by, a secret society, or two!! *(((YEAH! FUCK
THEM TOO!!)))*,
'CAUSE, that's what THEY do! *(i said, that's what THEY do!)*,

My shit is ALWAYS missing! *(((i'ma COME KILL ALL Y'ALL!!!)))*,
Replaced by bugged-replicas dude! *(((REPLICAS MY DUDE!!)))*,
'Cause, that's what THEY do! *(((i said, THAT'S WHAT THEY DO!!!)))*,

The room ALWAYS looks different *(((OH, i CAN'T IMAGINE WHY!!!)))*,
Step outside, AND shitz been MOVED!!! *(((don't u EVER let me catch u!!!)))*,
'CAUSE, i KNOW what i'LL do! *(((i said, i KNOW WHAT i'LL DO!!!)))*,

Being followed by the same, fixed-wing airplane! *(((the fix IS in!!!)))*,
AND HELICOPTERS TOO!!! *(((MOTHERFUCKIN' HELICOPTERS
MY DUDE!!!)))*,

'Cause, that's WHAT THEY DO!!! *(i said, THAT'S WHAT THEY DO!!!)))*,

CAN'T let my Nephew see me like this! *((((HE'D BE DISAPPOINTED IN me!!!)))*,
JUST QUIT this shit and BE THROUGH!!! *(((QUIT AND BE THROUGH!!!))))*,
'Cause, that's what I'LL do! *(I said, that's what I'LL do!)*,

I ain't come up here, to be *STUCK! ((((I'm fuckin' SICK of being stuck!!!)))*,
GOTS'TA get tha' fuck BACK on my giddy-up! *(((GIDDY-UP MOTHERFUCKERS!!!))*,
'CAUSE, THAT'S WHAT I'LL DO!!! *((((I SAID, THAT'S WHAT I'LL DO!!!)))*,

Each line of meth, IS my last! *((((i DON'T EVEN WANT TO DO NO MO'!!!)))*,
BUT the next one BECOMES - "This IS my LAST line!" - TOO!!! *(((Wanna know WHY??)))*,
'CAUSE, THAT'S WHAT IT DO!!! *((((i SAID, THAT'S WHAT IT DO!!!)))*,

i SAID, i remember food!!! *((((i said, i REMEMBER FOOD!!!)*,
Yeah, i remember sleep! *((((i said, i REMEMBER sleep!)*,
BUT, that WAS a long time AGO! *((((such a long, long, time ago!)))*,
'CAUSE, i'VE BEEN UP FOR WEEKS!!! *((((i SAID, i'VE BEEN UP FOR WEEKS!!!)*,

'CAUSE, that's what it do! *((((i said, THAT'S WHAT IT DO!!!)))*,
That's what it do! *(i said, that's what it do!)*,
That's what it do! *(i SAID, that's what it do!!)*,
That's what it do! *(i said, that's what it do!)*,

i've been up FOR WEEKS!!! *(i said, i've been up for weeks!!!)*,

i've been up for weeks! *(i said, i've been up for weeks!),*
i've been up for weeks! *(i said, i've been up for weeks!),*
i'VE been up for weeks! *(((i SAID, i'VE BEEN UP FOR WEEKS!!!))),*

It's the night of the freaks! *(i SAID, IT'S THE NIGHT OF THE FREAKS!!!))),*
It's the night of the freaks! *(i said, IT'S the night of the freaks!),*
IT'S the night of the freaks!! *(i SAID, it's the night OF the freaks!!),*
It's the night of the freaks!!! *(((i said, it's THE NIGHT OF the freaks!!!))),*
AND, WHEH I TELL U, THAT DIRTY LITTLE WHORE, IS THE DEVIL *(((SHE IS!!!))),*
ALL Y'ALL BEST BELIEVE THAT SHIT!!! *(((WHAT THE FUCK i JUST SAY!!!))),*
'CAUSE, THAT SHIT IS TRUE!!! *(i SAID, THAT SHIT IS TRUE!!!)))*.

And, though, IT'S ONLY BEEN ONE NIGHT!!!(((TOLD Y'ALL HE WAS *SPUN* THE FUCK OUT!!!)))(((Y'ALL BETTER START PAYIN'-THA-FUCK-ATTENTION!!!)))...TO, Mr. Trife's - *Tier-Three-Mind* - IT FELT LIKE - *he WAS spun-out* - FOR TEN DAYS!!!

And, (((AFTER ALL THAT!!!))), he MAY not know, which end is up, OR, what the fuck WAS real, AND, WHAT THE FUCK WAS NOT?!?!?(((AFTER ALL, WHAT THE FUCK DOES A CLONE KNOW, ANYWAY?!!?)))(((HMM)))...

However*(AND REGARDLESS!)*...

That dirty little CUNT OF A WHORE, (((THAT CRYSTAL BITCH))), worked HIS MIND good!!

'CAUSE...

That WARM WASHRAG, from his Tier-Three-Mind, HAS been lifted!!((((FROM the psychosis of BEING meth-crazed!!!)))...

FOR(YOU SEE!)...

His Tier-Three-Memory, HAS been jump-started!!!(AND, YES, his voice-of-intubation, is STILL GUARANTEED TO AMAZE!!!)...

And so...

"Fuck!! THAT'S right!! I'M A CLONE!!! FUCK THA' BULLSHIT, I'ma fig'out, WHERE THA' FUCK, is MY home!! OH SHIT! THAT'S RIGHT!! I REMEMBER now!!! *...OF WHEN, I broke the hell out, FROM THEE below-levels, UNDER THE GROUND,...in a hallway... made of white jade.*"

*(Old habits die hard)...*Ya' dig?

Chapter Eighteen

NO ONE EVEN CARED

And so, after a hurried (((and freezing-cold-shower!))) in the darkness of an abandoned rowhome. And, mind you, he DID SO,... listening for AND HEARING the sounds, OF PEOPLE on ALL THREE FLOORS, (((in the DARKNESS OF ABANDONMENT!!!))),... sneakin' tha'-fuck-around!! And then, once in, a fresh black suit and, in some brand new black Stacy Adams shoes, Mr. Trife, STEPPED ON OUT of that abandoned house at night...

FOR...

HE AIN'T TRYNA' BE *STUCK!!!*

And so...

HE'S BACK on his MUTHAFUCKIN' GIDDY-UP!!!

As...

He's, back ON HIS his grind! (To pay HIS "music industry dues"!)...

STILL a bit tweaked. (Though, HE AIN'T been up for weeks!)... ((((THAT SHIT just made for A GOOD HOOK!!!)))). AFTER ALL, Pockets, told him so, THAT, *"He'd have a 'lil time on his hands!"*

AND SO...

He wrote himself, A COUPLE OF RHYMES!!

And so(NOW!)...

He's got TWO NEW SONGS, in that, *once virgin,* black and white, composition song book!!

With, suitcase in hand, Mr. Trife, is steppin' hard down these city blocks. And, he does it wit that, *OL' BROTHA TRIFE STROLL!!!* STEPPIN' HARD, down THESE city blocks! STEPPIN' HARD, down these UNEVEN sidewalks! AND, HE'S DOIN' IT WIT, a bloodsoaked red hat, COCKED HARD to the side on top of his head...affixed wit a bullet hole!

Steppin' hard, TO, make it cross town. *Gotta' 'member HOW to get to Legs' place!* To, lay-low and lay-up. (For, Anna Mossitti), HE KEEPS his head on a swivel!! TEETH CLINCHED, *(((from the meth))),* GOT his jawline chiseled!!

(And so), and so while...

(He GOTTA' maintain, a low-profile!)

AND SO...

He's steppin'. Swivellin'. AND, he GOT ON his stroll! Seeking refuge and a bad-bitch, that kicks-it like a gun, behind and beneath, a bullet hole!

And so...

Mr. Trife, is lookin' up from under, that hat's bloodsoaked brim. Gonna give his Nephew a big ol' pound! AND, a big ol' bear hug!! WHEN he sees him again!!!

And so...

(It's: So Far! So good!)

FOR...

AIN'T nothin' FUCKED-UP GO DOWN, while strollin' THROUGH the hood!(((AWE FUCK!!!)))...Come! LET'S take a look...

FOR, JUST UP AHEAD...

(Mr. Trife, *peeps-out* a mother and, her teenage son, having just stepped outta' an old green Chevy Nova, *from just having found a spot, from having just parked, from having just pulled over)*...

And, as Mr. Trife approaches the mother, she begins to frantically scream, "MY BABY!!! MY BABY'S STILL IN THE BACK!!!" A '73 Nova. AND her seven month old baby!!!!!! JUST LIKE THAT! GONE in a flash!!

AFTER...

(Just having, some asshole-loser. SNATCH her car keys! Hop in. And. SPEED the-fuck-off!)...(JUST LIKE THAT!!!!!!!)...

"Ain't THIS a MOTHER!!", Mr. Trife, thinks!!

AFTER...

(Just having just, BORE WITNESS. To a mother. Just having, her '73 Nova. WITH, STILL, her baby in it! CARJACKED!!!)...(JUST LIKE THAT!!!!!!!)...

"DOIN' this shit IN FRONT OF me??", Triflin', belts out!! (((Oh, and PLEASE DO, don't have NO doubts!!!!!!!)))...

For...

Mr. Trife, BEEN ON his giddy-up!

And(NOW!)...

GETTIN' on HIS steeze!

For...

HE 'BOUT TO get on BOTH THEM SHITZ, (at the same mutha' fuckin' time!!)...

And...

(DO IT WIT ease!!).

"WHO tha' fuck, YOU think, YOU IS!?!", Mr. Trife, shouts-out, (far BEYOND miffed!!).

FOR...

(Triflin's GONNA' fuck-up YOUR WHOLE ENTIRE WORLD)... (((IF you fuckin' 'round wit kids!!!)))(((BELIEVE THAT SHIT!!!!!!))).

And so...

WITHOUT a second thought, (for, Mr. Trife, HE AIN'T GOTTA' contemplate, for what, HE'S GONNA' do!), and, well,...he ran OUT INTO traffic! (AND, WELL, as for, his FIRST thought?). WELL, he left that back on that uneven sidewalk! (WHERE, he thought to...leave his suitcase:)

And, well, AS FOR, Mr. Trife...

WELL, he caught up WITH that car! AS, it got stuck in traffic! JUST up AT the NEXT light!

And, well, AS FOR, THAT asshole-loser carjacker...

WELL, HE got caught-off-guard! When, he HAD his car door RIPPED OPEN!!! And, well, AS FOR, THAT asshole-loser carjacker...well, he got caught. (BUT, his breath got away!) WHEN, Mr. Trife,...PROCEEDED to choke him!!!

(And, well, SEEING AS, *old habits DIE hard and,* so on and, so forth)...

AS FOR, Mr. Trife, *(A Being Of: Brotha Trife!)* Well...HE CHOKED THAT MOTHERFUCKER, (seated right there in the car!), right in traffic, right up at that next light!

And, well, AS FOR, Mr. Trife...

WELL, he WAS fully enjoying himself!!! WHEN, he watched, (through those 24 karat golds!), THAT MOTHERFUCKER'S FACE...turn FROM blue TO purple!! AND, when HE SAW that asshole-loser carjacker's EYES...roll up!! RIGHT up there! RIGHT UP AT the red light!!

And, well, AS FOR, Mr. Trife. (WELP!) THIS is what HE chose...

For, Mr. Trife, he LEFT his left hand ON that (asshole-loser's) throat! THEN, with his right, Mr. Trife, LEFT that asshole-loser motherfucker, WIT A shattered eye socket, uneven jaw AND, wit a - pushed-to-the-other-side-of-his-face - BROKEN nose!!!

And so and so well, AS FOR, Mr. Trife. (((I told y'all already! HE AIN'T gotta' think twice!)))...

(WELP!!) Mr. Trife, LEFT that asshole-loser motherfucker, IN THE MIDDLE of the street, (((WIT A DIET OF SOUP AND RICE!!!))).

And, well, the only reason why, Mr. Trife, stopped choking that guy, wasn't 'cause his face was turnin' purple and, those sittin' in traffic, could only see, the whites of his rolled-up-eyes. And, well, it was, but, yet, it wasn't 'cause, Mr. Trife WANTED, to unhinged his motherfuckin' jaw and, PUSH his nose, TO the other-mother-fuckin'-side! Well, it WAS 'cause of those at the red light, in traffic, sittin' stopped and in shock, were all yellin' out their car windows, at Mr. Trife, *"Yo! Just whoop his ass! That mutha' fucka' always be jackin'! But, DON'T choke him, like some PUSSY-COWARD-RACIST-COP!!! OR WE ALL GON' BUM RUSH AND MAKE IT STOP!!!"*

And, well, Mr. Trife, well...

HE RETURNED that car! (He simply got in and, BUSTED a U-Turn!) (It really wasn't too far!).

AND, well, YOU would think THAT, it WOULD BE the mom, THAT would be IN FOR a surprise! BUT, it was Mr. Trife, THAT WOULD BE in for a surprise! (WHEN he stepped outta' THAT ride!).

(Tier-Three-Mind, knowing ENOUGH to know, THAT, the cops, WOULD SOON BE showing up!) AND SO...

Mr. Trife, he hands the mother back her car keys. And then, POST-HASTE, grabs his suitcase, FROM off that uneven sidewalk! (And, WAS just 'bout to get BACK ON his giddy-up!) WHEN, the mother's teenage son, BLURTS OUT, to his mom's "MOM, 'DAT'S HIM!!! 'DAT'S THA' MAN 'DAT, BEAT ME UP!!!"

"AND, THIS is the thanks, I GET???", Triflin', asks, "WHAT THE FUCK!?!"

"Boy! Whatchew talkin' 'bout?? DON'T BE RUDE!!! I KNOW you got BETTER HOME TRAININ', THAN that!! I taught you myself! THIS MAN, JUST brought my car back! AND, YOUR baby brother! Boy, don't make me HAVETA' give you a smack!", the mother, claps back!

"Mom! 'Dat's what I'M talkin' 'bout! *DIS IS THA' MAN 'dat, SMACKED-tha'-crap outta' me N' Roger, a few years back!!* I TOLD you! 'Member??? I TOLD you, 'BOUT 'dat! 'Member!?! *'CROSS from the post office? On tha' corner??* 'Member??? *...UP ON THA' NORF Side!!! HE crossed tha' street n' smacked tha' crap outta' me N' Roger!* I 'member, 'DAT ISH!! *HE WAS parked at tha' post office!* YOU was! Facts, dawg! DON'T try n' deny!! *'CAUSE, me n' Roger WAS fightin' over, who "called it" first!* 'Cause, I "CALLED IT" first!! Facts, dawg! 'Cause, I SAW IT FIRST!! I straight pointed n', said, *"DAT'S MY black Bimmer - "Seven-Fiddy" - BIG BODY ride!!!"*, her teenaged son, animated, provides!!!

And so(Then)...

(The three of them, all stand there, looking cockeyed at one another, on that uneven sidewalk. In the hood. At night)...

AS...

It *DAWNS* on the mother! (as, she *exclaims!!!*), *"THAT'S the brother from THE STATUE!!!* Oh shit! HE'S BACK!!! My son,...you're right!" (And then, the son, provides HIS *REAFFIRMATION!)*, "TOLD you, mom!!! *Tha' ish went down, in front of 'dat 'partment buildin' 'dat, err'body swears be haunted!! 'DIS man, came walkin' cross tha' street and, just straight smacked THA' CRAP OUTTA' me 'N Roger, 'dat day, we WAS, gettin' READY TO fight!!"*

Hmm??...(MORE information gained!)...(((FOR, Mr. Trife's, TIER-THREE-BRAIN!!!)))

THOUGH...

Mr. Trife, don't *know nothin'* 'bout HIS statue! (IN AND OF...*old SYKE Park fame!*).

BUT...

He NOW knows, WHICH WAY to go! (And, BESIDES all that!). *Triflin' KNOWS, Heavy Duty, BE 360! (And so, HE KNOWS, HIS NEPHEW WILL KNOW, WHAT he NEEDS to KNOW!!)...*

AND SO...

IT'S GIDDY-UP TIME!!!

And, with suitcase in hand. And, with gold karat 24's over his eye, Mr. Trife, COCKS HIS BULLET HOLE HAT at the mother, as he, then, makes his way ON UP TO...the "Norf Side"!!!

And, UPON his arrival, at the 'partment building, (CROSS from the post office!), Mr. Trife, DOES SO smile! As he, stands there on the corner, looking up, at that window, *WHERE, once, HIS Nephew, once dropped the key, (out of to him), waiting on HIS Uncle to catch down below!* ...*(OH, ABOUT...1,260 DAYS AGO OR SO!!!).*

And then, JUST LIKE THAT, *Tier-Three-Memory,* of he, *KICKS in!* AS HE, dips down a tight alleyway. AS HE, makes his way 'round back! AND, WELL, as for THIS triflin' mutha' fucka', well, HE DON'T NEED NO key! (For, THIS HERE triflin' mutha' fucka', KNOWS HOW to, gain entry!!!). Back door opened, *movin' like Nigerian incense smoke* and, HE don't make a sound, though, from *the creeking* from those old back wooden steps, *there's a warning being spoken. AND, they're saying* FOR YOU *to turn back!* AIN'T NO FUTURE DOWN them loooooong white halls! YOU wasn't put on THIS earth,...TO BE LIVING LIKE that!!!

(YA' GOTTA' RECOGNIZE THE SIGNS!!! AND HEED THE WARNINGS!!!)...(YA' DIG!!!)

BUT...

Old habits DO die hard. Weirdo fucking halls! Swear for God. These bricks, painted white, LOOK OF - they-should-*or-used-to-be* - OF SOME, outside wallz! And, as Mr. Trife, keeps makin' them rights, (of halls that abruptly end!). The rights, he makes, ARE hard. BUT, it AIN'T hard TO DO what's right! AND SO, Unc AIN'T GON' stop! 'TIL he has his Nephew IN HIS sights!

("And, OH YEAH!!! That's RIGHT!")(AS, Tier-Three-Memory, KICKS BACK in!!!)...

Nephew SAID, for him, "TO NEVER knock on THIS door!" (BUT, I'll be damned! THE motherfucker has been left ajar!)

(Hmm. Legs left HIS door ajar??? Hmm. Something must not be right!)...

Come...let's have A LOOK AROUND INSIDE...

And so, Mr. Trife, doesn't kick-in no open door. Nope. (Triflin' gonna do HOW Triflin' do!). AND SO, he gon' creep in Legs' place...NICE AND SLOW!!! And, the first person THAT he sees, IS HIS...bottom bitch, GIDGET COLE!!! (WITH her head BETWEEN her knees!!!). AND, the ONLY thing, THAT GETS kicked open IS,...*HIS Tier-Three-Memory!!!*

MY *old hookers!* AND some,...NEW hookers!!! Wait? What??? ALL WITH their...heads? BETWEEN their knees??? What the fuck IS going on!?! DIDN'T expect to see THIS shit! (on the closed-side, of the door now open!). Hmm?? MAYBE, JUST MAYBE, they all heard me creepin' in AND,...they ALL BE, JUST jokin'!!!

Maybe? (I said, MAYBE!!!) COME with, Mr. Trife! LET'S take a CLOSER LOOK...

And, as Mr. Trife, gains entry he's, movin' light on his toes, and he's, closing that door, nice and slow. And he's, continuing to silently-tread, as he's, lookin' past the centerpiece on the table, of the table, that's just straight ahead. *Oh, THAT table, will, AND, DOES turn, to BE sure!* And, THAT motherfucker is, just a few paces, from the door! *(THAT table! YES! THAT TABLE THAT, Unc and Legs, and Nephew, once sat at!)...(oh, 'bout, three and a half years or so back!).*

And, of that centerpiece, of that small oval wooden table, of which is, a still sealed, uncracked and untapped bottle, of Sailor Jerry Spiced Rum! Of which is, surrounded by the *"works"*, of some - *used-to-be-the-mob's-muscle-in-this-town* - turned - strung-out - *JUNKIE BUM!!!*

AND, DON'T NOBODY MAKES a move. And, don't nobody makes a sound. As, Unc, stands there, *TRYING TO get it all worked out, in his Tier-Three-Mind,* as he's, lookin' tha' fuck around!

And, off to his right, in the living room, seen thru the large and high, arched and wide, and white-enough doorway, of no doors - with dirty-handmarked-smudges runnin' - up-and-down both sides... Wait!? What?? COULD this REALLY be??? For, it's Gidget and, a WHOLE BUNCH of hookers, LOOKIN' AS IF THEY BE...eatin' THEY OWN pussy!! As they, ALL BE, sittin' on the sofas. As they, ALL BE, STILL not movin'! As they, ALL BE, STILL not makin' any sounds! As, they and, ALL THE WHILE, (between their knees),...their heads BE hangin' down!!!

BUT...

(Trife's focus, IS: WHAT he CAME THERE for!)...(The same very same reason, WHY he looked past, that centerpiece on the table)...

WAIT!? WHAT?? Could this REALLY be?!? My...MY...Nephew's on the floor!?!

FOR...

ON the floor. On the OTHER SIDE of the table. THERE'S LEGS!!! AND HE'S...kneeled down OVER Nephew! And, there's Nephew! LYING ON HIS BACK!!! And, there's Legs! And he's, ALL FUCKED-UP-ON-BENZOS and, shooting-up MY Nephew, WITH a LETHAL DOSE of smack!!!!!!

(Wait?)((What??))...AND...(((What The FUCK!!!)))...

STARTLED FROM the sneak-up! (Benzoed-up!!) Legs, to his feet, stumbles up.

AND...

PUNCHES, Mr. Trife, RIGHT IN THE MOUTH!!!

((((Go 'head motherfucker, KEEP ON fucking up!!!!!!)))).

Coming cross, Mr. Trife's face, IS the same face THAT the face, IN the cloud DID make!!! The very same very look. (((That being, a look, of: PURE RAGE AND HATE!!!))). Tier-Three-Memory takes him back, (oh, to 'bout, three and a half years ago - being the year of the date). Of when, Unc, FIRST WALKED into Legs' place,..."JUST KNEW THIS MOTHERFUCKER was bad news!!...I SHOULDA' killed Legs, FROM the gate!!!!!!"

(Taken aback)((Ready TO lose HIS shit!))(((AND SNAP!!!)))...

But...

He don't.

As...

He can't.

As...

He stands helpless to and to prevent attack.

For...

(Unc, stands there, lookin' 'round the room)...

AS...

His thoughts, and actions, HAVE BEEN slooooooowed down!

AS...

(With the sounds, within the scene, within YOUR TUMBLING car, IN WHICH, therein, there's plenty - of YOUR car's contents - floatin' 'round!)...

AS...

YOU REMAIN hog-tied and HELPLESS, RUMBLING TOWARDS YOUR DOOM!!!

AND(MAKE NO MISTAKE!)...

THIS PLACE is fuckin' weird! *(Unc's shadow, moves in slooooow-motion time!)...*

(His sight, and sounds, have been slooooooowed down!)...

AS...

With screeching tires...ENROUTE TO A DEER!!!

AND(MAKE NO MISTAKE!!)...

(Unc's shadow, AIN'T GOT NOTHIN' to do wit - his mind - TELLING - his vision - EVERYTHING IS - AND - HAS - BEEN - SLOWED - DOWN!)...

AS...

With that impending IMPACT, with that bridge abutment, (((TUMBLING IN A CAR))), YOU CAN NOT STEER!!!

For...

His own weird-shadow casts, upon the white wall he faces.

AND(MAKE NO MISTAKE!!!)...

It AIN'T got NOTHIN' to do wit - *the flicker - of the candle's flame!*

AND(MAKE NO MISTAKE!!!!)...

(It AIN'T got NOTHIN' to do wit - what his - one - good - eyeball - is seeing - from his brain!)...

FOR...

Unc, sees *his shadow,* from cross the room. And with his right hand, *of it,* he traces.

And...

HIS SHADOW, IN REAL TIME, *IT REFUSES TO MOVE!!!*

(((OUTTA' SHEAR - AND - BLATANT-DEFIANCE!!!))).

Rather...

(IN slooooooow-motion-moves)...

IT MORPHS!!!

For...

HIS SHADOW, IS DELAYED!!!

((((OUTTA' SHEAR - AND - IN PURE - HUMANLY - NONCOMPLIANCE!!!)))).

AND SO...

Upon the wall he faces, to be sure, *his shadow, it laps like the ocean,... upon the sands of the shore.*

And...

(Unc, he places his right hand, over his heart. *As, his Tier-Three-Brain is, thinkin', "I'll be darned!")...*

AS...

...He watches,...on the wall,...*the shadow,...of his arm,* of which, in which, in real time, in and of the body shadow, OF WHICH AND IN WHICH - *his shadow arm* - IS STILL NOT APART!!!(((OF WHICH, OF COURSE, WOULD BE, OF THE NATURAL TREND!!!)))...*Rather, ((((ON IT'S OWN TIME!!!)))), the shadow,...on the wall,...OF HIS OWN ARM,...does so, as it does so, moving towards,...the body shadow,...of which, to which, well,...it slooooooowly bends!* (And, TO BE SURE!). UPON the wall, he faces, *his shadow, IT laps LIKE the ocean,...UPON the sands of the shore!* (As with, the ocean's breakers, the remnants,...filter down,...as it absorbs)... *((((AND, THAT'S EXACTLY WHAT THE FUCK UNC'S SHADOW IS DOING!!!)))).* As he, currently, uncovers his heart. And, then, again, when HE QUICKLY COVERS HIS HEART AGAIN!!! (((And, don't YOU ever, EVER, make the mistake, of thinking, *of the arm shadow,* of the body shadow, OF THEM connecting - FOR - *the arm* - it - DON'T connect... *IT ABSORBS!!!)))*.

...*"Is THIS shit, REALLY, real? Wait?? What???"*, Unc, *thunk, (((BACK FROM the lapse, from being TAKEN ABACK!!)))* and, looks into the eyes of, that: "JUNKIE-MOTHERFUCKER!!!". *(KNOWING of NO DOUBTS!)*... *(That, don't NOBODY GETS MY BENEFIT - OF - MY DOUBTS!!!),* as, Unc's, *MIND-SHOUTS, "MY NEPHEW - YOU KILLED!!!!!!"*

Oh fuck.

Unc picks up Legs. And, slams that junkie-motherfucker down! Slammed him down, RIGHT NEXT to his Nephew! (((GONNA' HAVE THAT JUNKIE-MOTHERFUCKER DIE ON THE SAME FLOOR!!!)))..."YOU GON' DIE, RIGHT HERE!!! YOU PIECE-OF-SHIT-JUNKIE-MOTHERFUCKER!!! DIE!!! DIE!!! DIE!!! RIGHT HERE, ON THE SAME FLOOR!!! THE SAME FLOOR, WHERE YOU KILLED MY NEPHEW!!! DIE!!! DIE!!! DIE!!! YOU GON' DIE, RIGHT HERE!!! ON THE SAME FLOOR!!! RIGHT HERE, *IN THE SHADOWS, OF..."THE TURNING TABLE"!!!"*

(Old habits DO die hard. And, tables DO turn). And, sometimes...

Mutha' fuckas GOTTA' die!!!!!!

Come. Let us ALL ENJOY, as Unc, KILLS THIS JUNKIE-MOTHERFUCKER!!! (Shall we?) YES!!! I THINK WE SHALL...

And, WITH BOTH of his hands, 'round the throat of Legs, Unc, begins to choke THE LIFE out, of: THAT piece-of-shit Legs! RIGHT THERE, on the SAME floor! RIGHT THERE, on top of that piece-of-shit carpet!*(((RIGHT THERE, WHERE, Legs SHOT-UP NEPHEW, WITH A LETHAL-DOSE OF SMACK!!!)))RIGHT THERE, WHERE, that junkie-motherfucker, placed HIS "WORKS", UPON the table and, TURNED NEPHEW ONTO THAT DOPE SHIT!!! RIGHT THERE, WHERE,... Nephew died.*

(AND, being the pussy THAT HE IS), Legs CAN, BUT WON'T, make eye contact WITH Unc. Though, HE WAS GIVEN HIS CHANCE, to do so. *For, his eyes, hadn't yet, rolled-up and, come to a stop, IN THE BACK OF HIS JUNKIE-HEAD!!!*

YET, this: NO-eye-contact - piece-of-shit - SO PROVIDED Unc with, SOME answers, to some DEMANDS, "He half-assed it. So, I shot-him-up a SECOND time.", *("Yeah, 'cause, YOU WANTED him to die!"),* (((*THAT*

IS the look, IN Unc's eye!))). But, ALL that, Unc, can see, IS Legs' collapsing-throat,...IN his hands!

And, right before Legs dies. Legs, looks up into Unc's flickering 24 karat gold eyes. (((And, the cocksucker, EVEN HAD THE GALL, TO crack a smile!))). And, that piece-of-shit Legs, HE TOLD UNC, with his LAST bit of air, "Heavy Duty, owed me money. Plus, he was never really big on doin' the dishes. But, that's neither...here nor there." Nodded-out on smack or not, no one checked for Nephew's pulse, no one dialed 911, no one even cared.

And, what WAS DONE had, ALREADY BEEN done, by the time that, Unc had gotten there. "DIDN'T I TELL NEPHEW, TO GET OUT OF THIS CITY!?! DIDN'T I TELL HIM, JUST TO GO TO MIAMI!?! DIDN'T I TELL HIM...to be happy?", Unc, thinks to himself, (as he, sat down at THAT table). As he, sat down in, the SAME VERY SAME chair. (His back to the wall!) Window TO his left! "Living" room straight ahead!!! (With, the: DON'T - EVER-knock-on-THIS - DOOR - TO HIS right!) Just as, AS HE, sat the FIRST TIME, that he came there.

"Really yo!? Really wit THIS SHIT, right now???", Unc, thinks to himself, (as he, contemplates of, what surrounds). As he, contemplates, why no one, opened the seal to that centerpiece? As he, contemplates, taking a BIG SWIG of, blood and rum! (((As he, got punched in the mouth!)))...(((And, IF NOTHING ELSE, of WHAT SURROUNDS, Unc COULD USE...a drink RIGHT ABOUT NOW!!!))). As he, sits there,...looking at HIS Nephew. As he, knows-he-just-knows, HE CAN FEEL IT, that, as he, knows-he-just-knows, that, upon him, HIS Nephew, IS looking down!

And, Unc *stares* at that bottle. The bottle *a thousand yards away.* As, Unc, *stares* at that bottle, *in his thousand-yard-gaze.* The bottle gracing dead-center of THAT table. And, Unc *stares* around that apartment. *ALL one thousand yards of it!* And, Unc, takes it upon himself...to open the seal. *('Cause no one else was able.)*

"AHHHHH, THE THINGS WE DO TO OURSELVES!!!!!!", (Unc's toasts TO his Nephew!). And then, he pours some out FOR his Nephew! And, then he, takes that bottle TO THE head! *((((((AS HE, SWILLS DOWN, BLOOD AND RUM, TO THE BEAT OF WAR DRUMS AND, A FUNERAL DIRGE, IN HIS MOTHERFUCKIN' HEAD!!!!!!))))))* And

then, he sits there. *IN his thoughts.* RIGHT THERE AT, the table, *THAT turned!* (As he, sits in an apartment...FULL of the dead!).

And...

Unc, ain't EVEN phased!

As...

Unc, begins to have visions:

Of lying room-by-room-by-room, side-by-side-by-side, (Of AND WITH: the essentially-dead!), JOINING him, IN the lower under the ground levels. Of hallways...made of white jade.

And...

(JUST AS, HE WAS, stirred-awake, in and, of hallways,...made of white jade)...

THERE'S stirring IN the "living" room!

(AIN'T NOBODY best be playin'!)...(For real, for real. AND JUST SAYIN'!!!)...

And so...

(As Unc, stands back up and, walks into the "living" room)...

HIS OWN shadow, it trails, slooooooowly behind him.

FOR...

NOT OUT OF HATE, THOUGH, *IN AND, OF DEFIANCE, THIS ANTI-SOCIAL SHADOW GETS PULLED TOWARDS* HIS BODY!!! Until, *(SLOOOOOOWLY&FINALLY),(AS IT TRIED TO FIGHT IT!!!), it* JOINS Unc in, the "living" room! *(The slooooooow absorption OF IT ALL!!!)* *SLOOOOOOOWLY.*

(A collection of connection)

BUT...

(THIS SHADOW DON'T LIKE IT!)

FOR...

This shadow MORPHS - in slooooooow motion - on the wall - BEHIND Trife's back! But, *it* don't move in real time with Trife. (Have you ever *seen a shadow, ever do this* before, ever in your life???)...

Well...

YOU HAVE NOW!!! *WELCOME TO TRIFE'S WORLD!!!* (Come!) ((NOW, let's all walk with Trife))...(((into a room full of dead girls!!!)))...

BUT...

(WATCH YOUR BACK!)...

'Cause...

This fucking thing MORPHS!!!

'CAUSE...

IT'S OF THIS *fucking evil apartment!*

FOR(YOU SEE)...

Mr. Brotha Trife ain't IT'S source!!

And so...*(A thousand yards away!)*...(IN the "living" room!)...

...((((*THAT FUCKED-UP SHADOW* HAS JOINED TRIFE AND YOU!!!))))((((*'CAUSE, THAT FUCKED-UP SHADOW, ENJOYS FUCKED-UP SIGHTS,* QUITE, RIGHT, FROM, LIKE, *a lethal-mixture, OF: SMACK. Acid. Bogus E-pills. AND shrooms!!!*)))...

AND...

Wouldn't you know?? (MOTHERFUCKIN' SHIT!!!) ((((((MY NEPHEW'S DEAD!!!))))))

BUT...

(Guess who's STILL alive???)...

THAT HOOKER-BITCH, GIDGET COLE!!!!!! (And, she's dressed JUST LIKE all the others!) (Wearing thongs and bikinis. And, lacey-white-swimwear-wrap-up-covers!). And, they're ALL dressed, *JUST AS THEY ALL WERE, WHEN they left! (WHEN, that anchor, left the seafloor!). WHEN, The: Doing-Big-Things-Yacht-Propellers - CHOPPED through - BIG-SEA-CREATURES - TURNIN' THEM MOTHERFUCKERS INTO - tiny-BLOODY-like-amebas! As THEY, set a course to the north! As THEY, chopped through the seas, TURNED TO BLOOD!!!!!!((((((FROM, ALL THE: cute, big-eyed - help-me-please - arctic baby seals...THAT BAD HABITZ CLUBBED!!!!!!))))))*.

"WELL, I SEE, THAT YOU SURVIVED!!! AIN'T YOU, GOT THE NERVE!!!", Unc, shouts, (laying it GOOD into her!), *"Y'ALL NEVER, LEFT TOWN??? ON MY WORD, YOU BEST TELL ME, NOTHIN' BUT THE TRUTH!!!"*, as Unc, goes through the ceiling, *shadow trailed up to the roof!*

"We...went...to...Miami. Just...as...YOU...said.", the OD'ing Gidget, strhuh-struha-struggles to say, *"I wanted...him...to...stay , because of you... he's dead.* You know...your...Nephew...gotta' hard head. *He...came...lookin'... for...YOU!"*, Gidget, tells Unc, over blue lips and puke.

("Old habits die hard.", is all of what Unc, can manage to mutter).

And then, Unc begins, to have *these visions:* (As if, he were seeing it FROM up above!)(As when, he saw himself lying there, under a white sheet, in hallways, made of white jade!). And, Unc, can *see, HOW* it went down! And, Unc,...smiled. *As he, saw Nephew, toss that pimp's Jordans! Suspending them, high above the shroud! (FOR, THE WHOLE DAMN MARINA TO SEE!!!). And, Unc KNEW, THAT, they all HAD, in fact, MADE IT OUT of the city and, MADE IT TO Miami!!!* (And, Unc knew, that, his Nephew, was happy...if only for a while:)

However...

(That smile disappears:(

AS...

Unc's vision, TAKES HIM to when, Nephew and Gidget,...showed up at Legs' place:

(Come). (Have a look, WITH Unc)...

...("You got that taste, kid. I KNEW you'd be back! Tables do turn, kid. Tables do turn. But, Duty, you're blowin' my cover, kid. You got my home lookin' like a whowaa factory! This AIN'T NO, "No-Tell-Motel"!!! THIS is MY home, kid! La Casa Secura!!! Remember? AND, where tha' fucks my taste, kid!?! Heard ya' came into some BIG MONEY! You forget 'bout ol' Legs, did ya', kid?? BUT, I know how, we can make things right, between me and you. Since you're back, and, ya' brought along your friends. Well, we might as well, all get good and fucked-up! Like old times! BUT, this AIN'T no soup kitchen, kid! MY shit, AIN'T for free!!! AND, looks ta' me, kid, you and your friends, ARE already into Legs HEAVY, for A GOOD BIT of money!! SO, this is what we're GONNA' do. YOU come work for me again, and, we'll turn all these whowaas, on ta' tha' "Turnin' Table". Make some money, kid. Less, of course, what ya' already owe me! Waddaya' say, kid? Sounds good, to you?", Legs, tells Heavy Duty, upon waking from his Benzo'd stupor)...

And, right before Gidget dies. She motions, *for her long-lost-friend,* Brotha Trife, to remove from his (those 24 karat lenses, of limited-edition) eyes. And, as a single trail of blood and weepings gives way, from the clone of Brotha Trife's, swollen and stitched-shut eye, Gidget, says, over blue lips, *(and with, The: Gray-Mist-of-Death's-Condensation - BEGINNING TO COAT her eyes!!),* "Your Nephew, *said,..."Nobody but you...could crack open that bottle". He said,..."That was only for you".* Your Nephew, loved you, Unc. He...*wouldn't let...nobody...look at or...touch...that bottle.* He said, *"That's for THE MOST TRIFLIN' motherfucker THIS SIDE OF the Mississippi!".* Brotha Trife, your Nephew,...*said, "Nobody,...was worthy,... to open...that bottle". He said,..."Only you,...could...do...that".* Brotha Trife, didn't NOBODY in...this...WHOLE...ENTIRE...WORLD...love you... more than your Nephew."

Chapter Nineteen

GASLIGHT

FAR-THE-HELL-AWAY, from North Juarez...

Pockets, ever the gambling-man (that HE IS!), *AND, drinker of drinks,* (and, NOT NEW TO MUCH!), BUT, *(NEW TO Mr. Trife's "MORGUE-LIFE"!), WAS IN NEED of some drinks, (after THAT experience!!). And, well, he IMMEDIATELY took himself, and his two newly-signed rappers, to...*(WANNA' TAKE A WILD-GUESS???)... (THAT'S RIGHT!), *Pockets, went to,...BITCHEZ!!!!!!*

'CAUSE...

There be BITCHEZ in Vegas! There be BITCHEZ on tha' South Side! The deep south got BITCHEZ! AND, YOU KNOW,...Philly got BITCHEZ! D.C. got their fair share of BITCHEZ! (DAMMIT!) *There's even BITCHEZ in The Hamptons!! THERE BE BITCHEZ FROM COAST-TO-COAST!!! 'CAUSE,...*(OH SHIT!!!)...(HERE IT COMES!!!)...*EVERYWHERE YOU LOOK,...THERE BE SOME BRAND NEW BITCHEZ!!! AND,...* (Oh-my-damn!)...*there EVEN BE some OLD BITCHEZ,...*(Oh FUCK!)... *IN DIRE NEED of an OVERHAUL!!! AND, WELL,* (DAMMIT!)... *these old BITCHEZ, be gettin'...*(YO! REALLY??)...(shall we say?...)...*a... FACELIFT!!!*(Renovated 'n shit!)(You know, gettin' they PLUMBING gutted-out 'n shit!!!). *FOR, YOU SEE,* (DAMMIT!)...*JUST WHEN YOU THINK YOU KNOW BITCHEZ,* (SHIT!)...*WELL, from coast-*

TO-coast...(HERE WE GO!!!)...(WAIT FOR IT!)...(WAIT FOR IT!!)... IT'S A MUST FOR BITCHEZ, ON YOU, TO GET BRAND NEW!!! (Shew!)...(That wasn't so bad...was it:)

(ANY-DAMN-WAY!)...

AND SO...

(After, Pockets, MC Busta-Nut and, False Profit, (DAMMIT!)...(er-ruh-uh), were done with BITCHEZ)...

Pockets, drove to and, parked that RV of his, in that humongous parking lot, of that 24-Hour Off-Track wagering establishment. That one, the one, not too far from, the Mark Meharg Memorial Hospital. That one, the one, with...THAT morgue! THAT one, the one, that's not a far walk, from THAT seedy-ass shitty-ass lime green Buena Vista! (And, why, would Pockets, set up shop, so close to all of that, YOU may ask?)...(Well, because, Pockets IS, a GAMBLING MAN, AFTER ALL!). *And, well, he HAD TO get up wit tha' ponies and, place himself a couple o' bets!* (And, OF COURSE!), *Pockets, TURNED his two newly-signed-rappers ON TO playing the ponies! AND, SO NOW, his two newly-signed-rappers, ARE in deep, to Pockets' pockets! AND, SO NOW, initial-album sales, merch sales and, so-forth,* (of MC Busta-Nut and False Profit's profits!), *MUST AND SHALL GO - DIRECTLY INTO POCKETS' POCKETS - TO PAY OFF THEIR GAMBLING-DEBT - TO POCKETS!!!* (TOLD Y'ALL, POCKETS, GOT SOME SHIT TO HIM!!!)(Y'ALL BETTER START LISTENING!!!)...AIN'T THIS MUSIC-GAME A MOTHERFUCKER!?!...(Don't answer that yet:)

And so...

(While, Mr. Trife, was gettin' all (((SPUN-THA'-FUCK-OUT!!!))) with McDusty, McCrusty and, with GOOD OL' SCABBY McKNEES!!!)...

Well...

Pockets, MC Busta-Nut and, False Profit, were gettin' (((GOOD-'N-SAUCY!!!))) ALL UP IN a BITCHEZ' V.I.P. (DAMMIT!)...(ER-RUH-UH!)...*area.*

And...

(While, Mr. Trife, was, (you know), (((STRANGLING-THA'-SHIT!!!))) outta' motherfuckers all night!!)...

Well...

Pockets, was also KILLIN' 'EM at tha' track! WHILE, (mind you!), gettin' a FIRM-STRANGLEHOLD, on 'Nut and Profit's - FUTURE PROFITS!!

AND(AS SUCH!!)...

BOTH, Pockets, AND Mr. Trife, were MAKIN' A KILLIN'!!!

...WHICH, (brings us to where, we're at RIGHT NOW!). Come! Let's listen in on the phone call goings-on, between Pockets, and Phillip Tate, shall we? (((YES, I THINK WE MUTHA' FUCKIN' SHALL!!!)))...

"...hang on a sec, would ya', Phil??", Pockets, at the helm, not wanting ANYONE to overhear his convo, tells Phillip Tate to hang on. Then, while seated in HIS Captain's chair, in HIS RV, Pockets, annoyed, leans 'round the side of his Captain's chair and, hollers back to the RV's kitchen area, at his two newly-signed-rappers, "Y'ALL TWO, KEEP IT DOWN!! Y'ALL SEE ME, UP HERE, ON THA' MUTHA' FUCKIN' PHONE!! DAMN, WHY DON'T Y'ALL, WRITE ME, A HIT SONG, OR SOME SHIT??? 'STEAD OF, SMOKIN'-UP ALL THAT GRASS!!!" (Not that, 'Nut or Profit, were really even making that much noise!!). But, Pockets, (BEING POCKETS!), just, wanted to check on them, making sure, they weren't listening in, and, GET them BUSY...DOIN' SUMFIN'!! (DAMN!)...(DO SUMFIN'!!!) Pockets, after (hearing himself!) giving orders, turns back 'round in HIS Captain's chair, to continue, his conversation with Phil, (under hushed-tones and hash!).

"Grass!", MC Busta-Nut, whispers to False Profit, (crackin'-himself up!), then, continues, (while he lights-up a blunt!), "Old, CRAZY-IN-THA'-HEAD, Old-Head! DON'T, he know, THIS-HERE-SHIT, be THAT *"GAS"!*"

Meanwhile. (Back up at the helm)...

"...yes, I am 100% certain, sir. I put all of said requested, reading-materials, in the back sleeping quarters of the RV, prior to, your departure.

Check the closet again, sir. I placed them on the floor of your closet. I remember, distinctly, sir. And, I was careful, not to stack the books and the 3-Ring Binders, up against your hunting rifle. I know how much you love, that weapon, sir."

"THAT AIN'T, NO WEAPON! THAT'S, A "THIRTY-AUGHT-SIX"!!!!!!", Pockets, hollering into his phone, (hoppin'-up from HIS helm!), then, with cell, pressed to ear, Pockets, begins his march, through the kitchen area, enroute, to the back of the RV!

And so(Back in the back private sleeping quarters)...

With door slammed shut and, with closet door slammed open and, with cell pressed to ear, Pockets, digs 'round in the closet, while, telling Phil, (all-sarcastic and shit!), "Ok, Phil. I'm back here. And, I'M looooKING!", (while, fixing his eyes, on everything, he AIN'T tryna' see!), rootin' 'round in the closet with one arm, Pockets, satisfied, (that, he's DISSATISFIED!), stands back-upright and, fixes his custom-made custom red hat, perched high upon his head, (while, fixing to dig, right into Phillip's ear!), "Guess what, PHILLIP?!? YOU'RE CRAZY!!! I DON'T SEE, SHIT!!! When I tell you to do something, PHILLIP, I expect you, to follow my word, to the mafuckin' letter!"

THEN...

Getting a bright idea, ('cause, you know, Pockets be IN LOVE WITH HIS MIND!)...

Pockets, goes runnin' to the kitchen area, (knocking 'Nut and Profit off'a the sofas!!) and, flipping the sofa cushions over! Pockets, NOT finding, what he came there to find, looks at 'Nut and Profit, but, doesn't ask them shit, (before, hustling back, to the back private sleeping quarters and, slamming the door shut behind him, once again!).

THEN...

('Nut and Profit - dually-do-and-do-not-do-dually - a very-non and a very-milliennial-thing!)...

THEY ACTUALLY STRAIGHTEN THE SOFA CUSIONS BACK UP AND, PLACE THEM BACK ON THE SOFAS...WITHOUT BEING ASKED TO DO IT!!!

BUT...

(They WERE *smoking gas,* WHILE they were doing it!)

SO...

(They were probably just HIGH!!).

Meanwhile(Back in the back private sleeping quarters, Pockets, questions Phil!)... (Come on YOU nosey-motherfuckers! Let us all eavesdrop!)(YOU KNOW YOU WANT TOO!!!)...(NOSEY-MOTHERFUCKERS!!!)(LOOKATCHA'!!!)...

(ANY-DAMN-WAY!)...

"Phil, *did Y.S., have her laptop with her, when she arrived, at Jettison Records???",* Pockets, urgently asks!
"Sir?", Phillip, poor-judgmentally asks!
"DAMMIT, PHILLIP!?!", Pockets, get-yo'-shit-together, asks!
"Sorry! Sorry!! Sorry!!! YES, SIR!!!! Oh, you mean, *the night you were out searching for C. Trife! YES! When, MC Busta-Nut, False Profit and, Y.S. showed up, I didn't see her with it at first. BUT, I DO remember, seeing her with it, while she sitting in the studio lobby, waiting for you to return.* You know, as well as I do, sir,...*she stays on her laptop!",* Phillip, apologetically-yet-informatively, provides!
"YEAH! You got THAT right!", Pockets, chuckles, then continues, *"AND, IN those HEADPHONES!* SHE AIN'T tryna' hear NUTHIN' from, NOBODY!! 'Specially, THEM TWO fools, out there! ...Damn..."
"So, what's the problem, sir? Did Y.S., lose her laptop, or something?", Phillip, inquisitively-yet-concernedly asks.
"Y.S. lost more than her laptop, Phil.", Pockets, vaguely-yet-confidentiality provides, as Phil, *on hold,* calls Pockets twice, *"Sir? Sir??",* as Pockets, looks 'round HIS mobile studio, *(where he once, checked guts!)* and, once, he sees that bullet hole, (in HIS *once-"buttery"-*mic!), Pockets, puts two-and-two together!! AND, THEN, reveals to Phil (his gut!),

"Shit. Phil. THAT CLONE-BASTARD, GOT Y.S.' laptop! AND that SUMBITCH probably got, her motherfuckin' thumb drive, too!!"

"I TRIED to TELL you, sir. *You NEVER, can be TOO CERTAIN about, THESE Tier Three's.* Especially, THE ONE, YOU got on the road, WITH YOU! I TOLD you, sir. *You never, can be too sure about, these Tier Three's.* AND, NOW, you have one, on the road,...STEALING from YOU!!!", Phil, *feeling*-himself - *from-confidence-provided-from-distance-and-a-telephone-provided* - *providently*-informs, (*Of: Suspecting-Pockets'-suspected - "AH-HA!" - moment!*).

"DAMMIT, PHILLIP! What I TELL YOU, *'bout TELLIN' ME, shit!?* DON'T be, TELLIN' ME, SHIT!! I'M POCKETS, DAMMIT! SO,...I got this,...too.", Pockets, trying-to-convince-Phil-AND-HIMSELF - quips!, (then, cools-himself-out and, says), "Sorry, Phil. It's just..."

Phillip Tate, not one to kick-a-man-when-he's down, (rather, to facilitate!), advises, "...it's just, YOU got BIGGER PROBLEMS than, Mr. Trife STEALING, Y.S.' laptop and thumb drive!"

"WHAT IS IT??? Swear fo' God, Phil! You GONNA' drive me *crazy,* WIT this shit! Don't EVEN tell me, the DUYU CREW came back and, YOU FAILED in keepin' them, OUTTA' my office,! Phil? ...Did YOU LET them, in MY office? ARE THEY DESTROYING, MY ALL-RED-EVERYTHANG OFFICE, PHIL?!? Philllllip, JUST hike up your trousers, like a big boy, and, finally TELL Pretty High, to leave YOU tha' fuck alone! And, do me a favor, huh? KEEP THEM THA'-FUCK OUTTA', MY OFFICE!!!! I really don't need no bad news, Phil. So, you gotta handle shit down there. Listen, Phil, THIS road trip,...HAS gone TO shit! Y.S., well, let's just say,...Y.S. is no longer with the label.", Pockets, of too-prideful-vagueness, provides.

"I see. Well, sir, besides the fact, that, the DUYU CREW have NOT returned. And, subsequently, HAVE NOT destroyed your office. The other lil' bit of good news that, I can provide you with, is you DID WANT to see HOW your new artists, could "hack it" on the road. And, I THINK, you've FOUND your answer! Relatively-early, INTO your trip, too! As you know, sir, not all can "hack it", in THIS business. SO, PLEASE, sir, CANCEL this "Meet & Greet/Road Trip", of yours and, get Mr. Trife, back down here, ASAP!!! IF he's stealing ALREADY, sir?

Then, there's NO TELLING WHAT he's capable, of doing NEXT! Both of us, together, sir, WILL carve-up, C. Trife, come May 1st!! If nothing else, *(NERVOUS WHISTLE!)*,...that SHOULD "stand us in good stead", with the REMAINING "powers that be".", Phillip, implores!

"ARE YOU *CRAZY, PHIL??* I THINK YOU'RE actually FUCKIN' *CRAZY!! YOU KNOW YOU'RE CRAZY,* RIGHT!?! You KNOW, I can't do that, Phil! THERE'S money TO BE made on this road trip!PLUS, I GOTTA' get MY WOMAN back!! AFTER THAT, Phillip? THAT clone-motherfucker, IS as good as CARVED!", Pockets, deplores!

"IF you INSIST, sir. Uh,...sir?", Phil, appeasingly-questions.

"WHAT is IT, Phil?", Pockets, appeasingly-asks.

"PLEASE, TELL ME, that, Mr. Trife, CAN'T overhear ANY of this! PLEASE ensure, that, he's NOT eavesdropping in, on THIS conversation, sir! WE can't afford to have, ANYONE EAVESDROPPING IN on, THIS COVERSATION, sir!!", Phillip, beseeches!

"No, Phillip. *I already dropped him off.* And, the motherfucker HASN'T contacted me yet, either. *Tier-Three-talkin'-BIG-SHIT,* motherfucker! I EXPECTED him, to have my woman to me, BY now! AND, I DON'T want to, be hittin' HIM up, either! JUST, in case, he GOT nabbed by the NJPD! Shiiiiit, I AIN'T givin' them, NO IDEA, that, *I sent THAT FOOL back into their city!!",* Pockets, provides, then, pauses, then, persists, "Damn,..."THEIR" town. AIN'T. THAT. SOME. SHIT! Damn, how *times,* HAVE changed, Phil. HOW *TIMES,* have changed!"

"I see, sir. ...Well, sir,...I hate to be the one, to have to tell you, that I have to tell you something. BUT, laptops and thumb drives, aside. Perhaps,...maybe,...I truly AM *crazy???* BUT, I'M going to HAVE TO INSIST, THAT YOU, *"swallow your PRIDE",* on this one! So as, to ALLOW ME, to tell YOU, what's IN those reading materials! BECAUSE, sir,...IF Mr. Trife, IS in possession OF THOSE missing reading materials? AND, worse yet,...HAS ACTUALLY READ THEM, BEFORE he delivers you, your lady-friend?? Well, sir, THERE'S GOING TO BE hell to pay, WHEN that TIER THREE goes off, the likes of which,... *(((nervous-whistling-intermission!)))*...HAVE NEVER BEEN SEEN BEFORE, HERE ON EARTH!!! IT'LL BE THIS COUNTRY'S WORST NIGHTMARE,...IF NOT THE WORLD'S!!!!!!", Phillip, emphatically-(and, yet, perhaps-a-bit-overdramatically)-theorizes! (YOU KNOW HOW PHIL IS!! ALL NERVOUS AND SHIT!!).

"THAT bad, Phil?", Pockets, underestimatingly-asks! (YEAH! THAT'S RIGHT! I'M MAKIN' UP WORDS!!!)...(IT'S MY BOOK, MOTHERFUCKERS:)

"WORSE than you could, EVER imagine. ESPECIALLY, with THIS PARTICULAR, Tier Three! *In all my years, of being involved in this, there has NEVER been and escape.* And, this NEW state-of-the-art building was, AS CLOSE to a slam-dunk-guarantee, AS it gets. *AND, C. TRIFE, did it, LIKE, it WAS nothing!* Sir, I'm sure you're in love with your lady-friend,...but,...you REALLY only have three options, with THIS Tier-Three...

1). Find him before he reads those reading materials. You HAVE TO find him, sir! Find him, cut your trip short, bring him back here. We'll heavily sedate him and, then carve him alive.

2). Just return to Atlanta, sir. Get as FAR AWAY as possible! YOU'D be *CRAZY,* not to, sir! LET the world deal WITH him!

3). Kill him up there. Or, what I would STRONGLY SUGGEST, have someone kill him FOR you!

...Sir? Pretty High and the DUYU CREW, would do that for you, wouldn't they, sir?? It's NOT LIKE, they're NOT *crazy*-enough, TO DO that FOR YOU, sir! Would you like for me, to attempt to contact Pretty High, and, have them meet-up with you, in Pennsylvania?", Phillip Tate, facilitates.

"*Swallowed-pride,* hurts like a motherfucker, don't it?? Damn. Ok, Phil. If you're able, get Pretty High on the phone. I'M JUST gonna' haveta' call ANOTHER audible on THIS road trip, THAT'S all.", Pockets, convinced,...concedes, (Erring on the side of judgement. That, at THIS point, Phillip Tate, MAY actually know better,...and the LEAST-CRAZY, of the two!!).

BUT...

(FUCKIN' WIT A MUTHA' FUCKA'S MIND IS A MUTHA' FUCKA'! AND FOOLISH-PRIDE IS WORSE THAN THAT!)

AND SO...

Pockets, after, *endulgeful-non-priortized-sidetracked-prideful-thought,* shouts at Phillip, of AND with, *FOOLISH-PRIDE,* "Yeah, "THEIR" TOWN!!! FUCK THAT!!! THIS HERE, IS POCKETS, PHIL!!! *I HAD THAT WHOLE FUCKIN' SHIT-HOLE-TOWN IN MY POCKETS* AND, WATCH ME, MUTHAFUCKIN' DO IT, AGAIN!!!"

"Uh,...sir???", Phillip, questions...Pockets' sanity!

"Nuthin'! ...JUST get THE DUYU CREW up here, A.S.A.P.!!!! I'LL have them create the "BUZZ" and, I'LL head INTO North Juarez AND get MY LADY out, MY-DAMN-SELF! Come back early?? AND, have NOTHING TO SHOW, for THIS business trip??? Are you fuckin' serious, Phil?! NO! *YOU'RE OUTTA' YOUR FUCKIN' MIND,* YOU KNOW THAT, PHIL!?! YOU think, YOU know BETTER, THAN me??? YOU, PHILLIP, DON'T KNOW SHIT!!! YOU KNOW, THAT??? YOU KNOW, THAT??? YOU GOT ME, FUCKED-UP!!! I'M, POCKETS!!! I got EVERYTHANG!!!!!! And so, I GOT THIS, too!!", Pockets, imposing, imposes HIS will!

"I got you.", Phillip Tate, facilitates, before he hangs up the phone (and, then, sits there at his desk for a moment), before, *thinking aloud,* *"A fool, has but, two posessions: Pride. And, Denial. And lacks, two others: Accountability. And, Shame."*

MEANWHILE...

(BACK IN NORTH JUAREZ!) BENEATH...THAT...ol' El Train Bridge!...

Mr. Trife, (after he got back on his giddy-up!), walked waaaaaay cross town, passing gas stations' "skimmer'd-up" gas pumps, skimmer'd-up from mafuckin'-punks, STAYIN' on they come-up! And so, after a looooong walk, with suitcase in hand, Mr. Trife, approaches his old haunts, (that being, and, that of)...THE ROXBURY 'PARTMENTS! Tier-Three-Mind damn-near back up to speed!...(Though, all things considered, that being, and, that, of: *the weed, rum, and, the speed!)*...Mr. Trife, UNDER THAT, bullet-hole-hat, BE STAYIN' on his steeze!! Though, *after leaving Legs' place,* looking for, during his walk, a pair of gator skin cowboy boots, hanging from a wire, in the dark!

And, (sho' 'nuff!)...

(FROM up-under that, bullet-hole-hat, Mr. Trife, looks up. And, through those 24 karat golds, he sees those 'skins that NOBODY DARED touch!)

BUT...

More fucked-up to him than that, (that being, and, that of), (a pair of tail-cut gator skin cowboy boots, that NOBODY dared touch!) IS, "WHY-tha'-fuck, ALL THESE "fancy-schmancy" 'spensive-ass-luxury-vehicles, KEEP cuttin' off!??", Mr. Trife, says to himself, aloud.

As...

All CROSS town, ALL THESE BRAND NEW (to him!) *cars and SUV's at red lights,* (to him!) *KEPT stalling-out AND, RUNNING OUT OF GAS!!!*

'Cause...

(TO HIM!), *HIS TIER-THREE-MIND, DON'T KNOW NUTHIN' 'BOUT, "start-stop" engines! (THAT BE cuttin' off, AT RED LIGHTS! TRYING TO reduce, gas consumption and emissions!).*

"THAT shit, AIN'T worth tha' money!", Mr. Trife, *says, (of a GLS450 4Matic Benz, a BMW X3, and, an Audi A4),* as he's, approaching, the Roxbury 'Partments front door!

And...

Just up ahead, there's a pimp standing up ahead, with those pimpin'-ass gator skin cowboy boots, hangin' over his head! And, the pimp's ONLY overhead, is his bottom bitch, "BIG HUSKY"! (And, she's a down-ass bitch!). *Tha' type-a-bitch, to place a fresh cigarette up to, a pimp's lips! Tha' type-a-bitch, to then, light-up that bitch, fo' a pimp! Tha' type-a-bitch, to do THAT shit, ALL night, fo' HER pimp! Tha' type-a-bitch, a pimp, AIN'T EVEN GOTTA' snap his fingers (AT a bitch!), fo' her, TO DO that shit! AND, IT'S JUST them two!! 'TIL mutha' fuckin' tricks come thru... (tryna' get lucky!).*

'CAUSE...

"Tha' Game" GOT thrown off track! (Oh, 'bout,...1, 260 days or so back!).

WAY-BACK-WHEN...

"Too Cold", held shit down! (rockin' them gator skins - hangin' overhead - of silver and black!).

WHEN-WAY-BACK...

(A slobber-mouth-morning DJ drivin' by - would see - NUTHIN'...BUT titties AND ass cracks!!!)

AND SO, (AND, BUT NOW!)...

OUT ON "THA' TRACK", IT JUST BE - "BIG HUSKY" - IN THIS TOWN!!!

And so...

(THIS big-thorough-ass-bottom-bitch, GONNA' hold it down!)

'CAUSE, (AS we, all know!)...

A pimp, NEED HIS money!

And...

THIS THOROUGH-ASS THICK-GIRL, she be goin' by the name of,..."BIG HUSKY"!!!

"What it do, pimpin'?...Oh, Oh, Oh, OH, Oh, OH, SO, *YOU BACK???*...DON'T BE servin' me, fo' MY stable of bitches! ...PIMP-ASS, nigga!", the pimp, (fly-as-fuck!), says, upon Mr. Trife's approach, between a couple of puffs!

(And, though, with Mr. Trife, the pimp, WAS ONLY fuckin' 'round!)...

BUT...

This here pimp, HE AIN'T NO - MUTHA' FUCKIN' - CLOWN! (And, fo' "THA' GAME" and, fo' THIS CITY, a pimp, TRYNA' hold it down!)...

Big gold crosses and, lion's heads layin' heavy, 'pon his three-piece-suit. And, they hangin' heavy from, gold ropes thick and busy like, sassafras roots! *Tha' type-a-pimp, TO STAY, well-groomed,* (BUT NEVER a groom!). *Tha' type-a-pimp, TO STAY, TRYNA' catch himself a bitch!* (*Fill'er-up wit drinks!*) *Then, seal tha' deal in the back, of the back, of a strip club's back private lapdance room! Tha' type-a-pimp, to let you know HE LIVIN' RIGHT,* (*BY his fingernail length!*).

FOR...

Long "Pimp Hand" fingernails, AIN'T FOR YOU SQUARES!

BUT...

(IT WORK FO' A PIMP!)

(And, wit them, Pampered - Well-Manicured, Clear-Finished-Nail-Polished - "Money-Counters" - a pimp, DON'T count HIS money, 'til tha' night IS FINISHED!!!)...

'CAUSE...

After a bitch, give A PIMP'S MONEY, to a pimp...a bitch'll BE empty-handed!

SO...

Get back-out-there, bitch! (*AND, DON'T BE comin' back EMPTY-HANDED!!*)

'CAUSE...

THEM EMPTY-HANDS of a bitch, a bitch,...GOTS'TA' REPLENISH!!!

Tha' type-a-pimp, THAT, STAYS wit, ridiculous-diamond-blingers, (*SITTIN' HIGH atop of EACH ONE of his fingers!*). *Tha' type-a-pimp, THAT STAYS, shaped-up wit, deep-rolling-waves, down to the root! Tha' type-a-pimp, THAT STAYS, FRESH from his big-brim Bailey, on down, to HIS OWN, tail-cut gator skin shoes! Tha' type-a-pimp, fo' a lonely-hungry type-a-bitch, a pimp, STAY - TRYNA'-BE - RECRUITIN'!*

And...

(HE DON'T don't pack no pistol!)

'CAUSE...

HE THA' TYPE-A-PIMP, THAT GON' LET HIS MOUTH DO THA' SHOOTIN'! (Tha' type-a-pimp, THAT, STAY shootin', his mouth-off instead!)...

And...

THIS-HERE-PIMP, be goin' by the name of..."WEEKEND FRED"!!!

And, Mr. Trife, just stands there - *tryna'-fig'a-out - WHAT-THA'-FUCK - 'DIS-HERE PIMP - is talkin' 'bout???* And, as he, stands there, (staring at the odd-pair), Mr. Trife's *peepin'* the pimp's angles!, (WHILE HE'S, *TRYNA'-fig'a-out - WHICH body part* of BIG HUSKY'S - *is lookin' THE MOST PAINFUL!!!*). Be it, her: ten *"sausage-links"* - strapped-down - in them open toes! OR, be it, the: *"SECTIONAL-BULGING", (from her knees down to her ankles!),* CAUSED BY, her: knee-high-high-heel-stiletto-Roman-Gladiator-cross-laces...*CUTTIN' OFF her circulation!!!*

(And, before Mr. Trife, can ask this pimp, *why's he talkin'* AS IF, *they be old friends!)...*

Weekend Fred, gets'ta SHOOTIN' HIS - MOUTH-off - again! (Come! Let's listen in!)...

"Shit, pimpin', I was jus' fuckin' 'round, 'bout, that stable, now! I don't NEEDS-NO stable, OF bitches!! Lemme' tell ya' sumfin', pimpin'. BIG HUSKY, be ALL-A-PIMP needs!! YOU unda' 'stand me?? Pimpin', pimpin', pimpin', she all YOU need too, pimpin'!", says, Weekend Fred, (then, gives Mr. Trife, the once-over), from his suitcase-in-hand, on up to the bullet-hole-hat (cocked hard to the side atop of his head!), then, says, "DAMN, PIMP!! YOU lookin' stressed AND distressed!! AND, you look like, you COULD USE - a "GOOD-go-'round" - WIT, tha' HUSKY ONE! Tell ya' what, *ya' pimpin'-muthafucka'*, go on upstairs in tha' 'partments wit 'dis BIG-HUSKY-WOMAN and, 'dis here pimp will cut ya', a "one-time-break" on them funds! Consider it,...a "homecomin' party",..."a gift",...SINCE YA' back in THIS-HERE town! PIMPIN', SHE'LL get ya' RIGHT, mane! *You know HOW, a pimp do!* Jus' spittin' FACTS, 'n GOOD GAME!!"

Then...

(Turning to, BIG HUSKY), Weekend Fred, says, "BIG HUSKY! Take tha' holmes-here, upstairs and, show pimpin', a good time!"

And...

Mr. Trife, just stands there, checking out BIG HUSKY'S, big ol' breasts!!, (proceeded by, her big ol' nipples - JUTTIN' through - her skin tight dress!!)...

And...

BIG HUSKY, GOT IT - FUCKED-UP! *For, that smile, that developed, on Mr. Trife's face, WASN'T 'cause, Mr. Trife, fell in love! (((HELL NO!!!)))*.

IT'S 'CAUSE...

(*He was smiling at his old cowboy boots - STILL suspended - up above!!*)

And then...

Mr. Trife, looks right past both of them, (losing his smile!), as he, checks out, the Roxbury 'Partments. (NOW, LOOKIN' run-down, abandoned and, condemned!!!).

And then...

Mr. Trife asks, Weekend Fred, *"What tha'-fuck HAPPENED, to THIS joint??? 'Cept, fo' that, rickety-ass elevator, tha' Roxbury 'Partments, WAS on point!"*

Put-off (AND, OUTTA' POCKET!), BIG HUSKY, adjusts her long blue wig!, (then, provides, Weekend Fred, a few - fresh-mouthed - outta'-

pocket - digs!), "'NUFF of, ALL tha', chit-chat! Y'ALLS can, have y'alls - "bromance" - 'nother time!", (then, turning her FULL ATTENTION, on Mr. Trife), BIG HUSKY, asks, all sweet 'n nice, "So, waddaya' say, pimpin'? Ya' ready fo' BIG HUSKY,...OR what!? 'Cause, I KNOW, I'M DOWN! *I ain't NEVER ride-a-nigga that, GOT HIS OWN STATUE N' SHIT!!!* Pimp, long as you IS hard AS a statue - ol' BIG HUSKY - WILL ride ya', fo' FREE!" ('CAUSE, FOR a brotha that gets - as-HARD-as-a-statue - ol' BIG HUSKY - is gettin' - "THIRSTAY-IN-THA'-WORST-WAY"!!!).

"BITCH!!! Now, YOU KNOW, YOU'S outta'-pocket! JUST light MY cigarettes! Get'a pimp, HIS money! And, HO, a pimp CAN speak-on WHAT'EVA' THA' FUCK a pimp, wanna be speakin' on! But, THAT SHIT, DON'T APPLY TO YOU,...'STAND ME!?! DON'T you EV'A let a PIMP hear yo' ass - SPEAKIN' ON - givin' ALL THAT "HUSKINESS" away, fo' FREE!!! YOU UNDA' 'STAND ME?? DON'T act like - YO' ASS - CAN'T get dismissed! AND, 'DAT SHIT, CAN HAPPEN, TOO!! Unda'stand 'DIS, ho! SOON AS I "pull" THAT - BADDEST-IN-THA'-CITY-SHAVED-HEADED-MOMMY, that be kickin'-it wit a HOUSE-ARREST-ANKLE-BRACELET, I be seein', walkin' these streets?? BIG HUSKY, YO' ASS JUST-MIGHT fuck-'round and, FIND YO' ASS, watchin' me COUNTIN' MY MONEY from tha', "NOSE BLEED" seats! DON'T BE, SPEAKIN' on, MY MONEY 'gin,...'STAND me?!?", Weekend Fred, in reply, says!

"Shaved-head, you say? Mommy's tha' "BADDEST IN THA' CITY",...is THAT right??", Mr. Trife asks, Weekend Fred, twice!!

"Tha' ABSOLUTE-BADDEST in tha' city! HANDS - MUTHA'-FUCKIN' - DOWN!!", Weekend Fred, replies, *(while, cupping the shape of an imaginary-ass, formed in thin air!!),* WHILE, UNDER cowboy boots and, from under BIG HUSKY'S stare!!!).

"And, you say, she be *KICKIN' IT* wit a...wit a...HOUSE-ARREST-ANKLE-BRACELET??? Lil' mommy's on house arrest, or some shit???", Mr. Trife asks, Weekend Fred, with haste! (AS, that: *"KICKIN'"* reference, GOT, Mr. Trife's, *Tier-Three-Mind, KICKIN' IN!).*

AS...

(Mr. Trife's, NOW puttin' 2 + 2 together!!)

THAT BEING, (AND, THAT OF)...

Pockets' reference, OF: "The BADDEST GIRL in tha' city", THAT - "KICKS-IT - LIKE MY GUN!!!"...(COUPLED-ALONG WITH, AND, that, OF: Tier-Three-Brain remembrances of...ANNA MOSSITTI'S - FACE!!!).

...FOR(YOU SEE!!!)...

(GATHERING INTELLIGENCE - ON ANNA MOSSITTI - TOOK MORE PRECEDENCE!!!)

INSTEAD OF...

(INQUIRING ABOUT "HIS STATUE", at this point-in-time - DIDN'T ENTER, HIS TIER-THREE-HEAD!!!)

AND...

BEFORE MR. TRIFE, CAN INQUIRE, ABOUT "ALL THIS - STATUE - SHIT", WEEKEND FRED, SHOOTS HIS - MOUTH-OFF FIRST, INSTEAD!!!

(Come!) (Let's listen in!)...

"NAH, PIMPIN'!!! GAME, RECOGNIZE GAME, PLAYA'!!! And, I SEE, ya' game! YOU AIN'T gettin', lil' mommy, befo' me! So, DON'T EVEN try it! *IT'S 'cause of YO' ASS* - "Tha' Game" - *DONE changed!! 'Cause of, YO' ASS*, THEY AIN'T NO bitches, in tha' city, NO MO', *down ta' GET a pimp, THAT MONEY!!* ME 'N BIG HUSKY, be tha' ONLIEST-TWO that, be STAYIN' TRUE to tha' GAME!! 'Stand me!? ...Well, me 'n BIG HUSKY,...fo' NOW!! But, WATCH-A-PIMP RETURN tha' game ta' what it NEED-TO-BE!!! So, from pimp ta' pimp, I'ma TELL ya' LIKE 'DIS, pimpin'! KEEP YA' funky-ass 'way from tha' SHAVED-HEADED MOMMY! 'STAND ME?!?! Tell ya' what, pimpin'. I'll serve ov'a this here HUSKY-JAWN, AFTER I "pull" tha' lil' shaved-headed mommy! Waddaya' say, PIMP!?!", Weekend Fred, proposes and provokes!

BIG HUSKY, (catching MAD-ATTITUDE at Weekend Fred!), QUICKLY-quips at Mr. Trife, "HEY PIMP, YOU can find her EVERY DAY at 12-Noon-SHARP,...STARIN' at YOUR statue!!"

(Weekend Fred, cuts his eyes HARD at BIG HUSKY, but, before he can shoot his mouth off!)...

BIG HUSKY, removes the nearly-finished cigarette from her pimp's lips. Then, places a fresh smoke in his mouth, lighting it up for him!! (THE "Pacification" of it all, fo' a pimp!)...(Ya' dig!).

And so...

(With, Weekend Fred's mouth reloaded, with a fresh smoke)...

Mr. Trife, seizes his opportunity, to shoot his mouth of first! (Figuring, yet inquiring, *'bout all, This - "My statue" - Shit - is but a joke!*)...

"What-tha'-fuck is EVERYONE keep talkin' 'bout!?! MY STATUE!!! MY STATUE!!! MY STATUE!!! That's all tha' fuck, I KEEP hearin' TONIGHT! OK,...I'LL BITE! WHERE tha'-fuck is MY STATUE??? 'Cause, IF there REALLY IS one? ...I'D like, to SEE IT!", Mr. Trife, calls their BLUFF!, (as, BIG HUSKY, ashes Weekend Fred's smoke)...(then, places it back up to his lips for a pimp, to take his next puff!).

(And, while Weekend Fred, is taking a puff)...

BIG HUSKY, seizes HER opportunity, to get in good with Mr. Trife! (And, she answers the call, *'bout all, This - "MY STATUE" - Stuff!*)...

"It's in "old" *SYKE PARK. Tha' city erected it fo' ya'!* You know, *SINCE YA' donated a lot of money to tha' city 'n shit.* You know tha' streets be talkin', pimp! Ain't no secret, *you had SYKE Park, bulldozed-over!* But, EVEN WIT all ya' GOOD DEEDS, ya' STILL ain't gon' be able to "pull" lil' mommy! SHE got this sadness, 'bout her. BUT, you can find her there, in "old" *SYKE PARK,* EVERY DAY rain or shine, at 12 Noon.", BIG HUSKY, informs,...showing some love on the streets!

"DAMN RIGHT, YOU AIN'T "pullin' her"! But, go 'head on down there, pimp...YA' STATUE-HAVIN' MOTHERFUCKER!!! Damn, pimpin', I CAN'T hate. DON'T HATE tha' playa',...OR "Tha' Game"! 'Stand me!?!", Weekend Fred, let's it be known...showin' hatin' AND love!

"*SYKE Park*, huh? High Noon? Word. Good looks, y'all.", a thankful, Mr. Trife, replies,...showin' tha' streets some love right back!

"Tell ya' what, pimp. *Ya' did ya' thing, here in tha' city.* AND, YA' LOOKIN' stressed! So, I'MA have BIG HUSKY here, break ya' off wit that "HUSKY-JAWN", fo' free! Me 'n YOU together, DAMN, PIMPIN',...WE'LL git 'dis game back-up *ta'-a-respectable-level,* fo' a pimp!", Weekend Fred, serves-up BIG HUSKY and...showin' love fo' "Tha' Game"!!

(Having gotten a "good enough" look at BIG HUSKY, Mr. Trife, DIDN'T REALLY EVER consider it, NEVER considered himself a coward, but,...*KNOWS* he ain't, THAT brave! And although, BIG HUSKY, looks "good enough"! Mr. Trife's, *Tier-Three-Mind, KNOWS* "enough" TO *KNOW, "She GOT THAT, inflamed "wassa' name"!!!")*(OY VEY!!!)

AND SO...

"Good lookin' out, pimp. But,...I'LL SEE MYSELF UP!!! And, oh yeah, my man, Y'ALL AIN'T seen me,...ya dig?", Mr. Trife, replies...rejectin' gettin' back in "Tha Game" and,...some late-night-BIG-HUSKY-love!!!!

"I AIN'T SEEN YA', pimp! BUT, think 'bout my offer, 'stand me?? Pimpin', I wanna' see ya' out'cheer PIMPIN' HOES, wit me! Holla'-back atta' pimp, we'll chop-it-up! ...Ya' STATUE-HAVIN', motherfucker!", Weekend Fred, tells Mr. Trife,...showin' love and respect fo' a pimp! *(THAT DID tha' damn thing!).*

And so...

Of Weekend Fred and THE HUSKY ONE, as Mr. Trife walks past, he sees his suitcase-in-hand, with bullet hole in his hat, with 24 karat golds of his reflection, in the Roxbury 'Partments' front door made of glass. (And, once again, Mr. Trife finds, *that some deja vu has set in!*)...

AS...

That reflection, in that glass of him, reminds him of, (AND FROM WHEN), he first saw himself, IN THAT glass,…kinda' lookin'…LIKE HIM! (With, the tips of his dreads, dyed a beaming golden!). As he, so endearingly-held the neck, (of HIS protector!), of THE ONE and ONLY Pain Stick! (((Wit dat EVIL-ASS-GRIMACED-GRIN!!!))).

And…

As, he takes hold of that door handle, to step inside, Mr. Trife finds, *that something has yet again, hit him on top of his hat, (((FALLEN from the sky!!!))).* And, as he steps inside, Mr. Trife finds, the lobby to be full of *darkness and musk.* And so, he's finding, that feeling his way, through the lobby's *darkness,* in order to find the elevator, is a must! And, as he feels, (what must be) an "OUT OF ORDER" sign, Mr. Trife, ALSO finds, DAT DEEZ 'PARTMENTS sure feel far more,…LIKE squalor this time!!

"YEEEEEAAAAAAH, WELLLLLL!!! WHAT other option, I got? These are the steps, I GOTTA' take, IF I wanna make it to the top!", Mr. Trife, says to himself, (prepared to take the steps!), with suitcase-in-hand, and with bullet hole of hat, and with his hopes and of his dreams, of bustin' up onto the music scene! *(And, yes, WITH intubation-voice,… STILL amazin'!!).*

And so…

Once on the third floor, Mr. Trife found himself, kept-on finding himself, keeping-on finding, something more! As, he finds that, IT'S dark and lonely at the top! *(in the darkness, of the top floor).* Until, he finds that, once he has finally taken the steps and, has made it to the top. That, he has been met by, AND confronted BY…confrontation! As, he finds himself, finding himself, being confronted by, the self-proclaimed: "Hallway Hannah"! (The 'Partments, version of: "profiling-paradigmatics"!) As, Hallway Hannah, HAS FOUND, HER SOLE-SELF-RIGHTOUS PURPOSE IN LIFE! As, she HAS TAKEN IT UPON HERSELF, to encounter AND enforce, HER OWN ideals, of who's IN THE wrong and, WHAT'S RIGHT! And, Hallway Hannah, NEEDS this confrontation IN her life! So, THAT she CAN feel IMPORTANT! And, OF her WILL, OF her confrontations, Hallway

Hannah, EXPECTS THE CONFRONTED, JUST TO ABSORB IT! As, HER entitled-ass, feels as though AND expects, ANYONE that SHE encounters, just to OBEY! As, Hallway Hannah, JUST EXPECTS, the confronted, JUST TO ROLLOVER, CONFORM TO AND, OBLIGE AS THEY ABIDE, TO ANY-DAMN-THING SHE SAY! AND SO, Hallway Hannah, ATTEMPTS to BULLY and, IMPOSE HER WILL, upon ANYONE she feels! As, she feels, as though, ANYONE of HER "SINGLED-OUT-SCHMOES", OF their OWN rights, WON'T and DON'T know! And, IF ANYONE "happens" to KNOW their rights, Hallway Hannah, feels that IT'S HER right, OF ANYONE'S RIGHTS, (of which!) she HAS the right TO REPEAL! (But, JUST TO CLARIFY, Hallway Hannah's "definition" of: "ANYONE", is as follows! ANYONE: That, DOESN'T LOOK like her! ANYONE: That, DOESN'T LOOK like they BELONG in the Roxbury 'Partments!)(AND, JUST to BE sure, JUST SO she can feel better 'bout HER lot-in-life and, to MAKE herself FEEL A LOT more superior!)(ANYONE: That, LOOKS LIKE they may have just about the same amount of money as she does and/or perhaps a little bit more, WILL AND SHALL BE chopped down, made to feel less than and, referred to as "The Poor"!)(And, MADE TO FEEL A LOT more inferior!) And so, as Hallway Hannah, gets into her self-serving-bullshit-of-expertise, "YOU DON'T live here! LET ME see YOUR I.D.!! I'M CALLING the COPS!!!", Hallway Hannah, (of Mr. Trife), demands, commands and, with her arms speadout, the top floor hallway (of Mr. Trife's rightful-passage), she blocks!!! And so, Mr. Trife, STRAIGHT-MUSHES that nutty-busybody in the FACE! STRAIGHT-MUSHED, Hallway Hannah's nutty-ass, straight down TO the FLOOR!! *(And, though, Mr. Trife's, recently-awaken-mind, don't know nothin' 'bout, how THESE NUTJOB "Hallway Hannah's" and "Karens" of The World", these past few years, HAVE BEEN likened to roll)(Oh, for 'bout, the past 1, 260 days or more or so!)(REALLY YO' ?!? Tryna' BULLY a BULLY BOY???) (What tha' fuck YOU think this shit is hittin' for!?!)* "YA' FUCKIN' NUT!!! CALL THA' FUCKIN' COPS!!!", of and at, Hallway Hannah, Mr. Trife yells, "GO ON AND TELL 'EM, I'LL BE IN 'PARTMENT No.12!!! AND YOU TELL 'EM FOR ME, I'LL KEEP THA' DOOR UNLOCKED!!!", Mr. Trife, yelled, at the busybody-nutjob, pissing herself, down on the hallway floor, as Mr. Trife, (who was just minding his OWN business, as and of, the busybody!), he was steppin' over top! (And, Mr. Trife, did it ALL, WHILE his *OL' BROTHA-TRIFE-STROLL,* he NEVER breaks and, NEVER stops!). And, once he's reached, reaches for and, has compromised, his old No.12 door. And once, entry has been gained. THE BEST that he can tell, *IN the darkness, OF his old apartment, IT basically STILL looks the same!* Though, *NO wild party goings-on! NO DUYU CREW!!!* And, *NO HOES!!! (And, he actually-kinda'-misses ALL THAT madness.)(AND them MADNESS-motherfuckers!!!!)* As, he stands in *reflection.* As, he stands with his back, to GOOD OL' DOOR No.12, now closed. And, as he walks cross, that living room's plush, *ol' nutbush dance floor.* And, walks past *where, he glared at Gidget Cole, (GRINDIN' THA'-FUCK-OUTTA', Dead Sexy!!!!), in that, oversize white plush leather chair.* Mr. Trife, strolls right on into, his old bedroom. And, sees that, his big ol' bed, (the size of California!), IS still there! And, he smiles, as he *reflects upon,* upon that big ol' bed, *that he once laid upon. Upon which, (AND him!), WERE NUTHIN' but hoes' butts, upon which those hoes, were NUTHIN' BUT more hoes' butts and MORE HOES!!!* UPON WHICH, THAT BED, MR. TRIFE, IS FAIRLY-CERTAIN, BIG HUSKY'S BEEN FUCKIN' UPON, GETTIN' THAT "WASSA' NAME" INFLAMED, GETTIN' MONEY IN THE THROES!!! Then, Mr. Trife, walks into the bathroom. And, in the *darkness,* he feels that shattered-broken mirror. Still posted upon the bathroom wall. Above the bathroom sink. *Down which his blood once flowed.*

(No time for sadness OR for gladness!)...

FOR...

Mr. Trife, GOTS'TA stay ON his grind!

'CAUSE...

(Business IS business!).

AND SO...

By streetlight, Mr. Trife, was 'bout open up his song book and, write himself a song,...'BOUT THA' CITY'S "BADDEST"!!!

BUT...

Gunshots outside, got Mr. Trife, hittin' the deck!!!

For(YOU SEE!)...

(The street gangs used to keep guns, from entering Parkinson's City!)...

SO...

(HE AIN'T USED TO HEARING GUNSHOTS, IN A CITY!)...

AND...

(He DON'T KNOW why!)...

BUT...

(His TIER-THREE-MIND, knows "ENOUGH" to know, to get under the windowline!)...

'CAUSE...

AIN'T GON' BE NO WITNESSES UP IN HERE, FOR NO GUNMEN, OR THE COPS, TO DETECT!!!

(And, as he lays, under the windowline, in the *darkness*, in his *Tier-Three-Mind, he's back in Legs' apartment),...*as he lays there, and *reflects:*

...And, as Mr. Trife lays there, he can see himself, as he prayed over his Nephew. As, his Nephew layed there dead! After, he placed that empty bloody-mouthed bottle of Sailor Jerry's Spiced Rum, down next to his Nephew's head, after he shot-up Legs, shot that punk-ass Legs up TWICE, (((JUST LIKE LEGS DID TO HIS NEPHEW!!))), SHOT-UP LEGS TWICE WITH THAT HEROIN, JUST TO MAKE SURE HIS PUNK-ASS WAS DEAD, before he threw Legs out the corner-bay-window, down to tha' sidewalk on the corner below, before he got his giddy-up on from Legs' place, after he lifted off Nephew's long silver chain and cross, after he removed his bullet-hole-hat at a loss, before he placed the chain and cross over his head, on his way out the door. And, with suitcase-in-hand, before he stepped out of "La Casa Secura", before he left ajar the door, after he placed his bullet-hole-hat back atop of

his head and, cocked it hard to the side, he TOLD Legs' PUNK-ASS, "THIS place is NO LONGER secure!" (And, as Mr. Trife, slips into some shut-eye, beneath the windowline, of the No.12's dark-ass apartment floor, his *Tier-Three-Mind,* wrestles with LOYALTY, as...*he dreams of Anna Mossitti!)*(((Oy Vey!!!))).

(And, as Mr. Trife, slips into sleep. HE DON'T even know, THAT, he's slippin'!)...(And, ON THAT, he's sleeping!!!)

FOR...

(((BACK UP IN LEGS' APARTMENT, THERE'S A WHOLE CRIME SCENE GOINGS-ON!)))

WITH news crews stagged out front! With news vans breaking to a screeching halt! With news van's antennas extended sky high! With each newscaster breaking rules, while jostling for position! With each news station wanting to be the ones, with the breaking story (((FOR this one!))). With a large crowd that has gathered! With the crowd extending for blocks! With a sea of red and blue emergency vehile lights blinking and flashing! With yellow "POLICE LINE DO NOT CROSS" crime scene tape (ceremoniously posted and displayed upside down!) quarantining the parked ambulances, Coroners vans, and the cars of the cops! With the green Chevy-Nova-mother and BOTH of her sons taking-in, the measurements being made and, the photographs being taken! With Legs laying crumpled - DEAD - on the sidewalk! (With his shattered-fractured skull AND HIS broken-neck ass!!). With Legs yet to be zipped-up in a white disaster bag! (With him laying there IN his own dead blood AND in shattered-broken glass!). With a Buick parallel parked there, on the street next to him. That, he FAILED TO land on, AS HE fell past! *(FOR, Unc, TOLD THAT punk-ass Legs, that he WAS GONNA' NEED A BUICK!)(SHIIIIIIT, IF Legs landed ON that Buick??? Shiiiiiit, IT MIGHT'VE SAVED his ass!!).* With that - dirty - greedy - on-duty - fuckin'-prostitutes- in that - Roadside-Buena-Vista - shitty-ass-lime-green-and-seedy - JOOP!-cologne-bottle-wearing - vice cop - , upstairs in Legs' apartment! As, he's kneeled down NEXT TO...Heavy Duty's head! With the dirty vice cop taking turns, looking back-and-forth, at Heavy Duty's face and that, empty bloody-mouthed-bottle of Sailor Jerry's Spiced Rum! With the dirty vice cop, trying to remember "investigatively", *why, how, when, he's seen this kid's face AND, the bloody-mouth of a rum bottle before!* With the dirty vice cop finally able to put 2 + 2 together!! With the dirty vice cop's "deductive reasoning" coming up with the reason why, THIS kid's face AND, THE bloody-mouth of a rum bottle, just JUMPS OUT at him!(in a room full of SO much carnage!). With the dirty vice cop now *recalling his brief interaction with, THIS kid and, THAT wild-ass motherfucker drinking a bloody-mouthed bottle of Sailor Jerry's Spiced Rum! OF WHICH, in front, of the WILI Building, THAT wild-motherfucker AND THIS kid, WERE both, posted up!(AFTER they left DJ Wood's "Morning Wood Show", full of SO much carnage!).* With the dirty vice cop now *remembering, THAT he remembers, copping "GOOD GAS", OFF THIS kid!*...(OH SHIT!!! WHEN THA' FUCK DID HEAVY DUTY GET BACK IN TOWN?!?)...With the dirty vice cop NOT SAYING SHIT as he stands up!(from his once kneeling position). With the dirty vice cop not even signing the CRIME SCENE LOG!(As, he walks out of Legs' apartment!). With the dirty vice cop FEELING NOTHING for Gidget Cole, as she remained dead in the "living" room, as he studied and deducted, that bottle of rum, of and in conjunction with, THAT dead kid's face! With the dirty vice cop STILL NOT SAYING SHIT to nobody and, AIN'T TRYING to listen! As, he makes his way, to and down, those - *BEST-heed-the-creekings'-warning-in-and-of-these-old-wooden-back-steps!* As, he slips out the back to, make his way to, his big-ass undercover Caddy (parked 'round back!). With the dirty vice cop *KNOWING* WHAT he HAS TO do! With the dirty vice cop HATING HIS LIFE!!! As, he *KNOWS, that he HAS TO leave here and, drive cross town and, PERSONALLY go and tell Skin's that, some WILD-MOTHERFUCKER named Brotha Trife, HAS beaten him to it and,...has killed Legs!*

(((OY TO THE MUTHA' FUCKIN' VEY!!!)))

Chapter Twenty

THE MIDNIGHT HOUR

A in't nuthin' LIKE waking up on the bathroom floor! (Oh, YOU KNOW, YOU HAVE, done THAT before!). As, Mr. Trife, does so, the next day. And, it takes him a little while,...to get his bearings. Though, HE *KNOWS, HE'S THE CLONE OF BROTHA TRIFE!!!* (And, YES, HE *KNOWS, THAT'S a FUCKED-UP pairing!!*). Though, *the meth and the rum,* are now out of his system. *(Though, he wanted to go clean and sober!).* Though, THIS "industry" GOT HIM! *(AND, has GOTTEN him!!)*...(GOTTEN HIM FOR, WHAT???) GOT HIM, of the drugs and of the booze,...MISSING THEM,...now that *the effects - of the liquor and meth -* ARE OVER!!!(((OY VEY!!!))).

With, head back and, with eyes closed and, with the odor, of and from, the strain, of and from, the pressure, of and from, the pain, of and from, the pleasing-release, of and from, a strong and long morning piss, (pissin' out a bottle of that brown liquor!), OF AND FROM, A HEALTHY-DOSE, WAFTING-THE-FUCK UP HIS NOSE!! And, with that, with like that delayed-reaction, of and from, gettin' hit in the nuts! Of and from, the pushin' and, of the straining, GOT Mr. Brotha Trife's head, starting to pound! And, IT'S GOT HIM, WANTING TO bite - The - mutha'-fuckin' - Dog - THAT bit him! And so, he heads towards the kitchen,...to have a look around!

Into the kitchen and, under the sink and, with all the cubboard doors flung open and, under the sounds of empty liquor bottles, (falling to, from being tossed and), from rolling cross the kitchen floor, Mr. Brotha Trife's, STILL after SUMFIN' to drink! "Ok. Ok. Let me think. Let me think.", Mr. Brotha Trife, says to himself, "Ain't no 'letric, up in this piece. So, if I'ma gamblin' man, like mutha' fuckin' Pockets? I bet, ain't NOBODY thought to check, the freezer. 'Cause, IF there's some liquor up in there, I'LL BET, they forgot it!" (And, WHEN Mr. Brotha Trife, found that skull-topped bottle of Padre Azul, oh please believe, THAT he was MOST PLEASED!!!).

"AHHHH, the things we do to ourselves!", Mr. Brotha Trife, says, after he poured some out for Nephew, 'bout to get bodied, after he removed the skull from the body, after getting "bodied", after taking that skull's forgotten about body to the head!

Ain't no running water. So, he can't freshen up. But, even still, WITH hot tequilla flowing through his Tier-Three-Veins, he's GOT TO get, on HIS giddy-up! So, it's back into the bedroom so that, he can collect up his stuff. (And, was 'bout to zip-up his suitcase that, *last night, he opened up),*...("Hmm. Should I write that song, 'bout Anna Mossitti? Or, should I flip open Y.S.' laptop?")...Decisions. Decisions. Nope. Mr. Brotha Trife decides, he's gonna' find out, WHAT the fuss is all about. And, SO...IT'S one of those, *"ALMIGHTY READING MATERIALS",* that Mr. Brotha Trife, HAS decided to open up!

And so...

He sits down on the bedroom floor. (Lotus style) And, takes a look inside. And, he gains some clarity. (As to why?) He keeps on getting hit with tiny stones...fallen from the sky! And, what it says to him, is that if stones, three or more, hit you that fell from the sky, that IT IS YOUR CALLING (TO BE SURE!!!), that YOUR PATH is THE ONE of a Shaman and, that you are to learn "the ways" to travel between the doors to find the cures.

And, (on that)...

Mr. Brotha Trife closes that book, and in the suitcase, he puts it back. ('Cause, to him, he don't need to read any more). 'Cause, he felt it. *He's*

ALWAYS felt it! And, while sitting *lotus style,* on the floor. *He closes his eyes. As, he meditates. As, he meets Brotha Trife, his Spirit Guide, up in the sky, between the doors. And, he has a deep talk with himself. IT'S JUST he and himself! Talking to himself. (((And, he's TELLING HIMSELF...TO WATCH HIS FUCKING BACK!!!))) And that, each time that he felt, a tiny stone, strike him atop of, his bullet-hole-hat. That, THAT DEJA VU, that he felt, WAS HIM, TALKING TO HIM! That, IT WAS, Brotha Trife, HIS SPIRIT GUIDE, FROM UP ABOVE, WATCHING HIS BACK!!! TELLING HIMSELF, TO FOLLOW HIS PATH! (((AND, BY ALL MEANS, TO WATCH HIS FUCKING BACK!!!))).*

And, (on that)...

Mr. Brotha Trife stands up, and removes that bullet-hole-hat. And, then he proceeds into the bathroom. And, stands before the mirror. Shattered. Broken. And, cracked. And, of that removed hat. He inspects that hat. *(Of, all the divots sustained). From, having been hit in the head. From stones. That, have fallen from the sky.* And, HE *KNEW* that, *THAT WAS HIM, UP THERE!!! CASTING STONES DOWN ON UPON HIMSELF!!!* ('Cause, HE HAD THE RIGHT to do that!!!). *AS, HE WAS TELLING HIMSELF, TO FOLLOW HIS OWN PATH!!! (((AND, TO WATCH HIS OWN, MUTHA' FUCKIN' BACK!!!))).*

And, (on that)...

Mr. Brotha Trife for the first time, removes from of his nose, those 24 karat golds! And, he leans into himself. As, he leaned forward. (To, get a better look at himself). *Looking at himself. Looking back at himself.* In the bathroom mirror. Shattered. Broken. And, cracked. And, for the first time, Mr. Brotha Trife, takes a look at his, swollen and stitched-shut eye socket. *(((Stiched AND swollen-shut!)))*. FROM MISSING AN EYE!!! HIS EYE!!! HIS MOTHERFUCKIN' EYE!!! THIS - MOTHERFUCKIN' - MUSIC INDUSTRY, HAS ALREADY...*TAKEN AN EYE!!!* "THIS-HERE-SHIT, BEST WORK-THA'-FUCK-OUT!! OR, ME AND THIS INDUSTRY, GON' BE ON SOME, *"EYE FOR AN EYE SHIT"!!!"*, Mr. Brotha Trife, says of himself, and *TO himself,* in that and of, *the "3 Hims",* (two in his face and, that of him, his guide, one above).

And, with a closed No.12 door at his back and, with his suitcase-in-hand and, with those limited edition Cazel's of, 24 karat gold, back covering his *taken-eye,* adorned on his nose, Mr. Brotha Trife, on HIS giddy-up IS back! (Back AT it!). GOT to keep his profile low. As he, GOTS'TA' trek-it cross town. *(To where, EVERY-DAMN-DAY, rain OR shine, Anna Mossitti, can be found!).* As, rain or shine, day after day, to stand before and look up at his statue, she goes. And, Mr. Brotha Trife, wasn't too impressed, with *all that reading materials stuff!* 'Cause, his *Tier-Three-Mind, WAS DRAWN to his twin!!* (OF HIM, *BEING HIM).* And, if he don't know NOTHING ELSE...he *KNOWS, HE GOT, HIS BACK, tonight!!* (So, him *KNOWING* that, *he HAS, HIS BACK - FROM UP ABOVE -* IS just a plus!!).

(And, it's a DAMN-SHAME, that it took, Mr. Brotha Trife, of Hallway Hannah's face, a straight-mush)...

'Cause...

As he walked past that busybody, (as he headed towards the stairs), for into Mr. Brotha Trife's business and affairs, Hallway Hannah, DID NOT DARE TO LOOK!

And...

With a head full of that skull-topped tequilla, Mr. Brotha Trife, heads down three flights of stairs. And, as Mr. Brotha Trife, strolled through that lobby, (to the outside world), he finds that, it ain't Weekend Fred nor Big Husky, rather, someone else, is standing there.

(Come. Let's *"peep the scene"* with Mr. Brotha Trife!)...

I'LL BE DAMNED!! It's THAT Cadillac - ride-share - driving man! Hey, my man, what time is it? Oh, shit! It's quarter-of??? Hey, my man, can I get a lift to the "old" SYKE Park? *Why you need to get there, in such a hurry?* Yeah, um, there's some statue there, I just wanna' checkout, that everyone keeps speaking of. *Yeah, hop on in. I'll get you there by noon, my friend. I just pulled over to check, my fuses and spark plugs.* And, after Mr. Brotha Trife, places his suitcase in the back seat, he hops on in up front.

And, then, Mr. Brotha Trife, gets TO doin', WHAT he do…*(Peeping - THA' FUCK - outta' shit!)*. 'Cause, oddly-enough *(OR NOT!!!)*, TO him, THIS '83 Cadillac Seville…*JUST FITS HIM…like a glove!!!!!*

And so…

(They boogied-on-down the road)…

WITH the ride-share driver man, driving like a nut! Speeding! And makin' unnecessary turns! (Hairpin turns at that!). UNNECESSARILY!!! And, don't you know, that "the tire squealer" drives that way while, ALL THE WHILE, while rollin' up some reefer!!

"Yo, holmes! IF I ain't have some place to be at, BY high noon?? My man, I woulda' BEEN whooped-yo'-ass, fo' drivin' like, a fuckin' nut!", Mr. Brotha Trife, says, *(then, plays it LIKE Pockets! AS, HE then, tells the ride-share driver man, of what he JUST cooked-up in his head!)*, "BUT, EVERYTHANG comes wit'a price, RIGHT!? So, pass me that joint before, you take this NEXT CURVE!! And, THAT WAY, I won't HAVETA' BUST-OPEN YOUR HEAD!!! 'CAUSE, IM'A NEED ME some of yo' weed, *to HELP SETTLE MY NERVES!!!*"

"Right on! It's casual. Here ya' go!", the ride-share driver, replies, passing Mr. Brotha Trife the joint, (then, continues, while laughing), "Listen, Daddy-O, I don't want no problems. I just NEVER drive SLOW!!"

Looking at the ride-share driver sideways, before lighting up that joint, STILL WANTIN' TO give his jaw a crack, Mr. Brotha Trife, takes a couple of puffs *(to settle his nerves!),* before passing the joint right back. (And, right before, an unnecessary tire yaw). (And, right before the ride-share driver, off that joint, takes a couple of draws)…he removes both hands from the wheel, while lookin' puzzled 'n frowned, at that joint that he had just, placed up to his mouth. (And, while looking at the joint, and, not at the road, the ride-share driver man continues speeding down, as he, continues to ignore the road, as he, continues to be perplexed, over the joint,…a lil' mo'!), AS THEN, at Mr. Brotha Trife, he points! And, he begins cracking himself up, (at what, he is about to say!), "I could TASTE IT on the joint, MAFACKA'!!! I KNEW that, you WAS gay!!"

AND SO...

THEY BOTH JUST CRACK-UP LAUGHING!! And, they both get to rapping. ('Bout music and, cars and, women and such)...

ALTHOUGH(ALL JOKES ASIDE 'N SUCH!)...

(It might be that bottle of tequilla, (on an empty stomach!), that Mr. Brotha Trife, polished-off in such a rush! OR, it might be, this meth-laced reefer, that GOT his Tier-Three-Mind feeling, A BIT touched!!)...

"BUT??? DAMN!!! DIDN'T I have THE EXACT SAME, Cherry Coke soda stain, RIGHT MOTHERFUCKIN' HERE, from my soda can, under my front passenger's seat that exploded, staining my Riviera's interior rug?!?", peeps, Mr. Brotha Trife's - TIER-THREE-MIND - (((DOIN'-WHAT-IT-DO - PEEPIN'-SHIT-OUT - THOROUGH-AS-FUCK!!!)))...

'Cause...

WHEN a can of Cherry Coke, in your car explodes, on a HOT SUMMER'S DAY...('Cause, you FORGOT about it, when you walked away!)...(AND, left that soda can in there!)...(AND, left the windows up - trapping in your car - the heat of an electric chair!!!)...(((WELL, GUESS WHAT???))))...THAT SODA CAN OF Cherry Coke, WHEN it explodes, its GON' soak down AND COOK INTO your car's interior carpet - AND - PERMANENTLY mark it!!

AND...

(((THAT'S JUST SOME SHIT - THAT AIN'T NEVER - GON' COME OUT!!!)))

AND SO...

(The ride-share driver man, as he drives, does some PEEPING of his own!)...

AS...

He's peeping, THAT, Mr. Brotha Trife, is *PEEPING-OUT HIS RIDE-SHARE CAR, PEEPING IT OUT TO SEE - IF IT IS IN*

FACT A CAR THAT - BROTHA TRIFE,...USED TO OWN!!!)))(((OY MUTHAFUCKIN' VEY!!!))).

(Come!)...(LET'S SEE how this shit plays out!)...

"NAH! IT COULDN'T BE!", (said, in the mind, of this-here TIER THREE), "'Cause, IF THIS WAS MY '83 Buick Riviera,...THAT WOULD MEAN,...there would be a cigarette burn,...IN THE FRONT PASSENGER'S SEAT!!!"

And...

As Mr. Brotha Trife, lifts up one ass cheek, to lean slightly to his right, to check and see, if there's a cigarette burn in the seat, (under his right thigh!), the ride-share driver guy, *(ON THE SLY!)*, passes that *meth-laced joint,* RIGHT BACK to Mr. Brotha Trife, *TO KEEP his mind - SPUN-THA'-FUCK-OUT-AND-FRIED!!!*(((COCKSUCKER!!!))).

"What's wrong, mafacka'?? Daddy-O, you buggin'???", this cocksucker, asks, (then, INSTRUCTS Mr. Brotha Trife), "HERE! *RELAAAAAAX YOUR MIND!!! AND, on THAT JOINT,* cool cat, JUST GET ta' tuggin'!!"

And so(AS, Mr. Brotha Trife, takes *that joint* to the face)...

YOU DAMN-RIGHT - NOW HE *KNOWS - THE WEED IN THIS JOINT - IS MUTHAFUCKIN'-LACED!!*

BUT...

((((OLD HABITS DIE HARD!!!)))

SO...

Mr. Brotha Trife, BULLIES the rest of the ride-share driver's shit! (So that the *"CRASH 'N COME-DOWN"* ain't so hard, YA' DIG!!!))). And so, as for, the ride-share driver guy's rolling papers, (AS, WELL AS), his "Weed Grinder" FULL of ground-up nuggz 'n rocks, Mr. Brotha Trife, did so, MAKE HIM give!

AND...

(SINCE it's the man behind the wheel's POSITION, to Mr. Brotha Trife, HE MAKES a proposition!)...

"SINCE you "bogarted" the rest of my rocks. Listen, mafacka', I KNOW you got a few numbers I could call, you know,...so I can make a few buys. I'm always lookin' for some new connects, groovy guy. Rocks, pills, weed and white, I'm always lookin' to cop a whole lot, I'm always in the market, for a big supplier, with a big supply. So, what's your bag? Why don'tcha' lay-it-on-me? And, after I make some BIG buys,...I'll come lookin' for you,...CATCH YOU on-the-flip-side."

And, (ON THAT!!)...

(What sounded like a tiny stone, fallen from the sky, was never even heard, by Mr. Brotha Trife, when it struck the Cadillac's roof!)...

FOR...

That: "WATCH-YOUR-MUTHAFUCKIN'-BACK!" *- Sound, was drowned out, by Mr. Brotha Trife's teeth, locked together being ground!*

As(A RESULT!)...

(Of the meth STRIKING the nerve in his jaw!)...(((SHOOTING UP thru his tooth!!!)))

"Yo, my man, ain't that "old" *SYKE Park,* just up ahead on the left?? Just drop me off here and, I'll walk the rest.", Mr. Brotha Trife, replies, (NEVER providing the guy with shit!).

"*Shit.*", the man, positioned behind the wheel, to himself, *thinks,* (and, while double-parking on the city street, *does so think,* to himself, *"I gotta' GET him TO BUY ME some more,...if NOTHING else!"*).

And so...

(As, Mr. Brotha Trife, steps outta' the ride)...

He leans back in the car door, to retrieve his suitcase from the back seat, that he nearly forgot(FROM his *Tier-Three-Brain,* gettin' *LACED-WEED-FRIED!!*). And, as he does, the man positioned behind the wheel, leans to his right, to lean to the side. So as, to do so, placing his right hand on the front passenger's seat. So as, to of, *a cigarette burn hole, (((in the leather seat!!!))),* he covers-up and hides!!(((COCKSUCKER!!!))).

And so...

As, Mr. Brotha Trife, begins to close the car door, the man, positioned behind the wheel, says to him, "Listen, mafacka', ALL THESE rides AIN'T free! *When I gave you a ride with those three foxy mamas, I "hooked-you-up" the first time. AND, DIDN'T YOU get - HIGH-AS-A-KITE - BOTH times, I'VE given you a ride?? AND, THEN, FROM ME, ALL MY SHIT, YOU STEAL!!!* But,...it's casual. SO,...I'll tell you what,...I'll stike ya' a deal. How 'bout you give me a coupla' names AND their phone numbers?? AND, I'll go make-some-tracks, cool cat, and get US some more! You won't even have to give me any "moolah" for the shit, 'til we meet up again. Wouldn't you say that's fair? I think, that's the least, YOU could do, for me!"

And...

Mr. Brotha Trife, just gets that look on his face. (((YOU KNOW THE LOOK!!!)))(((*THAT EVIL GRIMACED-GRIN-OF-THE-PAIN-STICK LOOK!!!*)))...

And, he removes those limited edition 24 karat golds, from off of his nose. And, he leans in close. (DAMN-NEAR touching, the man, positioned behind the wheel's nose, WITH his own nose!)...(YEAH! THAT MUTHAFUCKIN' CLOSE!!!). And, Mr. Brotha Trife, said, UNTO HIM, "I DIDN'T OPEN UP YOUR HEAD!!! AND, THAT'S THE LEAST, I CAN DO!!!"

And, with car door slammed. And, with, his: *ol' Brotha Trife-(((heels diggin'-in hard in the street, long-stridin')))-PISSED-OFF - Stroll,* Mr. Brotha Trife, HE DON'T GIVE A FUCK 'BOUT TRAFFIC!!! Cars nose-divin', *(((PROCEEDING screeching-tires halts!)))*. And, as he reaches the sidewalk cross the street,...he sees her.

And, she's oblivious to the sounds. As, she stands before and, looks up at his statue. *As, every day. At this time. AT High Noon. Rain OR shine. To him, she talks.* And, he's *mismerized* BY her. As, he takes in her curves.

As, he stands there on the sidewalk. (DIRECTLY BEHIND HER!!!). As, she stands BEFORE him!! As, he CAN'T do ANYTHING but watch! As, church bells in the distance toll, THAT it's High Noon on the clock!! As, she's well up in the park. As, she stands upon the gravel and of the stones, *of the former SYKE Park bulldozed!* As, HER beauty, in and of, the rubble, CREATED AND CREATES...a contrast that's stark! As, from him, of her, she's still a good distance away. As, she remains completely *entranced,* well up in "old" *SYKE Park!* For, upon the sidewalk, he remains frozen. For, as a statue, he remains as motionless. As, for her, beneath her, the rocks and rubble, provides her with the sweet-discomfort,...of a church pew. As, she looks up at him. (((TALKING TO HIM!!!))). As, she says UNTO HIM. As, she let's him know. She can't wait for THIS day! (Though, she DON'T know it!). THAT, THIS DAY, IS THE DAY, THAT, HE CHOSE...*to make her dream come true!*

And, as he approaches, neither one, hear ANY sounds! The irate motorists, of the traffic jam he created, yields to his heart that pounds. *(And, that's ALL, that HE, can hear!).* As, his approach to her, draws near. And, of that gravel. And, of those stones. And, of that, of his approach, he hears no tones. (For, as he walks, there might as well not even be a surface, beneath his feet). FOR, ALL that, this Tier-Three-Clone can hear,...*IS the POUND of HIS heartbeat!*

And, *DAAAAAAYUM!!! THERE she is!* (And, if I'M a gamblin' man!) *I'D BET, WE WOULD'VE HAD,...some beautiful kids!!* From under church bells, from under sacrilege, *from his imaginings,* from his one good eye, from undressin', from straight staring her down, *(((down to HER essence))),* from her soft exposed ankle on up, from up under that bullet-hole-hat, Mr. Brotha Trife, did so, as he persisted, as such. From behind sun blazoned eyes, from concluding, *from being mesmerized. OF. HOW. DAAAAAAAYUM!!! TONE. MUST. BE. HER. THIGHS!! ((OY VEY!!)).*

And, of him, she too, persisted. In, of, and from her deaf-tunnel-vision-view. Of which, at which, to look up, she continued. Deaf. Mute. And blind. Just like, to all, but his statue. And, all is but perfect. She...IS perfect! Why,...this has GOT TO BE HER!! (And,...SURE 'NUFF!) CLAMPED-DOWN-TIGHT, above her open toe sandal, (((RESTRICTED 'ROUND HER LEFT ANKLE)))...((((THERE IT IS!!!)))...a black house arrest anklet...IS CUFFED!!!

(((EXPOSED-MOST-GANSTA'-STYLE!!!))))

'CAUSE...

(((ANNA MOSSITTI, BEEN-DONE-HAD-STOP-GIVIN'-A-FUCK-WHAT - PEOPLE - THINK - FOR A WHILE!!!)))

For...

THE baddest in the city,...EXPOSES that bitch!!

FOR, TODAY...

(((Rockin' it rolled-up and cinched - to just below the bottom, of her left knee, is her pant leg - of her "Free People" CRUSHED-VELVET BELL BOTTOM!!!)))...

And, matching her robin's egg nail polish painted toes, Anna Mossitti, wears a high-neck - fluted-sleeved - laced-out-blouse - from "Free People - is what she chose! Adorned upon her left wrist, she wears a Movado. And, right at High Noon, is the ONLY time that, HER heart's NOT hollow!

And(YES!)...

(IT'S plain for HIM TO SEE)...

THAT, SHE IS, THE BADDEST IN THE CITY!!!

And(YES!)...

She STILL keeps her hair, CLOSELY shorn!!

And(YES!)...

As to why? She STILL keeps, her answer short:

"Did anyone ever ask Jesus, if it hurt, when they placed on, the crown of thorns?"

And(YES!)...

(There's only ONE thing, you need to understand)...

Anna Mossitti, rocks her hair closely shorn, like that...

(((((((BECAUSE SHE FUCKING CAN!!!!!!!)))))))

And, adorned upon, her beautiful nose(((HOLY SHIT!!!)))to wear today,...Limited Edition Cazel's of 24 karat gold lenses - IS what SHE chose! And, upon seeing that, Mr. Brotha Trife, is PROMPTLY *taken aback!* And, as such, *IT brings him back!* (Back, FROM WHAT??) (((AS, HIS *TIER-THREE-MIND,* GETS FIRMLY ROCKED!!!))). *OF IMPURE THOUGHTS, OF WHICH HE SHOULDN'T, OF HER FIRM THIGHS,* OF WHICH BELONGS,...TO POCKET'S WOMAN!!!((OY TO THA' MUTHA' FUCKIN' VEY!!)).

AND SO...

As, he's finally reached her. As, he's standing directly behind her! As, SHE STILL stands AS STILL AS HIS statue!! (As, she still has NO idea!). That, the man, standing before her. That, the man, that she wants TO HAVE stand BESIDE her. That, THAT man, that she wants to come back. IS, in fact, standing RIGHT BEHIND her back!

"Damn. THIS is SOOOOOO fucked-up! Smokin' on that laced-shit?? DAMN!!! I SHOULDN'T have gotten, SOOOOOO fucked-up!", said inside of, Mr. Trife's *Tier-Three-Head,* but, since he's SOOOOOO *fucked-up,*...HE SAID THAT SHIT, OUT LOUD INSTEAD!!!

And, as Anna Mossitti, snatches those 24 karat golds, from off of her beautiful nose, upon both limited edition lenses, gold tears flowed, as she stares up at HIS statue, as she, FOR herself, JUST HAS TO see, as she, NEEDS and WANTS OF HER OWN TWO EYES *TO PROVIDE AN EXPLAINATION,* IF SO, IN FACT, THAT STATUE, JUST SPOKE TO HER, *WITH A VOICE, OF INTUBATION, MOST AMAZIN!!!*

And, placed upon the backs of both shoulders - are both - of his large walnut-sized-knuckled-askewed hands. And, his breath on the back of her neck - sends her - to the promised land! And, of the gravel. And, of the stones. She spins 'round quickly, upon all of those!!. *'CAUSE, WHAT - she learned - from Brotha Trife, (oh, 'bout, 1,260 days ago or so!) - is that - SELF-PRESERVATION - IS the ZONE!!!*

And, as Anna Mossitti, holds her head high, *now, SHE'S the one, who's mismerized!* (AS, she SEES HERSELF, IN HIS 24 karat gold eyes!!). And,

(IT WAS!), HER ONLY WISH, FOR, TO BE HIS breath, on the back of her neck, *CREATING THAT VOICE - OF INTUBATION - MOST AMAZIN'!* AND, THAT WAS - THE LAST - THING THAT SHE SAW, (as, he caught and held her fall), were his eyes of, and, like, the sun, was BLAZIN'!

And, amongst the gravel. And, amongst the stones. And, amongst the big slabs of concrete, formed as toppled-over stalactites and stalagmites, *formed by a bulldozer's blade, hired by the city, paid for by the city, by that Gun Battle Bradley Bounty Money, to the city, Brotha Trife, did so donate, (oh, 'bout,...1, 260 - or-so-ago - days!)*, amongst all that, Mr. Brotha Trife, does so stand, under a bullet-hole-hat, with the dead blood of Y.S., soaked down into his hat band, all the while holding tight, the dead-weight, of a dead-lookin' body, IN THE MIDDLE OF A CITY PARK, UNDER NO LESS THAN, HIGH NOON SUNLIGHT!!!(((OY VEY!!!))).

"DAMN!!! THIS AIN'T-NO-WAY TO, GET ACQUAINTED!!!", Mr. Brotha Trife, says, out loud, (while lookin' the FUCK around!!), (while, holding the dead-body-weight, of Anna Mossitti, *whom fainted!!)*, "AND, I'm 'sposed to be keepin' a LOW profile! PLUS, I GOT SHIT ON ME!!! Holmes, YOU SLIPPIN'!! FUCKIN' COPS see me in this park, WITH her LIKE THIS, IN my arms??? Holmes, YOU AIN'T GON' SEE THE SUNLIGHT FOR AWHILE!!!"

And, though, he's trying not to rough her up, (((BUT,...DAMN BABY!!!)))(((WE GOTS'TA' GET ON OUR GIDDY-UP!!!)), Mr. Brotha Trife, rocks her gently in his arms. And, though, he's *peeping out* his whereabouts, *((((OF WHOM MAY BE PEEPING HIM THE FUCK OUT!!!)))),* in case, it becomes the case, she fails to be rocked awake, and HE'S GOT'STA' GRAB his suitcase in haste, (((AIN'T TRYNA' CATCH NO CASE!!!))), and with her in his arms, GET THA' FUCK UP OUTTA' THIS PLACE, IN THE EVENT, HE'S SEEN WITH, A DEAD-LOOKING-WOMAN IN HIS ARMS LIKE THIS, SEEN WITH A MAN, SHE'S NEVER BEEN SEEN WITH BEFORE, ROCKIN' HER GENTLY, *(((LIKE HE FELL IN LOVE WITH HER,... IN THE MORGUE!!!)))*, (and, all this time!), SHE'S HAD HIS FULL ATTENTION!! And, though, continually, as he does, of the gentle rockage, NEVER NOT ONCE, AT HIS OWN STATUE, DOES HE EVER LOOK UP, remaining fully attentive, to her current condition!

ALTHOUGH...

(There he stands! On a round - stacked-three-tiered-layered - MARBLE STAND!!! A GIGANTIC statue, carved from a single block of marble, CARVED BY HAND!!! In and of resemblance, OF the man, THAT,... once TERRORIZED and ROCKED THIS CITY!!! And, there HE stands! In marble. Holding oh so gently, AND, WITH REVERENCE,... the marble neck...OF THE PAIN STICK...IN HIS MARBLE HAND!!!)

(Come! Let's TAKE A LOOK AT THIS!!!)...

And, the DETAIL IS impeccable! *Though, the city had* (and, STILL has!) *NO LOVE - for the man,* (carved in marble, up above!). *BUT, taken into consideration was - ALL THAT MONEY - that the man, donated TO the city! (And then, there's the fact, that - "that man" - sent a bulldozer, to bulldoze over, THE SADDEST NUISANCE OF A SPECTACLE, that the city, has ever had!). And so, well, the city, for and of, "that man"....HAD TO do WHAT was respectable!*

(((And, the sculptor, GOT it down! EVERY last detail. From, what was described, to the sculptor, OF: "that man's" - MOTHER! FUCKING!! PEOPLE!!! FROWN!!!!)))

From, top to bottom. Back up to the top. And, back ON down. The detail, WAS impeccable!! THOSE MARBLE COWBOY BOOTS WERE TAIL-CUT!!! The bottom of that marble trench coat, NEARLY touched the round - stacked-three-tiered-layered - marble base!!! (AND, OF the base), though close, though, absent of touch, *(((FOR, "Pain-Stick-walkin'", though, there ARE three, though, doth solo - the PAIN STICK - DOES NOT TOUCH!!!)))*, THAT SCULPTOR, GOT THAT PART RIGHT*(((DON'T FUCK WIT THA' PAIN STICK, YA' DIG!!!)))*. AND, as too, *((((NOT TO FUCK WITH LUCK)))*, IN IMPECCABLE DETAIL, THAT SCULPTOR CAPTURED THE EVILNESS - OF THE PAIN STICK'S - EVIL-GRIMACED-GRIN-FACE!!!

And*(((((I WOULD THINK!)))*...

That, the sculptor, the city hired, DURING the commission OF (and or) BECAME sick!

'CAUSE...

Sculpted IN MARBLE, (((OF IMPECCABLE DETAIL))) *OF EACH AND EVERY DESCRIBED* (TO him!), *"TROPHIED"-PATCHWORK OF SCALPS.* WERE. EVERY. SINGLE. LAST. CATFISH. LINE. STITCH!!!

And, YES INDEED, the Pain Stick DID HAVE - A yard-long - thin leather strap! (MADE OF MARBLE!). AND, YES, A SHRUNKEN FEMALE BABY'S HEAD, (((SEVERED AT THE NECK!!!))), SCULPTED AND TETHERED-TIGHT (((LIKE KNOTTED WOOL!!!))), TO AND OF, THE BABY GIRL'S MARBLE HAIR, TO AND OF, THE END OF - THE YARD-LONG MARBLE STRAP,... IT WAS ATTACHED!!!

(And, NO, that statue, WOULD NOT be complete!)...(And, I AIN'T talkin' 'bout, the tail-cut leather cowboy boots, on "that man's" feet!!)

(((COME ON, YOU!!! THINK HARD!!! THINK!!!!!!)))

For, (YOU should ALREADY KNOW!!!)...

Artistically presented as "runny" (and, YOU JUST KNOW that sculptor was worth, EVERY CENT of that money!!), for, sculpted on that trench coat's sleeves, was the "bad-taste-in-YOUR-MOUTH-inducing" - sight, of - LIQUIFIED-"HUMAN-CHEESE" - TRACKING-DOWN BOTH OF THESE!!!

FURTHERMORE...

((((ADORNED ATOP - OF "THAT MAN'S" TRENCH COAT - SCULPTED FROM THAT SINGLE GIGANTIC MARBLE BLOCK - EACH ONE ON BOTH - SCULPTED ON THE SHOULDERS OF "THAT MAN'S" TRENCH COAT - *AS IF THE SCULPTOR'S ATTENTION TO DETAIL - WASN'T ALREADY ENOUGH...*WERE THE GRIZZLY-AFTERMATHS OF...SLICED-OFF AFRO PUFFS - FROM, THE ONE AND ONLY, GIDGET COLE, AND, IF YOU DIDN'T KNOW...KNOW YOU KNOW!!!)))(((((OY VEY!!!)))))

And...

THAT'S "THE MAN" THEY PAID HOMAGE TOO!!!!!!

(THOUGH, in love, and, love, FOR him, FOR HIM - TO GIVE - THEY HAD, NONE TO GIVE!!)(Bastards!). Though, (and yet!), homage WAS STILL PAID!!! And so, though, NOT IN LOVE, THOUGH, "the APPEARANCE OF LOVE", the city, TO "THAT MAN", they STILL gave!).

((((MOTHERFUCKERS!!!)))

'CAUSE...

((((THE WAY, BROTHA TRIFE ROLLED, WAS...IF HE DIDN'T HAVE YOUR RESPECT, HE DIDN'T WANT YOUR FUCKIN' LOVE!!!)))

And so, (AND, BUT, *EVEN STILL)...*

OF THAT STATUE. OF "THAT MAN". OF HIS, LONG DREADLOCKS. CARVED FROM A SINGLE MARBLE BLOCK. *THE SCULPTOR,...PAID HIS OWN HOMAGE!* AND, EACH MARBLE DREADLOCK TIP. RECEIVED, REFINED BY FIRE, A 24 KARAT SOLID GOLD DIP. OF WHICH, BEAM A GOLDEN HUE... FROM SUNLIGHT, FROM, OF, IF, AND WHEN, THROUGH, BIG FLUFFY WHITE CLOUDS, COMES BREAKING ON THROUGH, STRUCK UPON...AT HIGH NOON!!!

And, as Anna Mossitti finally, comes to. (She *KNOWS, SHE knows!)* *THAT, her one AND ONLY wish, HAS come true!* And, of that statue? *She, NEVER did touch! (For, she was SAVING her touch,...FOR HIS touch!).* The man, of her's, in his, OF THEIR's!! As,...they do so, both clutch.

(And, she didn't ask him why, he returned to her, on this day). And, as she, reached up and, removed his limited edition eyes of gold, from his face. "Horrible. Just...horrible.", is ALL, that she COULD manage to say!

"What? My EYE?? Oh, MY BAD!! *It got TAKEN out, from a rifle shot.* I just put things, into perspective. THIS, AIN'T PAIN! BEING *"stuck"*

IS pain! So, my "GIDDY-UP", IT CAN'T NEVER stop!", Mr. Brotha Trife, explains.

And, Anna Mossitti, replies, "No. No. NOT your eye! *Last night. IT WAS HORRIBLE! JUST, HORRIBLE!!* ...Stay with me tonight."

"Wait? What?? *WHAT HAPPENED!?!* YOU good?? I'LL KILL A MOTHERFUCKER *FOR FUCKIN', WIT YOU!!!*", Mr. Brotha Trife, speaking ONLY but the truth!

"No! Listen to me. Your eye,...it *sent* me some place...made me *think of last night!* I'm a prisoner in my own home...THAT, all red everythang apartment,...you know? I *KNOW,* you *remember me, opening the door for you,...at the top of those stairs.",* Anna Mossitti, says, with the first smile that has come cross her face, *(in, oh, 'bout 1, 260 or-so-or more days!:),* "Anyway, *something horrible MUST HAVE happened last night!* Because, down in the basement, of Precinct One, there's this...tiny-makeshift-morgue. THIS town is STILL dirty, you know! ANYWAY, they DON'T use that tiny morgue much. *BUT, last night, the City Morgue got filled up. So, all night long, 'round back, of Precinct One. From, my window, you know, up in - "my-prison-of-an-all-red-everythang-apartment",...I could see them. They brought ALL of these bodies, into that tiny-makeshift-morgue, last night. I couldn't sleep...I don't think I'll EVER sleep again."*

"Sorry, babygirl. But, I CAN'T stay with you tonight.", Mr. Brotha Trife, drops the bomb on her, (as her eyes and heart drop!), before he drops the knowledge on her, as to why, as he, lifts her spirits, "I'M gettin' you OUT of the city, under the *cover of darkness,* TONIGHT! ...BUNK THAT!! WE bouncin', RIGHT NOW!!"

"Uh, Brotha Trife, IF it were ONLY THAT simple.", Anna Mossitti, replies, directing his focus, off of her. As, they, both then, take a look at that house arrest anklet, constricting her ankle (AND the simplicity of their getaway!), AS the reason why!

"That's cute, babygirl! YOU think, that CAN stop ME from gettin' you, OUTTA' here??? What's the deal w.", Mr. Brotha Trife, begins, *(then - cuts-himself-off - in mid-sentence!). AS, he thinks to HIMSELF, "Oh, HOLD UP!!! WAIT!!! SHE just called me...BROTHA TRIFE!!! Oh, THIS is TOO fucked-up for ME!! Does she NOT KNOW,...that,...I'M a CLONE???"*

"What?? FINISH askin' me, *what you WERE 'bout to, ask* me! Hey, YOU KNOW WHAT,...it's cool. 'Cause, I GOT SOMETHIN' I WANT TO tell you! *WHOOOLE-LOTTA' grimy-shit went down, the last night YOU were in THIS town! ...Pockets,...LEFT ME here! YOU, left ME here!! This fuckin' dirty-ass police department, put some dirty-ass feds on "the payroll", SO, THAT, North Juarez PD could maintain, control of their city.* And, ALL OF THOSE dirty-motherfuckers, are using ME AS BAIT!!! Yeah, I'm allowed out of that all red everythang apartment. Yeah, I can walk around. YOU KNOW, go get my HOT fries! BUT, they keep me on this thing 'round my ankle,...they've ALL BEEN keepin' a close-eye on me. NJPD and some dirty feds are hopin', Pockets, will come back here one day, for me. And, if that day ever happens, NJPD 'sposed to hand him over, to the feds. But, THESE - dirty-mutha'-fuckas - AIN'T handin' ov'a shit! Brotha Trife, me AND you BOTH know, they GONNA' gun him down!", Anna Mossitti, looking up at "Brotha Trife", breaks it down, (then lets her head drop down, as she's, feeling down), then, lifts her head back up, (as her spirits rise back up!) and, speaks on as to why, her life no longer feels so fucked-up, "Pockets, never came for me,...but, YOU did. Stay with me tonight, Trife. *Remember the last time, that you saw me? We sat on that plush red leather sofa, smokin' those Lars Tetens cigars. And, we just talked to one another with no effort at all.* Wouldn't you like to be on that sofa, with me again?"

"Ooooooh, we got A WHOOOLE LOT, to talk ABOUT, babygirl! I DON'T think THAT red sofa is READY!", Mr. Brotha Trife, replies, (causing them both to embrace and smile:) But, then, that smile, of Mr. Brotha Trife,...*TURNS INTO THAT EVIL-GRIMACED-OF-THE-PAIN-STICK'S-EVIL-GRIMACED-GRIN!!!* And, of he of her. And, of her of him. As, they are in "the continuousness" of their embrace, (((AS, OF, AND-AND))), he KEEPS her there! *(((SO, ANNA MOSSITTI, CAN NOT SEE - THE EVIL LOOK - UPON HIS FACE!!!)))*.

FOR...

Mr. Brotha Trife's, Tier-Three-Mind, HAS JUST CAUGHT a hint of a trace.

Of...

(((an ENTIRE BOTTLE OF "JOOP!" COLOGNE!!!)))...(And, HE DON'T smell it on her!)

AND SO...

TO Mr. Brotha Trife, THAT COULD ONLY MEAN, THAT DIRTY-ON-DUTY-HOOKER-DISSIN'-NEVER-KISSIN'-VICE-COP, GOTS'TA BE HIDIN', UNDER OR BEHIND, ONE OF THESE PILES OF CONCRETE SLABS AND RUBBLE, SOMEWHERE, UP IN THIS PLACE!!!

And so...

Mr. Brotha Trife, whispers, "The midnight hour."

Then...

Slips out of the reluctance, of her, not wanting, to end their embrace. Although, successfully, he does so, and so, for it, he then, does so, as he, makes a break, after picking up his suitcase. Upon which, he plans to, as he, begins to, head back to, that apartment on the third floor, affixed with a No.12 on the door, to which, upon arrival, he plans to, break into. (Upon tonight's arrival, he will wait. And so, upon arrival, into that door No.12 apartment, he will break), for, to so, lay-up and lay-low. (And so, he got a suitcase in his hand. He got a trickle in his one good eye,...from that dead-blood-soaked hat band. And, these other three things this-here Tier-Three got on: 1). His way. 2). Edition's of limited gold. 3). And, a nice-eazy stroll).

And...

She too, begins, to head back, though, back to that - "ALL-RED-EVERYTHANG-PRISON-OF-AN-APARTMENT", of which, upon which, awaits...pain! Upon that plush red leather sofa, she will ache. (And, she WILL ache!)(AS, she waits!). As, she aches upon Brotha Trife as upon she awaits. (Paining!)...((Waiting!!))...(((ACHING!!!)))...Upon,... the midnight hour,...to draw near. And, the whole way there, Anna Mossitti, thinks more of the warmth, from the words in her ear. (More so, than what she was told).

Chapter Twenty One

'BOUT LAST NIGHT

And so, with a city - with and on - uneven sidewalks to cross, Mr. Brotha Trife, does so, with and on - a nice-eazy stroll - with and on - Stacy Adams soles...

FOR...

(He's in no hurry, to commit another burglary!)...

FOR...

(The shit that jumped-off in Legs' place, after he, at the very least, THOUGH, SHIT INCREASED, crept in, in violation, at the very least, of defiantly trespassin')...

OF WHICH...

(He AIN'T EVEN tryin' to be tied in!)...

SO...

(He's gonna' gotta' have'ta' stay tha' fuck away from Legs' place, for sure!)...

SO...

(That door No.12 apartment - he's gonna' gotta' have'ta' - break into, once more!!)...

FOR...

(He's gonna' gotta' have'ta' have - SOME PLACE - as to as to - lay-up and lay-low!)...

SO THAT...

(Upon the Midnight Hour, he'll come knockin' on that - ALL RED EVERYTHANG - apartment door!)...

And(then!)...

ONCE AGAIN, he'll be BACK UP TOP! (Up AT the top, of those ol'-musty-smellin' steps, OF WHICH, down below,...be a bunch of cops!)...

And(THAT'S RIGHT!)...

ONCE AGAIN, TRIFE, WILL BE,...ABOVE THE LAW!!! (ALL-UP-IN Precinct One!),*(JUST AS he had done)...(Oh, 'bout, 1, 260 days ago or so!).*

And so...

As, he walks, he's having *ALL KINDS OF THOUGHTS!!! ('Bout, LOYALTY, to Pockets!)...AND...(loyalty,...TO HIS OWN pockets!!)...*

FOR...

HE AIN'T TRYNA' BE *STUCK!!!*

HOWEVER(The more, he walks)...

(((The MORE, ANNA MOSSITTI, HE FINDS TO BE, IN HIS THOUGHTS!!!)))

And so, (TO HIM!)...

THAT'S what, HE'S *FINDING* to be - SOOOOOO - *fucked-up!!!* (Oy Vey!).

And, though, (DUE to him!), *smelling A FULL BOTTLE of "Joop!"* cologne, (self-preservation BEING the zone!), *though, whereabouts peeped of his own* - (but, yet, failed to find or spot - that "Joop!" cologne bottle wearin' dirty vice cop!) and, though, HE DIDN'T KNOW - IF - that dirty vice cop - SAW HIM - or not - (Oy Vey!) - and, though, he must walk back through the city, he finds that, he's beginning to get the runs, though, in his eye (the GOOD one!), that being, and, THAT OF, dead-bullet-hole-hat-blood, THOUGH, EVEN SO, Mr. Brotha Trife, is finding - of his best - he's trying, to keep that saturated hat band - and - his profile low! And, though, Mr. Brotha Trife's, *Tier-Three-Mind,* GOT HIMSELF *THINKING,* THAT, *HE INDEED, ALLOWED HIMSELF TO SLIP,* and, though, he WASN'T asleep, he indeed, *KNOWS he WAS SLEEPING!!!*

FOR...

(SURE-AS FUCK, HE WASN'T ALERT AND ON HIS TOES!!!)

FOR...

DUE TO THE BOOZE, THE DRUGS, AND HIS PAIN PILL ABUSE, OF CONSUMPTION OF SUCH, HE IS GUILTY OF!!!

AND(AS SUCH!)...

(ALLOWED himself to BE exposed!).

(((And, though, his Tier-Three-Mind, (to him!) is all-but-awake, and, HE believes, that, he IS, back-up-to-speed. And, though, (to him!!), he is well aware, of every one, and every thing, IN real time, that IS happening! ALTHOUGH,...it's the - *SIMPLEST-SHIT* - THAT - *gets IN his mind!* And so, it's his *qualia* that's *fucking-up* his *quality of life! OF WHICH IS,* MAKING HIM OF, WHAT HE'S SURE,...*TO BE UNSURE!!!)))* ...(Got it?)(Good!).

FOR...

(As, he walks - *HE BELIEVES* - he has, his bearings!)...

"Ok, yeah. NORTH JUAREZ! Yeah, THIS city - IS the ONLY city - out in the middle of wherever! YEAH, I *KNOW NOW, EXACTLY WHERE I'M AT!!!*"

BUT...

(As he, walks past, the huge parking lot, of the City Mall)...

Mr. Brotha Trife, bears witness to - the noisy-public-nuisance - created by the cup from Orange Julius, and the Auntie Anne's pretzel someone lazy, placed into it! And, as a result, the litter-strewn parking lot, is where - life vs life - gets fought and lost - by a large group of - SEAGULLS!!!

WHICH...

(((GOT Mr. Brotha Trife, OF WHICH, EXACTLY WHERE - THE FUCK HE'S AT - NOW - TRYING TO RECALL!!!)))

"Damn...I thought, I thought,...I was MORE "inland", than I am. DAMN! I MUST BE,...DOWN THE SHORE!!!", of Mr. Brotha Trife's, TIER-THREE-MIND, (OF his whereabouts, TRYING to absorb!).

AND SO...

As Mr. Brotha Trife, continues his stroll, cross town...

((((OF WHAT, he WAS, certain of - NOW - his TIER-THREE-MIND - certainly-ain't-so-certain - NO MORE!!!)))

Come! (LET'S GO WITH, Mr. Brotha Trife, AS WE TAKE THIS NICE-EAZY STROLL!!)...

And, as he strolls cross this city, he continues to bear witness to - all-sorts-of-things - that are, commonplace today - *that, became - common* (and, in place!) - *during his years, in the under-the-ground-levels of THAT hallway...(made from white jade!).* (((And, as such, became, CURRENTLY in place, *in and, of occurrence - DURING HIS - looooooong intubated-snooze!))).* So, as Mr. Brotha Trife, finds himself bearing witness to, a group of city youths, (he FINDS, THAT), he's actually - quite-saddened - FOR the group, (AS, FOR,...the way,...THEY walk!).

For...

"ALL these kids TODAY,...MUST BE malnourished!!!", of Mr. Brotha Trife's, ("Left-Behind-The-Times-Tier-Three-Mind"), thoughts, concludes!

BUT, (((IN ALL ACTUALITY!!!)))...

ALL "THESE KIDS TODAY", CHOOSE TO WALK THIS WAY!!! (((SO, AS, NOT TO PUT A CREASE IN THEIR BRAND NEW...$295.00 PAIR OF SNEAKERS AND SHOES!!!)))(((OY VEY!!!))).

And so...

(Movin' right along from that shock, Mr. Brotha Trife, continues, strollin' nice 'n eazy, straight down the main Boulevard of the city , block for block)...

Although...

(He's discovering, that, his stroll, though, nice 'n eazy, has become, more one, *of discovery)...*

For...

He's been discovered by post tramatic stress, and so, that blindspot sidestreet he just *peeped,* just right up ahead on his left, of it, he *discovers, compelling feelings, down which, to dip,* and, for this city's main strip, his *now urgent need, of getting the hell off of it,* to the backroads he'll stick, *discovering empathy, upon malnutrition joining in upon reentering,* upon jack shit, *(he just don't wanna see no more fucked-up-shit involving kids!).* Sadly, though, *that's EXACTLY what he takes along with him!*

FOR...

(((As, he dips, *joining him,* down that sidestreet that he's entering, *are kids conjoined with post tramatic stress, inside his Tier-Three-Mind, filled to to brim!)))*

And so...

With gettin'-tha'-hell-off-that-Boulevard done, with him under a high noon sky, with his limited edition gold eyes, blazin' like the blood of a custom-red-'n-saturated-sun, Mr. Brotha Trife, is pleased, feeling much relieved, as he sees, a group of little kids, ACTUALLY RUNNING 'ROUND 'N PLAYIN'!!!...*(UNLIKE THAT OTHER GROUP, OF THE CITY'S YOUTH, TAKEN ALONG WITH HIM, HAUNTING HIM, INSIDE THE MIND OF THIS-HERE TIER-THREE, TOO MALNOURISHED TO EVEN, BEND THEIR KNEES!!!)*...(((BUT, REALLY THOUGH, THEY AIN'T TRYNA' PUT A CREASE, IN THEIR BRAND NEW PAIR OF $295.00 SNEAKS!!!))).

FOR...

(What, Mr. Brotha Trife, just borne witness to, is a group of the city's youths, far from square, tryin' to "drain 3's" thru - a posted-up-on-a-telephone-pole-plastic-milk-crate - square basketball hoop!!!)...

And so...

(As to, NOT to disturb these kids at play!)...

Mr. Brotha Trife, crosses over the sidestreet, and, as he does, he bears witness to, some "grown ass men", with no care or concern at all, for the city's youth. 'Cause, these "grown ass men", have just split a "Dutch", (((GETTIN' READY TO ROLL-UP!!!))), dumping "Game" cigar "guts", right there in the street, right there...at the "YOUTH'S-AT-PLAY" FEET!!

BUT...

(Mr. Brotha Trife, just keeps it pushin'!)...

'CAUSE...

He's gotta' keep, HIS profile low!

For(YOU SEE!)...

(LAST NIGHT'S CARNAGE, he CAN'T repeat!!)...

Although...

(LEST WE FORGET!)...AND...(((SHAME ON US ALL, IF WE DO!!!)))...

Mr. Brotha Trife, *(Brotha Trife's, direct decendant of thee)*, walks back, as he calls for the ball, "Ayo, lemme' get'a shot, lil' homie!". And, with ball got. And, with a lil' shake 'n bake crossover of ankle breakin'! And, with his high-arcing "Fadeaway 3" taken. Mr. Brotha Trife, turns his back on his shot. (DIDN'T EVEN wait to see that, high-arcing 3-Pointer drop!!!). As he, crosses back over - back to - the other side of the sidestreet - that he just crossed over. (And, wouldn't you know!)...coming down outta' - Mr. Brotha Trife's - one good eye, was a single tear, as he walked away). FOR, he knew that, he had drained that "3"!!!, (from what all those "kids-at-play" all had to say!!!). For, WHEN he drained that "3", all those kids, shouted,..."KOBE!!!" (And, that's WHY Mr. Brotha Trife's - one good eye wasn't dry - as he walked away!). For, it warmed his heart to know, that - kids shooting "3's" - still all say, "KOBE!!!",...to this VERY DAY!!!

Though...

'BOUT LAST NIGHT!!!

(((HMM. I NEVER FINISHED TELLIN' Y'ALL, *'BOUT LAST NIGHT!!!*)))

SOOOOOO...

YOU KNOW, WE *'BOUT TO GET BACK INTO THAT,* RIGHT???

FOR...

(As that, dirty-on-duty-gettin'-brain-smokin'-weed-'n-doin'-blow-tryna'-maintain-vice-cop exited, Legs' apartment building, through the back door)...

WELL...

HE KIDNAPPED A MOTHERFUCKER!! (That, was snooping 'round the crime scene!).

That...

(In the darkness, behind that apartment, failed to keep HIS profile low!)...

That...

Saw, that upsidedown-displayed "POLICE LINE - DO NOT CROSS" yellow crime scene tape, (THAT, read that shit - DISPLAYED - UPSIDEDOWN!!!)...AND, STILL, LIFTED-UP THAT SHIT - UP ABOVE HIS HEAD - AND, ENTERED INTO THAT CRIME SCENE OF IT BELOW!!!

For...

((((That dirty vice cop, was in NO MOOD, (from here!), to go cross town and, HAVE TO inform Skins,...'BOUT YOU-KNOW-WHO!!!)))

SO...

He took out his frustrations! (On, THAT motherfucker, who was on the wrong-side of the crime scene tape, like, HE WAS INVESTIGATING!!!)...

So, he punched him hard in the gut! (AFTER, he maced him in the face!). THEN, LOCKED HIM IN THE TRUNK OF HIS CAR! And, figured, he'd rob him and, then kill him and, dump his body somewhere! (Perhaps, EVEN, pin Legs' murder ON the motherfucker!)...(((SO, THAT, HE COULD THEN, MAKE THE ARREST!!!))). SO, THAT, HE COULD GET A BUMP-IN-PAY!!! (((SHIIIIIIT, DOIN' IT THE NORTH JUAREZ WAY?? SHIIIIIIT, MAYBE ONE DAY, HE'LL BE WEARIN', THE COMMISSIONER'S STARS!!!))).

BUT...

THAT plan, went to shit!

'Cause...

(((THAT motherfucker, YOU just kidnapped,...KNOWS WHO YOU ARE!!!)))

For, (sneakin' 'round that crime scene)...

This cat, who got kidnapped, was rockin' a throwback Eagles jersey, and fitted-cap, of kelly green. (And, this kidnapped-cat - WAS DRAWN - TO that crime scene!). WHEN, HE SAW, FROM A DISTANCE - WHAT SEEMED TO BE - A FLASHIN' AND BLINKIN' AND STROBIN' BLUE AND RED LIGHT - SEA!! For, to THIS ('BOUT TO BE KIDNAPPED) CAT, NO OTHER SIGN, would be, MORE direct!! (AND, FOR THIS CAT to consider, ANYTHING else WOULD BE, an insult TO, HIS INTELLECT!!!). SO, on foot, he ventured that way! (((AFTER, cocking to the side, on his head, a fitted kelly green Eagles cap, HOW HE ALWAYS COCKS HIS CUSTOM RED, CUSTOM-MADE RED HATS, THE EXACT same way!))). FOR, TO THIS cat, THAT sea of BLUE and RED, could ONLY mean...THE CAUSE, OF that crime scene...HAS TO BE... THAT, CRAZY-MUTHA'-FUCKIN'-TIER-THREE!!!

AND SO...

NOT ONLY DOES, THIS - DIRTY - TAKIN'-LIBERTIES-ON-DUTY-BETWEEN-HOOKERS'-KNEES - VICE-COP, GOT TO - DRIVE FROM HERE, (IN HIS BIG-ASS-CADDY-WITH-BIG-ASS-RIMS!), STRAIGHT TO, SKIN'S COFFEE SHOP - NON-STOP!

BUT, (HE'S GOT TO DO IT WITH)...

POCKETS - IN THE TRUNK OF THE CAR - OF AN UNDERCOVER COP!!!

(((AND Y'ALL THOUGHT Y'ALL ALREADY KNEW THE WHOLE DAMN PLOT!!!)))

Chapter Twenty Two

CHRISTMAS MOURNING

And so, Mr. Brotha Trife, *after he shot that "3-Pointer-Crossover-Fadeback"*, finds himself back, at his door No.12 bungalow. And, once back, he finds himself, as Pockets, told him so. *(That, he would find himself, finding that he will, while, lying-low in the city, having some time to kill).*

And so...

Mr. Brotha Trife, retrieves his suitcase, from off the bedroom floor. And, once having retrieved his song book, from his suitcase, Mr. Brotha Trife, makes his way into the kitchen, post haste!

For *(AND WITH)*...

Thoughts of Anna Mossitti, songs of her, in his song book, he plans to fill!

AND...

(((THE REALLY FUCKED-UP PART IS!!!)))...

OF those songs, FOR Pockets, (((OF songs OF Anna Mossitti!!!))), Mr. Brotha Trife, is gonna' write them with,...a red feather quill! (Oy Vey!).

FOR...

Sitting atop of that kitchen counter, sits Mr. Brotha Trife. And, sitting next to him, is his bullet-hole-hat! (Which, sits on the kitchen's countertop, upsidedown). And, OF WHICH, the *"collected-blood"* from Y.S.' head*(((FROM WHEN SHE SHOT HERSELF DEAD!!!)))*sits, as it HAS - *"settled-in"* - THAT hat's band! *Tacky. Funky. Dank. Wet. Burgandy. And, brown!*

And, (sitting next to that!)...

Is Pockets', red feather quill! (And, it sits, in a tiny red bottle). *Where, prior to that, it sat, way in the back, amongst and with, the black mold and the rat shit, under one of those kitcken cabinets, just this morning, Mr. Brotha Trife, flung open!*

For(YOU SEE!)...

IT'S the VERY SAME red feather quill and tiny red bottle that,...Brotha Trife stole! (As it, sat on Pockets' red mahogany desk!), in that ALL RED EVERYTHANG APARTMENT! (((OH, 'BOUT...1, 260 DAYS AGO OR SO!!!))).

AND SO(YOU SEE!!)...

(For, Morris knew, he could do it with time. Tech knew, he could do it with a 9)...

SO...

Mr. Brotha Trife's GONNA' sit right here! (And, WITH THIS day, STAY ON his grind!!).

AS...

He *thinks* about, *"Pouring my soul INTO a song...ABOUT a girl...that AIN'T mine!"* (((DIPPING that red quill in the blood of Y.S. - writing lyrics in his song book - AS he composes a rhyme!)))

DOIN' IT FOR THE LOVE, NOT THE MONEY!!!

But...

OF THE song he writes, IF he can get rich with this,...even better! And, if not, Mr. Brotha Trife KNOWS that, he'll BE just fine! (For, EVERYONE'S got, a story to tell!). Mr. Brotha Trife, JUST WANTS to share - HIS WORDS - with the world. And, HE KNOWS, THAT, HE'LL DO IT... (all ON God's time!).

And so...

Of, thoughts of the future. Of, thoughts of Anna Mossitti. (A future, with her, that he KNOWS,...he can NEVER have!)...(((ALL DUE TO THOUGHTS OF LOYALTY!!!))) And of, thoughts of feeling blue. And of, thoughts in his head. Of, writting a blues tune. And of, thoughts of the day, that, he knows,...he'll miss her THE MOST!

AND, *(ON THAT!)*...

THIS IS WHAT, MR. BROTHA TRIFE, SITTING ATOP, OF THAT KITCHEN COUNTERTOP, COMPOSED:

CHRISTMAS MOURNING

No it don't look like Christmas morning,
When my baby's not around,
No presents under the tree,
'Cause, no tree to be found,
No snow,
Only tears fall down,
No it don't look like Christmas morning,
When my baby's not around,

No stockings hung up by the fire,
AIN'T NO Christmas lights to take down,
It DON'T EVEN FEEL LIKE it's Christmas,

AIN'T NO MISTLETOE TO BE FOUND!,
NO IT DON'T LOOK LIKE CHRISTMAS MORNING!
I'm just bending all these strings,
Tryna' DROWN OUT tha' sound,

SITTING by the fire WITHOUT YOU,
IT'S SO COLD!,
I see the flames glowing,
BUT YOUR SHADOW DOESN'T SHOW!,
NAAAAAAH!,
AIN'T NO CHRISTMAS MORNING!,
NO it don't look like Christmas morning,
WHEN MY baby's NOT around,
No snow,
ONLY tears fall down,
YEAH, GO ON AND GIVE IT TO ME ONE MORE TIME!,

No it DON'T feel like Christmas morning,
WHEN THE DEVIL RAT-A-TAT ON THE DOOR,
HE BEEN askin' me,
FOR my whiskey,
HE BEEN beggin' me,
For my soul,

NO IT DON'T LOOK LIKE CHRISTMAS MORNING,
WHEN THE DEVIL RAT-A-TAT ON THE DOOR,
He BEEN ASKIN' me,
FOR whiskey,
HE BEEN beggin' me,
FOR MY SOUL!,
NO IT DON'T LOOK LIKE Christmas morning...

And, (on that)...

Mr. Brotha Trife, of that red feather quill, in that tiny red glass bottle, he puts it back. *('Cause, "Christmas Mourning", IS THE ONLY SONG he'll compose - WITH Y.S.' blood - COLLECTED AND SETTLED in the band of his bullet-hole-hat!).* And, he gets to *thinking* 'bout, *sticking to the backroads. (And, affording himself a lil' extra time, in his travels).* 'Cause, before he goes to see, Anna Mossitti, (upon the midnight hour)...FIRST - he's GONNA' break INTO - that tiny-makeshift-morgue! *(((AND, HE KNOWS EXACTLY HOW HE'S GONNA' DO IT!!!))).* 'Cause, his Tier-Three-Mind, *IS PICTURING - Precinct One's - "Prisoner Release Door", ('round the back of the back!).*

"Yeah, THAT'S RIGHT! *IT'S THE SAME-DAMN-DOOR!",* as Mr. Brotha Trife, *is picturing it!, ('cause, Mr. Brotha Trife CAN picture it!),... ('CAUSE, HE'S SEEN IT BEFORE!!).*

FOR, *(it's the SAME-DAMN-DOOR!)...*

That, once upon a time, a recently-released prisoner - OF WHICH - stepped-out from the back! IN WHICH, Mr. Brotha Trife, pulled his car, up to him and distracted! (YOU REMEMBER WHEN!!!).

WHEN...

Nephew, came out the shadows! (((THEN, with the butt off his gun... PISTOL-WHIP CRACKED 'EM!!!))). Then, opened-up the trunk, and threw him in the back! (Then, drove his ass to Brotha Trife's BELOVED CEMETERY GROUNDS!!!). Then, drove down that winding-path and parked near, the pond in the back! THEN, "BOUND HIS HANDS AND TIED HIS FEET" TO THE TRUNK OF A TREE!!! THEN, LEFT HIS ASS - UNDER A PINETREE WITH HIS - ENTIRE HEAD - IN DUCT TAPE - WRAPPED IN!!! (((Yeeeaaahhh,...YOU remember THAT shit, DONT'CHA'!!!))).

AND SO,(the reason WHY, Mr. Brotha Trife, GOT TO thinkin' 'bout the backroads)...

IS because, (though, as of late, he HAS BEEN sticking to the backroads!), HOWEVER, something has NOW just dawned-on-him...and, HE knows! (THAT, IF HE WERE the ORIGINAL Brotha Trife - and, NOT - WORKIN' WIT THIS TIER-THREE-MIND)...THAT, what JUST dawned-on-him - WOULD HAVE - dawned-ON-HIM,...A LONG TIME AGO!!!

(((HMM!!!)))...

AND SO...

Mr. Brotha Trife, ponders, "HOW COME, EVEN OUT ON the main drag...AND, EVEN on these backroads,...I AIN'T SEEN - NOT ONE MARKED POLICE CAR - ((for TWO WHOLE days now!!)), IN THIS ENTIRE, fucking city!?!?!?"

AND SO!!!...

(((BY, A MAJOR FUCKING TASK FORCE, Mr. Brotha Trife, KNOWS THAT,...HE IS BEING FOLLOWED!!!!!!))) .

Chapter Twenty Three

A "FUCKING BIRDS" NIGHT

*A*nd so, Mr. Brotha Trife, laid-low, (until it was night!). *And, got back on his giddy-up, (when it was time to go!). AND, he did, IN FACT - STICK TO - the backroads!* (((AND, STILL, HE HASN'T SEEN, NOT ONE, MARKED POLICE CAR!!!))). *AND, YES, BY UNDERCOVERS AND SHIT, Mr. Brotha Trife, WOULD GUARANTEE, THAT, HE IS, BEING FOLLOWED!!!*

(But?)...*(((WHY???)))*

FOR...

(Mr. Brotha Trife's - Tier-Three-Mind - SHOULDN'T have ANY remembrances OF - ANYTHING that's OCCURRED - AFTER - the tips of Brotha Trife's dreadlocks, a beaming gold, were dyed!)

'Cause...

THAT'S WHERE his, DNA-Cloning-Sample, CAME from!

And...

ANYTHING that HAS OCCURRED, IN Brotha Trife's life, AFTER THAT POINT, Mr. Brotha Trife's Tier-Three-Mind, SHOULD NOT HAVE, ANY KNOWLEDGE OF!!!

BUT...

(AS TO THE REASON WHY-*TO-WHY, AFTER THAT POINT IN TIME, THAT BROTHA TRIFE'S DREADLOCKS WERE DYED, MR. BROTHA TRIFE'S TIER-THREE-MIND, CAN PICTURE AND, KNOWS CERTAIN SHIT..., IS 'CAUSE HE GOT A SPIRIT GUIDE... IN THE SKY!!! (((For, Brotha Trife, IS watching HIS back, FROM up above!!!))).*

BUT, *(((the question,...IT STILL REMAINS!)))...*

"*WHY* are THESE cocksuckin' undercovers,...FOLLOWIN' ME???", Mr. Brotha Trife, asks himself, "MAYBE they think,...I'M somebody else?!?", (and then, continues, to talk to himself), "Nah, it's THIS music industry! FOR, that's WHAT IT'S hittin'! I guess, I just GOTTA' GET USED to havin' NO privacy! THIS "INDUSTRY" IS RUTHLESS!!! *IT took my eye...IT TOOK MY HOMEGIRL Y.S.! ...AND, HER TWIN SISTER, TURNED-UP MISSIN'!!*"

And, even though, Mr. Brotha Trife, IS being crept on by his foes. He, with suitcase in hand and, with limited edition gold lenses on his nose and, with his bullet-hole-hat pulled down low, Mr. Brotha Trife, breaks into the back door, of Precinct One! Successfully! ('CAUSE he's inside!) And, FROM the outside THAT door,...JUST looks undamaged and closed!

And, once inside, Mr. Brotha Trife, immediately heads towards the stairs that'll, lead him to the precinct's basement. And, after going down that flight, he kills the basement's hallway lights. *And, in the basement's darkness,* he makes his way to the door, of Pricinct One's tiny-makeshift-basement-morgue,...(((*BY FOLLOWING THE SMELL OF FORMALDEHYDE!!!)))*)(((*OY VEY!!!*))).

And...

(YOU KNOW HOW, Mr. Brotha Trife's GONNA' do!)...

'Cause...

HE'S ALREADY INSIDE!!!

'CAUSE...

(((HE can break into a morgue,...A WHOLE LOT QUICKER THAN YOU!!!))).

And(once inside)...

He turns on the lights. (And, what he sees, IS WHAT he CAME there FOR!). THOUGH, WHAT he SEES, MAKES him (((RIGHT THEN AND THERE!!!))) CONTEMPLATE SUICIDE!!!

For*(IN there)*...

WITH that STENCH, OF deterioration AND decay. And, in there, WITH all those dead people (((that, had NO idea!!!))) *that, WHEN they PUT ON their underwear* (THAT morning!), *OR put that watch ON their wrist* (THAT, they're STILL wearing!)...(((DOING OF, WHAT they TOOK for GRANTED!!!!))), *THAT, THAT WOULD BE THE LAST TIME THAT, THEY WOULD, EVER DO IT!!!*...((('CAUSE, THEY'D BE DEAD,...LATER THAT DAY!!!))). And, IN THAT MORGUE, WITH a bunch of hookers *(((WHERE, THAT stench, JUST HANGS IN THE AIR, 'CAUSE, IN THERE, IT'S SO DAMN COLD!!!)))* and, RIGHT IN THERE, WITH THAT HOOKER, Gidget Cole, well, Mr. Brotha Trife, sees his Nephew lying there. Damn, homie. (We was 'sposed to be drinkin' 40's and talkin' shit...when we was old:(

And...

(What could be the reason why, Mr. Brotha Trife, broke into that tiny morgue?)...

Well...

He's GOT to bring himself TO DO,...what he COULDN'T do before!!

FOR...

(When he first saw, his Nephew lying dead, on Legs' apartment floor)...

Unc, was GONNA'...RUN THROUGH HIS Nephew's pockets! (But, the very THOUGHT of doing that, TORE HIM UP!!!)...

'CAUSE...

(((HE'S SEEN, POCKETS, DO SOME GRIMY-SHIT, LIKE THAT BEFORE!!!)))

And well(AND, BUT STILL!!)...

Unc, IS STILL, disgusted WITH himself, *(FOR JUST HAVING the VERY THOUGHT OF IT!!),* BUT, HE *KNOWS, HIS NEPHEW, (AS, TO WHY!), KNOWS THE DEAL,* THAT, HIS UNCLE, AIN'T JUST GOIN' THROUGH A DEAD MAN'S POCKETS,...TO STEAL!!!

And so...

ALTHOUGH, Unc, feels bad, (((YET, AND, BUT STILL))), HE... unzips that white disaster bag! And, RETRIEVES from HIS Nephew's pockets,...a pair of gold cufflinks, keys to a yacht, and a...docking pass!

And, as Unc, remains there in that morgue with his Nephew, he removes his gold eyes, (for, YOU SEE), he wants to look at his Nephew, with nothing, obstructing his view. And, as he looks at his Nephew, *AND upon the OUTCOME that this street life,* WILL bring you to, *(((AND, DO TO you!!!))),* Unc, *wonders* aloud, as he, *says, "Nephew, WAS soooooo in love WITH the streets! I wonder, IF Nephew, EVER knew love, IN this street life?* THE STREETS, AIN'T NEVER LOVED NOBODY, I EVER knew!"

And then, Unc, kissed his Nephew on his forehead. And then, zipped him back up. And, then said a prayer for his Nephew and, all IN there with him that were dead.

And then, as quick as Mr. Brotha Trife, had gained entry. THAT BROTHER SPLIT!!! Killed the lights, locked that morgue door back up tight, back up the stairs, EVEN turned back on the basement's hallway lights!

And, SINCE, IN the precinct, HE WAS ALREADY inside! IT WASN'T SHIT FOR HIM, ONCE AT THE TOP OF THE BASEMENT STAIRS, JUST TO GO UP THE NEXT FLIGHT!

FOR, Mr. Brotha Trife, MOVED LIKE a Nigerian incense smoke trail, through those doors! AND, up and down those stairs! AND, through Precinct One's halls! ARRIVING at HIS destination, that ALL RED EVERYTHANG apartment, upstairs...ABOVE THE LAW!!!

And, with cops downstairs, (doin' cop shit). And, with Mr. Brotha Trife with, suitcase-in-hand, stands before that all red everythang door, at the top, of a long flight of, old-musty-smellin' stairs, (in an upstairs hallway dimly lit). And, with bullet-hole-hat atop his head, cocked hard to the side. And, with limited edition 24 karat golds, obscuring his swollen and stitched-shut *FUCKED-UP* eye. And, with a deep exhale, from out of his lungs. And, with a rat-a-tat on, that red door. Anna Mossitti opens it up. And, though one ain't acting, THEY BOTH ACTING, LIKE they AIN'T NEVER SEEN THE OTHER ONE BEFORE!!

For...

Anna Mossitti, starts hitting his chest, after jumping into his arms, after she let out a scream, before she started crying, before she started kissing him, before she said unto him, "I've missed you so much!"

AS...

(((Mr. Brotha Trife, stands there, at the top of those long musty stairs, in a hallway dimly lit. AS, he *thinks* to himself, AS HE'S getting screamed at, JUMPED ON, HIT and, THEN finally KISSED, *"Yup! SHE THINKS, I'M Brotha Trife!!! MISSED ME so much??? I DON'T know WHAT tha' FUCK, SHE'S talkin' 'bout!! BUT, I'MA FIND OUT!! Yeeeeeeaaaaaahhhhh, weeeeeellllll, MIGHT be KINDA' shitty, BUT,... HEY, I'M DOWN!!!")))*

And so...

With both inside that all red everythang apartment and, with that all red door locked and closed, Anna Mossitti, takes her sexy walk cross that red shag carpet and, Mr. Brotha Trife's, JUST-STEADLY-WATCHIN'... THAT ASS AS it's thrown!!

"I've been SO lonely. And YOU'RE back! WE'RE celebrating ALL NIGHT!!", Anna Mossitti, says, grabbing two bottles of champagne from the 'fridge, adjourning to the all red everythang living room, placing both bottles on the red coffee table made of marble, sitting down on the plush red leather sofa, (patting the sofa cushion next to her), offering him to sit, (getting herself ready for a night of drinks and conversations and shit!).

Sitting down on the sofa, (though, not the cushion next to her). You DAMN right, Mr. Brotha Trife, IS up for a good night! (But,...would REALLY like to grab a shower AND put on some clean threads FIRST!) So, with a bit of a "stall-tactic", (PLUS, HE AIN'T TRYNA' BE *STUCK!* SO, HE CAN'T BE *GETTING BACK INTO THESE OLD HABITS* AND STUFF!!!), he says, to her, "Hey, listen. I don't drink or do drugs no more. I'm goin' clean and sober, love."

"OH, REALLY?? WELL, *YOU sure SMELLED like, YOU'VE BEEN GETTIN' IT IN, when I saw you at YOUR statue earlier!* SO, JUST KEEP DRINKIN', honey! 'CAUSE, if YOU DON'T get it in WITH ME,... YOU DON'T get it in WITH ME!", Anna Mossitti, tells him, (with a playful wink!).

Then...

Anna Mossitti, removes those 24 karat golds from his face and, looks him in his eye.

And...

(He looks right back with that - side-to-side - looking into both of her eyes - one eye at a time - type-of-look - with his one good eye - while looking into her eyes!!)...

And then, she says, to him, "HEY! YOU had those tats under your eyes removed! WHATCHA' do THAT for???", (Proverbs 15:3, Keeping a watchful eye on the wicked and the good, ARE the EYES of the Lord).

And(ONCE AGAIN!)...

HE just plays it like, he knows WHAT she is talking about! (ACTING like it's not AN act!).

'CAUSE...

(Tellin' her THAT HE'S a clone, PROBABLY GONNA' FREAK-HER-THE-FUCK-OUT!!!)...(((AND, THEN, HE'LL NEVER GET HER, OUT THIS CITY!!!)))

And...Yeah! (WHAT he's doin', IS shitty!)...

BUT...

HE AIN'T TRYNA' BE *STUCK, LIKE HE WAS, IN EMRALD HALL, LYING ON HIS BACK!!!*

And so...

Thinking fast, ('cause, he AIN'T quite sure, *WHAT Brotha Trife and her HAD goings-on, way back!!)*, Mr. Brotha Trife, snatches a bottle of that champage and, hops-up-off the sofa, pops that bottle and, Anna Mossitti, snatches that bottle RIGHT back!, (AIN'T GOT NO champagne glass!), so Anna Mossitti, STRAIGHT LOOKS HIM DEAD IN HIS EYE, as he in her eyes he looks RIGHT back, with that - side-to-side - looking into both of her eyes - one at a time - type-of-look - while looking into her eyes, as she licks the entire length of the side, (of that champagne bottle's neck and side!), as Mr. Brotha Trife, remains trapped in her eyes and, trapped between her, the red marble coffee table and, that big plush red leather sofa, as the bubbly bubbles over!

AND SO(OY VEY!)...(the next morning)...

Mr. Brotha Trife, wakes-up with Anna Mossitti, asleep on his chest, on that plush red leather sofa, AS SHE GETS AWOKEN, by his words being spoken, "Those FUCKING birds!!!", *(AS, THOSE FUCKING BIRDS, WILL LET, ANY LATE-NIGHT-DRINKER KNOW, THAT, YOU'VE DONE IT AGAIN!!! NOW, WAKE-YOUR-ASS UP!! YOU GOT SHIT TO DO!!)...(((THE PARTY IS OVER!!!)))*.

"SHIT!", Mr. Brotha Trife, says aloud, NOW realizing FROM her look (AND, those fuckin' birds!), THAT, HE'S got some explaining to do...(RIGHT NOW!), "No, listen, babygirl, I don't regret last night, one bit. But, *LAST NIGHT,...we SHOULDA' dipped!!* NOW, we GOTTA' wait 'til tonight!", as he, looks at those empty champagne bottles, (AND the morning sun, LOOKING HIM IN THE EYE!), before, continuing, "Like I said, love. I have no regrets, 'bout last night. BUT, I GOTTA' KEEP a clear head FOR this music shit,...FOR just LIFE in general."

And, Anna Mossitti, replies, (still lying on his chest!), "Honey, I have no doubts the two of us can make beautiful music together, we already have. But, IF you think you're gonna be or stay clean and sober, let ME, tell YOU, something, honey. You're gettin' into the wroooooong "game", EVEN with that *soothing-voice* OF yours!", (as she's, only trying to be as honest AS she can!), (*as she, kissed him on his chest, after each sentence that she said!*).

Sitting up, (the best that he can!), with Anna Mossitti, still lying on his chest, propping himself up, (as he bares, her weight and his), on his elbows and forearms, he says, to her, "Nah, love. YOU got it, ALL wrong! YOU WATCH! ...Im'a be iight."

Closing her eyes, she buries her face in his chest (kissing it, one last time), before, she, looks up into his one good eye, and, replies, "The "music game" and the "drug game" are one in the same. Where you find music...you find drugs...AND it's all just one big hustle!"

SPEAKING OF HUSTLE!

(LET'S HUSTLE ON OVER AND DROP IN ON OL' SKINS AND THAT DIRTY-DRINKIN'-N-SWEARIN'-PULLIN'-HOOKERS'-HAIR-ON-DUTY-VICE-COP)..(SHALL WE?)

FOR...

THEY HAD AN INTERESTING EVENING, AS WELL (TO SAY THE LEAST!), WHILE THOSE FUCKING BIRDS LAST NIGHT, WERE STILL ASLEEP!

SO...

(LET'S SEE HOW THAT SHIT PLAYED OUT, WHEN THE DIRTY VICE COP SHOWED UP AND MET WITH SKINS, SHALL WE???)...(YES, I THINK WE MUTHA'-FUCKIN' SHALL!!!)

AND SO...

As the dirty vice cop arrived at Skin's coffee shop, he parked his big ass undercover Caddy (with the big ass rims!) 'round back and, went in the back with, Pockets, locked in the back, in the trunk, in stowe! (Oy vey!).

And, with a few, "OOOOOOOH'S!!!" (and, with a few "three-fingered" points!!!), Skin's crew and Skin's muscle, LET'S that dirty vice cop KNOW, that ONLY "friends of theirs" are allowed, to come waltzing in unnanounced, (through the back door of THEIR joint!).

For Skin's, HAS been RUBBED RAW! AND, when THAT happens, (oh boy, here it comes…wait for it…wait for it…), as a result, usually, resulting in, ONE GETTING RUBBED OUT!!! (OY!).

BUT, Skin's don't want to give the order, (to one of his men), to rub out the man, sworn to keep peace and order. So, he orders his muscle, to unhand the man. And, Skin's himself, tells the unhanded-man, to have a seat at his round table, (ordering and causing disorder!), ordering one of his men, to give up his seat, to the unhanded-man and, for his own man to stand!

And so…

(The dirty vice cop, at Skin's round table, takes a seat, under heavy cigar smoke and guys packing heavy heat!)…

At which time…

Skin's, tells the dirty vice cop, "You's either DRUNK OR YOU'S HIGH, comin' in UNANNOUNCED, into THIS I.A. Club of mine! THIS SHIT, BETTA' be important! And, I don't know nuttin' 'bout, no gasoline taxes bein' extorted! You's sittin' here. But, DON'T YOU'S think, YOU'S playin' cards, wit US!! SO, you's BEST stop fuckin' playin' games! And,…SINCE my boys here, CAN'T seem to locate Legs,…YOU'S BEST-BE-HERE to tell ME, YOU'S KNOW WHERE, LEGS IS AT! SO, I CAN GO KILL HIM MYSELF! AND, THAT'S the ONLY thing, YOU'S BEST-BE-HERE, TO SAY!"

And so…

(Slammin' down the rock glass closest to his hand, after slammin' down the V.O., the dirty vice cop, tells Skin's the BAD news that, he had for him, before finding out THAT comin' here, WAS a BAD idea!)…

AS...

Gettin' gripped-up BY SKIN'S MUSCLE, let's him know!(Oy Vey!).

THEN...

The dirty vice cop, PLEADS for HIS life!! (THAT, he WASN'T IN ON IT!)((THE KILLING OF LEGS!!))...(((as he, snitches on the one, who's return to this city, has finally come,...the one and only, Brotha Trife!!!))).

THEN...

He's slammed back down into his seat! (After pleading to Skin's, "Wait a minute! I still got some GOOD news, you ain't hear yet!!)...

(Come. Let's listen in!)...

"Listen to me, Skin's! I DID what you been, payin' me to do! I DID, locate Legs! UNFORTUNATELY, tha' mutha' fucka' WAS dead! WHAT'S a brother, to do?!? ...Ain't like, Y'ALL, found his rat-ass first. FUGGETABOUTIT!!!", the dirty vice cop, tells Skin's, while HAVING a laugh, (at SKIN'S EXPENSE!).

'Cause...

The dirty vice cop KNOWS, (though, he AIN'T playin' cards!),('cause, he CAN'T play in THIS card game!),('cause, only "friends of ours" can play in THIS card game!),('cause, "friends of ours" AIN'T friends of "those"), and, even though, he can clearly see, that, with Skin's salt and pepper bangs hanging down over his eyes, Skin's is clearly peeved! Regardless, though, the dirty vice cop, POURS HIMSELF a healthy glass of V.O., so that he and Skin's can have drink. (((AND, HE'S BEING SO BOLD, 'CAUSE, HE KNOWS, HE'S GOT,...AN ACE UP HIS SLEEVE!)))...

"Raise you glass wit me, Skin's. Now, I know, you're all pissed-off 'n shit, findin' out 'n shit, killin' Legs yourself, is off tha' table.", the dirty vice cop, begins, before looking back up over his shoulder, (the one that Skin's muscle is standing over!), before, continuing, "YEAH, AS I was sayin'! AND, YOUR MUSCLE here, is makin' it pretty fuckin' crystal clear, I better find Brotha Trife FOR you, SO you can kill him, YOURSELF! BUT, what IF I told you,

I ALREADY found you,...SOMEBODY ELSE!!", (Skin's, just looks cross the round table, up at his muscle, prompting the dirty vice cop, from his place at the round table, to be muscled!), "YO', Skin's, I DON'T appreciate the treatment, brah!! I AM, THE LAW, AFTER ALL!!", the dirty vice cop, let's it be known, (in and from the clutches of the muscle's paws!).

"GET HIM OUTTA' HERE! GET HIM THE HELL OUTTA' HERE!! AND, DON'T YOU'S COME BACK 'TIL YOU'S, GOT SOME REAL NEWS!!!", Skin's, shouts back!, (before, the dirty vice cop, is muscled-out the back door, head under shoes!!).

Landing on his back, (after being thrown the hell out the back!), the dirty - gettin'-a-charge-charging-prostitutes-on-duty-gettin'-off-on-knockers-after-knockin'-prostitue's-charges-down-gettin'-a-charge-gettin'-prostitues-off - vice cop, drove back cross town, with Pockets, STILL in the trunk, IN STOWE!

And, since the dirty vice cop, has BEEN on the mob's payroll, trailin' Anna Mossitti, (((FOR THE MOB!!!))), EVERYWHERE SHE GO, the dirty vice cop, IN FACT, WAS at "old" SYKE Park earlier in the day, at high noon, layin'-low, under slabs of concrete, layin' on debris and rubble, as he lay!

UNFORTUNATELY...

(FOR the dirty vice cop, HE DIDN'T get the chance to tell Skin's, any of that!)...

'Cause...

Skin's, was trippin' ON his power!

AND SO...

(The dirty vice cop, after being thrown the hell out of the club, with Pockets, STILL LOCKED IN HIS TRUNK, drove back cross town...

And...

Was standing at the far end of a dimly lit hall, observing Mr. Brotha Trife, enter that all red everythang apartment,...UPON THE MIDNIGHT HOUR!!!

And so...

With his ear, pressed up against, that all red everythang's, red apartment door. The dirty vice cop, heard Anna Mossitti and Mr. Brotha Trife, recording "Christmas Mourning"!

As...

THAT DIRTY VICE COP, stood there, LISTENING TO THEM, doing that...(((AND MORE!!))).

And then...

The dirty vice cop, drove BACK over to Skin's...(You KNOW WHERE!)...

WHERE...

ONLY "connected guys", (((WITH IMPUNITY))) OR, "their friends", NEVER get ticketed for double-parking! And, NEVER get towed-off, (for parking, up on!), a city's street center-median! (FUGGETABOUTIT!!!).

AND SO, (ONCE AGAIN!)...

(The dirty vice cop, parked 'round back, of Skin's "coffee shop")...

And, (ONCE AGAIN!)...

HE walked right IN the back!

'Cause, (NOW!)...

HE'S GOT a ROYAL FLUSH up HIS sleeve!!!!!

AND, (THIS TIME!)...

He AIN'T here TO take NO crap!!

And(UPON THAT!)...

Polyester knees get banged together!! (As, wooden feet get slid back from the round table!!). As, the dirty vice cop, through the back, of La Alla Banca, walked back in!!

AND...

(YOU know that, he was met, with "stand up guys", standing-up, from Skin's crew!)...

AND...

(Skin's muscle did, WHAT Skin's muscle, was 'sposed TO do!)...

BUT...

(With THAT ROYAL FLUSH up his sleeve?)...

That dirty vice cop, just PUSHED-ON THROUGH!!!!! (Talkin' bout, as he, sat cross from Skin's), "Skin's, I's 'gwine double my normal fee, FOR tha' "411", I's GOT FOR YOU!!"

(Prompting, Skin's)...

To look up from the round table, at his muscle.

(Prompting, the muscle!)...

To reach inside his sports coat, pulling out a...

...white envelope to pay the brother! (GOTCHA'!!!:)

(Prompting, the dirty vice cop!)...

To riffle cash like cards, so as to inform, "THAT envelope's JUST for my leg work. I's 'gwine needs me ANOTHER one, JUST LIKE that one, for WHEN I bring YOU in, Pockets, unharmed!"

(PROMPTING, Skin's!)...

To the dirty vice cop, to retort, "You's tellin' me, YOU'S know WHERE Pockets, is at??? AND, he bet'ta' be unharmed! 'CAUSE, I'MA do THAT! And, you's BET'TA' know, WHERE he is! YOU'S bet'ta' NOT BE TRYIN' to extort! OR, I'MA cut your balls off!! AND, bury them WIT YOU'S, under concrete FRESHLY poured!!!"

(Prompting, the dirty vice cop!)...

To push up from the round table, sayin', "I's 'gwine be RIGHT back!", then, looks at the muscle, sayin' to him, "Get ready to pay me, paesan!", (WITH that, EXPENSIVE laugh!).

(PROMPTING, Skin's!)...

To laugh, (a very COSTLY rolling-laugh!!), "YOU'S so FULLA' shit!!", Skin's, begins, then his polyester pants pocket he digs in, then splashes the pot, with a fourfold knot roll, he pulled from within, "Ok, cop! I'll CALL you's bluff!! ALL that cash belongs to you's, IF YOU'S can REALLY do that!!!!"

And...

(A few mintues later, walkin' back in on Skin's card game)...

IS that dirty - on-duty-beatin'-the-mob-at-their-own-game - vice-cop, AND, TO Skin's, SOMEONE, THAT, resembled POCKETS! (THOUGH, NOT QUITE THE SAME!!)...

FOR...

(To the BEST OF, Skin's recollection, the man, standing by the man, by the looks of the man, by his namesake, bilaterial pants pockets of two-hundred grand, looked nothing, by which, he received, his name!!)...

FOR...

((((Pockets, looks exasperated, FROM BEING LOCKED IN A TRUNK!!! AND, he's got dried snot, under his nose! AND, he's got tear tracks, that have dried, under his eyes!! FROM being maced in his face! BEFORE being PUNCHED in his gut!)))...

AND, the LAST TIME, Skin's, got a look at Pockets, a custom-made custom red suit, with the matching custom-made custom red hat, cocked hard to the side, was what he was rockin'! (The brother stayed clean!).

BUT(NOW!)...

(So, that, he could move on foot undetected, throughout the city unsuspected, on a mission, OF: "See-And-NOT-Be-Seen"!), Pockets, IS

dressed in throwback Eagles gear, with a snapback Eagles cap, (cocked hard to the side!), of kelly green!

"Who's this guy?? You's playin' games!?! YOU'S, FUCKIN'-DICKHEAD-COP, YOU'S!!!", Skin's, yelled, at the dirty vice cop!

"Play YOU, Skin's!?!", the dirty vice cop, wisely-unwise-to-comprise-such-a-hustle-replied, then removed that fourfold knot roll from the pot, then wisely did not, riffle enough cash to make that, rubber band removed from 'round his wrist, wrapped 'round that knot roll pop! All before he then, took a seat back at the round table, in the very same spot! All before he then, motioned for Skin's, to lean in. All before he then, leaned forward cross the round table, himself leaning in. And, THEN, the dirty vice cop, whispered in Skin's ear, BEING WATCHED, by made men, that looked at him, like, don't fuck up 'cause, YOU'S AIN'T ONE OF "OUR FRIENDS"!!!

(Prompting, Pockets!)...

INCENSED, to glare into the eyes of the dirty vice cop!!

(PROMPTING, Skin's!)...

To look up from the round table at his muscle. (through bangs of pepper and salt!!).

(Prompting, cause)...

Of the resulted salt and pepper swipped, as Pockets, resulted the cause of his clandestine conversation to stop!

(Prompting, the muscle!)...

TO come down heavy, on Pockets, "The Boss offered you the chance to meet him. Sit down. OR I'LL sit YOU down!! DON'T embarrass the Boss. OR I'LL give you a beatin'!!", (under heavy cigar smoke, under heavy ballads, under heavy love notes, heavy heat under sports coats, under heavy frowns, all adds up to a lot of weight, and, it ain't gettin' any lighter, the balls on this fucking Pockets, is he actually gonna make the Boss wait, to take his place, to take his turn, to play his hand, at this - Poker-Game-Sit-Down - Meeting!?!)...

(PROMPTING, Pockets!!)...

To look down at the dirty vice cop's red-faced Rolex watch...and smile!

(Prompting, Pockets)...

To harken back a while...(to that shitty-ass lime green room, of the seedy Buena Vista Roadside Motel!)...

(FROM WAY BACK), WHEN...

His baby bro, (TOO COLD!!), told him that he was GONNA' peel that watch off that cop's wrist, AFTER he shot the teeth OUT his head!

((((PROMPTING, Pockets!)))...

To think,...(((("I SHOULDA' FUCKIN' LET HIM DO IT!!!"))))(((OY VEY!!!)))

HOWEVER...

Pockets, EVER the GAMBLIN' MAN, A Man, OF: ALWAYS jockeying FOR position, pulled a chair out for himself from the round table WITH force! (And, spun that bitch 'round!). Before, he did, in fact, took HIS seat, AT the round table! Though, seated in a position of that chair being STRADDLED, (stacked atop that chair's back are the forearms of this powerlifting avid!!), SEPARATED HIMSELF, WHILE seated AT the round table, indicated by his jockeyed-position, and, the position in which he cocked his kelly green brim, "Yeah, I'll sit down, but, I AIN'T down WITH them!!!"

BUT...

(business IS business!)

((((TOLD Y'ALL POCKETS GOT SOME SHIT TO HIM!)))... ((((Y'ALL BETTER START PAYING-THE-FUCK-ATTENTION!!!)))

And so...

As those fucking birds were still asleep. A Dirty. Grimy. Backstabbing. Rip-Off. Fuck YOUR Feelings, (in other words, a standard music industry deal was made!), between Pockets, Skin's and, the dirty vice cop! A three-headed monster! (I SAID COUNT THEM SHITZ!!!) (((THERE'S THREE!!!))). Come! Let's listen in on how THIS SHIT goes down, shall we? ...(YES!!!)...(I THINK WE FUCKING SHALL!!!)...

AND SO, (Skin's, begins!)..., "Tell Pockets, what you's just whispered to me."

And, (the dirty vice cop, complied)...(Telling Pockets, that, he heard this amazin'-soulful-voice,...of Brotha Trife!)

AND, (THAT!)...

What he heard, was Anna Mossitti and him, doin' a duet together, of this new Christmas song that, Brotha Trife wrote earlier that night. He said, he wrote it because, you, Pockets, was deep in this music game. And, could make him a big star. And, somethin' 'bout, havin' some time to kill. And, somethin' 'bout, Pockets givin' him, a song book. And, somethin' 'bout, it can be only hot fire songs, that Pockets, wanted him to write. (And, that, dirty vice cop, he was pretty sure, that, that's what he heard)...((BUT, he's DAMN SURE, that, Anna Mossitti's GOT, ONE helluva' SET of pipes!!)). And that, they recorded just the vocals, in just one take. And that, he ain't hear no more singin' after that(YEAH, SO, WELL, ANYWAYS:)they MUST have taken, a nice long break! (Oy VEY:) And that, they recorded it with, his homegirl's laptop mic. And that, the song was saved to, some singer Y.S.' thumb drive! And that, EVEN THOUGH, WHAT he heard, WAS through that all red everythang apartment door, pressed TO his ear, AS he was tryin' to be quiet. HOWEVER, he KNEW, THAT WHAT he heard, WAS A HIT SONG BEING RECORDED, ON THE OTHER SIDE!!!

Pockets, (staring blankly at the round table), shaking his head and, talking to himself in a haze, "I'll be damned. THAT Tier-Three-Motherfucker! It REALLY DID, ONLY take him,...a couple of days!"

"What's that?? Speak up! It only took you's goombata, a coupla' days, ta' fuckin' what? Write that hit Chrismas song?? Well,...I'M fuckin' impressed!", Skin's, says to Pockets, then continues, while scanning the room, (while shuffling a tall stack of his poker checks), "BUT, THAT'S the END of THAT, you's! RULE #2 in MY CLUB: Don't you's be talkin' UNDA' you's fuckin' breath!!"

"THAT'S RIGHT! You got somethin' to say? SAY IT!!!", the muscle, making his point, seconds the motion of RULE #2, at Pockets and, the dirty vice cop, by "three-finger-pointin'", (RULE #2: If it ain't whispered in Skin's ear, AIN'T NO whispering IN THIS joint!).

"Alright, you's pipe down, pipe down. Get our guests some drinks.", Skin's, tells his muscle, (as the dirty vice cop, slings his left arm, over the back of his seat).

(And, while drinks are being brought, Pockets, remained in deep thought)...

For...

There's poker chips on the table. (But,...AIN'T NO GAMES bein' played!).

FOR...

Seated AT THIS round table, is an old-school-hustler-and-playa'-turned-drug-kingpin-turned-music-exec., a dirty-fucking-bitches-on-duty-taking-chances-pictures-and-movies-vice-cop, and the "Skipper" in this town,...(and ALL HIS crew is made!).

(And, while liquor is being poured, into rock glasses, with no ice)...

Skin's, kicks it off, (by breaking the ice!), "Pockets, you's come into my fuckin' city,...a few years back. And, you's made out with a lot of money, the short amount of time, you's was here. But, you's never did clear that wit me. DID you's? Maybe you's didn't realize, that'a be a nice thing, for you's to do?? Maybe you's made a mistake? Maybe you's FUCKIN' greedy!?! Maybe you's didn't stop 'n think, there's things you could do for me?!? IF I'd EVEN LET YOU'S, FUCKIN' DO things FOR me!!! ...I'm going to decide that you's know the order,...that you's know how things have to happen. And, yet, you's NEVER DID make an attempt, for me, to extend my hand to you's, in friendship. What? I ain't gotta eat? Is that what you's think of me, ya' fuck?? I look like a man to you's that, ain't gotta eat too?? What? YOU'S think it's ok for you's, to not come to me in friendship, to extend YOU'S hand to me,...wit fuckin' street tax in it?? Let me ask you's somethin'...YOU'S think, MY family, WANTS for YOU'S, to fuckin' MAKE ME look bad??? YOU'S think, people

AREN'T gonna fuckin' talk??? YOU'S GOT ME lookin' like "Joe-Fuckin'-Jagoff" OV'A HERE!!! And, FOR THAT, AND, THAT ALONE, woulda' been enough for me ta' want ta' fuckin' clip you's! …You's got a lot of enemies in THIS town,…YOU'S KNOW THAT, right? You's got the NJPD,… excludin', this slimeball-fuck, sittin' here, that, wants'ta whack ya'! And, DON'T YOU'S EVA' QUESTION MY INTELLECT, JUST SO, that, YOU'S know! A coupla' years back, when Brotha Trife first showed-up in this town, IT'S 'CAUSE OF YOU'S! YOU'S brought him in here, WIT YOU'S, ya' motherfucka'! THEN, you's both "lambed-it" outta here, WHILE you's both STILL had the fuckin' chance!! And, NOW! …THAT psychotic-fuck, is back! And, YOU'S back! SO, that means, YOU'S fuckin' brought him BACK INTO MY CITY, WIT YOU'S!! So, appreciate my hospitality,…for even ALLOWING YOU'S ta' fuckin' sit here, at MY table. ACTUALLY, consider YOU'S-SELF FUCKIN' LUCKY, ya' prick! 'Cause, NOW, I DON'T wanna CLIP you's! The man, you's brought BACK into MY city, KILLED A MAN TONIGHT! IN MY FUCKIN' CITY!!! NOOOOOOOBODY in MY city, was 'sposed to touch THAT FUCKIN' JAGOFF MOTHERFUCKA', BUT ME!!! SO, Pockets,…if you's was in MY position,…WHAT would YOU'S DO,…IF YOU'S was ME?!?"

(And, Pockets, BEING Pockets, BEING a man, of: "already-been-done-had!" - HIS - "first taste" OF "big money" - AIN'T-GON'-GO-FO' - financially goin' below - that "bar" - that, he's set for himself, upon reaching that - "first taste of big money status" - that he reached, years ago!)…

ALTHOUGH…

Upon reaching his conclusion, of reachin' in his pockets this time, and payin' Skin's "monies owed" on that back street tax, OF THAT, Pockets, PAYS THAT,…no mind!!!

HOWEVER…

Pockets KNOWS, THAT TIER-THREE-MOTHERFUCKER, made for him, a - "precarious-position" - to be in!

NOTWITHSTANDING…

(Sitting in a position, of being seated at a round table, surrounded by "stand up" men, seated and standing!)(((FUGGETABOUTIT!!!)))...

BE THAT AS IT MAY...

(Pockets, NOW KNOWS, WHAT THAT dirty - ear-pressin'-all-red-everythang-on-duty-apartment-door-eavesdroppin' - vice-cop, INTO Skin's ear, WAS whisperin'!)...

And so...

(Pockets, BEING Pockets, he's got questions to ask. AND, he's got some questions to ask HIMSELF! AND, IT AIN'T NO QUESTION,...HE'S GOT TO DO IT FAST! SO that, the precarious-position he's in, he can, then assess. AND THEN, REASSESS!! IN RECORD TIME!!!)...

THOUGH...

Pockets, continued to not address Skin's question.

As...

(His Big-Hustle-Wheels, in his Big-Hustle-Mind...CONTINUED to grind!)...

AS...

(Pockets, in his own Big-Hustle-Mind, continued to contemplate)...

FOR...

HE WAS just thinkin' 'bout, HIS OWN ends!

AND...

(((HIS OWN-DAMN-FATE!!!)))...

(Come! Let's see HOW *Big-Hustle-Wheels,* in the music biz *GRIND)...*

"Ok. I'll LET Skin's clip that, Tier-Three-Motherfucker. Eh? What could that hurt? Hmm? I WON'T HAVE TO WORRY 'bout gettin' my hands on them reading materials, BEFORE THAT TIER-THREE-

MOTHERFUCKER, reads THEM SHITZ first! Hmm?? BUT, ACCORDING TO this-here dirty-fucking vice cop, THAT Tier-Three-Motherfucker's VOICE, IS STILL "intubation-voice-AMAZIN'"!!! BUT, his voice AIN'T GON' STAY like that forever,...SHIT! THAT intubation-voice, IS ON the clock! Hmm? Do I REALLY wanna serve-up THAT, Tier-Three??? Then again, talkin' to ME, like that? FUCK SKIN'S!!! BESIDES, I ALREADY GOT THAT TIER-THREE-MUTHA' FUCKA'S TRUST!!! I COULD MAKE ME A LOT OF MONEY WITH HIM!!! ...'SPECIALLY since, Y.S., got ALL flaky!!"

(And though, there's cards on the round table, and, the chips are stacked high)...

Pockets KNOWS, THAT, THE stakes ARE EVEN HIGHER!

'Cause...

(((HE AIN'T BEEN lifted clean-up-outta-his-chair - YET - 'round his neck - BY - a piano wire!!)))...(((FUGGETABOUTIT!!!)))

BUT...

Pockets, being the gamblin' man, (that he IS!), IS right IN HIS element!

And...

(((IN this, MUSIC BIZ, POCKETS KNOWS, that, Skin's WANTS IN!!!)))

'Cause...

Skin's POKER FACE, (OR LACK THEREOF!!!), IS tellin' it!!!

FOR...

(All this time, while, Pockets' *Big-Hustle-Wheels DID grind!*), *Pockets, did see, Skin's poker hand! For Skin's, been glancing over at a wall, (more specifically!), AT the picture frames that, they're hanging on)* (((With names like; Frankie Valli, Francis Albert and, Frankie Avalon!))) (((FUGGETABOUTIT!!!))).

And so...

Pockets, (EVER the GAMBLIN' MAN!), seated at the round table, KNOWS HOW he's gonna play, HIS poker hand!

FOR...

(HE'S GONNA' PLAY, the hand, HE'S BEEN delt!)...

'CAUSE...

((((The young fella positioned, standing behind Skin's, CERTAINLY appears to be, A music lover...HIMSELF!!!)))).

'Cause...

(Positioned WITHIN, Pockets, Big-Hustle-Mind, his Big-Hustle-Wheels, CONTINUED to grind!)...

"OK, Pockets, YOU GOT EVERYTHANG!! And so, YOU GOT THIS TOO!! SINCE, I've been here, that kid's been, singin' every song. Well, he's just been mouthin' the lyrics to himself. BUT, HE'S KNOWN the lyrics to EVERY song, THAT has, come on! And, since he's positioned that close to Skin's,...he's GOTTA' BE his son,...or his nephew,...or sumfin'! Ok, gamblin' man. It's TIME to PLAY, THIS hand!!!"

(Alright y'all! LET'S WATCH Pockets go to work!)...

"Ok then, Skin's. WHAT would, I do, IF I was in, YOUR position??? SHIIIIIIT, I WOULD ALLOW a man in MY position, TO MAKE HIM, A muthafuckin' STAR!", Pockets, says, of the lanky-loves-songs-love-songs-crooner-guy!(standing behind Skin's, but slightly off to tha' side, standing somewhere between the ages of 20-25, with jet black bangs that, just like Skins', when not slicked-back, hangs down into his eyes!!).

(FUCKING POCKETS YO!)

(Alright Skin's! Whatcha' got! For the gamblin' man, with the kelly green brim - to tha' side - FULLY cocked!)...

"You's know, Pockets, I was never THAT fuckin' impressed wit you's. You's fuckin' waltz into town, set-up fuckin' shop, and, in NO FUCKIN' TIME at all, GOT EVERY LAST STINKIN' COP, IN MY FUCKIN' town, IN you's pockets! And, why the fuck not!?! Fuckin' lookin' at THIS FUCKIN' FLAKE ov'a here, IT REALLY AIN'T too hard to fuckin' figure out, HOW you's fuckin' done it! BUT, I gotta hand it to you's, Pockets. You's a lot smarter, than I gave you's fuckin' credit for!", Skin's, explains to Pockets, (wit'a swipe at his bangs!), and, while he gives the dirty - (on-duty-you's-sittin'-here-outta-you's-element-seated-here-at-the-round-table-amongst-men-of-men) - vice cop, a swipe, (BY laughing at HIM, WITH THAT expensive laugh!). And then, Skin's, continues, after pointing his finger at the dirty - (on-duty-NOW-THINKIN'-HE'S-a-major-player-IN-THIS-MUSIC-GAME!) - vice cop, "This fuckin' cop sittin' here, at MY round table, sittin' here in MY club, tells me, you's some fuckin' "big shot" in the music industry now. Is that right? You's some kinda' fuckin' "big shot", ya' fuck ya'?!? Well,…you's motherfucka', I WANT IN!!! And, LET ME, TELL YOU'S somethin', you's know, 'CAUSE, I'm Italian. BUT, if not for US, there'd be NO FUCKIN' music industry, FOR YOU'S!!", Skin's, speaks on, (what's BEEN BURNING in his mind!),… (then, orders him, "Raise you's glass with me."), raising his glass to Pockets, (as Pockets, raises his glass back!), as the dirty-drinkin'-on-duty-vice-cop, raises his glass as well, (the poor soul, lost heavily at the poker table, in strong cigar smoke hanging heavy and strong sauce!!), as Skin's, addresses Pockets (and, ONLY Pockets!), "Well played, Pockets. Well played. I delt you's the fuckin' cards AND, you's played them…PERFECTLY. Salute!!"

And so…

(After, Pockets, took a taste of the toast)…

He KNEW BETTER, than to sit there, AT the round table, (amongst men of men!)…(EXCEPT for, THIS flaky-ass dirty vice cop!) and,…GET ALL FUCKED-UP!!!

REGARDLESS…

Of what Skin's prior preconceived thoughts were of Pockets' smarts, Pockets KNEW IT WAS A MUST, for him, to stay sharp!

FOR...

(HE ALREADY KNEW, IN his Big-Hustle-Mind, WHAT WAS TO COME NEXT!)...

..."Skin's, GOTTA' "EAT", TOO!! SO, SKIN'S, IS GONNA' WANT A BIG CUT, OF MY "TASTE"!!", (IS what HIS - Big-Hustle-Mind - SUSPECTS!!)...

SO...

Pockets, does what he LOVES doing and, that's ASKING questions, (to fig'a out the formula!), WHILE buying himself SOME time!

And so...

Pockets, looks cross the card table at the lanky young fella, who still hasn't left Skin's side, the one who's suit coat needs to be taken in and custom-tailored on the sides, the one who's continuously had a few strands of his jet black bangs, hangin' down over one of his eyes, and then, asks Skin's, "What's he sound like?"

(And, WHILE Skin's, is looking back over at the-skinny-lover-of-love-ballads-continuously-lip-syncing-love-ballads-standin'-over-his-right-shoulder, and, then, looking back at Pockets, Pockets' Big-Hustle-Wheels... ARE turnin'! And, as Skin's, then, looks over at the picture frames hanging on his wall, and, then, looks back at Pockets, Pockets, ALREADY knows, IN his Big-Hustle-Mind, WHAT Skin's answer IS GONNA' be for certain!)

And so...

Skin's, replies, "Who?? My son-in-law, Francis?? Would YOU'S fuckin' believe it, IF I told YOU'S, my daughter's husband, Francis, IS a DEAD-RINGER for "The Chairman" HIMSELF!!"

And, (ON THAT!!!)...

Pockets, raises his glass, while saying, "Salute!!", (((WHILE, AT THE SAME TIME, HIS Big-Hustle-Wheels, GOT HIM THINKING, IN HIS MIND))), "Ok, THIS is HOW, I'M GONNA' play it! It's MY label! AND,

THAT Christmas song was written BY MY signed artist! Soooooo, THAT MAKES THAT SONG,...MY SONG!! Shiiiiiit, I JUST GOTTA' get THAT Tier-Three-Motherfucker to re-record "final vocals" in MY mobile studio! WORSE-CASE-SENERIO...hmmm...I NEED TO get MY hands on that THUMB DRIVE! AND, THEN, I can just "mix and master" the-fuck-outta' it! AND, THEN,...VIOLA!! I GOT a version OF that song, WITH, THAT, INTUBATION-AMAZIN' VOICE ON IT! Yeah, so, well, ANYWAAAAAAYS, ol' Francis sounds like, "Sr.",...MY ASS!!! BUT, I'll appease Skin's! I'll "entertain" the THOUGHT, of Skin's son-in-law, Francis, recording "final vocals" on that Christmas song. AND, fuck-what-you-heard! ...I'LL put out BOTH versions!! AND, GET PAID OFF'A BOTH!! BUT, I GOTTA' GET my hands on Y.S.' latop AND thumb drive! 'CAUSE, THAT'S MY MUSIC ON THAT THUMB DRIVE!!! 'CAUSE, THAT'S MY MUSIC ON THAT LAPTOP!!! MY LABEL!!! MY MUSIC!!! MY STUDIO!!! MY CONTRACT GUY!!! MY SONG BOOK!!! MY THUMB DRIVE!!! MY ARTISTS!!! MY MAFUCKIN' MONEY!!! I'M POCKETS!!! I GOT EVERYTHANG!!! I'M ON TOP OF THE WORLD!!!!!! And so,...I GOT THIS TOO!!!" (And, ALL THAT, THAT FAST, IN HIS BIG-HUSTLE-MIND, ALL THE WHILE...just saying, "Salute!!").

"Ok, you's. Now, you's LISTEN to ME!", Skin's, begins, "I've WANTED TA' fuckin' clip you's for'a coupla' years now. SO, you's bet'ta say'a coupla' HAIL MARY'S...'cause, NOW,...I DON'T fuckin' want YOU'S clipped! BUT,...as you's know, THAT'S gonna fuckin' cost you's! ...I WANT you's ta' get "US", back IN the MUSIC BIZ!!! And, there's sumthin' else. That,... fuckin'...sociopath-artist of you's what-wrote that, fuckin' Christmas song,... HE gave you's life. 'Cause, HE'LL be THE ONE gettin' clipped, in place of YOU'S! He did, horrible, fuckin',...horrible-things, to...some - low-life-shit-bum - THAT,...he DIDN'T have NO fuckin' business touchin'! I dunno' if I'm more upset,...that,...he fuckin' did it,...or...if'e did it TOO fuckin' fast!!"... (For Skin's was gonna CLIP 'EM slow!)(FUGGETABOUTIT!!!)..."So, NOW, Pockets, there's "things" you's fuckin' GOT TO DO, ta' make things right. You's gotta make things right, Pockets. AND, YOU'S GONNA' MAKE THINGS, FUCKIN' RIGHT!!! Pockets, you's close to this guy, so you's gonna put this fuckin' maniac-songwriter of you's, in a place for me, ta' get close to him! ...And, I'll fuckin' take it from there,...fuggetaboutit. (then, pointing

cross the round table at the dirty vice cop), Skin's, continues,…"This prick cop ov'a here is gonna be you's driver, he's gonna be stuck ta' you's hip, until this gets done. So, DON'T let this take til' the middle of what'eva'. GET this motherfucka' close ta' me and, I'LL MAKE SURE, what's GOTTA' be done, IS done!" (afterwhich, Skin's reaches cross HIS round table, to extend his hand, to the music biz man, to seal the non-negotiable…music industry deal).

(While shaking hands, with Skin's),('cause, well,…NOW, THEY'RE BOTH IN IT TOGETHER!!)(FUGGETABOUTIT!!), Pockets smiles, while replying, "Ooooooooh! I SEE, YOUR HUSTLE, KNOWS NO BOUNDS, AS WELL!!"

(While pulling his hand out of Pockets'),('CAUSE, well,…THAT was, QUITE enough!), Skin's replies, with NOT THE LEAST BIT OF A SMILE, "Yeah. What'eva', you's. …You's NOTHIN', like me!"

And so…

(As, Skin's and Pockets discussed this music shit further,…they ALSO plotted!!)..

OF HOW: Skin's was GOING TO murder the muderer that murdered the man that got murdered, that NOBODY IN THIS CITY, WAS 'sposed to murder, BUT Skin's!(SHEW!).

And(EVEN THOUGH!)…

(It was, Pockets, who was gettin' Skin's INTO the "Music Industry Game"! IT WAS, Pockets, WHO WAS dealt a non-neogotiable hand by Skin's, SIMPLE AND PLAIN!)

EVEN SO…

(YOU SHOULD, ALREADY KNOW, that…THE RULES ARE THE RULES!!!)

AND SO…

(((Pockets, GONNA' MAKE-DAMN-SURE,…Skin's PAYS HIS MUSIC INDUSTRY DUES!!!)))

FOR...

AT THIS ROUND TABLE - NOT to be percevied - AS soft - IS a must!

But(For NOW!)...

((((Pockets, GOTTA' WORK ON CREATING - THAT - MC Busta Nut and False Profit - Meet 'n Greet "BUZZ"!!!)))

AND SO...

(As, Pockets and, the-dirty-(MADE-to-drive-Pockets-around-on-duty)-vice-cop, leave out the back door)...

Skins' Consigliere, seated, right-to-the-right of Skin's, leans over towards Skin's and, WITH concerns, (and, JUST TO MAKE SURE!), "advisitory"-asks, "Skin, YOU'RE not ACTUALLY goin' INTO business WITH this fuckin' guy,...ARE you???"

"ARE YOU'S FUCKIN' KIDDING ME!?! We're gonna' fuckin' "bust-him-out", LIKE WE always do! FUGGETABOUTIT!!! And, JUST SO, fuckin' Pockets KNOWS, WHO'S tha' fuckin' BOSS, and, who's ALWAYS been'da fuckin' boss, in THIS fuckin' town,...let's just fuckin' say, by'da fuckin'-time tha' 33 vinyl has cooled,...ol' Pockets' gonna-fuckin'-git some 22's, in'is fuckin' ear'ta listen to!! You's-a good Consigliere,...but, leave all the thinkin' ta' me, huh? I don't need YOU'S fuckin' help, wit this."

And...

Those fucking birds, continued to sleep.

ORANGE JUICE

And so, *as those night birds,* do so now chirp, those early fucking birds, do so set themselves up first, as to not be taken of their turn.

BUT...

THEY AIN'T the only ones fast at work!

For...

THEY AIN'T the only ones ON the hunt!

For...

THEY AIN'T the only ones looking for "food".

For...

Skin's and his crew, are out front, of La Alla Banca. (And, Skin's got his bangs in his eyes!!)...

FOR...

Skin's GOTTA' "eat" too!

(((FUGGETABOUTIT!!!)))

AS...

He and his crew, sit out front. (As, his strong muscle remains posted-up!). As, they sip from white porcelain cups, of strong-roasted brews.

But...

(THEY AIN'T the only ones "up and at 'em"!)...

FOR...

Those that got bills to pay (and, mortgages, lifestyles and, mistresses to maintain!), make that,...slow-rush...cross the macadam!

But...

(THEY AIN'T the only ones on the move!)...

For...

((((Pockets, is with that dirty vice cop and, he's MAKING HIM pay ON DUTY, his...music industry dues!!)))

FOR...

Pockets, is making him drive him all 'round town, making it out to be like, they're out lookin' to setup Brotha Trife, for "the close enough positioning", for Skin's to mow him down!

NAAAAAAH...

Pockets, lookin' to setup...a last-minute-Meet-'N-Greet-BUZZ-Event-venue!(OY VEY!).

SOOOOOO...

(FUCK SKIN'S!!!)

FOR(YOU SEE!)...

(SETTIN'-UP MR. BROTHA TRIFE - FOR SKIN'S TO CLIP - JUST GON' HAVE TO WAIT!!!).

But...

(THEY AIN'T the only ones that didn't sleep late!)...

For...

(((Pockets, been on his phone, MORE than he ain't!))).

For...

Pockets, has been blowin' up phones! (And, he's been giving directives!!). And, has FINALLY heard back, WITH SOME GOOD NEWS,...from Phillip Tate

But...

(THEY AIN'T the only ones that received good news!)...

FOR...

WHEN, it comes to turnin' THIS world ON IT'S ear?....((((For, WHEN IT COMES, to mayhem, mass destruction and mass SUFFRAGE????))))....For, there's only four.

For...

THEY AIN'T a fifth FOR A REASON!!!!....(from of which TO choose).

And...

THEY AIN'T goin' BY any other name, than....

(((((THE DUYU CREW!!!!)))).

For...

(Pockets, hit up Phillip)...(And, Phillip, hit up Pretty High)...(And, Pretty High, FINALLY hit him back!!!!)...

AND...

Phillip, told Pretty High, that Pockets, said, "That THEY AIN'T, NO ONE, that, DO what Y'ALL, CONSIDER "fun"!!!! For, Pockets, said, he GOT PLENTY of "fun" for y'all, as a matter of fact. And, IN RETURN, ALL he wants IS for y'all, IS TO WATCH his back!"

FOR...

THEY AIN'T SHIT, THAT, Pockets CAN give, OR offer, OR provide - THE DUYU CREW - TO GET THEM TO ABIDE!!!!((((For, they ARE in, and, of themselves!!!!))))((((And, they make life ON earth a LIVING hell!!!!))))....

BUT...

To, OFFER them, WHAT THEY CONSIDER, to be "fun"???? (SHIIIIIIT)...

((((IN AND OF, LIKE THEM, THAT DO WHAT THEY DO????))))....((((WELL, HELL,...THEY AIN'T NO ONE!!!!))))

And so...

Of the wishes of Pockets, they did so, abide. ((((FOR, RIGHT NOW, AT THIS VERY SECOND, THEY RIDE!!!!))))((((Two columns AT two abreast!!!!)))). With, one hand on a throttle WIDE-OPEN!!!! With, the other hand, MIDDLE FINGER IN THE AIR!!!! ((((WITH, THE WIND, beaten-off OF their WHITE, BRIGHT RED, BLACK, and PALE, vintage Prohibition Era-style gangster suits, and beaten-off OF their suspenders, and beaten-off OF their three-piece vests!!!!)))). And, they're traveling at BREAKNECK-BLINDING-SPEED!!!! ((((WITH, THE FOUR, TO - TROTTLES WIDE-OPEN - HANGIN' ON!!!!)))) AS, THE FOUR, ARE - STRAIGHT-UP-LIFTING-UP - CLEAR OUT OF THEIR SEATS!!!! ((((AND, DO NOT GET IT TWISTED))))... ((((THERE IS, AND, CAN BE ONLY ONE, TO THAT, AND OF, THEY LISTEN!!!!)))). AND, THAT IS, AND, THE ONLY WAY, IT IS!!!! ((((FOR, THEY ARE HERE, AND, THEY ARE REAL, AND, OF THEM, THERE IS NO PRETEND!!!!)))). AND, IT IS THE FOUR'S MISSION, TO MAKE YOU PRAY, THAT, "YOU" WERE NEVER BORN!!!! ((((AND, OF THIS, I DO NOT KID!!!!)))).

But...

(THEY AIN'T the only ones on the road!)...

For...

That ride share driver guy, KEEPS looping blocks after blocks in North Juarez City. Drivin' 'round in that 1983 Cadillac Coupe. (The one painted silver with the black ragtop roof!). The very same car, that Tier-Three-Motherfucker SWEARS, he's BEEN in before! *(WHICH, had Mr. Brotha Trife thinkin', "Maybe, this laced-up weed, just got my mind "THOAD"?!?").*

BUT...

(THEY AIN'T the only ones on their grind!)...

FOR...

Mr. Brotha Trife, FINALLY got showered-up (and, wearin' a fresh-set of "fines"!). And, to his song book, he's been on his grind, filling up those pages and filling up those lines, with a couple of songs and a couple of rhymes!!!

For...

He and Anna Mossitti, been sitting together, on that PLUSH RED LEATHER SOFA and, sippin' on coffee (and, been waitin' on some food to be delivered, ALL THIS TIME!)...

And...

They've been talkin' 'bout, how they made beautiful music together. (And, they're getting better re-aquainted!). And, they're talkin' 'bout, what took place yesterday, at high noon, (in "old" SYKE Park!), AT THE MOMENT, Anna Mossitti fainted!

HOWEVER...

(Mr. Brotha Trife, CHOSE NOT to discuss - THAT HE SMELLED THAT - Dirty-Wearin'-An-Entire-Bottle-Of-"JOOP!"-On-Duty-Vice-Cop's

Cologne - IN the bulldozed-rubble's dust, FROM WHEN THAT GUST OF WIND - OUT-OF-NOWHERE - KICKED-UP!!!).

AND SO...

(As they sip their morning coffee together, on that plush red leather sofa and chat)...

(COME! LET'S LISTEN IN ON THAT!)...(((YOU-NOSEY-MOTHERFUCKERS!!!)))...

"You know,...", Anna Mossitti, begins, "...I HAVE TO ask you something."

"Oh, yeah?", Mr. Brotha Trife, replies.

"Yesterday. AT YOUR statue. In "old" SYKE Park. I...I...I noticed something. You NEVER,...looked at it. *YOU NEVER ONCE, looked up at YOUR OWN statue!* BUT, I DID notice, it's because *YOU WERE ONLY...looking, AT me!* AND,...I don't know? ...MAYBE, maybe,...it's JUST me? BUT, did...DID YOU notice, that, *WHEN I turned around and,...saw you, that,...AT THAT EXACT MOMENT when I turned around and SAW YOU,...*it,...I don't know,...IT'S LIKE, *IT GOT REAL WINDY ALL OF a sudden???* I'm talkin' 'bout, *A HUGE GUST OF WIND,...came out...CAME OUT of...nowhere!!* I mean,...I KNOW *I fainted.* And, I...I'm not sure *how long...I was EVEN...out for!* And, honey, my memory's a lil' hazy ON...*some...of...that.* But,...I guess WHAT I'M TRYING to SAY to you, Trife, IS,...*you FELT that HUGE GUST OF WIND TOO,...*right???", Anna Mossitti, (of HER sanity!), inquires, (THEREOF!).

And*(JUST LIKE THE WIND!)...*

Mr. Brotha Trife,...*BLOWS HER OFF* - WITH a shoulder shrug!

AS...

(Anna Mossitti, NOW REALIZES - THAT - Mr. Brotha Trife, HAS opened-back-up HIS song book!)...

AND(ON TOP OF THAT!)...

HE'S GOTTEN RIGHT BACK ON HIS GRIND! As his NEXT fire song, HE HAS BEGUN to write!

FOR...

((((AS OF, their conversation's "subject", HE'S JUST STRAIGHT-SIDESTEPPED THAT SHIT TO THA' SIDE!!!))))(((OY VEY!!!))).

Ut-Oh.

(Let's see how this shit plays out!)...

"Uh, Trife? HELLOOOOOOO!!! YOU KNOW that's FUCKED-UP, right?? I WASN'T finished!!", Anna Mossitti, tells him, with voice raised! (And, in an attempt to turn his head towards her's, clips his chin with a graze!!!)(GETTIN', ALL: "Animositied"!!!)....(IS THAT EVEN a word???)(DOESN'T MATTER!!!)(I'M using it ANYWAY:)...(Let us move on!)...

"Hey! Hey! Hey! TAKE IT EAZY!!! LOOK,...I'm sorry. Yo, BUT, on-some-realness, YEAH, I *NOTICED THAT SHIT*, TOO! So, what's good?", Mr. Brotha Trife, replies, with an apology, (SEEING - the reason-why - he-TRIED-to-sidestep-the-rest-of-THIS-conversation - BY THE LOOK - IN her eyes!!).

"THANK YOU!!", she says, sarcastially, (AND with PLENTY of attitude!!), before, she continues, "ANYWAY! I wanted to ask you, something else.", (as she, begins, EVEN AFTER seeing him cringe!), *"WHAT were you lookin' AT yesterday,...after all that wind??* I mean, *YOU NEVER EVEN looked up at your OWN statue! And, other than,...lookin' DIRECTLY AT me, I saw you looking AROUND ME,...but,...it's like,...it's like, YOU WEREN'T LOOKING around!* SO!?! WHAT was it?? *WHAT WERE you LOOKING at?!?"*

And...

(Mr. Brotha Trife sighs, before, he removes those 24 karat golds from his eye)...

And, he explains, to her, that, in a way, (right before she fainted!), *the face that SHE made,....HE saw THAT face before! (When HE SAW, A FACE in HIS CEMETERY clouds!).* And, he goes on as he explains, *of how he felt. (Of how: When he looked-up at that face in the clouds, he felt the "presence of three").* And that, *she made the SAME EXACT FACE, AS THAT cemetery cloud made, (EVIL frown, BEFORE it smiled!!!).* And of, *HOW then, it scrolled-up and leveled-out flat like a shelf, before it drifted-off fast! (To the right! And out of sight!).* And how, he WASN'T going to tell anyone *about that!* ((('CAUSE THEY WOULD THINK HE WAS CRAZY!!!))). SO, he was just gonna,...keep *that* TO himself! And, he went on to say, that, *when the wind kicked-up at "old" SYKE Park yesterday, he saw a "hollow-transparent-tunnel" come down, COMING DOWN OUT OF THE CLOUDS!!! And of, HOW, it stop right over, her right shoulder. And of, HOW THEN, the "hollow-transparent-tunnel's" "end",* ("the end" that was, up in the clouds, from where it begin!), *RETRACTED-DOWN INTO ITSELF!!! And what remained, was a "circular-hollow-transparent-starburst", with rays like the sun, BUT, IT WAS the color gray!* And, he went on to say, that *he WAS looking around, CHECKING for trees, FOR loose papers, FOR...ANYTHING!!!* (TO confirm WHAT he suspected!)...THAT - *absolutely NOTHING ELSE - WAS being blown!!!* And of, *HOW THAT - "mighty gust of wind" - AND THAT - "grayish-hollow-transparent-tunnel" - WAS there FOR them!!* ((AND, FOR THEM ALONE!!)) BUT, he poses the question, *"Of that wind you felt, from when that "starburst" came from the sky flying down, it left a "grayish-hollow-transparent-trail" FROM the clouds, OF US,...WHY, were WE selected!?!"* And then, he went on to explain, *of how, that "grayish-starburst" about the size of a pancake remained. As if, it were there TO protect her! AS IT, traveled-down FROM THE "upper-world", TO PROTECT HER! AS IT, slowly-traveled behind her head,...IN PROTECTION OF HER!!* And how, *FROM hovering above her right shoulder, it traveled to his right, then,... hovered, THEN, slowly-passed behind her head, AS IT,* (then again!), *PROTECTING HER, it hovered over her right!* AND OF, *HOW WHEN, the "grayish-starburst" traveled behind her head, he knew it was still there, even though it was out of his sight.*

And...

To his "pleasant-surprise",...SHE DIDN'T CALL HIM CRAZY!!!

HOWEVER...

(Anna Mossitti, DID look at him WITH A "believably-crazy" - LOOKIN'-AT-HIM - kinda'-crazy - LIKE - HE-JUST-MIGHT-BE-KINDA'-CRAZY - kinda' - crazy-type-OF-look - IN HER EYES!!)... (Poor ol' Mr. Brotha Trife:(

And then...

She, asks, *"THAT'S what,...YOU SAW??? HOVERING?? Around ME!?!* I DIDN'T see it! BUT,...*THAT'S WHAT YOU SAW!!* Hey, Trife?...YOU EVER SEE anything,...LIKE...THAT...before??"

And, (after a bit of thought)...

He explains, "Ya' know? I DON'T know! ALL I know IS,...is *MY memory IS...REALLY FUCKED-UP!!* And, EVEN THOUGH,...it seems to...be...gettin' much better. THIS world, JUST...DOESN'T,...*it just doesn't, seem...the same."*

"Well, honey, WHAT do YOU, *THINK that was???"*, she, endearingly asks.

Thinking of, the presence, of: The "Possible-Three", (Of: WHO'S face IN the clouds, THAT could POSSIBLY be!), and, thinking, of: HOW SHE made, THAT SAME face, (((Poor Mr. Brotha Trife, REALLY AIN'T that sure!))). But, he goes on to tell her, *EXACTLY what HE thinks, "I THINK it was, a Guardian Angel...comin' down...from up above."*

And then...

She, asks, *"WHO do you think IT was THERE for??* ME??? Or..., for... FOR you?"

But...

(Mr. Brotha Trife, DOESN'T answer!)

FOR…

There's A KNOCK on that ALL RED EVERYTHANG'S apartment door! (YOU remember that, I mentioned they…ordered food, before:)

And…

After Anna Mossitti, took her sexy walk, cross that red shag rug.

And…

After she, opened that door up. (EVER so slight!).

And…

After she, gave the man some money. (She stepped, slightly to the side!).

And…

After she, DID THAT, Mr. Brotha Trife, said, "I'll be damned. THIS fuckin' dude!"

AS…

(It was THAT mafackin' ride-share-drivin' man!)…(((DELIVERING THEIR FOOD!))).

(COCKSUCKA'!!!)…

BUT…

(LIKE I SAID, THEY AIN'T THE ONLY ONES THAT GOTTA' "EAT"!)…

'CAUSE…

(Pockets, MADE that dirty-ass-vice-cop, drive him back over to Skin's coffee shop!)…

SO…

(((LET'S DROP BACK IN, ON OL' SKIN'S, SHALL WE??)))…

AND SO...

(OK!)...(ALL TOGETHER NOW!)...(((("YES!!! I THINK WE MUTHA' FUCKIN' SHALL!!!")))...

FOR...

(Back inside of La Alla Banca)...

Skin's, Pockets and, the dirty - (sippin'-on-Espresso-Martinis-ON-DUTY-with-his-pinky-up) - vice cop, sit down at the round table. And, at this "sit down", from his eyes, salt and pepper bangs are steadily being swipped - from being notified - from Pockets - from being FULLY in love with HIMSELF - from being able to look a man square in his eyes - AND LIE - from BULLSHIT provided - from "failing" to find Brotha Trife, though, insurances of provisions, of close proximities - of opportunities - to Skin's he will be given - to get close enough to Brotha Trife to clip him - from Pockets, being able!

Even so...

(Pockets, CAN'T WAIT TO get back TO HIS Jettison Records RV!)...

Though...

NOT due to Skin's aggistrations!

SHIIIIIIT...

(We talkin' 'bout Pockets, baby!)(Pockets ain't phased!)...

NAAAAAAH...

THIS hardworking - "man-of-leisure" - CAN'T WAIT to get back... AND GET OUTTA' THESE Throwback Eagles kelly greens! AND GET BACK INTO HIS ALL RED EVERYTHANGS! ((((OF: Custom-Reds!!!)))...((((OF: Custom-Mades!!!))).

For...

TO Pockets, (THESE "Made Men"!), THEY AIN'T, the only ones that, can rock Custom-Mades!

SO…

Pockets, GOT TO convince Skin's, (RIGHT HERE!)(AND, RIGHT NOW!!)(SEATED AT THIS ROUND TABLE!!!), THAT, LA ALLA BANCA, IS the PERFECT VENUE, (((the ONLY way HE KNOWS ABLE!!!))).

And so…

Pockets, (reaches in his pocket!), and, from one, a money clip made FROM one, of some - endangered-motherfucker - PEELS and THROWS that money down, LIKE he's playin' Spades!

(Looking up at his muscle, signal given - for - signal presented)…

Skin's muscle, collects and counts, that money off the round table, "Comes out ta' be, 100 Grand", Skin's muscle, says, after which, Skin's and Pockets shake hands.

(Looks like THAT kind of money, just got - Pockets' PERFECT venue - RENTED!!!)

"TOLD YOU'S BEFORE, Pockets, I AIN'T NO DUMMY! I'll TAKE you's money. YOU'S wanna' make it THAT EAZY for me??? TA' take YOU'S fuckin' money?!? WELL,…I have NO fuckin' problem at all IN takin' YOU'S money! You's got ONE HOUR in my joint,…for you's,…lil'…meet 'n greet. AND THEN, I want ALL OF "YOU'S" the HELL outta' my I.A. Club! YOU'S unda'stand me!?", Skin's, MAKES it clear! , (WHILE clearing his muscle's hand, OF THAT EAZY MONEY!).

"Loud 'n clear, Skin's. Loud 'n clear.", replies, Pockets, (then, takes a look 'round, still seated at the round table), and, then asks, "What kinda' sound system you got up-in-here, Skin's?"

"The kind that ONLY sounds good, for ONE hour! YOU'S got that?!? AND once you's lil' meet 'n greet is o'va?? MY club bet'ta' look the same way, AS before I let YOU'S come in here! Or? YOU'S gonna' have hot coals dumped all ov'a you's head…you's unda'stand me?", Skin's, giving directives, (of HIS own!).

"Skin's, I'll have my two, youngboy-artists, attend to the sprucing-up of the place. You won't even recognize it, after I'm gone.", Pockets, offers.

(Looking up o'va his shoulder at, his muscle standing there)...

Skin's, then looks back at, Pockets, and, says, "Yeah, ok you's. That'll be fine."

And then...

(Skin's, with a moment, of: "underestimation-perhapsation", continues)...

As...

He, says, to Pockets,..."And, let me tell you's sumthin', Pockets. I gotta' tell ya'. THAT'S showin' class, you's."

And then...

(Skin's, with a moment, of: "warm-'n-fuzzy-is-for-fuckin'-suckers!", continues)...

As...

He, tells Pockets, "...But, just so you's know. THIS big sumbitch'll be standing o'va them,....JUST how he does me! Justa' MAKE SURE, you's..."lil' artists"...DON'T GET ANY fuckin' "cute-ideas" AND think 'bout makin'-off with sumthin' FROM the I.A. Club!"

(Pockets, NOT taken aback. RATHER, repositions his back to rest comfortably, against the back of his chair!)...

And then...

He, tells Skin's, "Listen, Skin's. They got more concerns, THAN stealin' somethin' from you. LIKE, rememberin' tha' lyrics to their songs, for instance! They AIN'T thiefs, Skin's. THEY the NEXT TWO great rappers in tha' game!! Believe me, Skin's. My youngboy's are just waitin' on THIS buzz, to help blow them up!! BUT, if it'll make you feel any better,...'bout the situation. Sure. Have big-boy here, RIGHT next to them two, at all times."

THEN...

(Leaning forward, Pockets, with a smirk, at the start and ending of this next statement, continues)...

AS...

He, tells Skin's, "Personally, I think that's an excellent idea. NOBODY wants FOR SKIN'S to get IRRATATED,...FROM BEING RUBBED tha' wrong way!"

(Skin's, a made man. Sitting amongst made men. Get's into some MADE men shit!)...

"LISTEN, you's! All of this, comin' into MY club, for you's "buzz", WASN'T apart of our initial music-biz-conversation, last night! And,... yeah,...YOU'S paid me good. So,...THAT'S NOT the issue. And, throwin' in you's rappers...to,...freshin' up the joint, AFTER this lil'... meet 'n greet of theirs', ISN'T the issue,...either."

THEN...

(WHILE pile-driving HIS round table, WITH his right index finger!)...

Skin's, continues, "BUT, I WANT "You's" in-'n-OUTTA'-here FAST! THIS club...has standards,...rules,....you's know!?"

AND SO...

After, The: (Just-Looks-Like-ONLY-A-Man-IN-AND-OF-HIS-Position - BUT-You-JUST-Get-THE-INKLING - Skin's-Was "Gifted" - THIS) - Diamond-Pinky-Ring - (FOR - A: "Foolhardy-Jester-Of-Gaining-Points" - OR - (FOR - A: Debt-Collection-Payment-ON-Points!) - OR - (FROM: Taken-AT-Gun-Point!!!) - HAS met, the back of Skin's neck, (ENSURING, that, the salt and pepper of his bangs, HAVE BEEN swept-out of his eyes and SLICKED BACK!), Skin's, continues, "BESIDES,...I have a rep TO protect! I ALREADY got Philadelphia ridin' me...on this..."udder-thing",...FUGETTABOUTIT!!! AND, a whole lotta' "YOU'S" bein' IN the I.A., is jus' gonna' give 'em MORE, uh, "ammo". SO, "YOU'S" got today AND today ONLY, to hold "you's" lil' meet 'n greet. I'M givin' "YOU'S", ONE hour! But, HERE'S the thing, Pockets. SINCE, I'm allowin', ALL OF this to happen IN my club,...mind you's. So, NOT ONLY, DO I want MY son-in-law, to record ON THIS new Christmas song. BUT, WHEN the song DOES get cut? YOU'S GONNA' sign o'va ALL of this Brotha Trife's "writing credits" TO, MY son-in-law!"

THEN...

(SEEING Pockets, getting ready to object!)...

Skin's, tells him, "I'm NOT finished, YOU'S! Publishing rights. Recording rights. EVERYTHING involving THIS fuckin' song,...I GET a 51% split. And, that's NOT all!"

THEN...

(Leanin' forward, Skin's forearms, on his round table. His hands, before him, on the table, clasped. Lookin' INTO Pockets' eyes. STUDYIN' him HARD!)...

Skin's, continues, "YOU'S have any swag, you's tryin' ta' move? You's plannin' on sellin' merch, at this meet 'n greet?? IF YOU'S do? You's kick-up 51% of swag sales, TO ME! And, FROM HERE on out, you's got t-shirts to be printed for you's record label? Hats bein' made? I don't give'a fuck IF its'a - "beer-holder-spongie" - what'eva-tha'-fucks-dem-things-are-called - THAT'S - gonna' have you's record label's logo, printed-up on it. WHEN it comes'ta screenprintin' GARMENTS and, what'eva-the-hell-else - kinda' swag - YOU'S plannin' on sellin'. YOU'S come, TO me. And, it goes THROUGH ME! And, just you's rememba' this. This IS non-negotiable! SO, if I'M YOU'S?? I'D be on my way, ta' doin' ALL OF what you's fuckin' gotta' do..."

Then...

(Skin's, with hands unclasped. With, elbows on table. With, right pinky ring finger extended. With, right palm faced down. With, the tip of his right index finger, placed atop of, the tip of his left index finger, faced upward. With, Skin's right index finger, going from left index finger tip, to left middle finger tip, to left ring finger tip, to left pinky finger tip - in conjunction with - as it coincides with - the breaking-down - OF: The-Best-Sound-Advice-That-He-Can-Give-To-Pockets - (as much, as for himself!) - To: Get-Pockets-And-The-Rest - OF: "YOU'S" - The-HELL-In-And-OUTTA'-HIS-I.A.-Club - FAST!)...

Skin's, continues, "...to get'cha' rappers, here. GET THIS "buzz" of YOU'S, created. O'va. AND, DONE WIT!"

Pockets. The hustler. Who, defiled the odds. (yes,...defiled!). WHO, MADE himself into a drug kingpin. Who, defiled the odds. Who, made it out. (Without!)...GETTING himself locked up OR killed! Who, defiled the odds. Who then, made himself into a music-biz-head-honcho. Who, defiled the odds. Who, entered this city. The city of...North Juarez! Who, defiled the odds. Who, was WANTED DEAD by NJPD! Who, defiled the odds. (Who, not even the North Juarez Police Department knew, that the mob was plannin' on clippin' him FIRST!). Who, defiled the odds. WHO NOW, sits at the the head of the mob's round table,... WITH Skin's! Who, defiled the odds. Who, sits at that round table WITH - THE-DIRTIEST-OF-THE-DIRTY-ON-DUTY-VICE-COPS - IN THE ENTIRE CITY!!! Who, defiled the odds. WHO NOW,...sits amongst made men. Who, defiled the odds. This man. The hustler. The kingpin. (The: "Head-Honcho like a MF"!). THE...gamblin' man, WHO IS,...made for MOMENTS, like THESE! For, HIS Big-Hustle-Wheels, continue to grind, ALL THE TIME!

And so...

Pockets, gets into some Pockets shit!

(Come!)...(LET'S SEE how Pockets, goes to work!)...

"Ouch! 51% of the publication AND the recordings, Skin!? THAT would give you OWENERSHIP! Well, sir. SINCE, you're gonna be holdin' a "majority stake" in this Christmas song,...LET US NOT RUSH, THIS Meet 'n Greet. And, LET US, create THIS "BUZZ", for YOUR son-in-law,...INSTEAD!! So, tell you what, Skin's. You DON'T want JUST ONE hour, for YOUR son-in-law, do ya' Skin's?? With a 51% share in this song, NOW YOU have a "VESTED INTEREST" in THIS "BUZZ"! NOW, YOU'RE gonna want this DONE, the RIGHT WAY! Am I right!?! SO, we can sit here all day, hashin'-out and goings-over of this, that and, the third, in regards to, the recordings being handled by Sound Exchange, ASCAP handlin' the royalties - from radio air play and, 'bout Jettison Records handlin' the recordings. And, since you know enough, to know 'bout, publishing and so forth. THEN, you perhaps would know that, Jettison Records Publishing, would be handlin' the song,...ain't that right, Skin's?. WE CAN speak on THESE things,...you know? We can speak on these things, Skin's. BUT, there's MORE "pressing-matters", THAT TAKE precedence, OVER THESE, uh,..."minor details". BUT, oh-by-the-way! WHAT, I REALLY WANNA' DO, is, get back to MY Jettison Records RV. And, OH-BY-THE-WAY!! Mind you, that's, FULLY-EQUIPPED, wit'a mobile studio, in the back of that sumbitch!!! And, oh-by-the-way! PARK THAT sumbitch, RIGHT-OUT-FRONT of YOUR club, Skin's!! AND, get YOUR son-in-law, into MY studio and RECORD, HIS vocals! We'll do, a couple "rough takes". And, THEN get him singin' the "final vocal" cut. Yeah,... SO, well, ANYWAAAAAAYS, I'll get MY contract guy, drafting-up the contracts! HE'S the best, IN the business! But, FIRST, above ALL else, even before me servin' up Brotha Trife to you, we GOTTA' get our HANDS ON that, fuckin' Christmas song! I'M talkin' SONG BOOK and ALL!!! Yeah, UH, so, WELL, anywaaaaaays,...FOR your son-in-law to learn, AND KNOW, the lyrics. HE'S GOT to FEEEEEEL the song, Skin's! HE CAN'T sound like, he's TRYIN' to REMEMBER the lyrics AS HE'S singin' the song, Skin's! Or, THAT-SHITZ gonna come 'cross, ON the track! HE'S GOT to convey AND communicate "the meaning" OF what, HE'S singing! NOT, JUST, "remember" and "recite", the lyrics!! ...You feel me?? 'CAUSE, Skin's, WORSE than, SOUNDING like, he's soley "ATTEMPTING" to remember the words, Skin's,...is that, THAT-SHITZ GON' COME 'CROSS, TO THE LISTENER!!! AND, then, AIN'T NOBODY GON' buy THAT shit!!!"

And then...

(Pockets, cocks that throwback kelly green atop his head, harrrrrrd to tha' side!)...

And then...

(((SCHOOLS THA' FUCK OUTTA' SKIN'S!!!)))

(Come!)...(Y'ALL GONNA' WANNA' HEAR THIS SHIT!!!)...

(((AND FUCKIN' PAY ATTENTION!!!)))...

"YOU WANT 51%, Skin's?? WELL, let ME tell ya' somethin', 'bout THIS "music game", Skin's. IF you son-in-law DON'T sing this song, JUST RIGHT?? SHIIIIIIT, 51% OF nothin', EQUALS NOTHIN'!!! YOU feel ME???"

"Yeah. I "feel" you's. But, Pockets, you's CAN fuckin' try'n...dazzle me...wit...all OF you's, big soundin', music-jargon. WIT, you's, "ASS-CAPS" and,...you's BIG soundin' ...what-tha'-fucks... that..."Sounds Exchanged",...GIBBERISH! BUT, LET ME, TELL YOU'S, 'bout, WHAT I know 'bout THIS, music biz! AIN'T NO FUCKIN' WAY IN HELL, I'M USIN' ANY DOCUMENTS, YOU'S CONTRACT GUY, WRITES UP!!! I AIN'T fall off a tha' back, of some truck, YOU'S know! ...I KNOW a guy.", Skin's, replies, two untrusting-souls, (AND, for GOOD reason!), TRYING TO "out-play" the other, in THIS "music game"!!(OY VEY!)...(((AND FUGETTABOUTIT!!!))).

"Ooooooooh! YOU, KNOW a guy!", Pockets, replies, (with a, roll of his eyes!!), "NOT a chance! I AIN'T fall off the back of SOME-DAMN-TRUCK eve'r!!!"

"YOU'S don't rememba' TOO good, DO YA', Pockets?!? MY club! MY round table!!! MY son-in-law! MY RULES!!! AND,...BESIDES all'a THAT,...Pockets, YOU'S AIN'T in NO fuckin' position, TO be NEGOTIATIN'!!", Skin's, begins, (THEN, looks over at, the - dirty-DOIN'-dirty-deeds-ON-DUTY-vice-cop!), BEFORE, continuing..., "'CAUSE, if you's TRYIN' ta' negotiate on somethin' I made VERY CLEAR to you's, was NON-negotiable?? HE'S gonna clip you's! RIGHT here...and, RIGHT fuckin' now!"

(After a GOOD long laugh!)...

Pockets, STATES, WHILE, looking right into AND THROUGH, the dirty vice cop's eyes, *(A LOOK, that, GOES STRAIGHT back INTO the BACK OF his eyes!!),...* "HE'S dumb, Skin's. But,...HE AIN'T stupid! AIN'T THAT right, COP??"

(SEEING *that look,* Pockets, JUST gave him!)...

COUPLED WITH...

(((*WHAT* Pockets, told him, *WHEN* HE, GAVE IT!!)))...(Well, the dirty-on-duty-ain't-dumb-BUT-smart-enough-to-know-vice-cop, *KNOWS,* that)...

...*Pockets' MA'MA, AND, HIS - ON-A-TIGHT-LEASH-OFF-THE-CHAIN - BABY BROTHER, (TOO COLD), ARE STILL, locked-up IN THAT BANK VAULT CELL INSIDE OF PRECINCT ONE!!!*

And...

(((*THAT'S JUST SOME SHIT - the dirty-smart-ENOUGH-on-duty-vice-cop - AIN'T WILLING TO DEAL WITH!!!)))*

AND SO, (With "enough" GOOD sense!)...

"WHOA! WHOA!! WHOA!!! Skin's! Tell ya' what. HOW 'BOUT I drive Pockets, to go get his RV. IF he's WIT ME,...in the city,...HE'S good! AIN'T NOBODY 'gwine, clip 'em. NOT, even me! SO, I drive 'em, to get this RV. We bring it, back here. We park it, out front. AND, we-get-on-wit this buzz for...FOR, YOUR son-in-law! ...ALRIGHT, Skin's???", the - dirty - (showin'-an-ounce-of-GOOD-SENSE!) - on-duty - vice cop, advises, Skin's!

"Alright, you's two. Go take care'a, whatcha'-gotta', take care'a. All those cars double-parked out front will be moved, by tha' time you's two get back, wit this, RV of you's. Park it out front and, let's-get-on-wit this shit.", instructs, Skin's.

THEN...

(Leaning back in his chair. Comparable to the posture, and, feeling received, from, AFTER,...filling-up on Sunday's gravy!)...

Skin's, says, (WITH satisfaction!), "You's know, Pockets? FEELS pretty-damn-good TO BE involved,...IN the MUSIC biz!! I'LL MAKE SURE that there's a nice turnout, FOR MY son-in-law's EVENT, tonight. We'll pack THIS JOINT...the right-way."

(Seeing as Skin's, WAS receptive to, HIS suggestions!)...

The - dirty - NOW-feeling-AS-though - HE'S - a: "big-mover-'n-shaker" - IN THIS - music-biz-deal - (AND, DOIN' IT ON DUTY!) - vice cop, seizes HIS MOMENT - TO - jump IN the "music game" and, GET PAID!

AS, (he offers up, YET ANOTHER suggestion!)...

"Skin's. Pockets. I got a solution, TO y'all's, "contract guy", "situation". Everyone in this room knows, good-AND-DAMN-well, AIN'T narry-a-one of ya' gon' truss usin', tha' other one's "guy", to draft-up contracts on this Christmas song. And, BELIEVE ME, gentlemen. THAT Christmas song, IS a BANGER!! YOU'LL MAKE millions!!! SO,...Skin's? Pockets?? What YOU BOTH NEED, is,...an "impartial" guy. You know, someone... neutral!"

For (You see)...

Skin's and Pockets? Well,...THEY AIN'T the ONLY ONES to be layin' down cards, AT THIS-HERE ROUND TABLE!(Nope!).

FOR...

THIS-HERE - DIRTY-ASS-VICE-COP - IS gonna SHOW his hand, in THIS game!...(((an OPEN hand!))).

And so...

(Amongst, looks from Skin's and Pockets, OF: "AAAND???" - "WHAT'CHA' got FOR us??")...

The - dirty - with-open-right-palm-gon'-NEED-some-money-put-IN-it-ON-DUTY - vice cop, continues…, "Skin's, you know that guy,…that, you wanted me to look into?"

Pockets, explodes, "AWE,…NOW,…HOLD ON A MINUTE THERE, NEGRO! YOU, SAID, "NEUTRAL!", AIN'T THAT what, YOU said?? YOU, SAID, "impartial"! You TRYNA' pull SOME slick-shit, here!?! NOPE!!! I AIN'T down, wit-tha'-shit, ALREADY!!"

And…

(With a simple wave of his hand and, a slight - "No" - shake of his head, Skin's, has let his muscle know, THAT Pockets, DOESN'T require his "fully-juiced" arm wrapped-'round AND, squeezing the life OUTTA' HIS throat!)(Fuggettaboutit!)…

HOWEVER(Skin's, does so, inquire, further)…

"What guy? The guy, from the bus station? …THAT guy??"

"No, Skin's. NOT that guy.", the (dirty-on-duty-trying-not-to-reveal-TOO-much-TO-TOO-many-ears!),(fuggetaboutit!), vice cop, tells Skin's, before, continuing…, "You know, Skin's. That guy. The one, you wasn't feelin' for'a minute there,…bein' in the neighborhood."

"The food truck guy?", Skin's, asks.

"No. Not THAT guy. …He's iight, tho'. Skin's, that guy, that started hangin' out a lil' bit too much, for your liking, Skin's,…at the pizza parlor.", the - dirty - (keepin'-tabs-on-motherfuckers-FOR-Skin's-ON-DUTY!) - vice cop, ATTEMPTS, to inform!

"Who?? Sul? HE ain't Italian…,BUT, he KNOWS fine cuisine.", Skin's, answer given.

"NOT that guy, Skin's. Sul KNOWS, what a FUCKIN' napkin looks like! I'm TALKIN' 'BOUT, the one, YOU wanted ME, TO run some background checks on. THAT guy!…Remember???"

"HOOFAH!! Madone. *THAT fuckin' guy, USED TO irk tha' shit outta me!*", Skin's, begins, (swiping the bangs that fell into his eyes, AT the mere mention of "The Guy"!), then, Skin's, turns to Pockets, and, says, "THIS fuckin' GUY! Pockets, *couple'a years back,*…I don't know, BUT, *we're talkin'*

'bout six months or so, after you lambed-it outta town. So look, *this fuckin'
hippy-motherfucker, starts hangin' out at the pizza parlor*, right? Best fuckin'
pie in town, Pockets. It's the crust. Madone! FUGETTABOUTIT!!!
Anyway, listen to me. *THIS,…hippy-fuck,…shows-up and, he's keepin'
the pizza parlor in business ALONE, what-from ALL-THA'-FUCKIN'-
SLICES, he was gorgin' HIMSELF on!* I'm SURE, YOU'S know, HOW
IT IS, Pockets…, *some prick, shows-up, that, don't NO ONE know, but,
EVERYBODY'S talkin' 'bout!* WELL, somebody LIKE THAT?? NEEDS
some lookin' INTO!!! Am I, right??…Fuggettaboutit.", (then, pointing
cross the round table at the dirty vice cop, Skin's, continues),…"So.
Pockets. *I put THIS prick-bastard here, on 'em. You know,…keep an eye
on his "comin's 'n goin's",…who-tha'-fuck he associates with,…simple-shit.*
Shit, THAT, THIS prick, can handle!", (and, after Pockets and Skin's,
share that expensive laugh together. As, well as, Skin's crew, JOINING
in! As they, laugh a bit TOO-hard FOR, some minor-ball-breaking. AS
THEY, laugh that - suckin'-up-to-the-boss - laugh!), Skin's, continues…
"So. Listen to me. Turns out, Pockets, *this hippy-fucker, he AIN'T no…
uh…transient. HE'S actually GOT a job!* AND, he's got GOOD TASTE
in automobiles, too,…the hippy-fuck. But,…I digress. ANYWAY. Listen
to me! SO, Pockets, *this vice cop here, HE'S UNABLE TO find any-dirt on
tha' prick.* So. Pockets. This cop here. *I keep sendin' him down to da' pizza
parlor. Every-fuckin'-day! Ta' tryin' dig up some dirt.*", (then, again, "three-
fingered-pointing" at the dirty vice cop), Skin's, asks him, *"How MANY
pounds ya' start'ta pack-on, ya' prick ya'!?!"*, (and, AGAIN, after expensive-
laughter from Skin's crew, cumulated with a "sucking" sound!), Skin's,
continues… "Alright. Alright. I keep ya' around for'a reason. I'm JUST
breakin' you's balls! Anyway. So look. Pockets. *The ONLY thing, "Officer-
Thin-Skin" ov'a here, can find on tha' guy, ud'duh than the usual,…you's
know,…he'sa hippy-fuck.* SO, he likes to get all fucked-up!", (then, again,
givin' the dirty vice cop the "three-fingered-point", but, THIS TIME,
shakin' his hand VIGOROUSLY at the cop!), Skin's, DEMANDS,…"And,
YOU'S tell THAT hippy-FUCK, FROM ME…IF, HE KEEPS GETTIN'
LOADED AND KEEPS CIRCLIN' THE BLOCK, DRIVIN' LIKE-A-
NUT THROUGH THIS NEIGHBORHOOD,…I'M THE REASON
WHY, YOU'S WHACKED 'EM!!! …The hippy-fuck."

And...

(With the dirty vice cop topping off his martini ON DUTY!)...

He SLURPS-THA'-FUCK-OUTTA' his morning coffee and then, advises, Skin's, "YOU don't wanna do that. And, YOU DON'T want ME, DOIN' that."

And...

(With Pockets, and, with Skin's muscle alike, all looking at Skin's)...

Skin's, swipes back his bangs! (AND, does some "advising" of his own!), "Don't you's EV'A make the mistake, OF correctin' me!"

AND...

(With another - big-cocky-slurp - of his morning brew, the dirty - sippin'-cocky-on-duty - vice cop,...plays the game)...

The "game", OF: Keeping HIS bread buttered!...(THAT, dirty-ill-gotten-KIND-of bread!)...(((FROM an ill-gotten dirty butter knife!!!))).

AS...

He says, (helping he, AND SKIN'S out alike!), "Skin's,...with ALL DUE respect. WHY don't you FINISH tellin' Pockets,...whatchu' was 'BOUT to finish tellin' 'em?"

AND...

(((With another VIGOROUS "THREE-FINGERED-POINT!!!"))), Skin's, tells, the dirty vice cop, "Quiet, YOU'S!!! I DON'T NEED you's help!", (BEFORE, he DOES, in fact, DO JUST THAT!),(Dug out of the hole from looking bad!),...and...continues..., "SO. POCKETS. Listen to me. AS, I WAS SAYIN', BEFORE, THIS prick ov'a here, interrupted me!! I WAS 'BOUT ta' TELL you's, THAT the cop here, *he struck-up'a coupl'a conversations, ov'a a coupl'a Pepsi's and slices. And,* this JIT-BAG sittin' ov'a here, *tells me, that, the hippy, use'ta be in "the biz".* I mean, you's wouldn't think it, *if, you's ev'a watched this fuckin' hippy-cocksucka eat!*

BUT, apparently,...he's WELL-VERSED in music contracts. SO. Listen to me! Pockets. LET'S move on dis fuckin' 'ting! SO. Right here. And, RIGHT now! What's say, you's AND I, both agree, ta' have, this...hippy-motherfucker, draft-up contracts, on this Christmas song?? JUST SO you's unda'stand,...it'sa 51% split, in MY fav'a."

(Pockets, possessor of the Big-Hustle-Mind)...

OF WHICH, *(inside!)*...

(KNOWS ENOUGH TO KNOW THAT...AIN'T NO WAY IN HELL, a man, OF Skin's position, WILL trust him on, A: Hashed-It-Out - And-Now-Shaking-Hands-Over-Martinis - Our-Word-IS-Our-Bond - You'll-Have-To-Come-To-My-House-For-My-Next-Cookout - I-Cook-The-Best-Steaks - MUSIC BIZ - Don't-Worry-About-It - It'll-ALL-Workout-In-Your-Favor - Song Royalties - Did-I-Fail-To-Mention - My-Integrity-In-This-Business-Has-Never-Been-Questioned - Handshake - Deal)...(OY VEY!!!)...(Yeah,... THAT mother-fuckin' SHIT!)

AND SO...

(Pockets, the seeker-of-knowledge and, asker-of-questions)...

Decides, right then and, right there, *(in his Big-Hustle-Mind!), "Why-tha'-fuck-not-do-it!?!"*

HOWEVER...

(THIS, SEEKER-of-knowledge and, ASKER-of-questions, NEEDS TO ask, Skin's,...just A FEW MORE questions!)...

FOR...

((((IN that Big-Hustle-Mind of his, Pockets knows, that, Skin's 51% take, on his son-in-law's track,...AIN'T GOT SHIT TO DO WITH, the 100% take, THAT, Pockets GONNA' take, FROM that Tier Three's "intubation-voice-amazing" track!!!))))((((OY VEY!!!)))).

AND, *(BESIDES!)...*

Skin's ain't gon' know shit, about that!!...(And, IF he EVER does),...

THEN...

FUCK-UM ANYWAY!!! (I'LL BE BACK IN ATLANTA, WITH MY WOMAN BY THEN!!!). (((SORRY FOR YOUR LUCK MUTHAFUCKA'!!!!!!)))

BUT...

MONEY IS MONEY!

AND...

(business IS business!)...

AND...

Even though, Pockets, SAYS he's giving up 51% on a song to Skin's...

(YOU JUST KNOW HE'S GONNA' ANGLE IT TO GET THAT SHIT BACK!)...

'CAUSE...

(((THAT'S THIS MUTHA' FUCKIN' INDUSTRTY, YA DIG!!!)))

And so...

(Pockets, JUST HAS TO, ASK!!)...

"Skin's. Answer somethin', for me. THIS, "hippy-fuck", AS you've already SO-ELIQUENTLY called him. Well, I DON'T know tha' muthafucka',...AAAAANND, it - sure-AS-fuck - SEEMS to me, THAT, YOU AIN'T-GOT-NO love, FO' tha' muthafucka'! SO,...I'd have to say...that,...THAT, makes him..."impartial-enough". BUT,...BEFORE I say,..."yes" and, agree to this hippy-motherfucker,...answer me this,...why tha' fuck you wanna bring some guy in on this thing of ours,...handlin' contracts...AND, OH BY THE WAY, that, in your OWN words, MIGHT I ADD, *used to, "irk tha' shit outta me!".* So,...*what he do??"*

And so…

(With the dirty vice cop, dropping and shaking his head, KNOWING that, Skin's, FOUND THIS shit disgusting!)…(And, perhaps, "inexcusable" for a grown man to do, OR ALLOW to have happen!)…

Skin's, swipes the salt and pepper of his bangs, and, says, "Pockets! LISTEN TO ME! *This fuckin'-JAGOFF-hippy-FUCK, would sit right up there at the counter, eatin' slice afta' slice of pepperoni pizza. MUSTA' HAD'DA MUNCHIES…the fuckin'-hippy…from smokin' pot ALL day long! ANYWAY,…SOON AS you's would step in tha' pizza parlor, THERE HE WAS, foldin' anotha' big slice'a pepperoni pizza that just came out'da oven!! And, THIS SUMBITCH, would just LET that ORANGE GREASE collect in tha' palm of his hand, as he's blowin' on tha' slice'ta cool-it-off. AND, when tha' fuckin'-jagoff would go'ta FINALLY take'a bite,…ALL THAT FUCKIN'…ORANGE FUCKIN'…PEPPERONI-FUCKIN'-GREASE… WOULD… JUST…RUN-THA'-FUCK STRAIGHT-DOWN HIS ARM!!! THA' COCKSUCKA'!!!* Hippy…fuck. Pockets, *even on days, he DIDN'T have his sleeves rolled-up…or was, wearin' a jacket,…YOU'S JUST KNEW… that orange juice…was runnin' down his fuckin'-hippy-arms!!*"

Pockets, (spittin' his coffee ALL OVER the round table!), looks cross the table (AND the coffee!) at Skin's, with a look, of: "TOTAL-HOLY-FUCK!!!". And, in doing so, MASKS HIS LAUGHTER WITH HARTY-COUGHS, as if, the reason-being, he spit hot coffee ALL OVER Skin's round table, WAS for and due to the event that, he was choking! And then, Pockets, MANAGES to say, "And,…*THIS is who, YOU WANT to do,*…THESE CONTRACTS!?!?!?!"

Skin's, NOT EVEN bothered by this, but, rather, taking comfort that, Pockets, apparently found this sort of "eating-behavior" to be of a "barbaric-nature" and, NOT the table manners OF a man OF "dignity AND class"!! And so then, Skin's, says to Pockets, "You's know, Pockets. *Before my daughta' got married. IF my son-in-law…for'da first time…woulda' come'ta MY house…ON'A SUNDAY NUN-THA'-LESS and,…woulda' sat down AT MY table…AND,…woulda' ate LIKE THAT pig,…well,…MY daughta' WOULD'A been plannin' a funeral instead'ov'a weddin'!* But, FORTUNATELY-enough, FOR, my son-in-law, he'sa "crooner-wit-class" and, not some hippy that had his hand in the music biz and, what-knows-how'ta bang-out good contracts. So? YOU'S good wit dis guy, OR WHAT!?"

And, Pockets simply, states, "Skin's. If YOU'RE good wit 'em. I'M good wit 'em."

And then...

(The two of them stand up and, make their way 'round the round table to the other. And, with the sounds made, from, a couple of - heavy-pats - given, to each other's backs),(more so, than, an embrace!),(and, in doing so), Skin's, states, "Ok, Pockets, THIS is our guy. NO switchin'-up AND gettin'-cute, TRYIN' ta' bring in YOU'S contract guy!"

And, as Pockets, replies, (AS he's TRYING to hide HIS PLEASURE!!),(on which, "the hippy" THEY, BOTH UPON, DID NOW decide!!), "NO! NO! NO! SKIN'S! THAT'S the guy, YOU WANT! SO, THAT'S the guy, WE'RE STICKIN' WITH!"

(And, with a shake of the hands, the two, have entered into an agreement, with the another)(Hoofah!!).

(And so then, Skin's, motions for his muscle to breakout that - "dirty-butter-knife" - "dipped in" - "the-dirty-butter-of-a-finder's-fee" - and, "butter" that - dirty vice cop's "bread-of-an-open-hand" - and, yes,...it's all done ON duty!).

And, as Skin's is telling the dirty vice cop, to not take too long in driving Pockets to get his RV, 'cause, he's got to get up with that hippy-contract-guy and, not to be comin' back here without him. Pockets, is telling Skin's that, that coffee is running right through him and, that he's got to go hit the head. And, as Skin's is motioning for his muscle to show Pockets where the pishadoo is, the dirty vice cop is waiting for Pockets to be out of earshot. And, as the dirty vice cop is watching Skin's muscle leading Pockets away cross the room. And, as Pockets is getting out of earshot and out of sight, the dirty vice cop, is telling Skin's, that, he won't have no problem at all, getting the hippy "on board" to do the contracts, 'cause, the hippy has been working for him as a C.I. (Criminal Informant!). And, as Skin's is telling the dirty vice cop that, he wants him to get his hands on that song book, laptop, and thumb drive, BEFORE Pockets does and, to give it to him. The dirty vice cop is *thinking,* (but doesn't say!), *"I ALREADY GOT THAT SMASH-HIT OF A CHRISTMAS SONG RECORDED!!!",* (THROUGH THAT ALL RED EVERYTHANG'S RED APARTMENT DOOR!!!).

(BY WAY, AND, BY MEANS OF)...

Some - HIGH-POWERED - Undercover - Audio-Recording-Listening-Device - Vice - Shit!

(((OY MUTHA' FUCKIN' VEY!!!))).

Chapter Twenty Five

SPOKE 'N WORDS

And so, for Pockets, with shit to get done and, a couple of places to go, the dirty vice cop on duty, is driving too slow...
FOR...

Pockets, wants that cop to flick-on those lights in the grill. (And,...TO LET THAT SIREN SCREAM!!!).

For...

Pockets, don't want to do NUTTIN' but,...GET BACK to his RV! (And, by ALL means, for Pockets, a brother, HAS GOT ta' get CLEAN!!!)...

FOR...

He's GOTS'TA' BE LOOKIN' RIGHT (in his, ALL RED EVERYTHANG custom-made clothes!!), for tonight's (((FUCK SKIN'S!!!))) - MY Jettison Records - Meet 'N Greet Show!!!

And, (BESIDES!)...

There's a WHOLE-GAMUT of things (BEING SPOKEN ON!) inside - OF HIS Big-Hustle-Mind!

And, (at this point)...

Y'all should have not one doubt.

'Bout...

Pockets, BEING IN LOVE with HEARING A PLETHORA OF WORDS comin' outta HIS mouth!

And so...

THERE AIN'T GON' BE NO SHORTAGE OF WORDS, GETTIN' CRANKED OUT!!

AS...

POCKETS' - BIG-HUSTLE-WHEELS...(((GRIND!!!)))...

And so(AS SUCH)...

HIS placements ON priorities, (OF WHICH, and TO do it ALL IN!), HE'S only GOT BUT,...so much time! 'Cause, NOW, he's GOTTA' RECORD a singer THAT,...he AIN'T NEVER HEARD sing! And, (((BESIDES ALL THAT!!!))), NOT Pockets, NOR Skin's SON-IN-LAW, EVEN KNOW THE WORDS TO THE SONG,...OR KNOW... THE MELODY!!! (Oy vey! And, GOOD LAWD!!!). BUT, WHAT Pockets KNOWS, IS that - THOSE DUYU CREW motherfuckers - BEST NOT...LEAVE ME HANGIN'!!!! *(I NEVER miss 'em when they're gone!)*(But,...THIS TIME!!!!)...(I'm just sayin'!!)...I REALLY need the DUYU CREW TO show up! 'CAUSE, I NEED THEM to HELP ME "blow" - this "BUZZ" - THE FUCK UP!!!! *(And,...I'LL be damned!!)... EVEN THOUGH, I ain't heard from, Mr. Brotha Trife, SINCE I left him in a cemetery. I NOW know - that Tier Three motherfucker - DID follow MY directives. AND THAT he STUCK TO THE PLAN!!!* (((But,...THEN again,...THAT'S THE ONLY reason WHY,...*I...KEPT HIM ALIVE!!!*))). I JUST KNEW, THAT CLONE of Brotha Trife, COULD make his way TO the city!!! (((AND know WHAT to do...ONCE he GOT inside!!!))). So, so, so, hmm?? ...WOULD IT BE just best...FOR me...TO JUST let, THAT - JUST-PLAIN-TRIFLIN'-MOTHERFUCKIN'-TIER-THREE, just TO DO...his OWN thing??? Would it be best for ME, to not waste MY time worryin' 'bout him,...gettin' my lady outta tha' city? Amongst other things, oh Good Lawd, I DEFINATELY GOTS'TA' place priority ON recordin' Skin's son-in-law! Shiiiiiit, THAT: "sounds LIKE Francis Albert" mafacka, BETTER BE able to sing!!! 'Cause, NOW, all this GOT ME considerin',...would it be best just FOR ME, TO JUST keep,...MY CONTACT WITH Mr. Brotha Trife,...TO A...minimum?? 'CAUSE, I don't know, IF HE'S read any of THOSE reading materials... YET!!! 'Cause, IF he DID??? (Then,...IT'S a SAFE bet!)...That, WHEN he sees me again...HE'S GONNA' blow his MUTHA' FUCKIN' TIER THREE TOP!!! (((OY VEY!!!))) BUT,...I gots'ta' get my hands on Y.S'. thumb drive,...AND HER LAPTOP!!! (((Shiiiiiit!!!))) PLUS, I'MA NEED THOSE...*Christmas song lyrics that HE wrote!* AND I'M TAKIN' ANY NOTES IN THAT SONG BOOK, *that he MIGHT HAVE taken ON music notes!* But, but, but, but,... YEAH, YOU DAMN-MUTHA'-FUCKIN'-RIGHT, I GOTS'TA' KEEP MY CONTACT WIT THAT - MADMAN-OF-A-TIER-THREE - TO A BARE-MUTHA'-FUCKIN'-MINIMUM!!!

(YEAH, UM, so, uh, well, ANYWAAAAAAYSSS)...

As, far as, THAT CRAZY-TIER-THREE'S song book and shit???

Shiiiiiit...

I'MA LET THIS SLOW-ASS-DRIVIN'-DIRTY-ASS-VICE-COP GO GET 'EM!!!!!!

And so...

This wanted man, once again, travels these busy city streets in broad daylight. Though, this time, Pockets is on a - Time-To-Be-The-Fuck-Up-On-Out-Of-This-Town - Flight!! Big-Hustle-Wheels grind, got Pockets, *thinking, "Don't get TOO happy yet, my boy. Makin' it outta these waters of shark infestation,...AIN'T NO 'cause for celebration! When ALL I'M GON' DO, is just to, turn right back 'round and,...JUMP RIGHT BACK IN 'EM TONIGHT!! Shiiiiiit, ARE you fuckin' crazy!?!",* (OF WHICH, AIN'T NO *if's-and's-but's or maybe's!!!*), (As, Pockets, AIN'T tryin' to be seen!). As, he's a wanted man,...wanted BY the NJPD!!! WANTED STANDING ALIVE!!! ...((JUST TO BE DEAD ON HIS BACK,...BLASTED OFF

HIS FEET!!)). As, he positions himself, slumped down, deepseated, on maroon leather set deep, in this dirty-ass vice cop's undercover Caddy's front passenger's seat!

And, with this mind-set of his, that has set-in, as he sits on seats of no depreciation, there isn't and won't be a chance in hell, to mine that old-fine-leather-mint-condition-smell, to mind therein, for lack thereof, there isn't and won't be appreciation.

But, this old head's eyes froze, no longer checking for venues out the windows, though, now, checking out this Caddy's old school car radio, and, those, old school car radio pushbuttons! Which, instantly, it got this old head, *thinkin', "That's takin' me back to the '60s. I can still feel the tension in 'em when I was tryna find somethin'!"*, (you know the ones, the ones that get preselected and set, by pulling them out then pushin' them back in, from after your favorite radio stations you've picked, the ones to put the "herk-'n-jerk" in that lil' orange 'n plastic car radio AM/FM dial stick!). Plus, all those old school gauges and knobs, all over and on, the dashboard, got this old head, (reminiscin'-a-lil'-bit-more-now!), lovin' the old school manual-window-handles, that ya' still gotta' crank, to roll ya' windows down!

(And, Pockets,...got EVERYTHANG!!!). AS, his Big-Hustle-Wheels grindin' reminds him, of his: I-Gotta-Make-It-Outta-Town-Alive-Exodus, OF THAT, that, HE TO, GOT this! As, Pockets, chooses to relax. As, he turns his head 'round to inspect, this dirty-ass vice cop's rear window's deck. And, he's pleased to see, *what he used to place up behind his back seats,...*an "old school playa'" air freshener shaped like a plastic crown!

Choosing to take a few more moments, to soak in, some more old school shit, Pockets, is feelin' this Cadillac's classically-smooth path. (Fuck feeling a bumb in the road!). Classic look and lines, is what compliments THIS ride! And so, the path outta town, is as smooth as a Kobe free throw!

And, to get on down the road, it ain't no problem! (No key fobs!). And, AIN'T NO keyless entry bullshit! AND SO, to do it: 1). Just put your DOOR KEY in the door! 2). THEN, put your IGNITION KEY in the ignition! 3). And, BY ALL MEANS, just keep it old school - AS

YOU - aggressively grab hold, to that gear shift knob, and, into drive, that bitch is thrown, (straight from the steering column!).

AND, hangin' from that old school gear shift steering column? Well, there's a small forest of air fresheners, (about thirty of 'um!), of Black Ice trees!!! (WHICH, AIN'T doin' no good!). 'CAUSE, that shit ain't covering up shit! 'Cause, this-here dirty-ass vice cop, 'bout thirty clear-polyproylene-plastic-bags - OF - clear-your-nose-the-fuck-out-narcotics - filled to the zip-to-close top - THOUGH - dependant upon - the criminally-illinformed-viewpoints - kept by these - criminal informants - kept dependant upon - by-what-this-here-dirty-ass-vice-cop-got - THEREIN - GRACING - NOT - LACING - CONTAINING - odorously-potent-smellin'-weed,...(IS WHAT this-here dirty-ass vice cop got!!).

But, it's these Florida tints, hung on the windows of this undercover car, the type under bright sunlight, you might be able to see in, (but ya' gotta squint hard!), is what's really making Pockets feel better 'bout, gettin' out of the city,...WITHOUT him gettin' got! (More like,...making him feel better 'bout,...ridin' WITH a cop!).

But, what's fucking wit him, is that lil' crackle and squelch, from time to time, over a hand held police radio on the front seat laid out,...right next to him!

But, this-here dirty-ass fuckin' vice cop, AIN'T NEW to this dirty-ass-fuckin'-vice-cop shit! (So, he of them and them of he, are in the know, of the "know how's" on a "need to know basis", of HOW to link-up and get in touch with him!).

Dark window tints as seen through can not subtract nor add to North Juarez's already dim view. Hanging on the streets and corners and in the alleys, it's just the passing-perpetration-perpetuation-preview of social's maladies!

Of the city they continue to get through, this-here "boots-on-the-ground" dirty-ass vice cop and the man that prefers his view from the world's top, are worlds apart, but, there's not really all that much, separating THESE two!!

Both maintain a predatory and an opinionated point of view, both own their own, distinctly, separately, with too damn much pride, though, together, they both find, that together, they both have arrived, not at the city limits, but, at the same point in their own lives.

Finding, what we've both turned our lives into, that tonight, this "Buzz-shit" must AND gotta work! And, THE ONLY WAY it's gonna work,...IS THAT WE WORK together!! SO, DON'T start none WITH me. And, I WON'T start none WITH you!! So, don't get short with me and, I won't get curt with you and, together, LET'S go put in THIS work!! OR, OUR next ride, AIN'T GON' BE in no cop car. ...IT'S GON' BE ON OUR WAY to the morgue in a hearse!!

Pockets, driven, and this-here dirty-ass vice cop with drive, both continue makin' this ride. Looking forward to makin' money. Looking forward to seeing the city limits. Seeing the world as clearly as they want to see it.

And, with that viewpoint, distinctly, separately, both incapable of seeing the poignantly dim view. For, one, it's the handing out of tailored justice. And, the other? Hand-tailoring excessive! And they both get paid handfuls, perpetuating the existence of both!!

Both give: NOT a single-fuck 'bout YOUR worth!! Both know: hoes will make you kill. Both know: down-ass-niggas-turned-house-niggas-turned-bitch-niggas-turned-snitch-niggas are the worst. Both know: fuck all THAT insanity! MONEY comes first!!

As, they both, through this city, and, "the dim life", go on. And, giving NOT ONE FUCK, 'BOUT ANY of the injustices they've just passed, are passing, AND WILL pass, THIS-HERE dirty-ass vice cop,...turns the old school radio volume knob, turning up on the old school radio, an old school song!

And, in turn, Pockets, turns his attention back into the Cadillac's interior, of and on, the indecentcy that's on FULL display, (and hanging WAY-TO-DAMN-CLOSE to his head!), hung from this-here dirty-ass vice cop's rearview mirror!

And, (with NO doubts, ya' dig!), what hangs, swings, as it moves to the beat! As, the dirty-ass vice cop on duty does it smoothly - smooth-Cadillac-path-ridin'-street-bump-scootin' - bumpin' an old school jam, by Blackstreet!

'Cause, THAT'S HOW, THIS-HERE dirty-ass vice cop ON DUTY be rollin' RIGHT NOW! Car interior filled-up with that potent-smell, (permeating straight-thru clear-resealable-polypropylene-bags) of that "turnt up loud", with an old school song's volume-unreasonably turnt up loud!

And, what's that dirty-ass vice cop got hanging from his rearview? Well, it's just to let the NEXT prostitute *know,* (that he's got-up-in his undercover Caddy, ON DUTY!), *"HO! THAT'S TO LET YOU KNOW, YOU THE NEXT ONE, I'M FINNA' DO SUMFIN', WRONG TOO!!!"*

And though, the handling and drive on this Cadillac, makes for a smooth-riding path. EVEN SO, what hangs from the dirty vice cop's rearview mirror, (to the music!), SWAYS forth-and-back!

(Well, what the fuck is it already, you may ask???)...(Well, I'll fucking tell you!)...

It certainly ain't hung there, for the air to freshen. It's to teach, the NEXT hooker, up in his ride, *(that, just like the LAST hooker, UP IN this ride!),* YOU 'BOUT to be taught, a long-armed-heavy-handed-hand-tailored lesson!!!

And, from just once glance, *(of that rearview-warning and reminder!),* this-here dirty-ass vice cop takes THIS hard stance, *"I'm finna' drop these charges. But, FIRST, I'm finna' drop these pants!".* (And, get all up on and behind her!).

AND, just so, the NEXT ho, *know* HOW it go, (with THIS-HERE law!), *"You can START workin' off your charges, by START workin' your jaw!",* (OF-a-would-be-better-off-in-the-trash-laced-thong!)*(from the last prostitute!),* that the dirty - taking-tangibles-and-full-advantage-too(and-'bout-to-DO-THE-SAME-to-you!)-vice-cop manhandled, as he worked on duty, workin' them shitz down and off!!!

"So, uh, cop, uh, yeah man, you can't drive NO faster than this??? Like,...DAMN negro! We STILL in tha' city! You get me, to where I gotta be and,...yeah, so, well, anywaaaaaays, I MIGHT just, LET YOU in ON this "music-industry-shit"! I MEAN, that is, UNLESS, you WANNA' BE a cop, THE REST OF your life?? I mean, THAT'S cool an all,..THAT IS...IF, you wanna...BE THAT!?! Yeah, so, well, ANYWAAAAAAYS, you know,...there's SOME good ones out there,...I suppose. BUT, let's be HONEST,...YOU AIN'T ONE OF 'EM!!! I mean, JUST HOW

LONG DO YOU THINK YOU CAN keep gettin'-away WIT bein' THEE DIRTIEST ...fuckin'...cop - IN A sea - OF - dirty-fuckin' cops,... BEFORE - "tha'-shit" - CATCHES UP, WIT ya'?!?", an outspoken Pockets, spoke of, on,... AND, SPARKS SOME BULLSHIT!!!

"Oh. Ok. Ok, pot'nuh. I SEE WHAT'S goin' on here. Pockets, THIS "industry" GOT YOU, TOO!! GOT'CHA',...changin' ya' TUNE!", the dirty drivin'-his-undercover-big-ass-Caddy-with-big-ass-rims-slow-on-duty-vice cop, replies!

"THA' FUCK you talkin' 'bout?!? I AIN'T, FORGET shit! OH! SO, you THINK I forgot that, *YOU HAD TO mace me,...TO sucka' punch ME?!?* THAT'S some "PUSSY-shit", "12"!!! DON'T get-it-twisted, mafucka'! "12"! "12"!! "12!!!", YOU AIN'T shit, TO me!! SO, you can SAVE all that "partner" shit! You WANNA' pull this shit over, RIGHT now?? YEAH, GO 'HEAD!!! AND, pull THIS shit THA'-FUCK over and, WE CAN GET the "fair one" on! Mafacka', I AIN'T FROM HERE!!! *I'M FROM mafackin' "HARD-TIMES-VIRGINIA",* mafacka'!! I'LL SHOW yo' ass *how, WE do!!!",* Pockets, sayin' it, LOUD & PROUD!!, *(GOT Pockets thinkin' 'bout, HIS SOUTHERN ROOTS! GOT Pockets callin' the muthafuckin' cop "12"! GOT Pockets TAKIN'-IT-BACK to HIS SOUTHERN ROOTS! GOT Pockets speakin'-on tha' cops HOW THEY spoke-on DOWN SOUTH!).*

"Mutha'...FUCKA'. You IN, MY car!!! DON'T BE GETTIN' LOUD WIT ME, POT'NUH!! DON'T THINK YOU can jus', speak up and, SPEAK TO ME - ANY ol'-DAMN - WAY - YOU - MUTHA'-FUCKIN' - please!! 'CAUSE, you DON'T WANT ME pullin', THA'-FUCK over!!!", the dirty-vice-cop-gettin'-LOUD-AND-standing-his-ground-on-duty, spoke up!!!

"OH, REALLY! And, WHY'S that?!? OH? SO, SO, SO, YOU THINK...YOU GOT SUMTHIN' FO' 'DEEZ HANDS???", an outspoken AND NOT jokin', Pockets, replies!

(Accustomed to being the alpha, this-here dirty-ass vice cop speaks up, one not to mince words, he gives Pockets a mouthful!)...

"Don't try me, Pockets. You REALLY think, YOU got somethin' for a city FULL OF COPS, THAT WANT YOUR ass DEAD?!? Or DID

YA' forget 'bout THAT shit?? YOU gets NO sympathy FROM ME, POT'NUH! JUST WATCH what, I do! OH, I'LL pullover, ALRIGHT! And, I'MA-WATCH YA' ASS - get-tha'-fuck - on-out. 'Cause, Pockets, AFTER you step outta THIS car? I'M pullin' tha'-fuck-OFF FROM tha curb! AND, I'm leavin' YO' ASS, fo'a WHOLE GANG of cops - THAT YOU - pissed-tha'-FUCK-off!!! *The whole fuckin' department knows ya' TRIED to beat 'em for they pensions!* YOU AIN'T goin' in front of NO DAMN judge, ee'ver! TRUST ME…YOU DON'T want that!! *'Cause, ALL THESE judges KNOW you WAS TRYNA' BEAT 'EM FO' THEY, city pensions too!* EVERY-LAST-FUCKIN' officer AND official, in this city, KEEP waitin' day and night, fo' when they get notified, that YO' ASS HAS APPLIED FO' THEY RETIREMENT BENEFITS!!! WHERE'S tha' FUCKIN-SHIT at, pot'nuh?? And, DON'T gimme-dat - "look" ee'ver, Pockets. YOU KNOW what tha' fuck I'm talkin' 'bout! THE RECORDS FO' THA' CITY PENSIONS!!! *The "bankers'" records,* Pockets. *His "paper trail"! HIS "blood trail"!!* Pockets,…where they be? You CAN tell me, pot'nuh!!! It'll,…IT'LL be OUR lil' secret. Ain't nobody been able to find it saved on no "cloud". Soooooo? What?? *YOU put all of the banker's records on' a thumb drive,…DIDNT YA'!?!* So, WHERE IT BE AT, pot'nuh??? YOU KNOW ME, Pockets!!! …I'M 'BOUT MY MONEY!!! I just WANT a "taste". And, NOT NO 51% taste, Skin's be juicin' ya' fo'. 'Cause, right 'bout now??? I'M tha' only friend YOU GOT in THIS city! …They want ya' dead, pot'nuh…they want ya' dead. YOU AIN'T gettin' NO-FAIR-SHAKE in 'DIS HERE town! And,… yeah, *the feds tried to clean this bitch up,…after ya' beat-feet a few years back.* BUT, YOU KNOW HOW IT BE,…*North Juarez been grimy-as- fuck fo' dis' long,…FO' a reason!* And, I'ma hip-ya'ta-sum'fin, pot'nuh. YO' MOMS IS HEATED, SON!!! *NOT 'cause ya' got'er locked-up!* Shit, YO' MOMS IS A G!!! FIRST OFF, *it took damn-near half tha' station to get ya' nut-ass-brother back in that bank vault cell!* But,…ya' moms, yo'?!? *YO' MOMS, straight walked-tha'-fuck-on-in THAT bank vault cell, LIKE a G!! And, right befo' that vault door, got slammed shut behind her?? YA' MOMS turn't 'round AND said to EVERY LAST COP standin' there, "Any Y'ALL BITCHES, play "Spades"???"* YOOOOOO!!! HAD ME trippin'! BUT, ya' moms, yo'? YO' moms, BE HEATED like'a MUTHAFUCKA', pot'nuh!! *'CAUSE, YA' NEV'A DID GET AT THAT MONEY FROM THEM CITY PENSIONS THAT, YOU WAS 'SPOSED TO "KICK-UP" TO HER!!!* BELIEVE ME, pot'nuh, AS OF THIS very moment, YOU NEED ME MORE, than I NEED you!! What you NEED TO do, POT'NUH, is,...calm ya' ass down a lil' bit AND, LET ME get'cha' ass OUTTA' muthafuckin' North Juarez,...ALIVE!!! Pockets,...you KNOW tha' NAME of MY game,...I'M ALL 'BOUT GETTIN' MONEY!!!", the dirty-witholding-information-on-duty-vice-cop explains, to Pockets, (before, he continues...), "SO, if you got somethin' for me, on the "music tip", then, WHAT the fuck IS IT and, HOW MUCH money you GONNA' pay me TO do it?? 'CAUSE, I DON'T NEED ya' bullshit, pot'nuh!! And, I DON'T NEED tha' shady-bullshit OF the music industry, EE'VER!", the dirty-in-a-position-to-play-hardball-on-duty-vice-cop, tells Pockets, (((KNOWING-GOOD-AND-DAMN-WELL - HE'S GONNA' DO - SOME - DIRTY-MUSIC-INDUSTRY-COCKSUCKIN'-ASS-EATIN' - SHADDY-ASS-BULLSHIT - *WITH THE - SECRETLY-RECORDED-FIRST-AND-CURRENTLY-THE-ONLY-VERSION - OF - "CHRISTMAS MOURNING" - WHICH - CONTAINS THAT - AMAZING-VOICE-OF-INTUBATION - ON IT!!!)))*(((OY - TO-THE - MUTHA'-FUCKIN' - VEY!!!))).

And so...

"Shiiiiiit.", Pockets, *thinks* to himself, *"Money over pride...ain't THAT some shit!",* as, he's beginning to settledown,...(((BUT NEVER WILLING TO SETTLE!!!)))...

So...

Pockets, tells the dirty vice cop, "Look, I want you to be "Head of Security" for this "buzz" tonight. I want YOU right on the "frontlines" of this thing,...LIKE,...YOU COULDN'T EVEN IMAGINE! BUT, I gotta lotta'-shit to do AND TO handle, BEFORE "this buzz" CAN EVEN happen. MAINLY, I gotta get my hands on THAT song book,... you know,...the one with the lyrics to this Christmas song in it? Shiiiiiit, Trife's THE ONLIEST ONE, that's got ANY-KINDA' documentation, TO WHAT the actual WORDS ARE, TO THIS Christmas song! I mean,…I'M MUTHAFUCKIN' POCKETS! I GOT EVERYTHANG!!! BUT,…guess-tha'-fuck what?? I ain't GOT THE WORDS to this mafuckin' CHRISTMAS SONG!!! AND, SINCE I can't be in two places at once. I'MA NEED you to get up with that triflin'-motherfucker and, GET THAT song book FROM him! Just, tell 'em that I said, *"For him, to put everythang he's got, in that suitcase of his."* And, tell 'em that, *"your brother"* says, *"For him, to give it exclusively TO you. And, to give it, ONLY to you!"* And, listen cop. I'm talkin' laptop. Thumb drive. His song book,…yeah, so, well, anywaaaaaays, IF HE HAPPENS to have any other books lying around,…I'MA want ALL OF THEM BOOKS, TOO! Everythang. …You understand? I want it all! Don't worry 'bout it. HE'LL be cool wit it. BUT, IF HE gives ya' ANY shit, 'bout it. Tell'em… tell'em,…yeah, uh, er-rah, so, well, uh, ANYWAAAAAAYS, TELL'EM, *"I want the CONTRACTS, for "YOUR Christmas song", to be typed-up ON YOUR HOMEGIRL Y.S.' laptop!"* Got it?? And, you can even throw in there, that, *"AFTER the contracts been typed up that, Pockets, thought it would make for a nice gesture, for the contracts to be SAVED, ONLY TO Y.S.'S thumb drive!"* HE'LL like that! And, tell'em, tell'em, *"We need the song book, too. So, that,…so that, "the contract guy", can include "YOUR lyrics" IN the contracts…and, yeah, so, well, anyways, to allow "the contract guy" to get a head start, in the filing of a copyright ON "YOUR Christmas song",…FOR YOU!!!"* Look here, cop. Just, MAKE SURE you SAY, that, *"your brother",* wants it. OTHERWISE,…you can fuckin' forget it! HE WON'T give you SHIT!"

"You see, pot'nuh,…you DO, NEED me! YOU, got ya'self, "ALL-WORKED-UP-'n-heated" and I WASN'T EVEN talkin' 'bout "me", macing YO' ass! The "tune", I was talkin' 'bout, WAS, *you decided AWFUL-QUICK on this hippy-motherfucker, writtin' up the contracts for you and Skin's!* Soooooo, WASSAP wit 'dat??", the dirty-playing-BOTH-SIDES-of-this-music-industry-fence-on-duty-vice-cop angles, Pockets.

(Looking over at the dirty vice cop)…(sizing him up on HIS angles!)…

Pockets, replies, "Oh? THAT. Yeah, so, well, ANYWAAAAAAYS, I just figured that, SINCE you got your hooks in 'em already, seein' as, he's YOUR informant, and all."

Angles presented, for angles played, the dirty vice cop attempts to deflect game, "Informant??? He ain't my

(Pockets instincts on suspicions has him steppin' all over the suspected-bullshit-presented in mid-sentence!)

AS...

(Pockets, continues,...TO spit game!)...

"...THEN! He'd be LESS APT to fuck these contracts up! ...THAT'S all. SO, you know,...BEIN' tha' "gamblin' man", THAT I am,...I'M BETTIN' ON YOU havin' ENOUGH weight hangin' over him, that, HE WON'T be on "some-dumb-shit"! LIKE, tryin' to write these contracts up, SO AS, to work HIMSELF in AS, a co-owner OF the publishing ON THIS Christmas song. OR, be on some-slick-shit and, make-it-out SO that, HE ENDS UP WITH ownership OF the "masters",...OR some other "shit-stick" shit!! TRUST ME, ON THIS,... the devil's IN the details!"

(Looking back over at Pockets, the dirty - STILL-playin'-games-ON-DUTY - vice cop, speaks on: "The Game")...

"It's LIKE that!?! FUCK THIS "Music Industry" shit! I mean,...you HEAR stories and shit,...BUT, SHIT,...IF ya' GOTTA' keep ya' eye ON YOUR contract guy??? THEN,...I mean,...WHO'D EVEN WANT "IN" on "THIS" shit?!? Hey Pockets, YOU want me to be "Head of Security" tonight, fo' ya', pot'nuh? "THAT", I CAN do! BUT, mixin'-up in this "Music Game" ANY FURTHER??? YOU can FORGET THAT-SHIT, pot'nuh!! BUT, I'll tell ya' what,...I'll ONLY do this "security detail" for you tonight, IF ya' make me the "Head of Security" FOR ya' WHOLE-DAMN RECORD LABEL!! Yo',...Pockets,...*what was that you was tellin', Skin's, last night?? Jettison Records,*...right? DAMN, POT'NUH!!! YOU TELLIN' ME, I'M DRIVIN' tha' head OF...Jettison Records, around?!? Y'ALL BE PUTTIN' OUT NUTTIN' BUT THAT HOT FIRE!!! Jettison,...Jettison,...Jettison..., (OH SHIT!),...I GET IT! Y'all be: "DROPPIN' ALBUMS",...ain't that, right?!?"

"Yeah.", Pockets simply, replies, cockin' his kelly green Eagles hat to the side, while lookin' at the dirty vice cop,...(out tha' side of his eye!).

"So, pot'nuh? I'm now officially your "Head of Security" for Jettison Records!?!", the dirty-vice-cop-gettin'-delusions-of-grandeur-gettin'-sucked-into-this-"Music-Game"-BULLSHIT-on-duty, asks!

"Of course. Yeah? THAT'S ALL YOU!!! BUT,...ya' GOTTA' do somethin', fo' me first...", Pockets, replies.

"Whatchu' need me to do for you?? YOU can count on me, pot'nuh! I'M DOWN WIT THIS JETTISON RECORDS - SHIT!!!", the dirty - thinkin'-'bout-what-Pockets-said-'bout-how-much-longer-he-thinks-he-can-keep-gettin'-away-wit-bein'-THEE-DIRTIEST-of-the-dirty-vice-cops-on-(AND-OFF!)-duty-before-the-shit-catches-up-with-him - vice cop, replies!!!

(OH LAWD!!!)...(WHAT'S Pockets' Big-Hustle-Gears gonna' CONJURE UP NEXT???)...

"ROLL YOUR WINDOW DOWN, MAFUCKA'!!! YOU GOT THE WHOLE INSIDE OF THIS DAMN CADILLAC, SMELLIN' LIKE REEFER AND A FULL BOTTLE OF "JOOP!" COLOGNE!!!, Pockets, shouts!, (in the process of laughing out loud!).

"You, MUST NOT know!! ALL MY ladies LOOOOOOOVE this "JOOP!", shit!!!", the dirty-rollin'-his-car-window-down-on-duty-vice-cop, replies, (with a laugh and with pride!!).

"MAN, I was JUST fuckin' wit ya', "POT'NUH"! ..."JOOP!", THAT'S SOME "old-school-playa'-playa'" - SHIT, RIGHT THERE! *BACK in my "Playa' Dayz", I used to "douse-me-down" in a bott'll'ov' 'DAT-shit, TOO!!"*, Pockets, replies, (and, ALTHOUGH, his car window is down, he's STILL CONTINUING to roll!:)

AND SO...

(WITH car windows down and, with the dirty vice cop on duty reaching the city limits, THESE TWO MOTHERFUCKERS ARE ACTUALLY GETTING ALONG, as the dirty vice cop on duty has managed to get Pockets out of town!)...

AS...

(((The dirty vice cop, jumps up on Highway Route 36, giving his gas pedal a punch, MAKIN' that drippin' gloss black '60 Eldorado Brougham - sittin' on 120 chromed-out spoke rims - JUMP!!!)))...

"THAT'S MORE LIKE IT!!, Pockets, instructs, "THAT'S what-tha'-fuck I'M TALKIN' 'bout! DAMN, NEGRO! I got places to be! OPEN this bitch UP!!!"

"Hey,...pot'nuh. DON'T BE TELLIN' ME HOW TO BE DRIVIN' MY-MUTHA'-FUCKIN'-CAR!!! THIS-HERE; IS MY MUTHA' FUCKIN' CAR,...POT'NUH!!! AND, anotha' thing! DON'T tell me HOW to do MY job! And,...I won't tell you, HOW TO do YOURS! You DO NEED me to get up wit dat "hippy-contract-guy", A.S.A.MUTHAFUCKIN'.P.,...AIN'T THAT, RIGHT?!? Weeeeeell, THAT'S what-tha'-fuck, I WAS doin'!! KINDA'-HARD for me to pullover AFTER SPOTTIN' the contract guy's car, DON'TCHA' think, IF - I'm goin' "a-buck-five" THROUGH the city?!?", the dirty-vice-cop-AIN'T-'bout'ta'-be-TAKIN'-Pockets'-SHIT-on-duty, SPEAKS UP!!

(Pockets, AIN'T 'BOUT to take NO lip off'a some "DIRTY-ASS VICE COP")...

(((LOSES HIS TOP!!!)))...

AS, HE...

Leans his head out of the front passenger's window!

As, he...

(((POINTS EMPHATICALLY, at the spinning-spoked-up-chrome-rim beneath him!!!)))

AS, HE...

(Loses his kelly green cap in the process:)

As, he...

Speaks on (((and, GETS RAW AS FUCK!!!))), (as to), what he views beneath him!

(Come!)…(LET'S listen in!)…

"JOB??? "12"! "12"!! "12"!!! WAKE THA'-FUCK UP, "12"!!! YOU SEE DAT-OUT-DARE??? YOU AIN'T NUTTIN' BUT A SPOKE!!!!!! HATE TO break-IT-TO-ya', "12",…BUT, you AIN'T nuttin' BUT a "WARM BODY" IN A seat!!! THAT'S what-tha'-fuck, YOU IS,…TA' 'DEM!!!", Pockets, WITH THAT "DOWN SOUTH" SLANG FOR A COP ("12")…(AND, WITH TRUTH SPOKEN!!!).

And then…

(With his head back inside of the vehicle, Pockets, gets nasty!)… (WELP! SO MUCH for THESE TWO getting along!!)…

(COME!)(LET'S LISTEN IN!!!)…

"Job! Ain't that a hoot! OK, THEN,…I'MA help ya' out WIT, *"YO' JOB"!* Oh, SO, what?!? *YOU ain't NEVER HEARD OF a DAMN cell phone??? You got "paper" ON THIS hippy-motherfuckerfucker, DON'T'CHA?? HE'S "makin' buys" FO' ya',…AIN'T HE!?! So, so, so, so, SO, WHAT???* OH! I SEE!! *YOU "tha'-type"' TO JUST "HANDOVER" a STACK of "buy money" AND, just LET tha' "muthafuckin' DIRTBAG RAT-ASS criminal informant" have "FREE-reign",…AIN'T'CHA'!?!* Sooooo,… WHAT!?? *HE AIN'T gotta "check-in", WIT you???"*

THEN…

(Rolling his eyes all-sarcastic-'n-shit!)…(Pockets, speaks-on-it, SOME MO'!!)…

…"C'mon, "12", BE REAL!! *THAT'S what YOU'RE tellin', ME?!?* Shiiiiiit, SEEMS to me,…*I DO GOTTA'-TELL-YOU HOW to do YOUR job!* Lookie-here, "12",…YOU FUCKIN'-UP this "Head of Security" gig, that, I'M TRYING TO BLESS YOU with! And, I'M lettin' you know THAT shit, RIGHT NOW! *JUST hit the hippy-contract-mafucka' THE-FUCK-UP on your cell phone!* I GOT too-much-shit to do AND, NOT ENOUGH TIME to do it in!"

AND THEN…

(After some - "SERIOUS-FACE-WASHING" - from, his avid powerlifting hands, Pockets, DONE with, His: "Don't-BE-So-Thin-Skinned" - Ball-Breaking, spoke up on ALL HE REALLY EVER GAVE-A-FUCK ABOUT, THIS ENTIRE CAR RIDE!!!)...

(Let's listen in!)...

..."ARE YOU EVEN GONNA' be able to get WORD to this hippy-fuck, IN A "timely-business-fasion"? AND HAVE HIM there at Skin's place, when I get back there wit my RV?? *THIS AIN'T some "roll call" that, YOUR ASS can JUST come "strollin'-in-on" AT ANY-DAMN-TIME, you please!* THIS, is "BIG-MONEY-BUSINESS", YOU dealin' WIT, negro! And,..."12",...DON'T BE SLOWIN' ME DOWN!!! 'CAUSE, WHEN I get back with my RV, I'm parkin' THAT mafucka' out front of THAT I.A. Club!!! And, I'm gettin' Skin's son-n'-law IN tha' back of that bitch in tha' booth! And, I WILL BE recordin' him singin' that FUCKIN' Christmas song! ONE TAKE! ONE TAKE! That's ALL-THA'-FUCK it's GONNA' take! ALL I need from Skin's son-in-law is HIS "rough vocals" on tha' track. 'CAUSE, when it comes to ME bein' a sound engineer? When it comes to my skills at mixin' and masterin'?!? SHIIIIIIT!!!! One take, is ALL IT'S GONNA' take! I'LL MAKE HIS "rough vocals" SOUND LIKE "final vocals", AFTER I get done "WORKIN' MAH MAGIC" on THA' track. 'Cause, I'M that FUCKIN-GOOD!!!", Pockets, speaking-on-it, and, speaking FULLY, OF: "the love of being"...IN LOVE WITH HIMSELF!!!

"Fuck that shit, POT'NUH!! YOU tha'-one that NEEDS TO *"LOOKIE-HERE"!!!* YO' ASS CAN get-tha'-fuck-out RIGHT NOW and, WALK YO' ASS aaaaaall-tha'-way down to tha' NEXT exit! AND THEN, WALK YO' ASS ALL-THE-WAY-DOWN Business Rt. 36, BACK to ya' RV, SINCE YA' WANNA' KEEP "jumpin'-tha-gun" ON shit!"

THEN...

(After a lil'-subconscious "face-washin'" of HIS own!)...

The dirty vice cop, turns to Pockets, (with a chuckle) and, says,…"*CALLIN' me, "12"*,…WITCHA', country-ass!! We "5-0" UP HERE, POT'NUH!!"

Then…

(((With some VERY-CONSCIOUS "face-washing"!!)))…

(The dirty-vice-cop-washing-his-face-on-duty, spoke up, ON: "The Subject")…

"I'VE been in THIS "Music Game" for FIVE-FUCKIN'-MINUTES, and I ALREADY hate THIS shit! *YOU wanna keep on, ASSUMIN', shit???* WELL, HAVE-AT-IT, POT'NUH!! SEE HOW MUCH shit you gonna be able to get done, WIT OUT MY help!! Just,…settle-tha'-fuck-down,…for'a minute, WILL ya'? Like,…DAMN! YOU AIN'T tha'-MOST-EASIEST-person to work wit,…ya' know THAT!?!", the dirty - STILL-enamered-on-duty-with-the-idea-of-having-his-foot-in-the-ALMIGHTY-"Music-Industry-Door"-vice-cop, begins, telling Pockets,…

BEFORE…

(Coming TO the realization, that!)…

Having just one foot in the door of the music industry and having to deal WITH Pockets' shit IN this "Music Game", as "Head of Security" for a major record label, COULD JUST VERY WELL BE his WAY OUT of the - Dirty-Cop-In-A-Dirty-Police-Department - "CORRUPTION GAME"!! IN WHICH, the "door", of THAT "GAME", he has BOTH FEET FIRMLY-PLANTED IN!!((OY VEY!!)).

And so…

DEALING with "Pockets' shit", IS FAR GREATER than BEING DELT a lengthy prison sentence and,…HAVING BOTH FEET IN a jail cell and,… HAVING THAT jail cell door SLAMMED on BOTH of them shitz!!((OY TO THA' MUTHA' FUCKIN' VEY!!)).

AND SO…

(The-dirty-on-duty-STILL-WANTING-IN-on-this-"MUSIC-INDUSTRY-SHIT!"-vice-cop, continues)...(SCHOOLING POCKETS IN THE PROCESS!)...

..."Pockets, I WANT THAT "Head of Security" position! SO, I'm gonna' explain some-shit TO YOU 'bout, my CURRENT position as a muthafuckin' "spoke"!! *I get up wit all of my criminal informants in person,...face-to-face,...THAT'S tha' way I like it. THAT'S the way,... IT'S GOTTA' be! ANYONE of them fuck-heads CAN tell me ANY-'OL-SHIT, OVER tha' phone! I AIN'T fall'off a NO-DAMN-TRUCK, ee'ver!! And,...besides, pot'nuh,...I DON'T TRUST, my Department!* YOU EVER THINK ABOUT THAT??? YOU THINK those "department-issued" cell phones AIN'T BEING monitored...by,...WHOEVER-THA'-FUCK!?! *NO cell phones! I AIN'T "creatin'" THAT "paper-trail"!!!* I told ya' before to just relax 'n calm-ya'-ass-down a lil' bit, DIDN'T I?? *...I can get-up-wit that hippy-informant-of-mine at one of his, two jobs. If NOTHIN' else, tha' HIPPY mutha' fucka', DOES work! And, it WORKS-OUT-WELL, for me,...for, tha'-shit he HAS TO DO,...FOR ME,...to KEEP HIS ass OUTTA' jail! I'll be able to get-up wit 'em. That SHOULD ease-yo'-mind! ...HE just likes to take "long breaks" WHILE he's workin'. He just takes-off and gets lost, sometimes.* I don't know what to tell ya', pot'nuh. YOU KNOW HOW "it" be! *...HE's GOT his "own-way"...TO hustle muthafuckas...*"

(Pockets, coming TO A realization, of HIS own!)...

Considering the fact THAT, he CAN'T BE a "one man show" on the road!

(Considering the fact, THAT)...

((((He's far, far, away from, HIS: ON TOP OF THE WORLD - Corner Office Home!!!))))

AND...

(CONSIDERING THE FACT, THAT!)...

THAT: Nervous - Whistlin'-Jumpy-Jumpin'-Outta'-His-Socks - Phillip Tate, on his WORST day,...THIS: Dirtiest-Of-THEE-DIRTIEST - Vice Cop, AIN'T!!!

AND SO...

He's gonna HAVE TO GO-EAZY on the cop!

'Cause...

((((Pockets, "HAD-BEEN-HAD" his FIRST "taste" of BIG MONEY! And, HE HAS set that "bar", OF WHICH, NOT to let HIS money slip below, CAUSING his "money bar" TO DROP!!!)))(((OY VEY!!!))).

And, (OF: "Pockets'-considerations")...

Pockets, considers WHAT'S to follow as to be AT THE TOP!!!

For...

(HE'S STILL-GOTTA'-GET, Mr. Brotha Trife's, "final vocals" recorded!)

'CAUSE...

THAT - TIER-THREE MOTHERFUCKER'S - "AMAZIN'-VOICE-OF-INTUBATION" - AIN'T GON' stay THAT WAY forever!!

AND SO...

(((TIME IS MONEY, MOTHERFUCKERS!!!)))

FOR...

THAT: Voice - ((((CREATED-BY-THREE-YEARS-OF-INTUBATION!!!)))) - OF: Tier-Three-Trife's is,...STILL ON THE CLOCK!!! (((OY-TO-THA'-MUTHA'-FUCKIN'-VEY!!!))).

(Come!)(LET'S LISTEN IN ON POCKETS' REALIZATIONS),(YOU NOSEY MOTHERFUCKERS:)

"Alright. ...ALRIGHT!! Listen, "12",... (SHIT!), as,...MUCH AS, I, hate to...admit it,...(FUCK!),...I...I do need YOUR...assistance. THERE!! YOU HAPPY, NOW!?!", Pockets, replies, *of swallowed-pride!((RIPPIN' his throat RAW down the back,...AND BOTH SIDES!!))*, before, and, as he, continues..., "Alright, *findin' mafackas IS your bailiwick.* SOOOOOO,

I'MA just ease up on you, *on THAT tip*. You STILL AIN'T too much of driver,...if-you-ax me! BUT,...THAT SHITZ MOOT, at THIS motherfuckin'-JUNCTURE!! But, I WILL choose to agree, that, *you'll be able to track your informant down*. And, have his ass at Skin's place, READY to do-up these contracts for me, by the time, I get back. Just do me a "solid", huh? After you drop me off,...fuckin' get ON IT! I mean, YOU GONNA'-GOTTA' FLY YO' ASS back to your city AND, get that song book 'n shit, from Trife! JUST REMEMBER, if you tell 'em *"your brother"* said, *"It was cool to give it to you."*, then, YOU SHOULDN'T have much problems. ...Hang on a second."

Then, (Reaching for his cell phone)...

Pockets, scrolls through his contacts and, dials-up the "sensible-one", (of his two rappers). Pockets, turning into, His: "Big-Wig-Music-Biz-Mode", turns to the dirty vice cop, and, says, "YOU NEED to tell me more 'bout this Christmas song, that YOU heard. I don't have much time. But,...I'M MAFACKIN' POCKETS, YOU FEEL ME!!! So,...I GOT this! BUT, FIRST! It IS imperative, that, I make this call, prior to my arrival at my RV. Preparation is the key..."

And so, (as False Profit, answers his phone)...

Pockets, tells Profit, to put it on speaker and, for False Profit to MAKE SURE that, MC Busta-Nut, IS listening as well!!

For...

(Pockets, wants MC Busta-Nut to "dually-hear", HIMSELF speak!!")...

FOR...

Pockets, WANTS to make sure, THOSE TWO ARE listening!!

WHILE...

(((Pockets, IS listening TO,...HIMSELF speak!!!)))...(An "OV VEY!!!" IS fitting FOR right here,...dont'cha' know:)

And so...

(While the following telephone conversation is taking place, the dirty vice cop, continues driving on duty, *WHILE humming, whistling and, singing the Christmas song TO HIMSELF down low)*...

(Come!)(Let us ALL illegally eavesdrop in on Pockets' phone call, shall we??)...(((YOU "WIRETAP LAW" VIOLATING MOTHERFUCKERS!!!)))...

"Alright y'all, HUDDLE UP!!! I'm on my way back to the RV and time is imperative, gentlemen. SO, I'm going to place priority on the following "X's and O's" that, I'm going to go over with y'all, right now! In the future, gentlemen, Phillip Tate, will have all shows "booked" well in advance. And, notifications of same, provided to all, that it will pertain. And, in most cases, we WILL BE arriving at the venue, hours in adavnce for sound check, to "get your minds' right" and, for whatever else that, needs to be taken care of. BUT, THIS IS THAT "Road Life", gentlemen! SOMETIMES, gentlemen, on tha' road, you just gotta call an "audible"! SO, get freshened-up, clean't-up and, BE lookin' right! I want y'all in your "fliest-shit" tonight! I told y'all before we left, *I wanted to see HOW y'all could handle this "life on the road"*, didn't I? WELL, tonight IS "make-or-break", night! Sometimes, gentlemen, this "road life", DON'T ALWAYS GO according to plan. Sometimes, the tour bus might breakdown. OTHERTIMES, we'll land in Paris for a show, ONLY TO FIND that OUR LUGGAGE ended up in NIGERIA!!! BUT, it's HOW you handle "SUCH SITUATIONS", IS what MAKES YOU a professional!", Pockets, begins,...

BUT THEN...

MUST set MC Busta-Nut straight!

'CAUSE...

(ON speaker phone, Pockets can hear, THAT FOOL clowin'!)...

"YOU KNOW, FOOL!! *YOU remind me of my baby bro. HE TOO, was always clownin', WHEN he SHOULDA' been LISTENIN'!* I'll have you know, 'Nut. Nigeria is THE third LARGEST "music industry market", IN THE WORLD!!! So, GET'CHA' shit straight, son! And, YOU JUST MIGHT stick 'round in this industry TOO find, THAT SHIT out!! Speaking of gettin' YOUR "shit straight", THIS is "tha' shit" I HAVE TOO go over, wit BOTH ya'll! Now,...*we've done some shows together, in the past. ...Them little night clubs, in tha' hood. And, y'all did good,...for tha' MOST part.* BUT,...TONIGHT?? We GON' BE up in'a club that, "WE" ain't exactly the anticipated crowd's,...demographic. I ain't got tha' time, too slow down. SO, Profit, I'M delegatin' it TO YOU, TO EXPLAIN that shit to 'Nut, once I conclude this conference call. AND, since that IS THE CASE, I NEED Y'ALL to BE "on point" like a mafacka', tonight,...YOU FEEL ME??? So,...I'll START WITH you, 'Nut. AND, pay attention! 'Cause, this shit IS important! 'Nut,...*our last gig WAS an ABSOLUTE train wreck! YOU CAN'T BE gettin' soooooo smoked-up befo' tha' show, that YOU CAN'T EVEN remember tha' words, to YOUR OWN damn songs!!! And, you showed-up at our last production meeting, ALL-FUCKED-UP,...noddin' tha' fuck-out 'n shit!* ...WHY WOULD an agent want to "sign-on" TO, REPRESENT you??? I CAN'T have THAT, NO more! WE'RE gonna "tighten-shit up" 'round here, FROM HERE on out! When this "road trip" is over. And, we get back to the label. The absolute first thing that I'm GOING TO assist upon YOU BOTH do, IS TO fill out an "Weekly Itinerary"! And, IN THAT itinerary, YOU ARE going to make a "TO DO" list! Beginning, from 6:00AM to 9:00PM. And I want you to put in there, WHEN you SCHEDULED yourselves for meals, exercize, meditation, etc. And, YOU WILL "map out" what YOU WILL BE doing "musically" and "educationally", EACH HOUR, to hone your skills and your craft AND to better yourselves as artists AND AS MEN. WE ain't-got-time FOR "tha' bullshit", no more! YOU feel me!? WE WILL MEET, once a week. And, at this..."Itinerary Meeting", or, for-that-matter, AT ANYTIME DURING THE WEEK, I MAY ASK YOU,...WHAT DID, YOU do, TO better yourselves, this week? WHAT DID, "YOU",...accomplish, THIS week? Will YOUR answer be, *"I didn't do anything, all week??"* Or, WILL "YOU", ANSWER, *"This is WHAT, I'VE DONE, TO improve, MY life, AND MY career..."*. Now, with social media, I want y'all to keep up with your accounts. Simply, check-in. Like and share posts, from the other artists on our label. MAKE THE MOST OF EVERY OPPORTUNITY, TO promote Jettison Records AND YOUR fellow artists. WE JETTISON RECORDS, BABY!!! SHOW YOUR LOVE!!! We all in this together, not everythang gotta be 'BOUT YOU! Show love and support, for your other artists. If a mafacka' on our label, has a show coming up? BLAST THAT SHIT ALL OVER SOCIAL MEDIA!!! IF you squander such an opportunity? Then, YOU HAVE SQUANDERED potentially gaining a new fan! And, IN TURN, squandered them potentially buying merchandise, concert tickets, YOUR MUSIC,...AS, WELL AS, THEM PROMOTING YOU, the label...AND, your fellow artists, THROUGH, word-of-mouth, OR THROUGH, social media! YOU FEEL ME!?! Listen, y'all. If we "tha' shit" and we know that we "tha' shit"? Then, AIN'T-NO-SHAME-IN-OUR-GAME IN showin', a mafacka', some LOVE! You feel me??? Fuck ALL "tha' bullshit"! LET'A hater, STILL hate! BUT, AS FOR, US?? WE GON', SHOW LOVE!!! And, as far, as, this, social-media-shit goes? I WANT Y'ALL TO BEWARE, OF scammers contacting you THROUGH social media! YOU KNOW,...CORNBALL SHIT!! LIKE, texing your phone, hittin' you up on your email, etc., stating that, they are in the "music industry". OR, are WITH the media! And, they want to interview you and/or asking you FOR money. IF this happens! YOU contact me,... immediately!! And, I'll have Phillip Tate look into it. And,...*STOP POSTING EVERY-DAMN-WHERE, ya'll be at! If ya'll eatin' lunch somewhere,...WHO GIVES A FUCK?!? THA' WHOLE WORLD don't gotta know that!* YOU FEEL ME??? Safety first, gentlemen,...safety first. Now, WE GON' tight'n-up on our "lines of communication", too! Keep your cell phones on you. And, MAKE SURE that they're KEPT charged! Now, I understand that, y'all might wanna chill wit'a fine mommy or two. Go buy-up tha' mall. And, take yo' peoples wit ya'll to tha' dealership, so they can watch y'all buy that phat new ride! BUT, WHEN I HIT Y'ALL UP?? YA'LL BEST-BE hittin'-me-back, IN'A "timely-business-manner"!!! OR, I'MA START handin' out fines! YOU FEEL ME ON THIS?? Good! Common courtesy and respect, gentlemen. What you do on your own time,...is what you do on your own time. BUT, DON'T

Y'ALL EVER, EVER, EVER, MAFACKIN'-FORGET, THAT, BUSINESS IS BUSINESS!!! SO, give me "timely notification" if you got something goings-on, that may end up running later than initially planned. But, when it comes to "business", DON'T BE - MUTHA FUCKIN' - LATE!!! NOW. AT TONIGHT'S event and, for THAT matter, FROM-HERE-ON-OUT, I want y'all to be aware of YOUR SURROUNDINGS!!! EVERYONE'S a potential fan, OR A potential hater, you feel me, so, at tonight's event, I want y'all two to stay close, have each other's backs and, don't be wondering off separately...yeah, so, uh, um, well, anywaaaaaays, I wouldn't want nuthin' bad to happen to y'all tonight. SO, at tonight's event, stick close and, wait to be introduced to perform and, when it's YOUR TIME to take the stage,...*MAKE THEM REMEMBER YOU!!!* KEEP 'EM TALKIN' 'BOUT JETTISON RECORDS!!! Now, when I get back, after I get myself good-'n-cleaned-up, I'll hip y'all to what-all's gonna-be happening after I park this RV in front of tonight's venue. Yeah, so, well, anyways, *I signed a new artist to the label, while I was away.* And, I wanna get him in the booth and, see what he sounds like singing this song he wrote. So, False Profit, make sure that new mic is on point and, that everythangs ready-to-go in my studio. Time, gentlemen. Efficiency! WE got to make the most of our time today, 'cause, we ain't gon' have that much time to get it all done...BUT, WE WILL,...get it all done! SO, while I'm recordin' tha' "new guy", I want y'all in tha' back room of the venue. And, I want y'all to stay there 'til you're introduced to go on. And, I DON'T WANT Y'ALL, talkin' bout, thinkin' 'bout, doin' NUTHIN' that, AIN'T GOT NUTHIN' TO DO WITH MUSIC!!! NO idle chit-chat! NO goofin' off! Get focused,...and STAY focused. YOU feel me?? I want your fingernails clipped. And, I want your nose hairs trimmed. It's "MUTHA'-FUCKIN'-Showtime", tonight, you feel me!?! Attention to detail, gentlemen. I don't want no lint on your clothes. And, DON'T BE usin' that deodorant stick that's gonna be gettin' "white-shit" on your shirt! Attention to detail, gentlemen. Attention to detail. YOU'RE not just representing, YOURSELVES tonight! YOU'RE representing Jettison Records, tonight! WHICH MEANS, YOU'RE REPRESENTIN' ME, TONIGHT!!! SO, GET YA'SELF "ON POINT" AND, STAY THA' FUCK "ON POINT"!!! I know this "life on the road", CAN be a grind! ...It can really take a toll, on your body and mind. But, it's important THAT y'all take care of yourselves. GET your rest! Look AND feel right! YOU feel me? Profit, *I remember what you used to tell me, right 'round the time I signed y'all. NOTHING was EVER clear,...before I started handlin' EVERY ASPECT of your career. You NEVER KNEW IF it was a paid gig, or not? HOW MUCH you were, gettin' paid?? WHAT percentage, was going to the promotor?!? SHIIIIIT, Y'ALL DIDN'T EVEN KNOW what percentage WAS goin' TO Y'ALL!!! And, y'all remember? BEFORE, I signed y'all?? WASN'T y'all 'sposed to travel-cross-country wit some group??? And, "THAT SHIT" WASN'T MADE, TOO CLEAR, to y'all either!! WAS IT??? "It" was ALWAYS "some shit",...WASN'T IT!?!?!? FIRST! Y'all was GONNA' BE co-headliners. THEN! Y'alls was "'sposed to be" the opening act! AND THEN! Y'ALL was JUST "gon' be doin'" some "featured monolog", in between acts! ...OR some LAME-ASS horse-shit, to THAT affect!! AND THEN!!! YA' ASSES NEVER DID GO ON THIS "CROSS COUNTRY TOUR"!!! ...MUTHA' FUCKIN', DID YA'!?!?!?* My point being, fellas,...IS, GET'YA REST!!! 'CAUSE, maybe? JUST MAYBE!?! *IF y'all WAS GETTIN' ya' rest? And, NOT-SO-DAMN "green-'round-tha'-gills", ALL-THA'-MAFACKIN'-TIME!?! ...WHO KNOWS,..."tha' shit" might've worked-out, FO' YA' ASSES!!!!!!* MC Busta-Nut,...False Profit. Phillip Tate, IS A wealth of information! SO, when we get back to Jettison Records, I want y'all to feel comfortable in asking, Phil, ANY questions that you may have, ABOUT the business,...the industry. Yeah, SO, WELL, ANYWAAAAAAYS,...UNTIL we're back at the label? KEEP YA' MINDS' focused ON tonight's Meet 'n Greet! On...YOUR Meet 'N Greet!! ...Alright, 'Gents. Do either of y'all, have anything, for: "The Good of The Order"?...

And...

(Before, either False Profit, or MC Busta-Nut can answer)...

Pockets, ends the call.

'CAUSE...

HE'S the one calling the shots!

And...

(((HE AIN'T TRYIN' TO listen,...TO y'all!!!))).

'Cause...

Pockets,...GOT SOME shit TO him!!

(((YOU MOTHERFUCKERS, BETTER START LISTENIN'!!!))).

'CAUSE...

JUST AS, a boxer's coach, in between rounds, KNOWS that, he has JUST ONE minute! And, FOR THAT minute, WHAT that coach WANTS his boxer TO REMEMBER,...IS THE FIRST AND THE LAST THINGS(before the toll, of the bell, to the next round rings!)TO come out HIS mouth!!!

AND SO...

(BACK TO "the matter" AT hand!!!)...

FOR...

Pockets, mentioning that Christmas song to the dirty vice cop, as THE LAST thing THAT HE WANTED that dirty vice cop TO hear HIM say, right before HE placed THAT call! WAS ALL APART, OF: Pockets' - I'VE-BEEN-playin'-THIS-DIRTY-VICE-COP-for-a-minute-LOOOOOOONG-OF-WORDAGE-Phone-Call - Plan!!!(((ALL THINGS FOR A REASON,...YA' DIG!!!))).

FOR...

JUST, LIKE: Phillip Tate's - "Nervous-Subconscious-Non-Sensical" - Whistlin', Pockets, PLANTED that song and TOUCHED into that dirty vice cop's "Subconscious-Mind"!!!

And,(AS, SUCH!)...

Pockets, GOT THAT dirty vice cop...SUBCONSCIOUSLY hummin', singin', and whistlin'!!!

And...

(OF the WORDS to the song? And, OF HOW the MELODY goes??),...

(((YOU BEST-BELIEVE ME, WHEN I SAY!!!)))...

THAT...

THE WHOLE ENTIRE TIME,...POCKETS,...WAS LISTENIN'!!!

((((((I TOLD Y'ALL POCKETS GOT SOME SHIT TO HIM!!!))))))

Then...

Seeing that, humongous shared-parking-lot of the Walmart and of the wagering establishment. Where, gamblers can place bets, 24-Hours-a-day Off-Track. Where, Pockets parked his RV. Where, he left MC Busta-Nut and False Profit behind! WHERE, Pockets, tells the dirty vice cop to, "SLOW DOWN and bust this next right!"

Then...

Driving through, to the back of that humongous lot. The dirty vice cop, pulls his undercover Caddy, behind the RV, (I'll be damned!), JUST LIKE, he's making a traffic stop! ...*(Old habits die hard,...YA DIG!!).*

And so...

(Pockets, hops out, closes the door and, then, leans back down into his rolled down window)...

'Cause,(((YOU KNOW Pockets, AIN'T NEVER AT A LOSS FOR WORDS!!!)))...

AND SO...

HE'S GOTTA' give HIS "Head of Security", SOME MO' "X's and O's"!!!

..."Yeah, so, well, anyways, I got some guys from my label comin' up to assist you,...with this "buzz" and Meet 'n Greet Show. You know,...

security. NOW, I know WHAT you're thinking,...I'm FULL of shit, right? NOPE! YOU'RE "Head of Security", tonight! I WON'T take THAT away, from you! Like, I said, *I WANT YOU on the FRONTLINES of this thing!* BUT, as for me? AS, OF right NOW?? I GOTTA' go "prep" my rappers in this here RV of mine, for tonight. Since, TONIGHT'S event, WE GOTTA' expidite!! SO, the NEXT time I see YOU, you'll be positioned out front of Skin's club, for crowd control. You ain't gotta worry 'bout, my rappers. *My rappers are FROM tha' streets!* Busta-Nut and False Profit, DON'T NEED NO bodyguard!! SO, I'ma NEED YOU, posted-up in front of the door to this RV, while, I'm recording, Skin's son-in-law. Listen, "12", DON'T BE lettin' NOBODY in! After, I've recorded Skin's son-in-law,...we'll come outta tha' RV. And, WHEN that door opens, THAT'LL be YOUR que! I WANT YOU, specifically, "Mr. Head of Security!", to walk Skin's son-in-law in the front door of Skin's club! You know,...Skin's said, *he'd MAKE SURE there was a nice turnout, packin' his club "the right way", for tonight.* SO, stick-by Skin's son-in-law,...yeah, so, well, anywaaaaaays, SINCE, he's GONNA' BE a BIG STAR,...SOON AS THIS Christmas song drops! YOU know HOW, Jettison Records do! ...WE BE DROPPIN' ALBUMS!!!"

Then...

(After some shared-laughter, Pockets, reaches into his kelly green throwback Eagles sweatpants and, pulls out one of those endangered money clips, peels off a few bills and, reaches in the car, slapping the money down into the palm of the dirty-'bout-his-money-vice-cop!)...

And then,(continues)...

..."Get some bottles ta' pop, for this event tonight! And, pick up a nice bottle of somethin', for Skin's. ...I want Skin's to see, that we're doin' it "right", tonight! You feel me?"

And so...

(With, thoughts and, looks of concern, over Pockets', disconcern!)...

The-dirty-gettin'-MORE-and-MORE-hip-TO-the-placement-ON-priorities-OF-this-"music-biz-shit" - vice cop, asks, "Uh, AIN'T YOU forgettin' somethin'?? LIKE, ain't there ANYTHING ELSE, you wanna talk about??"

"What? MONEY?? Don't worry 'bout it. What? I'll pay you "Head of Security money", after tha' event is over.", Pockets, replies.

"OH, YEAHH!!! I'MA NEED MY MONEY!!! You AIN'T NEVER gotta worry, 'bout that! I'M ALWAYS, gon' be 'bout MY money! But, yeah,...that's cool wit me, pot'nuh. You CAN pay me AFTER the event, tonight. But,...no pot'nuh,...I WASN'T talkin' 'bout that.", the dirty-'bout-his-money-on-duty-vice-cop, explains.

"HEY, "12"! YOU slowin' me tha'-fuck down! WHAT is it, mafacka'!? What?? NO CELL PHONES??? I'M cool wit that! NO cell phones, IT IS! JUST handle yo' shit, YOU feel me! AND, be IN FRONT of Skin's club, by time I come pullin' up wit this RV. And, I KNOW you'll be there, 'cause, I KNOW YOU 'BOUT YO' MONEY!!!", Pockets, says, before her turns, (leaving the dirty vice cop with those final words!).

But...

(The dirty vice cop honks his horn, gettin' Pockets' attention!)...

THEN...

Calls out, his window rolled down, *"WASN'T you gon' ask me 'bout the Christmas song?? AIN'T THAT what, YOU forgettin'? 'Cause, THAT'S what-tha'-fuck, YOU mentioned!"*

And...

Pockets, just gives him a look. A *"look"*, OF: *"What tha' fuck, YOU HONKIN' for???"* - *"Just get yo' ass back to the city!"* - *"And you BEST find that, mutha' fuckin' hippy!"* - *"And I BEST find yo' ass, standin' in front of my RV!"* - *"'Cause, YO' ASS BE DRAWLIN'!!"* - *"WIT ALL 'DIS MUTHA' FUCKIN' HONKIN'!!!"* - *"And DON'T MAKE-ME MAKE-YOU FIND OUT - how gettin' to the top - AIN'T SO MUTHA' FUCKIN' PRETTY!!!"* - (AND, with NO words needed, *what ELSE WAS IN*, that *"look"*?) - ((("AND, YA' ASS BEST-GET-ME THAT, COCKSUCKIN' SONG BOOK!!!!!!")))(((OY VEY!!!))).

And so...

(As, the dirty vice cop, begins to drive)...

MC Busta-Nut, pokes his head out the RV's door! Makin' sure, that AIN'T NO cop car!

(((HEY, I DON'T BLAME THA' BROTHER! HE'S JUST TRYNA' MAKE SURE!)))

As, Pockets,...goes inside.

AND...

(AS, THE FLYIN'-BACK-to-the-city-ON-DUTY-dirty-vice-cop - FLIES BACK UP - Business Route 36!)...

MAKIN', His: THIS Is MY Shot TO Get - OUTTA' - Bein' A Dirty-Ass-Vice-Cop - GOTTA' - FLY BACK TO NORTH JUAREZ - NON STOP - GOTTA' - Prove To Pockets - I CAN Handle ALL Of - THIS - "Head Of Security" - SHIT - GOTTA' - Catch-Up-Wit - THAT - Contract-Draftin'-Criminal-Informant-Rattin' - HIPPY - GOTTA' - NOT-GET-MYSELF-KILLED - GETTIN'-THAT-SONG-BOOK - Trip - Back To The City, the dirty-vice-cop-talking-to-himself-on-duty, says, to himself, (AND, OF POCKETS - GOTTA' - FEW CHOICE WORDS!!), "THIS music industry, IS a motherfuckin' trip! Pockets, spoke 'bout, everythin' to me under-tha'sun, on tha' "music-tip"! HE'S GOTTA' BE tha' MOST "chattiest-motherfucker" I'VE EVER MET, IN THIS WHOLE ENTIRE WORLD!!! ...BUT, he ain't NEVER spokeon,...asked me 'bout,...or make mention of,...his girl."

<h2 style="text-align:center">Chapter Twenty Six</h2>

GOT BUZZED?

nd of, Pockets' girl??

Well...

SHE'S BEEN GETTIN' BUZZED!!!

For...

(A girl's gotta pass her time,...SOMEWAY!)...

SO...

GETTIN' BUZZED, has been her routine! (For, the past 1,260 plus days!).

EVER SINCE...

Pockets, blew town! ...(leavin' behind his love!).

FOR...

Anna Mossitti's, GOTTA' BE in that ALL RED APARTMENT, affixed WITH house arrest bracelet and all! (Though, she IS allowed out!)...(You know, to walk about)...

BUT...

At 11:11AM sharp! She's GOTTA' BE there! IN that apartment! ...(to answer the call!).

For...

THAT dirty-ass vice cop, HAS BEEN tasked, to call that old red rotary dial phone, (the one atop of Pockets' old red mahogany desk!) AND, ASK, if..."EVERYTHANG, BE EVERYTHANG??"

FOR...

(((She is JUST bait!)))

So...

AT 11:11AM AND 11:11PM sharp - (((AND, I DO MEAN, SHARP!!!))), SHE'S GOTTA' answer THAT phone!!

And(wouldn't ya' know??)...

These city cops ain't really got, NO problem WITH her!

BUT...

((((Those 11:11AM SHARP phone calls, are JUST TO let her know, that the North Juarez Police Department, is keepin' A CLOSE EYE, ON YOUR "Coming's-'n-Go's"!!!)))...

AND SO...

IF Pockets IS THINKIN' 'BOUT, comin' back FO' YA'?? (And, SNEAKIN' YA' outta town!?)...

WELP!(THESE-HERE 11:11AM SHARP PHONE CALLS!)...

(((ARE TO GIVE YOU SOMETHING TO THINK ABOUT!!!)))...

AND SO("BAIT"!)...

LET YOUR THOUGHTS,...marinate.

'CAUSE...

ALL THESE current judges, AND cops, AND EVERY city official, AND employee, (from the bottom, back up TO the top!), ALL KNOW, one thing...

(((Pockets' hustle, NEVER stops!!!)))...

And...

ALL OF THESE EMPLOYED BY THE CITY, GOT THEIR JOBS FROM being in "THE RIGHT" hunting cabins, WITH "THE RIGHT" people! (JUST LIKE, BEFORE THEM, WERE their parents AND grandparents!!).

And so...

(((WITH the corruption IN THIS city, RUNNING generations deep!!!)))...

And...

WITH, that banker, the cops shot dead, (back in the day!), OF: "the payoffs", OF: "the BLOOD TRAILS", (((OF: "THOSE records"!!!)))...

THAT banker, (TO THEM!), AIN'T HAVE NO business, TO keep!!!

And...

EVERY North Juarez cop AND judge knows, that Pockets, WITH THOSE records, LIVES WITH leverage, TO GET AT GENERATIONS of city pensions,...and "eat"!

AND SO...

Of North Juarez, (of Anna Mossitti!), THEY WON'T let her go!

'Cause...

If and WHEN, Pockets, comes for her?...

Then...

(((HE'S GOTTA' GO!!!))).

So...

Anna Mossitti, (BEING HELD in the city), ((((ALL THIS TIME!!!)))), has made,...but just ONE friend.

And(oddly enough!)...

Her "friend" ALWAYS seems to BE hangin' 'round, (oh, right around...11:11AM SHARP!).

WHEN...

That dirty-ass vice cop, rings that red rotary phone on her,...(((CHECKIN' IN!!!))).

And so...

WITH the time on the clock BEING 11:11AM SHARP, FLYIN' UP THE HIGHWAY, WEAVIN' IN-'N-OUTTA' TRAFFIC, SWITCHIN' LANES 'N MEARGIN' BADLY, IN THAT - SPOKED-OUT UNDERCOVER - WITH THE BIG ASS RIMS - CADDY(((ON DUTY!!!), OBEYIN' NO CONSTRUCTION ZONES, (((FUCK THEM ORANGE CONES!!!))), THAT dirty-ass vice cop DOES SO, as he rings that red rotary!(((FROM HIS CELL PHONE!!!))).

(ALRIGHT READERS, SHOW SOME GUTS!)

(((("ABUSERS-OF-POWER!" AND DIRTY-ASS COPS, DO IT AAAALL THE TIME!!!)))...

SOOOOOO...

(((Y'ALL WANNA' BREAK SOME MO' WIRETAP LAWS, OR WHAT???)))...

"...I KNEW you was gay! I could taste it on the joint!! AFTER you passed it back to me!!! BWHAAAAAA-HA-HA-HA-HA!!!!!!", (((IS WHAT, the dirty vice cop COULD hear!)))...

AS...

Anna Mossitti, picked up that old red rotary dial phone, (RIGHT AT 11:11AM SHARP!), placing that red phone up to her ear!

AS...

(Said by, THAT burned-out-HIPPY-food-delivery-man!), (AS HEARD IN THE BACKGROUND!)...

'Cause...

(((JUST LIKE CLOCKWORK, IT'S 11:11AM SHARP!!!)))

AND...

Anna Mossitti's, *ONE AND ONLY FRIEND IN THE CITY,...is* STILL hangin' 'round!!!

"Oh! YOU GOT jokes, HUH??", (Mr. Brotha Trife, tells, the-hippy-food-delivery-man!), "AIN'T NO thang! I CAN take a joke! But,...AYO!!! PASS THAT-SHIT back, my man! And, DON'T-BE-GETTIN' none of 'DAT ORANGE PIZZA GREASE on me! OR ON tha' fuckin' joint!! AIN'T YOU BRING, NO NAPKINS??? Lemme' take a WILD guess!?! Hmm,...YOU ONE OF THEM "IT'S-NOT-MY-JOB!", DICKHEAD'S,... AIN'TCHA'!?! "It" AIN'T, YOUR "JOB", to make sure the customers GET some MOTHERFUCKIN'-COCKSUCKIN'-NAPKINS WIT THEY ORDER, AIN'T THAT RIGHT, MY MAN??? 'CAUSE, YOU AIN'T GOT NUTHIN' BUT ORANGE PIZZA GREASE, RUNNIN' ALL DOWN YO' ARM, FROM YO' HAND!!!", (((IS ALSO WHAT, the dirty vice cop, OVERHEARD!!!)))...

AS...

(Anna Mossitti, stands there by Pockets' red mahogany desk, WAITING ON the dirty vice cop, to ask her, these NEXT THREE WORDS!!!)...

"Everythang, be everythang??", the dirty-ass vice cop, asks.

"YEAH! I'm STILL here!! Everythang, BE everythang!!! YA' HAPPY, NOW???, Anna Mossitti, replies, upon (YET AGAIN!) being, asked,

(((With PLENTY of ANIMOSITY!!!))) AND, with A-WHOLE-LOTTA' SASS!!!

"DAMN! *WHY you ALWAYS gotta be givin', ME attitude?!?* I'M JUS' doin', MY fuckin' job!! SHIT! ...So, uh, (heh!), (heh!), (heh!),...YOU wouldn't-of,...happened to-of,...come-cross them, "pension records" 'n shit,...WOULD ya'?? You know,...I COULD "shorten" ya' time in tha' city a GREAT deal,...IF YA' JUS' work WIT ME ON this! *YA' SURE, YOU DON'T know WHERE Pockets STASHED, that dead banker's records??* (Heh!), (heh!), (heh!),...JUS' askin',...YA' KNOW, (heh!), (heh!), (heh!),... Anna Mossitti, in tha' event, they was, to EVER surface!", the-dirty-with-a-lil'-nervous-laughter-of-HIS-subconscious-vice-cop, asks,...('Cause, IN ADDITION to ringin' that red rotary phone?),...(((CONSCIOUSLY-LOOKIN'-FOR-HIS-NEXT-ON-DUTY-"DIRTY-COME-UP!", IS HIS, NUMBER ONE TASK!!).

"I DON'T know WHAT you're, talkin' 'bout!!", Anna Mossitti, snaps!!

"JUS' PUT that hippy-mutha-fucka', ON tha' DAMN phone!", the dirty-ass vice cop, demands!

WHEREAFTER...

Anna Mossitti, takes her sexy walk, back cross that plush red carpet!, (sitting back down next to Mr. Brotha Trife, in that all red living room, of that all red everythang apartment)...

AS...

Mr. Brotha Trife, stays steadily-lookin'-back-over, the back of that big plush red leather sofa, (at the hippy-"IT-AIN'T-MY-JOB"-to-provide-you-with-napkins-SOLELY-a-deliverer-OF-food-driver-man!)...

AS...

He's TURNING that red phone orange!,...(FROM all the PIZZA GREASE on his hand!).

"Did ya',...take care of her?", asks, the dirty-ass-selling-drugs-on-duty-vice-cop!

"Yeah, I took care of her. She ordered two strombolis.", the hippy-delivery-driver, replies.

"NO, YOU FUCKIN' DUMB, BURNOUT!!! DID YOU "take care", of HER!?!", the dirty-ass-vice-cop-shouting-his-"clarification"-on-duty, shouts!

"Huh?? OH! OH! OH! OH! Ooooh, "TAKE CARE" of her, "take care" OF her! YEAH, MAAAAAAN!! I "TOOK CARE" of her,...sold her, an eigth.", replies, the hippy-delivery-driver-drivin'-Ride-Shares-on-tha'-side - (got-himself-in-a-jam!) - AND-NOW - GOTTA'-DO-some-"dirty-work"-FOR-"THE-MAN"!!!...

UNDER THE GUISE: ((((Of delivering pizza pies!))))

AND...

Being a legitimate "Ride-Share-Ride"!!

Although(((ALL-THE-WHILE!!!)))...

Being THEE-DIRTIEST - of - THEE-DIRTIEST - OF - the-dirty-ass-vice-cop's "criminal-informants"! (((WHO'S MAKING HIM DO ALL KINDS OF UNLAWFULLY-IMMORAL-SHIT!!!)))...

Such as...

KEEPING HIM WITH A HEALTHY-SUPPLY OF WEED! BOGUS-E-PILLS!! AND, BAGS FULL OF NARCOTIC ROCKS!!!... (so, as, TO: "FEED"!!!)...

(Feed to whom, YOU ASKED!?!)

Well...

((((I-AIN'T-GOT-NO PROBLEM AT ALL IN TELLIN' YOU!!!!!!)))...

TO: NEWCOMERS TO THE CITY ALSO REFERRED TO AS "NUBIES"! TO: THOSE CHOSEN AS "TARGETS" BY THAT DIRTY-ASS-VICE-COP AND THAT FUCKING-RAT-HIPPY! (((TO: MANIPULATE ONE'S MIND!!!))) TO: GET "CLEAR-THOUGHT-PROCESSES" TO STOP! TO: KEEP "FEEDING" THEM "THAT"

SHIT - PROVIDED TO THAT RAT - BY THAT DIRTY-ASS-VICE-COP! TO: GET A TARGET'S-MIND "ENTRAPPED"! TO: KEEP A TARGET'S-MIND SPUN! TO: GET A TARGET TO START BUYING - "THAT" SHIT - IN MASS VOLUME! TO: START SELLING MASS QUANTITIES OF "THAT" SHIT! (((TO: JUST-KEEP-UP WITH THEIR "ENTRAPPED-ADDICTION"!)))...(((THAT'S BEEN FORCED UPON THEM!!!))) TO: GET "UDDER-MUDDER-FUCKERS" - PUT AWAY - ON THA' INSIDE! TO: KEEP HIS HIPPY-RAT-ASS - STAYIN' FREE - ON THA' OUTSIDE!!!(YEAH!)...((((((THAT GUY)))))).

...."So, you blazed-up wit her again,...right? DID she get-to-flappin', her gums???", asks, the-dirty-fuckin'-shady-vice-cop-sellin'-weed-laced-with-Sodium-Pentothal-on-duty-TO-POCKETS'-LADY!(((YEAH!!!))) (((THAT GUY!!!))).

WHEREAFTER...

(The hippy, looks back over at the plush red sofa, to ensure, that those two, over there, in the living room, over the back, of that big plush red sofa, over at him, they weren't looking back at him over!)...

BEFORE...

...He says, (while TRYIN' to keep, his voice down a bit!), "No, maaaaaan! SHE'S good! She DON'T EVER, SAY shit! That laced-up weed, don't work on her, not ONE bit! BUT, I got this "udder-mudder-fucker" that's here, to take a couple of hits. But, REALLY,...FOR the most-part! WHEN, addressing me? ALL HE WAS DOIN', WAS MUTTERING 'bout, HOW HE COULDN'T WAIT, FOR THE DAY,...to carve me to lil' bits!"

"Good!", the dirty-ass vice cop, replies!

"Good?!? THIS fuckin' guy, IS crazy!! Like, listen, maaaaaan, *I drove him into the city, with McDusty, McCrusty, and Scabby McKnees, a few days back. He was a "Nubie", headed TO town, MAAAAAAN, so, I DID what you want me TO do! You know, maaaaaan, "feed 'em" the shit, you keep supplyin' me with, to feed all newcomers, comin' into town, that look like they party, and MIGHT BE down! Like, listen, maaaaaan, I left 'em with Scabby and them. But,...they disappeared, leavin' him in THAT "abando", ALL ALONE!! ...BUT, LISTEN, MAAAAAAN, I saw this SAME "mudder-fucker", walkin' 'round again! I was ABLE to get him back in the car,..."provided" him with ANOTHER "free ride",...tried to work 'em,...see if he knew of any "udder-mudder-fuckers", sellin', buyin',...USIN', MAAAAAN.* Like, HEY, maaaaaaan, I do a lot of shit FOR you. BUT, when it comes to THIS "mudder-fucker"!?!...MAKE Scabby McKnees DO the "follow up" ON him! Besiiiiiides, maaaaaan, I was gonna' meet up with you later. So, like, listen, HEY, MAAAAAAN,...WHY we talkin' all this shit OVER the phone???", asks, the hippy-informant, trying to speak of a "hushed-tone".

"SEE WHA' I'M SAYIN'??? *THAT'S WHAT got-ya'-ass "jammed-up" in tha' FIRST muthafuckin' place,* POT'NUH! YOU TALK, TOO DAMN MUCH!!! YA' DAMN, CHATTY-MUTHAFUCKER!! Yeah, WE WAS 'GWINE meet-up! And,...NO!!! NO, I DON'T wanna-be-havin' THIS conversation, OVER tha' phone! BUT, SINCE ya' "ramblin'-ass" GOT TO ramblin'! NOW, ya' OWE ME,...AGAIN!!! And, I'M "cashin' in" THAT-shit, RIGHT NOW!!! SO, what I NEED from YOU, is to make MY LIFE, a whooooooole lot easier. There's a biiiiiig event, goin' down at La Alla Banca, tonight,..."music biz" shit. JUST YOUR, *"wheelhouse"!* AND, ya' THINK, I never lookout fo' ya',...all dat much. And,...I DON'T!!! BUT, I looked-out for ya', THIS time! Skin's and Pock ...um, "another party", need a "contract guy" for some contracts they need typed-up. You know,..."music biz contracts",...for a song. And, SINCE *THAT'S what you USE TO DO, "Mr. Former-Music-Big-Wig-Contact-Man!",* I TOLD them, you WOULD do it. SO, GUESS WHAT??? YOU'RE BACK IN THA' "MUSIC BIZ", BITCH!!! ...Thanks to ME,...of course! Oh, and, Skin's wants his place packed for this event. Soooooo, guess what I's 'gwine ALSO make you do, pot'nuh? I'ma need you to bring Anna Mossitti and her, uh, "house guest", TO Skin's club. And, I'M talkin' MUTHA'-FUCKIN'-A.S.A.-MUTHA'-FUCKIN'-P, MUTHAFUCKA'!!! DO NOT be lettin' me down, now! And, YO' ASS, SURE-AS-FUCK DON'T WANNA'-BE-LETTIN' SKIN'S MUTHAFUCKIN'-ASS DOWN, POT'NUH!!! So, ALL I WANNA' KNOW is? WHY YO' ASS STILL on, tha' MUTHAFUCKIN' phone?!?", the dirty-ass - imposing-HIS-WILL-and-ABUSING-HIS-POWER-vice-cop-delegating-HIS-"dirty-work"-on-duty, informs!

And so...

(After, REALLY NO thought at all!)...

The hippy, (trying his best - NOT - to have - THIS - psycotic "house guest", BACK IN his car!), NOT WANTING to find out, IF today to IS the day "the mutterings" (((of him BEING carved TO lil' bits!!!))), is actually, GONNA' HAPPEN TODAY!!!(((OY VEY!!!))).

AND SO...

The hippy, replies, "Like, HEY, MAAAAAAN, THAT'S gonna be a problem! I HAVEN'T "done up" ANY music contracts IN years! Besiiiiiides, maaaaaan, I have nothing TO "do up" contracts ON! Like, listen, maaaaaan, AIN'T NO typewriters ANYMORE, officer! So, listen, maaaaaan, I'm sorry 'n all,...BUT, I CAN'T help you out, WITH THIS one!"

WHEREAFTER...

(The dirty vice cop, goes for his "ol' standby"!)...(Hmm)(((LIKE WHAT, YOU ASK???)))...

Well...

((((I-AIN'T-GOT-NO PROBLEM AT ALL IN TELLIN' YOU!!!)))...

LIKE: The bag of dope THAT, THAT DIRTY-ASS VICE COP KEEPS IN HIS SOCK, To: "conveniently" plant - (AND/OR!), To: drop! (((TA' GET YA' DUMB-ASS TO WORK FOR HIM!!!))), (((WEARIN' WIRES 'N SHIT!!!))), WITH: "promises" on "your-part", OF: NO "Testification"!!!...(Is that EVEN a word??)(((DOESN'T MATTER!!!)))(I'M USIN' IT ANYWAY:) BUT OUR "TARGET(S)", GOT TO GET LOCKED UP, BEFORE "YOU" can EVEN think 'bout, YO' CHARGES GETTIN' DROPPED!!! (((OY - TO-THE-MUTHAFUCKIN' - VEY!!!))).

And so…

…"Well, "pot'nuh", the dirty-ass vice cop, begins,…"YOU really ONLY GOT, two choices. But,…THEN AGAIN, ya' ass REALLY ONLY EVER HAD, TWO choices!! DO AS, I SO, muthafuckin'-please! OR, "EYES-'GWINE"-STICK-YO'-ASS in THAT, muthafuckin'-bank-vault-cell, WIT TWO baaaaaad muthafuckers THAT, YA' ASS DON'T-WANNA-BE IN THERE WITH!! SO?? You can "convince" your "house guest", TO ALLOW YOU to use his laptop to type-up these music contracts? OR? IT'S - "you-BEST-NOT-fuck-'round-AND-BEAT-MA'MA", - at "Spades"!!!"

And so…

(((AFTER REALLY NO THOUGHT AT ALL!!!)))…

The hippy, replies, "So, you SAY, YOU WANT me to bring these two to Skin's place, for that music event? AND have some music contracts drafted-up, A.MAFACKIN'.S.A.P.??? LIKE, hey, maaaaaan,…THAT I CAN DO, Daddy-O!!!"

"I KNOW, YOU WILL! DON'T fuck-wit-me again, "POT'NUH"!!! Get'em in THAT car! GET 'EM blazin' on THAT shit! Get 'em, TALKIN'!!! …I WANT more "dirt" on that "psycho house guest", OF YOURS!! Oh,…and, DON'T let him leave that suitcase of his behind! IF YA' ASS SHOWS UP WITHOUT DAT SUITCASE???", the-dirty-micro-managing-on-duty-vice-cop, threatens and demands!!

BUT,(EVEN THOUGH!)…

(This music-contract-fuckin'-rat-Ride-Share-food-delivery-hippy-driver-man, HAS his "OWN WAY" of "HUSTLIN' MUDDER FUCKERS",…it WASN'T gon' be THAT easy!)…

'CAUSE…

THIS-here TIER THREE, got OTHER plans!!!…(((OH-MY-LAWD!!!))).

SOOOOOO...

SHALL WE ALL SEE HOW THIS SHITZ GONNA' PLAY THA' FUCK OUT???

(OK! GOOD!! ALL ON THREE!!! ALL TOGETHER NOW!!!),...

"YES!!! I THINK WE MUTHAFUCKIN' SHALL!!!"

(Very good, y'all!)...(YOU'RE gettin' IT now:)

AND SO...

Once offered, Mr. Brotha Trife, "not-so" politely declines, the hippy-food-delivery-Ride-Share-driver's offer, for a ride!

FOR...

He DON'T know THIS, motherfucker!

SOOOOOO...

(((HE DON'T TRUST THIS, MOTHERFUCKER!!!))).

For...

He DON'T know NOBODY named, "Skin's"!

'CAUSE...

(JUST 'CAUSE Skin's is "your" friend)...(((THAT DON'T MAKE HIM "MY", muthafuckin' friend!!!)))

FOR...

THIS-HERE - "Tier Three" - MAY HAVE ONLY been "awake", FOR ABOUT a week...

BUT...

(Mr. Brotha Trife's - "Tier-Three-MIND" - KNOWS ENOUGH, TO KNOW)...

AS...

(((He LET'S IT, be known!!!)))...

..."JUST 'CAUSE, he's "your" peeps? THAT DON'T MAKE SKIN'S, "MY" MUTHAFUCKIN' PEEPS!!!"

BUT...

(MORE information WAS gained, IN his "Tier-Three-Brain"!)...

"Hmm. Some big "music buzz" event, in the city...TODAY?? GO 'HEAD, POCKETS!!! YOU RED-SUIT-WEARIN'-MUTHA'-FUCKA', BOOKED THE VENUE!!!", (as those, *Tier-Three-Thoughts,* continued!!!).

And so...

(((Mr. Brotha Trife, reaches for HIS cell phone! FINALLY gonna turn it BACK ON! GOTTA' LET POCKETS KNOW, HE WROTE SOME "HOT-FIRE-SONGS", FOR HIS DEBUT!!!)))...

BUT...

For, you see, well,...Anna Mossitti, she AIN'T READY TO BE... rescuded!

For, you see, well,...SHE WANTS to spend as much TIME, with the man, *that once, raised HELL in THIS city, WHILE rippin' lines, 'n smokin' blunts! (((The man, that once, reaped the scalps of...ANYONE HE WANTS!!!))). The man, that once, sewn said scalps, USING catfish line, TO a trench coat,...that HAD...DRIED "HUMAN CHEESE"! (((FROM ONCE, BEING LIQUIFIED, AND RAN DOWN, BOTH SLEEVES!!))) AND, the man, that once, SMELLED OF...pine treeline...*

FOR...

The deeds, OF human souls, of THE PAYMENT of dues!

And so...

(Anna Mossitti, takes Mr. Brotha Trife by the hand)...

'Cause(EVEN THOUGH!)...

Behind those, limited-edition-lenses of 24 karat gold, Mr. Brotha Trife, has JUST ONE eye! (THE *LOOK* in it, LET'S them BOTH know, *ain't nobody GOTTA' THINK twice!!*)...

FOR...

(THERE WILL BE, no bluff!!)))...

As...

She tells, that hippy-food-delivery-man, "My friend here, seems to think, you've been here loooooooong enough! SO, YOU-BEST-BE, on your way!", (but, THEN, *she DOES give it a SECOND THOUGHT!!*),..."Me and my friend here, WERE 'bout to go for a walk. BUT, come to think of it,...*I haven't been out to see a show IN years!* SO, stop 'round later,...IF you're free. And, YOU CAN drive us both there,...if you want!!"

AND SO...

(Anna Mossitti, with no hesitation, takes Mr. Brotha Trife by the hand!)...

AS(IF)...

HE WAS, HER MAN!!!...(oy vey).

And...

They both, (plus the hippy!), make their way out, that all red everythang apartment. And then, make their way down, those old musty-smelling wooden steps, makin' their way out, the back door of Precinct One. To where, the cop cars are parked on station. To where, a chain-link fence enclosure, encloses, seized vehicles of impoundment. To where, to Mr. Brotha Trife's astoundment, *he gets hit on top of his bullet hole hat...* (again!), *THINKING that, it might BE Heaven sent,* (OR at, the VERY least!), *KNOWING that, IT WAS meant FOR him!* (FROM, having read, the very little bit of, the reading materials that, he read!).

AND, (SO NOW!)...

From, (HAVING read!), Mr. Brotha Trife KNOWS that, WHEN he gets hit atop of his bullet-hole-head, WITH further deja vu, *that's HIS spirit guide, (((the MOST triflin' OF THE triflin', BROTHA TRIFE))), TELLING him, TO watch your FUCKING BACK!!*

'CAUSE...

(Someone IS TRYING to get you!!!)(((FUCK Y'ALL!!!))).

And so...

(From having been taken by the hand SO quickly!)...

TO(NOW!)...

Trying TO decipher the - latest-of-the-most-recent - deja vu "signs", Mr. Brotha Trife, AS he's being led, from back 'round the back of the precinct, TO the sidewalk AND those marble columns out front, *(FROM WHENCE, HE ONCE, OF PRECINCT ONE, STOOD OUT IN FRONT OF OUT FRONT!!!)*, TO Mr. Brotha Trife, NOT EVEN realizing, THAT, he left his song book AND HIS suitcase behind! ...(INCLUDING Y.S.'s LAPTOP!! AND, HER ONE AND ONLY PRIZED-POSSESSION, HER...$50,000.00 THUMB DRIVE!!). (((OY VEY!!!))).

AND SO...

As the two walk, (hand-in-hand) that hippy-delivery-driving-some-kinda-music-contract-man, hops into his silver, (with the black rag top) '83 Cadillac Seville...AND, goes TEARING OUT ON TO the city street, from 'round back of the back of the precinct, *(from whence, he was once parked)*, LEAVING THE TWO IN his rearview APPEARING far, as they continue to walk...(hand-in-hand!)...to "Old" *SYKE Park!*

(WITH the feel OF Anna Mossitti's hand, FIRMLY-LOCKED into his, as his, as she, IS FELT by her's, THEY BOTH finally feel, AS THOUGH, they've FINALLY GOT a handle on their worlds)...

AND SO...

As the hippy flies by,...they pay him no mind.

And so, as that criminal-informant-contract-writing-hippy, goes out into the world, to continue his mission, to meet up with that dirty-ass vice cop, to let him know - FACE-TO-FACE - (AND NOT OVER THE PHONE!) - so as, to so inform, *"Get them both in this "Ride Share" car? YOU can forget that!! Like, hey, maaaaaan, I ain't even got that laptop!"*, (KNOWING that dirty-ass vice cop, (on him!), gon' be trippin'!!!), Mr. Brotha Trife's, ONLY mission, as the two, AS their hands - hand-in-hand - of the continuance-of-the-holding-of-the-hands...continues,...IS to listen.

And so, as the - "walk-of-clasped-hands" - goes on, on...down...the sidewalk. Mr. Brotha Trife, though, he is, though, he isn't, of and for her's and OF attention paying. Though, he DOES hear, Anna Mossitti. Though, he don't. For, he ain't. Of, the paying of attention. OF, for, and, ALL the while, he really hasn't even heard, NOT one word, THAT she's saying! (BUT, ya' REALLY CAN'T blame tha' man!) FOR, ALL HE'S REALLY placing his FULL attention ON, of and as of, AS THEY, continue-the-continuance OF THEIR - "walk-of-clasped-hands-walk" - IS,...the sound OF her voice AS she talks!

And, as for being a prisoner OF THIS city, (((MORE LIKE BAIT!!!))), *for,* hmmm,...*OH, ABOUT 1,265 days, (WITH THAT DAMN house arrest bracelet AFFIXED TO the bottom of her leg!), she, JUST LIKE* him, *DON'T EVER smile when she walks. Passing her days and her time, walking IN captivity every day, RIGHT 'round this time. She, JUST LIKE* him, *AS she passes those, walking past her and or of those, THAT, for HER liking, BE gettin' MUCH TOO close, she,* JUST LIKE him, *for she NEVER, SAYS a word! FOR, SHE DON'T talk,* JUST LIKE him, *AS she, walks down... THESE UNEVEN CITY sidewalks.*

But, FOR her, on THIS day, IT IS quite different THIS time! *(FOR, SHE walks, ALL the time!)*(FOR, THIS IS HER daily grind!) And, Mr. Brotha Trife, CAN tell, THAT, SHE NEEDS THIS walk TODAY!!! And, HE'S just letting her vent! And, THAT MAY be a DAMN shame! 'Cause, HE'S JUST listening to THE SOUND of HER VOICE...and, NEVER heard, NOT a single word, THAT, she HAD TO say!!

And, HE CAN TELL, THAT, JUST LIKE HIM, *SHE STAYS ON HER "Giddy-Up"!* And, AS their hands, REMAIN - hand-in-hand

- with the other, HE tips his bullet-hole-hat TO her. AS, if to say, "I LOVE THAT IN YOU, LOVE!!" (((And, it's ALL because...))), JUST LIKE ME, (((FUCK Y'ALL!!! AND, FUCK LUCK!!!))), "YOU AIN'T TRYIN' to be...*STUCK!!*"

(And so, hand-in-hand, THEY...continued on)...

...AND, right about NOW, Mr. Brotha Trife, AIN'T EVEN concerned...'BOUT THAT Christmas song!

FOR...

(HE'S on, Some: "LATER for Pockets!" - WE'LL get TO that "Buzz Event" - WHEN we get to it - TYPE - Shit!!)...

For...

(((HIS hands GOT other plans!)))...

(THE VERY SAME HANDS, THAT, HE WROTE "CHRISTMAS MOURNING" WITH!!! OF THE VERY SAME SONG THAT, HE KNOWS, IS A HIT!!!)...

And since, it's almost JUST ABOUT high noon time. (And since, THROUGH those big fluffy white clouds, THAT morning sun, DOES shine!). And since, "Old" *SYKE Park,* IS just up ahead, ON the right. Anna Mossitti, hand-in-hand, takes Mr. Brotha Trife, BY the hand. And, leads him into the park, and of, that rubble, through. SO, that, he CAN take a good LOOK UP...at HIS statue! For, she WANTS, FOR HIM, FOR HIM, (TO dually see!), *AT HOW,...the tips OF HIS dreads GLOW, (AT high noon time!), A BEAMING GOLD,...SENDING shivers UP-AND-THEN-RIGHT-BACK-DOWN-TO-THEN-(((AGAIN!!!))) - JUST TO - SHOOT-AGAIN-BACK-UP - HER spine!*

And, AS the two, stand before HIS very own statue. AS, they stand, (AND, FOR WHICH THEY STAND!), amongst, THAT "Old" *SYKE Park* rubble. She begins...to read him. AS, a man, which IS...humble.

FOR...

HE would rather, (WHICH HE DOES!), WATCH HER quiver! FROM THE shivers!

((((WHICH SHE DOES!!!)))).

And so...

ALL THIS TIME, as through, THOSE big white fluffy clouds, THEE morning sun DOES shine. THE possession, OF THE NEED, TO speak on, (on, in and, OF him), he DON'T possess. (DON'T need to!) And so,...he WON'T. *(((For, HE WOULD RATHER, WATCH her quiver FROM, THE shiver!!!)))*. And, ALL THIS TIME, TO speak on HIS OWN statue, (AS AT HIGH NOON!), *OF WHICH the tips* (OF HIS dreads), *WERE shown, TO BEAM,...a BEAMING gold.* And so, WITH no need to,...he don't.

SO...

("WE'LL" just, leave THOSE TWO - hand-in-hand - BENEATH, THAT HIGH NOON SUN AND, AMONGST, THAT - "Old" *SYKE Park* - RUBBLE!!)...

AS...

Anna Mossitti, asks, the man,...(((OF WHICH!!!))), SHE HOLDS THE HAND, (((TO WHICH!!!))), she BELIEVES - TO BE - "HER" - "Statue Man" *(comissioned BY the city!)*(OY VEY!)...The statue of..."Too Cold".

EVEN THOUGH...

THE man, (((TO WHICH!!!))) SHE HOLDS the hand, (((OF WHICH!!!)))*(((she DOES NOT KNOW, IS the clone OF the man!!!))), THAT, DONATED ALL THAT MONEY, TO rebuild THIS city!*

((((THE man, THAT, IN THIS city, CAUSED SOOOOOO MUCH trouble!!!))).

...As she, asks, ""MY" Brotha Trife! ...What, ARE YOUR aspirations? WHAT'S, IN your future?? WHAT, do YOU WANT,...OUT OF life???"...

...(And so!), AS "WE", MOVE on...

...There's A swarm ON ITS way! OF flying BUZZING bugs!!!! ((((HOW MANY, YOU ask????)))). ENOUGH TO blockout the sun!!!! AND, THERE'S A storm,...AND DISEASE...AND a skelton CLUTCHIN' his rib bones, GETTIN'-BEATEN-UP - BY - THE WIND, ((((TO AND FROW!!!!)))), BEING THROWN, FROM AND OF, THE BLACK FLAG GETTIN' SHREADED-DOWN TO A RAG, ON THE BACK OF CHOPPER, THE COLOR IS BLACK!!!! FROM, POPPED-CLUTCHES AND FROM THROTTLES WIDE-OPEN!!!! Leaving YOU, WITH dispare, WITH NO hope...AND YET hoping!!!!!!! WITH,...FEELINGS OF anger!!!! Gonna-gotcha' QUESTIONING YOUR FAITH!!!! AS TO WHY YOU LOST, WHAT YOU LOST, AND ((((WHY????)))) IN YOUR MIND, YOU WERE ALLOWED TO BE SO WRONGED???? AND, FOR AND OF, IF you did and, IF you EVEN thought of, ((((HOW COME it ain't????)))) and, WHATEVER MADE YOU BELIEVE that,...YOUR FAITH was EVER STRONG???? ((((OH, YES!!!!)))) HAVE fear, my dear, *FOR,...they WERE put here!!!!* ((((TO CAUSE FEAR!!!!))))((((AND THEY'RE ON THEIR WAY!!!!)))) ((((THE END IS NEAR!!!!)))) TO, TAKE whatever!!!! AND, TO WITHOLD, whatever THEY WANT ((((FROM YOU!!!!)))). FOR, THEY DO WHAT THEY WANT TO DO!!!! AND, PLEASE, YOU BEST-BELIEVE, that,...THEY'LL DO IT TO YOU!!!! FOR, THEY ARE THE ONE AND ONLY....DUYU CREW!!!!

AND, WITH straight drag pipes, they RUMBLE the city's main drag!!!! And, these FOUR RIDERS are, HIGH AS THEY RIDE!!!! AND, they're DRUNK-AS-FUCK!!!! ((((FULLY in their bag!!!!)))). AS, the DUYU CREW, RUMBLES the main drag of North Juarez, BUZZIN' STRAIGHT-THROUGH!!!! For, that's HOW they ride!!!! And, OF HOW, they ride???? Two abreast. Two columns of two. Pretty High, front left. AND, he's WREAKING OF airline fuels. AND of....3RD-DEGREE SKIN!!!! ((((FROM charred - JAGGED AND SHARP - airline fuselage BURNS, that are CAUTERIZED 'ROUND THE EDGES, THAT YOU CAN SEE STRAIGHT-THROUGH... AND IN!!!!)). ((((OY VEY!!!!)))). Pretty High, ((((RIDIN' HIGH!!!!)))), ON his CHOPPER of white!!!! And, oh, please-BELIEVE, ((((WHAT

YOU'RE SEEING)))),.....it IS quite a SIGHT!!!! FOR, Pretty High, runs straight-through the city,....WITH PASSAGES....runnin' STRAIGHT-THROUGH his TORSO!!!! And, IF he had A soul? .... (((((YOU'D SEE IT!!!!)))). *From, ANY NUMBER OF TUNNELS (((((CREATED)))) FROM - ANY NUMBER, OF: PRETTY HIGH'S- (((((CAUTERIZED!!!!))))-YOU-CAN-SEE-straight-through-them - BURN HOLES!!!! AS, HOT airline FUSELAGE, passed STRAIGHT-THROUGH his white three-piece vest, (((((AS IT PASSED - ALL-THE-WAY-DOWN-INTO-GOING-STRAIGHT-THROUGH - HIS CHEST!!!!)))).* AND, WHEN HE RIDES, PRETTY HIGH, well, he....CONQUERS "SMOOTH"!!!! And, HE DOES IT WITH, a white chopper TO MATCH, HIS - vintage white Prohibition Era-style - GANGSTER SUIT!!!! Bad Habitz, front right. RIDIN' ON HIS RAKED OUT AND STRETCHED CHOPPER (((((of a COLOR)))) RED AND BRIGHT!!!! (((((And, "YOU" KNOW HOW, Bad Habitz, DO!!!!))))).... (((((FOR, HE GONNA' HAVE, ALL KINDS OF SHIT, STUCK TO HIS, BRIGHT-RED VINTAGE - PROHIBITION ERA-STYLE - GANGSTER SUIT!!!!)))). WITH, whale blubbers, OF WHICH, HIS SUIT, is covered!!!! AND, FROM, (((((those OH-SO cute)))) BABY SEAL'S BLOOD, OF WHICH, (((((MOST OF WHICH!!!!))))(((((from flying onto on-lookers!!!!)))), ALL THOSE snowy artic owl feathers, COULD NO LONGER HANG ONTO OF!!!! (((((OY VEY!!!!)))). Black bike, back right. CHOPPER throttle,....OPEN WIDE!!!! For,.... IT'S "THE DIET"!!!! AND, HE'LL LEAVE YOU DYING, WITH YOUR MOUTH WIDE OPEN, EMPTY AND, DRY!!!! And, when, The Diet rides, HE BE RIDIN', DRUNK AND HIGH!!!! And, THIS, BLACK-FLAG-FLYIN' RIDER, (((((OF the DUYU CREW!!!!)))), IS covered WITH, High Seas sea salts!!!! AND, The Diet's COVERED, IN THE salt OF the land, TOO!!!! *(((((THE TOILS OF HIS WORKS!!!!))))* Everything, FROM his suspenders TO his shirt(((((included BUT NOT limited to)))) IS - SALT-PEPPERED-CROSS - his black vintage Prohibition Era-style gangster suit!!!! And, WHEN The Diet comes-a-ridin', the ONLY forks YOU'RE findin', ARE the forks - ON HIS - raked out and stretched chopper!!!! (((((Please STOP YOUR cryin'!!!!)))). YOU WANT EMPATHY???? FROM The Diet???? (((((DON'T EVEN

BOTHER!!!!)))). AND,....THEN,....YOU GOT THAT "SICK-FUCK" IN PALE!!!! Dead Sexy, back left, OF THE left column, RIDIN' HARD ON'A PALE CHOPPER, ((((DRUNK-AS-FUCK!!!!)))),....bringin' up the tail!!!! AND, HE'S WEARIN', THAT, vintage Prohibition Era-style gangster suit. ((((The color IS pale!!!!)))). And, DON'T YOU EVER on YOUR LIFE, ((((TO DARE)))) tell, Dead Sexy, THAT, HE AIN'T "dead sexy"!!!! 'CAUSE,...((((OH BOY!!!!))))....((((HERE IT COMES!!!!)))). YOU wanna know why???? ....*Dead Sexy, DON'T find NOTHIN' TO BE, AS dead sexy AS, CHECKIN' HIS "dead sexy" REFLECTION,....IN YOUR OPEN DEAD EYES!!!!* And,....IT'S ALL because,....killing YOU AND ALL YOU LOVE...IS....Dead Sexy's ONLY tale!!!!

And, with WIDE OPEN THROTTLES, hangin' ONTO throttles WIDE OPEN, FLYIN' BY THE SEAT OF their ((((Prohibition Era-style gangster)))) pants, GOIN' SO DAMN FAST, ((((WHITE, BRIGHT RED, BLACK, and PALE)))) chopper seats OF ostrich skins, they're NO LONGER ABLE TO sit DOWN in!!!! And, AS for, their OTHER hand???? MIDDLE FINGER IN THE WIND!!!! And, FROM ABOVE, there COMES a rumble! (FROM THAT ol' El Train Bridge they're RIDIN' under!). BUT, IT'S the *THUNDER,* FROM their ((((CHOPPERS')))) straight drag pipes, THAT rattle Club Six-One-OH!'s *BOTTOMLESS* liquor bottles inside!!!! AS, that ol' El Train and the DUYU CREW, continues to rumble and *THUNDER-ON* thru!!!! *And, though, Club Six-One-OH!, IS the DUYU CREW'S old haunts.* They, keep it ROLLIN', breakin'-off from ONE'S-SELF, ((((like the bottomless bottles rattled and broken, *FALLING just TO REFORM back up on the shelf!!!!*)))). For, no sooner have they BUZZED past that wrought iron door handle, twisted and black, of Club Six-One-OH!'S tall and of heavyweight, Bavarian-Beer-Hall-style wooden door, intricately engraved. They are here, and there are four, *and they have been made to put YOU in a grave. Conqured. Starved. Fucked with. And a sinner slain.* For, ((((YOU SEE)))), at THE FOUR CORNERS of the city, POSTED-UP, ARE the DUYU CREW!!!! ((((AND THEY DOIN' WHAT THEY DO!!!!)))). A WHITE chopper. A BRIGHT RED chopper. A BLACK chopper. And, a PALE chopper's engine REVS!!!! *BADGERING WITH THUNDER!!!!* ((((OF WHAT LIES AHEAD!!!!)))). The city...it taunts.

And...

THIS IS CAUSING A PROBLEM!!! FOR SKIN'S...is FUCKING BEING bothered!!! For Skin's, at the ready, prepped and poised, just outside the entrance TO HIS domain's door. (((YOU SEE))) FOR, SKIN'S, IS FUCKING GETTIN' RUBBED RAW (((CREADTED BY AND,))) AS A RESULT, OF ALL THIS RAW-FUCKING-RUBBING-NOISE!!!(((OY VEY...AND OY!!!))). For, Skin's, this is and, THERE IS, just simply entirely WAY TOO MUCH, FOR SKIN'S!!! FOR, ALL THAT *THUNDER PIPE*, IS CAUSING TOO MUCH IRRATATION!!! (For, DON'T-NOBODY-LIKE for Skin's, to be gettin', all fucking-irritated, ALL OVER again!). For, Skin's, hates to wear a hat, (that's just a personal preference), *of which long ago, for Skin's upon decided.* For, Skin's, prefers TO FEEL THE...contact, OF the swiping OF the hair, FROM the face AND OF the eyes. For, Skin's, ALL THIS (er,..rah...) RAW-FUCKING-RUBBING, (((IS CAUSE!!!))), FOR Skin's,...TO COME INSIDE!!! (oy...vey!).

And so, (((YOU SEE!)))...

For Skin's, WASN'T playing games!

For...

Skin's, (himself!), OUT FRONT of La Alla Banca, was setting up,... the red velvet rope barricade!

For...

The crowd! And for, the BUZZ!!, (((ALREADY beginning to gather!!!)))...

BUT...

The rubbing of the raw and, (the subsequent noise, AS THEE result!), HAS MADE, for Skin's, to be gettin',...worked ALL-UP-IN a lather! (((OY VEY!!!))).

And so...

For Skin's, this "BUZZ Event", AIN'T no "play date"!…(((For "Skin's",…COMES ON the name plate!!!)))(((HOOFAH!!!))).

And so…

Skin's, swiped away the salt and pepper of his bangs, (in his face and eyes!!), AS frustration hangs!(((FUGGETABOUTIT!!!))) As he, stepped back inside of, his La Alla Banca I.A. Social Club.

Though*(((LEST WE FORGET!)))*…

Barring TONIGHT'S "BUZZ Event",…*no YOU ARE NOT welcome!!!*

And, though, it wasn't sign language, Skin's, WAS talking WITH his hands! (WITH his arms flailing-about!). Giving HIS, "5th Avenue Crew", HIS list, OF demands! Talkin' 'bout, *what he just saw, that lasted for but, just a split-second!* Talkin' 'bout, *these FOUR "Mezza Morta" RIDERS, that APPEARED to be "half-dead"!*, (is WHAT, he suspected!!!!). Talkin' 'bout, "Va fa Napole!!!!" - (wishes!). Talkin' 'bout, "WHERE A PLACE IS TO BE PREPARED!", *(for these FOUR RIDERS!)*…((((DOWN WITH THE FISHES!!!!)))). *"Gira Diment!!"*, (TO Skin's!), *Skin's, son-in-law, tells!!* "Yeah,…I MIGHT be "Goin' Crazy!!", (for Skin's, begins!),…"BUT, YOU'S GOIN' TA' help me, SEND those FOUR RIDERS, straight TO FUCKIN' HELL!!!!"

AND SO…

Skin's, tells, his Consigliere to stay. And, to get in touch with Pockets! (((("TO MAKE SURE, he's on his way!")))…

And, Skin's, tells his son-in-law, to "warm-up his vocals" - AND - "to drink, some hot lemon and tea!" And, Skin's, flails-his-arms-about (SOME MORE!)(((DEMANDING!!!))), that, ALL THOSE cars, "double-parked out front" - BE REMOVED - "to prepare a place, for Pockets' RV!"

And then…

Skin's, TELLS his muscle, "to come with him!"

AND…

Two of his soldiers are also TOLD, "to come along!"(The one, with the "Roman soldier", tattooed on his forearm!),(And, the other?)Well, HE WAS handpicked, FOR being handy, with'a Smith & Wesson! (((FUGGETABOUTIT!!!))).

FOR...

(Skin's won't tolerate all this noise, for when his son-in-law is in Pockets' RV studio, behind closed doors, with recording IN SESSION!!!)

And (SO THEN)...

The four of them, all walk out the back door, to go find AND teach,.. THOSE FOUR RIDERS,....a lesson!!!!((((MADONE!!!!)))).

And so...

(It's Skin's muscle, to be the first to leave (La Alla Banca), and, to be the first one, to walk out the back)...

FOR...

It's for, Skin's muscle to make sure, the coast is clear and to check. And, with the coast clear, Skin's, steps out the back, WITH his two soldiers (at his sides), THERE to protect!!

And(AS, they do!)...

Skin's muscle, then, opens the front passenger's door, for Skin's.

("WHY'D HE DO THAT?")...(I HEARD "YOU" ASK!),Well...

((((I AIN'T GOT NO PROBLEM IN TELLIN' YOU!)))...

FOR...

(Skin's muscle, opened his car door for him)...(((OUTTA' respect!))).

And, with the Roman soldier, sitting behind Skin's. The next one in the sedan, is the man, that's handy with a Smith & Wesson. And, once Skin's Smith & Wesson hitman, is seated to the Roman soldier's left. Skin's muscle, then, takes one last good look around, (just to double-check!!).

And, with Skin's muscle seated behind the wheel, of that, beautiful black, Cadillac XTS. Skin's, and his handpicked crew, go out in search of - *THOSE FOUR RIDERS - that - DARED TO BUZZ-BY - showing HE AND HIS "BUZZ Event" and HIS club,....NO respect!!!!(((HOOFAH!!!)))*.

BUT...

IN the city, THERE'S - A LOT - goin' down! And, the INSIDE of Skin's club, FOR the "BIG BUZZ" - IT'S ALL - decked out! FOR, THERE'S a large crowd (THAT has gathered!) out front, of Skin's I.A. And,...they're ALL DECKED-OUT - DRESSED UP LIKE - GANGSTERS AND GOOMAHS!!! And, they...*ALL HAVE HOPE!!!* (((SUCKAS!!!))). And, they're ALL TOO EAGER (to BUY INTO!) and, BELIEVE, *The - "Buggered" - OF - The-Blowing-UP-THEIR-ASSES' - OF - Smoke!* (((And THAT, *The - "Burglary" - OF - "THE-BIG-BREAKING-INTO" - OF - "The Music Industry"* - WILL HAPPEN TODAY!!!))).

FOR...

You got, young turks - and - wanna-be associates! And, SOME in the crowd (OF COURSE!!), JUST wanting TO BE jerks!!!

And...

((((They all - WANNA-BE - put on - Skin's, son-in-law's record!)))...

AND THEN...

YOU HAVE, some of THEM, that - WANNA-BE - "Put on", BY Skin's!

(((TO: PUT IN "THAT" kind of "WORK"!!!))).

FOR...

The word(((THAT'S been "BUZZING" AROUND TOWN!)))) is THERE'S some-kind-of "BIG EXECUTIVE EVENT"(((AT ANY MINUTE!)))THAT'S, ABOUT. TO. GO. DOWN!

HOWEVER...

(As, for the city's COPS 'n shit?),Well...

They DON'T like it! NOT. FOR. ONE minute!

FOR...

(A city FULL OF dirty cops, AIN'T TRYIN', TO direct traffic!)...

And, THEY - SURE-AS-FUCK - COULD GIVE - HALF-A-FUCK - 'BOUT TRYIN', TO MAKE (and/or TO GET) an, UNRULY mob TO stop!!

FOR...

Dirty cops, ALL they REALLY WANT is (TO TRY 'N MAKE 'N GET!), SOME "DIRTY MONEY", (before, THE END of their SHIFT!!!)...

FOR...

((((Dirty-Ass-North-Juarez-P.D. AIN'T TRYIN', to deal with NO "Music-BUZZ-RIOT"!!!)))

'CAUSE...

City traffic IS GETTIN' ALL fucked up! (((And, Skin's is GETTIN' ALL pissed off!))) For, Skin's, has been sittin' *STUCK* in "BUZZ Traffic"! For Skin's, FROM WHERE, he's *stuck*, STILL hasn't "fig'a'd out", FROM WHERE, all that *THUNDER*, IS COMING FROM!!!!

AND SO...

(((("FUCK", SWIPING the hair, FROM OUTTA' his eyes!!!))))...

"Va fangool!", says, Skin's, (OUTTA' frustration AND disgust!)... (((FOLLOWED UP: BY THE SWIPE OF HIS CHIN'S UNDERSIDE,...BY HIS FOUR FINGERS AND THUMB!!!!!)))...

And...

As traffic, for Skin's, FINALLY begins to move. Just for, Skin's, to find himself, *STUCK* AGAIN, sittin' at a red light, sittin' IN a foul MOOD!! And, as Skin's, is looking 'round, (tryin' to fig'a out his path, TO that *THUNDER* sound!), Skin's muscle, taps him on the shoulder, tellin', Skin's, "BOSS!!! FUCKIN' TAKE'A' LOOK AT THAT!!!".

(PROMPTING Skin's, to tell his muscle!), "DON'T YOU'S EVER TOUCH ME! AND FUCKIN'-ROLL YOU'S FUCKIN'-WINDOW DOWN!!!"

(And, as storm clouds, begin to roll in, if we're Blessed)...

...THROUGH big white fluffy clouds, WE'LL be alive to SEE... the Morning Sun...shine through again! And, WITH *peals of thunder*, (AS the sky begins to get prematurely-dark!)...GUESS WHO, SKIN'S MUSCLE, SPOTTED,...WALKING OUT OF "OLD" *SYKE PARK?!?*

AND SO...

Skin's, leans cross the front seat, SHOUTING OUT the driver's side window, "YOU'S ONE LUCKY-SON'OV'A-BITCH!!! YOU'S LUCKY, I GOT MORE PRESSIN'-MATTERS!!! *YOU'S LUCKY, I DIDN'T SEE YOU'S A-COUPL'A' NIGHTS BACK!!! OR EVEN, A-COUPL'A' HOURS AGO!!!*".

AND...

Mr. Brotha Trife, with Anna Mossitti, by his side, (SQUEEZING his hand tight!), well, of Skin's, he JUST HAS TO ASK, (as Mr. Brotha Trife, shouts back!), "OH! "YOU'S" THINK SO???".

AND...

Skin's, replies, "YEAH, YOU'S! I DO!! *I'DA' SHOT, YOUS' CANNOLI, OFF'A' YOU'S!!!*".

AND...

(Mr. Brotha Trife?)...(well?)...

HE looks at Anna Mossitti and, cocks his head, to the side. And, he gives her a smile, and a wink, WITH his one good eye!

And then...

(He looks back over at Skin's, who's still sittin' in "pissedoffness", STILL *STUCK,* AT the red light!)...

And then...

Mr. Brotha Trife, removes his 24 karat golds, from his eye.

And then...

(He cocks his BULLET-HOLE-HAT)...(((HARD to the side!)))...

AND THEN...

(Mr. Brotha Trife hollers-back, at Skin's, *WITH ALL OF his might!)* *(((MAKIN' DAMN-SURE THAT HE CAN BE HEARD!!!)))...*

"CANNOLI?? WHAT'S 'DAT??? A PIECE OF FRIED CHICKEN WIT-SOME "MOOT-ZA-REL-A" SPRINKLED ALL-CROSS-'DAT, YARDBIRD?!?!?!".

AND...

((("OOOOOOOOOOOOOOHH!!!!", IS the ONLY thing THAT CAN BE heard, from inside of Skin's ride!!!!)))...

AS...

Skin's, musclehead-driver, pulls off from the - from-red-to-green - light!!!!

And...

As Skin's, and his men, go in search of, *THE DUYU CREW'S THUNDER(((((CAUSING those DARK storm clouds TO roll in!!!!)))))*, Skin's, (STILL) sits, IN "pissedoffness", (YET!!)..., sits, WITH a...shit-eatin'-grin!!

AS...

(He *thinks*, to himself, *"I ALMOST hate TO admit it! ...BUT,... THAT, SON-N'OF'VA'-BITCH'S-VOICE),...(((IS PRETTY-FUCKIN'- AMAZIN'!!!")))*

And so...

(With, traffic in the city, movin' abnormally slooooooow!)...

With, MASSIVE-creations-OF-gridlocks, AS a result! (Of city traffic, *STUCK* in city traffic!). OF city traffic, TRYING to get TO this "BUZZ SHOW". Skin's, decided, just to head back to his club. *(((FOR Skin's, AND HIS arrogance, WITH this "Music Industry", now...IS IN love!)))*.

And so...

(By the time he made it back, there was a mob scene out front!)...

For Skin's, perhaps upon poor-judgement, *(or perhaps, it WAS upon ENVY!)*, tells, his musclehead-driver, "to park the car 'round back.", *(but, that!)*, "he was gettin' out, out front!" *(For Skin's, was feeling, LEFT out of the mix!)*.

FOR...

Out front, there were ASPIRING musicians! Singers!! And, rappers!!! (((And, motherfuckers from-and-not-even-from "the neighborhood" dressed up, as GOOMAHS and GANGSTERS!!!)))...

(And, perhaps, for Skin's, the ULTIMATE SIGN of respect? FOR Skin's, and for HIS "BUZZ Event"??)...

YOU HAD PLENTY of paparazzi and the press, shootin' videos and SNAPPIN' PICS!!!

For(by the time, Skin's got back)...

Pockets' RV, WAS parked out front, AMONGST the throngs!

AND...

((((Pockets, HAD ALREADY RECORDED "JUST ONE TAKE", OF SKIN'S SON-IN-LAW SINGIN',...THAT CHRISTMAS SONG!!!)))

And...

The dirty-FOLLOWING-directives-on-duty vice cop, was staged, just outside of the RV's door!

For...

(((There's - "RECORDING IN SESSION"!)))

AND...

(As, previously-directed, by Pockets, to Pockets' "Head of Security", Pockets, so directed)...

"NOBODY comes in this RV! And, under NO circumstances - NO interruptions - THERE ARE to be! So? SHOW-ME-whatcha'-got! ...It's YOUR JOB TO KEEP and ensure!!"

AND SO(under *"torn-pressure"*)...

(The dirty-vice-cop-*feeling-Pockets'*-AND-Skin's-*PRESSURE*-(on-duty!)...HAS, a decision, TO MAKE!)...

FOR...

The dirty vice cop IS between-a-rock-AND-a-hard-place...(on duty!),...(((MAKE,...NO mistake!!)))...

AS...

Pockets' "Head of Security" stands before, the RV's door!

AS...

(((HE stands BEFORE Skin's!)))

And...

As Skin's, approaches him, Skin's, is...*BEAMING WITH PRIDE!!!*

For Skin's, presses through the throngs. While hands shake under the pressure of pressed-skin, from, and, of, (and in!) the moment, FROM, when, FOR Skin's, (the neighborhood hero!), in and, OF the revel, SHAKING hands, with ALL that he can, (OF the throngs!), AS HE presses-on, plowing-past them!

BUT(YET!)...

(((AND, BUT STILL!!!)))...

As, far as, Pockets' "Head of Security" is concerned, there's STILL "RECORDING IN SESSION"!!!

(Psst!)...(HEY!)...((("Mr. Head-OF-Security"!!))), THAT MEANS...

NO one (((AND - I-MAFACKIN'-MEAN - NO ONE))) allowed!!!!!!

And so...

THIS - Dirty-Mutha'-Fuckin'-Vice-Cop - STILL - has, A decision, TO make!(((ON DUTY!!!)))...(AND, FOR HIS SAKE - the decision - HE MAKES - better be RIGHT!!!)...

And(he's UNDER *"torn-pressure"*)...

And, he's UNDER the approach OF Skin's! And, he's...UNDER the roar of the crowd! And, he's UNDER the SNAP OF THE FLASH, of a multitude of cell phones, news media, and paparazzi camera lights!... (oy...VEY!!!))).

But...

(Since the-dirty-vice-cop-on-duty-IS-playing-BOTH-SIDES-of-the-music-industry-fence!)...

...HE decided, to just let Skin's walk-on-up and, enter the RV!(UNDER CERTAIN and impending DOOM OF Pockets', ADMONISHMENT!!!)(OY VEY!!!).

HOWEVER...

TO the dirty-vice-cop-being-in-for-an-on-duty-surprise, Pockets, DIDN'T LOSE - HIS SHIT!(TO the dirty vice cop's, ASTONISHMENT!!!).

HOWEVER...

ALL WAS WELL! ...(*The recording session WENT well!!*)...

And...

(As the dirty vice cop, peeked-up-into the open door of the RV,...it wasn't too hard to tell!!!).

FOR...

Walking out from Pockets' private sleeping quarters, and, (AS IN Pockets' OWN words!),*(back where, he makes, "magic happen"!)*, back where, Pockets, has HIS soundproof mobile studio, back where, *he DID, IN FACT,* (JUST MADE!), *"magic happen!"*(((and, Pockets, TOTALLY *AND COMPLETELY - IN LOVE - WITH - HIMSELF!!!)))*, AIN'T too shy TO tell ya', THAT, *all IT did take him WAS, "JUST ONE TAKE!"*(And, that, *HE did it, "ALL BY HIMSELF!"*)...(and, THAT, *"HE DIDN'T NEED, NOBODY'S HELP!!"*), as Pockets, and Skin's son-in-law, step-out-from - having-just-opened, POCKETS' mobile studio door!!

Back where...

((((Pockets, "GOT IT ON WAX", IN JUST, ONE TAKE!")))...

Back where...

Skin's son-in-law, (UNDER Pockets' "studio-prowess"!!!), singing, that Christmas song (in acapella!), WAS recorded!!!

And...

...Seeing as, (between, Pockets and Skin's), there was nothing but hands under squeezing-tight-pressure,...(followed by, audibly-hard slaps and pats on the back!)...

(FOLLOWED BY!)...

Four cheeks being kissed-twice and a playful-punch to one's chin!

And...

(Between, the opening, of the RV's door, the dirty-vice-cop's-nosey-on-duty-envious-eyes, SEES ALL OF THIS!)...

As...

He decides, to abandoned his post. Closing the door.

As...

(((HE STEPS-UP INSIDE!!!)))

And, Pockets, as he sees the dirty vice cop, NOT at his post,...doesn't seem to care. As, Pockets, walking from the back of the RV, (back in one of his custom red custom-made red suits!), tells, Skin's, and his son-in-law, for him to excuse.

As...

Pockets, proceeds to the RV's kitchen area. (Cocking his custom red custom-made red hat, haaaaaard to tha' side, ONCE there!)...

WHERE...

Seated, sitting with his arms folded, at the fold out kitchen table,...is Skin's,...Consigliere!

(((And, I've BEEN TRYING to tell y'all, THAT, Pockets, GOT some shit TO him!)))

FOR...

Pockets recorded that Christmas song...*FROM memory!*

AS...

HE "played" that dirty-unbeknownst-to-him-that-he-"was-getting-played"-on-duty-vice-cop!

(((HAD HIM singing the lyrics to the song, AND humming the melody!)))

HOWEVER...

(((Skin's, Consigliere, GOT some shit TO him TOO!)))...

For Skin's, Consigliere, winks back at that cocked haaaaaard custom red custom-made red hat! For Skin's, Consigliere, *has BEEN* and, IS *down FOR,...the POWER move!!!*(((MADONE!!!))).

And so...

Entering the kitchen, is Skin's and, his son-in-law. And, Pockets, starts boastin'! *'Bout HOW impressed he was, (WITH, Pockets' coaching, OF COURSE!)* at HOW, the kid, IS A "natural"! *(And, AT HOW, the kid's singing voice SOUNDED singing, THAT Christmas song!)*.

And, as Skin's, begins, (going-on-and-on-and-in!), 'bout, "HEY! YOU'S!! WHERE'S the fuckin' contracts at?!?", (Skin's, Consigliere, chimes-in), "NOT to worry, BOSS! I got it ALLLLL covered! Skin's, *you left me in charge,...so, I signed your name!* And,...yeah,...SO, well, anywaaaaaays,...*TO "expidite" thangs!* IT'S ALL legit, BOSS! *WITNESSED by, THAT, "hippy-contract-trashcan-fuckhead-fuck", OF COURSE!!"*

"OH, REALLY??? *FUCKING DID YOU'S, NOW?!?* So,...WHERE THE FUCKS, HE AT???", Skin's, (swipes at his hair!) as, he snaps!!

And, Skin's Consigliere, (arms folded!), replies, "Take it easy, boss. *I ain't think, you would mind. All's I was, tryin' ta' do, was save you some time. The Christmas song, got done. So, WE took care'ov the contracts...* so, that, YOU could get YOUR "BUZZ EVENT" started, SOON AS, you got back, *from whereva', you was gettin' back from!* BUT, it's YOUR call, boss! So, IF ya' want? I'll take you to, the hippy, RIGHT now! BUT, just'a give-ya'-a head's up! ...HE'S baby-sittin', Pockets' two rappers, in your club, boss. NOT, in YOUR office! But, the room, IN the back. Yeah, so, well, anywaaaaaays, *I went 'head AND signed YOUR NAME on the contracts!* 'Cause, I KNEW, YOU WASN'T tryin' ta' BE 'ROUND, "all of that"!", then, (arms unfolded!), (layin' on a lil' charm!), Skin's Consigliere stands up, gives the boss' cheeks a kiss, one kiss on each, (((GOTTA' show, the boss respect!))), OR get clipped, by "our" CLOSEST of friends, (((BEFORE the end of the week!)))(((FUGGETABOUTIT!!!))).

"YOU'S, GOT THAT RIGHT! I ain't tryin' ta' be 'round that, undignified, greasy-handed-hippy! YOU'S, know me, too good!", Skin's, to his, Consigliere, begins, "TONIGHT'S, a one-time-deal! And, AFTER tonight?? I DON'T want, nobody IN MY club,...lookin' like "THEM"!!!

And so...

(As that, dirty vice cop, grabs that, "bottle of something expensive", from that, stop he made, to grab that!)...

A $300.00 bottle of Remy Martin's seal gets cracked!

And...

(As the son-in-law, the dirty vice cop, Skin's, Pockets and Skin's Consigliere, all raise their rock glasses, of that $300.00 bottle of Remy Martin, into the air)...

Pockets, says, to Skin's, "MY BROTHER!! MY BROTHER!! Yeah, so, well, anywaaaaaays,...HERE'S to you, my friend!"

BUT...

(As, the rest, sip. Pockets, hears)...

((((That THUNDER rollin' in!!!)))

SO...

Pockets, quickly-washes-down HIS Remy Martin! (Slammin' his rock glass down, on the fold out kitchen table!), talkin' 'bout, "Skin's,... gentlemen. Excuse me, if you would, for'a few minutes. I'M finna'-get-dis, party started! FOR YOU, SKIN'S, MY BROTHER!! I want, FOR YOU, to make, a GRAAAND entrance! So, Y'ALL, stay put! AND, DON'T open, that door!! Til' AFTER, I make, an announcement!!!".

And...

(As Skin's Consigliere, assures Skin's, that "everythang", is alright!)...

Pockets, opens the RV's door((((SEEING NOTHING BUT A MOB OF SCREAMING FANS!!!))))and that it's been raining lightly, however, at ANY-MINUTE NOW, LOOKIN'-LIKE it's gonna, start to pour!

And(once outside!)...

...with the RV door closed, Pockets, sees Skin's muscle, PUSHIN' 'N SHOVIN' his way THROUGH the throngs! (Lookin' like HE KNOWS that somethin's goings-on!)...

AND...

Pockets *KNOWS, THAT, IF* he gets to Skin's, his plans - *FINNA'-GO - all wrong!*

SOOOOOO...

Pockets, do - what he, ALWAYS - do!

(And, WHAT'S THAT???)...(I HEARD "YOU", ASK!!!)

Welll...

(ALL TOGETHER NOW!!!)...((((I-AIN'T-GOT-NO PROBLEM AT ALL IN TELLIN' Y'ALL!!!)))...

For(Pockets!)...

BUYS A MUTHAFUCKA'S SOUL!!!

((((BY PLACIN' PAPER IN THAT PALM!!!)))

And so...

As Pockets, follows the cleared path, to make it to the I.A. Club's room in the back, as HIS muscle NOW, clears a path, OF muscled-throngs!...

(LET US TAKE A LOOK in that BACK ROOM!),(at MC Busta-Nut and False Profit!!),(to see what the fuck is goings-on!!!)...

(AND, I AIN'T even gonna ask this time if "YOU" want too!)...('Cause, I know YOU WANT TOO:)

And so...

Having been sitting in that back room, (all this time), has been just those two, rollin' up, smokin' blunts and, spittin' tha' lyrics to all the songs they gonna do. False Profit, eyes closed, occupied in his mind, (of his DJ'in' techniques!), BLESSED WITH GOOD muscle twitch, GOT HIS HANDS GOIN', of which, his DJ'in' techniques, THAT he's rehearsin' 'n visualizin'! *And, False Profit, FOLLOWED Pockets' directives!*

(So, HE GOT dressed up CRISPY 'N STYLIN' rockin' "Rich N Rotten"! False Profit, humble?? NOT in the LEAST BIT!!! *Keepin' good "Company &" to finishin' off his ensemble, is a blulky-gemmed-up-belt-'n-buckle, THAT he GRIPPED-UP from "Lit"!).* And, False Profit, well, he's been lookin' at the good! *As, he's been tryin' to get through to 'Nut, tellin' him, not to stress shit, that, Pockets' long-ass-phone-call, prepped us for THIS VERY MOMENT!, (AS HE KNEW, POCKETS-IN-LOVE-WITH-HEARING-HIMSELF-TALK WOULD!!!).* (And, all the while, ALL THIS TIME, WHAT HAS BEEN occupying, MC Busta-Nut's, time???). *Well, MC Busta-Nut, HAS BEEN occupying two folding chairs,...goin' FROM buzzed TO fried!!* And, well, 'Nut, he's LEANIN' back with two syrofoam cups, WITH his feet propped up, WITH BRAND NEW SNEAKS WITH NO CREASES AND NOT laced up!! And, he got black - "manufacturally" - ripped-'n-frayed - skinny jeans on, IN WHICH, to perform,...with no shirt on! ('Cause, MC Busta-Nut's - GOTTA' SHOW - that - HE'S FULLY - tatted-up!!!). And, THAT'S HOW he's goin' out! ('CAUSE, he STILL AIN'T gettin', dressed up!) 'Cause, 'Nut? Well,...HE DON'T CARE!!! 'Cause, HE'S just gon' keep-on-keepin'-on tippin' 'n leanin', IN those two foldin' chairs!! (And, WHY is that, YOU ASK??)(I'll make it abundantely clear!)(((('Cause, *MC Busta-Nut, has an OVERABUNDANCE OF HATE!!!)*)))Due TO the fact THAT, *"Skin's kin be recordin' in OUR RV and, tha nigga Pockets, GOT BOAFF'OV-US SITTIN' OUT'CHERE!!!"* Then, 'Nut, *FULL OF HATE* and, feelin' tha pressure, of being pushed to the back, lights that "pressure", talkin' 'bout, while releasin' tha pressure from his lungs, "I'm finna show dem out'der on that concrete, where I'M from! Profit, WATCH what I DO!! I'M finna get 'um ALL-HYPED, my G! I'm talkin' CONCRETE FACTS!!!".

(Finally, PULLED-'N-MUSCLED through the PACKED I.A. Club, making it to the back, Pockets, enters the back room, assisted by Skin's paid-off-muscle, in his palm, Pocket's placed a CRISPY-Make-Your-Hand-Smell-Like-Freshly-Printed-Money-STACK!!!)...

Pockets, takes one look, at MC Busta-Nut, (and, snaps!), "Get THAT look, OFF ya' face! Later, FO' all dat!!"

And...

(While, False Profit BECOMES, full of smiles!!)...

'Nut, looks at, Profit, like, he don't know, ('cause HE DON'T!).

(And, poor 'Nut. Ya' gotta kinda feel for the kid)

For...

HE'S so full OF hate!!!(THAT, he CAN'T see the good before him...(And, sadly. He, probably,...never won't:(

'Cause...

(As, MC Busta-Nut, continues to lean back, *so full of hate,* emulating, LIKE he's hard)...

THAT'S, the attitude, that's GONNA' leave him, full of wounds, the kind-of-type-wounds, that run so deep,...(that won't give him the chance to even scar:(

BUT THEN...

MC Busta-Nut's, *hatin'-face,*...becomes a grin! As, he DOES FINALLY SEE why, False Profit, was smilin'! As, Pockets,...blesses them! As, they are both blessed!! WHEN, Pockets, places that - Cuban-link-drip - over their heads! WITH, that, Jettison Records heavy-weighted diamond-encrusted "JR" medallion, hanging on their chests!! (And, oh yes! THAT'S WHAT IT TOOK!!! *TO TURN THAT HATE* INTO A GRIN!!! *CASHED IN THE HATE, IN HIS SOUL,* FOR SOME JURRY AND DIAMONDS!!!). *EVEN False Profit WAS fooled!* It's all marketing. The beginning of the end.

And so(LET US ALL head back out front!)...

FOR...

(((The TIME has come! FOR Pockets, TO GIVE the people what HE *KNOWS* they want!)))

Unpacked, seldom-used, for parties and such, is the I.A. Club's PA-sound-system. Such as, for when, Skin's, wants to hold such a party and/

or a big event. Such as, for the Fourth of July and/or for Christmas. *And so, a good-while ago, taken from the room in the back, were four tall-standing all-black-and-boxey-Peavey-PA-Speakers, repositioned, double-stacked.* And, they grace the exterior. As, they're positioned, on each side of the front door. And, positioned next to one double-stack, are two turn tables, positioned on a black cloth. And, positioned under that, is a sturdy 6 foot foldout table. And, positioned under that, you got the sidewalk. And, positioned under a set of headphones, is the head of False Profit. And, with cordless mic gripped-tight, positioned in his hand, like a last-call-bottle, a shirtless MC Busta-Nut, graces his way out the front door. And, positioned ON TOP OF THE WORLD, with cordless mic in hand, Pockets, *FULLY IN LOVE WITH HIMSELF,* gets the masses hyped! And, as Skin's and, his son-in-law are introduced,...the RV door opens! *(((And, as it does, the masses, begin to roar!!!)))*. Then, Pockets, introduces, HIS two rappers! As, False Profit, positions the needle on the record, (for to show the masses!), WHAT those two turn tables ARE for!! And, it's really quite sad. The music starts off quite sad. With low, though, jumpy-strings, building, with woodwinds kickin' in, bringin' in with them, *heavy storm winds!* And, I would swear I heard a harp, right 'bout 'round the time, the heavy percussions start! And, pacing back and forth, MC Busta-Nut, yells into the mic, as the masses he tells, to count along, to and for the viral song, that 'Nut and Profit are known for!! And, as False Profit, goes off wit tha scratch 'n cut , MC Busta-Nut, gets the masses following his lead, as the masses all count along and jump! And, to the masses' count, MC Busta-Nut thrusts his pelvis *(with enough force, to make Elvis blush!)* as the masses count-off the viral hook, *(of MC Busta-Nut & False Profit's 400, 000 selling underground mixtape, "Tha' Spermicidal Tendencies"),* of their underground hit song, *"Drop 'Em And Give 'Em 10"*, as, Pockets, looks on, at his two rappers, *FULLY IN LOVE WITH HIMSELF,* with no need to pretend. And since, business is business, to be sure, Pockets, looks over at the son-in-law, over there, standing next to Skin's, both standing over there, by the RV'S door. And Pockets, gives them both a double-thumbs up!! Thanking them both through the jumping-counting-frenzied-masses, hey, take a look at US!!! WE just recorded a hit song!!! And Skin's, YOU DA' MAN!!! NOT ONLY did you LET ME rent your joint, but, "YOU'S" A MAN OF YOUR WORD, SKIN'S!!! LOOK AT ALL THESE MAFACKAS!!! YOU DID, IN FACT, PACK THE I.A. CLUB!!! And, over there, by that RV'S door, Skin's and his son-in-law, with the biz, with "THE BUZZ", with themselves,...*ARE FALLING IN LOVE!!* But,...business IS business. And so, Pockets, looks up at that sky of black,...that's 'bout to open up! Then, Pockets, cocks his custom red custom-made red hat, HAAAAAARD TO THA' SIDE, AT THEM TWO MAFACKAS, standin' over there together, OVER THERE, by the RV'S door!! And, then, Pockets,...SEEKS SHELTER LIKE A MAFACKA'!!! 'Cause, a WHOLE BUNCH of mafackas, finna GET WET!!! 'Cause,...IT'S ABOUT TO POUR!!!

AND SO...

Beginning the song off, with the count of the hook, *(with narcotics and confidence in his eyes being the look!!),* MC Busta-Nut GOTTA' get the masses RILED UP! And so, foregoes the first verse first! (BEING TOLD, to do so!), the masses,...DO SO JUMP!!! (As, they don't even ask!). "THEY" just jump AS HIGH as "THEY" can, do so vertically! (As, the masses, do so indeed!). AS, THE MASSES FOLLOW...(MC Busta-Nut's lead!). AS, he repeatedly JUMPS, up and down emphatically, elbows goin', chest nearly meeting his knees, as if,...it were all rehearsed! And then,...the music,...dramatically stops! AS, False Profit,...cuts in, the BASS DROP!!! (FOLLOWED-UP, with the selection!), to bring back in the strings, the percussions and, the woodwinds! And then, coming in last, *(as that sky of black opens up!),* ARE the blasts OF the trumpets!!!!!!!! ((((Orchestrated by False Profit TO perfection!)))).

And, Skin's is over there,...*BEAMING WITH PRIDE!!!* As, the masses, at "HIS" "BUZZ EVENT" block the street for blocks!((((JUMPING UP AND DOWN!!!))))SHOUTIN', *"DROP 'EM, AND GIVE 'EM 10",* to this FILTHY-SONG, (((AS the masses count!))). Paparazzi snappin' pics! Nothing BUT flashin' lights! (And MUCH TOO, Skin's Consigliere's, shagrin!), *(for MUCH TOO long!),* for Skin's, to HIM, *HAS BEEN slippin'!* ((((And, drawlin' WAY TOO MUCH attention!!!)))). For Skin's, as he stands OUTSIDE, *BEAMING WITH PRIDE,* you got gawkers, music lovers, the press, party-goers AND UNDERCOVERS INSIDE!!! But, Skin's,

HE DON'T SEE NOTHIN', but smiles on faces, (takin' up their whole entire faces!), smilin'-wide, from the left side to the right! But,...that ALL changed,...WHEN the DUYU CREW GOT everybody runnin', duckin' and TRYING TO hide!!!! When, *FOUR FLAMIN'-RED-HOT-TOMMY-GUN-MUZZLES,* causing burning sensation through the masses' hydes, when the DUYU CREW started dumping off these "cans" LIKE a food drive!!!!

And, MC Busta-Nut, he must be empervious, to the pain of the rain. 'Cause, he don't know he's been shot! *Perhaps, it's due to the "lean" he was drinkin'?* So,...FUCK IT!!! As, the rain and the winds become more strong, MC Busta-Nut, KEEPS rapping his song!(((FOR THE SHOW MUST GO ON!!!)))...

HOWEVER...

WHERE'S, the BASS DROP???

Maaaaaaaaan, False Profit's BEEN dead!!!!

(((((DON'T YOU SEE that EKG line-of-bullet holes punched in the front of Skin's I.A. Club????))))

And so...

MC Busta-Nut turns 'round, (from the lack of that bass drop sound!), seeing False Profit dead and, the bullet-riddled-EKG-line-level, punched through the exterior's front, of Skin's I.A. Club, *(the former-height of False Profit's former-head!!!),* MC Busta-Nut turns 'round, faces and solutes the crowd, then meets the rest of his blood, as he falls for his final rest upon the ground.

"THAT...mother...fucker.", Mr. Brotha Trife, to himself, under his breath, he mutters. As, he and Anna Mossitti, followed the sound of the *THUNDER. And, had been in the crowd, taking in "The BUZZ Show", standing holdin' hands, as if they were lovers.* But, from the ensuing stampede, *(those that weren't shot and killed),* found otherways...to die and bleed. And though, they were both knocked down to the street, Mr. Brotha Trife, shielded Anna Mossitti's body, of what seemed to be, the feet of wild beasts. And, in the street, as they lie, some girl lie dying next to them. And, you know what that triflin' Tier-Three-Motherfucker *thought* at that moment??

THAT...

(((Her and Anna Mossitti, ARE just about the SAME size!!!)))

And so...

That, Tier Three, placed that dying girl's foot, up on the curb. And then, placed Anna Mossitti's foot, up on the curb next to her's. And then, using that dying girl's blood and sweat, he worked that ankle bracelet down off of Anna Mossitti's leg! And then, that ankle bracelet, he slid and affixed, ONTO the leg of that, lying there DYING chick! ((((I HEAR YOU, MOTHERFUCKERS!!! AT ME, DON'T CURSE!!! FOR,... YOU'RE STILL READIN'!!! 'CAUSE, YOU LOVE THIS TRIFLIN' WORLD!!!))). And, then,..."Giddy-Up" time? YES, INDEED!! Taking her by the hand, that Tier Three, got Anna Mossitti to safety, (((pressed all-up-on her))), GOT HER pressed-up-against a buildin', shakin' at the sight, of watching that dying girl die, piled-high-beneath, dead bodies and feet, FROM the next wave, ...of the stampede!!! (((MOTHER... FUCKING...OY...VEY...YO!!!))).

And...

(As, the DUYU CREW'S THUNDER, traveled in peals)...

From that building side, ALL PRESSED-UP-ON ANNA MOSSITTI, that Tier Three sees, a PALE CHOPPER comin' his way!!!! ((((With, Dead Sexy perched, upon that!!!!)))). He saw Dead Sexy from behind those, limited-edition's of 24 karat golds. And, with his one good eye, *peeped* Dead Sexy perched, up on his pale ostrich skin seat, (from underneath his bullet-hole-hat!).

And...

(That, Tier Three, *peeped* people in the street)...

BEING RUN-THA'-FUCK-OVER, BY THAT PALE CHOPPER'S, FAT REAR TIRE!!!!...(((((from having been kicked over, by Dead Sexy's, pale reptillian-covered feet!!!!)))).

And...

((((*THAT, pissed that, TIER THREE off!!!*)))...

AND SO...

A roarin'-past them Dead Sexy, got CAUGHT IN THE FACE, WITH THE BACK OF A TIER-THREE-ELBOW!!!

And(AS THE RESULT!!)...

Off that pale ostrich skin seat and chopper, Dead Sexy, got LIFTED-OFF!!!!

And so...

(No longer pressed-up-hard against the side of that building)...

THOUGH...

Anna Mossitti, WAS STILL, pressed-up-hard AGAINST SUMTHIN'!!

FOR...

(((She was pressed ALL-UP-ON THE MOST TRIFLIN'!!!)))...

As...

WITH her face, buried in Trife's back! (And with her arms, wrapped 'round him tight!!). All while, (AND ALL THE WHILE!), perched-up-upon a PALE ostrich skin chopper seat, ((((GOIN' LIKE A BAT - STRAIGHT-OUTTA' - HELL!!!!)))), WAS THAT, rear tire, of PHAT!!!

And so...

Was it Giddy-Up time?

((((((YOU MUTHA’ FUCKIN’ RIGHT!!!!!!))))))

THAT TIER THREE, CHEATED DEAD SEXY, OUTTA’ THAT CHOPPER!!!((((HOPPED ON THAT BITCH!!!))))...AND, THEN,... RODE-THA’-FUCK-OUTTA’-THAT MOTHERFUCKER!!!!!!!!!!!!!!!!!

(That Tier Three, rode that chopper hard!),...((WEAVIN’ IN AND OUTTA’ CARS!!))...

And...

(((HE WASN’T STOPPIN’ for NO red lights!!!)))(((AND FUCK ALL THAT *THUNDER* AND THAT LIGHTNING!!!)))...

’Cause...

HE stuck TO the plan!

AND...

He wasn’t stoppin’ til’, (FROM this city AND the North Juarez P.D.), Anna Mossitti,...was FAR OUTTA’ SIGHT!!!

Chapter Twenty Seven

THEE "ASCENDANCY"

But, back in North Juarez...

(after, Mr. Brotha Trife and Anna Mossitti were, long gone)...

THERE WERE SCORES TO BE SETTLED!!!

FOR...

(((Motherfuckers, had to explain themselves!!!)))...

For, Skin's, was lookin' for the settle-up! For, Skin's, SON-IN-LAW was dead! (AND, MOST of HIS 5th Avenue Street Crew!). *HIS club got shot up! For, Skin's muscle, was one of 'em!((((THAT GOT SHOT DEAD!!!!)))). For, Skin's muscle,...GOT BUZZED too!!!*

(((For Skin's, HIMSELF, is LUCKY, that, HE AIN'T dead!)))

AS...

A bullet, had BUZZED, his head!

"And, where's-da'-fucks, MY Consigliere!!!", Skin's, shouts-out-loud, swipin' the salt 'n pepper out his eyes, (slickin' back all the blood in his hair,...THAT, he didn't know was there!),..."AND, WHERE'S-DA'-FUCKS, THAT, BLACK-ASS, POCKETS!!! *SHOULDA' KNOWN, doin' business wit "YOU'S", WAS gonna go wrong!"* And then, Skin's, with no song and no contracts, falls face-first-dead in the street. *Got shot in the head.*

AND(((WORSE THAN THAT!!!)))...

FOR...

The "Music Industry" took,...a BIG FAT BITE OUTTA' THAT ASS!!!((((BUTT-CHEEKS LOOKIN' LIKE RAW MEAT!!!!)))).

But...

(As, FOR Pockets??)...

There NEVER WERE no contracts!!!

(So, Pockets?)...

OWNS THE RIGHTS(((of the dead)))son-in-law's recorded version OF the Christmas song!

'CAUSE...(Well?)...

(((Pockets,...GOTTA' "EAT"!!!)))

And, Skin's Consigliere?

Well...

(I'll get ALL Y'ALL caught up - ON HOW - shit went down!)... *LONG BEFORE Skin's club got SHOT UP,...YOU know,...long before Skin's, got dropped off, and WALKED-RIGHT-ON-UP-IN the RV'S door,... YOU know,...long before Skin's, told his muscle to, "park 'round back."*

Well...

(((A WHOLE-LOTTA'-SHIT - WENT DOWN - BEFORE THAT!!!)))

And so...

(As, Skin's was still out, threatening to shoot off Mr. Brotha Trife's cannoli)...

Pockets, told the dirty vice cop, and Skin's Consigliere to huddle-up, in his RV. (And, as Skin's son-in-law, was in the I.A. club, warming-up his vocals, sippin' on lemon and hot tea!)...

The sharp mind of Pockets, (that devious-motherfucker!), cooked up a hustle quickly!

And...

(As for, Skin's Consigliere??)...

Well...

HE GOT PLAYED TOO!!!

For...

(((THIS Music Industry AIN'T IN LOVE WITH, AND,...SURE-AS-FUCK DON'T NEED YOU!!!))).

For(ALL he, WAS good for!)...

WAS, FOR some "diversionary-tactics", *(FOR WHEN, Skin's, got back!).*

AND SO...

WHAT-HAD-HAPPENED WAS!!!...(((YOU KNOW, *PRIOR TO THE "BUZZ")))...*

Pockets, delegated,..."Look-here,...ALL-THA'-FUCK YOU IS, EVA' GON' BE IS, SKIN'S No.2!! SOOOOOO, let me, ASK YOU, somethin'!? HOW-THA'-FUCKS THAT, SITTIN' WIT YOU??? IF YOU ain't tryin' TO move up...then, YOU might-as-well quit! Shiiiiiit, EVEN I, was tha' H.N.I.C, in this-here town! And,...I-AIN'T-HAVE'TA', DO much! ALL I HAD TO DO,...was reach in my pockets! But,...YOU ARE, HIS No.2!! SOOOOOO, Skin'll, LISTEN to you!! SO, when Skin's, gets back, I need YOU, to get Skin's, IN this-here RV! Just, tell 'em,…just, tell 'em,…"Pockets, wants for me and him, to have a drink." …YEAH, well, so, ANYWAAAAAAYS,…JUST make up some shit!!! 'CAUSE, unless YOU, ALWAYS wanna-be, his No.2?? Then, "BOAF-OF-US" NEED, him out front FOR this, "BUZZ HIT"!!".

And so(THEN!)…

(The dirty vice cop on duty, GOT LOOKED AT BY Pockets, LIKE, - uh - HEY - "Mr.-Head-of-Security!" - YOU-BEST - CO-SIGN - FOR ME, ON THIS SHIT!!)…

And, as such, the dirty vice cop, so stated, to Skin's No.2, "YOU even, said it yourself! "Skin's, BEEN slippin'!" - AIN'T THAT, what you said?!? - "Skin's, be ALWAYS flyin', off tha' handle AND trippin'!!"

And then(AFTER THAT!)…

(Pockets, cocked that custom red, custom-made red hat, hard to the side on his head)…

And, as such, so then, said, "If you tryin' to move up IN this world?? I CAN give YOU legs. And, I KNOW, YOU WANT, Skin's outta tha' way! And, I KNOW, that, YOU BEEN READY to be No.1, in THIS city! 'Cause,…crime PAYS!! Yeah, so, well, uh, ANYWAAAAAAYS,…stick wit ME!!! I CAN GET YOU IN the music industry! Don't ask me how,…BUT, I JUST KNEW, that hippy-contract-guy, WASN'T gonna come through! FROM, MY EXPERIENCE, MOST MAFACKAS IN "THE BIZ" DON'T DO, HALF-THA'-SHIT, THEY SAY, THEY GONNA' DO!!!"

For…

Pockets, IS a gamblin' man!

And so…

(HE rolled them bones!)…

AND…

(((Gambled ON the fact, THAT - THAT "hippy-contract-man" WAS - THE SAME - "hippy-contract-man" - THAT - Pockets knew,...FROM-WAY-BACK!! IN FACT, SINCE, THAT - "hippy-contract-man" - TOOK OFF on him, ONCE BEFORE, Pockets, gambled ON the fact, that, that hippy, the writer of music contracts,...WASN'T GONNA' SHOW!!!))).

..."Shiiiiiit, I'LL TEACH YOU how to, draft-up contracts! You'll be makin' BIG MONEY!!! STACKS ON-TOP-OF STACKS!!! And, yeah, so, well, anywaaaaaays,...IT'LL ALL be, legit.", Pockets, spins the "Music Game", to the FORMER Consigliere, of the FORMER Skin's!(((HOOFAH!!!))). (And, BIG MONEY, was 'bout ALL it took, for Sink's Consigliere, to be convinced!).

And so(THEN!)...

(The dirty-vice-cop-GETTIN'-looked-at-AGAIN-from-Pockets-on-duty, threw in HIS two cents!!)...

"How 'bout, now?? NOW'S, YOUR CHANCE, to get out!! EVEN I, went legit!! Ya' best GET OUT now, POT'NUH, OR Skin's, 'GWINE GETCHA' pinched!!!"

And so(Then, AFTER THAT??)...

Pockets and Skin's Consigliere, shake hands!

(FOLLOWED-UP!)...

BY a couple of - AUDIBLY-HARD - slaps and pats, on each other's backs!! (And, of course,...cheeks got kissed too!!).

But(THEN!)...

Pockets, got serious as shit!

(Cocked that, custom red custom-made red hat, haaaaaard to the side, on his head of his!)...

And...

(While, STRAIGHT-GRILLIN' Skin's Consigliere, IN his eyes, Pockets, spoke-on some TRUE "Music Game" TRUTHS)...

..."BUT, FIRST,...ya' gotta PAY YOUR,..."Music Industry" DUES!!!"

And, well?(NOW, that YOU ARE ALL caught up ON ALL of THAT shit?) Well...

Skin's Consigliere, WAS IN THAT RV, as Pockets, behind the wheel, pulled off from out front of Skin's GETTIN'-SHOT-UP club! As, Pockets, drove over motherfuckers AT WILL((((GETTIN' THA' FUCK OUTTA' THERE!!!!))))DURING, the "BUZZ KILL"!!!!(((FOLLOWED-CLOSELY BY BLINKING RED AND BLUE LIGHTS!!!))) - (IN THE GRILL) - OF THAT UNDERCOVER CADDY!!! DRIVEN BY, POCKETS' "HEAD OF SECURITY"!!!...(((THE-FORMER-DIRTY-ASS-COP-OF-VICE!!!)))).

And so...

Pockets, behind the wheel of that RV, made-his-way, onto the highway of Rt. 36. (As, HE TOO, evaded the North Juarez PD!!). As, HE TOO, made-his-way, OUT of the city! And then, once down, off the highway,... once down,...the road,...a-good-ways...

THISISHOWSKIN'SCONSIGLIEREGOTPLAYED:

(Right there, parked along the southbound berm, of Business Route 36)...

Pockets, in HIS mobile studio, before him stood, the Consigliere. And, next to him, stood, his "Head of Security". And, Pockets, in his hands, he held, that thirty-aught-six.

And, AS for guts??

Well...

(((HE WAS CHECKIN' IT!!!)))

FOR...

Pockets, STRAIGHT-UP FORCED his "Head of Security", TO the label, to SHOW that, he was LOYAL!!!

And so...

(The former-dirtiest-vice-cop-on-the-police-force)...

After drawing his gun, put one, in the Consigliere's gut!

AFTER WHICH...

The dirty-ass vice cop, stood there in, and with, his OWN DRAWS...

(((('BOUT TO BE SOILED!!!)))(((OY VEY!!!))).

And, after taking that swung deer rifle gun butt to the nuts, falling atop of the fallen. The "Head of Security", (fallen from GRACE!), tossed his gun over to Pockets and, begged and bartered for his life! He EVEN offered up, *his secretly-recorded Christmas song,* (((OF THE ORIGINAL-VERSION))), *sung by, Anna Mossitti and Mr. Brotha Trife!!*

And, Pockets, with that - *upper-hand-handed-over-version - (of the secret-recording!)* - in his pocket, decided, that, THAT...WASN'T enough!!! ('Cause, Pockets, BE DAMNED if, HIS "Head of Security" - *gon-be-tha'-type - to SOIL HIMSELF,* over some, "necessary" - "muzic-biz-tactics"!

For...

Pockets, NOW, got TWO recorded versions, OF that Christmas song!!

Soooooo...

(It's, NOW, a matter of)...

Pockets,..."Used-YOU-up!"

And...

(((HE DON'T NEED-YOU-NO-MO'!)))(((OH LAWD!!!))).

BESIDES...

The former-dirtiest-cop-of-vice, *went FROM: "Gut-Check-Time"*, TO: Layin'-There-Wit-Ya'-Draws-ALL-Shitty!

SOOOOOO...

Pockets, shot that former-dirty-ass-vice-cop in his temple, (WITH the-former-dirty-ass-vice-COP'S OWN GUN!!!).

Then, Pockets, rolled the Consigliere over and, peeled that concealed revolver, off the Consigliere's leg. And then, Pockets, shot 'em both a couple mo' times. He even shot that former dirty ass vice cop in his mouth! Blowing teeth and blood all over the former dirty ass vice cop's face! Whereafter, Pockets, did SOME MO' peeling!! AS, off that former dirty ass vice cop's wrist, a red-faced Rolex, he takes!! AND THEN, RIGHT THERE, on the side of Business Route 36, Pockets, opened that RV's door, bearing witness to the *THUNDER* and lightning storm!!! And, while looking down at the dark berm, windy, stormin' and, teemin', Pockets, kicked both them motherfuckers down to that dark-gettin'-rained-on-berm, (all shot up!), with their guns in their hands. *(((Lookin' like they both died tryin' their best to be the first, one to kill the other one, in a firefight in which, NEITHER ONE was waitin' they turn!!)))*. And, as Pockets, pulled off from the southbound berm, in his side mirror, it looked like what it appeared to be. *Two dead men that got lit up.* Under the red and blue blinkin' lights of,...that undercover Caddy's grill! AS, in THIS, *THUNDERSTORM,* AIN'T NOBODY ELSE (crazy-enough!), TO BE - out-about-'n-'round - in THIS - *THUNDERSTORM,*...to witness! And, if EVER questioned, Pockets, stickin' to THE STORY, Of: WHAT it looks like it TO be! *("Well, your Honor, some cop and some gangster, must'ov'-shot-up one another.")* Stick to that story? YOU know Pockets will!(((THAT IS, IF he CAN'T buy the motherfucker, reachin' in his pockets, pullin' out two endangered-money clips claspin' 200K in crisp $1,000.00 bills!))).

AND SO...

(With, two - used-up-bled-dry-bled-out-stepped-on-stepped-upon-stepped-past-and-kept-it-steppin' -, stepping-stones - "REMOVED", FROM POCKETS' WAY!)...

Pockets, heads on his way, (to find his own lay-up and lay-low spot!), TO clean up HIS mobile studio, OF BLOOD,...AGAIN!!! And to, buy himself some time, to let THIS *THUNDERSTORM* wash away, the blood on the front of his RV(((and, what's sure to be - ALL-UP-UNDER-AND-IN-THE-WHEEL-WELLS!!!))) - *as, Pockets, was at the wheel(((and, RAN OVER MAFACKAS AT WILL))), makin' HIS getaway!!!*

And...

(With two separate versions of that Christmas song, on two separate thumbs drives, in two separate custom red, custom-made red suit pants pockets)...

Pockets, heads towards a place, (driving at just the right pace!), as to, not catch the eye, of no "Johnny Law's", (ain't tryin' to increase THEIR heart rate!).

'Cause*(JUSTIFIED!!!)*...

IN Pockets' *MUSIC-GAME-HUSTLE-MIND*, this-here RV, *AIN'T the one, that, ran over a bunch of mafackas (((at will!!!))), MAKIN' an escape!!!*

AND SO...

(With no one else out on the roads, Pockets, knows EXACTLY where HE'S gonna go!)...

For...

Where he's gonna go, he *knows*, that once he gets there,...*he'll be alone!*

BESIDES...

There's, ONLY ONE other, that would, be: "crazy-enough", (Who, IS: "out-there-enough!"), TO BE, out there,...WITH THE SKY OF BLACK! (And, OUT THERE WITH all that lightning!)...((And, OUT THERE WITH these storm winds!!))....((((*And, OUT THERE WITH the DUYU CREW'S THUNDER!!!!*)))). And, as Pockets drives, fightin' his night vision, he AIN'T thinkin' 'bout those two that he dumped, on the side of the highway! (Shiiiiit, Pockets, thinkin' OF his two thumb drives!!).

(Can't barely see the road! Hands at 10 and 2!! And yet,...he cracks a smile!!!)

For...

WHEN he gets, to where he's goin', Pockets, gonna check...his email!

(((SHIIIIIIT, BUSINESS IS BUSINESS!!!)))

BESIDES...

(He ain't been able to check it in a while:)

And, though, Pockets, got them big-ass windshield wipers goin' and, with the time on the wheel, (no longer showin;) that RV of his, NEARLY slid-off the road! BUT, yet (and, but still!), THAT, custom red custom-made red hat of his, HARRRRD-TO-THA'-SIDE, IT GETS COCKED!

'CAUSE...

BUSINESS IS BUSINESS!

AND...

IT AIN'T ALWAYS PRETTY!!

But...

(((IT'S PRETTY AT THE TOP!!!))).

And so, Pockets, turns off of Business Route 36, travels down a long - no-other-cars-on-the-road - road, passing a gas station on his left-hand side, with just one car parked on the side with no lights. And, due to all of the wind and the rain, Pockets, couldn't tell, if there was a driver behind the wheel. (Or, if someone, were slumped down, tryin' to hide!). But, due to this *WICKED-THUNDER-STORM*, the gas station(and, the - surrounding-square-mileage - FOR MILES!)had no lights (and),... ((GASP!!!!))...(((NO WIFI!!!!))). So, Pockets, couldn't tell, if anyone was inside. (But, figured, due to the storm, the gas station was just closed). As he, kept fightin' his night vision,...the storm...AND the road!!!

And, then, Pockets, makes a right, at a 4-Way intersection with no functional traffic lights! And, then, Pockets, drives a-short-ways and,*((((NEVER HAS HE DRIVEN IN A THUNDERSTORM LIKE THIS, IN ALL OF HIS DAYS!!!!))))*. As he, makes another right. As he, cuts that Vegas RV of his, down a long-winding-paved-path, after cutting off his headlights!

And(once parked, waaaaay back in the cut!)...

Pockets, walked to the back of his RV, (TO HIS mobile studio!).

BUT...

(NOT to cleanup!)

FOR...

Business IS business!

For...

Pockets, GOTTA' check his email!

FOR...

(((Pockets, GOTTA' hit up PHILLIP TATE!!!)))...(For, Pockets, GOT "Hotspot"!!!)

For...

Pockets, GOTTA' checkout the news!(((((TO SEE, HOW MUCH OF A "BUZZ" - JETTISON RECORDS - NOW GOT!!!!))))

(((((TOLD YOU THIS SHIT AIN'T PRETTY!!!!))))

And so...

As Pockets, sits at the foot of his bed, on the very same bed, *where Y.S. blew off her head, in the very same mobile studio, where two others - too-eager-to-get-in-the-biz - got shot, (damn,...SURE SEEMS like, a lot of motherfuckers die, one way or another, in music studios...A LOT!).* In the flicker of the darkness, from the flicker of his phone, Pockets, put on his Hotspot and, put on the news. (And, as he held that phone in both hands, with both of his elbows, resting on both of his thighs)...(((YOU SHOULDA' SEEN the look in his eyes!!!)))...

THE INTERVIEW:

A "BUZZ-GOER", from under a sea of blinking reds and blues, from under the sexy-gaze of Mimi Johnson, (on scene news reporter), from under the blinding-white-spot-light, (of the cameraman's camera), from under pressure, from under the pressure of LIVE TV, from under TOO MUCH wind and the rain, and the lightning and the *THUNDER,* from under no helicopter blades to be heard over, as a "BUZZ-HERD" gathered 'round, with fresh blood gettin' smeared and streaked, under their feet, from the wind and from the wind-battered street, tried his best, FOR HIS WORD TO BE HEARD, "...we was at home and, we was 'sposed to head out some of'ver-place laid'r. But, we heard 'bout dis "Buzz Event" 'bout'ta pop-off, at any minute, o'ver here. So, we said, *"Bet".* We come down here, check-shit-out. Why tha' fuck not? OH! MY BAD! THIS be "Live TV" 'n shit! YOOOOOOO!!! I'm trippin'!" (And so, after some guidance and some help from Mimi Johnson, the "Interviewee", continues...), "...OH. So, yeah. The weather came outta NOWHERE! It was like a swarm of *BUZZING LOCUSTS!!!!* WE all out here, aspirin' artists, TRYNA' get this cheddar. It's tha' cheddar! It's tha' cheddar! KNOW WHAT I'M SAYIN'!? AIN'T NOBODY even realize we was gettin' shot OR shot at!! I ain't really see who was shootin' and, I'ma be real witchu', I WOULDN'T tell ya' IF I did! But, DEEZ "hitters", was "AIR 'N OUT" MF'S, ON-SITE!!! But,...GETTIN' that cheddar! GETTIN' OUR - "BIG SHOT" - IN tha' "Industry"! ...THAT, was our ONLY focus!!! (THEN, raising up his bloody hand to show for the camera, and, for the viewers at home, a FULLY-ENCRUSTED diamond Cuban-link chain and its "JR" medallion, THAT he "found" "near", the body of MC Busta-Nut)...(The "Interviewee", continues...), "Yeah, so, well, anyways,...I found this,...know what I'm sayin'? BUT, this-here medallion,...WATCH THIS! I'm finna' put this on RIGHT NOW!!! AIN'T-NEV'A-GON' take it off!! I mean,...check ME out!

I'M on TV, FLOSSED OUT, RIGHT NOW!!! (Then, lookin' down at that expensive-heavy-jury, hangin' on his chest, with the twinkle of the "JR" diamonds, from the camera light, giving and making him see, the stars that he ALWAYS wanted to see,...in HIS eyes, continues...), "...it's like,...it's like,...it's MINE! IT'S LIKE,...IT'S LIKE,...TO "JETTISON RECORDS"; I'M ALREADY SIGNED!!! SHOUT-OUT TO MY GUY, FALSE PROFIT!!! SHOUT-OUT TO MY GUY, MC BUSTA-NUT!!! AND, I ain't got all-dat-much cheddar, at tha' current moment, you know what I'm sayin'? BUT, but, but, but,...I'MA show dem LOVE and, PAY FO' all they downloads ON EVERY-DAMN streamin' site, out-dare,...NO MATTER WHAT!!!" (Then, lookin' back down at that "JR" medallion and, then lookin' into the sexy-gaze of Mimi Johnson, he looks straight into the camera on LIVE TV,...) and, says, "And, this here, "JR"-JETTISON RECORDS medallion,...I'MA cherish this-here shit,...fo' ev'a'."

And so...

Pockets, from within HIS mobile studio. And, from under all that loud wind and lightning and THUNDER. And, from under that custom red, custom-made red hat cocked hard to tha' side, Pockets, as he watched a "BUZZ-GOER" in North Juarez, being interviewed, NEVER heard OR saw, from under ALL that lightning, THUNDER and wind, nor, from under that cocked hard to the side, custom red custom-made red hat brim,... the other two pair of shoes, of Mr. Brotha Trife and Anna Mossitti, standing there, in that mobile studio the entire time,...looking down on him, watching him. As they,...watched him watch, that entire interview. As they, watched that ENTIRE interview,...WITH him!!!

And, as Pockets, holdin' that phone, with both of his hands, looks up from the foot of his bed from where he sat. And, from-up-under the brim of that hat, AS HE DOES, in the dark-flickerin'-blue, (of HIS, mobile studio!), *NEVER saw that, THEIR HANDS, WERE once clasped!!*(Oy VEY!!).

And...

UNLIKE, (at that statue!), there were NO jumping-hugs, INTO waiting-arms!

THOUGH...

(((Pockets, DID nearly jump-out-of his skin!)))

WHEN...

From-up-under that, cocked hard to tha side custom red brim, saw two-flickerin', 24 karat gold lenses, of limited-edition, flickerin'-back AT him!(((OY VEY!!!))).

And, Pockets, (recollecting HIS cool!), BEING, That - "playa' wit protocol" - *(FROM - the old school!!)*, KNOWS THAT, IT'S A MUST, too,..."lay on tha' charm"!!!

As...

He does so.

AS...

He scoops up, (layin' a big kiss!), on Anna Mossitti!...(AS, he holds her, laid cross, in his avid powerlifting arms!!).

And so...

(On her own two feet, placed back down, before, the animosity, began to show!)...

THAT...

Anna Mossitti, WANTED to be let down, *FROM, BEING let down, FROM, BEING left behind,*...(((TO BE TURNED INTO BAIT!!!))) (((MOTHERFUCKIN'OYVEY!!!)))...*FROM, WHEN, Pockets,...blew town!*

AND, (Anna Mossitti, ain't too happy. But, it's safe to say)...

FROM behind, those flickerin' 24 karat golds, to Mr. Brotha Trife, she's *lookin' like,* WITH Pockets, THAT, *SHE MIGHT, STILL BE DOWN!*...(Yeah!)...(((THAT shit!!))).

AND...

(((Mr. Brotha Trife, got a *look,* in his ONE GOOD EYE, *like, he wants Pockets dead!)))*

And, (it's safe to say)...

THAT LOOK, it could be from, FROM, Anna Mossitti, *LOOKIN' LIKE,* she might, STILL be down!

And, (it's safe to say!)...

IT COULD BE from, from, Pockets, FROM WHEN he parked that RV, (back in the cut!), in the back, OF Brotha Trife's beloved cemetery! (((FROM WHEN, he nearly, knockin' that parked PALE chopper and, BOTH OF THEM to the ground!!))).

And, (it's safe to say!!)...

It could be from, from him, having just borne witness, (TO THE aftermath!), of, that: "BUZZ-BLOODBATH"! *(((FROM, Pockets, "sacrificin'", FOR: "The Good of THE BUZZ", the young lives of, False Profit and MC Busta-Nut.)))*...(((From, HAVING THEM BOTH gunned down!!))).

And so...

Behind the guise, of: "MY BROTHER!! MY BROTHER!!" (And, other idle-compliments)...

Pockets, standing before, that Tier-Three, with HIS lady standing to his left, *CAN FEEL, the billowing smoke in the gaze,* behind those flickerin' gold eyes, IN those frames. (And, figuring that, IT WOULD behoove, FOR HIM TO lighten THAT, TIER-THREE'S MOOD!!!).

AND SO...

Pockets, blurts out, (in jest!), "I KNEW that, ONLY YOU, could do it! *And, I KNEW that it was ONLY RIGHT, to give you life AND, to keep you alive!* SHIIIIIIT, wit ALL this life-'n-death 'n shit!?! MY BROTHER!! MY BROTHER!! FINDIN' YOU, AND MY BABY, in THIS-HERE cemetery, ONLY makes sense!!!"

AND...

(As Anna Mossitti, is looking at Pockets, AFTER looking at Brotha Trife!)...

Pockets, in the flickerin' blue cell phone darkness, (of HIS lit up by HIS cell phone mobile studio!), Pockets, HAS *A LOOK* on HIS face, *like:* *"OOOOOOOOOW! Damn,...my brother,...my brother,...DID I REALLY, JUST...SAY,...THAT...SHIT???".*

And...

(Before, Anna Mossitti, can say a word!)...

That, Tier-Three DEMANDS, of Pockets, THAT HE explain HIMSELF! *(AND, AS TO, WHY, MC Busta-Nut and False Profit, HAD TO DIE!!)...*

'Cause...

On the news...

((((THAT'S WHAT THE FUCK HE JUST HEARD!!!)))

And...

Pockets, cocks that custom red, custom-made red hat of his, HARRRRRRD-TO-THA'-SIDE atop his head! And, as Anna Mossitti, stands between, the two of them, she stays looking-up-at, those flickerin' gold lenses, beneath that, cocked-hard-to-tha'-side BULLET-HOLE-hat's brim! (As, Pockets, of explaining, HIS: "Brutal-Business-Mind"),... begins:

"It's all, really quite simple. It's all, a matter, Of: "Activation to Relegation TO PARTICIPATION!" *I TRIED to tell YOU BEFORE, that,* 'Nut and Profit,..."THEY HOUSE FLIES!!" SO,...I squashed them. And, in turn, *that kid on the news tonight, he gave MC Busta-Nut, False Profit, AND JETTISON RECORDS, the kind of EXPOSURE,...*money CAN'T buy! You see, *by creating such a "BUZZ",* I'm actually bringing the people AND the world together. *THESE victims, of the concert shootings, the* *victims of these mass shootings, and of, mass violence, in turn, GET to be interviewed by these celebrity morning talk show hosts. THESE VICTIMS, they NEVER would have had the opportunity to have met, and or to HAVE been, INTERVIEWED BY, such celebrities!* YOU SEE,...in a way,...I'M fulfilling THEIR dreams, BY ME, putting THEM, IN A POSITION, to be, PUT in a position, TO meet AND speak with, SUCH celebrities! And, BY doing so, *CREATING, such a "BUZZ",*...I'M turning the artists up ON stage, INTO A celebrity!! I'm turning these people being interviewed INTO celebrities!! *It's JUST LIKE I told you, back in MY ALL RED EVERYTHANG - ON TOP OF THE WORLD - OFFICE,...'WHO people THINK they NEED IN their lives, TO BE a star, IS THEIR star!!!"*...I activated, a plan. 'Nut and Profit, were "relegated" to being a "participant", IN that plan! I DON'T know WHAT else, TO tell YOU! 'Cause, IT really IS ALL, quite simple. *ALL MC Busta-Nut and False Profit HAD TO DO, was,...NOT get shot and die!!* (AND THEN, Pockets, *FULLY IN LOVE WITH HIMSELF, PATS HIS OWN BACK,* THE ONLY WAY HE KNOWS HOW!!!)...*"Thing is,...they REALLY DID come into THEIR OWN tonight! YOU shoulda' seen tha' "BUZZ EVENT" THAT, I PUT ON, TONIGHT, you triflin' mafacka'! I'VE NEVER SEEN MC Busta-Nut with SO MUCH energy!! MUST'VE been from MY "pre-game" speech I gave them and, ALL THAT I SPOKE-ON, on my way back to the RV! They BOTH bought into it!!* Yeah, so, well, anyways,...*even if it WAS all bullshit!* 'Cause, *I knew,* they was gon' die tonight. I mean, *the advice that I gave them WAS REAL shit,* BUT, business IS business. IT REALLY IS ALL, quite simple, Mr. Trife. Time BE money! Shame for THEM,...*they showed me they wasn't "house flies"* just, a lil' too late. ...MY HUSTLE,...knows,... NO BOUNDS,...nigga."

And(UPON THAT!)...

THAT, Tier-Three removes those, 24 karat golds, so that, UNDER THAT cocked bullet-hole-hat's brim, THERE IS, NO MISTAKE, (in the darkness, of Pockets' mobile studio's blue-light-flicker), THAT, THAT Tier-Three IS, talkin' TO(((AND ABOUT!!!)))him,..."WHAT you, SHOULD DO, IS, cut off ALL your limbs and, put them in four separate suitcases. THEN, cut off your head and, put it in a fifth."

And, THOUGH, Pockets *KNEW*, that, that WAS some scary-ass-shit! (*And, EVEN THOUGH, Pockets KNEW, that, Triflin'-Tier-Three, MEANT that shit!*). Pockets, quips, "THAT don't EVEN make no sense! YOU FUCKIN' - Tier-Three - LOONEY-MUTHA'-FUCKA'!!! BUT, it WAS some scary-shit, IF you REALLY STOP and, think 'bout it! But,…I AIN'T SKURRR'D!! I'M POCKETS, BABY!!! *From, Hard Times, Virginia*, to,…ON TOP OF THE WORLD!!! SO, let's cut the bullshit, 'tween me and you. *A "MASSIVE-BUZZ", has been created. A "BUZZ"*, in which, IF YOU play YOUR cards right, you CAN benefit from! So, where's the suitcase? Let's start with that. And, NOT the one, I'm 'sposed to put mah head in! Y.S'. suitcase,…where IS it??"

"I AIN'T like you,…YOU…FUCKIN',…BLOODSUCKER!!! THAT suitcase, is back at THAT fuckin', ALL RED EVERYTHANG, apartment of yours! *WHERE YOU, kept THIS peach locked up, for three years!* What?? …You THINK, you can send me, back INTO North Juarez, TO GET that suitcase?? My man, I AIN'T doin' NO MO' of ya', dirty work. Let, Y.S. AND her music go, man! LET her rest!", (THEN, pointing at his temple, Mr. Brotha Trife, continues…), "I got my song book right-up-in here, my man. *I listened to Y.S'. tracks.* THEY right-up-in here, too! I got your woman, back for you. That's what you REALLY wanted, outta this whole "Road-Trip-Road-Life" BULLSHIT, of yours, AIN'T it???" (And, after a reassuring nod-of-the-custom-red-brim, as seen by the flicker, in Anna Mossitti's blue eyes, Mr. Brotha Trife, continues…), "Ok, then. We done. You DON'T need MY songs and,…YA' AIN'T gettin' 'em! AS IF,…you WAS eva' gon' get MY shit…on tha' mutha'-fuckin' radio! "Solo Dolo", baby. I'm out. (Then, placin' those 24 karat golds, back on, Mr. Brotha Trife, continues…), "I'MA do MY OWN thing, my man. And, DON'T YOU EVER IN YOUR WHOLE-ENTIRE-I-WANT-TO-KILL-YOU LIFE, LET ME HEAR, ANY OF MY SONGS OR THOSE TRACKS, BEING RECORDED OR PLAYED, WITHOUT MY EXPRESS WRITTEN CONSENT AND OR PERMISSION, AND WITHOUT ME GETTING PAID, AND MY, "DUE PROPERS"!!!!!! 'CAUSE, TRUST AND BELIEVE, YOU AINT GON' SURVIVE THE DOOM!!!!!! And, hey,…Anna Mossitti. If your smart? That is,…IF you're smart,…YOU'LL be on the back of that PALE CHOPPER, when I'm ridin', the hell outta this cemetery IN THAT, fuckin' downpour!"

And, Pockets, (((GETTIN' AS-INDIGNANT AS HE WANTS TOO!!!))), lays it, on thick, *"And, I thought, I TOLD YOU, ALREADY, MY STUDIO!! MY MUSIC!!!!!!"*

And, Anna Mossitti, (not ready, for Brotha Trife NOT TO BE, around!), fumbles around, in the blue-screen-flickering-dark, finding the light. And, (with a *look, of: Not the LEAST BIT surprised!)*, TO FIND, that, she's BEEN standing in fresh blood, *(IS the look!)*, Mr. Brotha Trife, sees *IN* Anna Mossitti's eyes. ...(*Think about THAT SHIT for a moment!*).

AS,(UPON!)...

Those mobile studio lights coming on, Mr. Brotha Trife, now realizes, as he surmizes, the blood that he and Anna Mossitti, have been standing upon, gettin' all-up-under - AND IN - the soles of their shoes, USED TO belong to,...the dirty vice cop!

'CAUSE...

((((The WHOLE mobile studio stinks of,...gunsmoke and "Joop!")))).

And so...

THEN, taking charge of the situation, Anna Mossitti, (being the strong woman that she is!), tells, Pockets to,...just listen.

As...

She takes Brotha Trife by the hand, (steppin' over fresh blood, gettin' soaked down into the rug!).

AS...

She holds Brotha Trife's hand tight, (AS ON fresh blood, she ain't tryin' to slip 'n slide!).

As...

(((She steps up to that..."buttery" studio mic!)))

AND SO...

(Looking up into, the beaming gold eyes, of "her" Brotha Trife)...

Anna Mossitti, tells him, "Just to relax. And, sing it to ME, JUST AS, YOU sung it before."

AND...

As she, BEGINS to sing, (THAT Christmas song!), Pockets, HITS... record! (And, then, in closing his eyes, in concentration, Pockets, places up to the bridge of his nose, his right index finger and thumb). And, as Mr. Brotha Trife, in so joins, Anna Mossitti, in the duet, as he, with her, does so sing, upon her request. And so, FOR her and, ONLY her,...it is done!

And so...

As they sing, Pockets eyes, remain closed.

WITH...

(His right index finger and thumb, in concentration, placed upon, the bridge of his nose!).

And...

With that, side-to-side, with his one good eye, behind those 24 karat golds BEAMING from the light, Mr. Brotha Trife, lost in meditation, lost in the melody, lost in the look as he looks into both, one at a time, as she looks back with that, reflection of beaming gold in her eyes.

AND...

(As the song ends, Mr. Brotha Trife, leans near, and, whispers, in her ear, "You wanna go for a ride?")...

HMM...

(Y'all wanna find out what happens next???)...

"MY BROTHER!! MY BROTHER!! YOU got that fire in your throat AND in your gut!", Pockets, OPENING HIS EYES, begins, (ending the recording, as the song ends!).

While(AND ALL THE WHILE!)...

(((FULLY IN LOVE WITH HIMSELF!!!)))(((BEAMING WITH PRIDE!!!)))...

While(AND ALL THE WHILE!!)...

((((((HAVING NO IDEA, that, the two, HAD BEEN staring into each other's eyes,...the entire time!))))))

...”WHAT I tell YOU, 'bout this shit, MY BROTHER!?! TOLD, YO' ASS!!! *JUST, WRITE ME SOME FIRE!!!* WAIT 'TIL YOU SEE what I do, WIT this shit! And, I gotta tell ya Mr. Trife, *YOU even put the MAIN INGREDIENTS in THAT song! YOU wrote about THE DEVIL and DRINKIN' WHISKEY!!!* GOTTA' KEEP THE MASSES, FUCKED!!! Shiiiiiit, AFTER I get done WIT this track!?! Mix! Master!! Music!!! *SHIIIIIIT, DONE-GOT THA' "BUZZ" STARTED 'N SHIT!!!* JUST YOU WAIT, 'til I get YOU, up on stage, singin' THIS shit! Tha' ladies, SHIIIIIIT, just gon' be throwin' they draws AT a nigga!!", Pockets, announces!!

And(ON THAT!!)...

Mr. Brotha Trife, (gets that "lil' smile of his" come cross his face!), (dips his head to tha' left!!), looks down, on Pockets, and, says, *"YEEEEEEAAAAAAHHHHHH, SUMFIN' LIKE DAT!!!", (VOICE-OF-INTUBATION-PANTY-DROPPIN'-AMAZIN:)*

(Strong woman, aside!)...

Anna Mossitti, GETTIN' jealous as she, asks, "HEY! WHAT ABOUT ME?? Ain't NO OTHER woman BUT ME, singin' with "MY" Brotha Trife!"

((ON-TOP-OF-THE-WORLD, ASIDE!!))...

Pockets, looks at her AS HE, ASKS, "WHAT'S this, *""MY" Brotha Trife!*", shit!?!".

(((ALL-feelings, aside!!!)))...

Anna Mossitti, replies, "Well,...you know? YEAH, SO, WELL, ANYWAAAAAAYS! ...SINCE you sent Brotha Trife, INTO North Juarez TO rescue me! THAT'S all!"

THEN...

With, that "ANIMOSITY of her's" KICKIN'-IN, (gettin' that neck side-to-side goin'!), ((AND WIT her eyes rollin'!!)), PLAINLY-states, "NOT sure WHY, YOU ain't come, for me?? *And THAT-THA'-SHIT TOOK, THREE YEARS!!! ...'GUESS, makin' YOURSELF, into some "big-music-man", WAS more important, huh??* Well, AT LEAST Brotha Trife CAME, for me!".

(((((ALL of, THAT: "MY-BROTHER!!-MY-BROTHER!!"-SHIT, ASIDE!!!!)))))...

Pockets, TENDS to, AS he, DOES-SO, (((AS HE, BURSTS, HER: "MY"-Brotha-Trife-BUBBLE!!!))), *"YEAH, SO, WELL, ANYWAAAAAAYS!"*, HUH??? IS THAT, RIGHT!?! ...Oh! ...I SEE!! Weeeeeell, AS MUCH, as I, HATE to break-it-TO-you, SWEATHEART! But,...THAT AIN'T Brotha Trife!! Well,...NOT really!!", Pockets, begins!, (AS, THAT: "expensive-laugh", AT HER expense KICKS-IN!!)... (((and, DOES SO, the ENTIRE time!!!))), AS HE'S, CONTINUING..., "THIS-HERE - TIER THREE - IS A CLONE OF BROTHA TRIFE!!!"

((((((ALL BURSTED-BUBBLES, ASIDE!!!!!)))))))...

Anna Mossitti, asks, "HER" Brotha Trife to remove, those 24 karat golds from his eyes!

(In which, FOR HER, he does so, abide!)

AS...

(((IN HER)))...

He DOES so,...confide!

"Listen,...yes,...it's true. But, this hasn't been a lie. I would never lie to you."

And, as he, gets into, explaining about, *how it felt, to have that HOT "wash rag" on his brain. (((And, of how, the "feeling" of STUCK felt!))). And, as such, from the under the ground levels, he broke the hell out! And, of how, Pockets, kept Clone-Trife alive, for him, to come rescue you. And, of how, Pockets, made him, an offer, to NOT be STUCK! And, of how, Pockets, told him, "BUT, FIRST,...you GOT TO PAY your "music industry" DUES!!!"*

And, as he, begins to tell her about Y.S. and, the bullet hole hat that, he wears cocked hard to the side upon his head, Anna Mossitti's reaction, to hearing about THIS homegirl Y.S.,...is to grin, happy and wide! (AS SHE, doubles that up, BY doubling-down!!). AS SHE, becomes "all-blinky-eyed"!! As she, TRIES to hide the jealousy, IN her jealous-eyes!! (AT. One. Blink. At. A. Time!!).

And...

(((GOD BLESS, THAT TIER-THREE!!!)))...

'CAUSE...

(He STOPPED short of telling her)...

That, *HIS ORIGINAL-MOTIVATION, for THAT Christmas song,... WAS Y.S.!!!*

BUT(THAT!)...

He wrote it, THINKING ABOUT YOU, instead!!!

(((OY VEY THA' FUCKIN' MUSIC GAME!!!))).

EVEN SO...

NOW, ANNA MOSSITTI, HAS THAT FIRE, IN HER GUT!!! (((OH, NO!!!)))

AS...

(((THE SCORCH, OF HER SCORN, COMES OUT!!!!!!)))))))...

And so...

With her finger-snap, Anna Mossitti, followed-up with that same index finger held high (FROM her waist!), BIG-ARCHING-SUNDIAL-MOTION, 360-degrees, (down to her OTHER side!!), followed-up, with, that SAME index finger STICKIN' IN HIS FACE, followed-up, with, lettin' that neck go, *(((lettin' that, ANIMOSITY FLOW!!!)))*, followed THAT up with, lettin' out a BIG OL', *"OH, HELLLLL NO!!!!!!"*

AS...

(Of, Mr. Brotha Trife!), she, ASKS, "SO?? *WHAT was that, THEN,...the other night!?! You KNEW, I DIDN'T KNOW, THAT, you,...WEREN'T BROTHA TRIFE???"*

"Wha? What?? WHAT??? WHAT'S that, NOW?!? *EXACTLY, what-THA'-HELL was THAT, BETWEEN Y'ALL, THA' OTHER night!?!"*, Pockets, with a series-of-questions, QUESTIONS QUICK!!!!!, (WHILE, glancing-over-REAL-QUICK, over AT, his closed closet door!).

OF WHICH...

Behind which, IS his Thirty-Aught-Six!!!

(All and, all the WHILE!)...

OF thinkin', OF guts!

AND...

(((("CHECKIN'" it!!!))).

And so...

Muttered-under, that, Tier Three's breath, to himself (and, NOT-so-much in jest!), OF the part, OF answering, (((OF referring, To: "BETWEEN Y'ALL!"))), *"NOT much!"*

'CAUSE...

(((("BETWEEN" THEM, there wasn't...NOT MUCH...AT ALL!!))))

EXCEPT...

(OF COURSE - (((OY VEY!!!))) - some SWEAT:)

THEN...

Pockets, (OF COURSE!), thinks, OF himself!(And, OF: The "Acquired") - ((AND/THE: "Sustainability-REQUIREMENT", *OF: "The FIRST TASTE of BIG money!!")*) - (((AND, OF: "THE NEED" - SINCE, IT'S NEVER ENOUGH!!!))) - ((((TO: AMASS great wealth!!!!))))...

AND SO...

Pockets,...keeps it STRICTLY BUSINESS!!!

'CAUSE...

Pockets, INTENDS TO keep HIS place, (((AT THE TOP OF THE WORLD!!!))), IN THIS music business!!!

And so...

He tells, Mr. Brotha Trife, "COME with me AND Anna Mossitti!! 'Cause, NOW that you've brought MY woman, back TO ME? SHIIIIIIT, WE headed back down TO, Jettison Records! And,...WE LEAVIN' TONIGHT!!! SHIIIIIIT, WIT THAT TRACK the two of you, JUST SUNG together?? SHIIIIIIT, I'M GONNA' make YOU, a BIG RICH STAR!!! I'm GON' put music to THAT track and, mix and master the HELL outta that sumbitch, THE MINUTE we get back!!! And, DON'T YOU WORRY, 'BOUT-A-THANG!!! ...Yeah, so, WELL, anywaaaaaays,...I KNOW A GUY, that'll do-up, a "fair-'n-legit" set, of contracts!"

But...

(Pockets KNOWS, he DON'T mean, NOT A SINGLE word, THAT he's sayin'!)

'CAUSE...

HE just wants to serve-up, Clone-Trife, TO them "People"!((("WE LEAVIN' TONIGHT!!!"))).

'CAUSE...

("I'M POCKETS, BABY!!! I'M ON TOP OF THE WORLD!!!")...

And...

(((THAT'S WHERE-THA'-FUCK - HE INTENDS - ON STAYIN'!!!))).

And so...

..."YOU KNOW, a guy?? MY MAN, I KNOW you ain't talkin' 'bout *that clown-muthafucka' that be tellin' some crony-ass jokes and STAY WIT pizza grease all ov'a his damn hands!! YOU talkin' 'bout that hippy-fool that you was tellin' me 'bout that hipped you to tha' "Music Game"??* Small fuckin' world, holmes. *I met ya' boy!* HE straight , "CLOWN-MATERIAL"!!! ...Nah. I'm good, on that, my man. LET ME, TELL YOU 'BOUT THA' "MUSIC GAME"!!! *SINCE, I've been in "The Game", I had my rib broke, my eye took, found Y.S., AND MY Nephew dead!! AND, YOU HAD, 'Nut and Profit, shot up!! AND YOU PUT EVERYBODY'S LIFE, at that "BUZZ Event", IN jeopardy,...*JUST SO, that, YOU, COULD get ahead! *AND, YA' GOT ME BACK ON, "THAT SHIT", pain pills and got me back drinkin'!!!",* Mr. Brotha Trife, begins, (then, speaks on, what will be forever *STUCK, IN his TIER-THREE-MIND!!!*),..."Tha' "Music Game" AND the "Drug Game", ARE one in the same.",...AIN'T THAT, WHAT YOU SAID!?!", (THEN, GETTIN' PISSED!!! Mr. Brotha Trife, continues, gettin' into the "REALNESS"!!),..."Gettin' signed, and, then, havin' to put MY-MUTHAFUCKIN'-TRUST in YOU, "MUSIC-BIZ-FUCKHEADS"?? REALLY YO'??? I'm 'sposed to believe, "EVERYTHANG'S", JUST GONNA' WORKOUT?? EXACTLY AS, YOU SAID??? C'mon, holmes. 'Cause,...IT REALLY AIN'T TO VERY-FUCKING-REASSURRING, when,...*EVERYWHERE I BE, I GOT, SOME SQUIRREL-ASS CARS ALL TINTED THA'-FUCK-OUT, FUCKIN' FOLLOWIN' ME!!! Like, it MUST, be: "BIG-BLACK-CELL-PHONE-DAY", OR SOME SHIT!!!* 'CAUSE, IT REALLY AIN'T

TOO-DAMN-HARD FOR ME, TO PICK-UP-ON-THE-FACT, THAT, *ALL THESE "CLEVER-MOTHERFUCKERS", DRIVIN' 'ROUND, EVERYWHERE I BE, ALL BE WEARIN' THE SAME EXACT FUCKIN' BLACK BASEBALL CAPS!!! AND, THEY ALL BE WEARIN' THE SAME EXACT FUCKIN' BLACK SUNGLASSES!!! AND, THEY ALL BE TALKIN' TO EACH OTHER, AND I KNOW THEY ALL BE TALKIN' 'BOUT ME!!!* 'Cause, *THEY ALL BE ON THE SAME EXACT FUCKIN' BIG BLACK CELL PHONES!!!!!!* CORNY-ASS, MOTHERFUCKERS!!!!!! ...Pockets, my man, call it my *"Clone-Powers"* or some shit, but, *I can read their minds, it's like, I know, EXACTLY what THEY'RE sayin':* "HEY, THERE HE IS!!! THAT'S, AN AFFIRMATIVE!!! THERE HE IS!!! 10-4!!! YOU WERE RIGHT!!! HE'D BE COMING MY WAY!!! AND, I CAN CONFIRM, YOUR DESCRIPTION, OF HIS "PHYSICAL-APPEARANCE" TODAY!!! ALL UNITS, BE ON THE LOOKOUT FOR, THE GUY DRESSED IN ALL BLACK, ROCKIN' GOLD SHADES AND, WEARIN' A BLACK HAT COCKED HARD TO THE SIDE!!! HE GOES, WHEREVER HE WANTS, TO GO!!! HMM,...MAYBE, JUST MAYBE, HE REALLY ISN'T COMMITTING ANY CRIMES??? 'CAUSE, HE WALKS WHEREVER, HE WANTS TO WALK!!! IT DON'T LOOK LIKE HE'S EVER SCARED!!! ALL UNITS, HE AIN'T EVEN TRYING TO HIDE!!!" ...Pockets, *all that creepin' 'n sneakin' 'n followin' me bullshit,* DON'T FUCKIN' IMPRESS ME, IN THA' LEAST!!! FUCK Y'ALL!!!!!! *And, every other day, IT'S "LOW-FLYIN'-AIRPLANE-DAY"!!!* BWWHAAAAAAA!!!!!! GET THA' FUCK OUTTA' HERE, *WIT THAT WEAK-SHIT!!!!!!* Pockets, *I KNOW these muthafuckas be FLYIN' "ORBITS" 'N POSITIONIN' THEIR FIXED-WING PLANES, FOR CAPTURING "INDENTIFIABLE AERIAL PHOTOGRAPHS", OF ME!!!* Tell me, holmes, what's up with, *THAT shit?!?* THESE MUTHAFUCKAS BE DIPPIN' 'N TIPPIN' THEIR WINGS 'N SHIT, ON SOME "SIGNALING SHIT", WHEN THEY FLYIN' BY ME!!! I mean, I figure YOU would know, but, *AIN'T THERE some kind of laws against airplanes flyin' JUST ABOVE BUILDINGS AND TREETOPS???* Holmes, *I even got HELICOPTERS, hoverin' overhead!!!* You tellin' me, holmes,...*THAT'S WHAT* comes along *WITH* bein' IN "The Biz"?!? Naaaaaah, my man,...I'M GOOD, ON *ALL THAT!!! THIS shit,*...AIN'T worth it! SO, BEFORE I FLIP-THA'-FUCK-OUT,

AND DO SOME SHIT, TO THESE SQUIRRELY-MUTHAFUCKAS THAT STAY FOLLOWIN’ ME AROUND?!? Listen, holmes, from THIS “Industry”,...I’M just, GONNA’ dip! I’M just gonna do this shit, FOR the love, OF it! I’ma put that Christmas song out, MYSELF! AND if I make a couple of bucks? Great! And, IF I get rich from it? THEN,... EVEN better!!! But, I’M TELLIN’ YOU STRAIGHT-UP, Pockets,... DON’T FUCK-UP!!! DON’T fuck-up, AND, LET ME hear, OR findout, THAT, you used ANY of MY lyrics, MY recordings, OR ANY PART OF THOSE THUMB DRIVE TRACKS!!! ‘Cause, ON God,... YOU AIN’T gon’ like WHAT WILL, COME your way! And with that, “MY BROTHER!”,...I’m out.”, Mr. Brotha Trife, spoke HIS Tier-Three-Mind!!!

AND, (upon that!)...

(He spins on his heel, (((ON THAT bloody mobile studio rug!))), as he’s, gettin’ ready to walkout of their lives. But, THEN, ON his sleeve,... he feels, a gentle tug)...

AS...

IT’S Anna Mossitti!

And...

(SHE’S *looking* into his 24 karat golds, with *a look, LIKE: “YOU gotta BE, kiddin’???”*)...

AND SO...

Mr. Brotha Trife, removes those, 24 karat golds, TO REVEAL, his one good eye! AS he, THEN, gives her, that - looking into both of her eyes - side-to-side - one at a time - kind-of-type-look - (WITH a look IN his eye, LIKE: “I’m headed out, THAT door!”) - So - (“ARE YOU down with me?”) - ‘CAUSE - (“Babygirl, out there? IN THAT world??”) - IN - (“A world, THAT’S after me???”) - AFTER ME - ((((“Babygirl,...THA’ PICKENS IS SLIM!!!”))) - KIND-OF-TYPE-LOOK - while - (AND, ALL THE WHILE!!!) - SEEING, the equallity OF love and pain - ((IN BOTH OF HER EYES!!)) - one at a time - and - side-to-side - BUT - in them both - of - THAT LOOK OF THE PAIN,...of him going - (And, of the love?)...OF WHICH - SHE AIN'T kiddin' - OF which - (AND, THAT),...she ain't tryin' to hide!!

And so(UPON THAT!)...

(((Mr. Brotha Trife, a Tier Three Clone,...KEEPS IT REAL AS-FUCK!!!)))...

AS...

HE, ALL UP IN POCKETS' MOBILE STUDIO, ALL UP IN FRONT OF POCKETS, DOES NOT FRONT!!!

AS...

He, with his one good eye, (NO MORE side-to-side!!), as he, straight up remains locked ON AND IN the true person, and, HER TRUE soul, (BROUGHT to the surface!) from within Anna Mossitti's right eye, *as he, asks her, ((WHAT HE KNOWS, THEY BOTH WANT!!)),*..."Do you wanna be my fuck up??? And, NO, I don't think, I'm pushin' my luck up! 'CAUSE, with *THAT look* in your eye. And THE WAY, you got your bottom lip, in your teeth, clinched tight. I don't think, you're gonna tell me, TO shut the fuck up! So? Do you wanna be my fuck up?? Yeah, I KNOW you gotta man. BUT,...I GOT OTHER PLANS!!! So, put YOUR hand inside MY hand! WE both GON' BE FUCKING UP TONIGHT!! ...YOU understand!? So, tell me,...do you wanna be MY fuck up?"

AND SO(UPON THAT!)...

Pockets,...KEEPS IT, STRICTLY BUSINESS!!!

AS...

(Pockets, BREAKS-IT-DOWN)...(((('bout,...BUSINESS!!!))),...

"Right about now? ...YOU soundin' pathetic! AND, you STILL don't get it!! THIS-HERE is tha' MUSIC INDUSTRY!!! THERE AIN'T NO ETHICS!!!!!! *THOUGHT I told YOU, already? WEREN'T YOU payin', attention??* There's a BIG DIFFERENCE between, hearin' and LISTENIN'!! I'M ON TOP OF THE WORLD!!! And, MY hustle NEVER stops! Yeah, *ALL THAT "squirrel-shit" COMES* with this "biz"! And,...it DON'T EVER stop! Business AIN'T pretty, but,...IT'S pretty AT the top! And so,...I'm STRICTLY business! And, WHEN you're IN business? YOU gotta be ALL THE WAY in, or,...you'll soon FIND YOURSELF,...OUTTA' business!!" (Then, AS indignant, as he WANTS TO BE, Pockets, starts in on Anna Mossitti!),..."And, TRUST AND BELIEVE, I'M finna'-find-out, *WHAT-tha'-fuck did, or, didn't go down, 'tween you, AND, THIS-HERE, TIER-THREE!!!"* (Then, *IN LOVE* with hearing the sound of HIS OWN voice, Pockets, goes in on THEM BOTH!!)..."And,...IN CASE Y'ALL FORGOT, OR SOME SHIT?!? ...THIS is business. I'M, STRICTLY BUSINESS!!! It IS, *and, has ALWAYS BEEN,* just 'BOUT business! *SO,...IF y'all, CAUGHT feelings?* Well,...fuck YOUR feelings!! *SHIIIIIIT, ANNA MOSSITTI, KNOWS WHY I WANTED, HER BACK!!!* And, I ain't gon' tell YOU, THIS shit, NO more! I'M, STRICTLY BUSINESS!!! This IS, A: "BIG MONEY", business!! *And I've BEEN-DONE-GOT MY "first taste", OF "big money"!* And so,...NOW?? SHIIIIIIT, I'M out to get MORE!!! *SOOOOOO,...if YOU, caught feelings?* MOTHER. FUCK. YOUR. FEELINGS!!!!!! As, FOR me? ...WHEN IT, comes to,...MY money??? WHEN IT COMES TO ME,...GETTIN' EVEN MORE???", (of, the one, behind those 24 karat golds, of, the two, in which, of the reflection of them both, of, the three, of Pockets, of a cocked harrrrd to the side custom-made custom red brim, of essentually, all three OF them!!!),(of what's to come next),(of what's yet to be told),(on the blood stains, of a studio floor!),..."I swear fo' GOD, from tha' GATE, 'TIL I SHOW YO' ASS THA' DOOR,...I DON'T GIVE A LOVELY-MOTHER-FUCK,...IF you're IN love,...OR IN the morgue."

And...

(As, Mr. Brotha Trife, walks through that RV's dark kitchen area alone, to head out alone, into the night, all he said, to Pockets, was)...

"You've been warned."

And...

As he, keeps it pushin'(Back on HIS giddy-up!), Trife, AIN'T DOWN WIT all this DRAMA AND BULLSHIT!!! And, as, far as, IF(((AND,... THAT'S A BIG-FAT "IF"!!!)))contracts, WERE TO BE EVER DRAWN-UP???

Well...

As, FOR Trife, and, some BULLSHIT-RIPOFF-SHADY-ASS-ONEWAY - MUSIC-BIZ - CONTRACT???

Well(IN that!)...

TRIFE, AIN'T TRYNA' BE, MUTHA' FUCKIN' *STUCK!!!*

AND SO...

AS HE, keeps it pushin', through, that, dark RV, (with THE LIGHT of that studio upon his back), Anna Mossitti, asks, "What would you have named, that song, you sung to me?"

And...

(Not even breakin' stride and, with no looking back), Trife, replies, "You already know, babygirl,..."Christmas Mourning"."

And, Pockets, *TOO full of PRIDE, (as he's), (FULL of Trife's rejection!) and, waaaaaay TOO FULL OF HIMSELF,* begins to go off, as Trife, begins to go off,...in his OWN direction! As, Anna Mossitti, slams that DAMN mobile studio door shut, figuring that Trife, (of Pockets' shit!), has ALREADY heard enough! As, Pockets, with that taste of big money, HAS FORGOTTEN,...WHAT it's like to taste,...his OWN medicine, "...MY MUSIC!!! MY STUDIO!!! MY MONEY!!! Just YOU, remember that! So, if YOU leave tonight? Don't you ev'a let me see you come 'round! BUT, IF you DO come 'round,...JUST BREAK YOUR FUCKIN' NECK, LOOKIN' UP AT THE OTHER-LEVEL, ON TOP OF THE WORLD, BEST BELIEVE, WHEN YOU COME LOOKIN' FOR ME, THAT'S. WHERE. I'LL. BE. FOUND!!! YOU HEAR ME, YOU TIER-THREE, MUTHAFUCKA'!?! 'CAUSE, I STAY AFTER, KEEPIN' THAT, "BIG-MONEY-TASTE", IN MY MOUTH!!! 'CAUSE,...MY HUSTLE, KNOWS, NO BOUNDS!!!".

And, as that chopper fires-up, drivin'-off, in that *SEVERE THUNDER* storm, TOO SEVERE FOR the month of May. Trife, pulls-off, on that pale chopper, headed into a storm that's, lookin' like the end of days. And so, Pockets, the "playa' wit protocol" figures, that, with Anna Mossitti, he BETTER make-up! As,...he beings to take his custom red, custom-made red suit AND her clothes off!!

(And, as God as MY witness, Pockets, TRULY IS,...strictly business!)

AS...

Anna Mossitti, (TO Pockets!), HAS BEEN bait, a tool, and,...a MULE!!!

For, (you see!)...

Hiding for the past 1, 260 some-odd-days...or so, (plus two or three!!), have been those city pensions, that the North Juarez PD could NEVER find, *(THOUGH, they looked, for ALL THOSE PAPER RECORDS, but,...COULD NEVER find!),* 'cause, Pockets, (That - Big-Hustle-Mind - Mafacka'!), *HAD ALREADY destroyed ALL THOSE PAPER RECORDS, but, NOT BEFORE, he converted them ALL to, and,...saved them on a thumb drive!*

For, (YOU SEE!)...

Anna Mossitti, FOR Pockets, was TO smuggle that thumb drive, out of the city, hidden inside of,...her body cavity!

AND...

(If YOU could JUST IMAGINE - *"the look"* - AS IT - came upon, Pockets face!)...

WHEN...

He DISCOVERED, THAT "FUCKING" TIER THREE - *had gotten to that thumb drive first,...ALL UP INSIDE,...*HIS ALL RED EVERYTHANG PLACE!!!

(((OY-MOTHERFUCKING-TIER-THREE-VEY!!!))).

Chapter Twenty Eight

THE SENTIMENT IN SUNFLOWERS

O f the month of December, Trife, having dropped all that "Mister" shit (and, for that matter, his pursuit in music!), having returned to his old city, *(of the former moniker: Parkinson's City)* and, as such, DID SO, AS HE, began, referring to himself, simply, as "Trife" (and, at times, "T"), FOR the pleasing, to HIS ear's-version, of his name.

For,(you see)...

(((AFTER, *all THAT "music shit",* he DON'T like being around... NOBODY!!!)))...

AND...

HE aint EVEN tryin' TO hear the sound, of NOBODY'S voice!, (singing OR not!).

And, he DON'T like nobody talking TO him and, even if they choose too, (which, is something, he strongly recommends that YOU DON'T do!), simple and plain, he won't AND don't give-a-fuck 'bout, WHAT YOU ARE saying!

And so...

Out of, (((AND, DUE TO!!!!))) - *"Music-Industry-Let-Down-Misery"* - Trife, has shortened his name to, "T".

For, you see(NOW!)...

(((HE HATES sounds!!!))).

AND(AS SUCH!)...

Trife, HAS shortened HIS-OWN-DAMN-NAME to "T", JUST to get the sound coming OUT OF HIS OWN mouth,...OVER WITH quick!

For...

(((The motherfucker IS mad!)))...(SOME, may even classify him, AS: "ANGRY"!!!)))

SO...

THIS angry motherfucker HAS SHORTENED HIS NAME to, "T"!!!

'CAUSE...

AFTER, THAT: *"Music Industry BULLSHIT" experience?!?*

Well...

He aint even trying to hear, even the sounds, of ANY voices!... ((INCLUDING his own!!!)).

AND SO...

Back in the month of May, as he arrived in "Old P.C." (Parkinson's City), riding in the driving rain, NOBODY really was outside! SO, NOBODY really knew, THAT THUNDER, was coming from him! Coming into town!! ON THAT PALE CHOPPER!!!!

So...

Nobody really could see HIS pain.

OR...

Where he stashed that chopper!

OR...

Where he was laid-up,...IN a deep depression,...thinking of Anna Mossitti,...AND thinking of, THAT: "Music-Bullshit-Waste-OF-Time!"... (wishin' that he die).

And so...

Every once in a while, out from, his: "place to fall back FROM y'all",...he would creep. But, he wouldn't stay long. Church bells got him hatin' that church bell song! (The brother was lost!)...(((BUT, HE FELT HIS BEST, WHEN HE WAS, WAY-THE-FUCK-AWAY-FROM,...ALL OF Y'ALL!!!))). So, of his, old abandoned church, (surrounded on three sides by a century's old cemetery), though, *through and by, his: "Gun Battle Bradley donations"*, the church, was refurbished. (And, with a new generation of parishoners, it does flurish!). BUT, when the parishoners come?? THAT'S WHEN he hates HIS LIFE, the worst!! SO, he goes and, hides in the attic. (AND, AT TIMES, in the undercroft!). BUT, when he hears, the singing of the hymns, he doesn't...feel so lost.

And so...

One time, (for, a time) and, at times, (NOT for, a full time AT ALL!!), Trife, (or, "T")(BUT, he would FULLY understand IF YOU, called him "Angry"!), crawled-out, from that undercroft, to take a walk. (But, ONLY when it was dark!). For, he didn't want to see that sun at high noon. *For, it would remind him of that time, those times, of for, his time, and, times together, that, he spent, with Anna Mossitti at "Old" SYKE Park.*

And so...

When he would go for these walks, he could feel it, he could sense it, that, the city, wasn't the same. The city, had lost it's *"Old Soul"*. (For, it had become modernized!). For, the city, was *NO LONGER LOST,...in it's OWN TIME!* For, there were, no little old ladies, no longer to see, walking up the sidewalk, or crossing at an intersection, *while pulling behind them, That - Two-Wheeled-Lightweight-Stainless-Steel-It-Was-Empty-On-My-Way-To-"Da'-Stowe"-But-NOW-On-My-Way-Back-It's-Full-Of-Groceries-Big-Black-Rubber-Wheeled-Lil'-Old-Lady-"Grocery-Getter" - Basket!*

FOR...

((((THEY ALL NOW JUST GET - "Uger" EATS!!!))))(((OY VEY!!!)))

And,...it was a damn shame!

THOUGH...

(From the donated Gun Battle Bradley money, the city,...WAS THRIVING!)

AND...

(((NOBODY GOT BULLIED NO MORE!!!)))...

BUT...

Gone were, The: "Mom 'n Pop's"!

AND...

(IN PLACE were, The: "Convienently-Gettin'-Your-Money" Stores!!!)...

Family doctors, were no longer APART of your family! (((And, they SURE-AS-FUCK weren't making NO house calls!!!))). BUT, you can feel free, to use your CELL PHONE,...to locate a "participating-family-practice" on one of YOUR one billion Apps and,...THEN call!). THEN, go through the prompts. And, THEN,...leave a voicemail! (Hope yo' ass AIN'T waiting ON a quick response!)...(And, in YOUR section of the city,...HOPE the WiFi aint shitty!). 'CAUSE,...things done changed! FOR, this city,...AIN'T-GOT-NO PAY PHONES!!! But, THE MAJORITY of the citizens, WERE happy!! (Except, for...the street gangs!).

For...

(((THEY TOO, had,…lost their soul!!!))).

FOR…

Long-gone were the days, of outside marauding gangs, (TRYING to enter the city!).

For…

There was NO bounty money, (FOR,…to stole!).

FOR…

(THERE WAS, NO Gun Battle Bradley!)(((HIS head, AND THAT Bounty, HAD BEEN claimed!!!)))…

The streets were clean! *THAT "10th Floor Holocaust" was gone!* (Praise Jesus!).

(And,…so was,…Heathen:(

The gangs, didn't even rock their colors no more. (But, no guns, still never, entered the city)('CAUSE, the gangs, were still itchin' to bust your head open!)(Ain't? THAT?! SOME?!? shit?!?!). *OLD HABITS DIE HARD, YA' DIG!!!* …(Funny,…ain't it??)…I guess, SOME things,…JUST DON'T change!

BUT(ONE TIME!)…

FOR, A TIME, AND, PERHAPS, JUST 'CAUSE HE WAS ANGRY, (AND, PERHAPS, FOR THAT, HE WAS LOOKIN' FOR A FIGHT!!!), T, decided to take a walk,…while it was STILL daylight! BUT, there would be NO fight! For, the city, DIDN'T recognize! For, the city, IN BROAD DAYLIGHT, DIDN'T know, it was him

For, HE TOO, wasn't rockin' no "BULLY BOYZ" colors! For, T, was still rockin' that, designer suit of black, behind those, limited-edition lenses of 24 karat gold, beneath that custom-made custom red hat - comin' equipped and FULLY-AFFIXED - wit'a BULLET HOLE, (and, still rockin' it wit, that - cocked-hard-to-tha'-side - brim!).

For, HE TOO, the city no longer, was the same! *(And, even though, that hot wash rag, had been far removed, from his Tier-Three-Brain!!!).* Though,

T knows, FOR A FACT, that, *back upon his arrival in Parkinson's City, back in May, he ain't never not once before, in THIS city, had he, ever spot, an infestation, of NO DAMN spotted-red-and-black-flying pest-invasion!!!!!!*

AND SO...

(*NO LONGER, FULLY COOKED*, though, more like pan seared, is the brain, of this-here Third Tier)...

(And, as he, reflected back),...*back to, the month of May. Back to, as he sat, IN HIS beloved cemetery - at that - picnic table bench - AMONGST - AND - WITH - Seven Fucked-Up Memorials - AND - the spirits - that come and go from their graves.* (And, in reflection), *OF: "HIS-OWN-DAMN-LIFE" - THAT BEING - AND - THAT OF - The MOST Triflin' Motherfucker THIS SIDE of the Mississippi - THE ONE - MUTHAFUCKIN' - B. MUTHAFUCKIN' TRIFE - (THAT BEING) - (AND) - (THAT OF) - (the one) - before, he brokeout, of: That - Under-The-Ground-Levels - Spot - HOW - HE HAD - NEVER-NOT-ONCE-BEFORE-SPOTTED-AT-ALL - (IN "HIS MUTHAFUCKIN'" LIFE!) - ALL OF THOSE - WINGLESS-SPOTTED-CRAWLING-BLACK-BUGS-SPOTTED-WITH-SPOTS-OF-RED-AND-WHITE!!!*

And so, on this particular, Takin' - An-Out-Amongst-Y'ALL-IN-THE-MOTHERFUCKING-DAYLIGHT - Walk, T, in thought, *reflects back, on those crawling-spotted-bugs, that he spotted, crawling cross that cemetery picnic table - IN HIS - beloved cemetery!* And, T, decides, that, since he, is not, he. (HE'S NOT gonna place blame!) Rather,...(((GASP!!!)))...TAKE ACCOUNTABILITY!!! (FOR, the things, THAT, he's seeing IN THIS CITY, THAT, JUST DON'T SEEM THE SAME!!!). And, as a result, IT HAS TO be, (at the VERY least!), in part, DUE TO: *HIS - three-PLUS-years - UNDER the ground!!!*...(((And, DUE TO: HIS CURRENT - TIER-THREE-BRAIN!!!))).

AND SO(AS, FOR!)...

(*THIS INVASION, OF: ALL-OF-THESE-CRAWLING-BACK-IN-MAY-NOW-FLYING-BUGS-THAT-HE'S-SPOTTED-DURING-THE-MONTHS-OF-FALL-WHEN-HE'D-BE-OUT-FOR-ONE-OF-*

HIS-"FUCK-Y'ALL"-WALKS - THINKIN' - WHAT-THE-FUCK - ALL-THESE-FUCKIN'-BUGS - IS JUST TOO MUCH - SPOTTING 'EM - FLYIN' EVERYWHERE IN SIGHT - SPOTTED WITH SPOTS - OF RED - BLACK - AND OF - SPOTS OF WHITE)...

T, (((GASP!!!))) TAKING ACCOUNTABILITY, THAT, IT MUST BE, AT, THE VERY LEAST, IN PART, AND, DUE TO: HIS - "TIER-THREE-AND-REMAINING-EYE!!! (Poor ol' T,...ya' GOTTA' feel FOR the guy!)...AS, HE has, NO idea, THAT THEY ARE...Lantern Flies! (((MOTHERFUCKIN'-TIER-THREE-BRAIN-OY-VEY!!!))).

And so(THIS, ONE TIME, FOR, A TIME!)...

T, crept out from under that undercroft, for the first time, in six weeks, headed to a bar he hates, (((NOBODY there, BETTER DARE, to EVEN speak!))). ONLY THERE, TO refill, his busted heart, 'cause,... (((THE MOTHERFUCKER LEAKS!!!))),...."Hey, barkeep. Give me the STRONGEST shit you got! KEEP 'EM, comin' straight up! ...I DON'T need them, on the rocks.",...{"You want a menu, with that?"},..."Nah! I AIN'T here, to eat, no food. ONLY here, TO forget ABOUT the shit, THAT, I ALREADY, forgot!!",...(THEN, T, while standing up at the bar!), He looks to his left, looking down at the barfly, seated to his left!),..."Listen, mama. I DON'T want YOU, sittin' next to me! You, MIGHT be, real nice? BUT,...I DON'T want, YOUR company!!!",... {"Some woman, fucked you up!", WAS, the barfly's ONLY reply!},... (And, Trife, told her, as he, removed those 24 karat golds!),... "Look-here, mama, I-AIN'T-GOT-NO tears, left TO waste! ALL, I GOT LEFT,... ARE these, wounded eyes!!",...{{{And, the barfly, sang:, "WOUND, WOUND, WOUND,...WOUNDED EYYYYYES!!! I SAID, HE GOT, WOUND, WOUND, WOUND,...WOUNDED EYYYYYYES!!!"}}}...

AND SO...

T, snatched that bottle straight-outta' that barkeep's hand, and, whipped-it AT the television screen!

'CAUSE...

(((HE HATES THAT FUCKING TEAM!!!)))...

And(THEN!)...

He put his fist through the JUKEBOX!!!

'CAUSE...

(((HE HEARD,...HIM AND ANNA MOSSITTI SINGING!!!)))
((((OY VEY!!!))))...

THEN...

He ripped that barfly's line, she just finished choppin'-up on the bar!

((((OLD HABITS DIE HARD!!!))))...

'CAUSE...

(((THE DRUG GAME AND THE MUSIC GAME...PLAY FOR THE SAME TEAM!!!))).

And so...

T, says, (to the Barkeep), "Save it, barkeep! I AIN'T, payin' for shit! YOU MIGHT, think YOU'RE hard. But, TRUST ME, holmes,...YOU DON'T want to, get into it!",...{AND, don't YOU KNOW, the Barkeep's ONLY reply, was, "Some woman, fucked YOU over! ...YEAH, WELL,... THAT ain't, NO surprise!!}...(And, T, all calm 'n cool, pointed at his own face, and, said),..."Barkeep. I-ain't-got-no tears, left to waste. All, I got left, are these, wounded eyes."...{{{AND, THE WHOLE BAR, SANG: "WOUND, WOUND, WOUND,...WOUNDED EYYYYYYES!!! I SAID, HE GOT, WOUND, WOUND, WOUND,...WOUNDED EYYYYYYYES!!!"}}}....

And(on that note)...

T, was done with people.

So...

He headed to where, he could be with, and amongst, HIS people.

THAT, (WOULD BE!)...

(THOSE, that, he CAN relate to, THE most!).

Those...

That, have their heads in silence bowed low, as though, they were beneath, a church steeple.

For...

(Trife, goes through his days, trying to see, IF he, can go ALL day,... without talking to anyone! And, at THIS point, he's AT, the point, WHERE, he doesn't EVEN WANT to talk to HIMSELF, anymore!)

FOR...

He doesn't want to hear the sound, OF ANYONE'S voice. (Period.)

REGARDLESS...

(If they're talking to him or not!)...(((AND,...IT'S A DAMN SHAME!!!)))...

FOR...

(REGARDLESS, of WHAT section of the city, HE WALKED, (be it; Belmont Heights, "Tha' 'Burg", "Tha' Land", Port O' Bridges, the Caley Section of The City, and, even WHEN he WALKED through the Bully Boyz' old rival's territory of Candlebrook!), THOSE limited-edition gold shades STAYED on!!!).

FOR...

He of them.

OR...

They of he.

(((Fuck-A-Look!!!))).

'CAUSE...

TO HIM, after, That: *"I'll-have-a-go-at-this-music-industry - Shit!"*, his Tier-Three-Brain, is reminded, (((ONCE AGAIN!!!))), *of HOW, disgusted Brotha Trife,* (((HIS DONOR-SELF!!!))) *HAD become, WITH people!!!* And so, after such, A: "Reaffirmation", T, now knows, that, (Tier-Three-Brain aside!), that, he is, in fact, MOTHER FUCKIN' BROTHA TRIFE!!!(((BECAUSE, HE TOO, CAN'T STAND THE SOUND OF ANYONE'S FUCKING VOICE!!!))). ...And, that, if, in fact, he does happen to hear, the sound of anyone's voice? Well, THEN, that sound of someone's voice, ONLY STRENGTHENS the fact, that,...HE'S ENTIRELY TOO CLOSE TO PEOPLE!!! And, that, he knows, THAT, he's NOT doing enough, (((IN HIS OWN MOTHERFUCKING WORLD))) and, (((in HIS OWN MOTHERFUCKING LIFE!!!))), to be, all just that, he wants to be. And, THAT BEING,...a motherfucking recluse. For, this once "lover of music", can't even stand the shit no more! For, NOW he hates music! And, that's what, the music industry,...did to him.

In his ears, T walks 'round, with a pair of headphones that he found, plugged into the cell phone that he found. (And,...HE AIN'T EVEN got the fucking thing turned on!). HE just wants to make it LOOK LIKE,... he WON'T be able to hear you! SO, DON'T EVEN SAY HI TO HIM, (during YOUR, brief encounter with him!), as, he WALKS BY YOU on the sidewalk! (((OF WHICH!!!))), FOR, T,...CAN'T come and go, AND, be over with, TOO soon. And, that's what, the music industry,... did to him.

And, on his face, as he walks, he keeps on, those 24 karat gold shades. ((((OH, GOOD LORD!!!)))...(((THERE'S, some pleasant-looking old lady, up ahead, on the corner,...I hope...she doesn't...even wave!!!))). And, that's what, the music industry,...did to him.

BECAUSE, he AIN'T even TRYIN' TO BE mean,...or nice. (Or, EVEN look at THAT sweet-pleasant-looking old lady!). And, BEFORE, he even, gets to her? HE MIGHT, JUST,...lie down in traffic. And, IF he, GETS lucky? MAYBE, JUST MAYBE, one of THESE cars(((('CAUSE, HE ONLY NEEDS ONE!!!)))MIGHT NOT swerve! And, that's what, the music industry,...did to him.

And, as he continues to walk, down those even sidewalks, steppin' on cracks, (((FOR, IT'S, fuck YOUR mother's back!!!))), THOSE 24 karat golds, STAY ON! (So, THAT, he CAN'T, make NO eye contact!). For, HE DON'T WANT no contact! *For, OF his Tier-Three-Mind, HIS RELENTLESS-THOUGHTS ATTACK,...(((("WHAT THE FUCK AM I EVEN DOIN' OUTSIDE???))))((("I DON'T WANT IT!!!)))(((YOU can HAVE IT!!!))))((((I think,...YOUR world,...IS motherfuckin' WHACK!!!")))*. And, that's what, the music industry,...did to him.

And, as, he walks, these are his thoughts,...("Wait a minute!") (..."WASN'T there some nazis, in THIS building???") (..."What-the-fuck!?!") ("I REMEMBER them, NOW!!")("THEM, motherfuckers, were...BLACK!!!") ("YEAH!") ("THAT'S, RIGHT!!") ("There WAS a bullhorn, affixed up here!"),...And, as T, reflects upon it,...*(Trife, WAS DOWN WITH that BLARING-BULLHORN'S-MESSAGE!!))*...that, IN T's Tier-Three-Brain, HE, can NOW hear!!!

AND SO...

Trife, walks up to the now-vacant-Headquarters of the B.N.S.M., (that, one wouldn't even know, was once there!).

FOR...

(There are no B.N.S.M's signs of warning displayed!)...

FOR...

There are no messages, teachings, and ways, for to, out that, missing bullhorn, to blare into YOUR ear! (TO WHICH, TO leave you with MORE,...than a hearing aid!!)...

And...

(Though, the Headquarter's windows, were ALREADY painted black, since way back!)...

It just has the look, and feel, of an abandoned building.

(Yeah. It's lookin', and feelin', JUST like that!).

And so...

Trife, pushes open that door. (And he, actually misses, *NOT having answers, demanded of him!*). For, there's no one standing in that vestibule,... BUT him! For, there's no one there to provide a demanded answer, to a demanded question. For, his Tier-Three-Mind, NOW *remembers Lil' Bad Ass!* (And, he actually, misses *that lil' bad ass motherfucker!*).

For...

((((Lil' Bad Ass, has BEEN dead!!!)))).

AND SO...

He AIN'T 'round NO mo'! (*TO demand, answers, TO demanded questions, AT GUNPOINT, THAT HE just asked!!!*).

And, Trife, in that dark vestibule, where he stands, stepping to the side, as he places his hand, slipping it in between, where those two black curtains still hang, separating the vestibule, from that lil' bullhorn announcement room, *where announcements were made, actions, teachings and, ways, loud and obscene!* (As, Trife, moves to the side, one curtain, to the side!). AS HE,...sticks his head inside!!

And, Trife,...actually misses *the sound, of the voice of, That: "Devoted-WITH-Anger!" - light-skinned girl! (The one, with the mermaid-like hair, long, brown, and full of curls!).* JUST LIKE, Y.S., his Music-Industry-Homegirl!!).

And, Trife,...HAS TO let out a lil' laugh! ('CAUSE, when it COMES TO playing WITH Coupe d'etat?!?)...TO THIS DAY, Trife KNOWS, Coupe d'etat, DIDN'T PLAY!!! *For, she was down WITH The Message, The Teachings, "The Cause" and, The Ways!!!! ((('CAUSE, she was OUTTA' THIS WORLD!!!!)))...(((And,...SHE WASN'T,...fuckin' 'round!!!!))).*

FOR...

(Coupe d'etat, WAS THE TYPE, TO press a Desert Eagle, UP TO YOUR temple!)...

AND...

(((LET OFF A ROUND!!!!))).

And, as Trife, backed his head out from between those curtains of black, he stands facing that heavily locked and secured door, which separates the vestibule, from the B.N.S.M.'s main room. And, upon facing that, Trife, actually *misses the sound of, the locks': "CLACK! CLACK! CLACK!"*. And, Trife, ACTUALLY FINDS, that, HE EVEN *MISSES Blaqqq!!!*

And, Trife, HAS TO let out a lil' laugh! AS, NOW, he CAN *STILL HEAR, that unchained hyena, as it sat up on that stage next to Blaqqq, (((and AS TO WHY, it laughed!!!)))*.

And, as Trife, pushes open the inner door, *(no longer, bolted and secured!)*. Of which, to which, opened up to, the opened-up hardwood floor room. *Of which, to which, was created by* (and, with!), *the knocking down,...of the walls of structure. Of which, to which, failed to compromise their message, teachings, ways, and cause!* ('CAUSE, the B.N.S.M's message, *teachings, ways, and THEIR CAUSE, REMAINED SECURE!!!!).* Of which, to which, led to that opened-up hardwood floor room! (OF WHICH, TO WHERE, Trife, ACTUALLY *misses THE SOUND!!!). TO WHICH, OF WHERE, W@R, put the B.N.S.M.'s through their paces!*

OF WHICH(TO WHICH!)...

(((THE B.N.S.M's BIG BLACK BOOTS REIGNED DOWN!!!))).

And so...

Trife, entered.

And, he walked cross that hardwood floor. And, he took a look, around inside. (And, in there, it's dark enough). Though, Trife, can see, that, there's a layer of dust everywhere. And, up on stage, under, that, highback wicker chair, *where, Blaqqq sat, of which, to where, next to that, where that hyena sat, and, let out a laugh.*

BUT...

(((WASN'T NOBODY PLAYIN'!!!)))...

SOOOOOO...

(((TAKE A GUESS, AT WHAT, TRIFE FOUND!?!)))...

FOR...

Under, a thick layer of dust, Trife found, and, picked up, *an old B.N.S.M.'s propaganda pamphlet,...tucked into an old note book of Blaqqq's!!!*(((OF WHICH, TO WHICH, CONTAINED,...*the B.N.S.M.'s...Rules and Regulations!!!*)))(((OY VEY!!!))).

AND...

Therein, it contained, *the B.N.S.M.'s Chain of Command. AND,...their Method OF Operations!!*

AND...

Therein, it contained, *the B.N.S.M's Revolutionary "Fallout" Plans! AND,...their "Fallout" Plan's LOCATIONS!!!*(((OY VEY!!!))).

AND...

Therein, it contained, (IN regards to Blaqqq and W@R!!), THERE WERE, some *NOTEWORTHY notations!!*

AND...

(If you, YES, "YOU", WANT TO KNOW, WHAT TRIFE READ IN THAT NOTEBOOK???)...(((YOU'RE GONNA' HAVE TO BUY AND READ - BOOK No.3 - OF - THIS-HERE TRILOGY!!!)))... (MOTHERFUCKERS,...LEARN SOME PATIENCE:)

AND SO...

Trife, left.

And, he left, with that propaganda pamphlet. And, he left, with that notebook, as well! (To do, his OWN research!!!). And so, with bullet hole hat and, with those gold shades on, Trife, did so, as he, DOES SO, AS HE, CARRIED-ON!!! (FOR, ALL HE'S REALLY TRYIN' to do,... IS get back TO "HIS" people!),(THE ONES, with their heads bowed so low, be it, in prayer, shame, or out of disgrace!),(BUT, they ARE happy "enough"!),...(FOR, they, HAVE FOUND "their place!"). AND SO, AND, (BUT, THEN!), Trife, damn-near-ripped THOSE, limited-edition lenses of 24 karat gold, FROM OFF OF his face!

AS...

He looked upon, (in the Belmont Heights Section of The City), a school yard's brickwall's side. (AND, EVEN THAT, heartbroken,... miserable,...motherfucker,...HAD TO smile!). As, he looked upon, a multicolored, vividly-colored, spray paint abstract mural of,...himself standing tall!, (with the Pain Stick held by the neck, oh-so-endearing, by his right hand!). *And, that graffiti artist got that Pain Stick's evil-grimaced-grin and all!!! For, someone had spray painted that mural, oh, about 1,260 days ago or so, AFTER Brotha Trife, had gone! For, THAT ARTIST,...*"got" *him!* (((AND, IT'S A DAMN-SHAME!!!)))...

...'Cause, Trife, never knew...that artist...at all.

And, as he continues to walk, Trife, bears witness to, too many, too emotionally-sensitive, too emotionally-draining, too-dismissive (to, and), OF: VALID points, BEING, (and), TOO bullheaded-upon, OF: ONLY what they, WANT to do!! (((OF WHICH))), These, too-damn sensitive and TOO-DAMN DRAINING YOUTHS, ARE NOT WILLING to do, The Things: They GOT TO do FIRST, (((IN ORDER))), TO GET to THAT POINT IN LIFE, OF: NOW, I can do, WHAT I WANT, to do!!! (((FROM, NOTHING MORE AND NOTHING LESS, THAN, DUE TO: Puttin' in that HARDWORK first!!!!)))(((OY-HARDHEADED&LAZY-VEY!!!))).

AS...

(Trife, has in his sites)...

TOO many "Self-Entitled-Sensitives", giving EVERY EXCUSE, as to WHY, they CAN'T work! AS THEY, PLACE BLAME, UPON YOU, AS TO WHY, YOUR guidance and advice,...WON'T work!! ...(Yeah,... sadly:(...(THAT BULLSHIT!!!).

And*(UPON THAT!)*...

(SEEING as, HOW fast, the world (((FOR the worst!))), HAS changed!)…

Jade forms from within.

And(((lines the halls, OF: His - HALLS-OF-WHITE-JADE-TIER-THREE-BRAIN!!!))).

AS…

Trife IS done WITH the city!

AS(((WELL, AS)))…

(((The City's: FREE-of-Forming-Calluses(((ain't-got-none!!!)))Lumberjacks-of-Man-Buns - AND - The: Eyebrows-on-Fleek - Employment-and-Common-Sense - NEVER-Seek - COMMUNITY!!!((((((OY-TO-THA'-FUCKIN'-VEY!!!!!!)))).

FOR…

AFTER, three some-odd-years. Under the ground. "The World". (((As HE, remembered it!))…IS,…nowhere to BE found!!! AS, Trife, DIPS-THE-FUCK-OFF, of these even sidewalks, CHOCK-FULL OF: "Self-Entitled-Playin'-Make-Believe-Masses!" And, runs as, fast as he can, DOWN and THROUGH, an embankment, (steep and full), of: tall-and-all-bent-over-dead-December's-weeds-and-grasses!

All the way down. Trife, runs.

And…

(He AIN'T lookin' back!).

And…

He keeps running, until he reaches and meets up, with a set of train tracks!

(As, for people?)…(He, IS done!).

(Away FROM people!)…(((HE AIN'T tryna' be 'round NONE!!!))).

And...

Trife, he walks, up on those train tracks,...(((FAR - THE-FUCK - AWAY - FROM PEOPLE!!!))).

Back to his church.

For...

(ALL, he wants, to do, IS TO, make his, way back!)...

Look back, FOR people?

(((NAAAAAH!!! HE AIN'T-GON'-DO-'DAT!!!))).

Walking WITH the cold of December. He walks WITH his head down. And, he walks WITH the hope, (TO HIM!) a *"PLEASING-vision"* upon, his back's approach. *((((THAT BEING, OF: HIM rollin' n' tumblin' AND BEING CHEWED UP by a train!!!))))*...(WITH, and from,...lack of NOT feeling). FROM, (OF HIM,...God willin'!!) NOT hearin', (FOR, he AIN'T listenin'!), FOR-NO-DAMN train's warnin' whistlin' sound! And so. He walks. (((And, he AIN'T lookin' back!))) And so. He walks. With his head down.

And as, he walks. In walks, his thoughts. Of? *His ol' beloved pinetree line...he burned down. (And, of his beloved weeping willow...HE BURNED DOWN TOO!!:)* And, in thought, OF thoughts, of AT times LIKE these, that, BRING forth thoughts...*OF the Kraken...SHOWIN' HIS TEETH!!!* And of. *THAT peace. HE found there. Amongst the dead. From within. His beloved cemetery.*

(For)(You)(See)(It's)(That)(Peace)(Within)(Him)(That)(   )(Is) (Missing;)

And as, he walks. In walks, his thoughts. Of thoughts. Of? *The talks! THAT HE HAD. WITH,...ripplin' tentacles! Ripplin' in. His beloved. Cemetery pond.* And, he reflects. Back, of how. *The Kraken. Granted him the power. To see. From the Bishops to the Knights. To the Pawns. To the Queens. Who, was? And, who WASN'T! On his. Mutha'. Fuckin'. Team.*

As...

He. Reflects. Back upon. *THE CRISIS!!! As, it WAS! Bestowed upon!* *...HIS MENTAL HEALTH!!!* Upon, which. He. Dissects. Of, the lining. Of, Tier-Three-Brain. As, ONCE AGAIN!! There is a breach. Of white halls of jade! Upon. Dissection. He. Puts. A. Check. *Face-to-face-ripplin'?* (Yup!)(Dissected. AND, CHECKED!!). *"DON'T SLEEP ON MIDNIGHT!!!"(OF, The: TWELVES),*(Yup!)(Dissected. AND, CHECKED!!). *Of, "granted power"...OF, "DAY OF BLOOD!!!"(OF, KILL EVERYBODY!!!)(FOR, thine own-self-worth and love?)...(YUP!!)* (DISSECTED. AND, CHECKED!!!). *OF, Kraken's: "Clarity",...OF, third-eye-vision....OF,...thyself??(((OY VEY!!!)))(((CHECK IT OUT!!!)))...* *(((HE WAS TALKING TO HIMSELF!!!))).*

In and upon the surface, of his beloved cemetery pond, Trife, walks. As, he walks back. IN thought. AS thoughts,..."Walks" in. *Of, meditation's black. (From WAY back!). (Of, and as,) HE was gripped!(((WITH MEDITATION'S BLACK!!!)))...(IN it!)((OF it!!))(((AND, AS!!!))), trailing, trailing, trailing-off, Brotha Trife, so sat. (Upon!)((HIS BELOVED!!)) (((Cemetery Bench!!!))).* Far from the physical. Far,...from a picnic. *Finding peace. NOT panic! Of, next moves. And, of, WHO'S movin' AGAINST you! Kings to Pawns. Day of Blood. MOST will be gone. (((The Kraken)))...* *(((HELPED HIM plan it!!!))).* Off balance. And,...off balance. *Tips that weep and lock get wet. Ripplin', ripplin', ripplin'.* IN reflection, *in THAT reflection, "Brotha Trife, meet the Kraken. Kraken, meet Brotha Trife!"* He of the Kraken. The Kraken of HE. *(((THE WORST, IN him, HE met!!!))).*

And as, he walks, with head held low, (walking in, *His: "Fuck-The-Music-Industry - hopes-'n-dreams - turned-out-to-be - SUCH-a-bummer - FULL OF CROOKS - left-with-empty-pockets-of-pissedoffness - Sorrows"),* THOSE railroad spikes, (to him!), BEGIN, TO *LOOK* like a...*comfortable pillow!* (As he, continues to wrestle, *in his switchblade mind, sharp on BOTH sides!!).* As he, continues to walk, *BEGINNING TO GET,* YET, TRYING, TO GRAPPLE-OFF, *SUCH EVIL-THOUGHTS!!!* (((AS he, walks, WITH thoughts, *OF: "JUST, letting shit go.")))*(((And, of thoughts, that, he IS the type...*TO BURN MOTHERFUCKERS DOWN)))*...(((HIS - "Day of Blood" foes!!!)))...(((SINCE, he IS the type, TO burn down TO the ground...*A CEMETERY'S...weeping willow))).*

And, up ahead, from up under the brim, of his BULLET HOLE HAT, UPON HIS LOWERED HEAD, Trife, can see, that, up on his left, is WHERE, he left,...that, stashed PALE CHOPPER!!!(Amongst, AND WITH, to him, his,...ONLY friends!). For, he knows, WITH THEM, HE FEELS, AT HOME!!! (And, why, YOU asks?!?)...

FOR...

IT IS a place prepared! Many won't acknowledge it's there! To venture forth, most wouldn't dare! IT'S beneath that "Fog of Depression" layer! WHERE, the "don't-want-to-be-bothered", can't. And so,...won't.

For...

Down a slight embankment, (from the train tracks), are rows upon rows, for, as far, thru that fog, AS, his one good eye goes! And, beyond the mist and paleness of THOSE rows? Are, EVEN MORE rows! (Of WHAT, YOU ask?!?)... OF,...DEAD SUNFLOWERS!!! And, beyond that, is the Bully Boyz' old club house! (That being, that stubborn old bat's,...old wearhouse!). THAT BEING, the NOW abandoned warehouse, of: "Scratch and Dent"! (YOU remember the one!) *The one, of: "Furniture and Major Appliances"! THAT, (before he froze to death, in HIS OWN-DAMN URINAL TROUGH!)...was once, OWNED BY... Zinn!*(((OY VEY!!!))).

And, AS FOR those sunflowers...

(Planted in a large field, abutted - between the train tracks and that warehouse - of that, old stubborn bat)...

WELL...

EVERY spring, Zinn, would get out there, in that field. And, for rows and rows, would plant sunflowers seeds amongst the dead sunflowers, that NEVER got mowed down! (And, if the city's zoning board, had their way?)...*(You know, WAY, WAY, BACK, in the day??).*

WELL...

Zinn's sunflower field, WOULD BE BY NOW, one of, THOSE: New - Luxury/Apartment/Townhouse/Condo/Restaurant/Quaint-Little-Businesses - With - EVERYBODY-ALL-UP-IN-YOUR-BUSINESS

- (AND-NOT-JUST-A-LITTLE-BIT!) - Communities, POPPING-ALL-UP-IN-AND-GROWING EVERYWHERE,...in EVERYBODY'S town!!!

SO...

(Trife HAS, that: "stubborn ol' bat", TO thank FOR, HIS: "Rows-Upon-Rows-OF-Dead-Sunflowers-FOR-AS-Far-AS-HIS-One-Eye-Goes!")...

And so...

Trife, (down off those train tracks,...down there,...AMONGST AND WITH, the dead sunflowers!),...FEELS RIGHT at home! (And, TO HIM, THOSE dead sunflowers ARE...art!).

For...

TO HIM, they remind him, of...him! (FOR, JUST LIKE, HIM, those sunflowers stand tall, yet,...flawed!).

For...

TO Trife, THOSE sunflowers, IN DEATH, ARE looking REGAL! (YET, with, within, in and, upon DEATH, THOSE sunflowers...lower their heads).

For(you see!)...

TO TRIFE, HIS friends, ARE THERE, TO remind him, that, *EVEN something so magnificent, as a sunflower,...this world and life...can and will...deplete you.*

AND...

JUST LIKE, HIM, their heads,...hang low.

FOR(YOU SEE!)...

(Trife, HE CAN SEE the beauty IN that!)...

FOR...

HE IS,...amongst HIS friends!!!

And(THAT being!)...

THEE: "Sunflowers of Depression"

And...

As Trife, stands there, IN that field, (((IN, of, WITH and, amongst, THAT FIELD'S MISTY-PALE-DEPLETION))), OF THE SCENT OF DECAY, *(OF TIRE TRACKS, OF HIS - "I'LL-TAKE-A-RUN-AT-THIS-MUSIC-INDUSTRY" - SHOE-PRINTS, IN THE EARTH, IN THE DRIVING RAIN, IN THAT FIELD, HE RODE IN FIRST, AND WALKED AWAY)*, OF THE FUNGI, OF NO TEMPERANCE, OF MENTAL HEALTH, OF THE DAMP-COLD-MUSK, OF ALL OF THEIR HEADS HUNG LOW,...AS IF,...IT WERE,...A MUST, OF AND WITH THE GRAYS-'N-BROWNS, OF AND WITH THE FOG OF DEPRESSION, for, you see, Trife, begins TO feel, THAT PEACE, FROM WITHIN, THAT, (HE), HAS BEEN MISSING!! AS HE, begins to feel, that, *THERE IS a presence, THERE WITH HIM,...* OTHER THAN,...himself!!!

And so...

Trife looks up and thru that hanging layer of fog, up at that December's cold overcast sky. *And, in two gigantic clouds, Trife knows, THAT, HE KNOWS, THOSE two...sets of eyes!! Set in the faces...((OF TWO gigantic cloud faces!!)). And, he knows that, he knows, that, those clouds ARE,... looking at him!! And, he knows that, he knows, that, they know, that, he's... looking back up at them!!*

FOR(UP there!)...((IN the sky!!))...

((LOOKING BACK at him, ARE...HIS *Nephew AND HIS donor-self Brotha Trife!!))...*

And, he begins to pray.

For(and upon)...

(Meditation's black TO TAKE HIM!)...(((INTO,...deep meditation!)))...

And, as he prays, his prayers are answered!

AS...

He DOES, SO PRAY,....*(((IN deep meditation!)))...*

As...

His head leans, all the way back. With his arms, stretched out, shoulder height. WITH, his palms, facing upwards, TOWARDS the sky!

AS...

(He begins to wrestle, with and upon,...FORGIVENESS), and,... (((((((VENGEANCE!!!)))))))

AS...

Prayer, enters in, (and upon), deep meditation...

As(prayer and deep meditation, enters)...

((HIS: Sharp-On-BOTH-Sides,...Switchblade-Mind!!)).

And(FROM within, that)...

(((THAT, BEING: MEDITATION'S BLACK)))...

Trife, begins to see, COUNTLESS stab wounds. ...Bloody. And, seeping.

(((Put there!)))...

IN HIS back, (in part!), BY, his OWN,...poor judgement! (The judgement, of: HIS "underestimation"!). OF: The WORST kind, OF lack, IN judgement!! ("THAT": HE COULD have, EVER possessed!!!).

AND...

(((WHAT COULD "THAT" POSSIBLY BE, YOU ASK!!?)))... (((WELL, I'LL FUCKING TELL YOU!!!)))...

"THAT", BEING: GIVING,...a motherfucker, TOO MANY chances,... TO prove THEMSELVES,...TO BE honest, AND,...not cruel.

AND...

(((WHY THE FUCK, WOULD HE, DO SOMETHING, LIKE: "THAT", YOU ASK???)))...

SOOOOOOO...

"THAT", HE, COULD prove, TO HIMSELF, "THAT", The: "Shady-Fucking-Shit", "THAT" he, WAS seeing, (((IN people!))), WAS: ONLY due to, HIS: "trust NOBODY attitude"...(((And, "THAT", and, so for, and, as, far as, WHAT, HE WAS SEEING, (((IN THEM!!!))), WASN'T, what,...he WAS seeing, at all!)))...(Yeah!)...((("THAT" shit!))).

And so...

(AND, but, YET,...*HE SAW IT,...all along:(*

And so*(NOW!)*...

((((IN: DEEP MEDITATION'S BLACK))): HE KNOWS, "THAT", from ALL of THOSE stab wounds, TOO, TOO, MANY, TO count(((IN his back!!!)))"THAT" - IT WAS - FROM, HIS: poor judgement, IN: NOT WANTING, TO BELIEVE,..."THAT",...HE WOULD EVER LET, SUCH: a snake(S) in the grass,...get "THAT" CLOSE to him and, (((("THAT", SUCH a snake, WOULDN'T...stay, SO LONG! KNOWING "THAT", Trife HAD,...GOOD INTENTIONS!!!)))(((CAN I GET A MUTHA' FUCKIN' "OY VEY!!!")))...(Thank you:)

FOR(EVEN, a snake IN the grass!)...

CAN'T,...stab YOU in the back, BECAUSE,...it's hands, to hold, "THAT" knife, they lack!

BUT*(It WAS!)*...

Due, TO: Trife's,...POOR JUDGEMENT!!!

AND...

(((GASP!!!)))...(((TAKING ACCOUNTABILITY FOR HIMSELF!!!)))...

("THAT": HE, EVEN PUT HIMSELF,...IN a position,...TO trust:(

And(((AS SUCH!!!)))...

(GOT stabbed, IN HIS motherfucking back:(

AND SO...

With head held back, standing in there, amongst and with, beneath and in, that low lying layer fog shelf and mist, Trife, stands there with, and, amongst, HIS friends, of FREE-STANDING, DEAD SUNFLOWERS!!! As, he stands, amongst AND WITH, The: "Heads of Depression", (of, dead sunflowers drooped),...drooped,...AT Trife! (Looking down on him!),(Though, NOT looking down ON him,...YA' DIG!). And so, Trife, in the - Deep-Prayer-Deep-Meditated-Shaman-Trance-State, Of: "I'M-GONNA'-HAVE-TO-PRAY-AND-MEDITATE-UPON-THIS-SHIT!" - (type-of) - "I'MA-NEED-ME-SOME-STRENGTH-LORD!" - (type-of) - "LORD-HAVE-MERCY-SO-I-KNOW-HOW-TO-MOVE!!!" - Meditated-Prayer-INDUCED-Shaman-Trance-State, Trife,...receives a vision! Of, How: IF he, WERE to do it!(that is, and, THAT BEING),...OF: REVENGE ON THIS MUSIC INDUSTRY!!! THIS: IS, the way! THAT: HE would, WANT TO do it!! As, THE VISION, of: HIS - BLOODY - Stabbed-Up - STABBED-IN-THE-BACK - Back, BRINGS - Trife's,...ancestors back!!! (((And,... THEY ALL HAVE BLOODY BACKS!!!!!!!))). AS, shirtless, UPON that chopper of PALE, Trife, WOULD RIDE!!! And, beside him, WOULD BE,... one of his ancestors,...shirtless,...BACK BLOODIED,...ridin' on a raked-out chopper. AND, for two columns, taking up the left lane of a highway, ((((for, as far back as, YOUR - OH-MY-GOD-I-COULDN'T-ENVISION-A-MORE-TERRIFYING-IMAGE-THAT-YOUR-EYES-WOULD-DARE-TO-SEE - EYES - WOULD SEE!!!)))), ridin' at A - GET-THE-FUCK-OUTTA'-MY-WAY - SPEED, WOULD BE,...his ancestors,... shirtless,...ON raked-out choppers!!!!!!! (((And, THEY TOO, WOULD HAVE, their backs bloody!!!))) AND, JUST LIKE BROTHA TRIFE,

THEY ALL HAVE THAT LOOK(((YOU KNOW THE LOOK!!!)))THE LOOK, OF: "I'M GOING TO FUCKING KILL YOU!!!!!!"

AND...

(((Back down to Jettison Records,...THEY WOULD ALL GO!!!)))...

AND(ONCE they got there!)...

THEY WOULD, free those in bondage,...in the underground.

And(then)...

They would, brutally kill EVERYBODY THAT STABBED THEIR ANCESTOR, TRIFE, IN HIS MOTHERFUCKIN' BACK!!!... (((TURNING HIS BACK BLOODY!!!)))...(And,...of course, anyone that did them, and those, in the underground wrong!)....(of course:)

And(then)...

THEY WOULD,...burn that fucking record label to the ground!

And...

(((("THAT", my friends, IS: *"Trife's VISION!!!"*))).

And, upon that, with his head still held back, *still within meditation's black*, still with his one good eye closed, still with his arms in the palms-up position, still held at the same shoulder-height, (from when, they rose), *down from the sky, landing in his left hand, falls a tiny white stone. And, Trife knows, that, that stone came from Brotha Trife, up there, in that cloud's face in the sky. (And, Trife, still positioned, the exact same way, though with, left fist clinched). Of, left fist clinched, clinching, that white stone. Of, still, being in the black of meditation, still, as he, prays. And, of his vision. And, of his approval from Brotha Trife, up there, in that gigantic cloud's face in the sky. Trife, agrees with Brotha Trife! That, he should ride and storm, Jettison Records,...THEE. EXACT. SAME. WAY!!! And so, in meditation's black, in that trance, in his mind, he does, so say, "Fuck it."(((('Cause, BAD* SHIT, IS coming, THEIR way!!!))).

But then(being, *RIGHT NOW!*)...

FROM, way up above! FROM, that other cloud! (And, though, Trife's Nephew a.k.a. Heavy Duty, between he and bad things, there was no shroud). In Trife's right hand, a white stone, does so land! (((And, WITH right fist clinched!!!))). Trife, KNOWS that, THAT'S HIS NEPHEW,...TELLING HIM "NO!!!" (((And,..."JUST TO, LET SHIT GO!!!"))).

FOR...

You see, his Nephew WANTS TO SEE, his Uncle, (((THIS-HERE: Tier Three Motherfucker!!!))), *UP there, (((WITH him!!!)))...ONE DAY!!!*

For*(Nephew, NOW KNOWS!)*...

*(TO live, A life OF vengeance,...*well,...WHEN, YOUR TIME IS UP ON THIS EARTH,...it AIN'T up!)...

FOR...

IT'S the OTHER WAY(((((((DOWN)))))))YOU'RE GONNA' GO!!!

AND SO...

Trife, standing in a field. Standing with, and amongst, his friends. Thee: "Sunflowers of Depression". Head, held back. Still, rockin' that black suit. (((And,...THAT bullet hole hat!))). Still, with those, 24 karat gold lenses, of limited-edition, resting upon his nose. AND, WITH, his one good eye, STILL closed! Still, with, his arms at shoulder-height, *(from whence, they rose!!). (((Still, in the DEEP, OF: MEDITATIVE BLACK!!!)))* Still, with, clinched fists!! Still, clinching white stones!! And so, and, as such, and (AS, HE DOES!), Trife, a.k.a., (((THAT: TIER THREE MOTHERFUCKER!!!))) *knows, that, "HE'S GON' HAVE TO PRAY UPON, SOME SHIT!!!" (OF: FORGIVENESS OR VENGEANCE!!!)))*. And OF, that prayer?

Well...

HERE'S, the way, it goes:

"You look, upon me, with, eyes of scorn. I'm, me. That's ALL, I'm trying to be. So, I don't know, what, your looks of scorn, are for? You, judge me!

WHEN,…YOU shall not! YOU'RE NOT, THE ONE,…approved, to DO so!(((LET, the sinking begin - OF - that thought!)))Against ME, YOU cast, stones upon! In, doing so. Me or you? WHO'S, in the wrong!?! With two ears. And, with an eagar brain. Left, TO do. AS, sheeps. AND, robots DO!! …All the same. Believe and do, based on, what you hear. Well, let me, make THIS, very clear! My fists, ARE clinched. As, I too. Hold the rocks. 'Cause, I too, CAN CAST, STONES UPON!!!(((Now, LET the sinking begin - OF - THAT thought!)))Should I, cast stones? …As, YOU do? Should I, judge?? WHEN, I shall not!!! TO judge??? AS, YOU do!!! BUT, my head, looks North, as I, pray on it. My rocks fall South, from my clinched fists. As I, release my grip. Because, I KNOW, there's ONLY ONE, TO judge! THIS, I know, IS true!!! So? I cast. NO stones. And, IT'S because,…I don't want to be like you. Amen."

And(upon that)…

Trife, opens his one good eye. To find, both his arms down by his sides. And, he looks, at his palms. Now, free of those stones!! And, he looks up, *to find, both faces in the clouds,…rolling up like a scroll!!* And, he watches *them both, level out flat.* And, he watches *them both, drift off to his right.* And, he watches *them both go until, they both, are no longer in his one good eye sight. As,…they traveled on.*

And(upon that)…

(((IT'S BACK TO THE CHAOS!!!)))…

AS…

He hears,…*a familiar voice*…(((CALL OUT, TO HIM!!!)))…

(((*"LOOKATCHA'*!!! Standin' there, LOOKIN'-ALL, *"Sentimental-'N-Shit"*!!!")))*.*

AS…

Trife, turns 'round, to find, that,…it's BROTHA JESTER!!!… (((Trudging through the mist and the fog, AS HE TRUDGES out into, TRIFE'S: BELOVED - "Sunflowers of Depression" - DEPRESSION - GROUNDS!!!)))(((OY VEY!!!))).

AND…

He AIN'T rockin' no Bully Boyz colors! And, Jester's tall-spiked mohawk, dyed: "Bully-Boy-Green" is,…NOWHERE to be seen! *(As, Jester, has cropped his mohawk down to a "Shark's fin", frosted blonde, on the end!).*

"Jester??", THAT, Tier Three Motherfucker, begins, "Tha'-fuck, YOU doin' here??? And, DON'T BE knockin' over, MY muthafuckin' sunflowers, HOLMES!!!".

Jester, lookin' LIKE, he's been goin' through it, (well, 'cause,…HE HAS!!), still, trudging through Trife's dead sunflower field, replies, *"That old abandoned church, AIN'T abandoned, NO more! AND, WE done-burned-down, THAT 10th Floor, OF the parking garage! SO, THAT PLACE, up at, the: "end of the line", AIN'T there, NO MORE!!* And, I just-got-me a ride back from that cemetery, *YOU-DONE-BURNED-DOWN a coupla' years back!!!* …Triflin', *I always-be-lookin' for ya' there!* JUST TRYNA' see IF you'd, show tha' fuck back up! But, YOU wasn't, there either! BUT, I KNEW, I'd find ya' here! EVERY fall, T! *Every fall, after the sunflowers, Zinn planted, in the spring, would die,…YOU'D be out here, in THIS field! NOT when they, WAS alive! ONLY,…AFTER they die!!!* T, what tha' fuck is it witchu',…and, THESE DAMN sunflowers!?!".

(UT-OH!)…

AS…

Trife, replies, "First of all! These ain't DAMN sunflowers! They "damned" sunflowers."

"Tha'-fuck, you, mean, T???", a perplexed, Jester, questions.

T, then, takes a look around, at all of those rows and rows of dead sunflowers, ALL with thier heads drooped forward and hanging low, for, as far, as, his one eye goes. And, WHAT he sees, is what, HE *ALREADY KNOWS!!* (ALL THESE DEAD SUNFLOWERS, *LOOK DOWN AND DEPRESSED,*…with their heads hangin' low:(

Then, T, steps forward, (away, from his boy) and, WITH ALL CERTAINTY, at one sunflower, in particular, he points, saying, "Jester. You see, THIS ONE?? THIS ONE, RIGHT HERE!! YOU SEE, HOW, THIS ONE, is leaning forward more than, all the rest? Take a look around. I'm SERIOUS, Jester! DON'T give me THAT SHIT! SERIOUSLY, holmes. DAMN!! ...I want YOU to seriously take a look, at ALL these sunflowers, with me."

And(Jester)...

(((BEING JESTER!!!)))...

Just shakes his head, with a smirk, saying, "There you go again, T. Bein' all *sentimental* 'n shit!"

And(T)...

(((BEING BROTHA TRIFE LIKE A MOTHERFUCKER!!!)))...

Wants to shake the teeth outta Jester's head! But, INSTEAD, he says, "OK, HOT SHOT!!! YOU TRYNA' TELL ME, THERE AIN'T *THA' LEAST-BIT-OF-NUTHIN'* IN YOU, THAT YOU *HOLD ON TO?!?*"

And(Jester)...

Not holding on, *for a beating,* 'cause, he *knows, his ol' buddy Trife don't really wanna swing on him,* though, holding on to that class-clown-smart-aleck-smirk, Jester, simply says, "I hold on to *Ice Girl.*"

And(T)...

STILL PISSED, says, "THAT'S NOT WHAT THA' FUCK, I'M TALKIN' 'BOUT!! Look, holmes,...ain't you got a *lil' voice in your head,* that, *no matter how sappy tha' shit might be, it shows up outta nowhere,* and, chokes you tha' fuck up???"

And(Jester)...

(((BEING JESTER!!!)))

Keeps it *"100"* with Trife, and, says, *"The little voice in my head, committed suicide."*

And *(with that!)*...

T, says, "Dig that!"

(Before, *getting back*, to the matter-at-hand!)...

"Check it, but, I STILL want YOU, to take a look at MY sunflowers, ANY-FUCKIN' way! ...Take your time. GET a GOOD look. Just look through tha' fog for a-fuckin'-half'a-fuckin'-minute, FOR me! Thanks, my man. Go 'head. ...Ok. NOW,...you ready, FOR this?!? IT'S like they're ON a march. You see that "body lean", ALL THESE sunflowers, GOT?? THEY ALL GOT THAT slight "body lean" to them! And, they ALL leanin' in the SAME direction! One by one. They all stand on their own. BUT, TOGETHER, they're all tilted forward, like, they all got a some sort of slight-forward-lean to them. It's like they're ALL on the SAME mission! They,...they LOOK LIKE AN ARMY, or some shit,... MARCHING TOWARDS death!! BUT,...they're ALREADY dead! And,...they know it. They stand tall on their own,...together,...when they're fully alive in the sun. BUT, when they know it's time to die? They all lower their heads! AND,...lean towards death. But, it's not until THE LAST sunflower HAS dropped it's head, that, it LOOKS like, they're ALL taking that march together! Jester,...they wait. They wait UNTIL, THE LAST ONE, HAS dropped it's head IN death. And, then? IN death, THEY ALL march TOWARDS DEATH, TOGETHER!!! NOW, look back at THIS one! YOU SEE HOW, it's head, is heavier,...FULLER, THAN all the others??? Jester, when THIS ONE FINALLY decided to bow it's head, and die, the body of THIS sunflower, COULDN'T take it! It HAD TO lean forward MORE than the others, LIKE this! 'CAUSE, there was WAY TOO MUCH STRESS on its neck! It looks like,...it looks like,...like, it NEVER HAD its head up, at all. It looks like, it probably went through its whole-entire-short-life, JUST LIKE THIS,...WITH its head down, LIKE,...it COULDN'T WAIT to die. HE AIN'T, EVEN AS TALL, AS all the OTHER sunflowers!! HE NEVER GREW!!! Jester, THEY didn't HAVE TO wait ON HIM, to begin, THAT "DEATH

MARCH"!! HE'S, BEEN WAITIN', ON THEM!!! LOOK HERE, JESTER!! HIS head is ALL FULL OF SEEDS that, died too soon! AND, his head, EVEN looks MORE yellow, than ALL THE REST!! HE just dropped his head, way too early in life, AND,...GAVE-THE-FUCK-UP!!! Jester,...TELL ME,...tell me, you SEE THAT,...right?".

"Uh,...yeah?? AND!?!", Jester, questioningly-answers.

(T, STILL *"taking in"*, THAT sunflower!)...

...Tells, Jester, "This one, right here, reminds me, of...*me. Me,...when I was a kid.* LOOK! LOOK at THAT sunflower, Jester!!! That, RIGHT there?? Jester, THAT'S: *"The Art of Depression"*.

(IT'S Jester, NOW, WITH HIS head TOWARDS the sky!) & ((Rollin', HIS DAMN eyes!!))...

THEN...

...Looks-back-down, looking-up, at Trife, saying, *"THAT'S, WHAT, tha'-fuck YOU SEE,*...WHEN you look at THAT dead sunflower?!?".

(Trife, NOT 'bout to HAVE - HIS BELIEFS - QUESTIONED!) & ((AS A-Matter-of-Fact??)) - (((DON'T BE judgin' ME, EITHER, MOTHERFUCKER!!!)))...

...TELLS, Jester, ((Matter-of-Factly!!)), "Yeah! ...*I DO!!*".

(Jester, one to ALWAYS have Trife's back!) & ((Bitter AND angry AT the world!!))...

SOOOOOO...

(((One TO always have, a NEGATIVE comeback!!!)))...

...EXPLAINS, to Trife, "Well, let ME, TELL YOU sumfin'! T,...BEING SENTIMENTAL, IS A WASTE, OF FUCKIN' TIME!!! Look, at me, T. Shit, after you left? *And, THIS whole-damn-city lost it's heart?? ...I lost, my love, FOR these streets. Couldn't even think 'bout the streets.* BUT, you know me, T. I fell back in love wit it,...*old habits die hard! I had me a good "run" goin', for a bit,...you know,...smokin' whateva' I got my hands on. I WAS doin' bad, T. After, you left,...a few years back,...I-ain't-gon'-front, T. I was depressed, as a muthafucka',...started hittin' tha' pipe,...CONSTANTLY.* This city, *lost its soul, T. After you, cut Gun Battle Bradley's head off??* ...THIS city, *LOST its soul,...ITS fightin' spirit!* Shit, T, you think I *was* depressed, *after YOU, cut THAT motherfucker's head off, AND, THEN DIPPED??* ...T, YOU-AIN'T-GOT NO IDEA, *HOW depressed, I muthafuckin' was,* WHEN, I SAW YOU a week ago, in YOUR cemetery,...talkin' 'bout, *"Oh, you IN tha' "Music Game", NOW!".*

THEN...

(Jester, gives Trife, the "once-over"!)...

AND...

(SEEING how, he's still dressin' sharp, 24 karat sunglasses, a black designer suit, etc.)...

HOWEVER...

((Lookin' FAR, FROM: "put together"!!))

FOR...

(Trife, IS NOT "fresh",...NOR "clean"!!)...

FROM...

(NOT having had another change of clothes!)((SINCE THE MONTH OF MAY!!))(((SINCE HE stashed that PALE chopper!!!))))((((IN THE DRIVING RAIN!!!!)))))(((((IN THIS sunflower field!!!!))))))((((((JUST STRAIGHT TRIFLIN' YO'!!!!!!))))))

AND SO...

...Jester, continues..., "SO? *...How'd THAT shit TURNOUT, fo' ya'??* YOU some BIG STAR now,...AIN'TCHA'!?!".

Trife, just shakes his head, saying, "Nah. *Shit ain't workout."*

(Jester, pissed AT his boy!)((FOR, *falling victim, TO the "Music Game"!!))(((LET'S HIM HAVE IT!!!)))...*

..."Well, THAT AIN'T, too-damn-hard, TO see! 'MEMBER, *back when I saw you, in your cemetery?* LOOK AT ME, T! NOW, I'M tha' one, of the two of us, THAT'S gonna be yellin' AT the other!! *THAT NIGHT,* when your "BIG SHOT" music-whoever-tha'-fuck-that-was, *dropped you off in a dark-ass cemetery,...AND, left yo' ass there!* WHAT WE, talk 'bout, T??? *...ICE GIRL!!!* AIN'T THAT RIGHT, T?!? *WE TALKED 'BOUT,...Ice Girl.* AND, what *WAS* tha' last thing, I said to you, *right before I dipped-tha'-fuck outta there??* I COULDN'T EVEN LOOKATCHA', NO MO', T!!! WITCHA', GOLD GLASSES 'N SHIT!!! *I couldn't have been, MORE disgusted, WIT you, T.* But, I'm STILL ya' boy!! SO, I asked you, "IF YOU remembered that *"Ice Girl Story"* we was, JUST talkin' 'bout?" And, I'MA LET'CHA' KNOW WHY!! 'Cause, I *WAS LETTIN' YOU KNOW,* T,...that, *THAT'S HOW the "Music Industry" WAS GONNA' DO YOU!* JUST LIKE, Ice Girl, DID TO Cash and Tatum!! *Ice Girl, laid-up, HIGH-up, on that sofa! And, JUST LET THEM do, ALL OF the hard work, DOWN on the floor! JUST FOR, ICE GIRL, to SWOOP down AND, snatch that rawhide bone FROM them!! BUT, NOT UNTIL AFTER, THEY made it easier, FOR HER, TO EAT!!!"*

"Damn. ...That's, *EXACTLY HOW* THA' FUCK Pockets and Jettison Records, *DID ME!!! USED ME, to write HIM, A HIT FUCKIN' SONG!!!* ...And,...I ain't-got-shit, to show for it! *EVEN heard MY SHIT PLAYIN' on tha' jukebox, up at that bar I hate!* Gotta admit, though, MY song turned-out to be FIRE!!! Yeah, holmes,...THEY *did* me wrong."

Disgusted...

(Trife, reaches in his inside suit coat pocket, pulling out that cell phone Pockets gave to him)...

Pissed...

(Trife, goes to put that cell phone, in his mouth)...

And...

((BITE that fucker IN TWO!!))

"WHAT THA' FUCK YOU DOIN', TRIFLIN'!!! YOU GON' CUT'CHA' MOUTH, ALL-THE-FUCK UP! GIMME, THAT THING!!", hollers, Jester!, (SNATCHING, that cell phone FROM Trife!!).

THEN...

(Jester, takes notice, to something...different,...'bout his ol' buddy, T!)...

...And so, then he, asks, "Yo, T? Where's your "FUCK Y'ALL" - Grill, son?!? What? Lemme' guess,...*tha' "Music Industry" TOLD ya', YOU COULDN'T rock ya' gold grill, NO mo'!?!* YOU SEE, T,...THAT'S, THA' SHIT, "THEY", be doin'! YOU, CAN'T EVEN BE "YOU", NO mo'!".

And(upon that)...

"Mr. Brotha Trife", takes off his 24 karat gold shades, flips them shits around. And, checks out his mouth. In the reflection. *And, in reflection. And, HIS Tier-Three-Mind is, NOW just reminded THAT,...THOSE "CLONIN' motherfuckers", NEVER gave him a gold grill, in that emralde hall, made of white jade, in...the underground!!!*

And(upon that!)...(BEFORE Jester, CAN beat him to it!)...

"Mr. Brotha Trife", in that reflection, of those 24 karat gold glassess, *gets flashes of his past life, as it flashes!*

THAT...

((THOSE COCKSUCKERS, NEVER tatted "Proverbs 15:3" under his eyes sockets!!))

HOWEVER...

(((HIS TIER-THREE-MIND, don't know that, THEY DID!!!)))

'CAUSE...

(((HIS TIER-THREE-SKIN, HAD ALREADY SOAKED, THAT TATTOO INK IN!!!)))

And((UPON THAT!!))...((AFTER Jester, had received the answer, TO his question!!))...

((Jester, turns that cell phone on ((amidst, T's protest!!)) and,...CALLS POCKETS!!))...

"NAH! NAH! NAH, SON!!! I'M hittin' this, Pockets motherfucker, up! Lemme' tell ya' sumthin', T,...*YOU'VE been playin' by the rules,* in'a game...THAT AIN'T-GOT-NO RULES!!!", Jester, laments, as he, begins! (AS, Trife, just shakes his head. And, turns 'round. And, looks back up into the sky!).

SO(Let's checkout HOW, THAT phone call went!)...

..."DID THAT MOTHERFUCKER JUST HANG UP ON ME??? I'VE, been hung up on BEFORE. ...I KNOW, WHEN A MOTHERFUCKER, HANGS UP ON ME!!! THAT, MOTHERFUCKER, JUST HUNG UP ON ME!!!", Jester, snaps!... (BEFORE, calling RIGHT BACK!!).

AND(UPON THAT!!)...

THAT Tier Three Motherfucker, SNATCHES the phone!

And...

(((BARKS AT Phillip Tate!)))...

AND...

THAT - *Subconscious*-Whistlin'-OF-Nervousness - BEGINS, to kick-in!!(((*KNOWING WHO'S VOICE of - amazin'-intubation - THAT IS - on the other end!)))*, "GET Pockets, BACK on tha' phone, holmes!!!"

And(well)...

Phillip Tate,...FACILITATES!!!

"WHERE'S, MY MONEY!?! I heard, MY SONG, on'a jukebox!", Trife, shouts, at Pockets!

(PROMPTING!)...

((((Pockets,...TO SHOUT BACK!!!)))),..."*Thought I, TOLD you, ALREADY!?! ...YOU...TIER-THREE...MOTHERFUCKER! MY STUDIO! MY MUSIC!! MY MONEY!!!* MY HUSTLE, KNOWS NO BOUNDS!!! And, IT DON'T EVER STOP!!!"

And(UPON THAT!)...

(Pockets, after enjoying THAT "Laugh of Expense", EXPLAINS, to Trife, OF: "*The EVIL Mist"!)*...

...*"REMEMBER, those phone calls, I told you NOT TO worry ABOUT??* THAT, was FOR a reason, "MR. TRIFE"!! In THIS "Industry", IF you AIN'T ON the INSIDE,...THEN,...THOSE phone calls, AIN'T NEVER GON' COME!!!!!! *THIS "INDUSTRY", IS like, ITS OWN "BEAST", out there! AND, IT'S JUST WAITIN' TO pass OOOOON through, AND intercept, ANY AND ALL progress, you THINK, you MAY BE makin'!* And, THAT, "MY brother", IS: "*THE EVIL MIST"!!!!!!"*

And(on that note!)...

Triflin', replies, "You know what, motherfucker!?! YOU always laughin' AT someone's expense! *BUT, you know what I'VE learned, from hangin' 'round you,...if I AIN'T learned, NOTHIN' else?? IT AIN'T 'bout HAVIN', tha' last laugh. IT'S 'bout, NOT givin' A FUCK, 'BOUT HAVIN', tha' last laugh! 'Cause, NOBODY really gives A FUCK, ANYWAY!!* Shitty-people, KNOW they're shitty. So? WHY then waste your time, SPENDIN' YOUR TIME, ON that laugh?? 'Cause, ALL you're REALLY doin' is, spendin' YOUR OWN TIME! BY wastin', YOUR OWN TIME!! WITH, THAT bullshit "Last Laugh"!!! And, YOUR "WASTED TIME", IS WHAT makes it HAVE "thee" expense. An expense, that,...YOU'LL NEVER get back."

And(on THAT note!)...(Triflin', hands Jester back the phone).

And...

(As Pockets, keeps goin' ON-'N-ON, not knowing that it AIN'T Triflin' on the phone!)...

Triflin', turns 'round, looks back up at the sky *and, gets back in his zone!*

And...

(As Pockets, keeps talkin' ALL THIS SHIT!!)...

Jester, silently,...keeps listening!

And, as Trife, looks up at that sky, he thinks, of Y.S. (And, he gets to thinking about, the last thing that she said to him, before she pulled the trigger, PUTTING AN END to, HER: "Music-Biz-STRESS"...((("Yeah, so, well, anywaaaaaays!!!"))), IS what, Trife, hears Y.S. say, IN his Tier-Three-Mind!!!...(And, he gives thought to that!). Of which, upon which, Trife, NOW KNOWS Y.S., was trying to hip him TO that! (And that, beyond her year's, she was wise!). AS, in his Tier-Three-Mind, THIS is what, Trife is NOW realizing,..."EACH and EVERY time, Pockets, said THAT shit,...IT was FOLLOWED-UP BY,...some BULLSHIT LIE!!!"

AND(ON THAT SHIT!)...

Comin' cross Trife's face, was...THE PAIN STICK'S EVIL-GRIMACED-FACE-GRIMACE!!!((((OY VEY Y'ALL!!!)))...

AND SO...

Trife, turns back 'round. And, Jester, *UPON SEEING that face,* damn-near shits his pants! (AS, that cell phone in his hand, hits the ground!). And, Jester, picks it up, just to find that, the call has been ended.

And so...

(Jester, proceeds to tell Trife, of some of the shit, that, Pockets, was saying)...

"Yo, T. ...Uh,...you know some chick, named Anna Mossitti?? Well, Pockets, was sayin', she", (And, Trife, TOO-DAMN-DISGUSTED - WITH ALL THIS - "MUSIC-INDUSTRY-BULLSHIT", CUTS JESTER OFF!!!)...

FOR...

(At THIS POINT??)...

(((T, COULDN'T BE, MORE disgusted, WITH people!!!))).

For...

(The mere mention of her name - he merely no longer cares for).

For...

(To Jester, in reply, these were the only words required, by Trife, no less, and, no more)...

..."My man, I don't care if she's in love,...or in the morgue."

Chapter Twenty Nine

THE STATE OF THE ARTISTS

Of, Christmas morning. Under an overcast December's sky. An *"Evil Mist"*((((OF THEIR OWN RIGHT!!!)))DOES,...so ride! As, JUST AS, IN *"Trife's VISION"*, IT'S Trife, ON a PALE chopper, in the lead, (though, NOT the leader of the pack!). And, they're BARRELIN' DOWN THE STREET AT A BREAKNECK - GET-THA'-FUCK-OUTTA'-OUR-WAY - SPEED, FOR AS, FAR AS, THE EYE CAN SEE!!! !!!!!!!!!!!!!!!!

THOUGH...(up ahead!)....(((((JUST WAITIN' ON HIM!!!!))))....

Pretty High and Bad Habitz, sit perched and poised. (((((Upon, a WHITE chopper! AND, one of BRIGHT RED!!!!))))).

And(FOLLOWING that pack, is)...

THE DIET!!!! (((((RIDIN' ON HIS BLACK CHOPPER OF THE DEAD!!!!))))....

And(FOLLOWING BEHIND THE DIET??)...(Hanging waaaaaay back!)...

Well...

((((IT'S THAT MUSIC-CONTRACT-WRITING-HIPPY, THAT *NEVER SHOWED!!!*))))

FOR...

((((HE'S *BEEN* PLAYIN' EVERYBODY, *FROM THE GET-GO!!!*))))...

FOR...

((((HE AIN'T NO RIDE-SHARE-DRIVER!!!))))...

AND...

((((HE AIN'T REALLY EMPLOYED BY NO DAMN PIZZA SHOP!!!))))...

AND...

((((THAT AIN'T NO '83 CADILLAC SEVILLE!!!))))...

FOR...

((((THAT'S BROTHA TRIFE'S SEIZED '83 BUICK RIVIERA!!!))))

AND...

((((IT'S BEEN WIRED FOR SOUND!!!))))...((((FRESH OUT THE F.B.I.'S CHOP SHOP!!!))))...

AND...

((((THAT'S SPECIAL AGENT CHILLWELL, BEHIND THE WHEEL, OF THAT SEVILLE!!!))))...

AND...

((((HE'S BEEN *SHADOWING POCKETS FOR YEARS*, JUST LEAVING HIM OUT THERE!!!))))...

'CAUSE...

((((HE'S TRYING TO GIVE POCKETS, AND ALL HE'S INVOLVED WITH, TOO MUCH ROPE, AND TOO MANY YEARS!!!))))...

AND SO...

The city's citizens, of the city, *FORMERLY known, as Parkinson's City,* are all bearing witness to, the city's *FORMER street soldiers,* ridin' out of the city, on two wheels, as one, two columns of two!!

And...

They all have on their old colors.

THOUGH...

(ENTIRELY sprayed painted black!)...

Though...

Cross their backs, are red spray paint stripes, (that, have plenty of drips and runs!).

FOR...

Those of them that have choppers and cycles, were absolutely down for THIS run!

And(those of them, that didn't?)...

Well...

THEY STOLE some choppers and cycles!!

'CAUSE...

((((THEY WASN'T 'bout to miss out on THE fun!!!))).

And(what fun, would that be???) Well...

((((I'LL FUCKING TELL YOU!!!)))...

The fun of ridin' through those emrald halls made of white jade!

AND...

((((FUCKIN' SHIT UP WITH IMPUNITY!!!))).

FOR...

They AIN'T worryin' 'bout gettin' caught!

FOR...

THEY AIN'T goin' before NO judge!

FOR...

THEY AIN'T goin' behind NO DAMN prison bars!

FOR...

(((The MOTTO OF, The: "Bloody Back MC'S")))...(((IS: "Coffin Nails Over Jail")))...

FOR...

THIS ride,...IS STRAIGHT SUICIDE!!!!!!

And...(THEY AIN'T worryin' 'bout makin' it back!).

HOWEVER...

(Let us, *take it back, to what, led up to that,* shall we?)...(((YES!!!)))(((I THINK WE MUTHA' FUCKIN' SHALL!!!)):)

AND SO...

Back in those dead sunflower rows. Back, when, Jester saw, that evil-grimaced-Pain-Stick-face come twisting and forming cross Trife, gettin' locked in place, WITH, that look, (((YOU KNOW "THE LOOK"!!!))), "THE LOOK", Of: (((NOW YOU'VE PISSED ME OFF!!! NOW I'M PISSED OFF!!! AND, SO NOW,...ANYTHING GOES!!!)))(((OY VEY!!!))). And so, after that, Jester and Trife, had a talk. And, Jester, explained to Trife, that the Bully Boyz, still rule the streets! BUT,...with no Gun Battle Bradley! And, WITH NO BEEFS!!! The city and the city's street gangs,...lost its identity. SO, the Bully Boyz decided, they was gon' "shake it up" a bit! SO, the Bully Boyz decided,...to START SOME SHIT!!! And, how they went 'round the whole city. And, recounts how they stripped, EACH AND EVERY STREET

GANG, OF their colors!!! AND, how they spray painted EACH AND EVERY vest, ENTIRELY black!!! And, cross the backs of the vests, the Bully Boyz, spray painted fast and haphazardly, seven red stripes exactly!!!!!!! BUT, on some of the backs of each, some received, seven shots of rapidfire red spray paint spots, like a hole, JUST TO LET that red paint flow, to run down, and streak!!!!!!! BUT, REGARDLESS, be it, red stripes, or those short bursts of red spots, each set of the gangs' colors, on those black backs, each got, seven each!!!!!!! And then, the Bully Boyz gave the gangs back their colors! But,…they didn't even care. FOR, there was no Gun Battle Bradley for to beware! 'Cause, most of these gang members, if not all, have just been lookin' for somethin' to get into. Like,…TROUBLE!!! BUT, this fist fighter's town, NO LONGER had anyone TO fight! THOUGH, THESE street soldiers, STILL HAD the mentality of soldiers,…they just NEEDED "A CAUSE" TO stand behind! For, THESE SOLDIERS STILL HAD THEIR FIGHT!!! However,…they just needed something to do. And so, Trife, asked Jester, "Why seven stripes? Why seven spots?? Why NOT,…I don't know, man,…shit, 66? WHY didn't y'all, just spray paint a big fuckin' red "X" cross tha' backs? THEN, the only stripes needed, woulda' been two." And, Jester, told him, "That was my idea! Lucky #7, son! Just to send a message! That,…YOU MOTHERFUCKERS LUCKY, THIS IS ALL WE GONNA' DO!!!!!!!"

And so…

(Trife, told Jester, to "Gather up all those down 'n out, who just be exsisting, out on the block. Tell 'em, if they ain't got a bike? If they know how to ride a motherfuckin' motorcycle or not?? TO GO GET ONE!!! AND, meet me at Zinn's old wearhouse, tomorrow at high noon! And, YOU tell 'em FROM ME, those spray painted up colors, I want them to rock!")…

AND…

The next day, at high noon, as through big white fluffy clouds, beneath that high noon sun, as it came breakin' on through, Triflin', took a deep breath, as he stood on the top step, of and with, that abandoned Zinn's Warehouse at his back, head-to-toe in black, of him, it did protect, in the distance, in the mist, in of and with the fog, one-by-one - HIS sunflowers marched towards death - and, for them, they ain't comin' back, for them, *there WILL BE no comin' back, as the already dead, march towards death - one-by-one - together - step-by-step. Triflin', with that damned abandoned wearhouse at his back, wherein, oh 'bout 1,260 some odd days back, that stubborn ol' bat, Zinn, froze to death, in HIS OWN-DAMNED urinal trough, ON HIS OWN-DAMNED BACK!!! Triflin', head-to-toe, dressed in ALL BLACK, OF him, TO protect,…'cept, for his back, ('CEPT, FOR, THE SEVEN red spray painted stripes, STRIPED CROSS HIS DAMN BACK!!!!!!!). For him, before him, in the foreground, Triflin', addressed the gathered masses, sittin' or standin', on or next to the cycles, choppers, and trikes, they have "gathered". And, just like, Trife, they're ALL dressed in ALL BLACK, for, to, and, as to protect,…('CEPT, FOR THE SEVEN red stripes, or the SEVEN RED SPOTS, SHOT CROSS THEIR BACKS!!!!!!!). And, as Trife, stands there, facing the crowd, he gets into explaining of how, from here on out, those seven red stripes, will represent the wounds from lashes! And, of how, if you happen, to be one of those, of your set of colors, that have on the backs of those, of those red spots, of the seven of those, that, those, ALSO represent the wounds, PUT THERE BY THOSE BASTARDS!!!!!!! And, of how, those red drops and, of that red spray paint run, represent the pouring out, from and of, the wound's blood!(((FROM GETTIN' STABBED IN THE BACK BY THE SYSTEM, BY TRUST, AND, BY LOVE!!!)))(((OY VEY!!!))). And, Trife, that angry motherfucker, went on to explain, of HOW, it DON'T MATTER what color your skin is. 'Cause, EVERY MAN HERE, HAS BEEN A VICTIM, OF: "THE SYSTEMIC SYSTEM"!!!!!! And, that, "IF YOU GOT MY "BLOODY BACK"??????? I GOT YOUR "BLOODY BACK"!!!!!!!" (((And, then, ALL DECLARED, "I GOT YOUR "BLOODY BACK"!!!!!!!"))). And, Trife, let's 'em all know, "WE THE "B.B. MC'S"!!!!!!!" And, that, there will be no rank. That, each man IS a man! That, each man wears the same colors. That, we ride in together. And, we ride out together. That, each man, will be able to call, what "The Cause" is, THAT, we ride on. And, that, EVERY man here, will go with THAT man, on THAT man's run! And, that, every man here, WILL HAVE, that man's "Bloody Back"!!!!!!! And then, Trife, asked, the gathered masses, "DO YOU GOT YOUR BROTHER'S "BLOODY BACK"???????" (((And, then, ALL DECLARED, "I GOT MY BROTHER'S "BLOODY BACK"!!!!!!!"))). And, then Trife, gave his revelation, OF HOW, EVERY MAN, whether, they realize it or not,*

HAS a mission, and, "A CAUSE", TO right!! And, that, every man, of the "B.B. MC's" WILL have the back, of EVERY "BLOODY BACK", IN THE RIGHTING OF, THAT "CAUSE"!!! And, of how, "You can do ANYTHING, you WANT TO DO, in this world,…just, as long, as YOU'RE WILLING, TO DEAL, WITH the consequences! …COFFIN NAILS, OVER JAIL!!!!!!! YA' DIG!!!!!!!" And, Trife, explained, of how, "WE SHALL, ride out, and ride, like, a swarm of locusts, rippin' shit up, doin' whatever tha' fuck we want,…UNTIL, WE'RE ALL DEAD!!!!!!" And, of how, "THIS might not be long term,…BUT IT WILL BE ON OUR TERMS!!!!!!" And, Trife, went on to explain, that, we gon' ride, FOR "The Bloody Back"! A back,…that's been whipped by the system in place. A back,…that's BEEN stabbed in it!!! A back,…that's had a knee in it!!!!!!! And, Trife, asked, "Do each one of you men, have a personal wrong, that, YOU feel THE NEED, to right??? A wrong, THAT, you would do ANYTHING, TO right, THAT wrong, NO MATTER WHAT, YOU might HAVE TO DO,…even die for??????? Do each one of you men feel that you have been ripped off? …Ripped off like the whip ripped the flesh? Men, some of your ancestors couldn't do shit about that. They couldn't right their wrongs. They couldn't,…WE CAN!!!!!!! WE CAN DO WHATEVER THE FUCK WE WANT!!!!!!! AND, WE GON' DO WHATEVER, THA' FUCK WE WANT!!!!!!! Call it reparations,… call it whatever the fuck YOU want! Forty acres and a damn mule! Some of y'all gathered here today, OUR ancestors NEVER GOT their forty acres and a damn mule! BUT, THE "BLOODY BACK MC'S", OUT TO GET IT!!! And, it ain't even 'bout, EVER BEING ABLE TO, enjoy OR prosper, FROM, WHAT, WE'RE OUT TO take back, from, what, someone ripped off of us. IT'S JUST, ABOUT,…TAKING IT BACK!!! WE'LL LEAVE IT FOR FAMILY OR LOVED ONES!!!!!!! WE GON' TAKE IT BACK!!!!!!! 'Cause, it AIN'T their's TO have! And,…I'LL die for WHAT'S mine. You see, men. The music industry, IS the founder OF the "B.B. MC'S". I am NOT your founder. The music industry IS the founder. For, if not for them, RIPPING ME - THE FUCK OFF,…none of y'all, would be gathered here today, talkin' 'bout, WHAT WE'RE talkin' 'bout!!!!!!! SO, the music industry, IS the one TO THANK AND BLAME, FOR a horde, a swarm, of pissed-off angry black men and, men of many backgrounds and races, who feel ripped off, RACING TOWARDS YOU, BLAZIN' TWO COLUMNS, FLYIN'

COLORS with, red whipped, and stabbed in the back marks, and, with, red spots shot on our backs, held by the hand of the man that ripped off our ancestors' freedoms, and, ripped the skins right off their backs! THAT'S THE PAIN I FEEL FROM THE MUSIC INDUSTRY!!!!!! It's all just modern-day tied to a tree WHIPPING!!!!!!! "BLOODY BACK MC'S",…THAT. SHIT. STOPS. TODAY!!!!!!! AND, IF YOU AIN'T READY TO RIDE WITH ME, IF YOU AIN'T READY TO DIE WITH ME, THEN, TAKE OFF YOUR COLORS, TAKE THEM OFF YOUR BACK AND, DON'T YOU EVER IN YOUR LIFE, DARE TO PUT THESE COLORS BACK ON!!!!!! HE, WHO IS NOT WITH ME, IS AGAINST YOU!!!!!!! HE, WHO IS NOT WITH ME, IS AGAINST ME!!!!!!! SEARCH YOUR HEART AND MIND!!!!!!!"…(And, as Trife, searched his own heart and mind, he finds himself in that emrald hall, those halls of white jade,…and, he's ridin' free, freeing the artists from the under the ground levels of Jettison Records, in his heart and mind,…he finds!)…And, after some time, Trife, provides, (what would come to be known, cross the globe, as "The Triflin' Address")…"Our first march will be upon the state of the art titan building of Jettison Records. 'Cause,…I was there. Been there. Seen how they did me. And, THAT DON'T sit too well WITH ME!!!!!!! And, WHAT REALLY don't sit TOO WELL with me,…is the CURRENT "State of the Artists", that ARE BEING CLONED and, the one's THAT ARE being "housed" there! So? WE MARCHIN' ON THE MUSIC INDUSTRY!!!!!!! I'M doin' THIS, FOR the ARTISTS!!!!!!! I'M doin' THIS, FOR MY homegirl, Y.S.!!!!!!! … AND her TWIN SISTER!!!!!!! WE DOIN' THIS FOR OUR SISTERS TOO, Y'ALL!!!!!!! SOMEBODY GOTTA' HAVE THEY BACK!!!!!!! THE "BLOODY BACK MC'S" GOT, Y'ALL'S BACK!!!!!!! I'M doin' THIS, FOR EVERY LAST ARTIST, THAT GOT used, THAT GOT played, THAT GOT chewed tha' fuck up AND SPIT tha' FUCK OUT by THIS, "ASS-EATIN'-INDUSTRY"!!!!!!! The DEVIL, IS a "fooler"! And so,…the devil IS a fool! …Taken many forms. DON'T be fooled BY these fools, y'all! Only a fool, full of foolish-pride, will fully fail to take accountability, for their own actions, as the fool continues, to take kind hearts and, TRUE ARTISTS, and, TRUE businessmen and women, DOWN to their pre-planned fool-ass destination, with empty pockets, AND discard them,…a shitty-fool, shittin' all over REAL PEOPLE,…REAL PEOPLE THAT ARE REALLY ABOUT

SOMETHING, that, HAVE BEEN really fooled, as they've, really just tried, to work with, to, help a fool, BEING FOOLED, as THEY'VE BEEN GRINDIN' HARDER, THAN, the fool, AS THEY'VE been grindin', MORE FOR THE FOOL, THAN, THE FOOL,…for, the fools, ARE full of themselves, THEY'LL LET YOU do ALL the work, they'll let you burn up ALL YOUR money, KNOWING, they were NEVER about it,…the fool with foolish-pride. THIS IS A DEVIL INDUSTRY, Y'ALL!!!!!! DON'T BE FOOLED!!!!!!! DON'T BE A FOOL!!!!!!! But,…as, for me? "They", got ME TOO!! …I'm a clone, y'all. "They" cloned me. Right down there IN the under the ground levels OF Jettison Records! THIS SHIT, IS REAL!!!!!!! …I ain't, EVEN alive,…I'm ALREADY dead, I'ma kill 'em all, anyway,…so, it really don't, fuckin' much matter! So,…what DOES that mean??? It means,…I AIN'T GOT SHIT TO LOSE!!!!!!! It means, I DON'T GIVE A FUCK!!!!!!! JUST, like YOU!!!!!!! Or, else? Y'ALL WOULDN'T BE HERE WIT ME, ROCKIN' THA' "BLOODY BACK"!!!!!!! KILL THE DEVIL!!!!!!! SEND THE DEVIL BACK TO HELL!!!!!!! 'Cause, THIS SHIT, STOPS TODAY!!!!!!! And, THAT'S WHY, y'all are gathered here, WITH ME today!!!!!!! IT'S time, TO TAKE a stand, y'all. Live by the sword, and, die by that bitch. IT'S TIME!!!!!!! If YOU WILL have my back, how I WILL HAVE your back, LET'S RIDE!!!!!!! Look to your right, and, ask the man, to your right, "Do you got my "Bloody Back"?" (And, upon, an uproar of, "I GOT YOUR "BLOODY BACK"!!!!!!!"), Trife, tells them all, look to your left, and, ask the man, to your left, "Do you got my "Bloody Back"?". (And, upon an UPROAR OF, "I GOT YOUR "BLOODY BACK"!!!!!!!"), Trife, stepped down, off the top step of the warehouse. Hopped on that PALE CHOPPER. And, FIRED IT THE FUCK UP!!!!!!!

And so…

Then, Trife, said, "Fuck it."

And…

Bad shit came their way.

www.ingramcontent.com/pod-product-compliance
Lightning Source LLC
Chambersburg PA
CBHW070149310726
48976CB00001B/32